Wide Place In The Road

A Great Generation Love Story

by
Richard C. Kirkland

ISBN: 1463649347
ISBN 13: 9781463649340

To my wife, Maria,
for her continued encouragement and inspiration.

FORWARD

Wide Place in the Road is a story that for the most part, I lived or had first hand account. So after the years went by and the bad memories faded, I realized that it was a story to be told and I'm probably the only one left to do it. Based on real people and real history, it is a heart warming love story that begins during that era in American history fondly depicted as a more innocent time, followed by the dedication and sacrifice of America's youth who fought World War Two, the deadliest war in history. It is a period often referred to as "The Greatest Generation" and will bring back memories to seniors and for younger folks a refreshing glimpse of that unique era.

Richard C. Kirkland

*The book jacket was created from a painting by Author Richard C. Kirkland, and can be seen on his website, richardckirkland.com, along with other oil and watercolor paintings.

Chapter

~1~

It was called "the Grapevine."

In California's early days, it was an Indian trail that wound up the slopes of the Tehachapi Mountains from the San Joaquin Valley, through the Tejon Pass and down into the San Fernando Valley. In the late eighteen hundreds, they made it into a bona fide road with teams of men and mules. Then came automobiles and it was paved with cement using chain-driven Ford and Mack trucks.

The Mono Company got the cement contract because their plant was right there in the mountains. After it dried, Mono cement had a chalky-white cast to it. If you climbed a Tehachapi Mountain and looked down on the ridges and canyons where the road ran, it would appear as a narrow, convoluted vine, winding its way through the patterns of earthly greens and browns. They say that was how it came to be called the Grapevine.

The road reached its highest elevation at Gorman in the Tejon Pass. The pass was named after the Tejon Indians as was old Fort Tejon. It was originally located there to keep an eye on the Indians and protect the old California Overland Stage when it traveled through the pass. If you climbed one of the mountains and looked down at the road, most everything else you would see would be on Grapevine Ranch property, including the mountain.

The Ranch grazed thousands of white-faced, red-coated Herefords over its vast stretches of prime land in the green valleys and rolling mountains of the Tehachapi. That required a lot of cowboys in the early days since quite a bit of cattle rustling was going on then. But shortly after the Grapevine Road was paved, Prohibition became the law of the land, and most of the cattle rustlers turned to bootlegging.

After that they didn't need as many cowboys, but the Grapevine road did cut through a big chunk of the ranch, so to discourage trespassers, they put up a barbed-wire fence with "Keep Off" signs- and assigned one of their cowboys, Juan Martinez as sort of a watchdog.

Juan was called a breed because his mother was Indian and his father Spanish. Juan's father came from Old Monterey to work as a cowboy on the ranch. One day, while trailing cattle rustlers high in the Tehachapi Mountains, he got caught in a winter blizzard and took refuge in an Indian village. As the story goes, he fell in love with one of the Indian maidens and traded his horse for her. When he finally showed up back at the ranch with his bride but no horse, the foreman docked his pay ten pesos. However, he got his job back as a rider, and he and his Indian bride took up housekeeping in a tepee alongside Grapevine Creek. That's where Juan Junior was born.

By the time President Franklin Roosevelt's New Deal had repealed Prohibition, the cattle rustlers-turned-bootleggers were too fat to return to their old profession, so cattle rustling sort of died out. Other than an occasional automobile traveler who stopped and crawled through the fence to pick wild flowers, trespassers weren't much of a problem either so Juan's watchdog duty, which he now performed in a pickup truck, was a far cry from the old days when his father chased rustlers on a stiff-legged horse down a dusty trail.

These days, there was only one fly in Juan's ointment. It had to do with a group of young boys whose families lived along the Grapevine. They ignored Juan's keep off signs, crawled through his barbed-wire fences, climbed his mountains, and swam in his cattle watering troughs.

"Hey look, guys, our watchdog just drove up to the store in his truck," exclaimed one of those boys, standing on a rock outcropping on the side of a Tehachapi mountain and jabbing his index finger toward the canyon below.

The boy was tall for his age, which made the bib overalls he wore appear to hang on his thin frame. A mop of disheveled, sun-bleached hair fell across his forehead just above a set of intense green eyes, which were focused on the object of his attention: Juan Martinez's pickup truck. It appeared as a toy on the Grapevine road far below.

"You sure it's him, Jess?" asked one of four other boys who lay on their backs in a carpet of grass and wildflowers. All wore bib overalls and "Monkey Ward" (Montgomery Ward) tennis shoes. Some of the overalls had holes; others had patches over the holes. None wore socks or shirts, and their arms and faces were a golden brown.

"Yeah, it's him all right, Alvin. I can tell his truck." Alvin, the same age as Jessie, thirteen, scrambled to his feet and climbed up on the rock beside his friend. He was a head shorter but stocky, with broad shoulders and a shock of raven- black hair that shrouded his face. He stood for a moment squinting his eyes, which were as black as his hair. "Yep, yer right it's our injun watchdog."

The two boys looked at each other. "Wanna take a dip?" asked Jessie with a grin.

"Yah-Hoo! You bet I do!" replied Alvin, returning the grin. "Come on, guys, let's go swimmin'."

The other three boys raised to sitting positions, looking skeptical. "I dunno. I'm still in big trouble from the last time he caught us at the trouth," worried one, a tall, freckled boy with bushy red hair that jutted in all directions.

"Aw, come on, Gerald, don't be a scardy cat. He ain't going to catch us," assured Alvin, jumping off the rock.

"How you know he ain't?" asked another of the three skeptics, a chunky boy with a round face, close cropped sandy hair, and protruding front teeth. "That breed is a sneaky one- I'll tell ya."

"Yeah, but when he goes to the store, he always gets a bottle, goes back to his cabin, and gets drunk. You know that, Bobbie," said Jessie, climbing down off the rock and walking over to where a homemade knapsack lay in a bed of blue and purple lupines. "An' that means he'll be out of it for the rest of the day," he added, picking up the knapsack.

"I know, but just what if he don't?" worried Bobbie, shaking his head and climbing to his feet.

The last of the skeptics, a gangly youth with large, smoky-grey eyes and the same color hair that hung down over his face, reached up and pulled a sticker burr from his hair. "My dad says the next time I get caught on the ranch, I'm getten' the razor strap."

"Well, yer on it now, so what's the difference if yer on it here or over at the water trough?" said Alvin, unsnapping the metal fasteners and pulling down his overalls.

"The difference is that he ain't gonna catch me up here cause he can't drive that pickup truck up the side of the mountain. But he sure as heck can drive it over to the Rose Station trough."

"Aw, he don't know we're up here," replied Alvin, pulling out his penis and sending a stream into a bed of golden poppies. "He always knows when we go to the trough. That breed got some kind'a secret way of knowing stuff," declared Gerald.

"Aw, he'll be down there for hours. We got plenty'a time to hike over and take a swim. Whatta ya say?" pleaded Jessie, pulling on his knapsack.

"Just think how good that water is gonna feel," encouraged Alvin, maneuvering his stream over the tops of the poppies to assure that each got a share.

"Tell ya what. Let's flip for it, okay?" suggested Jessie. He was the unofficial gang leader but always managed to make it seem as though all members of the group were involved in a democratic decision making process. Jessie didn't do it because he wanted to be boss. It was just natural that he could make things come out to the benefit of all and more importantly, the most fun.

The three skeptics Bobbie, Jack and Gerald, looked at each other for an indication of the other's resolve. Someone blinked, and all three heads nodded in agreement.

Jessie dug into his overall pocket and pulled out a coin. "Okay, if Injun head comes up, we go." He flipped the coin, caught it, and covered it with his other hand. When everyone had gathered in close, he jerked the covering hand off the silver nickel. Although worn thin, the Indian head was plainly visible. Jessie was pleased because he wanted to go swimming, and he knew Alvin did. So he was gambling the coin would come up heads.

"Yea! Let's go!" shrieked Alvin, pulling up his coveralls as he started off down the trail in a fast walk. With reservations relegated to history, at least for the moment, the others fell in line.

There were numerous watering troughs on the Grapevine Ranch, any one of which was acceptable for a dip on a hot summer day. But the only one big enough for a little swimming and splashing around was over at the old Rose Station stage stop. It was a circular, galvanized iron tank almost three feet deep and fifteen feet in diameter. The only problem being that it was a pretty good hike over there. And it was down off the mountain where Juan Martinez could drive his pickup.

Old Rose Station had been the last stop before entering Tejon Pass on the overland stage route back in the 1800s. The route started at Sacramento, and went south through the San Joaquin Valley to Bakersfield and over the Tehachapi Mountains to Los Angeles. Time and the elements had taken their toll, but the old adobe stage house, minus its roof, still stood beside the water trough. The water was piped down to the trough from a spring on the ridge just above the station. Where it overflowed and seeped into the ground alongside the old stage house ruins, a vine of wild roses grew, which was why they called it Rose Station.

There was a romantic tragedy told by the Grapevine folks about Old Rose Station. It involved a dashing young rider who stopped there one day to water his horse and was smitten with the station keeper's daughter. He saw her standing beside the rose bush, and when they looked into each other's eyes, it was love at first sight. The stranger stayed at the station that night, and in the moonlight beside the rose bush, he and the girl kissed passionately and professed their love.

The next morning, a posse arrived on the trail of the notorious California outlaw, Joaquin Murieta. His description fit that of the handsome stranger, but before they could capture him, he escaped on his black stallion. A few nights later, he slipped back to the station and met his love at the rose bush. The station keeper overheard their plans to elope, and not wanting his daughter to be involved with an outlaw, he tipped off the posse.

That night when the lovers met at the rose bush, the posse was waiting. After a gun battle, the stranger escaped, but the girl was killed by a stray bullet. There were rumors that Joaquin Murieta was later gunned down by the posse. Another version held that he escaped, and sometimes on a moonlit night, he could be seen standing beside the wild rose bush at Old Rose Station with tears in his eyes.

On this afternoon, the good part of a century after the tragedy, about a dozen white faced Herefords were in the yard of Old Rose Station. Some were drinking from the trough or licking the yellow salt licks, while others just stood switching their tails contentedly; and rightly so, since it was their water trough and their salt licks. But on occasion in the summer, they were forced to relinquish their rights to a strange group of trespassers who always came charging down the trail screaming like banshees.

When they heard the first screech, on this hot summer afternoon, their white faces jerked up as they wheeled pretty much in unison, and scrambled off to a safe distance, turned, and watched the invaders leave a trail of overalls and tennis shoes along their route to the trough.

A few of the Herefords flinched at a new series of shrieks and whoops that came from the intruders when their naked bodies hit the cold spring water. But other than an occasional bawl of protest, they stood switching their tails and watching as the five boys laughed and romped in the water trough.

They had been watching for almost an hour when their resident bull came plodding down the trail. He was a big curly- faced fellow with long sharp horns. Shouldering his way through their ranks, he halted and surveyed the scene before him. A couple of heifers bawled and snorted to let him know they expected him to do something about the situation.

"Hey look, big daddy's arrived and is given us the evil eye," said Jack, pulling himself up to the rim of the trough.

"Yeah an' he looks pretty darn mean," observed Gerald, edging up beside Jack and looking at the bull, who had began to snort and paw the ground.

"Well let' em look. He can't get us in here," scoffed Alvin, playing with the stream of water from the pipe that fed the trough.

"I don't know about that. He could jump right over this trough if he wanted to," worried Bobbie.

"He can't do that," assured Jessie, holding the edge of the trough and kicking the water.

"He might. Remember that bull last summer that jumped the fence and chased us up a tree?" recalled Jack.

"He didn't jump the fence. He ran right through it," corrected Jessie.

"Well, he could probably run right through this trough too."

"Sometimes you guys act like a bunch of sissies. That ole bull is just showin' off for the heifers. I could run him off easy," proclaimed Alvin, putting his hand partially over the water pipe and squirting a stream of water at Jack.

"Yeah, sure you could," challenged Bobby.

"Wanna bet?" accepted Alvin, redirecting the squirting water at Bobbie.

"Sure."

"How much?"

"I'll bet ya a nickel."

"You got a nickel?"

"I can get one."

"Sure you can."

"You got a nickel?"

Both boys glanced at Jessie. Everyone knew that he possessed the only nickel among them. Jessie shook his head. "I ain't loaning my nickel for no dumb bet like that."

"Don't matter. I'll chase him off anyway," said Alvin, standing up in the trough, with water up to his waist.

"What ya gonna do?" worried Jack.

"I'm gonna run him off just like I said," replied Alvin, moving over to the rim of the trough that faced the bull.

"Alvin, come on, don't mess with that ole bull," counseled Jessie.

"Just watch me, Jess!"

Leaping over the rim of the trough, Alvin raised his arms over his head, let out a blood-curdling yell, and ran headlong at the bull.

The bull may have hesitated a fraction longer than the heifers, but give or take a second or two, he turned in panic and scrambled off in the same cloud of dust with his harem.

"Gosh, ya gotta admit, Alvin ain't scared of nothin'," admired Gerald, as they watched the naked, grinning Alvin plod back through the scuffed turf and cow dung on his triumphant return to the water trough.

"It's probably the injun blood in him," said Bobby.

"I'd bet," agreed Jack.

"Yeah, his grammy was full-blooded Tejon injun, ya know."

When Alvin arrived back at the trough, he washed the cow dung off his feet, and then jumped over the rim into the water.

Bobbie said, "Alvin, I owe you a nickel. You really did scare that ole bull."

"Naw, you don't owe me. We didn't shake on it."

"We made a bet."

"But ya gotta shake on it ta make it official."

"Alvin's right, Bobbie. Ya gotta shake on it," confirmed Jack.

"Do you think you're brave because yer part injun?" asked Gerald from where he sat on the bottom on the trough, which brought the water up to just below his chin.

"I guess so," Alvin replied, then lowered himself into the water and let out a whoop. "The water is colder when ya get out then back in."

"Oh no, look! A rider's comin!" warned Jessie, hunching down in the water.

"Where?" asked Gerald, as the others ducked down in the water also.

Before Jessie could answer, they all saw the rider come around the old adobe stage house and into view- and they knew they were trapped. The rider was between the trough and their clothes- there was no escape. All they could do was duck down and hope that he was blind or something and wouldn't see them.

The rider was small framed and slender and wearing a wide-brimmed, black Stetson hat with a silver-studded band. He sat in the saddle in a way that marked him as an expert rider.

The boys pulled their heads down as far as possible behind the rim of the trough and watched him rein his glistening Palomino to a halt a few yards from the trough. Slipping out of the saddle in a graceful, easy movement, he reached back and pulled a .30-caliber rifle out of its scabbard.

"Okay, come on out of there," said a voice, so different from what those hunched in the water were expecting, they were speechless. It was a girl's voice!

The girl pumped a cartridge into the chamber of the rifle. It sounded like she was loading cannon. "We can't," croaked Jessie. "We don't have any clothes on."

"Well, isn't that a shame," said the girl.

She wore grey jodhpurs and a bright orange shirt with a matching kerchief around her neck. The Stetson was pulled down low on her forehead, and with the sun at her back, her face was in shadow. Raising the rifle to her shoulder, she said, "You realize that I have the right to blow your dumb heads off because you're trespassing on private property."

"Yes, uh, we know, but if you'll let us get our clothes, we'll leave real quick," promised Jessie.

"Oh, you're going to leave all right, one way or another," said the girl, now sounding like an executioner. "What I don't understand is why you people don't have any respect for the property rights of others. Why is that? Would you tell me?"

The trespassers, huddled behind the rim of the water trough, looked at each other. Finally, Jessie spoke. "Well, it ain't that we don't respect your property rights. It's just that..."

"Oh'sure. How many times has our Mr. Martinez chased you off our ranch? Huh?"

"Well, we ain't hurtin' nothin', Just takin' a little swim," voiced Alvin.

"Oh, we ain't hurtin' nothin'," she mimicked. "What about those poor cattle standing out there dying of thirst?"

"They ain't dying of thirst. We only been here about an hour," replied Alvin.

"My father has been patient with you locals, overlooking your violations of our property rights. But he is running out of patience' and I don't blame him. Now you little ruffians get off our ranch and you stay off, or I promise, the next time I will shoot you."

The ruffians watched with open mouths as the girl turned on her heel and walked back to her horse. She slipped the rifle back into its scabbard, then pulled off her Stetson, and shook her head. A batch of yellow blond hair fell down around a face that was so beautiful it took one's breath away. The only mar any of the ruffians could see was that she had something in her mouth that glistened: like she had some kind of silver on her teeth. But it was of small consequence compared to the rest of her awesome beauty.

After the girl rode off, the boys got out of the trough, put on their clothes, and fell in line on the trail with little conversation. It was as though each wanted to savor his own private thoughts about the girl. When they reached the summit of the trail, just before it started down into the canyon where they all lived along the Grapevine, they halted and flopped down into the grass.

"That's the prettiest girl I ever seen!" declared Gerald.

"Yeah, she is something again!" agreed Alvin.

"She's a gillion times prettier than any of those dumb looking girls at our school," pronounced Jack.

"Yeah, but she wasn't so pretty when she was fixin to shoot us," reminded Bobbie.

Alvin shook his head. "Aw, I knew she wasn't gonna shoot us, did you think, Jess?"

Jessie shook his head. "No. She's too pretty to shoot somebody. That girl is probably the prettiest girl in Kern County."

All heads nodded because Jessie's opinion usually carried the most weight.

"Where do ya suppose she came from? I ain't never seen her around here before," said Bobbie.

"Me either," agreed Jack.

"She probably lives at the new Ranch headquarters. My dad says they just built a big hacienda out there for the big shot that runs the ranch," informed Gerald.

"No foolin? Ya suppose she's the big shot's daughter?"

"I bet she is," agreed Bobbie.

"If she is, she'd go to Grapevine School in the fall," declared Jack.

"I sure hope so," sighed Jessie.

Chapter

~2~

One of the reasons they paved the Grapevine road was so oil companies could construct pipelines through Tejon Pass from the San Joaquin Valley oil fields to the refineries in Los Angeles. These new refineries needed all the oil they could get to make gasoline, as Los Angeles was fast becoming the automobile showcase of the world.

Now, that didn't all happen by accident. "The City of the Angels" was the perfect place to show off the modern, mass-produced automobile, thanks to a modest climate and, of course, Hollywood. Now that "talkies" were the rage, movie goers could not only see Douglas Fairbanks or Jean Harlow driving their shiny new cars down the palm-lined streets of Beverly Hills, they could hear them talking about it.

Through a covert payola arrangement between a group of enterprising Los Angeles politicians and some imaginative marketing gurus in Detroit, they ripped up one of the most advanced and efficient mass transit systems in the country, the "Red Car Electric Railway," and built highways and then "freeways."

The pipelines were constructed alongside the Grapevine road and ran from the oil fields like Kern River and Lost Hills, over the Tehachapi Mountains to Los Angeles. The crude oil was heated and pumped by huge Allis Chalmers steam pumps, housed in pumping stations along the pipeline.

Other than the Ranch folks, hardly anyone lived along there before the pipeline came. But a twenty-four-hour crew was required to run the pumping stations, so the General Petroleum Oil Company and the Pan American Oil Company built a half dozen houses for their employees and families at each station every five or six mile along the pipeline. That resulted in the birth of a small community.

About half way up the canyon was "Grapevine Store." Mr. Switzner, the proprietor, sold a little bit of everything. He also served as the U.S. Post Master and when they paved the road, he put in two gas pumps. All the local folks traded there because Bakersfield, the closest town, was way off down in the valley.

Jessie's father worked at one of the pumping stations called Rose Station, named after the old overland stage stop. Jack's father worked at Grapevine Station, and Alvin's father was at Emidio Station. It was named after an Indian chief, but no one knew if Chief Emidio was any relation to Alvin's grandmother. Gerald's father was in charge of the state road maintenance facility at Wheeler Ridge. Bobbie's father worked at the Lebec Station which was just before the top of the pass and supposedly was named after a French trapper.

The elementary school for the children who lived along the Grapevine was down the canyon a couple miles from the store at a place where the road crossed Grapevine Creek. Its official name was Kern County Grammar School #34, but everyone called it Grapevine School.

It was a square, red-brick building, with one large classroom and a small apartment on one end that served as the lone teacher's living quarters. The teacher was Miss Abigail Trembell. It was her first job, and she came directly from college to Grapevine after the previous teacher, Mr. Hubbard, was killed when his car went through the railing on Dead Man's Curve. Four other drivers had met the same fate on that curve, but poor Mr. Hubbard was the only local ever killed there.

Miss Trembell was a pretty young woman with pink cheeks, violet eyes, and wavy brown hair. Some folks said they didn't think she would like being stuck out on the Grapevine and probably wouldn't last long. They also doubted she could handle some of the older boys, being so young and all- but as it turned out, Miss Trembell did just fine. She was a dedicated teacher, and since all the boys, young and old, were smitten with her, she had no trouble with them.

The requirement to teach all subjects in eight grades simultaneously was not easy, but Miss Trembell established a system that worked well. It was based on a simple method, long lost to modern teaching, called discipline.

Miss Trembell caused a stir in 1933 when she bought herself a Model-A Ford. This changed her image some, and it was even rumored that when she drove off down the road on a Friday afternoon and didn't return until Sunday, she was having an affair with her lover in Bakersfield. If she was, no one ever caught her.

Since it was a county school, the Kern County School Board approved the purchase of a small bus that went up and down the Grapevine picking up the children and depositing them at the school. The bus driver was Quincy Carver. He was tall, dark, and handsome. There was even a rumor for a while that something might have been going on between him and Miss Trembell, but Mr. Switzner said that wasn't true because Quincy was totally dedicated to his wife and children. Being the owner of the country store, Mr. Switzner's opinion carried a lot of weight, so the rumor died out.

After Labor Day of 1934, Miss Trembell began her sixth year at Grapevine School. She had started there in 1929 just before the Great Depression. This year, thirty-eight pupils enrolled for the fall semester.

Across the Atlantic Ocean in Germany thirty eight thousand Nazis gave Adolph Hitler a standing ovation after one of his tirades. It was on Movietone News reel in the new Fox Theater in Bakersfield. Nobody paid much attention to it though because everybody said there was no way America was going to get involved in another European war. It had only been seventeen years since World War I, the last European war.

After the bus arrived that morning and Mr. Carver and Miss Trembell smiled at each other and talked for a while, Miss Trembell got out her brass bell and rang it crisply. This was the signal to assemble at the front door. Then at her command, all the students marched up the cement steps into the classroom and took their assigned seats in one of the eight rows. Sometimes, when there were too many in a grade, some pupils would have to sit in the row with another grade. This year it came out just right, and each grade had a row of its own.

"Class, we have a new pupil," Miss Trembell announced after the Pledge of Allegiance. "Please say hello to Miss Michelle Parker- she's in the seventh grade."

Everyone said hello in chorus and looked at the new arrival, who sat in the third seat of the seventh row. That was across from Jessie and directly behind Alvin.

It was a big disappointment to Jessie and his friends that the new girl was not the beautiful girl from the Grapevine Ranch. But Michelle was pretty and had one rather noticeable feature: early mammary gland development. Some of the seventh and eighth grade girls had sizeable bumps at the top of their dresses, but not like Michelle: hers stuck way out.

"Before we have our vacation report, I have a few announcements," said Miss Trembell after Michelle's introduction. "I'm sure everyone noticed that Mr. Carver has built some outside tables where we can eat lunch." Besides driving the bus, Mr. Carver did things like that around the school house.

"I expect everyone to use them. He also put up brand new blackboards. Isn't that nice?" Everyone nodded. "I've gone over our rules with Michelle, and I'm sure the rest of you haven't forgotten them, but there are a couple that seem to dim over the summer so I'll briefly review them. Number one: no talking in class without permission. Two: raise your hand if you wish to speak. Three: only two at a time in the lavatory. And finally: no animals, reptiles, or birds in the class room. Are there any questions?"

There weren't any.

"All right then. Jessie, as the oldest boy in the eighth grade this year, you will be responsible to supervise the boys recess recreation program. (He was the only boy in the eighth grade that year) And Irene, as the oldest girl, you will supervise the girls. And when I ring the bell, I expect immediate termination of activities. Now, who would like to tell their vacation experience?"

Several hands went up. Miss Trembell picked one of the third graders who marched up to the front of the room and began to babble something about visiting her aunt in Cucamonga, wherever that was.

Without turning his head, so it would appear that he was listening, Jessie glanced across at Michelle Parker. After the Ranch girl, she looked kind of plain, but he had to admit she had the biggest titties of any girl on the Grapevine.

Jessie and his friends had always considered girls a pain in the neck for the most part. But lately, for some unknown reason, they seemed to be talking about girls. When his older cousin Glenn showed him a secret picture of a naked girl, it had stirred up some excitement Jessie hadn't experienced before. As he looked at Michelle now, trying to imagine what she would look like naked, he felt a touch of that same excitement.

It concerned Jessie that he had begun thinking these kinds of thoughts lately. He was pretty sure it was a violation of his Boy Scout oath which required that you keep yourself morally straight at all times. So he told himself he should stop it, but he wasn't having much success as thoughts about girls kept popping into his head.

He forced himself to turn his eyes back to the third grader who was still babbling on about Cucamonga. He decided he would have to talk to Alvin about it at recess. He and Alvin were best friends, and Alvin was not only the bravest of all his friends, but he also knew a lot of stuff.

The school playground extended back to a fence along the edge of a ravine where Grapevine Creek ran. The girls played games on one end of the playground, and the boys had a baseball diamond on the other end. Most of the boys wanted to play work-up baseball at the mid-morning recess, so Jessie gave his approval.

When he saw Miss Trembell headed for her bell about a half hour later, he gave Alvin a secret signal, and he slugged the ball over the fence, as Alvin could always do. That meant he and Alvin were allowed to go out through the gate and down the hill to the creek to find the ball- while everyone else went back to class. Miss Trembell was wise to their little ploy, but she let them get away with it on occasion because they maintained a good deal of control over the other boys.

It only took a couple minutes to find the ball, as usual, so that gave them at least ten minutes to throw rocks at the Pollywogs- all there was in Grapevine Creek. But on this day the Pollywogs got off easy because both Jessie and Alvin had other things on their mind.

"Alvin, why do you suppose that Ranch girl didn't come to school?" asked Jessie as soon as they reached the place in the creek where the school house was out of sight.

"I dunno, Jess. But I bet she's in high school," replied Alvin, picking up a rock from the creek.

"Yeah, that's probably why," agreed Jessie with a sigh of disappointment. "I was sure hoping she'd be in Grapevine School. She is the prettiest girl I ever seen."

"That's for sure. But I kind of figured she was older. I mean, she's got that older girl look- know what I mean?"

Jessie nodded. "She does all right. I'll ask my cousin Glenn if she rides on the high school bus."

"Good idea," agreed Alvin, throwing his rock into the creek.

Jessie recovered another rock and weighed in his hand a minute. "Alvin, what do you think of that new girl, Michelle?"

Alvin glanced across the creek at Jessie with a sparkle in his dark eyes and the hint of a smile. "Well, she's not as pretty as the Grapevine Ranch girl, but she's got big titties."

Jessie grinned. "Alvin, she's got the biggest ones on the Grapevine."

"Yeah you can say that again, Jess."

Both boys threw rocks at the pollywogs.

"Alvin, would you like to see Michelle Parker's titties in the raw?"

Alvin's black Indian eyes met Jessie's intense green eyes. "I would, that's for sure... Wouldn't you?"

Jessie nodded. "Yeah, I would too. But I think that's against the Boy Scout Oath."

Alvin looked down at the creek, thought for a moment, then nodded. "I think so, Jess."

Jessie sighed, picked up another rock, and studied it. "Well, I wonder if it would be all right if ya just looked at 'em an didn't touch 'em?"

Alvin juggled his rock for a minute. "I kinda think that if ya looked at 'em, you'd want to touch em...Don't you?"

Jessie hurled his rock into the creek. "Yeah...I guess." What'a ya suppose it'd be like to touch 'em?"

"She probably wouldn't let ya."

"Probably. But high school girls will, if ya kiss 'em good."

"If ya kiss em?"

"Yeah. My cousin Glenn told me a high school girl in Bakersfield let him touch hers after he kissed her good."

"I guess high school girls will let ya do stuff like that. And just think, Jess, you'll be in high school next year."

"Yeah, I wish you were too."

Although Alvin was the same age as Jessie, he'd lost a school year when he caught typhoid fever in 1931.

"Alvin, you ever kissed a girl?"

"Naw, have you?"

"Naw."

"Would you like to kiss that girl, Michelle?"

Jessie looked across the creek at Alvin and, after a hesitation, nodded. "Yeah, I think I would. You think she would?"

"Well, if she liked ya, she might."

"You think she likes me?"

Alvin hesitated. "Well, I seen her lookin at you."

"Ya did?"

"Yep."

"I wish I knew something about kissin."

"Aw, that man stuff comes naturally Jess," declared Alvin.

Chapter

~3~

It was a Saturday morning custom for the Grapevine gang to have a meeting at their secret cave in the canyon behind old Fort Tejon. The cave was far enough up the canyon that nobody ever went there, and it was big enough after you crawled in to sit around a bonfire Indian style. It got a little smoky sometimes, depending on which way the wind was blowing, but most of the smoke was drawn out through an opening in the top of the cave, just like an Indian tepee. It was a great cave and in a perfect location: about halfway from where all the boys lived along the Grapevine.

Transportation was not a problem for the boys. California State Route 99, "The Grapevine Road," was the main artery between the San Joaquin Valley and Los Angeles, so there were always trucks going both ways. The highway had a six-percent grade from the top of Tejon Pass at Gorman, down to the foot of the mountains at Wheeler Ridge.

In 1934, the trucks going up the grade moved along at about ten miles per hour in low gear. It was as fast as they could go, and since most of the trucks were open in the back, it was a lead pipe cinch to jump on one, ride to wherever you wanted to go, and hop off. The truck drivers just ignored the boys riding on the back of their trucks because it was too much trouble to stop and chase them off and then have to shift through all those gears to get going again.

Going down hill was even worse because if a driver missed a gear, the truck would run away and crash into Grapevine Creek because those old band-type brakes wouldn't hold a loaded truck on a 6 percent grade. So the drivers had to keep it in low gear no matter which way they were going, which was great for the Grapevine boys.

This Saturday the gang had invited a guest, Danny Switzner. Danny was a skinny little sixth grader who wanted desperately to become a member of the secret cave club, but the qualification for membership was to go swimming in one of the Ranch water troughs without getting caught and, of course, keep it secret. Danny hadn't passed that test yet.

He was invited to the cave on this Saturday because the boys had asked him to see if he could find out something about the Ranch girl. Danny could find out stuff like that since his father ran the store and post office and knew about everything that went on up and down the Grapevine.

"Her name is Hallie Lamont," Danny announced proudly after he, Jessie, and the rest of the gang assembled in the cave and had the bonfire going.

"Hallie Lamont," repeated Jessie reverently. "Wow, what a neat name."

"It is a neat name," agreed Alvin, poking a stick into the fire.

"Sounds kinda like one of those girls in King Arthur and Knights of the Round Table," said Gerald.

"Well, I like Penny better, but Hallie is a pretty name all right," agreed Bobbie.

"I don't know why you like Penny, Bobbie. She's in high school, and besides, she's going with Bud Carver," said Jack.

"Who says she is?" flared Bobbie.

"Frank Grover says so. And he knows cause he goes with Virginia, and her and Penny are best friends."

"Aw, that don't mean nothin'," scoffed Bobbie.

"Oh, yes it does. High school girls don't like grammar school guys. And she sits beside Bud all the way to Bakersfield on the high school bus. So you ain't got a chance," proclaimed Jack.

"Yeah, well, just wait till I get in high school you'll see."

"So what else did you find out, Danny?" asked Jessie. "Well, her father is the big shot at the Grapevine Ranch, and they live in that new hacienda they built over at the new ranch headquarters."

"No foolin'?"

"Yeah. You know they got a real swimming pool out there?"

"Wow!" exclaimed Jack.

"I ain't ever seen it, but my dad went over there once, and he says it's really something," informed Gerald.

"Don't she have to go to school?" asked Jack.

"Oh, she goes to a private high school in Los Angeles," said Danny, pleased that he was the primary source of authoritative information.

"Well, how can she do that if she lives there on the ranch?" asked Jessie, sensing the bad news of Danny's report was about to come.

"Oh, she lives in Los Angeles where she goes to school. She only lives up here in the summer time."

Jessie's spirits took a nose dive. He'd been disappointed that she wasn't the new girl at school, and now to find out that she only lived there in the summer was a real bummer.

It was quiet for a moment in the Indian cave. "That girl is prettiest girl I ever seen," mused Jack.

"She is that all right," agreed Alvin. "But ya gotta face it, she is a rich girl, and she ain't gonna have nothin to do with guys like us."

"Yeah, and remember, she said she would shoot us if she ever caught us on the ranch again," reminded Gerald.

"But that girl is so pretty I bet the bullets in her gun wouldn't even hurt ya," declared Jack.

That brought a guffaw as a piece of live oak popped loudly from the bonfire sending a fiery little comet shooting across the cave.

Miss Trembell always had a Christmas play at the school house, and it was a major social event. Every boy and girl in all eight grades had a part, and everybody on the Grapevine attended except the on-duty crew at the pumping stations.

The gang all agreed that plays were sissy stuff, but they liked it because school work went on the back burner during that whole week before the play. Miss Tremble said that if something was worth doing, it was worth doing right.

This year, Miss Trembell chose Jessie to play the role of Joseph because he was the oldest. It turned out that wasn't as bad as he first imagined because she chose Michelle to play Mary.

Since Jessie had resolved to forget beautiful Hallie Lamont, he had been looking for some way to get friendly with Michelle. But up to the time they began practicing for the play, he'd not made much progress. At recess the boys didn't mix with the girls, and Miss Trembell was death on talking in class, so all he'd been able to do was give her an occasional admiring glance. And he'd been encouraged because she had smiled back at him sometimes.

Jessie's first opportunity to talk to Michelle privately came when Miss Trembell sent them out to the lunch tables to practice their lines for the play. It was the chance Jessie had been waiting for, butonce he sat down opposite her, he'd become paralyzed and tongue-tied.

After they stared at their scripts for a while, Michelle finally said, "Are you glad you're Joseph, Jessie?"

He looked up at her. "Oh,- yeah. I'm glad. You glad you're Mary?"

"Oh yes, I'm glad. Aren't you?"

"Yeah. I'm glad you're Mary."

"I'm glad you're Joseph."

Both looked at the scripts on the table in front of them. "I was one of the wise men last year. It was easy," said Michelle.

"Hey, so was I... Where'd you go to school last year?"

"At Standard School in Oildale."

"Where is that?"

"You don't know where Oildale is?"

He shook his head.

"It's not too far from Bakersfield, in the Kern River oil fields. At Standard School, they have a teacher for every grade."

"You're kidding."

"No. And they have a different room for each grade."

"You're kidding."

"No. And we had movies in the auditorium every week."

"Real movies?"

"Yes. I didn't want to come here, but Papa got transferred."

"Oh. Well, it's neat here on the Grapevine. We do a lot of neat stuff."

"Not like in Oildale."

Silence. "Well, uh, I'm glad you came."

"You are?"

"Sure."

She smiled. "I might like it better after a while."

"I'm sure you will. Hey, you want me to pass you a note?" Sensing her uncertainty, Jessie explained. "It's okay. I know how to pass a note without getting caught."

Even though Michelle appeared apprehensive over Jessie's proposal, a sparkle in her blue eyes said she would like very much to get a note from Jessie.

"I'll do it after lunch," promised Jessie.

One of the more daring and exciting things to do in Miss Trembell's school was writing and passing a note. If you got caught, it was big trouble, and it seemed that Miss Trembell had eyes in the back of her head. So Jessie's promise was dangerous because he didn't want to jeopardize his special status. But he was proficient in note passing, and it was a chance to really impress Michelle- and suddenly, that seemed important.

She might even be impressed enough to meet him on Saturday afternoon and they could walk down to the creek and under the bridge over the Grapevine Road. Then, well, if she really liked him, maybe she would even let him kiss her.

The thought of kissing Michelle Parker aroused some exciting feelings in Jessie Rascoe. He wanted to kiss her all right, yet it was scary. But if Alvin was right and you had to do it to get anywhere with a girl, then he had to do it. And for reasons Jessie didn't quite understand, he did want to get somewhere with a girl. So it was settled: he would write Michelle a note after lunch period.

It all worked out pretty well. Jessie's note passing was up to par, and Michelle, although nervous, was thrilled at receiving it. In the note, he asked her to go for a walk to the creek on Saturday. Michelle wasn't quite brave enough to answer the note, but at their next Christmas play practice, she radiantly accepted.

Jessie decided to keep his plan a secret except to tell Alvin, who was almost as excited about it as Jessie. All through the rest of that week Jessie's thoughts centered on what he was going to do on his first "date." But even after many discussions with Alvin, he'd not settled on a specific plan. He'd decided to trust in Alvin's advice that it was man stuff and he would know what to do when the time came.

When Saturday finally arrived, Jessie's mother wanted to know why he'd put on his best pair of jeans and a clean shirt. He didn't like to fib to his mom, but he'd made Alvin take a vow of secrecy so he couldn't tell his mother. His dilemma was solved by his younger brother, Billy.

"I know where he's goin'," sing-songed Billy. "He's goin' to see Har-ee-ut."

Jessie gave his brother a dagger look there in the bedroom the brothers shared.

Eula Rascoe smiled and said, "Oh? Are you going to practice the Christmas play?" Everybody on the Grapevine knew that Jessie and Michelle had the lead roles in the play.

"Uh, well, we're gonna talk about it." They probably would, so it wasn't an out-an-out fib.

"That's nice. But we're going to Bakersfield this afternoon after your father is off work, so be here by five and not a minute later," instructed Eula, a tall, willowy woman with the same intense green eyes as her two sons.

"Aw, Mom, do I have to go?"

"Yes, you do. Your aunt Myrtle invited us to dinner, and she expects the whole family."

After his mother had left the bedroom the two brothers shared, Jessie whirled and glared at his brother. "You see, Billy, that's why we won't let you sixth graders go to our secret cave. You can't keep secrets!"

"Oh yeah. How come you let Danny go? He's only in the sixth grade."

"That was a special deal, but he ain't gone with us to the ranch yet. I'm tellin' ya, you ain't never goin' with us if you can't keep secrets."

"It ain't no secret. Everybody knows yer gonna go see Michelle today," replied Billy, flopping down on his bed and tossing and catching a baseball. At eleven, he wasn't as tall as his brother, but he was huskier with darker hair and eyes. The two brothers had played together as children and were compatible, but now Jessie and his friends considered sixth graders just too young and silly to share in their secrets.

"Everybody knows?"

"Yeah."

That upset Jessie because he knew Alvin wouldn't have told, so it could only mean Michelle was a blabbermouth. That was bad, but not bad enough to overcome the urgent necessity to make his first attempt at kissing a girl. That had become paramount on Jessie's agenda.

He hopped a truck at his favorite spot: just as it started around Dead Man's Curve. That was where several drivers had met disaster including two runaway trucks. It was the sharpest curve on the Grapevine, and the trucks were at their slowest there. The drivers had to watch the road intently as they steered around it, so it was easy for Jessie to swing onto the back.

The truck was carrying burlap sacks full of grain. They were soft and pliable, so it was easy to scoot down into a comfortable position so no one could see you and you could just lie there and look up at the mountains and sky.

Jessie loved riding a truck up the Grapevine. The whine of the engine had a special sound that was like music to his ears and gave him a warm, good feeling. He also liked watching the changing colors and silhouette shapes of the mountains passing across the blue sky as the truck labored up the Grapevine. Jessie had always been fascinated with those things, and he guessed that was why he was sure he wanted be an artist someday.

On this day, however, Jessie had other things on his mind. He was thinking about the momentous event that lay ahead, still trying to visualize just how he was going to proceed in the business of kissing his first girl. By the time he had swung off the truck about twenty minutes later, he'd built up a good deal of apprehension.

But Jessie was determined. He marched up to the Parker house there at the Lebec pumping station where Michelle's father worked and knocked resolutely on the front door.

Mrs. Parker answered the door. She had a nice smile and seemed friendly. She said something about how nice it was that he had come to visit, but Jessie wasn't listening. He was looking at Michelle, who was standing beside her mom dressed in a red-and-orange pleated skirt and a matching frilly blouse. Her light brown hair was in long curls with a red ribbon at the back. She seemed to sparkle, and when she smiled at Jessie, he felt that same excitement that he'd experienced lately whenever he was around a girl.

After promising to be back in two hours, they walked off with Jessie leading the way down the hill to the Grapevine road. The bridge Jessie had in mind was about a mile up the road from the Lebec pumping station.

"I'm glad you came, Jessie," Michelle said, stepping up next to him. They were walking along on the grassy trail that ran between the road and the Grapevine Ranch barbed wire fence where the Keep Out signs was posted.

"Me too," agreed Jessie.

They walked around an oak tree, Michelle on one side and Jessie on the other side.

"Bread and butter," said Jessie.

Michelle looked confused. "What does that mean?"

"When you walk around a tree like that you gotta say bread and butter or you will get bad luck," explained Jessie.

"Oh. They don't do that in Oildale."

"Well, I guess it's kind of different up here in the mountains."

"I guess so."

"Me an my friends hike a lot on the Grapevine Ranch."

"You do?"

"Yeah. Nothin' to it if you know how."

"Elinor told me they got a breed guard that will cut you if he catches you on the Ranch."

"Aw, that's ole Juan. He won't cut you even if he catches ya. And he can't catch us like he used to, now that we're bigger," said Jessie stopping to pick up a rock. "He only caught us once all summer," Jessie explained. Taking aim, he threw the rock at the nearest keep off sign.

"You hit it dead center!" Michelle exclaimed.

Jessie smiled. "I've had a lot of practice."

A truck loaded with machinery slowly passed by on the road, its engine screaming as it labored up the grade. It was one of those open cab Mac Trucks that had a big chain driving the wheels. The truck driver waved from his open cab. Jessie and Michelle waved back.

"How long did it take you to walk up to my house, Jessie?"

He glanced across at her, not sure if she were serious. "I didn't walk."

She looked puzzled. "Well, how did you get here?"

"On one of those," he said, pointing at the truck.

"You came on a truck?"

"Sure. On a grain truck."

Michelle looked skeptical, so Jessie explained how all the guys rode up and down the Grapevine on trucks- that was just the way they did it.

"Your parents let you do that?"

Jessie hesitated. "Not really. But all the guys know how to do it without getting caught. So nobody says anything."

"Golly. Isn't it dangerous?"

"Not if you know how to do it." Jessie was still explaining how things were done on the Grapevine when they arrived at the bridge. It was made of Monolith cement like the highway. Grapevine Creek ran through it, but there was plenty of room to walk in there beside the creek.

Michelle followed Jessie inside and they came to a halt at about the middle where it was darkest. It was quiet except for the soft gurgling of the creek. They stood looking at each other with an instinctive understanding that something special was about to happen- something daring and exciting.

Jessie sensed that Michelle was willing to do some things and despite the uncertainty of how to proceed, powerful forces were urging him on. He'd seen kissing in the movies, but something told him that's not how it was really done. Michelle had the same problem. She wanted to be kissed, but she too was unsure of how it should happen. Her instinct told her that Jessie was supposed to make the first move, so all she could do was wait and see.

"You can smell the wild mint from the creek real good in here," he said.

"Yes, it smells good," she agreed.

Another silence except for the creek sounds. Then suddenly: "Uh, Michelle, I...like you."

Surprised, but recovering quickly, Michelle said, "I like you too."

"Michelle?"

"Yes?"

"You want to kiss?"

There! He'd said it. He stood petrified, waiting for her answer while his heart pounded and the bridge rumbled from a truck passing overhead.

"If you want to," said Michelle softly.

Jessie felt an instant excitement. She had agreed! Now all he had to do was do it. He took a moment to compose himself and then stepped across the creek to where she stood. She was poised, waiting, and even in the semi-darkness he could see that she was watching him intently. He put his hands on her shoulders gently, leaned forward, and pressed his lips to hers.

It was the first kiss for both and produced all of those marvelous sensations that came with the first kiss of a teen age boy and girl.

Jessie had never experienced anything quite like what he felt when he kissed Michelle Parker. He had sensed that it was going to be something special when he kissed a girl, but this was beyond anything he had imagined. He could feel his heart beating faster, and there was a strange stirring down deep in his belly.

Perhaps not quite as intensely, but Michelle, too, was experiencing some exciting new feelings from her first kiss.

"Did you like it, Jessie?" she asked.

It took Jessie a moment to find his voice. "Uh, yeah. I did, Michelle. It was real good. You want to do it again?"

Eyes turned down. "If you want to."

He nodded and put his hands back on her shoulders, leaned over, and kissed her again, only this time a little longer. Then he moved closer to her and put his arms around her. She responded by putting her arms around him, and now the full impact of her touch, her warmth, and that unique girl fragrance that he'd only had hints of before, engulfed him.

This time they kissed like in the movies: holding each other and keeping their lips together longer. When they separated, both stepped back and stood silently for a moment with some powerful new feelings burgeoning inside.

After a moment, Michelle said, "You kissed girls before?"

He shook his head. "You kissed boys?"

She shook her head.

"It's great ain't it?"

She nodded.

"You want to do some more?"

"Do you?"

"Yeah."

"Me too."

They embraced again even more vigorously with their arms around each other and their bodies pressed together. This time Jessie could feel Michelle's breasts pressing against him and suddenly he became feverishly aware of a new burgeoning sensation.

Michelle, too, liked the exciting new feelings she was experiencing, but the caution flag went up when she felt something hard pressing into her. As much as she liked Jessie's kisses, instinct told her that hard thing was something she wasn't prepared to deal with, at least not at this point in time. So she tactfully backed away with the excuse that it was getting late and they had better start back or she would get in trouble.

So, savoring the wondrous experience of their first kisses, the two young lovers made their way out of the culvert and back down the road to the Lebec pumping station.

After he'd said good-bye to Michelle, Jessie hopped a truck carrying sacks of oranges and settled in for the ride back down the Grapevine. It wasn't as soft as the ride up on sacks of grain, but Jessie was in such a state, he hardly noticed. He could only think about the wondrous experience and the revelation that he'd just discovered a whole new world.

Jessie usually dropped off to sleep the minute his head hit the pillow, but that night he had trouble...a lot of trouble. He couldn't get Michelle off his mind, and each time he thought about kissing her, he got that same feeling he'd had in the culvert.

Jessie and Alvin had their own secret meeting place under a big oak tree on Grapevine Creek. It was where they met to discuss secret stuff they didn't want anybody else to know about. So the next day they met there and Jessie told Alvin the story of his momentous experience.

Alvin listened intently to every word, interrupting often with eager questions. Finally, when Jessie was finished Alvin said, "I guess that makes Michelle your girl-friend."

Jessie hesitated. "You think so?"

"Well, you kissed her and she kissed you back, right?"

Jessie nodded. "Yeah, she sure did."

"Well, that means she's yer girl friend."

Jessie nodded again. He wasn't sure if Alvin was right this time, but then, what he said made sense. So Jessie took Michelle Parker to be his girl friend and began to make plans to go on another date with her to the bridge. But fate stepped in, and things didn't turn out the way Jessie had planned.

First, the snow came right after Christmas that year, which foiled his plans. But the school play was a great success, and everybody on the Grapevine said that Jessie and Michelle were sensational in their parts in the 1934 Christmas play at Grapevine Grammar School.

Then right after Christmas, tragedy struck. The Pan American Oil Company had to lay off some workers because of the depression, and Mr. Parker was one of those. So the Parker family had to move to Los Angeles to live with relatives while Mr. Parker tried to find another job, except there wasn't any.

Chapter
~4~

The Great Depression had been going on for four years when 1935 rolled in. Millions in America were out of work and struggling to stay alive. "Hobo" camps had sprung up everywhere in Kern County, particularly along the Kern River.

Many of those in the camps were poor farmers from the Mid-west who had come to California in search of jobs on fruit and vegetable farms. But there were only so many jobs to be had, so when they couldn't find work, they built shacks out of cardboard, old rusted corrugated iron, abandoned car parts, or anything else they could find. They drank the river water and lived on carp fish, crawdads, and ground squirrels.

Scrawny, starved dogs and half naked children wandered around the filthy camps, looking for something to eat. Many slept in abandoned cars. In the summer, the camps were infested with flies and mosquitoes, and in the winter, a layer of wood smoke from camp fires burning old tires covered everything with soot.

There was no Social Security and no welfare available to those folks. The Salvation Army ran a soup kitchen, but even it was sporadic as donations were few because no one had any discretionary money to donate.

President Franklin Roosevelt, elected in 1933, finally got some things going like the Work Projects Administration (WPA) that began repairing buildings, parks, roads and such and they hired workers for a dollar a day. It was mostly unskilled, pick and shovel work, but it kept people from starving.

Fortunately, most of the folks on the Grapevine worked for the oil pipe line companies, and most were able to keep their jobs. The pay was only six to eight dollars a day, but that was sufficient to keep a family in the basic necessities, and the companies furnished living quarters. But there was little discretionary money and few luxuries.

The rare treat for most of those families was a drive to Bakersfield to purchase basics and attend a moving picture show, and perhaps even a Chinese or Italian dinner. A movie ticket was twenty five cents, and a Chinese dinner or Italian dinner for the Rascoe family of four, about a dollar and a half.

The primary adult social activity on the Grapevine was being associated with the PTA and school programs. The primary organized activity for boys in 1935 was the Boy Scouts of America.

All the boys who were old enough belonged, and those who weren't could hardly wait to turn twelve so they could join. The parents on the Grapevine also could hardly wait because it seemed that when they put on the scout uniform, an overnight transformation occurred in their sons: they magically discovered responsibility, discipline, courtesy, and all the other things their parents had been striving to teach them.

The General Petroleum Oil Company gave Boy Scout Troop 34 an old storage building there at the Grapevine Station for their barrack. The boys painted it and put displays of scout crafts and things on the walls. They held their weekly meeting there and once a year a "Court of Honor." All the parents came to admire the displays and see their sons receive the awards and merit badges they had earned during the year.

Jessie Rascoe, now fourteen, had earned the rank of a first class scout and was the Bear Patrol Leader. He took that responsibility seriously and conscientiously and since he didn't have a girlfriend anymore, he threw himself into his patrol leader duties. As soon as the snow was gone that spring of '35 he asked the scout master for permission to take his patrol on an unsupervised overnight camp out.

In addition to being the school bus driver, the school custodian, and a loyal husband and father, Quinton Carver was the Scoutmaster of Grapevine Troop Number 34. Quinton had his own style of running a scout troop, which was to give the boys plenty of latitude, while requiring strict adherence to the scout oath, the scout laws, and particularly the scout motto: "Be prepared."

"Okay, Jessie, you're old enough now to take your patrol on an unsupervised overnight," agreed scout master Carver. "But remember you have a couple of Tenderfoot scouts in your patrol, so keep that in mind in making your preparations."

"Yes sir. Bobbie and Danny are almost ready to pass their second-class tests, and I'll have three older first-class scouts: Alvin, Jack, and Gerald."

"All right. Where do you plan to go?"

"We'd like to hike into Bear Trap Canyon. Uh, would you get us permission from Mr. Martinez?"

Scoutmaster Carver hesitated. "Where in Bear Trap Canyon did you want to go, Jessie?"

"Oh, we'll just go to the Pete Miller Meadow and camp there."

Mr. Carver nodded. "Okay, that's a good place to camp. I'll get Mr. Martinez's permission for you to cross the ranch, but I don't want you to go any farther up the canyon than the meadow, okay?"

"Sure, Mr. Carver, that's as far as we'll go."

There were peculiar circumstances surrounding Bear Trap Canyon, which everyone on the Grapevine knew about. The canyon was on a parcel of government land that, for some unknown reason, had been excluded from the giant Spanish Land Grant that established the original Grapevine Ranch.

One of the cowboys who worked for the ranch, Jayson Hunter, had somehow discovered that fact, and when the ranch laid him off after the depression started, he filed a homestead claim in Bear Trap Canyon with the federal government and settled there with his family. There wasn't anything the Ranch could do about it, but the result was bad blood between Hunter and the ranch because Bear Trap Canyon was right in the middle of their finest grazing land. To make matters worse, the Ranch was forced by law to give Huntington an easement across their ranch land to get to and from his homestead.

Although the easement was nothing more than a cattle trail, it cut across the ranch and out to the state highway. That made it legally an open road, but the ranch maintained control over access with a fence and a locked gate at the entrance to the canyon. That's where Juan Martinez lived in a small cabin and, among his other duties, acted as gate keeper.

To maintain good relations, Mr. Carver would always ask Mr. Martinez if the Boy Scouts could go camping in Bear Trap Canyon even though they had a legal right to do so.

The other complication involving Bear Trap Canyon was about the Hunters themselves. They were mountain people who didn't mix with the Grapevine folks, and their ongoing feud with the ranch made them suspicious of anyone who came into the canyon.

Since the Hunter's homestead was on the upper end of the canyon, Mr. Carver would always have the boys camp on the lower end to make sure there were no problems. Naturally, this was intriguing to the boys, so an overnight in Bear Trap Canyon had a lot more going for it than just a plain camp out.

When Jessie marched his Bear Patrol up to the Martinez cabin dressed in full uniform and back pack that following Saturday morning, the breed came shuffling out of his cabin and looked them over silently.

"Hello, Mr. Martinez," said Jessie pleasantly.

"No swim in cattle trough. Keep off ranch property," he muttered in response.

"Yes sir. Don't worry, we're in uniform today, Mr. Martinez," replied Jessie.

Martinez looked at Jessie and nodded. Jessie had the impression that he saw the hint of a smile on the old breed's leathery face as he turned, opened the gate, and motioned for them to pass.

Indeed, Jessie had seen a smile. The boys may have been a fly in his ointment, but what no one on the Grapevine knew was that secretly, Martinez enjoyed it. He loved matching wits with the boys and the challenge they had given him over the years. It added a little spice to his otherwise mundane job of gate keeping and repairing fences and "Keep Off" signs. They also didn't know that he'd lost his wife and both sons in the great flu epidemic of World War I.

Jessie's Bear Patrol hiked to the Pete Miller Meadow that spring morning in a little over two hours, and that was record time. It was a challenging hike with a full pack on a trail that cut across ridges and down the side of steep canyons for nearly seven miles. It wasn't much of a trail, but after a hard winter, it was even worse.

"Okay, guys, that was a great hike. Let's set up camp first then we'll eat our lunch," instructed Jessie, after they'd all had a drink of the ice-cold water that bubbled out of a spring on one end of the meadow.

Pete Miller Meadow was named after an early California explorer who, as legend had it, was another of those who fell in love with a Tejon Indian maiden, married her, and lived there at the meadow in a tepee for many years.

Nestled in a narrow part of the canyon, the meadow was small but perfect for camping. In the springtime, it was always covered with lush green grass, batches of yellow buttercups, blue-violet lupines, and red-orange poppies. A grove of live oak and a thicket of willows rustled their leaves in the breeze that came down Bear Trap Canyon.

The scouts pitched their pup tents in a line on the grassy knoll at the south end of the meadow where the water ran down from the spring. Jessie and Alvin were in one tent, with Jack and Gerald in another, and the two tenderfeet, Bobbie and Danny, in the third. After their camp was in order, they flopped down in the grass and wild flowers to eat their lunch and plan their activities for the balance of the day.

"Boy, that's a rough trail! I don't know how the Hunters get that ole wagon of theirs in and out of here," observed Gerald, taking a bite of a peanut butter and jelly sandwich.

"I don't either," agreed Jessie with a mouthful of meat loaf sandwich. "But I guess they do because they come out to the store to get supplies once in a while, right, Danny?"

"Yeah, I've seen 'em, but they don't come very often."

"I was at the store once when Mr. Hunter came in his wagon to get supplies," added Jack, biting into an apple. "An' his two boys were with him. I tell you they are big, tough-lookin' guys."

"Whatta ya mean, Jack? What did they look like?" asked Gerald.

"They are huge guys, an' they got long hair like girls."

"Hair like girls!"

"Yes. And they got big, long guns."

"That's true," confirmed Danny. "They are wild-lookin' and they always carry those big long rifles. My dad says those are army guns like the ones they used in the war."

"Real army rifles?" asked Bobbie.

"Yeah," confirmed Danny biting into a candy bar.

"Have you ever seen them, Jessie?" asked Gerald.

Jessie shook his head as he put the last of his sandwich in his mouth.

"Me either," said Alvin, squinting his eyes as he contemplated the Hunters for a moment. "Jess, we gotta do a trail-following test. Let's do it up the canyon, and maybe we could see one of them."

Jessie shook his head since he had a mouthful of sandwich.

"Aw come on, Jess, we won't get too close to where they live."

"Can't do it. I told Mr. Carver we wouldn't go any farther up the canyon," Jessie explained when he'd finally swallowed the last bite.

The other scouts were curious about the Hunters. But they were secretly glad that Jessie had vetoed Alvin's proposal. Besides, they all knew they had to do what they promised, especially since they were wearing Boy Scout uniforms.

"Well, maybe they'll come down here," said Alvin. "I'd sure like to see one of them."

They flipped Jessie's Indian head nickel to see if they would do nature study or trail following that afternoon. Nature study won the toss. Being the patrol leader and having earned a nature merit badge, Jessie was the instructor and took pride in knowing the names of all the different flowers, trees, and weeds in the meadow. After that, he showed the Tenderfeet how to start a fire with flint stone and dry wood shavings. When the fire was going, he then demonstrated how to make a scout's stew.

Scout's stew was the Bear Patrol's favorite camp out dish because it was easy to fix and tasted great. You just throw the meat, potatoes, carrots and onions all in the pot of water, boil it for a while, and presto! It's ready to eat.

After the Scout's stew was all gone and their mess kits cleaned and put away, they gathered around the campfire. By now the canyon had turned to pitch black and the symphony of fascinating and mysterious sounds that always came at night on a camp out began to play. It was one of the best parts of being on an overnight camp out.

"Boy, it really gets black in this canyon at night," said Bobbie.

"Does Bear Trap Canyon really have bears in it?" asked Danny.

"I ain't ever seen any bears," replied Alvin. "But me and Jess saw a big wild cat the last time we were here, right, Jess?"

"Yeah, we did and you should'a heard him scream at us."

"What'a ya mean scream?" asked Bobbie.

"You know, like a house cat does when he's mad, only a lot louder."

"Do they attack people, at night?" asked Danny anxiously.

"No, they won't bother ya," assured Jessie.

"My dad says there's cougar in these mountains too, and they are really big and mean," informed Gerald.

"Well, that's what they say, but the scout manual says that wild animals won't bother you unless you bother them. The exception is a mother bear with cubs. You want to give her a wide berth," informed the Bear Patrol leader.

"Do mamma bears come out at night?" asked Bobbie.

"Yeah, they prowl around at night lookin' for something to eat," Alvin replied watching the affect on the Tenderfoot.

The Tenderfoot Scouts' eyes grew large.

Then Alvin added, "But they don't come here to the meadow."

"How come?" asked Danny and Bobbie in unison.

"Don't you know the legend of the Pete Miller Meadow?"

Both boys shook their heads.

Alvin got up, threw more wood on the fire, and sat down Indian style: cross legged. Squinting his dark eyes, he told the story. "When ole Pete Miller was exploring this canyon a long time ago, he saw a bear and decided to camp here and trap them. That's why they call it Bear Trap Canyon. One day he accidently stepped on one of his own traps, right here in this meadow. With one leg caught, there ain't no way you can open the jaws on a bear trap. So he lay there help-less and in awful pain for a long time until a Tejon Injun girl came along and found him. She got him out of the trap and fixed him up. When he was okay, they went over to her vil-lage and Pete bartered for her, and they got married, Injun style. Then they came back, built a tepee and lived here at the meadow. Knowing what it was like to get caught in a bear trap; Pete Miller made a promise that he would never trap bears again. And when ya make a promise Injun style, the bears know about it, so this meadow now has a bear King's X."

The fire crackled for a while before Bobbie said, "Aw, come on, Alvin. You really believe that?"

"I don't have any reason not to believe it," said Alvin grinning.

"He knows that stuff cause he's part Injun, huh, Alvin?" said Gerald.

"Yeah, I guess so," admitted Alvin.

"You think those Hunter guys have a bear King's X?" asked Danny.

"They don't need a King's X cause the bears wouldn't mess with those guys anyway on account of those big guns they always carry," advised Jack.

"You think those Hunters might sneak down here and shoot us while we're sleeping?" asked Bobbie.

"They wouldn't do anything like that," assured Jessie. "Besides, walking around at night, you could step on a rattler."

It was quiet for a moment at the Bear Patrol campfire, and then the night stillness was shattered by a loud, yapping bark. All heads jerked around, and enlarged eyes probed the darkness in the direction of the bark.

"Aw, that's just an ole coyote," assured Jessie.

"Yeah, that's all that is," agreed Alvin.

Then a couple of the coyote's partners joined in a chorus of yapping barks, which prompted Gerald to throw more wood on the fire and the Tenderfeet to move in closer.

They had all heard coyotes barking before, but in Bear Trap Canyon on a black night with bears, cougars, wild cats, rattlesnakes, and the strange Hunter boys on their minds, it seemed a little different. The talk around the campfire focused on experiences of hearing animal wails in the night on other camp outs until eyes began to droop and the coyotes got tired of barking and went to bed too.

The boys awoke to a bright, crisp morning at the Pete Miller Meadow. The blue jays were squawking, and several red-headed woodpeckers were already hard at work on a dead oak tree.

Dressed in full scout uniforms, they lined up in front of their pup tents and raised the Bear pennant on a willow pole. Some patrols didn't wear uniforms on camp outs, but the Bears always did because Jessie said it made you feel more like a scout.

After the pennant raising, each boy set about his assigned chores to prepare breakfast and get ready for the day's activities. Jack was chief chef that morning, and he cooked scrambled eggs. The eggs had been broken into a fruit jar for carrying so he just dumped them into the skillet and scrambled them over the camp fire.

When breakfast was finished and the campsite shipshape, Jessie held a class in trail following. He had a merit badge in that too. After he'd explained the procedure, he assigned Alvin as the official judge, and the rest of the patrol was to follow a trail Jessie would mark.

"Okay guys, the trail will lead to six markers I'm gonna put out." He showed them six pieces of colored paper. "They will lead you to where I'll be waiting. If ya get them all in two hours, ya pass the test. I need about fifteen minutes' head start. Alvin's got a watch, and he'll tell you when to go."

"Ya gonna lay the trail up the canyon?" asked Alvin.

Jessie grinned. He knew Alvin's curiosity over the mysterious Hunters was still gnawing at him. "Nope. Can't do it. We gotta stay in the lower part of the canyon."

"Okay," said a disappointed Alvin as he watched Jessie start off toward the thicket of willows on one side of the meadow.

Jessie not only knew all the trail signs by heart, he was an imaginative scout who loved to mark a trail that required sharp eyes to follow. After almost an hour of meandering through the willows and live oaks, leaving signs with broken twigs, pointing arrows made of small pebbles, and notches on willows, he'd placed all the markers that led back to the meadow. He then sat down on a rock beside a clump of willows to listen for sounds of his pursuing patrol. Other than a crow cawing, it was quiet.

After about a half hour, a covey of quail scurrying from the willows drew Jessie's attention. He scanned the bright green and yellow willow leaves but saw nothing unusual. Then a movement caught his eye. There. It moved again, and he got a glimpse of an alien color. It must be one of his patrol. It surprised Jessie that they had found him so soon.

He was waiting for them to emerge from the willows when suddenly there was a commotion, and an instant later a shrill scream pierced the stillness. Jessie's first thought was that it was a big wild cat or a cougar. He jumped up from the rock and watched the willows thrash about, and whatever it was came charging out on a dead run. After a few leaps it stumbled and fell into a writhing heap directly in front of where Jessie stood.

But it wasn't a wild cat or a cougar. It was one of the Hunter boys with the long hair. It took a moment for Jessie to recover from his shock and react. He leaped across to where the boy lay, writhing in the grass and moaning and holding his leg. It had to be one of the Hunters, but he wasn't nearly as big as Jack and Danny had claimed. Jessie leaned over to see what hurt him. When he saw the telltale fang marks on his leg, Jessie knew what had happened.

"A rattler bit you!" he blurted, dropping to his knees.

Out of a grimacing face, the boy looked at him with dark, frightened eyes.

"I gotta put a tourniquet on your leg," said Jessie, jerking off his scout kerchief. The boy tried to pull away, then went into another fit of pain.

Jessie's first aid training clicked off in his head the procedure for poisonous snake bite. The first class scout quickly set about the task at hand.

The Hunter boy had bare feet and wore only a pair of coveralls that had the bottom of the pant legs cut off, or worn off. It was hard to tell which. The fang marks were on the lower calf, so Jessie put the tourniquet on the upper thigh and tightened it with a willow stick. He checked his wrist watch to note the time, then pulled his first aid kit off his belt and removed the razor blade. He glanced at the boy. His long dark hair was tangled around a face grimacing with pain.

"I got to cut your leg. It's gonna hurt," Jessie explained urgently. The reaction he got was huge, frightened eyes and tight lips.

Jessie stared at the fang marks on the boy's leg. He had the razor blade in his hand; poised to do what he knew had to be done. Hesitating, with his heart pounding in his ears, he glanced at the boy's face. Tears were streaming down his cheeks, but he'd clamped his lips together to keep from crying out. Their eyes met, and as though he understood Jessie's dilemma, he nodded his head and closed his eyes tightly.

Jessie made the cut across the fang marks in one swift movement. The boy flinched, gritting his teeth. The cut spouted blood, and Jessie bent down and began to suck the blood and spit it out, which was how the Boy Scout first aid manual instructed to remove snake poison.

The boy was trying not to cry out, but Jessie knew he was in awful pain. A worker at Rose Station got bit by a rattler and he said it was the worst pain he'd ever experienced.

After about five minutes of alternately sucking out the snake poison and spitting it out, Jessie paused and glanced at the boy to see how he was doing. He had twisted around so that the bib part of his overalls had unhooked and fallen down. And there in the Pete Miller Meadow in the spring of 1935, Jessie Rascoe experienced one of those rare, emotional moments that he would remember the rest of his life: The Hunter boy wasn't a boy; he was a girl. And Jessie had his first look at a girl's bare breasts.

Chapter
~5~

With the realization that the big, mean Hunter boy was actually a small girl, Jessie experienced conflicting emotions: he was shocked, but thrilled with the sight.

After a bit, he realized that he must do more than just stare at her. He couldn't help look, of course, and if he hadn't been in his Boy Scout uniform, he might have feasted his eyes a little longer. But about that time, the girl, despite her pain, realized she was exposed and jerked the bib back in place.

That somehow reminded Jessie that in his preoccupation he'd forgotten all about the scout manual's instructions to signal for help in an emergency situation. He fished his patrol leader's whistle out of his shirt pocket and blew it loudly. After several blasts, he glanced at the girl again. He could tell from the look on her face and the tears streaming down her cheeks that she was in agony, but she didn't let out a whimper. She just gritted her teeth and held on to her leg with both hands.

She looked to be about his age. Her face was tanned, but appeared pale in contrast with her long dark hair and eyes. All she wore, as far as Jessie could see, was a pair of short- legged overalls.

"Do you hurt bad?" he asked sympathetically.

She looked at him with pained eyes and nodded.

"I think I got most of the poison out, but we're gonna have to get you to a doctor."

Her eyes opened wide, and she shook her head vigorously. Then another wave of pain from the snake venom struck her, and this time a cry escaped her lips. Before Jessie could blow his whistle again, he heard Alvin's reply signal off in the distance. Being the assistant patrol leader, Alvin had a whistle too. Within minutes, the rest of the patrol arrived and stood gawking at the girl.

"Good grief, what happened to him?" blurted Alvin, recognizing the long hair as a sign that it was one of the Hunter boys.

"He got bit by a rattler. Only he's a girl," reported Jessie.

Now the Bear Patrol moved up closer to where she lay and looked at her with disbelieving eyes.

"A girl?" croaked Gerald.

"Yeah. A girl," confirmed Jessie.

"I didn't know the Hunters had any girls. Are you sure he's a girl?" asked Jack.

"I'm sure, Jack," replied Jessie climbing to his feet.

"I knew they had a girl, but I ain't never seen her," said Danny.

"She's hurt bad. You can see that," observed Alvin. "Did you do the snake-bite procedure, Jess?"

"Yeah, but the first aid manual says you gotta get 'em to a doctor quick."

"How we gonna do that?" asked Bobbie, staring wide-eyed at the girl.

"We're gonna make an Indian sling and take her to Grapevine."

"Don't you think we ought to go get her dad and their wagon?" said Gerald.

Jessie shook his head. "It would take too long. Their homestead is another three or four miles up the canyon."

"Jessie's right. It would take over an hour just to walk to where they live at the other end of the canyon," said Jack.

"Well, what's she doin' way down here?" asked Gerald.

"Probably spying on us," said Bobbie.

"I don't know about that, but you can see she's really hurtin' and we gotta get moving. Alvin, you and Bobbie go cut a couple willow poles. Everybody take off your shirt. Jack, you collect them. I'll need them to make the sling. Gerald, you and Darwin get some rope from our tents. Okay, let's move!" barked the Bear Patrol leader.

And they did. Within minutes they had fashioned a stretcher with the willow poles and their scout uniform shirts. But when they tried to lift her onto it, she recoiled and kicked at them with her good leg.

"It's okay. You're gonna be all right. But we got to get you to a doctor, Okay?...Please... We won't hurt you. I promise," pleaded Jessie.

Either Jessie was convincing or the snake venom was taking its toll, because finally she stopped kicking at them, and they put her in the sling. With a scout at the end of each pole, they struggled off on their mission of mercy.

It was far more difficult than Jessie had calculated. The girl was small but heavier than she appeared and seven miles was a long way to carry someone in an Indian sling, particularly on the Bear Trap Canyon road, which ran down craggy gullies, wound up the side of steep slopes and along the rim of rocky ridges where footing was precarious. To make matters worse, Jessie had to dispatch his strongest scout, Alvin, to hike up the canyon to the Hunter homestead and tell them about their daughter. He'd rather have had Alvin to help carry the sling, but Jessie was secretly concerned about the Hunters' reaction, so he'd had no choice: Alvin was the bravest scout in the whole troop; everyone knew that.

Bobbie slipped and fell twice and Danny once, which caused everyone to lose their grip and fall down in a heap, dumping the poor girl onto the ground. Once she rolled halfway down the hill before Jessie could catch her. By this time, she was in sort of a daze anyway and just groaned a little when they scooped her up and loaded her back into the sling.

When they were too exhausted to go any longer, they would stop and rest a while, and Jessie would loosen the tourniquet for a few minutes and then tighten it again, as the scout manual said to do. Then they would struggle on.

It took over three hours, but they finally reached Juan Martinez's shack. Fortunately, the ole watchdog was at his cabin that day, and after he'd looked at the girl and saw the tourniquet on her leg, he nodded, turned to Jessie, and said, "You did the snake-bite medicine good, kid."

Jessie was surprised. How did the old breed know that it was he who did the snake-bite procedure?

As though he knew what Jessie was thinking, Martinez added, "You got Injun spirit, kid."

The strange compliment had an emotional effect on Jessie. It was like his arch enemy for all those years had suddenly pronounced him his blood brother.

Juan Martinez was a big man with a face that looked like it had been chiseled from a big hunk of tarnished copper. His thick, black hair was showing streaks of grey now, but the dark eyes were clear and sharp. He narrowed them and said, "Come on, gotta get'er to Doc Veeyon pronto." Then he scooped the girl out of the sling as though she was a rag doll.

With Jessie holding her in the front seat Martinez drove his pickup down the road in a cloud of dust, leaving the other scouts at his place to intercept Alvin and the Hunters and tell them where they had taken their daughter.

Doc Veeyon lived in a rock house beside the Grapevine road at "Oak Glen." He was retired now, but he'd practiced medicine in Bakersfield for years.

Ole doc was one of those who believed in the legend of the "Lost Padre Mine," and he was convinced that it was right there somewhere in Tejon pass. So when he retired, he moved up to the Grapevine and built his house out of the rocks that he dug up searching for the mine. Doc even searched for the Lost Padre on the Grapevine Ranch. The story was that he'd saved the life of a Ranch big shot, so he had permission to go on ranch property.

Now there was some historical fact to the Lost Padre legend. But it wasn't actually a mine; it was a fortune in gold ingots collected by the Spanish padres at the California missions.

Although the purpose of the twenty-one missions built in early California was to solidify Spanish claim to California, it was also to bring Christianity to the Indians. Now, one of the plus by-products was the element Au: good ole gold! It was brought to the missions by the Indians, where the Padres melted it into ingots. According to the legend, a large shipment, which had been collected over a period of time, was to be transported overland by mule train to old Monterey, where it would then be loaded on a ship for Spain. Led by a padre and guarded by Spanish cavalry, the group was last seen heading south into the Tehachapi Mountains. Then the entire party of cavalry, padres, mules, and gold just vanished, never to be seen or heard from again.

The reason Doc Veeyon had become interested was because one of his patients had told him a death-bed story about the Lost Padre. It involved an old sourdough miner back in the 1800s who turned up at Rose Station stage stop with a gold ingot. He claimed he'd found it at the foot of a giant rock slide in Tejon Pass. Assuming the gold was from the Lost Padre and buried beneath the rock slide, the stage station folks agreed to help him dig it out for a share of the gold. But the day he was to guide them to the place where he'd found the ingot, his horse threw him off, and he broke his neck. Doc believed the story and had been looking for the Lost Padre ever since.

Lately, however, Doc spent more time sitting on his front porch than he did looking for the Lost Padre. So if somebody needed doctoring, he was generally available to provide medical assistance. No one was even sure he still had a license to practice medicine, but it didn't matter since he was the only doctor between Bakersfield and Los Angeles.

When Doc looked up from where he sat reading on his porch and saw Juna's pickup speed up the road and skid to a stop in front of his rock house, he knew his medical services were needed.

"This kid's in bad shape," he grumbled when he examined the girl after Juan had carried her up the long column of rock steps and into the parlor where Veeyon did his doctoring business. Actually, it wasn't a business because doc hardly ever charged anybody for his services.

"Yeah, I seen that when the Rascoe kid brung 'em in," grunted the breed.

"How long has it been since she got bit?" asked Veeyon, leaning over the girl with his stethoscope.

Standing beside Juan shirtless, Jessie looked at his wristwatch and said, "Uh, almost four hours, Doctor Veeyon. We had to carry her out of Bear Trap on a stretcher."

The doctor glanced at Jessie, frowned, and turned back to his stethoscope.

"Kid do Injun medicine, doc," grunted Juan.

"You lanced the bite and did the suction?" Veeyon asked Jessie.

"Yes, sir."

"How soon after?"

"Right away, Doctor Veeyon."

Veeyon nodded, flipped the stethoscope off his ears, and moved quickly across the room to a medicine cabinet.

"She's had a violent reaction to the venom. All I can do now is give her a shot of anti-venom and hope for the best," he said, removing a syringe and vial from a cabinet next to the table where the girl lay.

Heavy set, with long arms and a cherub-like face, the old Dutchman still had a full head of grey hair and wore a classic Van Dyke beard, which made him look aristocratic. He filled the syringe from the vial, cleaned a spot on the girl's arm with alcohol, and injected her.

"Juan, you better high-tail it up to Gorman in your pickup and tell Fred Bartling to get down here quick with his ambulance," instructed Veeyon. "This girl's got to be taken to the hospital in Bakersfield as soon as possible."

There were no private telephones on the Grapevine, and Fred Bartling had the only ambulance. He kept it in an old barn at Gorman, which was at the top of Tejon Pass. That way, whichever direction he went, it was all down hill.

Martinez nodded and left the room.

Jessie glanced at the pale face of the Hunter girl lying on the table. Her eyes were closed, and she was quiet but breathing heavily. "Do you think she'll be all right, Doctor Veeyon?" he asked.

"Hard to say. But I can tell you one thing: if she survives, she'll owe you her life."

That night was another time that Jessie didn't go to sleep the minute his head hit the pillow. He tossed and turned thinking about Doc Veeyon's words: "if she survives." He couldn't understand why he was so affected by someone he didn't even know, but for whatever reason, he felt it deeply. When he found out the next day that she would be all right, it was as though a huge weight was lifted from his shoulders.

"I'm sure glad she's okay, I was really worried," he confided to Alvin the next morning at school before Miss Trembell rang the assembly bell. It was the first time they'd had a chance to talk privately since their Bear Trap adventure.

"Me too. And I'm glad for Mrs. Hunter. She's a nice lady, and I thought she was gonna die when I told her what happened to her daughter."

"What did Mr. Hunter say?"

"Oh, he got mad. He thought I'd done something to hurt his girl, and for a minute I thought he was gonna shoot me."

"No foolin'?"

"Yeah. He grabbed me and started yelling, but Mrs. Hunter told him to let me alone. Then after I explained it all, he calmed down and was okay."

"That must have been pretty scary."

"It was for sure. And so were those brothers of hers. They are just like Danny said, huge, tough-looking guys with long hair and big guns."

"Well, I had to send you Alvin. You know that."

"I know, and I'm glad I went there cause they're really pretty nice folks. Oh, a little strange, but I think people say stuff about them just because they live over there and don't mix with the folks on the Grapevine. Mrs. Hunter was real nice to me, and they let me ride up on the wagon seat all the way out of Bear Trap. Course, I could have walked faster. I didn't think those poor ole horses of theirs would ever pull that wagon out of the canyon. It took forever."

"I know. I thought you'd never get there." Jessie then told Alvin what the old breed had said about his doing the snake bite procedure.

Alvin thought a moment and then nodded. "Yep, that was sure enough an Injun compliment, Jess."

"Ya know, ole Martinez is not such a bad guy. He took us over to Doc Veeyon, then went and got Bartlett's ambulance. And when the Hunters came, he drove them all the way to Bakersfield in his pickup."

Alvin nodded. "Yep, yer right. He ain't as bad as we thought."

"Well, I'm sure glad the girl's all right. Uh, Maria? Is that her real name?"

"I guess so. That's what they called her."

"Sure a funny name for a girl, ain't it?"

"Sure is. But she don't look like other girls. Maybe that's why they named her Maria, you think?"

Jessie had seen that part of Maria that sure enough made her a girl and he wanted desperately to tell Alvin about it. He and Alvin shared all secrets, so it would be natural to tell him that he'd seen her bare titties. But for some strange reason, he couldn't tell Alvin. It seemed like he now had some kind of a special relationship with the Hunter girl, and if he told, he would be violating a trust they now shared. It was a feeling that Jessie had not experienced before.

Everybody on the Grapevine said the scouts were heroes. Scoutmaster Carver made a speech at the next scout meeting and told the boys their action exemplified the scout motto: Be prepared. Miss Trembell made a speech too, and all the scouts stood up in class and everyone clapped. Jessie's father and mother were so proud they celebrated by taking him and his brother Billy to Bakersfield in their 1929 Chevrolet for what was a rare treat: a moving picture show and a Chinese dinner.

Although it all worked out okay, Jessie was left with some feelings he didn't understand. He wished he could discuss it with Alvin, but he just couldn't. Maybe it had to do with Doc Veeyon saying that he'd saved her life. Whatever it was, Jessie knew he had to see the Hunter girl again.

Chapter
~6~

Jessie saw the Hunter girl again all right in a way he could never have imagined. And a picture of their meeting was on the front page of the Bakersfield *Californian* newspaper. It was the biggest thing to happen on the Grapevine since a Ford tri-motor-Trans-Western Airliner crashed near Lebec in 1931. That was on the front page of the Bakersfield *Californian* too.

How it all happened was that a reporter, Jim O'Day, found out about the snake-bit girl from a nurse over at the San Joaquin Hospital. That was where Tom Bartlett had taken her in his ambulance. Because of the severe snake poison reaction, she had to stay in the hospital for a while, and O'Day convinced his editor that it was a great human interest story.

O'Day then got the regional director of the Boy Scouts of America in the act, and he made a big deal over it. Members of the Bear Patrol of Grapevine Troop 34 were all declared heroes and received special awards at a big ceremony at scout headquarters there in Bakersfield. Of course, Jessie was the star hero since he was the one who had saved the girl's life by his quick action in administering the emergency snake bite procedure.

It took some convincing, but O'Day got the girl, whose name was Maria Hunter, to put one arm, kinda, around the hero's neck for the picture. The chief editor at the newspaper thought the picture was great and put it on the front page. That got a lot of attention on the Grapevine.

A couple weeks later on a Saturday afternoon, Jessie and Alvin were lying in the grass at their secret place beside Grapevine Creek when Jessie suddenly said, "Alvin, I'm gonna hike to Bear Trap tomorrow."

Alvin raised up on one elbow and looked at him. "You are? How come?"

"I gotta go see that girl."

Now Alvin came to a sitting position and looked at his friend curiously. "You gonna go see that Hunter girl, uh, Maria?"

"Yeah, I am."

Alvin's eyes narrowed. "You like that girl?"

Jessie rose to a sitting position too, looked at Alvin solemnly, and said, "I don't know. It's real strange. I don't even know her, but I gotta go see her again. I just got to."

Alvin nodded. "Well, she ain't very pretty, so it's probably on account of your savin' her life."

"Maybe so."

Two crows landed in the oak tree across the creek and squawked at each other for a while then flew off.

"You want me to go with you to the Bear Trap?" said Alvin.

"No. I got to do this myself. But if anyone asks, you and me went hiking down to Wheeler Ridge on Sunday, okay?"

"Sure. It's a long hike to the Hunters' so you better start early."

"Yeah, yer right. I'll get an early start."

On Saturday, when Jessie told his mother and dad at the supper table that he was leaving early the next morning to go hiking with Alvin, there was no objection, but later he ran into trouble with his brother. "Why can't I go with you, Jessie? I'm gonna join the scouts in just three more weeks."

"Because this ain't a scout hike. This is personal."

Billy looked at his big brother suspiciously. "You and Alvin ain't goin' to Wheeler Ridge. I can tell."

"How do you know we ain't?" flared Jessie.

"Cause it's easy to tell when you're fibbing. You get a dumb look on yer face."

Standing before his brother in the room they shared, Jessie was at a loss for words. Billy's revelation that he could tell when Jessie was fibbing was earth shaking. He really didn't like to fib, and he knew it was a violation of the scout law, but sometimes it just seemed like a little fib was the best way to avoid complications. Now, to learn that his brother could detect it was calamitous. "Aw, yer full of it Billy. You can't tell. You're just guessing," he retorted. It was all he could think to say.

"No, I'm not. And you know I'm not, don't you?"

Jessie diverted his eyes, and his brother grinned. Billy's eyes were darker than Jessie's and when he smiled, they sort of sparkled.

Jessie brought his eyes back to meet his brother's. "You wanna be in my patrol when ya join up, right?"

"Sure! All the guys say your patrol is the best."

"Okay. But like I been tellin' ya, ya gotta keep secrets."

"I can keep secrets, but you never tell me any."

"Well, I'm gonna tell ya one now. I ain't going to Wheeler Ridge, but don't tell anybody, okay."

"I won't. Where ya goin'?"

"I can't tell now, maybe later."

"Okay, Jessie, I won't tell anybody."

Jessie slipped out of the house the next morning before daylight. There weren't many trucks on the highway at that hour, but he finally caught a big flatbed carrying some kind of machinery. He rode it up the grade to just past Lebec pumping station where the Bear Trap Canyon road connected with the Grapevine. He hopped off the truck and started down the road just as daylight began to filter across the Tehachapi Mountains. He cut away from the road as it approached Juan Martinez's cabin, crawled through the barbed-wire fence, and rejoined the road farther down where he was sure the breed couldn't see him.

Although he'd thought a lot about hiking to the Hunters', he'd not been able to resolve just what he was going to say to the girl when he got there. He thought about it the whole time he was hiking into the canyon, but when he finally arrived at the Hunters' place, he still didn't know what he was going to say to her.

It took him over three hours to make the hike, counting a stop at Pete Miller Meadow where he'd slipped off his backpack, got a drink of cold water from the spring, then lay down in the cool grass, and rested a while.

Alvin had told him what to look for, so when he finally arrived at an old red barn in a grove of oak trees, he knew he was there. It was easy to find because all he'd had to do was follow the road to the end of the canyon. The Hunters' homestead was up on the side of the hill, so you couldn't see it from the barn.

It was a dilapidated barn with big cracks in the side boards and a rusted, corrugated iron roof. As Jessie stood there looking at it, wondering what kept it from falling down, a small door in the side opened, and Maria Hunter stepped out.

She looked the same as the first time he'd seen her: Long dark hair hanging in crazy folds about her tanned face. She wore the same threadbare overalls with short legs, and no shirt. The only difference was that she now had on a pair of men's high-top shoes.

They stood for a moment staring at each other uncertainly.

"Uh, hello," he finally managed to say.

"Hello," she replied, staring at him intently with huge, dark eyes that sparkled with little specks of silver. He wondered if her eyes were that big all the time or just when she was startled, or snake bit.

"You okay now?" he asked.

She nodded, still watching him intently.

"I'm glad."

Her eyes dropped, and after a hesitating, she said, "Ah'm obliged to ya."

"Aw, that's okay. Scouts do stuff like that."

She raised her eyes. "Thet's the first rattler ah ever stepped on."

"I guess it hurt pretty bad, huh?"

She nodded. "Papa makes me wear these ole shoes now."

They both glanced at her high-top brogans several sizes too large for her.

"They're ma brother Jake's. He growed out of 'em. Papa says a rattler'd have a tough time bitin' through 'em."

Jessie nodded. A blue jay landed in the oak tree next to the barn and started squawking. They watched until he flew away.

"Blue jays sure are loud," he said.

"Ya hike all the way into Bear Trap Canyon?"

"I sure did."

She looked at him suspiciously. "What for?"

The question was a surprise. "Oh, I just like to hike."

Her dark eyes examined him intently, and he was reminded of his brother's claim that it was easy to tell when he was fibbing. Could she tell he was fibbing? She sort of nodded knowingly.

"Boy Scouts do a lot of hiking, ya know. I hiked to Pete Miller a bunch of times."

"Ah never seen ya befo, ah mean, befo the rattler bit me."

"Well, we only hike as far as the Pete Miller Meadow. It's a neat place to camp."

"Ah know. Ah go down there sometimes ta watch the doves."

"You come to see the doves when the rattler bit ya?"

She nodded. "But Pete Miller ain't as pretty as Marble Springs. Ah go there most."

"Marble Springs? Where is that?"

"Oh, it's just over thet ridge," she said pointing. "Ya want'a hike up ta Marble Springs?"

Jessie hesitated. After already hiking over ten miles, it wasn't exactly what he wanted to do.

As though sensing his reluctance, she said, "It's mighty pretty up there and it ain't very far."

"Well..." He glanced at his wristwatch.

Her eyes went to the watch. "Ya got a wrist clock?"

"Yeah, I got it for my fourteenth birthday." Seeing her staring at it, he held out his wrist for her to see. "It's an Elgin watch. They're real good."

She advanced cautiously and looked at the watch. "It shore looks nice. Ma uncle Bob got one. He lives down south. But ah don't need a clock on account of ah tell time by where the sun is. Come on, ah'll show ya Marble Springs."

"Okay, if you want to."

"Jus' follow me," she instructed, then turned, and started off across the canyon, her brogans clopping and kicking up dust as she walked.

"You have to tell your folks or something?" Jessie inquired as he fell in behind her on what appeared to be an animal trail.

"Not long as ah get back befo dark," she replied over her shoulder.

She was a good hiker, even with the oversized brogans. Jessie had to hustle to keep up. The trail was steep, winding up the side of a ridge, and then dropping off into a small valley that cradled a meadow at one end. Water trickled out of a giant outcropping of grey rock that looked like marble but was actually granite. Whoever named the springs probably thought it really was marble. The trickling water formed a little stream that ran down and disappeared into the grassy meadow that was ablaze with the vivid color of spring wild flowers.

Jessie was breathing hard when the girl finally came to a halt at the edge of the meadow where a light breeze rustled the willow and silver aspen leaves.

"Ain't that purty?" she asked, looking at him expectantly. It was her first words since they left the barn.

Jessie nodded as he caught his breath. "It really is."

"Ah come here all the time ta see ma friends. Come on. Ah'll show ya." She turned and started off toward the meadow. He followed along behind, glad that it was only a short distance.

On a grassy area laced with yellow buttercups and violet paintbrushes, the girl collapsed into a sitting position and pulled off the brogans. "The grass feels good on yer toes. Ah shore hope Papa don't make me wear these ole shoes all summer."

Jessie slipped off his Knapsack, dropped it into the grass, and sat down beside her. He unlaced his tennis shoes and pulled them off. "Yeah, it does feel good on your toes. Me an' Alvin got a secret place like this down on Grapevine Creek. It ain't as pretty though."

"Is Alvin yer friend?"

"Yeah."

"He the one come told Mama and Papa ah got bit?"

"Yes. He's real brave. This where you meet your friends?"

She nodded. "But they don't come much if ah'm with someone."

"Your friends only come when you're alone?"

She nodded again. "Ma friends are the birds and animals."

"Hey, that's neat. I like birds and animals too."

"Ya do?"

"Yeah."

"Well, most of ma friends are squirrels and chipmunks, but sometimes a possum or a deer."

"You got a deer for a friend?"

"Well, deers ain't real friendly, but sometimes they come an get a drink while ah'm sitting here. Course, ah sit right still. Squirrels and chipmunks will come right up ta me when ah bring 'em some bread crumbs. They really like thet."

"Don't you have any other friends? I mean, people friends?"

"Sure. I got friends on the other side of the ridge. I hike over there with ma brothers sometimes. And ma friend Carlo comes over ta see me right often. He goes ta the Injun school. He's a breed an they're real strong. But sometimes he acts a little tetched."

"Tetched?"

She looked at Jessie incredulously. "Don't ya know what thet means?"

Jessie shook his head.

"Thet means he's tetched in the head, sort'a like a horse after he eats loco weed."

"Oh."

A pair of doves swooped down over the meadow and landed on the rock outcropping near the trickling spring water. The girl put a finger to her lips, signaling Jessie to be quiet. He nodded, and they sat still for a while watching the doves as they bobbed their heads and dipped their beaks into the pools of spring water.

After the doves had flown away, she looked at Jessie and said, "Ain't they purty? Ma brothers shoot animals an birds and ah hate it. But Mama won't let em shoot up here."

"Oh."

"But ah don't care if'n they shoot rattlers cause ah don't like them," she said, flopping down on her back in the grass.

"Me either. But they ain't animals."

"They ain't?"

"No. They're reptiles."

"Oh."

"Uh, how come you don't go to school at Grapevine, Maria?"

She flopped back down and said, "There ain't no way ah can go ta Grapevine School livin' here in the Bear Trap."

"Oh."

She was lying on her back, and when she raised one arm over her forehead, it pulled the overalls up so that a portion of a bare breast was visible. Instantly an excitement shot through Jessie. It gave him that same thrilling sensation he'd experienced the day he'd seen her at the Pete Miller Meadow.

But an instant later, as though she sensed he was watching her, she pulled her arm down and sat up. They stared at each other for a silent moment.

"Ah been ta Grapevine, and ah don't like it. It ain't near as purty as Bear Trap. 'Sides, ah go ta school right here ever day, exceptin Sunday," she announced defensively.

"You go to school here, in Bear Trap?"

"Sure. Ma mama teaches me real good."

"Your mama is the school teacher?"

"Yes. My mama is real smart."

Jessie was having trouble imagining that someone's mama could be a school teacher.

"We used ta live on the other side of the ridge befo Papa got laid off, and we had ta move over ta Bear Trap. What ya got in yer carryin, bag?"

"Oh, I got my compass, first aid kit, and my lunch." He reached over and opened up the knapsack, pulled out the items, and showed them to her. He saw her eyes lock on the candy bar.

"That's a Baby Ruth, ain't it?"

He nodded and glancing at his wristwatch. "Hey, it's getting pretty close to lunch time. I got enough to share. Would you like some lunch?"

She looked at him uncertainly. "Well..."

"Here, take half this meat loaf sandwich. My mom makes it, and it's really good." He took half the sandwich and laid it in the grass, handing her the other half in the wax paper he's wrapped it in. "And you take the Baby Ruth cause I like the apple just as good," he said, offering her the candy bar.

"Oh no, ah couldn't take all of it," she protested, but he forced it into her hand anyway because he could tell she wanted it.

She laid the candy bar next to the sandwich and leaped to her feet. "Ah'll get some cold water ta drink," she said and dashed off across the meadow.

Watching her run through the grass, her overalls flapping and her long dark hair dancing across her back, it occurred to Jessie she was like one of her little wild animal friends. She returned a few minutes later with a rusted coffee can full of spring water and sat down beside him.

"Marble Springs water tastes the best in the canyon," she declared as they both bit into the sandwich.

She devoured her half in short order and said, "That were a larapen sandwich. When Mama makes bread, ah fix a bean sandwich and bring it up here ta eat. Ya like bean sandwiches?"

"I haven't had one of those," Jessie admitted. Seeing her look at the candy bar, he added, "I'm a slow eater. You go ahead and eat your Baby Ruth."

She looked at him and smiled, and it was as though a bright light suddenly illuminated her. She seemed to glow, and her huge brown eyes flashed those little specks of silver. It gave Jessie a good feeling, and he was glad that he was there with her.

"Ah don't get candy bars much, but ah shore like 'em," she said, tearing the paper off the bar and biting into it. That she enjoyed the candy was evident, and she ate it even faster than she had the sandwich.

"Thet were real good," she said, then lay back in the grass, and was quiet while Jessie finished his sandwich. When he'd finished his last bite, he picked up the rusted coffee can and took a drink from it. It was great-tasting water.

"Jessie?" she suddenly said. It was the first time she'd called him by his first name, and he liked it.

"Yeah?" he answered, glancing over to where she lay on her back.

"Ah'm obliged to ya fer fixing me up when the rattler bit me and thet's fer sure. Mama says you saved ma life."

"Aw, that's okay, Maria."

She sat up and looked at him determinedly. "No. Ah got a obligation. If ya want ta see me, ah'll take ma overalls off."

Now Jessie was struck with more than a good feeling: he was speechless. For his age, Jessie Rascoe was pretty quick reacting and not too often caught off guard. In this instance, he was. He didn't have the slightest idea what to say or do. Oh, he'd love to see her with her overalls off all right, and the secret truth was that he'd hoped he might get a peek at her titties again. But what she had just offered was so beyond his comprehension that he heard himself say, "You ain't obligated, Maria. I'm a Boy Scout, and I help other people at all times. It's part of the scout oath."

She looked at him curiously for a moment. "When Carlo hikes over ta Bear Trap and brings me somethin', he always wants ta see me. How come you don't?"

She was watching him with a puzzled expression on her face while Jessie struggled with an emotional dilemma: He knew instantly that he didn't like Carlo, what a jerk! But how could he answer Maria's question honestly without being a jerk too? It put him in a terrible quandary, and he just sat there staring at her.

"Ya don't want ta see me?"

"Oh, no! I mean, yes. I'd, uh, like ta see you, but..."

"Ah'm glad ya do cause it's only proper ta do somethin in return when someone has favored ya," she said solemnly. Then jumping to her feet, she unsnapped the metal hooks on the straps and let the overalls fall to her feet.

And so, on a beautiful spring day in 1935, in the meadow at Marble Springs in Bear Trap Canyon, Jessie Rascoe feasted his eyes for the first time on a naked girl. It was one of those wonderful moments in his life that he would never, ever forget.

Maria Hunter, age fourteen, stood naked in a sea of nature's color: her petite torso appearing milk white in contrast to her tanned arms and face. She sort of posed like a little nymph who hadn't quite reached maturity. But her pink-tipped breasts, and the small, darkened crevice below her belly revealed a blooming maturity that would soon be full.

Whatever the thrill and excitement Jessie had experienced the day he got a glimpse of Maria's breasts, multiply it by ten, and that was what he felt as he sat spellbound in the grass at Marble Springs. Then, as quickly as she had dropped them, Maria pulled the coveralls back up.

"Did ya like seeing me?" she asked as she fastened the metal hooks on her overall straps.

It took a minute or two for Jessie to pull himself out of his trance and find his voice. "Uh, Yeah, I sure did," he croaked.

"Ah'm glad ya did because ah didn't know how to meet ma obligation to ya cause ah didn't know if you would come to the Bear Trap again."

"Well, like I said, Maria, you didn't owe me, but I'm real glad I came."

She dropped down into a sitting position beside Jessie. "Ah'm real glad ya came too," she said with sparkling eyes.

Needless to say, Jessie was experiencing some powerful new feelings, and she was sitting really close, and he desperately wanted to do something with Maria. Since he knew how to kiss a girl, he blurted, "You like to kiss, Maria?"

A strange look spread across her face, and she drew back.

"You don't like kissing?"

She shook her head.

"Don't you kiss Carlo?"

She shook her head vigorously, and Jessie felt a touch of satisfaction at knowing the jerk at least hadn't kissed her.

Then she said, "Ah don't let nobody grab me, Jessie."

It was a big disappointment because Jessie wanted desperately to kiss Maria. But he told himself to stay calm and figure out a way to overcome this latest hurdle.

"Uh, Maria, kissin' ain't like grabbing."

She looked at him skeptically, her eyes narrowed. "Ya kissed girls?"

"Oh, sure. I done it. Ain't you ever kissed a boy?"

She shook her head.

"It's easy and it's fun."

The look on her face told him she wasn't convinced.

"Everybody does it, just like in the a motion picture."

"Ah ain't never seen no motion picture," she said, diverting her eyes.

"Oh, Well, they do it a lot."

She looked at him curiously. "Why do they kiss a lot?"

Something told Jessie that if he could come up with a good answer to that question, he might just convince her. "Well, uh, what do you like to do best of all?" She looked confused. "I mean, what makes you feel real good...better than anything else?"

He could tell by the look in her eyes that she was thinking intently. "Ah like it best when the sun comes up here and all the birds are wakin' up and singin'."

"Well, that's what it's like to kiss, only better," declared Jessie, pleased with his analogy.

She studied him a moment. "Jessie, you tell fibs?"

Diverted eyes. "Uh, I'm not fibbing. Scout's honor."

"What do that mean?"

"When a scout says somethin' on his honor, you know it's true."

She appeared to be considering that answer favorably so Jessie went for broke: "You want me to show you?"

She sat motionless for a moment, then nodded her head ever so slightly.

She agreed! Jessie's spirits leaped, but as he prepared to kiss Maria, it occurred to him that he might have been a little hasty to promise on his scout's honor that she would like kissing. What if she didn't? But she would, he was sure of it. He wanted to put his arms around her, but decided it best to do this one step at a time. So he just leaned over and gently kissed her on the lips.

She jerked back, her eyes rounded.

"Ain't that good?" he asked hopefully, since it didn't appear that she thought it was all that great.

"Is thet all ya do?" she asked, sounding somewhat disappointed.

"Well, no. I mean that's just the first part."

She looked skeptical.

"Want me to show you some more?"

Hesitation. "Okay, a little."

He scooted over closer to her and put his hands on her shoulders. She kept her eyes on him, open wide. "Now ya gotta close yer eyes," he instructed.

"Close ma eyes?"

"Yeah, that's part of kissing."

She closed them, but peeked out of one as Jessie kissed her again, this time longer. When he finished that kiss, he noticed that her eyes were closed, and he was certain she liked it better this time. But she twisted out of his arms and jumped to her feet.

Jessie was acutely distressed at his failure. It was true he'd only kissed Michelle, but when he had kissed her, she had swooned and said it was real good. What was he doing wrong with this girl? All Michelle let him do was kiss; this girl had just shown him her whole naked body and she didn't like to kiss? It didn't make any sense.

"Ah have ta be excused fo a minute, but ah'll be right back," she said and dashed off across the meadow into a stand of willows.

Jessie felt a warm flush cross his face. He'd never thought about it before, but he guessed that girls had to go too out on a hike, just like boys. She came dashing back in no time and flopped down close to him. "Let's kiss some more, okay?" she said eagerly.

It was a boon to Jessie's ego, not to mention his passion, and it got him off the hook, so as to speak, about violating his scout's honor. Now he really got into some kissing. He put his arms around her and gave her a long movie kiss. He was certain that Maria liked it because she put her arms around him and kissed him back pretty good.

After they kissed a while, Jessie began to feel that same stirring down deep in his belly that he had with Michelle, only a lot more. So much so that he wanted to do some other things. But when he slipped his hand under her overalls to feel her titties, she pulled away abruptly.

"Ah don't want ya ta grab me, Jessie. Mama says ah shouldn't let boys touch ma private parts."

It was a major setback and just when he was certain that at last he was going to get to feel a girl's titties in the raw.

"But yer right about kissin'-it's fun and ah like it. Ya like kissin' me?"

"Oh, yeah. I sure do. Uh, Maria, it's not grabbing if you touch a girl a little bit when you're kissing. Touching and kissing is kind of like, uh, bread and butter. You know, they go together naturally."

Jessie thought it was pretty good logic, but Maria wasn't buying. She did give his argument some thought, and then said, "Well, ah shore enough like the kissin' part. But ah guess

I'm like ma little animal friends. They don't like ta be touched neither. But ah'll think on it, and maybe next time..."

Time! He'd forgotten the time. He glanced at his wristwatch. It was two o'clock. Disaster! He'd never make it home by five as his mother had instructed. "Criminey! I forgot the time, Maria. I'm in deep trouble!"

Chapter
~7~

It was a disaster for Jessie all right. He got restricted for the rest of that school year. He didn't make it home to Rose Station till almost seven o'clock that day, and to make matters worse, he got his brother in trouble too.

Billy had told his worried parents that Jessie was with Alvin. The only method of fast communication on the Grapevine was the company telephone, but they didn't allow personal calls except in emergency. So Mr. Rascoe declared an emergency and called Alvin's father at Emidio Station. When he found out Jessie wasn't with Alvin, Billy was in as much hot water as Jessie. The only good part was that Jessie found out his little brother could keep a secret, and it cemented a bond between them that they kept from that time on.

Mr. Rascoe, however, gave both boys an indefinite restriction and assigned additional chores for their dishonesty. In addition, Jessie got the lights out punishment at the weekly boy scout meeting where the scout master told the troop in the dark, that one of their members had broken a scout law. He wouldn't say who, but the guilty boy knew. And it made an indelible impression on Jessie Rascoe. He swore that he would stop telling fibs forever.

But Jessie also had an indelible impression of Maria Hunter, in the raw, and he wanted desperately to see her again. But since his restriction prevented that, he wrote his first love letter:

Dear Maria,

I was late getting home and got restricted, so I can't come to see you. But I will come to see you as soon as I can. Marble Springs is really neat, and I sure liked it because it was fun to be there with you. I liked it best when we kissed. Did you like it too? Do you think you would want to be my girl? I would like it a lot if you did. Please write to me and tell me. Your Papa could mail it when he goes to the store.

Very fondly, Jessie Rascoe

It cost three cents to mail a letter. but it was worth it. Mr. Switzner said that the Hunters only got their mail once in a blue moon, so Jessie didn't know when Maria would get his letter. He was pretty sure that she liked him better than Carlo now. But did she like him enough to stop letting Carlo see her? For some reason, that upset Jessie a lot. He just didn't want that guy to see Maria any more because, well, he just didn't. Even when he thought about Carlo seeing her, it reminded him of the time the heifer kicked him in the stomach.

The biggest event on the Grapevine that summer was when Mr. Switzner put in a giant root beer "barrel" in front of his store. It was a big round wooden structure shaped like a barrel that sold root beer through an opening in the front. Many of the Grapevine folks thought he was crazy because in those depression years a lot of the travelers were poor folks driving broken-down old cars looking for work. These folks sure couldn't afford to buy root beer. They would stop at a place about halfway up the Grapevine where the state had piped water down from a spring on the mountain side. There they could get a free drink of cold water and pour some in their overheated old cars.

But Mr. Switzner felt that there were enough travelers that would pay ten cents for a cold glass of root beer. He also decided that his son Danny was still too young, so he hired Jessie to run the stand. Jessie was happy to get the job because it paid a dollar a day. Big money! There would be jingle in Jessie's jeans when he went to high school in the fall. He was ecstatic when he told Alvin of his good fortune.

"I'll be rich by the time school starts!" he exclaimed as he and Alvin waded barefoot in Grapevine Creek the day after his big June graduation ceremony from Grapevine Grammar School, and the day before he started his first job.

"Yer really lucky, Jess. What ya gonna do with all that money?" asked Alvin.

"I'm gonna buy Bud Carver's Model A Ford."

"Wow!" exclaimed Alvin.

"Bud said he'd sell it for thirty dollars cause he wants to buy that big Durant that Mr. Switzner's got for sale. I figure by the end of the summer I'll have enough. My dad says I gotta put half of my pay in the bank, but I can spend the other half."

"Do you think your dad is gonna let you buy a car?"

"I think he will if I stay out of trouble for the rest of the summer. I been real good lately, and I think I'll be off restriction soon."

"That would really be neat. Just think, you'll be in high school and have your own car."

"Yeah, and I can drive over to Bear Trap and see Maria."

Alvin climbed up out of the creek and sat down on a rock. "You really like that girl, don't you?"

Jessie followed and sat down next to him. "Yeah, I like her."

"She's strange, and she ain't very pretty. How come you like her?"

For reasons Jessie didn't understand, he still couldn't tell his friend about how he felt about Maria and about seeing her in the raw. To do so seemed like some kind of breach of trust. What he wanted to say to Alvin was: *She's prettier than you think, Alvin. You ought to see her in the raw!* What he said was, "Yeah, she's a little wild looking, but she's a neat girl once ya get to know her."

"Does she like you?"

"I think she does."

"She should because you saved her life."

"Well, I know. But all of the Bear Patrol, Mr. Martinez, and Doc Veeyon helped save her life, Alvin."

Alvin nodded. "That's true."

The sound of a Mack truck laboring up the Grapevine echoed across the canyon, and a couple of grey squirrels scampered up an oak tree.

Alvin looked at his friend. "It's gonna be tough, Jess, to have a girl that you gotta walk twenty miles to see."

Jessie nodded. "But it's only ten miles to her house, Alvin."

"Yeah, but it's ten miles in and miles out. That makes twenty."

Jessie grinned. "She's worth it, Alvin."

It turned out to be a hot summer that year, and travelers going up and down the Grapevine road did stop and pay ten cents for a glass of ice-cold root beer. Mr. Switzner was pleased with his investment, but more pleased that he was right and those who said he was crazy were wrong.

But Mr. Switzner was in the minority that year as the depression continued despite President Roosevelt's best efforts. Even Gerald's dad had to lay off some of the state highway maintenance workers. One of the workers who lost his job was killed when his car crashed through the railing on Dead Man's Curve. He'd gone around that curve hundreds of times, so most folks figured he did it on purpose so his family could survive on the small life insurance policy he had.

Jessie was one of the lucky one's that year. He was getting rich. He was pulling six dollars a week. That was the good news. The bad news was that he ran the root beer stand all day every day except Sunday, and that was taken up with various family obligations. Those obligations included going to Bakersfield to visit relatives and sometimes to attend church.

There wasn't any church on the Grapevine, so if you wanted to go, you had to drive to Bakersfield and that cost money. Gasoline was expensive. It cost fifteen cents a gallon.

They did have a preacher drive out from Bakersfield for a while in 1933 and hold services in the old volunteer fire house. His name was Mr. Brown, and everybody liked him. But he couldn't see very well, and one Sunday he ran his car off Dead Man's Curve too. He survived the wreck, but he never came back.

Besides not getting to see Maria, Jessie's other big problem was that he had no time to do all the fun things he'd always done with his friends in the summer time.

"We went over to the trough yesterday, Jessie, and took a swim cause we saw Mr. Martinez going down the road to Bakersfield," Jack said when all the gang gathered around the root beer barrel on a Saturday afternoon.

"Yeah, it was great. Ya should'a been with us, Jessie," added Gerald.

"Well, I'd like to go swimmin' at the trough all right, but I'm runnin' this root beer stand all by myself. Mr. Switzner has me do everything."

"How many root beers you sell in a day?" asked Bobbie.

"A bunch," assured Jessie proudly. "Last Saturday I took in almost seven dollars."

"Seven dollars!" exclaimed Gerald. "It must be awful good root beer."

"It's real good, and it's ice cold," assured Jessie. "Tell ya what. I'm gonna treat you all to a glass."

All eyes widened. "That'd be great!" said Bobbie.

"Yeah!" agreed Gerald.

"Can you give root beer away?" asked Alvin.

"No, I can't do that. I just put a note in the cash box of what I drink or give away, and Mr. Switzner takes it out of my pay. But he only charges me a nickel a glass. I did that for my brother Billy and for Bud Carver and Frank Grover when they come by in Bud's Model A," explained Jessie as he opened the ice box and took out four glass mugs.

The boys gathered close to watch as Jessie, dressed in a bright red cap and serving apron, filled the mugs from the spigot in the side of the root beer barrel and handed them out one at a time.

As each boy tasted the cold root beer, he exclaimed in turn as to how great it was, and Jessie felt good at pleasing his friends. It sort of made up some for missing out on all the summer fun.

"Drinkin' this root beer is as good as goin' swimming at the Rose Station trough!" declared Alvin.

Jessie grinned. "Well, when it gets hot in this ole barrel, I sure wish I was over there with you guys taking a swim."

About that time, a sparkling, cream colored Packard convertible pulled up beside the root beer stand. All heads turned and all eyes focused on the two occupants. The driver was a handsome athletic-looking guy dressed in a white tennis outfit. The girl beside him was also dressed in white except for a red-and-blue ribbon in her hair. When she stepped out of the car, they could see she wore a short tennis skirt. Her legs were long and tanned. She was beautiful.

"It's her! It's Hallie Lamont!" whispered Alvin as the two dressed in white approached the root beer stand.

They were conversing and ignored the four boys as though they were part of the fixtures. When they stepped up to the small counter at the front of the stand, Hallie looked at Jessie, who was staring at her. She held his eyes for a moment, as though she wasn't sure if he were someone she should recognize. Then she turned back to the convertible driver and laughed at something he said. Her large, sky blue eyes sparkled and her laugh sounded like beautiful music.

Jessie vaguely heard the guy order two root beers. He nodded, opened the ice box door, and took out the glasses. He held one of the glasses up to the spigot and turned the handle. She called the guy George and was telling him something about the tennis game they had played in Bakersfield. Then she laughed again, and he noticed that she had a beautiful mouth and lips and the silver stuff she'd had on her teeth when he'd seen her at the water trough was gone.

She turned and looked at Jessie strangely, smiled, and said, "Excuse me, your root beer is running over." George laughed.

Jessie felt a flush on his face as he turned off the root beer spigot. He wiped off the spilled root beer with a cloth and handed her the glass. But he was so flustered, he let go of it before she had a firm grip, and it fell, struck the edge of the counter, and tipped over, dumping the entire contents down the front of Hallie Lamont's beautiful white tennis outfit.

Chapter

~8~

"Aw, don't worry about it Jess," consoled Alvin the day after the root beer disaster, which was Sunday and Jessie's day off.

"I can't believe I did that. How dumb can you get," groaned Jessie.

"It was just an accident."

"Yeah, by an incompetent jerk."

"She said you're an incompetent soda jerk. That's different than just a plain jerk," said a grinning Alvin.

"Not much different," said Jessie despondently, as the two sat in the grass at their secret meeting place on Grapevine Creek.

"Well, you said you'd pay for having her clothes washed. That's all you could do."

"Yeah and then she called me stupid."

Alvin nodded and tossed a rock into the creek. "Yep, she did say that."

"How was I to know you don't wash tennis clothes?"

"But ya know, she's even pretty when she's mad, huh, Jess?"

Jessie sighed. "Yeah, she is Alvin. But one thing for sure, she ain't never gonna speak to me again."

"Well, she said she was gonna bring you the cleaning bill for her clothes. She'll have to speak to you then."

"Yeah, but it won't be very friendly speaking."

"You think that guy George is her boy friend?"

"I guess so. Danny said he's a rich guy from Bakersfield."

"Boy, how'd you like to have the car he's got?"

"I sure enough would."

"With that car, you could get any girl you wanted."

"If I get Bud's Model A, I'd bet Maria will like it just fine."

Alvin narrowed his eyes and thought for a while. "Yeah, but when you get the Model A you can get a zillion girls."

Both boys glanced up when a woodpecker tapped his beak loudly on a black oak tree above where they were sitting.

"Ya know, Alvin, Hallie Lamont is beautiful all right, and I sure would like to have that guy's car. But I'll be happy with Bud's Model A, and the only girl I want is Maria Hunter."

When he arrived at the root beer stand on Monday morning, Jessie was feeling much better than when he'd closed it on Saturday.

He did his usual thing, which was to go into the giant root beer barrel through a rear access door. Once inside, he busied himself with the preparations that were necessary before he opened for business. When he was ready, he pushed the front door up, latched it in place, and found himself looking into the face of his first customer, which was as shocking as when he'd seen Hallie Lamont on Saturday.

It was Maria Hunter, and for a moment, he just stared at her incredulously. She was spotless clean and dressed in real girl's clothes. She had on a pretty blue taffeta dress and real girl's shoes. Her hair was in two long braids with ribbons in each one. She was stunning!

"Hello, Jessie," she said with a big smile and her huge brown eyes sparkling.

"Maria!" he blurted. "I...I didn't know it was you."

"Ya didn't?" she replied, obviously pleased with the effect her appearance had on him.

"Gosh no, You...you look different, I mean, in a dress, You look real nice."

She did look nice. In fact, Jessie was astonished. It was hard to believe his eyes. It was like he was looking at a different girl. But as his eyes traveled over her petite figure, Jessie experienced that same excitement when he'd seen her naked at Marble Springs.

Maria dropped her eyes coyly. "Ah thank ya fer the compleement."

"You really surprised me, Maria. What are you doin here?" he asked then glanced around expecting to see some of her folks, but she appeared alone.

"Ma uncle come over ta see us, an he carried us out ta the store ta get some groceries and mail." She turned and pointed. "Ya see thet Dodge Brothers motor car over there by the store? That's ma uncle Bob's. It goes right up thet ole road in the Bear Trap like nothin'."

"Golly, I'm glad you came, Maria."

"Me too. I got yer letter, Jessie, and I liked it real good. I wrote you a letter to, but I ain't got no stamp. Sides, Papa hasn't gone out ta the store so ah couldn't send it. But when ya come ta see me, I'll give it to ya... When are ya comin' ta see me, Jessie?"

"As soon as I can! I got me the job running this root beer barrel, and I don't get much time off."

"Ya work in there all the time?"

"Yeah. All day long till dark, and every day cept Sunday. And I sell a lot of root beer. You like root beer, Maria?"

"Oh, yes. Ah had some once, an it was good."

"I'll get you a glass," said Jessie eagerly.

"Oh, ah ain't got no money, Jessie. How much does it cost?"

"It cost a dime. But this is gonna be free."

Maria smiled warmly. "Thank ya, Jessie."

"Well, I'm coming to see you too, Maria, real soon," promised Jessie, deciding on the spot he was going to make an appeal to his parents to lift his restriction so he could go see her.

"Ah'd like thet, Jessie," said Maria. Then glancing around to see that no one was listening, lowered her voice, and said, "Ah do want ta be yer girl, and ah want ta kiss some more."

"Well, I'm coming over this next Sunday, Maria. That's for sure!" declared Jessie, as he handed the glass of root beer to Maria, making sure he didn't drop it.

She grasp the glass and took a big drink. "Thet sure is good!" she exclaimed, pausing, then tipping it up again, and drinking more. "Ah swear thet's the best root beer ah ever tasted," she declared, her eyes sparkling.

"I'm glad you like it, Maria," said a pleased soda jerk as he watched the girl in the blue dress drain the root beer glass to the last drop. As his eyes again passed over those contours at the top of her blue dress, he felt another surge of that same excitement. Oh, he'd go to Bear Trap next Sunday all right!

"That were larapin."

"Golly, Maria, you really look great in that blue dress."

She smiled and dropped her eyes again. "Ah don't have much occasion ta dress up. But when Uncle Bob said he'd drive us out ta Grapevine in his car, ah begged Mama to let me wear ma party dress. Ya want me ta wear it next Sunday, if Mama will let me?"

"Sure, that would be great."

"When ya get there, we'll go up ta Marble Springs, okay? I think Mama's baking this week, so ah'll fix us some bean sandwitches."

About that time, a big black Pierce Arrow pulled up in front of the barrel, and a group of finely dressed folks got out and came up to the stand to purchase root beer. Maria stepped off to one side and stared at them for a while. Then she turned her attention back to Jessie and watched admiringly as he did his business, serving the customers and looking professional in his red apron and cap to match.

Jessie was aware that Maria was watching him, so he was particularly careful to do everything right. He'd just finished serving the group from the Pierce Arrow when another group of thirsty travelers arrived, and before he knew it, Maria and her folks were getting into the car to leave. They exchanged waves as the Dodge Brothers motor car drove on up the Grapevine road.

"I'm pleased you're asking our permission, son. It suggests you have learned the valuable lesson about being truthful," his father said when Jessie asked for an appeal of his restriction.

"Oh, yes, sir. I know that scouts have to be truthful."

"Yes, but honesty is the best policy, Jessie, in or out of your scout uniform. You can't just turn honesty on and off to your liking."

"I know that too, Dad. I mean, I do now. And now that I'm fourteen and got a real job and everything, I understand those things better, and I'm just not gonna fib any more. I mean, even if it gets me in trouble, I'm not gonna fib."

Mr. Rascoe wasn't as tall as his sons, but he had the same light hair and complexion and the same broad smile. He nodded, gave his son one of those smiles, and said, "That's good to hear. All right, to go visiting the Hunters, you have to be invited."

"Oh, I've been invited. Maria came to the root beer barrel yesterday and invited me."

"What about her parents? Did they invite you?"

Jessie thought hard for a moment. "Well, when I fixed her up from the snake bite, they said I could come and visit anytime."

Mr. Rascoe nodded. "That's an invitation. Okay, it's a long walk into Bear Trap, so you better get an early start, and you know the rules about Sunday supper."

"Thanks, Dad. I'll be here. You can count on it. Like I said, I'm older now and a lot more responsible. I bet before long I'll be able to get my own car...don't ya think?"

Will Rascoe gave Jessie another of those broad smiles because he could relate to his son's imagination.

Will had been an adventurer in his youth, traveling around the country working at various jobs and experiencing both the thrills and the pit falls of that life. He had served in the Army during WWI including the horrors of trench warfare in

France. Despite his lack of a formal education, that experience had provided him with instincts and understanding of the realities of life that he applied to his relationship with his wife and sons.

Will gave his sons a good deal of freedom in their youth, encouraging them and participating with them in the many fascinating adventures available in a rural, mountain environment. There were certain logical rules of course, and those were strictly enforced.

"Jessie, I'm pleased with the responsibility you have shown lately, and you have done well saving the wages from your summer job. But owning and operating an automobile is serious and expensive, and there is no economic necessity for you to own one. These are very difficult times, son. Many people don't have jobs, and others have no homes or even enough food to eat. My advice to you is save your money until you have a real need to own a car."

It was a major disappointment for Jessie, but he resolved to stay out of trouble and keep his promise of no more fibs.

Grapevine parents didn't approve of their sons riding trucks up and down the Grapevine highway. But since the trucks moved along so slowly there wasn't much danger and the boys were careful not to get caught. But on this Sunday morning Jessie decided he couldn't take the chance, so he got up at four o'clock to go to Bear Trap Canyon, since now he had to walk all the way.

But it was worth the walk when he saw Maria running down the road to meet him when he finally reached the old red barn. She wasn't wearing her party dress, but she did have on a nice pair of snug-fitting blue jeans and a clean white shirt. Her hair was in braids again, tied with bright red ribbons. She was barefoot, and Jessie thought she looked terrific.

She ran up, stopping just inches in front of Jessie. "Hi, Jessie! Ah seen ya comin' up the canyon!"

"Hi, Maria."

"Ah'm awful glad ya came."

"I told ya I'd be here today."

"Ya shore did! And ah got us a lunch all fixed up ta go ta Marble Springs."

"That's great. You look real nice, Maria."

"Mama says ya don't wear party clothes on a picnic, so she wouldn't let me wear mah blue dress. But she let me wear ma best jeans and shirt. Ya like 'em?" she asked, whirling around to show him all sides.

"Yeah, they look real good," admitted Jessie, noticing that the snug jeans revealed some nice curves that the overalls didn't, and so did the shirt. "You don't have to wear the brogans any more?"

"Yeah, ah still gotta wear 'em. But Papa said ah could go barefoot today on account of yer callin' on me. Come on, let's go up ta the house fer a minute so ma folks can greet ya proper, an' then we'll get our lunch and go ta Marble Springs. Okay?"

Jessie had met the Hunters when Maria was bit by the rattler. He'd heard so many stories about them that he'd been surprised they weren't the mountain monsters he was expecting. Oh, they were a little strange, but nice and appreciative of his part in saving Maria's life.

Their homestead house was made of unpainted, rough-cut wood and sat on a fill of leveled dirt dug out of the side of the ridge. A rock retaining wall held the fill in place. Jessie followed Maria up a long rock staircase that breached the retaining wall and led to a leveled yard area where the house sat on one side. On the other side of the yard was a woodshed, a huge pile of split firewood, and a big oak tree. A shaggy, rust-colored dog got to his feet from where he was lying in the shade of the oak tree and let out a token bark.

"Quiet, Sam," said Maria. Sam barked once more and lay back down. "Sam's a shepherd an used ta be a pretty good stock dog, but he's getten a little decrepit now. Papa still uses him ta help round up the hogs now and then," Maria explained.

They entered the house through a framed wooden door that had a handle made from a deer's antler. Inside, a large room served as a combination kitchen, pantry, living, and dining room. Three doors led to the bedrooms on one side. At the front end, Mrs. Hunter worked over a wood-burning cook stove with a black stovepipe that ran up between the open rafters and out through the roof.

On the other end of the room, Mr. Hunter sat in a dilapidated overstuffed chair, smoking a pipe. In the center, there was a long wooden table where Maria's two big brothers sat on benches looking at out-of-date magazines. Two windows on the outer wall were covered with bright frilly curtains. A number of religious pictures in home-made wooden frames hung on the boarded walls. On one of the walls were several stuffed deer heads and a gun rack that held three World War I Springfield rifles.

Like her daughter, Mrs. Hunter was petite with big dark eyes. Her hair was also dark, but streaked with grey. She gave Jessie a nice smile, wiped her hands on her apron, and offered a hand to him. "We're glad ya came, Jessie."

"Thank you, Mrs. Hunter," he said, accepting her hand.

"Yer always welcome at our house, young feller," said Mr. Hunter in his gruff voice. He got up from his chair and shook Jessie's hand firmly. He was big and huskily built with thick bushy eyebrows and a mop of shaggy dark hair, also streaked with grey. Maria's brothers were carbon copies of their father, except their hair was coal black and long, and they were even bigger and taller than their father.

The men were all dressed in faded, but clean, blue overalls and long-sleeved shirts. Mrs. Hunter had on a faded green dress, but it too was clean and pressed.

The two brothers got up from the table, and when they shook Jessie's hand, it was like a giant vice had clamped his hand.

"We're beholden to ya fer savin' our sister," said Jake in a deep but friendly voice.

"We sure are," said Gene in a similar voice.

"Thank you. It was a team effort," replied Jessie.

"Yer welcome ta sit a spell," offered Mr. Hunter. "We don't never work on Sunday."

"Stephanie and Jessie are going up ta Marble Springs on a picnic, Jayson," interjected Mrs. Hunter.

"Ah know thet, Lydia. I jes' want him to know he's welcome," replied Mr. Hunter, sitting back down in his dilapidated chair.

All in all it was a nice welcome for Jessie. But he and Maria were anxious to depart, so as soon as they could, they packed the lunch into Jessie's knapsack and hurried up the trail to Marble Springs. When they reached the meadow, Jessie squirmed out of his knapsack, and they dropped into the soft grass and started kissing.

"Oh, Jessie, ah like kissin' ya, and ah swear ah would'a died if'n ya didn't come today," declared Maria after they had kissed for a while.

"Me too, Maria," croaked Jessie. "I'm really glad you're my girl now."

"Jessie, do ya like me a lot?"

"Oh, yeah, I like you a real lot." That prompted some kissing that was more like movie kissing.

After a while, Jessie's passion was such that he just blurted out: "Maria, can I see ya?"

Without answering, Maria leaped to her feet, unbuttoned her shirt and jeans, and threw them off into the grass. Then, as she had the time before in the meadow at Marble Springs, she posed for Jessie. Only this time Jessie thought she looked more like a beautiful goddess than a little naked nymph.

Jessie's passion exploded as he feasted his eyes, and he wanted to jump up and grab her. But caution prevailed, and as quickly as she had undressed, she dressed and flopped back down into the grass. "Did ya like seeing me, Jessie?"

"I surely did Maria. Uh, you think it might be okay if I touched your top part just a little bit?" he whispered hoarsely.

She pulled back abruptly and thought a moment. "Ah don't never do nothin Mama says not to. But I'll think on it and maybe after we have our lunch...?"

"Oh, okay." Jessie's appetite certainly wasn't for a bean sandwich at that point, but something told him not to rush this momentous event. So he got the sandwiches from his knapsack while Maria ran up to the spring and filled the old rusted coffee can with ice cold Marble Springs water.

"Ya like it?" she asked when they had settled next to each other in the grass and wild flowers, and Jessie had taken a bite of the sandwich.

"Oh, yeah, it's good," he replied absently.

"Papa likes hot peppers in his beans, and they shore will set yer mouth on fire if ya bite inta one, so watch out."

Maria's warning came an instant late as Jessie suddenly felt like someone had turned a blow torch into his mouth. He refilled the coffee can with spring water twice and drank every drop before he could even talk again.

Maria was apologetic and picked out the remaining hot peppers in Jessie's bean sandwich, but he decided to wait and finish his sandwich later. So after a while, when some feeling had returned to Jessie's lips, they started kissing again. And a while after that, when passions had again risen, Jessie took the plunge: "Maria, could I uh, touch you, just a little?"

She hesitated. "Ah shouldn't. Ah know thet, but ah promised. Just touch me a little bit, okay?"

"Oh, sure. Just a little."

At last the time had come for Jessie to feel a girl's breasts, and he was feverish with anticipation. He scooted a little closer to Maria, who was watching him with obvious apprehension. He put his arms around her and kissed her some more as he began to fumble with her shirt, trying to get it out of her jeans so he could put his hand underneath.

After some struggling, he finally got the shirt up far enough to get his hand inside and just the touch of her bare skin was sensational. But then, when his hand finally moved up and over the soft swell of her breasts, Jessie experienced his most explosive sensation so far.

Chapter
~9~

As Jessie reveled in the long-awaited moment of touching a girl's bare breast, he knew the explosion that echoed across the Marble Springs meadow was not his emotions: it was the sound of a big Army Rifle! His instincts told him that Mr. Hunter or one of Maria's brothers had followed them and had seen him put his hand under Maria's shirt.

Maria jumped to her feet with her hands on her hips. "You get out'a here this minute, Carlo! Ya hear me!" she shrieked.

"Ah seen ya kissin' that Gringo, Maria!" came a voice from the direction of the willow trees. "Ah got a good notion to blow his damn haid off!"

Maria glanced down to where Jessie crouched. "Stay down, Jessie," she warned.

"Ah'm not foolin, Maria. Ah'll shoot him!"

Jessie tried to scoot down lower in the grass.

"Carlo, ma brothers will skin you alive if ya hurt Jessie!"

Maria glanced at Jessie, her eyes had a strange look. He couldn't tell if she was afraid or just angry. "Jest stay still, Jessie," she cautioned in a whisper. "Ah kin handle Carlo. He's the one ah tole ya is a little tetched in the haid."

"Ah'm warning ya, Maria. I'll shoot him deader'n a doornail!"

"You ain't gonna shoot nobody, Carlo. Put thet gun down and come on out of there right now, ya hear?"

No answer.

"Carlo! Ya hear me!"

Jessie lay in the grass frozen with uncertainty. It was hard to grasp that this crazy, unreal thing was actually happening. A "tetched" breed was getting ready to blow his head off, and brave Maria was standing up to him while he hid in the grass like a lily-livered coward. It made him ill, but what could he do?

The willows parted, and Carlo emerged holding his gun at a sort of present arms.

He was Jessie's height and looked to be about the same age, but he was heavier in a bull-like frame. His coal-black hair hung down on his shoulders and around his dark-complected, bluntly chiseled face. His thick arms bulged with muscle.

Maria stood there watching Carlo as he walked toward them. He halted a few feet away and raised his gun. It was one of those big Springfield Army rifles, and from the expression on Carlo's face, it looked as though he intended to use it.

"How come yer kissin' thet guy, and you won't even let me touch ya?" he asked in a demanding voice.

"It ain't none of yer affair, Carlo!" she snapped.

"It is ma affair! Ya been ma girl fer a long time now."

"Not no more, I ain't."

Carlo's dark eyes narrowed, and he raised his gun some more.

"Carlo, I'm tellin ya! Get on out o' here or ma brothers are gonna skin ya alive!"

"Get out'a ma way, Maria. Ah'm gonna blow his haid off!" growled Carlo.

A cold terror gripped Jessie as he lay in the grass and watched the breed raise his rifle, with brave Maria standing directly in the line of fire. Then suddenly his dad's words came to him so clearly it was as though he was standing there speaking to him: "You should always avoid a physical confrontation, if possible, Jessie. But when the time comes that you know it has to be done, do it fast and do it with all your might."

Jessie came up from the grass in a rushing charge, and before Carlo could react, smashed headfirst into his mid-section. The force of his charge sent the breed reeling backward and falling heavily on his back with Jessie on top.

Jessie quickly untangled himself and got to his feet with his fists raised, but Carlo just lay there groaning and writhing. The force of his fall, with the added weight of Jessie on top, had knocked all the wind out of him. But what really hurt the breed was the rifle had somehow gotten under him when he fell and one arm was all twisted.

"Oh, Jessie, are ya all right?" asked Maria.

"Yeah. I'm okay, Maria. But I don't think he is."

"It serves him right. Thet was real brave of ya, Jessie."

Jessie was experiencing some pretty ambivalent feelings about this time. He'd had some playground scuffles with bullies, but this was his first physical confrontation and he was repulsed by it. On the other hand, he felt a keen sense of satisfaction that he'd overcome his fear and responded to his dad's counsel and the Boy Scout code of bravery. And he was confident it had been necessary because the breed might well have shot him or, worse, shot brave Maria.

Jessie turned and looked at Maria and was instantly filled with an emotion he hadn't experienced before. It wasn't like when he kissed her or wanted to feel her titties. He just wanted to take her in his arms and hold her. And he could see in Maria's eyes that she felt the same.

They were distracted by a sharp cry from Carlo as he tried to get up then fell back into the grass holding his arm and grimacing.

"You broke your arm," said Jessie as he bent over and saw the way Carlo's arm was twisted.

He looked up at Jessie with hate-filled eyes and growled through clenched teeth, "You sunafa bitch, Ah'm gonna kill ya."

"You're not gonna kill anybody, and you need to get a splint on that arm," said Jessie kneeling down beside the breed.

"Get away from me!" he said, kicking at Jessie.

Jessie backed away and said, "I'm telling you, Carlo, that arm is bad broken and needs a splint, or you're gonna be in real serious trouble."

"Carlo, ya better listen ta what Jessie says," said Maria.

"I know how to put a splint on your arm," added Jessie.

The breed tried to get up again and fell back down in another fit of pain, holding his broken arm.

Maria and Jessie stood for a moment watching the breed writhing in the grass. Maria kneeled down beside him and said. "Carlo, Ah'm sorry yer hurt, but ya gotta let Jessie fix yer arm. He knows how."

Carlo refused to answer, looking away while holding his arm tightly.

"Jest do it, Jessie," instructed Maria.

Using the sheath knife he always carried when hiking, Jessie cut splints from the willows. Then he removed his shirt, and Maria helped him cut it into strips of cloth. He then knelt beside the breed. "It's gonna hurt, Carlo, but I gotta set it straight."

Carlo continued to look away refusing to answer. When Jessie pulled the arm straight, the pain had to be intense, but the breed gritted his teeth and clamped his mouth shut, refusing to cry out. Using the cloth strips, Jessie bound the broken arm to the willow limbs, then secured it to the front of Carlo's shirt with a sling.

"That will hold your arm in place until the doctor can put a cast on it," said Jessie as he grasped Carlo and helped him to his feet.

"Ah don't need no doctor," he hissed through clenched teeth.

"Yes, you do," said Jessie.

He picked up his rifle with his good hand, stumbled across the meadow, and walked off down the trail.

"You better get to a doctor!" Jessie shouted after him.

"Ain't no use talking to 'em, Jessie," said Maria as they watched Carlo disappear into the woods.

Jessie shook his head. "That splint is only temporary to keep the bone in place until a doctor can put a cast on it."

"They're real poor folks, Jessie. Ain't no way he's gonna see a doctor."

Now Jessie felt worse than ever. As though she sensed his feelings, Maria put her hand on his arm and said, "It were Carlo's own fault. Ya were right brave ta do what ya did, and if'n you hadn't, he jus might have shot ya. Ah never seen him like thet before. Oh, he's a little tetched sometimes, but never like thet."

Jessie had an instinctive feeling he knew why the breed had acted that way. It was plain ole human jealousy - even at age fourteen, Jessie knew that was potent stuff.

"Ah'm awful sorry are picnic got spoiled. Ya want ta go kiss some more?"

"I kinda think I should get started back," he said, glancing at his wristwatch. "If I don't get home in time for Sunday supper, I'll be in trouble, and..."

Maria dropped her eyes and nodded. "Ah know. Ya don't want to get in bad wif yer mama and papa."

Jessie nodded, picked up his mutilated shirt, and put it on. He had cut off the sleeves and the tail to make the splint and sling so there wasn't much left to wear.

"Ah'll get ya one of ma brother's shirts ta wear, and ya can bring it back next time ya come, okay?"

"Oh, I'll be all right," Jessie said with a little forced smile. Then they gathered up the remnants of their picnic, stuffed it into the knapsack, and headed on down the trail.

There wasn't much conversation until they got to the old red barn, and Maria invited Jessie to the homestead. But he again said he had to get on home.

They stood there beside the barn for a moment looking at each other, both uncertain of what to say or do. As he had back at the meadow, Jessie wanted to hold her, but he couldn't bring himself to do it. And Maria wanted desperately for him to hold her and kiss her, but she too could only stand there too, mute.

It was as though they both had accepted that their love making at the meadow was responsible for what happened.

"Bye, Maria."

"Bye, Jessie."

Jessie made it home on time for supper that Sunday. He'd decided it was best not to tell his parents about the calamity in Bear Trap Canyon, so he hid the torn shirt. But it was another of those nights where he didn't go to sleep the minute his head hit the pillow. He felt sorry for Carlo, but he knew it had been a dangerous situation because the breed was acting crazy and might even have shot him or brave Maria. It was his first real confrontation, and although he didn't like it, he felt that he had acted pretty well. He was sure that brave Alvin would have done the same. He wished, though, that he had kissed Maria good-bye. He hoped she didn't think he was blaming her for what happened. Of course, he knew they shouldn't have been doing what they did, but it wasn't her fault. If there was any blame, it was his. Brave Maria...He really did like her... He liked her a lot...He would write her a letter tomorrow and tell her.

So in the summer of 1935, some good things and some not-so- good things happened to Jessie Rascoe and his friends. Jessie had some exciting adventures, made love to a neat girl, learned a lot working in the root beer barrel, and certainly his financial plan was a bonanza: he put fifty-three dollars in the Bank of Italy in Bakersfield. It was the biggest bank in town and looked like one of those buildings in Rome in the history books. Later on, after World War II started, Mr. Giannini, the owner, changed the name to Bank of America.

On the down side, he didn't get to see Maria again before school started, and he really hated that because he did want to see her, but that's just the way it worked out. Of course, both Jessie and Alvin were upset because Jessie was going off to high school and Alvin wasn't.

But Jessie and Alvin weren't alone. Lots of people were upset that fall of 1935. President Roosevelt's New Deal wasn't doing all that well. The Depression was still going on, and he was having trouble with a Supreme Court that didn't always see things his way. The WPA (Works Projects Administration) was helping some folks, and they had started the big Bolder Dam project over in Arizona. That provided some jobs, but there were still lots of desperate people without jobs.

Things weren't going well in Europe either. President Paul von Hindenburg died, and Adolf Hitler became the undisputed ruler of Germany, giving himself the title of "Fuhrer." In Spain, a full-blown civil war had erupted. Both Nazi Germany and Fascist Italy supported the rebels, and Communist Russia aided the Loyalists. So Spain became a proving ground for war machines.

In Italy, "Il Duce," Benito Mussolini, was tuning up for his invasion of Ethiopia, while on the other side of the world things weren't going any better, at least not for the folks who lived in Korea and Manchuria. The Japanese had seized control of that part of the country and set up puppet governments. It was evident to those who thought about it that war clouds were also gathering in the Pacific as Japan obviously had plans for conquest.

These events weren't things Jessie Rascoe and his friends worried about that fall, but they would eventually affect their lives profoundly.

Chapter
~10~

Kern County, California, was the site of one of the biggest oil strikes in California history during the early part of the twentieth century. So during the boom days they built a beautiful new high school: Kern County Union High School. But when the depression hit, there was no money to build more high schools, so they just enlarged KCUHS by adding "Tent rooms" and bused the students from all over the county.

Going to KCUHS was a whole new world and a shocking transition for students who came from the small, grammar schools like Grapevine. Having spent eight years in a one room school, Jessie was initially overwhelmed by the swarms of students, the confusion, and the enormity of the whole thing. But having grown to maturity in an environment that emphasized self reliance and flexibility, Jessie adjusted rather quickly.

"What's it like, Jess?" asked Alvin when the gang all gathered in their secret cave behind old Fort Tejon.

"You never seen so many kids- There are thousands of them," Jessie answered, waving his arms.

"Is high school hard?" asked Bobbie.

"Yeah, it sure is, and they give ya homework every day."

"Homework? Every day?"

"Yeah, I gotta read books and write stuff every night at home."

"I wonder if ya gotta go to high school?" mused Gerald.

"Yeah, I think ya do," said Danny.

"All I want is to be a mechanic and work on engines, so I don't see why I need to go to dumb ole high school," complained Gerald.

"Yeah, I don't need no high school either," agreed Bobbie. All I want to do is go to work for the GP like my dad."

"Well, I gotta go cause I want to go to art school, and ya can't go to art school unless ya graduate from high school."

"You still want to be an artist, Jessie?" asked Jack.

"Yeah, I sure do."

"Well, you drew some great pictures at Grapevine school, Jessie," praised Danny.

"Yeah, Jessie is a good artist. He can draw anything," agreed Jessie's brother Billy, now a full fledged member of the group.

"I want to go to college too, but it cost a lot, and my dad can't afford it," said Jack.

"My dad can't either. But I'm gonna join the Army Air Corps and fly one of those fast-pursuit planes. I can get all the girls I want then," said Alvin.

"Alvin, I thought you liked Agnes?" said Danny.

"Well, I do. But if you got silver wings, you can get any girl."

"You got a new girl yet, Jessie?" asked Jack.

Jessie shook his head. "No. Ya gotta have a car to get those high school girls."

The truth was that Maria Hunter was on Jessie's mind a lot. He'd not seen her since the calamity at Marble Springs, but he thought about her and wanted desperately to go see her. But it seemed that something always prevented him from going, apart from the logistical considerations of a twenty mile hike.

"Are there any girls there as pretty as Hallie Lamont?" asked Gerald.

Jessie hesitated. "Well, there's a lot of pretty girls there, but I ain't seen none as pretty as her."

"Yeah, you ain't gonna see many girls as good lookin' as she is," declared Bobbie.

"Do you like high school, Jessie?" asked Jack.

Jessie thought about the question for a minute. "Well, it's okay. But I'll like it a lot better when you guys all get there."

Other than not getting to see Maria, the rest of 1935 went pretty well. Mr. Rascoe did start teaching Jessie to drive in the family Chevrolet. They would drive out on the cow trail that went up Salt Cheek where Mr. Rascoe liked to hunt quail. It was a big boost to Jessie's morale. He learned quickly and could imagine Maria's reaction when he came driving up Bear Trap Canyon to see her in a car.

Jessie did his homework and managed to get good grades. He got an A in art because he liked it best of all. His art teacher said he had natural talent and should pursue it as a career. But she admitted there weren't too many jobs for artists, and folks didn't have much money to buy art these days.

Winter came early again that year with heavy snow on the Tehachapi, so Jessie never got back to Bear Trap to see Maria. But he did write her a letter and mailed it at the Grapevine Post Office. He knew that eventually one of the Hunters would come to the store for supplies and get the mail.

Dear Maria,

I am in high school now. I am taking history, algebra, English, social science and art. I like art best. I ride on a school bus that goes all the way to Bakersfield and back every day. The high school is really big. The Drillers football team has won all their games so far, but I don't get to go. My dad is teaching me to drive now, and when I get my car, I can drive over to see you. When spring comes, I'll come if you want me to. You want me to come don't you? I hope you are fine, and I hope you write me a letter soon.

Very, very fondly, Jessie Rascoe. P.S. Do you know if Carlo got his arm fixed?

As Jessie had told his friends, high school was hard, and it required a lot of work. That, Boy Scouts, and family obligations didn't leave much time for anything else. He caught the high school bus early in the morning and rode it to Bakersfield, went to class all day, and then rode it back to the Grapevine after the last class.

Riding the school bus was fun, and he made some new friends. But the bus driver, Johnny Lashburn, had strict rules: you had to stay in your seat at all times. So the socializing was limited. A couple of times he did sit next to a pretty girl who got on the bus at Digeorga Farms. She was friendly but all she talked about was herself.

There was another girl in his art class who was friendly, until she found out Jessie lived out on the Grapevine. But Jessie had already decided he didn't want any other girl anyway, because he was pretty sure he was in love with Maria.

As usual, Miss Trembell's 1935 Christmas play was the biggest event of the season on the Grapevine. The surprise was that Miss Trembell picked Alvin to play Joseph because everyone knew that Joseph was tall and Alvin was a little on the short side. Jack was the tallest eighth grader and was expected to get the part. But if he was miffed, he didn't show it. Agnes was selected to play Mary, so she and Alvin got to practice their parts together.

"You were great, Alvin," complimented Jessie, after the play was over and everyone stood around the punch bowl and visited and had Christmas cookies and punch.

"He got to play Joseph because he's the teacher's pet after you left Jessie," explained Bobbie.

Alvin grinned. "Just following in yer footsteps, Jess."

"I get to go with Alvin now when he hits the ball over the fence," informed Jack proudly.

A little later, when Alvin and Jessie went to the lavatory, Alvin confided, "Agnes and me are goin steady now. She has really growed up since you were at Grapevine School."

"She sure has, Alvin. She's a neat girl now."

"Yeah, I've kissed her a lot!"

"You like kissing Agnes?"

Alvin smiled. "Oh, yeah, I like it a lot, Jess."

"Me too. But I don't get to do much kissing any more."

"You still like Maria, huh?"

"Yeah, I do."

Alvin shook his head. "I still think you ought to get another girl, Jess. I mean, havin' a girl you don't get to see can't be much fun."

"Yeah, I know. But I just can't stop likin her."

Chapter

~11~

The Depression didn't get any better in 1936. "Happy Days Are Here Again," President Roosevelt's campaign song sounded good, but that was about all. He convinced a lot of people he was doing a good job, and he got reelected in a landslide of 523 electoral votes to poor Mr. Landon's eight. Fortunately, the oil pumping business was going okay, so most of the workers on the Grapevine kept their jobs.

To add to the misery caused by widespread unemployment and the terrible drought in the Midwest the poor folks, whose farms had become sand dunes, continued to migrate west looking for work on California's fruit and vegetable farms. Since Kern County was a big agricultural center, a lot of them came there.

When they came through the Tehachapi Mountains, many of their overloaded old cars would overheat or break down. Without money for repairs, they would take what personal belongings could be carried and leave the broken-down cars sitting alongside the road.

The law in those days called for Gerald's father, the state maintenance supervisor, to tow abandoned vehicles to a storage yard at Wheeler Ridge. If an owner didn't claim his car in thirty days, it was sold to the highest bidder. But there weren't many buyers for much of anything in those days, particularly old cars that wouldn't run.

Watching a Model T Ford being towed down the Grapevine one day gave Jessie an idea of how he could get a car before his sixteenth birthday and drive over to see Maria. He could buy one of those old cars and fix it up. He figured that his dad couldn't very well object if the car was a partnership deal with all the gang. That next Saturday when the gang met at their secret cave, he told them his plan. "Wouldn't it be neat to have a car of our very own?"

"Hey that's a great idea!" exclaimed Alvin, and the others agreed, but there were some reservations.

"We can't drive it on the Grapevine cause none of us have a driver's license," cautioned Jack.

"We don't have to," replied Jessie. "There's a jillion cow trails and dirt roads all over the foothills we can go on. I know how to drive now, and Gerald is a good mechanic."

"How much is it gonna cost?" asked Bobbie.

"Ya gotta put in a bid to the state," said Gerald.

After a good deal of discussion, it was unanimously agreed they would buy a car. Jessie agreed to bankroll the deal because he was the only one who had any money. Gerald would be the chief mechanic because he'd worked around his dad's cars and trucks and knew all about how to fix them.

When Jessie explained it to his dad, he pointed out that it was a joint enterprise and that it only cost him a dollar because each of the other six owners owed him a dollar, payable when they got that much. Mr. Rascoe was skeptical, but Jessie assured him he wouldn't drive on the highway, only on the back roads, summarizing his plea with: "An' you know I'm a pretty good driver, Dad, cause you taught me good." What could Mr. Rascoe say?

When the gang went over to the state storage area that following Saturday, they couldn't find a single car that would run so they choose two Model T Fords with the idea of making one from the parts of two. Gerald's father said he thought five dollars for the two was a fair price, and the deal was consummated.

Gerald's father also agreed to let the boys work on their car in the back of the state maintenance yard. It wasn't quite as easy as they had anticipated, but what Gerald couldn't figure out, he got one of his father's mechanics to help with, and after a couple of weekends of work, the "Tin Lizzy," was ready for a test run. It was the same weekend that Jessie finally got a letter from Maria. It was his first letter ever from a girl:

Dear Jessie,

I was real glad to get your letter. I thought you didn't like me any more because you didn't come to see me. I was looking for you every day for a long time. I'm sorry Carlo was going to shoot you. You was real brave. I don't like Carlo anymore. I like you. Will you come to see me soon?

Very, very fondly, Maria Hunter

P.S. I don't know if Carlo got his arm fixed.

Jessie was pleased to get Maria's letter, and he could tell she had taken great pains to write it correctly. It was special for him because she said she liked him, and despite a lingering concern over the confrontation with Carlo, Jessie knew he liked Maria a lot. He resolved to go see her as soon as he could.

The Model T Ford didn't run too well at first, and it was awful hard to get started. It ran on a magneto and had to be hand cranked. That was hard to do, and if the spark lever wasn't set just right, the hand crank would kick like a mule and break your hand. But after one of the state mechanics got it timed right, it sounded pretty good.

Shifting gears was different than on the Chevrolet, but the state mechanic showed Jessie how to do it, and after a few practice drives around the maintenance yard, Jessie was ready for a trial run.

"All right, guys, jump in and let's go!" As it was his idea and he was the financier, he got to drive it first.

Their Model T had a "touring car" body style, so it carried five of the seven partners easily. Mr. Switzner had Danny working in the store that Saturday, and Bobbie was on restriction for something.

"Okay, guys, what say we take a spin over to Bear Trap Canyon?" said Jessie when everyone was aboard and the Model T was running like a top.

"We can't do that cause we can't drive on no state roads," reminded Gerald.

"We don't have to drive on the Grapevine," said Alvin. "We can take the back way over the mountain and get there without going on any state road."

"That's a pretty steep mountain," cautioned Jack. "You think this car can climb up there?"

"Sure this car can go up there!" assured Gerald.

"Yeah, and that wagon road goes right on over and comes out in Bear Trap Canyon just below the Pete Miller Meadow," added Alvin.

"But ya gotta go on the Tejon if you go that way," reminded Jack.

Everyone looked at Jessie. Thoughts swirled in his head. It was a chance to see Maria, but he sure didn't want to get caught on the ranch because he'd stayed out of trouble all year.

Then Alvin spoke up and saved the day: "Come on, let's go! Ole Juan can't catch us. He got drunk and wrecked his truck. They had to tow it to Bakersfield to get if fixed."

"Hey, that's right," confirmed Gerald. "I saw Andy's tow truck takin' it down the Grapevine."

That was enough for Jessie. It was worth the gamble. "Let's go to the Bear Trap!" he said, and off they went in a cloud of dust, the Tin Lizzy giving off that popping sound peculiar to her little four-cylinder engine. The boys laughed and shouted and hung on tight as they bounded down a cattle trail that meandered across the Tehachapi foot-hills.

By the time they reached the higher mountains and started up the steep, winding wagon road, which was nothing more than two tracks in the grass, wisps of steam were coming from around the Model T's radiator cap. Jessie stopped beside one of the ranch water troughs, and everyone climbed out to let the engine cool.

"She runs like a top!" exclaimed Gerald, proud of his accomplishment.

"It does run good," agreed Alvin, drinking from the water pipe that fed the trough. "You're really a good mechanic, Gerald."

"Well, you guys did a lot too," replied Gerald modestly.

"Not as much as you. I don't know how you know all that stuff about mechanics," said Jack.

"I like doin' it, an' after I get out of high school I'm gonna join the Army Air Corps and work on those big airplane engines."

"Hey, Gerald, maybe you will work on the engine of my pursuit plane." Alvin said.

"Yeah, wouldn't that be neat? - Uh, ya gotta be careful when ya take this radiator cap off cause the steam will burn ya," cautioned Gerald as he gingerly began to unscrew the radiator cap. Everyone jumped back when Gerald pulled it off, and sure enough, a geyser of steam shot up into the air. After the Ford spewed steam for a while, Gerald filled the radiator with water from the ranch trough, and they were ready to continue their journey.

"I'll crank 'er, and when she starts, pull the spark lever down a little, Jessie," instructed Gerald. When everyone got back into the car, Gerald gave the hand crank a whirl, and the Model T jumped to life.

It was a steep road up the mountain, and by the time they reached Bear Trap Canyon and the Pete Miller Meadow, the Ford was steaming again. Jessie shut off the engine, and they all flopped down in the grass to wait for it to cool.

"Who would'a ever thought we'd be comin' to our ole scout camp in our own car?" said Jack, the long stem of grass he was chewing dancing as he talked.

"Yeah, we drove up here in less than an hour, and it used to take us almost three hours to hike in from Juan's place. This is the way to go camping," proclaimed Gerald.

"You can say that again. But I wish we'd of thought to bring some lunch," said Jack.

"Me too," agreed Alvin. "I guess you forget to be prepared when yer not on a scout trip."

"This is where you come on yer Bear Patrol campouts?" asked Billy.

"Yeah. We come here a bunch of times," confirmed Jessie.

"It's a neat place. This where that girl got snake bit?"

"Yep. Right over in those willows," said Alvin pointing.

"Where does she live?" asked Billy.

"Oh, the Hunters live up the canyon about three miles," said Alvin, glancing at Jessie. "Hey, why don't we drive up there and see them?"

"Aw, I don't know about that," cautioned Jack. "Those Hunters are mighty strange folks."

"No they ain't," defended Alvin. "They treated me real nice. And they said us scouts were welcome any time we wanted to come on account of we saved their daughter's life."

Jessie had been waiting for an opportunity to suggest they go on up the canyon, so he supported Alvin. "That's right, they are good folks. I been there and they said to come any time." Watching the others exchange glances, he added, "I'll bet Mrs. Hunter would give us some pie or something if we went up there."

Jessie could tell that bait was working, and after a few minutes more of discussion, it was decided they would drive on up the canyon and say hello to the Hunters.

When they arrived, Jessie parked the Ford at the old red barn, and they all followed him up the hill to the Hunters' house. The ole shepherd dog got up from his favorite spot beside the oak tree, walked over to the edge of the rock retaining wall, and let out his token bark. "That's ole Sam. He won't hurt you," assured Jessie.

"Yep, he's a friendly dogger," added Alvin.

About that time, Mrs. Hunter appeared at the retaining wall beside Sam. She was wearing the same dress and apron she'd worn at Jessie's last visit. At first she looked uncertain, and then upon recognition, she broke into a warm smile and said, "Oh, Jessie, it's you. This is a nice surprise."

"Hi, Mrs. Hunter. You remember Alvin and the other scouts?"

"Why of course. It's good to see you boys. I thought I heard a car coming up the canyon."

Jessie explained they had come to the Bear Trap in their newly constructed car. Mrs. Hunter invited them into the house and, as Jessie had anticipated, offered them all a piece of freshly baked apple pie. Her invitation was eagerly accepted.

"Maria is going ta be disappointed. She decided just a few minutes before you came that she was going to hike up to Marble Springs. Jayson and the boys are gone too. They hiked up to look in on old man Pretty. He's really getting too old to live alone way up there on the ridge."

"Uh, I ain't very hungry," Jessie fibbed. "I'm gonna run up an say hi to Maria while you guys have yer pie. I'll be back in a bit."

Alvin gave Jessie a little secret smile.

"That would be nice, Jessie. I know she would like ta see you," encouraged Mrs. Hunter.

Despite some anxiety over facing Maria again, Jessie found himself hurrying up the trail, not stopping until he topped out on the ridge and could see the meadow below at Marble Springs. There, he halted, out of breath, and looked down on the vivid colors of the grass and wild flowers. From the view of an artist, it was a beautiful sight, but in the same thought, Jessie was reminded that it was also where Carlo had threatened to blow his head off.

When he spotted Maria, those thoughts vanished. She was lying on her back among the wildflowers, dressed in her Sunday jeans and shirt. Her feet were bare with the brogans lying in the grass off to one side. Jessie could see her long dark hair shining in the sunlight where it lay entwined with the yellow, blue, and violet flowers.

Maria was an even more beautiful sight than the flowers, Jessie decided as he raced down the trail. When he reached the meadow, he slowed his pace and quietly slipped up to where she lay, unaware of his approach.

"Hi, Maria," he said when he was close enough. She leaped to her feet in one swift movement.

She looked at him incredulously for an instant with those huge dark eyes. Then recognition exploded, and she threw herself into his arms crying, "Oh Jessie!"

All of Jessie's reservations evaporated the instant Maria came into his arms. It was a rather mature scene for a boy and girl who had turned fifteen. There wasn't a lot of conversation. They stood there clinging to each other for a while, then they dropped into the grass and began to kiss and embrace quite passionately.

"Oh, Jessie, ah thought ya would never come ta see me again," she whispered emotionally at their first break from kissing.

Jessie preferred kissing to talking, but he managed to mutter a response: "I wanted to come Maria, but I... He returned to embracing and kissing.

"Ah was afraid ya didn't like me no more on account of thet dumb ole Carlo."

"I still like you, but when yer goin' to high school, ya don't have much time."

"Ah'm shore glad ya came today," she said and they went back to more kissing.

After a while, when Maria felt Jessie fumbling with the buttons on her shirt, she pulled away. "Jessie, ah got to know: ya don't got no other girl, do ya?"

It caught Jessie off guard, but he regained his composure quickly and replied, "Oh, no. I don't have any girl but you, Maria." It was true. He hadn't done anything with the art class girl, except have lunch and talk, so his conscience was clear.

"Oh, thet's good. Ah ain't got no other boy either, and ah like ya so much, ah'll do anything ya want," she declared, then pulled away from him, unbuttoned her shirt, and threw it off into the grass.

Maria displayed her pink-tipped breasts as though she was well aware of the effect on Jessie, and he was indeed intoxicated with the sight. They were like wildflowers, so beautiful he had to touch them, and when cupped in his hands, they had to be kissed. His reward was more than he could have imagined.

Maria too, having surrendered to the emotion that filled her young mind and body, experienced sensations she hadn't when they were just kissing. When Jessie caressed her breast with his lips, those sensations intensified. When he stopped, she said, "Oh, Jessie, do it some more."

Although it was Jessie's first such experience, he caught the emotion in Maria's voice and eagerly continued. A while after that, they both knew that it was time to do some other things.

When Jessie began to struggle with her jeans, Maria voluntarily unbuttoned and pulled them off. He quickly followed with his. The two fifteen-year-old lovers lay in the grass and wild flowers at Marble Springs experiencing, for the first time, that unique thrill of embracing a naked body of the opposite sex.

A desire mushroomed within Jessie so acute he was desperate to proceed to the next step, even though he wasn't sure just how to go about it. Maria was feeling some pretty strong desires too and wanted to please Jessie. But when he rolled over on top of her and she felt that hard thing pressing into her stomach, she knew she had gone as far as she could go.

"Jessie, ah'm your girl, but ah cain't do no more," she said, pulling herself to a sitting position, her long hair tumbling over her bare breasts.

It was a setback for Jessie. He lay there in the grass beside her for a moment with racing pulse and a raging desire. "How come you don't want to do any more?" he croaked in a hoarse voice.

"Well, ah want to, but ah cain't."

"How come? You said you would do anything I wanted."

She hesitated.

"Don't you like kissing and doin, things with me?" he asked, sitting up beside her.

"Oh, ah do Jessie. Ah like it, but..."

Mrs. Hunter, being old fashioned, had told her daughter that sexual relations were reserved for marriage, and her private parts were off limits to boys. So Maria's only real knowledge of sex had come from her observations in nature, primarily watching the cattle. She had paid little attention to their mating process until recently when it began to interest her. She would slip up close and watch, fascinated, as the bull's big thing came out and he would mount a heifer and thrust it into her. Maria realized that humans did it somewhat differently, but she sensed the basics were the same.

When she felt Jessie's hard thing poking into her, Maria knew that he wanted to do her like the bull did the heifer. And she was tempted to let him, because there was some acute feelings deep in her belly that were urging her on. But Maria knew that she had already bent the rules badly. "Ah want ta do it all the way, Jessie, but ah just cain't."

It was a big disappointment for Jessie. Although he knew little more than Maria about the actual procedure, he'd also watched the bulls and heifers so he had a pretty good idea of how to proceed, and he wanted to proceed something awful, even though he knew that it was morally wrong and in violation of the scout law.

"Ya gotta be married ta go all the way, Jessie."

"Well, yeah. I know ya do. But being my girl, don't ya think it would be okay to do it just a little bit?"

Maria thought about Jessie's proposal for a moment. Besides her own feelings, she wanted desperately to please him, but she too knew that it was immoral, and she couldn't imagine how you did it just a little bit. She glanced down at his penis. It was standing up from the forest between his legs.

Jessie saw her looking and it gave him an idea of how to proceed. "It's okay if you want to touch it."

Jessie's invitation was uniquely inviting. "Ya want me ta touch it?"

"Yeah, I want you to," he said in a low voice. Then he took one of her hands and gently placed it down there, and Jessie experienced another of those marvelous sensations that are so exciting the first time.

Maria too, felt a similar sensation when she touched Jessie's penis. It's hard, but velvet, feel fascinated her, and as she caressed it with her fingers, a new and sensational feeling burgeoned within Jessie. His arms went around her and he began to kiss and embrace her feverishly. It was like nothing he had ever experienced, and the more Maria caressed, the more intense the feeling became.

When Jessie's penis pulsed in Maria's hand, she instinctively squeezed it, and Jessie abandoned his kissing and grabbed her in a vice grip. Then a sudden cry escaped his lips, and he began to squirm around and gasp as though someone was torturing him. Maria glanced down and watched, fascinated, as a stream of fluid came out all over her hand and belly.

Maria had once seen a bull slip off a heifer when he was doing it, and his thing squirted juice just like Jessie's was now. So Maria knew what had happened, even though she didn't know why. But she knew that Jessie's squirming and groaning was pleasure, not pain, and it gave her a good feeling. It also made her wonder if she would feel the same pleasure if they'd gone all the way. She was pretty sure she would; the sensation in her belly told her so.

But Maria knew she'd done right by not doing it. She just couldn't. She had already broken the rules, but that was because she'd promised Jessie and because he did things to her, things that made her forget the rules. But she knew she couldn't go any farther, not until they got married. Bulls and heifers could, but not humans.

Maria gathered Jessie in her arms and held him tenderly as his quickened breath gradually subsided. She knew that he would want to come see her more often now because they had a secret bond between them that would last forever. She was sure of it. And she was just as sure that she would love Jessie Rascoe forever and ever.

Maria was right: Jessie had experienced the emotion of his first orgasm. And although he'd had no idea that it was going to happen, he knew now that it was an experience that surpassed anything he'd ever known before, and it happened with Maria.

So, Jessie too was overwhelmed and certain that it was a true indication of love. What else could it be? He'd had a special feeling whenever he kissed Maria, and he'd sensed there was more to come, but he'd never have guessed it would be like that. It had to be true love all right, and Jessie was certain that he would love Maria Hunter forever and ever.

"I love you, Maria," were Jessie's first words after his first orgasm.

"Ah love ya too, Jessie," replied Maria.

After their confession of love, they held each other tenderly in the meadow at Marble Springs.

Chapter

~12~

When Jessie heard Alvin shout, it brought an abrupt termination to the most important event so far in Jessie Rascoe's love life.

Alvin knew that Jessie liked Maria a lot, and he figured that something might be going on. So his shout was a warning to Jessie that he and the gang were coming up the Marble Springs trail looking for their absentee leader. It was a good thing, because Jessie and Maria barely had time to scramble into their clothes.

One look at Jessie told Alvin that sure enough, something big had happened, and he could hardly wait to hear Jessie's story. The girl, Maria, seemed flustered, but since the guys didn't really know her all that well, no one thought anything about it.

It all worked out okay. Jessie took some guff for being gone so long, but that was soon forgotten and everyone agreed that Marble Springs was even prettier than Pete Miller Meadow.

After they trooped back down the trail to the Hunter homestead, everyone thanked Mrs. Hunter for the pie, and they climbed into their Model T Ford. Jessie only had a chance to whisper to Maria that he would be back to see her as soon as possible. He wanted to kiss her, but he couldn't do that of course. He did have a chance to squeeze her hand, and she gave him such a loving look, he knew she felt the same.

Gerald cranked up the Ford, and they bounced off down Bear Trap Canyon with Maria waving from beside the old red barn.

They weren't in a particular hurry because it was still early enough in the afternoon to give them plenty of time for their return trip to Wheeler Ridge. Jessie wasn't speeding, but as he steered the Ford around one of the sharp curves on the old wagon road, he came face to face with a bunch of Grapevine Ranch cattle standing in the middle of the road. Since this was ranch property, the cattle had a perfect right to be there.

Jessie instinctively swerved to miss the cattle, but in doing so, he went off the road and straight down the mountain side. He applied the brakes, but they did little to slow the Model T as it gathered speed, plunging down the side of the Tehachapi Mountain.

"Jump! Jump out!" he shouted. It took a moment for his warning to register, but they all got the picture and jumped out of the plummeting Model T. The five of them bounced and tumbled down the mountain until they finally came to rest in the dirt and grass.

There weren't a lot of trees on that side of the mountain, so the Model T just kept gathering speed until it hit a rock big enough to turn it over. By that time, it was going fast enough to hurtle broken Ford parts another quarter mile on down the mountain before the last piece came to rest.

Jessie's first bounce when he jumped out of the Ford knocked all the breath out of him, and it was several minutes before he got it back. When he finally did, his first thought was of his brother Billy. He pulled himself up on one elbow and tried to look around. He couldn't see very well, and his mouth was full of dirt and grass. When he tried to wipe his eyes he realized there was blood all over his face.

Then he heard someone moan. "Billy!" he rasped. "Billy, you okay?" He heard another moan off somewhere else.

Jessie swiped his hand across his eyes again and tried to stand up. It was difficult. He hurt everywhere. When he finally got to his feet, he saw someone lying a short distance away. "Billy, is that you?"

"No. It's...me...Jack...I think I'm okay."

"Jess? You all right?" came another voice from behind.

Jessie turned and saw Alvin stumbling toward him. He had blood all over his face too. "Alvin, have you seen Billy?"

"Yep, he's up the hill a ways. I think he broke his leg."

Jessie tried to hurry up the slope, fell down, pulled himself up again, and stumbled on. "Billy, where are you?" he cried.

"Here, Jessie," came a weak voice from farther up the hill.

When he reached the prone figure lying in the grass, Jessie knew at first glance that his brother had sure enough broken a leg. "Does it hurt, Billy?"

"Yeah, it does," replied Billy in a pained voice.

"Is it broke?" asked Gerald, appearing with a big knot on his forehead and a cut on his cheek.

Jessie nodded. "Anyone else hurt?" he asked, glancing around. One by one, everyone checked in, and other than cuts and bruises, all seemed okay, except Billy.

"I'm sorry, fellows...It was all my fault," said Jessie.

"It wasn't your fault, Jess," said Alvin. "You didn't have any choice."

"That's right. There was nothing else you could do," agreed Gerald, spitting blood from a cut lip. "But it's a good thing we jumped out when we did."

"Yeah, just look at our car. That's the worst wreck I ever seen," said Jack, glancing down the mountain at the scattered wreckage.

"There ain't nothing left but junk," added Alvin, massaging one arm where his shirt was torn.

"The important thing now is we gotta put a splint on Billy's leg. See what you can find," instructed Jessie, trying to assume his Boy Scout patrol leader mode. But it didn't come off too well because he was so upset.

"Maybe we can use some of the parts from our car for splints," suggested Alvin.

"There's no parts left that ain't broken," said Jack, as he picked grass and dirt from his hair.

"How we gonna get him home?" asked Gerald.

"Were gonna carry him, just like we did Maria that time," replied Jessie as confidently as he could sound.

"It's a good fifteen miles from here to Wheeler Ridge, Jessie," said Gerald.

"And there ain't no willow poles on this side of the mountain," added Jack.

"A couple of us will go find some," Jessie responded.

"Maybe we should go over to the ranch and get some help," suggested Gerald.

Everyone exchanged glances. They all knew it was a good idea since it wasn't far from where they were to the ranch headquarters. Of course, that would bring even more trouble than they already had and they realized that too.

"Yeah, you're right," agreed Jessie. "Billy needs to get to a doctor as soon as possible, and that's the fastest way."

"I know where it is. I'll go," volunteered Gerald.

"No. It's my responsibility. I'll go," Jessie said. "Alvin, you're real good in first aid, so you put on the splint. The rest of you look around and find something to use." Turning to his brother, he added, "I'll be back with help as soon as I can, Billy."

"All right, Jessie," said Billy, grimacing.

"Ya take that road east at Old Rose Station," instructed Gerald. "It's about three miles on down there."

Jessie nodded and started off down the road limping. His head ached. He still had dirt in his mouth, blood on his face, and he couldn't raise his left arm. But those were small concerns compared to his distress over what had happened.

Wrecking the Ford was understandable. But Jessie couldn't shake the awful feeling that it was punishment for what he and Maria had done at Marble Springs just like the disaster last summer with Carlo when he and Maria had been doing immoral things. What possessed him? It was as though he had no control over his behavior. He knew it wasn't sweet Maria's fault, but it seemed that when he was with her, he was unable to control himself. Their love making this time had been the most exciting experience of his life, but it obviously came with consequences.

The new ranch headquarters was a big impressive-looking building with a big, impressive-looking sign out front. It was also closed for the weekend. After pounding on the front door for a while, Jessie walked on down a road lined with trees, which led to the sprawling hacienda where the ranch big shot lived.

The hacienda was a ranch-style, white adobe structure with a red-tile roof. There was a white adobe fence all around the compound with a fancy iron gate at the entrance. He opened the gate and followed a path made of brick that wound through a garden patio filled with flowers and shrubs. Jessie was nervous and intimidated, but he was also desperate and determined.

He walked up to a huge wood and wrought-iron front door that had a branding iron for a door knob. After knocking three times, each knock louder than the last, it appeared that no one was home. He couldn't imagine there wasn't someone there somewhere, so he followed another brick walkway around the hacienda to the rear area. Gerald had said they had a real swimming pool in their back yard. Since it was a warm spring day, maybe someone was out there.

A tall hedge ran alongside the walkway, and when Jessie came to an opening, he stepped through onto a cement pool deck.

For the third time that day, Jessie Rascoe experienced something that he would never, ever forget.

A naked man was lying with a naked woman on a lounge sofa beside the pool. They were embracing and kissing passionately just as he and Maria had been doing at Marble Springs. It was shocking, yet in a strange way exonerating to see someone else doing it. He just stood there, fascinated and speechless.

Suddenly the woman looked up, saw Jessie, and let out a shriek, "Jesus Christ!" She jumped up from the lounge, grabbed a towel, and quickly wrapped it around her naked body. It was the body of the most beautiful girl in the world: it was Hallie Lamont. And she was even more beautiful naked.

"Who are you, and what the hell are you doing here?" she gasped while her lover scrambled up and grabbed a pair of swimming trunks lying beside the sofa.

It took a minute for Jessie to compose himself and find his voice. "Uh...I'm sorry. I didn't mean to...I need help."

"I'll help you, you little son of a bitch growled the lover, whom Jessie recognized as that older guy, George, who owned the white convertible. Pulling on the swimming trunks, George dashed across to a small dressing enclosure and came out a second later with a revolver in his hand. "I'm gonna blow your sneaking damn head off!" he yelled.

"George, no, don't!" shouted Hallie. "Don't shoot him!" she pleaded as George raised the gun and took aim.

As Jessie stood looking down the barrel of that huge hand-gun, he could only think that this was more punishment for his evil behavior. He promised himself that if he survived this day he would change his evil ways forever.

"Please, George, don't!" Hallie coaxed as George thrust the gun barrel up against Jessie's head and cocked it.

"What the hell are you doing here?"

"I...I need help." It was hard for Jessie to think with the gun barrel pressed against his forehead. "My brother is hurt. We had an accident down the road."

George hesitated, his handsome face twisted in anger. "I don't believe you. You're here spying on us!"

Hallie stepped up and pushed the barrel of the revolver off to one side. "I think he's telling the truth, George. There's blood all over him, and I recognize him now. He's the kid that works in the root beer stand at Switzner's. Remember, he's the one that dumped the root beer on me." She turned and looked at Jessie. "Isn't that right?"

Jessie quickly nodded.

George looked at Jessie with narrowed eyes. "So what happened to you?" he demanded, still suspicious.

"We wrecked our car comin' down the Old Rose Station road. My brother got a bad broken leg."

"What were you doing there? That's our property," snapped Hallie.

"I know. I'm sorry...I-"

"Oh, shut up!" she snapped.

George turned and looked at her. "What'a we gonna do? You know he'll blab all over the place."

"I know, but..."

"I say we shoot him. It's perfectly legal. He was breaking and entering on private property. That way, no one will know."

"George, be realistic. We can't do that."

George looked at Jessie menacingly. "I can," he said.

Jessie looked at Hallie pleadingly.

"Well, I can't," the girl said, looking at Jessie. "If George lets you go, would you promise not to ever tell anyone what you, uh, saw here?"

Jessie nodded. "I give you my word on my scout's honor."

They both looked at each other, and then at Jessie. "On your what?" asked George.

"On my Boy Scout honor," Jessie repeated.

George sneered, "Gimme a break!"

"Hold on. That's important to these locals. They take that stuff seriously," Hallie advised, looking at Jessie. "I want you to say it again. What's your name?"

"Jessie...Jessie Rascoe."

"Okay, Jessie Rascoe, look at me and say it."

Jessie looked at her. Her disheveled, hair made her blue eyes even more blue, but they weren't friendly blue eyes. "I promise on my scout's honor that I'll never ever tell anyone what I...saw here today."

The girl nodded. George put the barrel of the gun back to Jessie's forehead and leaned forward so that his face was just inches from Jessie's. His breath smelled like whiskey. "And if I ever hear anything about this, I'll know who told, and I'll find you, kid, and blow your fuckin' head off. Do you understand?"

Jessie nodded.

"You say your brother has a broken leg?" asked Hallie.

"Yes, he does."

"How do you know he's got a broken leg?" demanded George.

"I know because-"

"Because you're a Boy Scout," interrupted George sarcastically.

Jessie nodded. "Uh, could you go get my brother and take him up to Doc Veeyon?"

"Take him where?"

"There is an ole geezer up at Oak Glenn who does bootleg medical for the locals," explained Hallie. "We can drive him up there in Dad's pickup."

"I think we ought to just shoot 'em all. They're trespassers," grumbled George.

"Be realistic, George," said Hallie.

Apparently everyone at the ranch had gone somewhere, and Hallie had stayed home because George, her rich boyfriend from Bakersfield, was coming to visit her, and do things... immoral things- just like he and Maria had done.

Reluctantly, George drove Mr. Lamont's pickup to the old Rose Station road and picked up Billy and the rest of the battered accident victims. Then he drove them to Doc Veeyon's place at Oak Glenn.

A short time later, everyone on the Grapevine knew the story, and the five Boy Scouts were in deep trouble, particularly Jessie.

Chapter
~13~

Mr. Rascoe recognized that it was an accident. But the disturbing thing was that his son, who was going on sixteen years old, was still doing irresponsible things. Jessie knew that he was not allowed to drive on ranch property. Now how could he expect to own and operate a motor-car if he continued this behavior? Jessie had no choice but to agree, and he took an oath to himself that this time he really would change his evil ways. But he still had trouble getting the whole thing sorted out in his mind.

He wished he could tell Alvin about what happened at the Hacienda, but he couldn't. He'd given his word on his scout's honor. Besides, he didn't doubt for a moment that George would shoot him. George was a tough guy and probably would have blown his head off if Hallie hadn't interfered, and that meant that Hallie Lamont had saved his life. Strange, it just showed that she wasn't really like that mean boyfriend of hers. So why did she like that guy? Well, even though he was almost a sophomore in high school, Jessie recognized there was a lot about people and life he didn't understand.

One thing Jessie did know for certain: he was in love with Maria. There was just no other explanation for what had happened. Yet he had to admit that twice now he'd nearly got his head blown off after making love with Maria. But then he'd seen with his own eyes, Hallie Lamont, the most beautiful girl in Kern County, doing the same things with George that he and Maria had done. And she was a rich girl and went to a big private school in Los Angeles and everything. Could it be that he and Maria weren't all that bad after all? The idea was an island of hope in a dark and stormy sea.

Jessie was a model of deportment for the remainder of his freshman year of high school. Mr. Switzner hired him again the summer of 1936 to run the root beer stand, and he figured that was a pretty good way to do penitence. He worked in the stand all day, six days a week, and did chores at home the other day.

He wrote Maria a letter and explained about the accident and all and that he would come to see her just as soon as he could. And of course, he told her he loved her very much, but before she received the letter, her Uncle Bob came to visit again in his Dodge Brothers motor car and brought her to the store.

Jessie experienced some pretty acute emotions when he saw Maria. She was wearing her party dress and looked just wonderful. This time her hair wasn't in pigtails; it was combed out long and gleamed in the sun. It reminded Jessie of when they were lying together naked that day, and he could feel her hair all around him.

Standing in the root beer stand looking at Maria, Jessie wanted to reach out and grasp her, kiss her, and do what they had done that day in at Marble Springs. He couldn't help it; that was just the way he felt, oath or no oath.

"I'm real glad you came, Maria," he whispered emotionally after her papa and Uncle Bob had gone into the store leaving her alone there in front of the root beer stand.

"Me too, Jessie, it was so long befo ah heard from ya." She glanced around to see if anyone was listening, and then added, "Ya still love me, don't ya?"

"Yeah, I do," he replied without hesitation. "I love you a lot,...a real lot," Jessie emphasized.

"Oh, ah love ya too, a real lot."

They looked at each other lovingly from across the counter of the root beer stand. "You want a root beer?" Jessie asked.

She hesitated. "Oh yes, but ya know Jessie, ah can't pay."

"You don't have to pay as long as I'm workin' here," he said. Pulling a glass from the ice box, he filled it from the spigot and handed it out through the opening to her.

"Thank ya, Jessie, ya always give me things," she said and took a long drink of the root beer.

Watching her, Jessie wanted to give Maria something more than a root beer or candy bar. He wanted to show her how he truly felt. He would like to climb over the counter of the root beer stand and kiss her. That was what he'd really like to do, but since he couldn't that, he had to give her something. Something of importance. Something that would tell her how much he really loved her. He glanced around the inside of the root beer stand. There wasn't anything there. Then it came to him. Yes. It was one of his most prized possessions, and that made it important to give it to Maria: his Elgin wristwatch.

"Oh, thet were good," she said when she'd drained the mug and handed it back to Jessie. "Mr. Switzner shore makes good root beer."

"He doesn't make it himself. He buys it from a company in Bakersfield," said Jessie as he leaned out through the front of the stand and looked around. There was no one else in sight, so he said in a low voice, "Come up close." She stepped up next to the opening. "Now close your eyes and give me your left hand."

She looked at him curiously. "Ya want me ta close ma eyes?"

"Yeah, please." She hesitated and then obeyed. He took her hand, slipped the watch on her wrist, and fastened the leather band. "Okay, now you can open them."

She looked at her wrist, and those big dark eyes grew even bigger. She glanced up at him uncertainly.

"It's yours, Maria. I'm giving it to you, he explained.

"Jessie!" she shrieked. "Ya... can't do thet! Ya need your clock in your business here."

There was a lot of truth in what she said. He did need it. But he'd made up his mind. He wanted her to have it so that was that. "I want you to have it, Maria, because, well, I just do."

"Oh, Jessie, thet's real nice of ya, but ah can't take it. It's too valuable an ya need it."

"Please, Maria, I really want you to have it."

She looked at him strangely for a moment. "This be kinda like you're engagin' me?"

Engagin' her? That took Jessie by surprise and required a moment of thought. It was in a sense like an engagement, wasn't it? He did want Maria to be his girl because he was sure that he truly loved her. Finally, he nodded. "Yeah, that's kinda what it is. But Maria, I don't think we should tell anybody. Let's keep it a secret, okay?"

"Oh, yes! Ah can keep our engagement a secret. And ah'll never take ma new clock off," she said.

"Well, ya gotta take it off when you wash, or you'll get it wet and that ruins it."

"All right, ah'll jest take it off when ah wash. Oh thank ya, Jessie. Ah'll love this Elgin clock forever, jest like ah'll love ya forever."

It was a pretty dramatic moment for Jessie and Maria, and they had started to lean over the counter to kiss when Mr. Hunter and Uncle Bob walked up to the root beer stand.

Although Jessie and Maria didn't get to kiss the day he gave her his wristwatch, they both felt good over the secret knowledge that they were now engaged. Jessie's explanation to his parents didn't include that secret, but he did tell them he'd given Maria his wristwatch because he liked her a lot. It was his parents' first experience of realizing that suddenly their son wasn't a little boy any longer, and they, too, had trouble getting to sleep that night.

The rest of the summer was pretty dull for Jessie and Maria, as they didn't get to see each other until just before Labor Day.

Maria showed up at the root beer stand on the Thursday before Labor Day in her party dress, but with tears streaming down her cheeks and her eyes red from crying. She sobbed out the story while her uncle Bob waited in front of the stand in his Dodge Brothers motor car.

Having completed Maria's elementary home school lessons, her parents decided she should go to high school, and the only way she could do that was to live with her Uncle Bob in Los Angeles during the school year. Maria was devastated, and so was Jessie. But they reaffirmed their love and promised to write letters to each other, and Jessie promised that the minute he got his car he would come to Los Angeles and see her. Maria said she would be waiting and that she would even wear her Elgin clock to bed to remind her of Jessie.

They waved good-bye as Uncle Bob drove up the Grapevine road toward Los Angeles. They didn't see each other for quite a while after that, but they did write letters, always professing their undying love.

The big event that Labor Day weekend for the folks on the Grapevine was the big annual General Petroleum Oil Company picnic. It was always the most fun event of the year, and in these austere times, it was really enjoyed by everyone because the GP went all out with lots of great barbeque, hot dogs, salads, ice cream, soda pop, and all kinds of cakes and pies.

The picnic area was in a grassy grove of oak trees in, appropriately, "Oak Glen." There was a wooden dance stand in the center with the picnic tables scattered around in a kind of circle so everybody could eat at the tables and watch the dancers. They had a live band and all the keg beer you could drink, which made for a pretty lively picnic.

The Boy Scouts helped get things ready and then, when the cars started arriving, directed traffic and stuff like that. It was a small way to show the Boy Scouts appreciated the GP giving them a scout barrack for free.

Abigail Trembell even had a beer and looked radiant in a pretty summer dress. Of course, she was the prettiest lady on the Grapevine anyway. Most of the scouts agreed to that as they sat at one of the picnic tables eating their barbecue after all the work was finished.

"Look at Miss Trembell dance! She is really good," exclaimed Alvin, watching her swing around the dance floor with one of the young men.

"She sure is. You ever dance, Alvin?" asked Jessie.

"Naw, but if I could, I'd sure go and dance with Miss Trembell."

"You'd go dance with Miss Trembell?" asked Bobbie, with a mouthful of barbecue.

"Yeah, I think she is really neat."

"I think she's mean as a snake," said Gerald.

"She's not mean. You're a great mechanic, Gerald, but you just don't understand girls," replied Alvin.

"Holy moley, look! It's Hallie Lamont!" said Jack suddenly.

All eyes followed Jack's line of vision, and all eyes landed on what Jack saw: Hallie Lamont, dressed in a beautiful yellow dress with a violet scarf at her throat. She was stunning, and every eye at the picnic was on her as she and some adults walked up and sat down at one of the picnic tables near the scouts. Jessie nearly choked on his barbecue.

"That's her dad, and those other guys are oil company big shots from Los Angeles," said Danny. He always knew that stuff.

Jessie couldn't take his eyes off Hallie. It was as though she hypnotized him, and he couldn't help seeing the image of her naked at the swimming pool. She was beautiful, with or without clothes.

"Wow, she's even prettier than Miss Trembell," said Jack.

"Yeah, yer right," agreed Bobbie.

"How old you reckon she is?" asked Jack.

"She's probably about twenty," Gerald guessed.

"She ain't that old," Danny said. "She's still in high school."

"You sure, Danny?"

"Sure I'm sure."

"She looks like a movie star," said Billy.

Jessie couldn't stop staring at her, and suddenly she looked across at him and their eyes met. At first, she appeared puzzled as though she didn't recognize him in his Boy Scout uniform. Then surprisingly, she smiled, which left Jessie momentarily flustered. But he recovered quickly, and since George wasn't with her, he returned the smile.

About that time, some of the other scouts came up to the table, and Jessie was distracted. When he had a chance to look back at her, he was disappointed to see that she was gone. He was looking around for her when a voice said, "Jessie, would you help Miss Lamont?" It was Mr. Carver, the Scoutmaster, standing beside the table with Hallie. Jessie leaped to his feet while the rest of the scouts stared incredulously.

"Oh, sure...sure," Jessie stammered.

"Miss Lamont would like you to help her get an earring that fell down behind the seat of her car," said Mr. Carver, smiling admiringly at Hallie, who stood back a ways looking demure.

"Thank you. I would appreciate your assistance, Jessie," she said in a nice voice.

"Yeah, sure."

"Can you believe that?" muttered Alvin as Jessie and Hallie Lamont walked off through the picnic tables with every eye following them.

They walked silently down toward the car parking area for a ways, and then she said, "I hope you don't mind doing this for me."

"No, I don't mind."

"It's very nice of you."

"Oh, that's okay."

They walked on.

"I see you're still in Boy Scouts."

"Yeah, I am," he said distractedly. It was exciting to be walking with Hallie Lamont, but Jessie was wrestling with the question of why she had picked him to get her earring.

"Did your brother get over his broken leg?"

Jessie took that question as a clue that she sure enough wanted to say something about Black Sunday. "Oh, yeah, he was one of the guys sitting there at the table."

"I'm glad."

When they arrived at the parking area, Jessie came to a halt and asked, "Where is your car?"

She looked at him and said, "I didn't lose my earring. I just wanted to talk to you a minute in private."

Jessie just stood there. He didn't know what to say.

"It occurred to me when I saw you there a few minutes ago that...Well, we treated you rather badly that afternoon at the hacienda. I also realize that you are to be trusted."

Jessie still didn't know what to say.

"Anyway, the purpose of this little charade is for me to tell you that I do appreciate your discretion. Not that I give a damn what people think about me. But I do give a damn about my father. He matters to me very much, and that incident at the pool came close to being a real mess. Well, you know."

Jessie found his voice. "Yeah, I know," he muttered.

"I'm sorry. I really am. I wanted to say that to you, and that's unusual for me. I rarely regret anything I've done, and I do pretty much what I please. For some impulsive reason, I needed to tell you that."

Again Jessie didn't have a clue of what to say to Hallie Lamont. She looked at him strangely for a moment, and then a little smile formed. "Well, maybe I do know why. How old are you, Jessie?"

He had to stop and think a minute to even answer that question. "Uh, I'll be sixteen in April."

She looked at him strangely. "You look older than that. In fact, I'm surprised you're still doing the Boy Scout thing."

"I like being a Boy Scout, Miss Lamont," he said, a touch indignantly.

She turned on a beautiful smile. "I didn't mean to criticize. It's just you look to be past the Boy Scout stage."

Past the Boy Scout stage?

"Don't look so surprised. You're a good-looking guy, Jessie."

A good-looking guy? This from Hallie Lamont, the prettiest girl in Kern County? It was hard for Jessie to comprehend. To be told by anyone that he lo oked older and was good look-ing would have surprised Jessie. Coming from Hallie Lamont, it was astonishing! He'd never thought much about what he looked like. He and his friends never talked about that. It was always about how girls looked, not guys. All guys looked about the same. At least to Jessie they did.

"And if I was sixteen instead of twenty-nine?"

"You're twenty nine!"

She laughed. It was like beautiful music. "No, I'm eighteen, going on twenty-nine."

It made no sense to Jessie, and he was having trouble believing he'd heard her say that she would like him if she wasn't older than him. Could that be true?

She smiled. "Anyway, I appreciate your discretion and don't pay any attention to my babbling. Come on, Jessie, let's go back to the picnic."

Jessie managed to satisfy the barrage of questions that came from his friends about his encounter with Hallie Lamont. He hated to fib because he'd taken an oath to stop all fibbing. But what could he do? He couldn't tell them the whole truth without breaking his scout's honor oath. He just stuck with the story that she'd lost an ear-ring, but when he and Alvin met at their secret place on Grapevine Creek the last Sunday before school started, he ran into trouble.

"Jess, you know I can keep a secret. You got one about Hallie Lamont?"

The question jolted Jessie, but it wasn't surprising that Alvin could tell when he had something on his mind. "Yeah, I do."

Alvin raised up on one elbow from where he lay on his back in the grass. "Yeah?"

"I think Hallie Lamont likes me."

"You do? How come?"

Jessie rose up too. "Well, she said I was good lookin'."

"She really said that?"

Jessie nodded. "And she said I looked a lot older than sixteen."

"But you ain't sixteen."

"I will be next April."

Alvin squinted his eyes some and said, "It sure sounds like she likes you. And if you get her, Jess, you got the best-lookin' girl in Kern County!"

"That's the truth. But, Alvin, I think she was just messing around."

"Ya think so?"

"Yeah."

Alvin looked at Jessie and squinted his eyes. "Why would she do that?"

Jessie hesitated. He was on delicate ground because he couldn't tell the truth without breaking his scout honor. "Well, I think she kinda says what she wants, and she was just playing around with me. It's okay though, Alvin, because I don't want any other girl but Maria, anyway."

Alvin looked at his friend with wide eyes.

"I'm gonna tell ya a really important secret, Alvin."

Alvin held up his hand with the three-fingered scout sign.

"I'm in love with Maria."

Alvin nodded knowingly. "Yep, I sort of figured you might say that. But how do you know you are, Jess?"

Jessie wanted to answer Alvin's question because they had always shared their deepest personal secrets, but this time he couldn't. He knew deep down that his intimate relations with Maria could not be shared, even with his best friend. "I just know, Alvin," he said, and flopped back down in the grass.

Alvin pondered Jessie's answer for a moment. "Well, it's like I told you when we were little kids at Grapevine School: Ya gotta do what comes natural. It's man stuff, and I guess you just know when the right girl comes along."

"Yeah, I think yer right."

Alvin flopped back down in the grass too, and they watched a grey squirrel racing through the big oak tree jumping from branch to branch with another squirrel right behind him. The two scampered through the branches, and then both leaped across to another tree and disappeared.

"Jess, it's a sign of true love all right: You givin' up the rich princess for that poor little hill-billy girl."

"I guess so, Alvin."

"The problem you got now, though, is that they both live in Los Angeles, so you ain't got either one."

Jessie always admired Alvin for telling it the way it was, but in this instance he didn't exactly like what he heard.

Chapter
~14~

Jessie stayed out of trouble that whole 1937 school year, and got pretty good grades. It was great having Alvin, Bobbie, Gerald, and Jack all in high school with him. It made for a lot more fun. Only two of the gang, Danny and Billy, were left at Grapevine School. They were now eighth graders, and it was their turn to get the baseball from Grapevine Creek when it went over the fence.

Jessie and Maria exchanged letters regularly that year. She was homesick at first and wanted desperately to come home. And to make matters worse she had to go to a special school for a year before she could go to high school. She didn't like Los Angeles and missed her little friends at Marble Springs. But she admitted she missed Jessie the most and looked at her Elgin watch a lot to remind her of him.

But after a while, her letters began to change, and Jessie could tell she was adjusting.

Jessie thought of a way to get his dad to let him purchase Bud Carver's Model A Ford. He wrote a letter to Mr. Randolph Hearst who owned the *Los Angeles Examiner newspaper,* and asked him to start a rural delivery service on the Grapevine and Jessie would deliver the papers in a model A Ford. To everyone's surprise Jessie got the job. That pleased Mr. Rascoe and he gave his permission for Jessie to purchase the Model A for $35,00.

Jessie got his driver's license, then went to all the houses on the Grapevine and managed to get 65 subscriptions for the morning addition of the Los Angeles Examiner.

The Model A was a dark-green roadster with red spoke wheels, a cloth top, wind wings, and a rumble seat. The rumble seat was perfect for carrying the papers. Jessie stacked them back there so he could reach through the canvas window, grab one, roll it, and put on the rubber band while he drove. He got so proficient at throwing that he could put a paper right at the customer's doorstep going down the road in his Model A at thirty miles per hour.

The newspapers came by truck from Los Angeles and were dropped off in a big bundle at Rose Station at four o'clock in the morning. Getting up that early was hard at first, but once he got used to it, Jessie loved it. There was something exciting about getting up before everyone else and driving out on the Grapevine road in the early morning darkness when there were hardly any cars or trucks. He delivered the papers from Wheeler Ridge to the top of the Tejon Pass at Gorman. He would finish his paper route just in time to grab his books and a piece of toast and catch the High School bus at seven o'clock.

Hearst Newspapers Inc. paid him five cents for every paper he delivered, and a dollar a day gasoline allowance. Mr. Switzner even gave him a special price of fifteen cents a gallon for gas because Jessie was performing a community service.

His newspaper business occupied much of Jessie's time and thought, but as the school year came to a close, this thought went to Maria's return from Los Angeles for the summer. His love life had been zero since she left. He sat next to a new girl on the high school bus a few times, but she was so shy she didn't talk. It wasn't that Jessie wanted to get another girl. He loved Maria and was loyal, but it was tough not having a girlfriend for so long.

So Jessie was about to explode with anticipation the day Maria came home. They had arranged by letter that her uncle Bob would stop at Switzner's store. So there Jessie waited in his best shirt and jeans standing beside his Model A in front of the root beer stand. He had the Ford polished and his silver newspaper sign on the front windshield: EXAMINER.

It was a shock when Jessie saw Maria step out of her uncle's car. She looked so different he hardly recognized her. She seemed taller and wore a beautiful powder-blue dress with real silk stockings and ladies high healed shoes to match. And the mounds at the top of her dress were noticeably larger. They approached each other cautiously, stopping a few feet apart.

"Hello, Jessie," she said softly. Even her voice seemed different, but her smile was radiant and her dark eyes sparkled like always.

"Maria, ...you...you look really great!"

"Thank you, Jessie. It's awful good ta see you."

"Oh, yeah. It's good to see you, too. You're a lot taller."

"Ah'm wearing high heels and they make me taller."

"Oh. Uh,...that's my car," said Jessie, turning and pointing at the Model A.

"It's a beautiful car, Jessie. Is that your paper sign on the front?"

"Yeah. That tells ya it's an official *Los Angeles Examiner* newspaper car."

"Thet's a real important lookin' sign."

"Yeah. Everybody on the Grapevine knows my car now."

Maria glanced back at where her uncle Bob waited impatiently in the Dodge. "Uh, Jessie, ah gotta go. Could ya come and see me?"

"Oh, yes, Maria. Now that I got my car, I can come a lot."

"Ah'm real anxious ta see you. Can ya come today?"

"Sure. What time you want me to come?"

Maria grinned and raised her hand. "Ma Elgin wristwatch says it's almost one o'clock now. Can ya come at three o'clock?"

"I'll be there!"

Jessie was pleased that Maria was wearing the wristwatch he'd given her, but he was more pleased at seeing her. It was hard to believe how beautiful she had become and how much she'd changed in just a year. She even seemed to talk different.

As he watched her walk back and get into her uncle's car, it occurred to him that next to Hallie Lamont, she was the prettiest girl on the Grapevine. He wished all the guys could see her now.

Jessie also realized from the feelings that raced through him when he saw her that it was going to be real hard to keep his oath of being morally straight.

When Jessie pulled up at the ranch gate a couple hours later, Juan Martinez came out of his cabin, walked up to Jessie's new car, looked it over, and nodded. "Purty good car," he grunted.

"I bought it from Bud Carver, Mr. Coonyo."

"Me know."

"I got a paper route now."

"Me know."

Impulsively, Jessie said, "Mr. Martinez, you want me to bring you a newspaper every morning?" It wasn't good business for Jessie to drive an extra five miles for just one newspaper, but for some unknown reason, he felt good about making the offer.

"Sure. That be good. How much it cost?"

"They got a special introductory offer of $2.65 per month."

"Hokay. I pay now?"

"Oh no. I come and collect at the end of the month."

"Hokay."

"I'm goin' into Bear Trap to visit the Hunters."

"Me know. Wild one. She not look so wild anymore, huh, kid?" said the ole breed with the hint of a smile as he opened the gate. Jessie smiled, and waved as he put the Model A in gear and headed down the road to the Bear Trap.

Mr. Rascoe had taught Jessie how to drive on rutty, dirt roads. But the road into Bear Trap wasn't much more than a cow trail over craggy ridges and steep hills littered with rocks and logs. So it was an adventure for Jessie, but he enjoyed the challenge. He stopped at the Pete Miller Meadow, had a drink of cold spring water and looked at the place where his Bear Patrol used to camp. But he didn't dally because he was anxious to be with Maria, even though he felt a little nervous over her new image. She looked so grown up, and it was hard to believe how pretty she'd become in just a year. That thought quickened Jessie's pulse, and he instinctively pushed down more on the accelerator.

Jessie was pleased when all the Hunters came down to the barn and looked at his new car. Even Uncle Bob, who owned the big 1934 Dodge, said it was a fine car. Then Jessie took Maria for her first ride down the canyon to the Pete Miller. It was a big thrill for both of them.

By the time they reached the meadow and Jessie parked the Ford beside the willows where Maria got bit by the rattler, they both wanted to switch their emotions to other things.

Jessie could hardly wait to take Maria in his arms and kiss her, and she was eager to have him do it. But having not seen each other for so long, they both felt somehow restrained.

Jessie liked Maria's new image, but it seemed almost like he was with a different girl, and although Maria's feelings for Jessie were stronger than ever, she too felt an unexplained reserve.

"Maria, I really missed you," said Jessie after an awkward silence.

"Ah missed you too, Jessie. Ah missed Bear Trap so much ah almost runned... ah mean, ah almost ran away."

"Ya did?"

"Oh, yes. Ah hated it in the city at first, but ah had ta stay. Ma aunt and uncle are awful good ta me, and ah got a good friend down there now."

"Ya do?"

"Yeah. Her name is Patsy Cline."

"Oh."

"It was real hard for me at first cause I was so homesick, and then some of the boys made fun of the way ah talk. I worked real hard ta try ta talk like everbody else, but it weren't easy. I passed all ma test though, so ah get ta go to high school next year."

"Hey, that's great, Maria. You do talk kind of different now, and you sure look different...You really are...beautiful."

She beamed. "You like me better, Jessie, when ah'm wearing a pretty dress?"

Jessie hesitated. Emotion suddenly overwhelmed reserve, and he blurted out, "I love you, Maria, whatever yer wearing."

Those were the magic words, and all restraint collapsed. They grasped each other in an eager embrace, and within a few minutes, their passions were soaring as they kissed and whispered words of endearment.

After a while, it became evident that making love in the confinement of a car wasn't the same as in the grass at Marble Springs, and Maria still had on the pretty blue dress with silk stockings and high-heeled shoes. That created a problem because Jessie was feverishly anxious to get to some more intimate lovemaking, but there was no way to get his hand inside her dress. He did get a thrill from the feel of her new silk stockings, but when he moved his hand up her leg, he got a shock. There were all kinds of things under there that he'd never felt before.

Sensing his concern, Maria said, "Ah got on real ladies' underclothes, Jessie. Ma aunt showed me how ladies is supposed ta dress."

Jessie was puzzled. "Well, what does it do?"

"Ah'll show ya, she said, squirming out of his arms and pulling up her dress. "Thet's called a garter belt. It holds up yer stockings, and this is an underskirt. See these?" She glanced at Jessie, who was somewhat bewildered. "These are real silk underpants. And let me show ya this." She pulled her dress back down and unbuttoned it at her neck. When she'd wiggled the top of the dress down over her shoulders, there was a sort of cloth harness thing cradling her breasts. "This is called a brassiere. It holds up my tit... uh, excuse me, ah mean ma breasts. Ma aunt says titties is only on sows. Ladies have breasts."

Jessie was at a loss for words.

"A brassiere sure makes ma breasts stick out, don't it?"

Jessie could only nod. But now he knew why her...breasts looked so much bigger.

"Ya want me ta take off ma brassiere?"

Jessie snapped out of his trance and nodded. She reached back over her shoulder, unfastened the brassiere, and slipped it off, and there they were: her beautiful, pink-tipped breasts. And actually it did seem they had grown, but it didn't really matter. Just the sight of them sky-rocketed Jessie's pulse, and the instant he took them in his hands he got that feeling, big time!

Jessie knew that he was in trouble. The way he felt it was going to be all but impossible to keep his oath, and he decided on the spot that he would take Alvin's advice and do what came naturally. So he went back to kissing Maria passionately and sort of scooting around there in those cramped quarters on the Ford's front seat. After he'd kissed and fondled her breasts, Jessie's passion was such that he could hardly wait to get Maria's clothes off like they had at Marble Springs. But it appeared that was not going to be easy because of all the encumbrances of her new ladies' clothes.

Being the perceptive girl that she was, Maria knew what Jessie wanted to do. But before they proceeded, Maria had to explain some things she had discovered in her new life in the big city.

"Jessie?" she whispered. "Ya said ya love me?"

"Yes! I do love you, Maria," he whispered eagerly.

"Ah love ya too with all ma heart, and I want ta do it too but we can't."

Jessie hesitated. What Maria had said surprised him. "You want to do it too, Maria?"

She nodded.

"You mean...all the way?"

She nodded again. Jessie pulled himself up in the seat and looked at Maria. The pink nipples of her bare breasts were pointed straight at him. He hadn't really expected her to agree to go all the way. Just do what she'd done the last time. So what did she mean?

"Ah want ta go all the way, but it's immoral before ya get married."

Yes, he knew that, and he knew it was wrong but-

"And ah also found out some other things in Los Angeles thet ah didn't know before."

"Well, what Maria?"

"When ya do it all the way, that's what makes babies."

Jessie was shocked. He sat there staring at Maria. It wasn't that he didn't understand where babies came from, and he knew the process involved sexual intercourse. But it hadn't occurred to him that he and Maria could have babies. He just assumed that was only true when you got to be an adult. "Are you sure, Maria?"

"Oh, yes, ah'm sure. Ma aunt told me all about it."

It was quiet in the front seat of the Model A Ford for a minute or two. Then Maria pulled herself up to Jessie and kissed him passionately. "Ah love ya, Jessie, and ah'll do anything you want, but ah don't think we should have a baby right now, do you?"

Jessie could only agree, even though he wanted desperately to go all the way with Maria.

"But we can kiss a lot and do other things," she whispered, pushing her bare breasts up against Jessie, which got his attention again and launched them into another session of embracing and kissing. After a while, Maria took off her ladies' clothes except the silk panties, and Jessie took off his, too, and put them all in the rumble seat so they wouldn't get messed up. It was a lot better hugging and kissing naked in the front seat of Jessie's new car, although still not as good as the grass at Marble Springs.

When Maria sensed that Jessie's passion had pretty much peaked, she did what she'd done at Marble Springs. Within seconds she could tell that Jessie was going to experience another love spasm. She watched fascinated, wishing that she could share in the pleasure. Then suddenly, she felt an urge. An urge to participate and experience the same pleasure as Jessie. She was certain it was because of their love, and she was desperately in love with Jessie. But then her aunt's caution about babies cut into her thoughts. If she did it all the way with Jessie now, she would have a baby and she knew they shouldn't have babies—not yet anyway-and that put a damper on her temptation. So again, Maria restrained herself and watched Jessie have another love spasm.

As she held Jessie in her arms afterward, Maria knew she'd done the right thing. She felt some disappointment, all right, but giving Jessie such pleasure was more than compensation. She knew that her time would come later, after she finished school. She hated being away from home and Jessie and all her little friends at Marble Springs, but as her mother said, she had to get an education if she wanted to have a boy like Jessie. Otherwise, it would be someone like poor Carlo and although Maria felt a fondness for the breed, she recognized the difference between fondness and love. She tightened her arms around Jessie, promising herself that she would get her education. Then nothing would ever keep her and Jessie apart, nothing!

But Maria didn't know about some things that were going on in other parts of the world. Adolph Hitler was gathering speed with his Nazi war machine as he prepared to plunge Germany and the world into war. He had already absorbed Austria and a good portion of Czechoslovakia. His Nazis had also taken over the press and radio and flooded Germany with their propaganda. The Reichstag only met now when Adolph told them to, and even then, it was just to listen to him run his big mouth.

In Italy, Mussolini was strutting around running his mouth too. He'd overrun poor little Ethiopia by pitting machine guns against bows and arrows. Over on the other side of the world, some others were also making trouble. Japan's military leaders, now in firm control of the government, were well into their agenda. Their war machine had conquered Korea, Manchuria, Northern China, and the major Chinese city of

Canton. President Roosevelt wanted to begin preparing for war, but people just didn't want to hear it, and you couldn't blame them. It hadn't even been twenty years since World War I, the war to end all wars.

Chapter

~15~

Jessie drove his Model A into Bear Trap Canyon to see Maria almost every day that summer of 1937. He would visit with the Hunters for a while, and then he and Maria would go for a ride because he was teaching her to drive. Maria loved driving and took to it like a duck to water. Sometimes they would drive to Bakersfield, see a movie, and get hamburgers and milk shakes at a drive in. Almost always afterward they would park at Pete Miller Meadow or walk up to Marble Springs. And after they made love for a while, Maria would do the thing that gave Jessie such pleasure. But she remained firm in her resolution not to have a baby until she finished school and Jessie was an artist. Then they would get married, make love all the way, and have babies.

It was a wonderful summer right up to the last week before Labor Day. Then disaster struck.

On a Saturday, Jessie had spent most of the day collecting for his newspaper delivery service. He finished by mid-afternoon and was headed home when he got a strong urge to be with Maria, so when he came to the turnoff, he nosed the Ford down the road and headed for Bear Trap Canyon. He knew it would make him late for dinner, but it was only a few days before she went back to school in Los Angeles, and now that he was sixteen and had a paper route, his folks were a little more flexible about his being home by a certain time.

When he pulled up beside the old red barn, Maria came running down to meet him. But he could tell by the way she looked that something was wrong.

"What is it, Maria? What's the matter?" he asked as she ran up and threw her arms around him.

"Oh, Jessie, ah'm glad ya came. Ma brothers got themselves in a heap of trouble."

"What's happened?"

"They got thet girl locked up in the smokehouse and they won't let 'er go, and we're all gonna get in bad trouble!" she cried.

"Maria, calm down and tell me what's goin' on."

"She rode up on 'em while they was skinnin' out a deer, and she said she was gonna have 'em arrested for poaching, so they grabbed her and locked her up."

It didn't make sense to Jessie, but he knew that Maria was generally cool under fire so it must be serious.

"Who have they got locked up?"

"Thet girl lives over at the Ranch in the summer time."

"Hallie Lamont?"

"Yeah, thet's her. She rode her horse over ta Bear Trap."

Jessie was having trouble comprehending. "Yer brothers got Hallie Lamont locked up in the smokehouse?"

She nodded.

"I don't understand Maria, why do-"

"Jessie, ma brothers were huntin' on Ranch property, and it's against the law anyway to shoot deer outta season. But we been doin' it fer years. And thet girl, uh, Hallie, she says she's gonna have ma brothers thrown in jail."

Jessie was getting the picture, but it was hard to believe.

"They said they ain't goin' ta jail, and she says they are. She's as lamb-headed as ma brothers."

"Well, what's yer mom and papa say?"

"Mama is havin' a tizzy, and Papa is thinkin' on it."

Jessie took a deep breath. "Okay, let's go."

As they climbed the stone steps to the homestead, Jessie tried to imagine beautiful Hallie Lamont locked in the smokehouse. He couldn't. The whole thing was unreal. He suspected the Hunter boys could be stubborn, and Hallie? His thoughts went to that the day he spilled the root beer on her tennis outfit... Yeah, he could imagine a caged wild cat. Maria was right. This was bad trouble.

When they got to the top of the rock steps, they were met by a couple of token barks from ole Sam and by the two Hunter boys, who were carrying their army rifles.

"You best get on outta here, Jessie," said Jake.

"Ya better listen ta Jessie, Jake, or you an' Gene are gonna be in a heap'a trouble," Maria shot back.

"An you stay out'a this, Maria," growled Gene.

"Look, fellahs, I'm yer friend. You know that. Why don't we talk about this a little, and maybe we can figure out something."

"Jessie's real smart. He knows how to figure things out," encouraged Maria.

About that time, Mr. and Mrs. Hunter came out of the house. Mr. Hunter looked grim and upset, and it looked like Mrs. Hunter had been crying because her eyes were all red.

"Ah don't think you should get mixed up in this, Jessie," said Mr. Hunter, furrowing his bushy eyebrows.

"Uh, Mr. Hunter, I know Hallie Lamont, and maybe I could talk to her."

"Ya do? You know her?" said Maria.

Jessie picked up on Maria's reaction, from both her voice and her eyes. "Well, I don't know her real good. She came to the root beer stand last summer, with her boyfriend."

"Oh," said Maria. "Jessie will get her ta take back what she said, and then you boys ken let 'er go."

"We ain't lettin' 'er go til she gives 'er word," growled Jake.

"Thet's right. She'll stay in thet ole smokehouse till she rots if'n she don't give us 'er word," confirmed Gene.

"Tell ya what. Let me talk to her for a minute, okay?" coaxed Jessie.

"There can't be any harm in that," said Mrs. Hunter.

"If Jessie knows 'er I think we outta let 'em talk to 'er, boys," put in Mr. Hunter.

After some more haggling, it was agreed, and everyone followed Jake and Gene up the trail to the smokehouse, which was about fifty yards back in the woods behind the homestead. It was just a shed made of heavy timber and wedged into the mountain side.

Jake lifted the two-by-four that barred the door and stepped aside, holding his rifle at sort of present arms, an indication that he would be standing guard. The others stood around the entrance watching as Jessie stepped through the door and into the darkened interior.

It took a moment for his eyes to adjust to the darkness, but Jessie could see that it was Hallie Lamont all right, sitting on the earthen floor with her hands tied behind her and a cloth gag over her mouth. She was dressed in riding clothes: grey jodhpurs, matching silk blouse with a scarf, and spurred, polished boots. Her hair hung down around her face in a disheveled, entanglement. But despite all that, she was as breathtakingly beautiful as ever.

She shouted something unintelligible. Jessie dropped down on one knee, and when he leaned over her to remove the gag, he caught the surprised look in her magnificent blue eyes.

After he removed the cloth gag, she coughed and sputtered a moment, then looked at Jessie, and snapped, "Christ! It's my Grapevine Boy Scout! You show up in the damn-dest places. But this time I'm glad to see you."

"Hello, Miss Lamont. Are you okay?"

"No, I'm *not* okay! These damn morons hog-tied me and threw me into this smelly place like a sack of meal. Untie me!"

Jessie glanced out at Jake who stood at the door entrance. He shook his head. Hallie Lamont caught the exchange, scowled. and spat, "I don't know what your connection here is, unless it has to do with that little split-tail, but let me tell you what I told the rest of these stupid clods. When I don't come home, my father will scour these hills and tear this place apart until he finds me. Then all of them will go to jail for not only trespassing and poaching, but for kid-napping as well. And you, my little hero, will be charged with complicity, which will change your- pretty Boy Scout uniform to one with black-and-white stripes, comprendo?"

Jessie understood all right. He realized that if he couldn't talk the Hunters into letting her go; they were all in a heap of serious trouble. His father always said that Jessie had a knack for getting into trouble, but could usually figure a way out.

Jessie knew, however, that this time he was dealing with a serious situation and some very stubborn folks. He got to his feet and stepped out of the smoke house. "Could I talk to her alone for a minute?" he asked.

The two boys looked at each other. Maria said, "Why do ya need ta talk ta her alone?"

"Please, Maria. This is very serious."

"Ah think Maria is right. You don't need ta talk ta her alone," growled Jake.

"For heaven's sake, let Jessie do what he thinks will help," pleaded Mrs. Hunter.

"Ma's right boys. Let 'em talk to 'er," said Mr. Hunter.

Reluctantly, the two boys and Maria agreed and backed off down the trail a few yards and waited while Jessie returned to the smokehouse and Hallie Lamont.

"Your little mountain honey is jealous," she said with a smirk as Jessie re-entered.

"Look, Miss Lamont, I don't think you should take all this so lightly."

"Hey, who's taking it lightly? I'm the one that's been pulled off my horse, thrown into this stinking place, hog-tied, and gagged! But the bright spot in this fiasco is to discover that my goody-two-shoes boy scout has his own little game going. How long you been diddling the wild stuff?"

Jessie felt the blush come over his face, and his tongue suddenly failed to function.

"I see you still blush."

"That's not very nice of you, Miss Lamont." Composing himself, Jessie added, "Maria is a real nice girl."

"Oh yeah? Doesn't it bother you to share her with a loony breed?"

Now Jessie was speechless.

"Come on! Everyone on the ranch knows the breed Carlo has been diddling that little bitch for years."

"That's not true!" flared Jessie angrily. "She never let him touch her!"

She snickered. "Oh sure. I suppose you know that because she told you so, right?"

"No! I know it because, well, I just know it's true."

"Sure you do."

"You're acting like a really mean person," snapped Jessie.

"One of my better traits is that I tell it exactly like it is."

"Well, you're wrong."

She studied him a moment. "You know, when I talked to you at the picnic last year, I thought you were a pretty sharp kid, but you're sure acting dumb now. You better listen to me or you're gonna get into some real serious trouble here."

Jessie hesitated. "Well, I'm trying to figure out how to get you out of here, but you're not cooperating."

"I'll cooperate, but you better untie me pronto and let's get out of here before this thing really gets out of hand."

"I can't untie you until you promise not to tell anyone what you saw here today."

"I'm not gonna be blackmailed by a bunch of damn ignorant hillbillies! And I'll tell you again, when my father hears about this, he will tear these people up and you with them!"

"Well, I didn't like being blackmailed by that big ape boyfriend of yours with a gun at my head either, Miss Lamont."

Her eyes widened as she stared at him. Then a little smile formed. "Hey, that, my little Boy Scout, was a pretty good card to play. Some of the sharp stuff coming out."

"All I want is your word that you won't tell anyone about all this. Please?"

She looked at him silently for a moment. "Even if I agree, how do you know I'll keep my word?"

"I don't think you're nearly as bad as you put on."

"Unh huh. And that's another pretty good card to play."

It had been hard for Jessie to keep his thoughts straight when he was around Hallie Lamont. It was like she almost hypnotized him. He knew she was smart and probably used to doing pretty much as she pleased, so she was no doubt seething over how the Hunter boys had treated her. The big question in Jessie's mind is would she really do what she said and put him and the Hunters in jail?

"All right," she suddenly said. "I'll agree on one condition."

Jessie breathed a sigh of relief. "Oh, that's great."

"I assume you drove over here?"

"Yeah. I got me a Model A Ford now."

"I want you to take me home in your Model A Ford."

It was such a simple request it surprised him. "Uh, that's all? Just take you home?"

She smiled. "That's all,... for now."

Although Jessie felt as if a big weight was lifted from his shoulders, the way she said "for now" gave him un uneasy feeling.

After he untied her and they came down the trail from the smokehouse, both boys blocked the path, holding their guns at present arms. Jessie explained the terms of the agreement he'd made. There were mixed reactions.

"Ah don't see why ya gotta take her home in yer car, Jessie. Her horse is right there in the coral," said Maria, obviously upset.

"Ah don't know if'n we ken trust 'er," grumbled Gene.

"Yeah! What if she's jest sayin' thet soze we'll let 'er go, then she'll tell the law and they'll come after us," added Jake.

"Do you people trust Jessie?" cut in Hallie Lamont.

All the Hunters looked at her suspiciously. Mrs. Hunter said, "Yes, we do."

"If I tell the law, they will come after Jessie too, as an accomplice. So he has as much to lose as you, and he is willing to gamble on my word to protect you people. As far as I'm con-cerned, you're just a bunch of ingrates, and I don't know why he's doing it unless..." She hesitated, glanced at Maria, and added, "Well, I guess I do know."

"We aren't ingrates, Miss Lamont. I'm sorry fer what hap-pened, but we're just poor people who do the best we ken," said Mrs. Hunter in a quiet voice.

Hallie stood there in her expensive riding habit and stared at the grey haired -woman in her worn, chintz dress. "I'm sorry too, Mrs. Hunter," she said, then turned, and took Jessie by the arm. "Come on, let's get out of here."

Jessie could sense the agony Maria felt as he and Hallie walked off down the smokehouse trail.

"Turn my Palomino loose. She'll find her way home," said Hallie Lamont over her shoulder.

Chapter
~16~

Jessie hated leaving without saying good-bye to Maria. He knew she was real upset, but he'd had no choice. His instincts were screaming at him to get out of there and do it quickly.

He drove rapidly down Bear Trap Canyon for a while, as though the Hunter boys might be chasing them. Hallie sat beside him in the bouncing Model A, holding on with both hands.

Eventually his racing pulse slowed, and so did the Ford.

He glanced across at her. She was watching him curiously. "That was an admirable performance, Jessie. It would appear I got it right the first time. You are pretty sharp for a sixteen-year-old."

Jessie was surprised and pleased at her praise, but he still felt a gnawing uneasiness. He glanced at her again. She was watching him with the hint of a smile on her beautiful face. A lock of her blond hair had fallen down and was bouncing across her forehead while her cerulean blue eyes seemed to sparkle mischievously. "I'm sorry that all happened. I'm sure they wouldn't have harmed you."

"I wouldn't put anything past those morons."

"They aren't morons. They are just poor mountain folks."

"You know, Jessie, your problem is that you've been in the Boy Scouts too long. You got this thing of being considerate of other people and doing good deeds. It may be an admirable trait, but it gets you into all kinds of trouble. You need to get into the real world."

Jessie attended his driving for a while so he could think about what she had said. It was hard to think rationally when he looked at her. It was pretty easy to understand Maria; she was what she was. But Hallie Lamont was different. "I think you're wrong. Being considerate of other people is the right way to be."

She looked at him with narrowed eyes. "Sure, and aren't you always in some kind of trouble?"

It stopped Jessie cold. It was true. He did get into a lot of trouble. "Yes, but I don't think it's because of being considerate of other people."

"Yeah, it is...a lot of it anyway. You gotta start thinking more of ole numero uno."

"Is that what you were doing when you said that awful lie about Maria and the breed, Carlo?"

"I tell it the way it is!" she snapped.

"I'm not saying you're purposely lying, but someone is, because I know for a fact it's not true."

"How do you know that?"

Jessie hesitated. He'd heard Carlo say it himself, that day at Marble Springs, that Maria would never even let him touch her, only look at her. But as much as he would like to prove this to Hallie by telling her, he couldn't. "I...I can't tell you, but I know, believe me."

She looked at him intently. "You're covering for her, or someone. But I suspect that in a way you're a lot like me: you tell it straight except when you're trying to protect someone. The big difference in us is I only protect one person, my father, from me, strangely enough. But Jessie Rascoe protects whoever needs protecting."

"I'd do a lot to protect Maria all right, but in this case it's not necessary, because what you said isn't true."

"It's common knowledge among the ranch hands."

"I don't care. You may think you're telling it right, but you're wrong."

"No, I'm not. She's nothing but a scheming little wench. She's letting you play with her, and you probably think it's love. Sooner or later you'll knock her up and be stuck with the little bitch."

All Jessie could do was look straight ahead while the flush moved up his neck and over his face.

"Cat got your tongue?" she asked, looking across the seat at him.

When Jessie could finally trust his voice he said, "Hallie, that was really mean. You ought not say things like that."

"You're not denying it."

No, he couldn't deny it, not morally anyway. He didn't like the crude way she'd said it, but it was true, at least it was true that he and Maria were doing things, intimate things. But the other wasn't true. "She's not a tramp or a bitch. She's a real sweet girl."

"Yeah, while she baits the trap."

Jessie had taken the back way down the old Rose Station road because it was the closest way to the ranch. He was coming down the same hill where he had wrecked the Model T, so he had to pay close attention to his driving. But Jessie was stinging from her blunt accusations. Not that he didn't deserve it, because he did. But Hallie was blaming the wrong person. He was the guilty one. Poor Maria didn't even know how to kiss until he came along.

By the time he had reached the bottom of the hill, he'd decided that he had to set it straight. He turned off at the old Rose Station Stage stop and pulled up to the water trough where he'd first seen Hallie that summer of '34. He shut off the engine, looked at her, and said, "Hallie, please believe me, Maria is a nice girl. You're wrong about her. It wasn't her fault all this happened. I really don't think the Hunters would have harmed you. But they did do wrong, and it was real good of you to forget about it. I'm the one that-"

"Hold. I haven't forgotten it," she interrupted.

Jessie looked at her incredulously. "But...you gave your word."

She gave him one of those sly grins. "No, you did."

"But-?"

"You still don't understand. I'm capable of most anything, if I believe I'm right, and I do in this case."

Jessie was astonished. He couldn't believe, or didn't want to, that this beautiful girl, whom he'd practically worshiped all this time, could be that devious. "You gotta be kidding, aren't you?"

She hesitated a moment. "No, I'm serious. But I will say that I haven't decided yet just what I'm going to do about it. You know, Jessie, what happened over there was pretty serious, and I don't mind admitting that I was really scared there for a while. Not a hell of a lot ruffles me normally, but getting pulled off my horse, hog-tied, gagged, and dumped into a smelly old smoke house got my attention."

"That wasn't right, and they shouldn't have done that."

"In any event, it's not something you can just brush off. And I suspect the Hunters not only poach deer, they probably help themselves to our steers every now and then, which is cattle rustling."

"Oh no! No, they don't. I'm sure."

"How do you know they don't?"

"Well, I just know."

"Sure you do."

Jessie looked at her for a moment, and she held his eyes unwaveringly. "What are you gonna do?" he asked in a concerned voice.

"Like I said, Jessie, I haven't decided yet. The problem is that whatever I do, it will implicate you. Since you might well have saved my life today, I don't want to send you to prison, if I can help it."

Jessie sat staring at her in the front seat of the Ford as the setting sun cast its last rays over the Tehachapi. He could only hope that she was saying all this just because she was still mad over the whole thing, and she would suddenly give him one of those great smiles and say that she was just kidding.

Sure enough, she laughed and suddenly leaped out of the Ford. "Come on, we'll worry about all that later. Let's you and I take a dip in the trough. Last one in is a sissy!"

Jessie was too stunned to do anything but watch her begin to peel off her clothes.

"Come on, Jessie! I don't have anything you haven't already seen," she said, flinging her clothes in all directions.

Jessie's shock was overrun by a surge of excitement. It was as though a switch was thrown somewhere in his circuitry and all modesty evaporated. He leaped out of the car and tore at his clothes. They finished undressing at about the same time and ran side by side toward the water trough. A few Herefords were standing around, but when they saw the human intruders bearing down on them, they let out a few bawls, wheeled, and ran.

Both humans let out bawls too when they leaped over the side of the tank and their naked bodies hit the ice-cold spring water. "Christ! I'd forgotten how cold this water is!" Hallie gasped as she jumped and splashed in the trough.

Jessie was in double shock: the cold water took his breath away, while his pulse skyrocketed over the excitement of swimming naked with Hallie Lamont. And right there in the same watering trough he'd skinny dipped with his friends for so many years.

After a few moments of shouting and splashing, they paused and stood facing each other in the icy water that came up to their waists. "Cold or not, this is fun. Right?"

"It's great," Jessie managed to reply, trying not to stare at her beautiful breasts, but unable to pull his eyes from them. They were larger than Maria's, and the nipples stuck straight out. She reminded Jessie of one of those magnificent Greek goddesses in his art history book.

She smiled at him, knowingly. "You like what you see, Jessie?"

"Yeah, I do," he admitted hoarsely, his pulse racing.

"Better than the little hillbilly?"

"Hallie, you're beautiful. You know that."

She laughed. "You think I'm beautiful?"

"I've thought you're beautiful since the first time I ever saw you, right here at this water trough."

She looked at him, uncertainly. "You saw me here?"

"Yeah. You rode up an' caught me an' my friends skinny dippin'."

She thought a moment. "Oh! I remember now. You were one of those little ruffians?"

"Yes, and that's exactly what you called us."

She laughed. "It doesn't seem possible that was you."

"That was a long time ago."

"Yes, did you think about me a lot since then?"

He nodded. "Yeah."

"Have I changed much?"

"You're even more beautiful. You had braces on your teeth then," he said grinning.

With that mischievous smile on her face, she moved through the water toward him until she was just inches away. The sun had dipped below the horizon, casting a reddish gold tint over her curvaceous body. She put her arms around his neck gently and then pressed her swollen lips to his.

Jessie's emotions exploded. His arms shot around her, and he grasp her tightly, eagerly responding to her kiss. They stood in the water trough, embracing and kissing until their passions rose to a feverish pitch, while the impatient cattle waited to reclaim their water rights.

Hallie suddenly pulled free of the embrace and backed away. The setting sun gave her face a flushed look. "Christ! You're a tiger incognito," she said in a husky voice.

Jessie just stood there breathing deeply, with his penis standing straight up out of the water. She glanced at it, turned, and made her way to the edge of the trough. "But when we make love, Jessie, it's not going to be in the Hereford's water trough."

She jumped out of the trough and walked over to where her clothes lay. "Come on, let's go on out to the ranch and get something to eat. I'm starved."

Chapter
~17~

Jessie stood naked in the ranch water trough at Old Rose Station with his pulse racing and his thoughts swirling in disarray. Kissing naked Hallie Lamont was something he couldn't have imagined in a zillion years, but he had, which signaled complications and consequences beyond comprehension.

Hallie picked up her jodhpurs and pulled them over her wet hips. "Come on, tiger, the night is young, and we gotta have sustenance," she said, laughing.

Jessie tried to say something, but his voice choked off. So he got out of the water trough and struggled into his clothes. After dressing, they got into the Ford and he drove off down the road toward the Ranch headquarters.

"That little interlude puts a different spin on things, doesn't it?" she said after they had driven a while silently.

He glanced across at her. It was almost dark now, but he could see that she was watching him with a curious look on her face. "It sure put me in a spin," Jessie admitted.

"Don't feel like the Lone Ranger," she said. "I got a little more than I bargained for too."

"I don't know what I bargained for, or what it means."

"You liked it, didn't you?"

"Yes, I did."

"So did I," she said and gave him one of those smiles that he didn't understand.

It only took a few minutes to reach the Ranch, so Jessie was still in a dither when he pulled up and stopped in front of the Lamont Hacienda. He had only been there once, that fateful Sunday when he'd also been in a dither after seeing her kissing another naked guy.

As they climbed out of the car, she took his hand as though it was a natural thing to do and said, "Relax, Jessie, I'm calling a King's X for now."

"What does that mean, Hallie?" he asked as she led him up to the big wood-and-iron front door.

"It means I want you to forget about the Hunter thing for now, okay?"

Jessie knew the rules of a King's X. It was kinda like Indian giving: you can take it back whenever you want. But her declared truce, and the way she held his hand did ease Jessie's concern some.

He had never been inside a house so huge and so splendid as the Lamont Hacienda. It was built in sprawling western style with so many rooms you couldn't count them all. In the center there was a giant living room with a huge rock fireplace at one end. All the rooms had beautiful furniture and polished tables and chairs, and on the walls hung genuine oil paintings.

"This is really nice," he said as Hallie led him through the interior.

"Thank you. Dad and I decided on a whole new decor when we moved here from our old hacienda."

"It's beautiful, and the paintings are really good. Specially this one," said Jessie, stopping before a large oil painting of a western landscape.

"You interested in art?"

He nodded as he looked at the painting. "Yes, I am. I want to be an artist."

"You want to be an artist?"

He glanced at her. She seemed surprised. "Yeah. I know it sounds dumb, and everybody says you can't make a living bein' an artist."

"But you're going to do it anyway?"

"I'm gonna try."

She smiled. "You're full of fascinating surprises, Jessie."

A short, dark-haired man entered the room and said, "Pardon me, señorita. Señor Lamont say you join him on patio, por favor?"

"Si, Miguel. This is Señor Rascoe," said Hallie. Then she and Miguel engaged in a conversation in Spanish. When it was finished, Miguel departed, and Hallie said, "Miguel speaks a little English, but he understands better if I speak to him in Spanish."

"You really speak Spanish good."

"Thank you. I just told him you would be staying for dinner."

"Oh."

"Come, Señor Rascoe, I want you to meet one of the good guys." She took Jessie by the hand again and led him out of the room and onto a lighted patio where her father sat reading at a wrought-iron table.

Mr. Lamont was tall and handsome with graying hair and, like his daughter, striking blue eyes. He was dressed in a cream-colored western style suit with a string tie and tan cowboy boots. When Hallie introduced Jessie, Mr. Lamont got up from the table and shook Jessie's hand warmly.

After they were seated, Mr. Lamont said, "It's cocktail time for me, and Miguel makes a fruit drink that Hallie claims is quite tasty. Would you care for one, Jessie?"

"Sure. That would be fine, Mr. Lamont."

Mr. Lamont gave the order to Miguel in Spanish and then turned to Jessie. "It's a pleasure to have you, Jessie."

"Thank you, sir. Hallie was showing me your house. It's really nice."

"Gracias. When we moved over to this new hacienda from the old ranch headquarters, Hallie did all the decorating herself. She selected every piece of furniture and the paintings."

"You're kidding!" Jessie blurted before he could catch himself.

Mr. Lamont smiled. "No, I'm not kidding."

Jessie felt his face flush.

"Among her other talents, she is quite artistically inclined," he added, looking at his daughter admiringly.

Jessie's eyes met Hallie's across the table. "You'r full of surprises too," he said, grinning.

She laughed and turned to her father. "Jessie and I have discovered all sorts of interesting things about each other today," she explained.

"Sounds like you two had a good day. Did you go riding together?"

Hallie hesitated and then looked at Jessie. "Yes, I guess you could say we did some riding together, and as for the quality of the day, it was uniquely fascinating, although the last act is still pending."

Her message was clear to Jessie. Despite the pleasantry and her Kings X, there was some serious unfinished business to be settled before this evening was over. But he still believed that, despite her threats, that Hallie would not go back on her promise not to prosecute the Hunters-and him-especially after what had happened at the trough. He was still in a spin over that-so much so, it was difficult to concentrate on the conversation.

"Do I detect some intrigue, daughter?" asked Mr. Lamont, smiling.

"You know me, Dad- I've always got something going."

Her father chuckled. "Yes, so you do."

"Jessie is going to pursue a career in art," she said, changing the subject.

"Oh, really? Are you studying art now?"

"Uh, sorta. I mean, I'm still in high school."

Mr. Lamont looked surprised. "Oh, I see. Well, I think it's important to pursue a career in whatever field interests you."

"I'm glad to hear you say that, Dad," said Hallie.

Mr. Lamont smiled and said to Jessie, "Hallie and I have a slight disagreement over her most recent interest."

"I'm going to learn to fly," announced Hallie.

"You're gonna learn to fly airplanes?" said Jessie incredulously.

"I had the same reaction when she told me," admitted Mr. Lamont.

Miguel arrived with a margarita and two glasses of punch. After he'd departed, Mr. Lamont held up his glass. "Whereas I don't approve and Hallie knows it, I'll stand by our agreement. And here's to both your successes." They touched glasses and took sips of their drinks.

"Dad and I made a deal," explained Hallie after the toast. "I'm going to continue my study at UCLA, but I will start flying lessons this fall."

Jessie could understand why Mr. Lamont was not pleased with Hallie's decision to fly airplanes. Except for Amelia Earhart, he'd never heard of a lady airplane pilot, but on second thought, it was something she would do all right.

"Actually, I've been fascinated with flying since I was a little girl, and this year when the university announced an elective course in pilot training, I tried to sign up. Naturally, it's for males only. But I found a flight school there at Santa Monica Airport that isn't prejudiced. As long as you bring money, they will teach you to fly."

"I still don't approve, mind you. But as long as she keeps up her grades, what can I say? She speaks fluent Spanish and French has completed Shakespeare and Chaucer, calculus, and Physics." Mr. Lamont paused and smiled. "And she's never got anything but a straight A."

"All A's? Jessie croaked.

Hallie looked at him and smiled. "Oh, I think I got a couple of B's along there somewhere, when I was in high school."

Although Jessie was surprised that anyone could get straight A's he was again reminded that he shouldn't be surprised at anything this girl did. He could tell that Mr. Lamont felt that way too, as the loving relationship between them was evident. He remembered Hallie saying she didn't care what anybody thought of her, except her father. But strangely, she'd never mentioned her mother, and Jessie couldn't help wonder if the way Hallie was had something to do with her mother.

"Do you live in the area, Jessie?" asked Mr. Lamont.

"Yes, sir. At Rose Station on the Grapevine. My dad works for the G.P."

"I see. Well, it's important to our economy to get the oil to Los Angeles, but I must admit that I was one of those who didn't want to see the pipelines built. I guess I'm just old-fashioned and didn't want the change. Running cattle on the Grapevine in the old days was certainly different than it is today." Mr. Lamont paused and took a sip of his drink. "Nowadays our fence rider does it in a pickup truck," he added, shaking his head.

Jessie smiled and said, "Yeah, I know."

"Do you know Juan Martinez?"

"Yes, sir."

"Old man Martinez would turn over in his grave if he knew his son was riding fence in a red pickup truck," said Mr. Lamont, pulling a sack of Bull Durham tobacco from his inside pocket. "And I can't get used to these new tailor made cigarettes either. I still have to roll my own."

While Jessie and Hallie watched, he rolled the cigarette, licked it, and put it to his mouth. "I drive a Cadillac and wear a fancy suit, but I'm not giving up my Bull Durham," he said, snapping a kitchen match with his thumb nail and firing the cigarette.

"You can smoke your Bull Durham all you want, Dad," said Hallie lovingly.

Mr. Lamont smoked, drank his margarita, and told stories about the old days, including his version of the romance between the girl from Rose Station and the bandit Joaquin Murieta. His story was that Joaquin and the girl escaped the posse and rode the outlaw's black stallion down to Baja, California, where they lived happily ever after.

"I like your version of the story best, Mr. Lamont," said Jessie. Glancing at Hallie, he added, "I like happy endings better, don't you, Hallie?"

Hallie laughed and said, "It depends on the plot."

While Mr. Lamont talked, Hallie gave Jessie little secret glances. Glances that left him wondering just what this strange girl was thinking, and more important: what kind of a game was she playing?

After a while, they went into the dining room and had a grand dinner at a huge oak table beneath a sparkling chandelier. The table was set with fine china and silverware on a linen tablecloth with Miguel serving from silver trays. It was a unique experience for Jessie although it would have been better if he weren't so anxious about what lay ahead.

After dinner, Mr. Lamont excused himself and retired into another section of the hacienda. Jessie followed Hallie into the huge front room that had stuffed deer heads and antique rifles on the walls. The mammoth fireplace wasn't burning since it was summer, but they sat down in front of it anyway in two overstuffed chairs opposite each other.

"That was a great dinner, Hallie, and your father is real nice."

"Thank you. He is great, and I love him dearly. I try hard to make him believe I'm the person he thinks I am, but it isn't easy, since I'm not."

"I still don't think you're as bad as you pretend," said Jessie, with the secret hope that he was right.

She smiled. "Wishful thinking, Jessie?" He couldn't help smiling.

She was silent for a moment. "I do things...things that... well, I try, but...I guess I'm just too much like her" She abruptly cut herself off, and a distressed look crossed her face.

Jessie had the impression she was referring to her mother, but she said no more, got up, and walked across the room to a wooden cabinet. She opened the cabinet and took out a bottle. "Once Dad goes to bed, he stays, and I help myself to a little of his private stock. Would you like to try some?"

"What is it?"

"Cognac. It's expensive and it's great, as long as you don't drink too much. It will wipe you out."

"No thanks, Hallie, I uh, don't drink alcohol."

"You don't even drink beer?"

Jessie shifted in his chair. "No."

"Well, that'll change when you get to college. Just about everybody drinks there."

"Everybody drinks at college?"

"Yes. The guys carry flasks of whisky. I love this stuff although I can't afford it at school. Dad is generous but insists I stay on a budget." She returned to her chair and poured a small amount of the Cognac into a glass and held it up as though examining it. "I'm sure Dad knows I imbibe now and then, but I don't do it in front of him, so it doesn't become an issue." She paused. "And I don't drink like some college kids. They really get soused and act pretty stupid."

"I've seen some drunk people, and you're right they do act pretty stupid."

"Anyway, here's mud in your eye," she said and took a sip of the Cognac. She didn't speak for a moment, and her beautiful blue eyes turned misty. She put her glass down on an end table, reached into the drawer, and took out a package of cigarettes and a lighter. Putting a cigarette between her lips, she said, "Want one?" Jessie shook his head.

"I didn't think you would," she added, lighting the cigarette.

After she had blown out a cloud of smoke, she picked up the glass of Cognac and leaned back in her chair. "You already know I'm not a very nice girl, so another of my evil habits shouldn't surprise you."

Jessie grinned. "I don't understand you, Hallie, but you're right, I doubt you could surprise me any more."

"I wouldn't be too sure about that," she said smiling. Then, turning somber: "Okay, King's X is rescinded. Try this on for size: I'll honor your word to the Hunters, but in turn, I want something from you. I want you to forget the mountain twit. What's her name? Maria? If you give me your word of honor that you won't see her again, I'll promise not to have the Hunters prosecuted."

She was right: she had surprised him again. He sat dumbfounded, watching her tip the glass of Cognac at him and then take another sip. All he could comprehend was that this was just more of unpredictable Hallie Lamont.

Jessie shifted in his chair and said, "Hallie, would you explain that to me again, please?"

"It's simple enough. I'm making you a deal. I'll forget about what happened today if you promise not to see that little bitch any more."

Jessie nodded, saying to himself. *Okay, just hold for a minute and sort this out. But* it was just too crazy to even comprehend, let alone sort out. "Ya know what, Hallie, you may be right. Trying to help other people does get you into a lot of trouble."

She laughed. "Now you're getting the picture."

"I don't understand. Seriously. Why is it important to you that I not see Maria again?"

"Didn't what happened at the water trough tell you something?"

He stared at her a moment, trying to grasp her point. "I don't know. It's really difficult to know just what you're doin' or why. It was pretty obvious how you affected me. But weren't you just, well, teasing?"

"It doesn't matter if I was or wasn't. The point is that you responded eagerly, and you know and I know, we would have done it right there in the trough if I hadn't backed off. Isn't that true?"

The question went around a couple times in Jessie's head, but the answer came out the same each time. It was yes,- and there was no way he could deny it.

"I'm not blaming you. I was the instigator, and I well, my point is that you think you're in love with that girl because you've been intimate with her. But in reality, how could you be in love if just a couple hours ago you wanted to make love to me?"

How could he deny that either? He sat quietly for a moment, trying to focus on some kind of rationale. Finally he said, "I admit my weakness when it comes to you, Hallie. You do things to me that I can't seem to control, but I still don't know why you're doing this or what you really want."

"Oh? Come on now. If you're going to be an artist, you gotta have more imagination than that."

"What?"

"Use your imagination, Jessie. What do you think I want?"

He shook his head.

"I want you."

Jessie's jaw dropped. "You're kidding!"

She laughed. "No, I'm not kidding. If you remember, I told you last summer I thought you were handsome, and if I was sixteen instead of twenty-nine, I'd be after you."

It seemed like just too much to comprehend. "But you're not sixteen, Hallie."

"No. But I'm not twenty-nine either and you're even more handsome than you were last summer. And you got a car now."

Jessie stared at her.

"Don't you think you should say something when a girl tells you she likes you?"

"Yeah, but I don't know what to say."

"Say what you feel," she said, with a little smile and a puff of her cigarette.

"Uh, I like you too, Hallie. I have since the first time I ever saw you. But I'm just a high school guy. You're in college, and you got that rich boyfriend, George."

The smile dissolved, and she took a big gulp of the Cognac. "Not anymore...I hate him!"

Jessie was struck with a sudden ambivalence. Her pronouncement that she hated that jerk George pleased him, but it also told him why her sudden switch in affections.

"We broke up, and I mean it this time. I've said it before, and then we would always make up. But not this time."

Conflicting thoughts galloped through Jessie's head as he considered Hallie's declaration. It told him why her sudden interest in him all right, but her advances at the water trough, although teasing at first, had resulted in some pretty supercharged emotion for both of them. He had to admit that in a sense he'd been in love with Hallie Lamont from the first time he'd ever seen her. And that attraction remained powerful.

Could that mean that Hallie was right? That he really wasn't in love with Maria? Wonderful Maria? Did he really want to switch from her to Hallie Lamont? How could he after all he and Maria meant to each other?

"I'm serious, Jessie. I'm through with George, and I really do like you."

"I like you too, Hallie, and...I'd like to go with you all right. Golly, what guy wouldn't? But Maria, she and I-"

"Jessie, you don't owe her anything. That's the nice guy in you feeling sorry for her. You have already agreed that you couldn't be in love with her, not after what happened at the trough. So your conscience has to be clear. Isn't that right?"

Jessie diverted his eyes. What she said was true, wasn't it? It had to be true, but something deep down told him it wasn't.

"Jessie?"

"Yes?"

"I'm not gonna share you. I want all or none. It's your choice."

He glanced across at her. She was leaning back in the chair watching him, with the glass of Cognac in one hand and a cigarette in the other. She appeared a little flush-faced now. He guessed it was from the Cognac. But she was so beautiful: her cerulean blue eyes sparkling, her red lips beckoning.

"I don't know what to say, Hallie. I really am confused. Just looking at you turns me inside out, but..."

She took the last sip of her Cognac, put the glass down, and ground out her cigarette. Getting up from the chair, she walked across to where Jessie sat, took one of his hands, and pulled. "Come here," she said in a husky voice.

Then she kissed him even more passionately than she had at the water trough. Jessie's pulse leaped, and he was powerless to do anything but return her kiss with the same vigor and emotion he had at the water trough, or maybe even more.

Chapter
~18~

That night Hallie gave Jessie her ultimatum was another of those where he tossed and turned for hours before he dropped off to sleep. Then he had bizarre dreams that were all mixed up with Hallie Lamont and Maria Hunter playing alternating roles in a crazy, disjointed script that went around and around and got nowhere.

When he got up at four o'clock the next morning to go on his paper route, he felt as though he hadn't been to bed at all. He drove up and down the Grapevine delivering his papers in a sort of daze as the crazy episode of the day before replayed itself over and over in his thoughts.

When he finished the paper route and parked his Ford back in front of his home at Rose Station, he'd still not reached a decision on what he was going to tell Hallie at noon. That was the deadline she had given him for his answer.

That last kiss at the hacienda had been a replay of the one at the water trough, and again, after a passionate embrace, she'd abruptly pulled away. Then she'd told him to go home, think about it, and give her an answer by noon tomorrow. It was all so distressing that Jessie decided to go back to bed. He fell into a deep sleep, and it was late morning when his mother finally awakened him.

"Jessie, don't you have some things to do today? School starts tomorrow, you know."

He glanced across at the alarm clock. It read eleven o'clock. "Oh, no!" he groaned and leaped out of bed. Now he would barely have time to get dressed and drive out to the hacienda before the deadline. And he still hadn't decided what to do.

It came to Jessie as he dressed, that Hallie was blackmailing him, plain and simple. What he should do is tell her to go fly a kite. Yeah, and then he and the Hunters would end up in jail. But would she really call the sheriff? It was hard to believe she would after the way she kissed him last night, but there was no telling what that girl would do. Of course there was also the question of how he really felt about Hallie Lamont.

After promising his mother he would be back in time for Sunday supper, he crawled in the Ford and headed down the Grapevine to deliver his decision to Hallie. The only problem was that he'd not made a decision.

As he drove down the old Rose Station road, he kept thinking of the terrible disappointment Maria would suffer when he didn't show up to say good-bye before she went back to Los Angeles. He knew she was upset anyway over his driving away in the Ford with Hallie. To make matters worse, they'd planned a last picnic at Marble Springs.

Miguel answered the door at the hacienda and gave him a big smile. "Hola, Señor Rascoe. Señorita Lamont, she wait for you," he said and led Jessie through the house and out onto the pool deck. There, Hallie was sprawled in a lounge chair reading. She wore white tennis shorts and a matching blouse, which made her tanned arms and legs look like they'd been painted a golden brown.

She glanced up when he approached and gave him one of her mesmerizing smiles. "Good morning, Jessie. You look a little haggard. Didn't you sleep well last night?"

He couldn't help but grin. "Not too well."

She laughed. "If it's any consolation, neither did I. Come sit," she added, moving her shapely legs over and patting the lounge chair.

When he sat down beside her, she gazed at him a moment and said, "My dad couldn't believe you're only seventeen. You're so handsome, Jessie, even when you're haggard. It's those intoxicating green eyes that sends this girl's pulse up a notch."

"I never know for sure if you mean what you're saying or just teasing, Hallie. And I'm only sixteen."

"I gave you an extra year, and I'm not teasing. You really do turn me on."

He grinned. "It's pretty neat to have the prettiest girl in Kern County say that, but I'm having some trouble believing it's all real."

"Oh, it's real enough. You know, Jessie, there's some potent chemistry between us," she said as Miguel came out onto the patio and placed two glasses of the fruit punch on a patio table.

She smiled, picked up a glass of the punch, and leaned back in the lounge chair. "So, you made your decision?"

Jessie looked at Hallie Lamont, the most beautiful girl in Kern County, and heard himself say, "I can't deny how you affect me, Hallie, but I love Maria."

Hallie looked surprised for a moment, and then a little smile formed. "Well, you can't have it both ways, Tiger. But you got the character to call it the way you see it, even though that's pretty stupid since it will land you in jail."

"I'm sorry, Hallie. Every guy on the Grapevine would give his right arm to have you for his girl, but I can't."

"Okay, Jessie. Then it's the calaboose for you and those morons in Bear Trap."

"Well, you have to do what you have to do, Hallie, but I think you're wrong. I know the Hunter boys shouldn't have done what they did. But they are just poor mountain people, and taking an occasional deer for food ain't gonna hurt nobody."

"We've discussed all this, Jessie, and you made your decision, so now you have to accept the consequences."

Jessie nodded. "I guess so."

She hesitated. "You know, you're the first guy that ever turned me down. And strangely enough I really am attracted to you, even if you are only seventeen."

"Sixteen."

"Stop correcting me. I'm trying to figure out how to get you off the hook without too much damage to my ego."

"Oh."

It was quiet on the Lamont pool patio for a moment.

"Tell you what, since I have to go back to Los Angeles today anyway, a new boyfriend down here isn't going to do me much good. So if you give me your word of honor you won't see the little bitch till I come back next summer, I won't call the sheriff."

"You won't call the sheriff if I don't see Maria till next summer?"

She nodded. "That's the deal, and you better grab it before I have an ego attack and change my mind."

Jessie hesitated.

"I'm doing a Jessie Rascoe: I'm going to protect you from yourself whether you like it or not."

Jessie smiled. "You see, Hallie, you're not nearly as bad as you claim."

She laughed. "You're going to do okay, Jessie, but I'm serious. I'm taking your word of honor you won't see her for the whole year."

"You have my word, Hallie."

"On you'r scout's honor?"

He smiled. "On my scout's honor."

"Okay, Tiger." She jumped up from the lounge chair and took his arm as Miguel appeared and announced lunch.

"Come on, let's join Dad."

They joined Mr. Lamont at a table on the veranda, but Jessie was so preoccupied he was having trouble concentrating on the conversation. He was pleased and relieved that he wasn't going to jail, of course. But not seeing Maria for a whole year? But then he wouldn't have seen her for a lot longer than that if he'd gone to jail.

Jessie was vaguely aware that Mr. Lamont was asking Hallie why her horse came home still wearing its saddle. She made some excuse that seemed to satisfy her father, and the conversation for the rest of the lunch was taken up discussing details of her going back to college. After lunch, Mr. Lamont bade Jessie goodbye, because he and Hallie had to get ready to leave for Los Angeles.

A short time later, as they stood beside Jessie's car, she took his hands in hers and said, "You really want to be an artist, right?"

"Yes, I do."

"Okay then, don't get sidetracked."

He nodded. "I won't. Good luck with your flying lessons. I'd bet you're gonna be a good pilot."

"You can count on it, Jessie," she said, then kissed him hard on the lips, and ran back into the hacienda.

Jessie drove up to Switzner's store, got an ice cream cone, then went down, and parked the Ford on the last big hill where he could see the cars going down the Grapevine toward Bakersfield.

Jessie had to admit that the whole thing came out pretty well, much better than he had imagined. In a sense, he was pleased with himself, except for the way he'd acted with Hallie at the water trough. That wasn't too keen for a guy in love with another girl. But Hallie was...Well, like she could cast a spell on a guy. On the plus side, he'd managed to defuse what could have been a real bad for situation for the Hunters, as well as himself. Actually, he'd cheated a little bit with Hallie when he promised to not see her until next summer, because he was pretty sure she didn't know that Maria would be gone all the school year anyway. In a way, he'd kind of snookered her, which wasn't easy with that girl. He grinned and took a big bite of the ice cream cone.

Chapter
~19~

Jessie began his junior year of high school with his love life on hold. But things weren't going well around the world either that fall of 1937.

The Depression was still going strong with lots of people out of work. Desperate men "rode the rails" under railroad box cars from city to city trying to find jobs that didn't exist. Bums went from door to door begging for food, and there were hobo camps everywhere, filled with destitute people living in cardboard shacks and eating ground squirrels.

President Roosevelt was doing his best, but his economic stimulus plan just wasn't cutting the mustard. To make matters worse, the winds of war were blowing stronger and stronger across Europe and the Far East. In Germany, the Third Reich had taken total control of Germany, and Hitler, Der Fuhrer, had sent his troops into the Rhineland in violation of the Versailles Treaty. England and France fussed at him some about breaking the treaty but didn't do anything but blab, so he got away with it, which brought the world one step closer to war.

Down south, Mussolini's troops had swept across Ethiopia easily. Then he and Hitler helped dictator Francisco Franco's rebel forces overthrow the Spanish government. In the Pacific, the Japanese were buying up all the scrap metal anyone would sell them and turning it into war toys. They also got around to signing treaties with Nazi Germany and Fascist Italy.

Despite the world muddles and Jessie Rascoe's absent love life, the Works Project of America (WPA) began to widen the Grapevine road from Bakersfield to Los Angeles. That was a big deal that not only put some people to work, but it also helped the economy of the area and got Jessie some additional customers for his newspaper route.

Danny and Billy graduated from Grapevine School, so now all the gang rode the bus to high school in Bakersfield. On Fridays that fall, Jessie would drive his car to Bakersfield, and he and some of the gang would stay in town after school, get hamburgers and milk shakes at a drive-in, and go to the Drillers football game.

Alvin and Agnes had a falling out, and she started going with Jack and Alvin with Elinor. Billy still wasn't all that interested in girls, but once in a while he would date Ruth or Patty. Bud and Penny and Frank and Virginia were seniors and going steady. Jessie's cousin Glenn was going with Penny's sister Bubbles and they got engaged. Both Bobbie and Danny liked Andrea, but she played both ends against the middle. A girl that got on the bus at Greenfield liked Gerald, but he still shied away from girls, preferring to work on cars and motors.

Since Hallie hadn't mentioned letters in her deal, Jessie wrote Maria a long letter professing his love and explaining what had happened that day with Hallie, leaving out certain details, of course. And she had written back also proclaiming her love and thanking Jessie for saving her brothers from jail. Jessie could tell she was still a bit miffed over his driving off with Hallie that day, but there was no doubt she still loved him.

Jessie did well in high school that year, and his art teachers continued to encourage him. They had a spring show at the art department, and one of Jessie's oil paintings won first prize, which was two free tickets to a movie premiere. He felt obligated to invite a girl who was the runner-up to go with him.

They went to the big new FOX Theater there in Bakersfield and saw *"Lost Horizon."* It was a good movie, but the girl turned out to be a blabbermouth, mostly talking about herself. So that was Jessie's only date that school year.

Jessie counted the days till summer when his promise to Hallie would be fulfilled and Maria would come home to the Bear Trap. Then he got a letter from her saying that she couldn't come until later in the summer. Her aunt got her a six week speech course, and although she wanted to see Jessie, she couldn't disappoint her aunt. As always, she said she loved and missed him terribly, and her uncle Bob promised to bring her down as soon as the course was over.

Jessie was disappointed and decided he couldn't wait to see her and would drive to Los Angeles. As soon as school was out. His promise to Hallie was fulfilled, and he could go see Maria with a clear conscience.

Jessie made his first long-distance telephone call from the pay telephone at Switzner's store. It was on the wall of the store, so everybody could hear what he was saying. But it was the only public phone on the Grapevine, and it didn't matter anyway because Jessie spoke to Mrs. Hunter, Maria's aunt. He told her he was coming to see Maria. She didn't sound all that happy about his visit but said it would be okay.

He left that next Sunday morning right after he finished his paper route and headed for the big city. It was Jessie's first long trip by himself other than to Bakersfield, so it was a major adventure.

The Grapevine highway wound around and across the ridges of the Tehachapi Mountains with hundreds of switchbacks, dozens of bridges, and a couple tunnels. It finally came down off the mountains into the sprawling San Fernando Valley. Jessie thought there was a lot of traffic in Bakersfield, but when he got to Los Angeles, he couldn't believe all the cars going every which way.

The Model A ran like a champ, but he got lost twice and had to stop at gas stations and get directions. The city was spectacular. He'd seen it in movies, but to actually see the activity and look up at those tall buildings was exciting.

He finally found the house where Maria lived with her aunt and uncle. It was in a quiet neighborhood that had sidewalks, green lawns, and shade trees in front of fine houses that were much larger than those on the Grapevine.

Jessie parked the Ford at the curb in front of the Hunter house, went to the front door, and nervously knocked. The door opened instantly, and he found himself staring into Maria's sparkling eyes. A surge of emotion shot through Jessie like a bolt of lightning. It was all he could do to keep from grabbing her and it was obvious that Maria felt the same. He could tell by the way she looked at him.

She wore a pretty green dress with silk stockings and matching green shoes. He could tell she had on one of those brassiere things too because of the way the top of her dress stuck out.

"Hello, Jessie," she said, smiling demurely. "Ah'm real glad you could come."

"Hi, Maria. You look great," he replied in a voice heavy with emotion.

"Thank you. You look fine too."

They stood staring at each other for a moment. Then she pulled her eyes from him and said, "Please come in."

Jessie walked through the door and into a living room where he was surprised to see several people sitting around on sofas and chairs and dressed in their Sunday best.

"This is ma friend, Jessie Rascoe," Maria announced properly to the group. It seemed to Jessie that Maria had changed even more than when she came home last summer.

Maria's uncle Bob, who looked kind of like Maria's father, except that he was dressed in fine clothes, got up, shook Jessie's hand, and introduced him to Maria's aunt. She was a nice-looking, grey-haired lady, dressed similarly to Maria. Then Uncle Bob introduced another adult couple, the Larsons, as good friends who lived nearby, and their son, John. John was a handsome boy, about Jessie's age, with wavy brown hair and a dimpled chin. He had on a suit and tie. Jessie wore jeans, but they were his best pair. Jessie's instincts told him right off that he probably wouldn't relate well to John.

After Jessie was seated in the group, Mr. Hunter explained to the Larsons that Jessie had once saved Maria's life when she was bitten by a rattlesnake.

Jessie blushed, Maria beamed, and John said, "How long did it take you to drive over the Grapevine?"

"I left at six this morning."

John glanced at his wristwatch. "Seven hours? I made it clear from Bakersfield in less than that."

"Well, I kinda got lost."

"What kind of car you got?"

"A Model A Ford."

"I got me a '34 Nash. It really goes."

"Well, now that Jessie's here, let's all go into the dining room and have dinner," said Maria's aunt pleasantly.

It was a nice dinner, but Jessie was uncomfortable. He was seated on one side of Maria, and John was on her other side. Maria was acting very proper and ladylike. They did exchange a few secret glances, but there was hardly any conversation between them. John did most of the talking.

"I'm going to UCLA next year. Where you goin'?"

"I got another year of high school."

"Oh, yer only a junior? I'm a senior. I'm gonna be an engineer. What are you gonna be?"

"An artist."

"You mean the kind that draws pitures?"

A nod.

John shrugged.

After dinner, they all walked down the sidewalk a few blocks to the town square, which had a bandstand in the center. Iron benches were scattered around, filled with many finely dressed people who had come to hear the music. The band was a mixture of old and young musicians who wore bright red uniforms and played loud music.

Jessie and John again sat on each side of Maria and listened to the band play. It was agony for Jessie to be sitting so close to Maria without being able to touch or kiss her, which he desperately wanted to do. Between the loud music and bigmouth John, he hardly got a chance to speak to her.

When the concert was finally over, everyone got up and walked back to the Hunter home where they all sat down again in the living room. Maria was across the room from Jessie. It was agonizing, and whenever their eyes met and she smiled at him, his pulse leaped.

Most of the time John was blabbing about something. Then some radio program came on that was important and everyone listened. It had to do with the deteriorating conditions in the world and the rising threat of war and stuff like that. Finally, Jessie was happy to hear the Larsons announce they had to leave, but he wasn't happy to hear John Larson say, "Maria, your uncle says it's okay for you to go to Janet's party with me next Friday, so I'll pick you up in my Nash about seven."

It was Jessie's first real taste of jealousy, and it reminded him of the time he and Alvin were teasing an ole Hereford steer and he kicked Jessie in the stomach. That was exactly the way he felt. His Maria going out with that jerk? He couldn't believe it. His eyes darted across to her, and he could see the flush move over her face.

After the good-byes were completed and the Larsons had left, Maria's aunt said, "When we have a late Sunday dinner, we only snack at supper time. Would you care for something before you go, Jessie?"

"Oh, no thank you, Mrs. Hunter. I'm still full from dinner. Thank you anyway."

"Well, we're glad you could come, and I'm sure Maria has enjoyed seeing you. Please come again," she said, pretty much telling Jessie to hit the road.

After saying good-bye to the Hunters, Jessie walked out to his car with Maria. By this time it was dark outside, but the porch light was shining directly on them. They stood for a moment there beside the Ford, looking at each other.

"Jessie, a'm sorry we didn't get to be alone for a while," Maria said in a low voice, as the Hunters were conspicuously visible through the open front door.

"Yeah. Me too, Maria. I really miss you."

"Ah know, Jessie. When ah come home after this speech course we'll go ta Marble Springs and kiss and make love all day, okay?" All Jessie could do was nod his head.

"Oh, Jessie, ah love you and miss seeing you so much it hurts."

"Well, how come yer going on a date with that guy John?"

"Because ma aunt says thet at ma age ah have to date proper young men to get perspective."

"Oh."

"Ah don't like him very much, honest. And ah'm for sure not gonna kiss him or anything like that."

Jessie nodded. He was still feeling pangs of jealousy, but that declaration blunted the intensity somewhat.

"Jessie, that boy don't mean anything to me. But ah'm going to become a lady, and ah'm gonna get educated so you will always love me."

"I love you the way you are, Maria."

"Ah know you do. But if ah don't become a lady now, someone like thet Hallie Lamont will steal you away. Ah just know it. Ah'll make you proud of me. You'll see." Glancing back at the house, she suddenly blurted, "Ah gotta go, Jessie." She put her hands on his cheeks and kissed him passionately on the lips, then turned, and ran back into the nice house.

Chapter
~20~

Jessie had to drive back home from Los Angeles that night because he had to run his paper route the next morning. It was a long, tiring drive on a winding two-lane highway, which he drove in a depressed state of mind. He knew that Maria loved him, but it was almost as though he hadn't even seen her. He'd wanted desperately to do what they always did when they made love and, instead, listened to John Larson run his mouth. It was upsetting to know that Maria was dating the jerk to get perspective. That, in Jessie's view, was a bunch of baloney, but he was sure Maria was telling it straight. She was only doing it to please her aunt.

After several hours of thinking about it, steering the Ford around the Grapevine's endless switchback turns, he decided to write Maria and tell her he didn't want her going out with that guy. She didn't need any more perspective. He'd just settled on that course of action when he suddenly realized he was going around Dead Man's Curve, and he was going too fast.

He crashed through the railing and went down the hill head on into an oak tree. He became another of the Grapevine locals who fell victim to Dead Man's Curve. Fortunately, he only got a bump on the head, but his car was wrecked pretty bad.

The accident almost put Jessie out of the newspaper delivery business. The cost to fix the Model A was more than he'd paid for it, and it took a lot of convincing to get his mother and father to let him continue. They finally relented, but only after he agreed to some restrictive rules, like no more long trips to Los Angeles.

Lying in the thick grass at their secret hiding place on Grapevine Creek, Jessie told Alvin all the details of his Los Angeles venture. After some thought, Alvin said, "An' besides all that, you got your car wrecked. I don't know, Jess. You might ought to think about gettin' yourself a girl that lives closer."

"It would make my life a lot easier."

A couple of crows landed in the oak tree and squawked at each other for a while then flew off.

"All I can say is that you must really like Maria a lot to pick her instead of Hallie Lamont," said Alvin.

"I do. I love Maria."

"Yep, I know ya do and she is a real sweet girl. But that Hallie Lamont, she's got it all."

"Yeah. Besides bein' rich and beautiful, she's real smart too. You know she got all A's in high school?"

"That's unreal, but it doesn't surprise me."

Jessie reached out, pulled an orange poppy, and examined it. "I like Hallie, a lot. The only problem with her is ya never know what she is thinking or what she is gonna do next. I saw Mr. Lamont at Switzner's the other day, and he told me she came to the store last weekend with that big ape boyfriend, George."

"I thought she dumped him."

"See what I mean?"

Alvin nodded, and pulled a poppy. "Well, he is rich, and he's got a convertible."

"I guess. Mr. Lamont said Hallie already knows how to fly an airplane and got her pilot's license."

"Isn't that somethin'!"

"Yeah."

"That's what I want to do, Jess. I can hardly wait till I'm old enough to join the Army Air Corps and fly those fast pursuit planes."

"I'm sure you're gonna be a good pilot, Alvin."

"Yeah. And you're gonna be a good artist, Jess."

"I think I will if I don't get sidetracked."

"Sidetracked?"

"Yeah. Hallie says I'm gonna get sidetracked by Maria."

"How can she sidetrack ya, Jess? She lives in Los Angeles now, and you live on the Grapevine."

That summer a businessman from Bakersfield opened "The Tavern" at Frazier Mountain Park. It was about five miles on up the road from Lebec in a lovely canyon that had lots of pinon pine and cedar trees. A few people even came up from Los Angeles and built summer cottages there, and since Prohibition was over, little places that served beer and high balls were popular.

The Tavern was built out of logs and rocks and had a small dance floor. What made it popular with the high school crowd was that on Saturday nights Frank Grover's dance band played there. Frank played the saxophone and organized the band with Bud Carver, who also played sax. Jessie's cousin Glenn played drums, and the new girl Ruth, who Billy liked, played piano and her brother Dick played the base fiddle. It was a great little band that played songs like "Alexander's Rag Time Band," "In The Mood," and "Green Eyes."

None of the gang knew how to dance, but it didn't take them long to learn. Waltzing was easy, and girls like Virginia and Penny knew how to do the new "Jitterbug." It became the big event of the week the summer of 1938, and everyone showed up on Saturday night at the tavern in Frazier Mountain Park. All the high school group drank soft drinks, so there were no big problems. It was just a lot of fun dancing and being together.

There were, of course, numerous romantic entanglements and intrigues going on, which added plenty of spice to it all. Virginia got a crush on Glenn, and someone saw them kissing outside in the dark at intermission. That was a dynamite scandal because Glenn was supposed to be engaged to Bubbles, and Frank and Virginia were practically engaged. Then once Agnes and Bobby disappeared for a while, and when they came back, Bobby had lipstick all over him, and Jack was really mad.

Jessie wasn't involved in any scandalous entanglements until the Saturday night that Hallie suddenly showed up. That turned out to be something more than a scandal.

He was standing beside the dance floor talking to Alvin, who was waiting for Elinor to come back from the ladies' room, when suddenly Alvin's eyes grew large, and at the same time, a voice at Jessie's ear said, "How about a dance, handsome?"

He spun around and looked into the most beautiful set of blue eyes in all the world.

"Hallie!" he blurted. "What? What are you doin' here?"

"I came to dance with you, Tiger. What else?" she said with a smile that sent shock waves through Jessie.

Every eye in the place focused on her. She wore a beautiful, off-the-shoulder white evening gown that accentuated every marvelous curve in her sensational body. Her striking yellow blond hair fell in waves over tanned shoulders. Even the band had trouble getting the next piece started.

"You sure surprised me, Hallie. Uh, this is Alvin Pyeatt, my best friend." Hallie said hello, and Alvin sort of croaked hello.

The music started, and Hallie held out her arms, and there was nothing Jessie could do but dance with her. Hardly anyone else danced; they all just watched.

Jessie had just learned to dance so he was a little self-conscious, but from the moment she came into his arms, he was unaware of anything except beautiful Hallie. The effect of holding her closely with that special fragrance she always had was so intoxicating he just floated around the dance floor in a in a sort of daze with his pulse gaining speed with every step he took.

"You get more handsome every time I see you, Jessie," she whispered in his ear.

"And you get more beautiful every time I see you, Hallie."

"You think of me much?"

"Yeah, I do."

"I'm glad."

"You think of me?"

"Now and then," she said, smiled at him and then snuggled back into his shoulder. "But there were a lot of nows and thens."

"Nows and thens in between George?"

She turned back again to face him and laughed one of those great laughs of hers. "Are you jealous?"

"Well, you said you hated him and you were through with him forever."

She laughed again. "Hey, Tiger, you turned me down, remember?"

Jessie smiled. "Yeah, that's true."

"You keep your promise?"

"What?"

"You're promise not to see the little bitch."

"Yes."

"Good. And are you still in love?"

"Yes."

They danced without speaking for a moment.

"You got a lot going for you, Jessie, but you're gonna piss it all away if you're not careful."

Jessie danced in silence before saying, "Ya know what, Hallie? I think you're jealous of Maria."

She pulled back and looked at him. "You know what, Jessie? You're right."

Jessie grinned. This girl sure didn't mince words, no matter what.

"You still want to be an artist?"

"I'm gonna be an artist."

"Good. Then remember what I told you last summer: don't get sidetracked."

"I won't. Your dad told me you got your pilot's license."

"Oh yes, and I love it, Jessie. It is just as exciting and fulfilling as I knew it would be. It's the challenge that bad Hallie Lamont needed."

"That's great, Hallie. And I still say you're not as bad as you think you are."

She laughed and squeezed him.

"Okay, Hallie, you've played your little game. Come on, let's get out of here," interrupted a gruff voice.

Jessie turned and found himself looking into the angry face of Hallie's lover, George. He looked just as big and mean as he had that day when he was gonna blow Jessie's head off.

"I'm not ready to go yet, George," snapped Hallie.

"You're going, or I'll pick you up and carry you," growled George, glaring at Jessie.

The music had stopped, and they were standing in the middle of the dance floor with everybody watching.

"George, don't make a scene. Go on out to the car, and I'll be there in a moment."

"Now! Hallie!" he said and grabbed her arm roughly.

"Hey! What'a you think you're doing?" said Jessie and then he felt like a freight train had hit him head on. There were flashing lights and bells ringing and all kinds of noises, and then everything faded to black.

It was another of those experiences that Jessie would never, ever forget. It took two weeks for the black eye to go away, and his jaw never did seem to go back to normal. George was not only a big ape, he was a big, strong ape, and he'd laid a real haymaker on Jessie.

Since Jessie was sprawled on the dance floor in a daze, he wasn't aware of what went on after George hit him. He found out later that no one there was willing to take on tough George except brave Alvin. He jumped right into it, but George knocked him across the dance floor too. Jack told Jessie later that Hallie was real upset, and she and George had a terrible fight right there in the Tavern. But after she was sure that Jessie was all right, she went on home with Georgeanyway.

Jessie didn't see Hallie any more that year, but surprisingly, she wrote him a short letter:

Dear Jessie,

I'm sorry about what happened at the Tavern.

It was my fault. I know George is jealous, so I shouldn't have been flirting with you. I guess it's just the nature of the beast. But some powerful things seem to happen when I'm around you. Who knows what the future holds?

Remember, you are going to art school!

Love, Hallie

Jessie read the letter several times and discussed it at length with Alvin. They both came to the conclusion that it was vintage Hallie Lamont.

"And that boyfriend of hers is one tough ape," admitted Alvin feeling his nose and grinning. "I don't think my nose will ever be the same."

"That was real brave of you, Alvin."

"You'd do the same for me."

"Yeah, I guess I would, and the result would be the same."

The two friends laughed.

Chapter
~21~

So Jessie's love life went on the back burner again. He ran his paper route and went skinny dipping with his friends a couple times at the old Rose Station water trough. But other than that, it was pretty dull on the Grapevine, right up to the annual PTA summer box social.

The box social was always held at Grapevine School, and everybody went: students, parents, and the one teacher, Miss Trembell.

The ladies brought picnic dinners for two in a box. The boxes were all decorated with bright paper and ribbons, and they were auctioned off to the highest male bidder by Mr. Switzner, who was always the auctioneer. The identity of the box maker was secret, so to have dinner with a certain lady required some sleuthing.

Now, if a certain lady wanted to have dinner with a certain gentleman, she dropped some clues as to which box was hers. That led to some lively bidding, particularly when the clues were known to several bidders. It was great fun, and it helped the PTA coffers.

Alvin and Agnes were back together again, so he knew which box was hers, but somehow Jack found out too and he had more cash. So he won, and Alvin ended up with Patty and not too happily. Billy got Elinor's box and Bobbie Irene's. Gerald got Ruth's, and Danny got Patty's. Frank always got Virginia's, and Bud always got Penny's. Jessie didn't want to bid against any of his friends, so he just bid on one they didn't. He got it for a dollar fifteen, and it was made by a new girl: Mary Jane Brown.

Jessie wasn't thrilled about it because Mary Jane was fat and dumpy and not very personable, but Jessie felt sorry for her because she was new and didn't know anybody. Her father worked for the Griffith Company, which got the construction contract to widen the Grapevine road. The Browns rented an old house in Oak Glen, just up the road from where Doc Veeyon lived.

Mr. Carver had arranged the desks in the schoolhouse so that after the bidding was all over, the couples sat facing each other to eat their box dinner. Mary Jane's box had fried chicken, potato salad, dill pickles, and apple pie. As soon as they opened it, Jessie took a bite of the chicken and said, "This is really good chicken, Mary Jane." It wasn't as good as his mom's, but he said that anyway.

"Thank you," she said with a cherub-like smile. She was wearing a yellow dress with red flowers all over it, which made her look even fatter than she was. She did have a pretty face, but the way her curling-iron curls hung, you could hardly see it.

"Do you like it on the Grapevine, Mary Jane?" he asked between bites.

"It's okay."

Another bite of chicken. "What year are you in high school?"

"I'm a senior."

"Hey, so am I."

"I know."

A bite of potato salad. "Where did you live before you moved to the Grapevine?"

"Up the valley in Tulare."

"You did?"

"Yes."

A drink of orange pop. Mr. Switzner always contributed the orange pop to the box social for free.

"You like Tulare?"

"Yes."

So it went until the box social was over and Mr. Switzner announced that it was a great success.

"That was a real nice box dinner," Jessie said as he got up from the desk, eager to join his friends.

"Thank you," she murmured.

"See you later," he said as he turned to go.

"Jessie?"

"Yeah?"

"Would you take me home?"

For a moment he wasn't sure if he'd heard her right. Then he saw the pleading eyes peeking through the dangling curls, and he knew he'd heard right.

Jessie didn't want to take Mary Jane home. He figured he'd done his duty just getting through the box social. It was tough talking to her, and he sure didn't feel any attraction. But he did feel sorry for her, so he agreed. Since the folks that brought her to the social knew Jessie, they said it would be all right for her to ride home with him. Of course, everybody knew that Jessie Rascoe, the Los Angeles *Examiner* paper boy, was a good driver because he drove the Grapevine every morning, rain or shine.

The gang all gave Jessie strange looks when he left the schoolhouse with Mary Jane, and he knew he would take some razzing over it. Surprisingly, she talked better on their drive up the Grapevine to Oak Glen. Jessie figured she was probably a little shy around people she didn't know.

When he pulled up in front of her house, he left the motor running as an indication that he wanted to leave. She turned to him and said, "Could we, uh, sit here for a little while?"

"Well…yeah…Okay." He had removed the Ford's isinglass windows for the summer, so when he shut off the motor, they could hear the crickets chirping.

After sitting in silence for a while, she said, "Thank you for buying my box."

"That's okay. It was great chicken."

Crickets chirping.

"They don't have box socials at Tulare."

"They don't?"

"No."

Silence.

"I had a boyfriend in Tulare."

"You did?"

"Yes, and we were almost engaged."

"You were?"

"Yes, but my stepfather got a job down here, so we had to move. I hated to come."

"Yeah, I don't blame you."

"I don't like my stepfather."

"Oh."

The scream of a truck engine grinding up the Grapevine drowned out the crickets for a while.

"You live on the Grapevine a long time?"

"All my life. It's a neat place."

"Tulare is a neat place too."

"Well, I think you'll like the Grapevine after you get acquainted."

"I guess. I'm glad I know you, Jessie."

"Uh, yeah. Me too, Mary Jane."

The mating call of a hoot owl up in one of the oak trees echoed through the darkness.

"Do you go to the dance at the Tavern, Jessie?"

"Yeah, I go almost every Saturday."

"I like to dance."

"I'm not a very good dancer."

"I…wish I could go."

"Yeah, you should go Mary Jane. We have a lot of fun."

"I don't have anybody to take me."

"Uh, ... I guess you could ride up with me." It just came out before Jessie could stop himself.

"Okay," said Mary Jane quickly.

"You're gonna take Mary Jane to the dance?" croaked Alvin the next day when Jessie told him.

"Yeah, I am. Sometimes I just don't understand myself, Alvin. I don't know why I do these things that always get me into trouble. I feel sorry for Mary Jane, but not sorry enough to want to take her to the dance."

"Well, how come you're doin' it then?"

"You tell me, and we'll both know."

When Mary Jane opened the front door at Jessie's knock that Saturday night, he was pleasantly surprised. She looked kinda nice in a pretty skirt and blouse that sort of camouflaged her. As they drove up the Grapevine on the way to the Tavern, she talked pretty well too, which gave Jessie some hope that the evening might not be as bad as he'd imagined.

But it turned out about the way he'd figured. Poor Mary Jane just didn't mix with the Grapevine girls, and she danced sort of club-footed, spiking his feet several times. So it was a long, difficult evening for Jessie. He got Alvin to dance with her once, but the rest of the time he was stuck with her.

When the dance was finally over, he could hardly wait to take her home and get it over with, but Mary Jane wasn't ready to call it a night. "Let's sit in your car for a while, Jessie," she said when he pulled up and stopped under the grove of oak trees in front of her house.

Although she became more personable and talkative when she was alone with him in the car, Jessie had pretty well expended his good-Samaritan efforts and was anxious to leave. After a few minutes, he said, "Well, I have to get up real early to run my paper route so..."

"Just for a little while longer, please?"

What could he say?

"The crickets are really singing tonight, aren't they?"

"Yeah, they are."

"I liked dancing with you, Jessie. Did you like dancing with me?"

"Uh, yeah, sure."

"I like you a lot."

Jessie sensed things were getting out of hand. He would just tell her he had a steady girl, and that would cut her off at the pass. He glanced across the seat. It was dark, but he could see her. "You're...a nice girl, Mary Jane, but I got..."

She abruptly scooted across the car seat, snuggled up to him, and put her hand on the back of his neck. "I'll do things if you want, Jessie."

Her offer took Jessie by surprise, and the next thing he knew, they were kissing. Shy Mary Jane's wasn't shy any more, she was soft and warm, and there was lots of her. It didn't take long for Jessie's sexual appetite to mount, and instinctively his hand went to her breasts. Mary Jane obediently unfastened her blouse.

Like the rest of Mary Jane, her breasts were large, soft, and warm. As Jessie's passion mounted, he moved one hand under her dress and up her leg. Now he was sure she would object and want to leave, but she didn't.

Something down deep told Jessie to stop. This was wrong! He didn't even like this girl. He heard the warnings all right, but suddenly he felt reckless. If she didn't care, why should he? So he moved his hand up until it was inside her panties. She would call a halt now for sure.

She didn't. "You wanna do it to me?" Before Jessie could even answer, she reached down and pulled her panties off.

Jessie knew he'd gone too far, but there was no turning back now. It was sort of like a wrestling match, but there on the front seat of his Model A Ford, parked under an oak tree, Jessie Rascoe experienced his first sexual intercourse with a girl he hardly knew and didn't even like.

It was, of course, a momentous event in his life, but he could never have imagined how awful he would feel afterward. It was hardly over when Jessie wished he could take it back. He'd finally done what he'd wanted to do ever since discovering girls, but he felt awful and was desperate to get away from her. He realized it was a terrible way to feel, but he couldn't help himself. All he wanted was to get out of there quickly.

"Did you like it, Jessie?" she asked as she retrieved her panties from the floorboard of the Model A.

"Uh, yeah," muttered Jessie, pulling up his jeans while Mary Jane was pulling her panties over her large hips.

When she got them on, she scooted over close to him and put her hand up on the back of his neck again. "I liked it too, Jessie, and I like you."

"I really gotta go, Mary Jane. I got to run my paper route in a little while."

"Will you take me out again next Saturday?"

"Well, I..."

"I'll let you do it again, if you take me out."

"Well I...Mary Jane, I gotta tell you something: I got a girl. I'm in love with another girl." There! He'd said it. It was out in the open, and that settled it.

But it didn't settle it.

"You did it to me!"

"I...I know. I shouldn't have. I'm sorry."

"Saying you're sorry isn't going to change it, Jessie. You did it to me, and now I'll be pregnant."

Pregnant! She'll be pregnant? Oh Jesus! What had he done? What had he been thinking? He hadn't, that's what! And he had a rubber in his wallet. His cousin Glenn had given it to him and said he should always be prepared, but he didn't even think about it. Jessie, you really did it this time!

"I'll be pregnant, and you know what that means."

Yeah, he knew what it meant. It meant he would lose Maria, and he wouldn't become an artist and...

"It means you gotta marry me."

"I know. I know."

And the world came crashing down! All in just a few minutes, a few thoughtless minutes.

So what else is new on planet Earth?

It was another one of those mornings that Jessie ran his paper route in a daze. He was so preoccupied over the terrible consequences of what he'd done, he missed several customers and completely forgot to leave the usual stack of papers at Switzner's store. When he finally finished, he didn't even want to go home. He drove on down to that last curve on the Grapevine, parked the Ford, and tried to think of what to do.

Jessie was certain he'd never felt worse in his whole life. How could he have done that? How? It was stupid and dumb, but there was nothing he could do about it - nothing. He would never be an artist now. He would have to drop out of school and get married to Mary Jane, and loose Maria forever. That hurt the most. He would be eighteen in April. Maybe he could get on with the oil company. The paper route probably wouldn't support a wife and baby. And what would his folks say? What could they say? They would be awfully disappointed, of course. And what would all his friends say? He would be the disgrace of the Grapevine. That's what he would be.

Jessie suffered through the following week in a state of despair. The big event he'd thought about all this time going all the way with a girl- had finally happened and left him with an awful feeling of remorse. He would have given anything to tell Alvin and get his good advice, but he knew he couldn't. It was too awful to even discuss with Alvin. To make matters worse, he had to promise Mary Jane he'd take her out next Saturday night. He'd had no choice as she had threatened to tell her stepfather what had happened.

The following Saturday, he drove her to Bakersfield to a movie and hamburgers at a drive-in. That way he didn't have to face any of his friends, and that was okay with Mary Jane because she admitted she didn't like his friends anyway. When he got her home that night, they parked under the grove of oak trees next to her house, and she said he could do it to her again if he wanted. He didn't want to.

She got miffed over that, stormed out of the Ford, and slammed the door. Then she yelled at him that he'd better take her out again next Saturday or he'd be in big trouble.

So the following week was even worse for Jessie than the week before. He'd been waiting anxiously for Maria's letter that would tell him when she would be coming up from Los Angeles. He got it that week, but the joy that should have been wasn't. Uncle Bob was bringing her that next Saturday, which was the last Saturday before school started. But it wouldn't do Jessie any good because he had to take Mary Jane to Bakersfield or get in even more trouble.

After hours of agonizing thought, Jessie concluded he had no alternative but to do what she wanted and take her to Bakersfield. This whole mess was his fault, so he would have to pay the piper. He was sure Maria would be hurt when he didn't show up to see her at Bear Trap, but what could he do? He didn't know if he could face Maria now anyway. Not after what he'd done. Besides, he didn't deserve Maria, not any more. Maria's aunt probably knew best after all. Maria would be better off with one of those guys down there in Los Angeles- Guys with character, proper guys who didn't cheat on their girls like he'd done. Jesus, what a jerk he turned out to be!

When Jessie knocked on the front door of Mary Jane's house that Saturday evening, a big tough-looking guy wearing a soiled undershirt answered the door. His hair was messy, and he had a beard stubble and a cigarette hanging from the side of his mouth.

"Yeah, what'a ya want?" he growled.

"I come to pick up Mary Jane."

The rough-looking guy just looked at Jessie.

"Who is it, Clyde?" came a voice from inside.

"Some guy wantin' Mary Jane."

A haggard-looking woman, wearing a threadbare terrycloth bathrobe came out from behind the door and looked at Jessie. Her hair was messy too. She stepped in front of the big guy, who turned and disappeared back into the house.

"Are you Jessie?" she asked with a weak smile.

"Yes, ma'am."

She pulled the door almost closed as though she didn't want Jessie to see inside.

"I'm Mary Jane's mother. She'll be ready in just a minute. I'd invite you in, but..."

"That's okay, Mrs. Brown. I'll wait in the car."

She gave him another weak smile, backed into the house, and closed the door. A few minutes later when Mary Jane came out of the house she looked upset. "I hate my stepfather!" she hissed as she got into the Ford.

Jessie didn't know what to say, so he just started the Ford and headed down the Grapevine toward Bakersfield.

"He beats up on my mom."

"You're kidding!"

"No, I'm not."

"He beats up your mother?"

"Yes, all the time," said Mary Jane. "I tell her to leave him, but she's afraid to."

Jessie couldn't help feeling sorry for Mrs. Brown. "That's terrible, Mary Jane."

Mary Jane sat quietly for a minute, and Jessie just steered the Model A down the Grapevine since he was at a loss for what to say. He'd never even heard of such a thing as someone's dad beating up on a mother. It was beyond comprehension.

"I wish I could get my mom to leave and go back to Tulare."

Jessie still didn't know what to say, but he did wish that Mary Jane would get her wish.

"Jessie?"

"Yeah?"

"I'm sure I'm pregnant, so why don't we just go ahead and get married and then Mom and I would have a place to go."

Now Jessie was really at a loss for words.

Mary Jane looked across the seat at him. "We're gonna have to get married anyway, so what's the difference?"

"Mary Jane, I'm not even out of high school yet. I can't take care of a wife and baby and your mom."

"You got your paper route job."

"I don't earn that much money."

"It would be enough."

"I don't think so."

"Well, you better think of something Jessie. Because when Clyde finds out you got me pregnant, he might kill you."

Chapter

~22~

Maria Hunter's best friend at Lincoln High in Los Angeles was Patsy Cline. She was a feisty little Irish girl with red hair and nice features, except for her freckles, which of course, she hated. Patsy was also smart as a whip and helped Maria a lot to learn the big city ways. They had become close, sharing secrets and discussing problems, particularly about their love lives.

Patsy knew when Maria burst into her room one day with tears in her eyes that this would be the next chapter in the her friend's love saga.

"Oh, Patsy, ma heart is breaking!" she wailed, throwing herself down on Patsy's bed.

Patsy knew that Maria had been struggling with a pretty serious dilemma: she was in love with the boy back home, but was trying to do what her aunt and uncle wanted, which was to date other boys so she could get perspective. It was good advice, and Patsy told Maria that it was and encouraged her.

Even though Maria wasn't crazy about it, she dated John Larson, whom she didn't like, and a few others to satisfy Patsy and her aunt and uncle. And so it worked out okay, until Kevin Blake took a tumble for Maria.

Kevin Blake had everything. He was handsome. He was from a rich family, and he was captain of the football team. Girls would kill to date him, and there were lots of pretty girls at Lincoln High. But to everyone's surprise, Kevin fell for Maria, and that was the crux of Maria's dilemma.

Although Maria herself had blossomed into one of the prettier girls at Lincoln High, Kevin told Patsy privately that it wasn't just her looks - although those sparkling eyes made his heart skip. He said the reason he fell for her was because she had a way about her that other girls just didn't have. He couldn't describe it, but whatever it was he loved it, and Patsy wished she had it.

After a few dates with Kevin, Maria told Patsy she was going to break it off because he was getting serious and she didn't want to hurt him. She was in love with the boy back home, Jessie Rascoe, and there wouldn't ever be anyone else for her.

But Kevin was persistent, and even after Maria told him she was in love with another boy, he said he would take his chances. Maria liked Kevin. He was nice and very considerate, and she had to admit it was fun dating the school football hero.

Although she didn't kiss him like she kissed Jessie, she also had to admit she liked kissing Kevin.

It was about that time in the relationship that Maria had gone home for a short visit after summer school. It had been almost a year since she had seen Jessie last, and she told Patsy that she was desperate to see him. Patsy suspected that Maria was struggling with some doubts about her old boyfriend, but just wouldn't admit it.

So it didn't surprise Patsy that something had gone wrong at that reunion. "Okay, calm down, Maria, and tell me what happened."

"Oh, Patsy, he didn't come ta see me!" sobbed Maria.

"He didn't show up?"

"No, and ah was there all day Saturday and part of Sunday."

"Well, it's like I told you, Maria, he's probably got another girl now, just like you got another guy."

"No, he doesn't. Ah know he doesn't. Ah can tell from his letters."

"Come on, Maria. Have you told him in your letters that you been dating Kevin?"

Hesitation. "No."

"Yeah, and he's not gonna tell you. I'd bet you a fudge Sunday that he's got another girl, just like you got Kevin. It's natural, cause he lives down there, and you live here now. You gotta face what it, Maria. You and him live in different worlds now, an that's that. You got to go on with your life here, and he'll do the same down there."

"He doesn't have another girl."

"How do you know that? Didn't you tell me that other girl, Hanley, was after him?"

"Hallie."

"Yeah, her."

"She didn't get him."

"You don't know that either. The truth is, it wouldn't be natural for him not to have a girl down there. I mean you said he's real handsome and has a car? And he's been sitting around all this time twiddling his thumbs? Gimme a break, Maria. You're not being honest with yourself."

Maria sat up on the bed and wiped her eyes with the back of her hand. "Ah don't know what ta think, Patsy. But Jessie loves me. Ah just know it, and ah love him. But ah guess you're right. Ah have to face what is."

"You do. And look at it this way. It does solve one of your problems."

Maria looked at Patsy with teary eyes. "It does?"

"Sure. Now you won't feel guilty anymore when you kiss Kevin."

When Kevin drove Maria to Lincoln High in his Pontiac convertible on the first day of school, it pretty well told all the hopefuls that he had picked Maria again that year for his girl.

And despite some misgivings, Maria had pretty well decided that, sure enough, she was now going steady with Kevin.

On the other side of the Tehachapi Mountains, Jessie began his senior year of high school with some misgivings too: big ones. And his misgivings were made even worse because he had to drive Mary Jane to Bakersfield High. That pretty well told everybody on the Grapevine that Jessie had lost his mind.

But the way Jessie figured, it was better than having to sit with Mary Jane on the high school bus, which she'd made clear she expected. He knew he couldn't afford to drive to school every day, so eventually he would have to face the music and ride the bus. But he would put it off as long as possible.

Jessie avoided his friends like the plague, but Alvin finally cornered him and wanted to know what was going on. He said he just couldn't talk about it yet.

"Golly, Jess, you ain't never had a problem before that we couldn't talk about," Alvin had said with deep concern.

"I'll tell ya as soon as I can, Alvin," Jessie promised.

The truth was that Jessie was so upset, he wasn't even acting like himself. Mrs. Rascoe told Mr. Rascoe that she was sure that Jessie was coming down with something.

Jessie drove Mary Jane to Bakersfield High all that first week of school. Everybody on the Grapevine was talking about it and wondering why Jessie had taken such a tumble for Mary Jane Brown. No one knew much about the Browns, except that Mr. Brown worked on the highway construction crew and they lived in that old house up the road from Doc Veeyon's place.

What no one knew was that Jessie was at his wit's end. He'd thought of nothing else since that disastrous night. It all came to a head that Saturday when Jessie took Mary Jane home after a movie in Bakersfield.

"You're gonna have to marry me, Jessie. We can drive down to Tijuana, and it only costs five dollars to get married down there. And if you don't, I'm gonna tell Clyde you got me pregnant."

So there it was. Now he had no choice.

Jessie tossed fitfully all that night, ran his paper route the next morning in a daze, and then went back to bed and slept till noon.

"Jessie, are you all right?" His mother asked when he finally got up and came into the kitchen.

"Yeah. I'm...okay, Mom."

"Well you haven't been yourself lately. Is there something you would like to talk about?"

"No. Thanks, Mom. I have to make a decision on something, that's all."

His mother nodded. "Well, if you do what is right, son, things will generally come out right."

Yes, but what was right in this case meant that he had to marry Mary Jane. That was that. And he had no one to blame but himself. He did it to her, so he was responsible and had to pay the penalty.

"Okay, Mom, I will," he said and headed for the front door.

"Aren't you going to have breakfast?"

"No, thanks. I'm not hungry. I'll see ya later."

When he pulled into Oak Glen a few minutes later and parked under the oak trees, it was crystal clear in Jessie's mind what he had to do. He forced himself to not even think of the consequences. Just tell her he would marry her and get it over with.

When the door opened to Jessie's knock, it was Mr. Brown, and he looked just like he always did, only worse. This time Jessie could see that he was drunk. He grabbed Jessie by the front of his shirt and shook him.

"You had something to do with this, didn't ya?" he shouted in Jessie's face.

The smell of whiskey and the indignity of being manhandled by a woman-beater struck a chord in Jessie Rascoe that rarely surfaced: he was infuriated. "Let go of me, Mr. Brown!" he shouted, jerking himself free.

Jessie's abrupt reaction seemed to surprise the big bully, and he stared at Jessie for a moment with bloodshot eyes.

"Don't get smart with me, kid, or I'll beat you to a pulp," he growled.

"You keep your hands off me, and I don't know what you're talking about!"

"I'm talking about those two bitches running off in the pickup- that's what I'm talking about!"

A sudden glimmer of hope shot through Jessie. "Mary Jane and her mom ran off in the pickup?" he blurted.

"Yeah and don't act like you didn't know anything about it, you little shit! I know yer in cahoots with those two bitches."

"I'm not in cahoots with anyone, Mr. Brown. I just came to see Mary Jane."

"Yeah, yeah, I know. You been fuckin' her, haven't ya?"

A flush swept through Jessie.

The bully sneered. "Well, you didn't get no cherry. She fucked every dick head in Tulare!"

Jessie was struck with an acute ambivalence. The sudden possibility that he wouldn't have to marry Mary Jane filled him with earth-shaking relief, while a deep anger toward Mr. Brown made him want to strike out with all his might.

"If they ran away, Mr. Brown, it was your fault for the way you treated them!" shouted Jessie.

"Oh yeah? It's none of you goddamn business and I'm gonna knock yer fuckin' head off!" Mr. Brown lunged out through the door, but missed the step and fell heavily onto the ground.

The fall knocked the wind out of him, and he lay there on the ground a moment trying to gain his senses.

"You hurt, Mr. Brown?" asked Jessie.

He looked up. His eyes glazed. "I'm gonna...knock yer... head off," he muttered as he struggled to his feet.

"You better go back in the house and lie down, Mr. Brown." Jessie turned and walked back to his car.

Mr. Brown stumbled into the house and slammed the door.

Jessie started the Ford and drove off down the road. When he pulled out onto the Grapevine and headed up the canyon toward home, he felt like a tremendous weight had suddenly been lifted from his shoulders. It sure enough appeared that Mary Jane and her mom had left the bully for good. It was as though the dark clouds had parted and Jessie could see blue sky above. Like his mother often said, "The Lord works in mysterious ways."

Chapter

~23~

Although Jessie felt as though he'd been given a last-minute death-sentence reprieve, he continued to worry about Mary Jane and her mother. He worried about Mr. Brown finding them and beating them up, and he worried about Mary Jane showing up on his door-step, pregnant. Then one day about a month later, he got a short letter from Mary Jane, postmarked Tulare, California.

Dear Jessie,

Me and mom are living in Tulare now. I quit school and got a job as a waitress.

I'm lucky. Jobs are hard to get. The guy that runs the cafe likes me, and we're going steady. You are a nice guy, Jessie. I'm sorry I lied to you about being pregnant.

Fondly,

Mary Jane

That letter from Mary Jane was wonderful news, and Jessie knew that he had been given another chance, which he also knew he didn't deserve. But it was a lesson that he swore he would never ever forget. The downside was that, in the process, he'd probably lost the girl he loved.

The Saturday after Jessie's nightmare ended, he and Alvin drove up to the new diner Fred Bartling had opened when the crews started work on the new Grapevine road construction.

The diner was made out of an old Pullman railroad car. There was a long counter down one side and a few small tables down the other. Jessie and Alvin went inside and took one of the small tables where they could look out a window and see the cars and trucks going down the Grapevine.

On weekends, Bartlett's daughter, Andrea, was the waitress. When she saw Jessie and Alvin, she dropped what she was doing and came over to their table. She greeted them warmly, but smiled the most at Jessie. Andrea, like everybody else on the Grapevine, knew Jessie had his own car.

The two guys ordered hamburgers, french fries, and vanilla milk shakes. She wrote it down on a little pad, smiled some more, and departed.

"Andrea is a pretty cute girl, don't you think?"

"Alvin, I ain't even looking at girls anymore, except Maria. That is, if she will even speak to me anymore."

"Ah, she will, Jess. I'm pretty sure."

"I hope yer right."

Jessie had told Alvin the Mary Jane horror story at their secret place on Grapevine Creek.

"When you goin' to see her?"

"Tomorrow morning soon as I finish my paper route."

"Does she know yer coming?"

"Yes. I wrote her a letter and told her."

"You gonna tell Maria the real reason why you didn't come to see her?"

"Yes. I've turned over a new leaf, Alvin. Nothing but the truth from now on. If she loves me, she will understand."

"Uh, I don't know about that, Jess. I ain't knocking truth. But my experience with girls is that they don't understand too good when it comes to messing around with another girl. And you sure messed with Mary Jane."

"That worries me too. But I made up my mind. I'm telling her the truth," pronounced Jessie as Andrea brought their hamburgers, french fries, and milk shakes, and smiled some more at Jessie.

When Maria received Jessie's letter that he was coming to see her, she had mixed emotions. On one hand, she felt that same thrill she always got over seeing Jessie, and it pleased her to know that something serious had kept him from coming to see her that day. On the other hand, she was going steady now with Kevin.

"What're ya gonna do, Maria?" asked Patsy as they sat across from each other having root beer floats at the local soda fountain on a Saturday afternoon.

"Ah'm not sure. Deep down, ah know ah still love Jessie as much as ever, but like you say Patsy, it's hard when you're separated a whole year, and ah gotta admit to likin' Kevin a lot now. He is such a nice boy, and it's fun goin' out with him. Ah don't know. Ah'll just have to wait and see how ah feel when Jessie comes ta see me."

Jessie made another long-distance telephone call from the pay phone at Switzner's store to make sure that Maria got his letter and knew that he was coming to see her. He talked to Mrs. Hunter who didn't sound all that pleased about it but said that Maria was expecting him.

Jessie left for Los Angeles right after he finished his paper route on a Sunday morning. He practiced what he was going to say to Maria all the way down the long winding Grapevine. If he was turning over a new leaf, he had to tell her the truth. Alvin said no, and Alvin was smart and knew a lot of stuff. He said what she don't know won't hurt her, and if he'd really reformed, then she didn't need to know anyway, as long as he didn't do it again. It made sense all right.

This time he didn't get lost and made it to Los Angeles in less than five hours. By the time he pulled up in front of the Hunters' nice house, he was pretty excited and nervous. But that was nothing compared to the shock he got when the door opened, and he saw Maria for the first time in a year.

Facing Jessie in the open doorway, Maria was experiencing the same emotion. For both, it was the result of a long separation and, of course, a guilty conscience over their infidelities. For a moment neither spoke. They just stood looking at each other, not knowing quite what to say.

"Hi, Jessie."

"Hi, Maria."

"You...look different," said Maria.

"Yeah, so do you."

"Ah guess we both changed in a year."

"Yeah, I guess so."

"Ah think you got a little taller."

"I did?"

"It seems like it."

"You look really nice, Maria."

"Thank you. Please come in. My aunt and uncle had some business to do, but they'll be back after a while."

"Oh, okay."

Jessie stepped into the house, and Maria closed the door and walked into the living room with Jessie following. Just watching her walk sent a thrill through him. She had on a pretty blue dress, with silk stockings and high heels. It looked to Jessie like she'd become more beautiful than ever.

They sat down in two overstuffed chairs opposite each other. "It's good to see you, Jessie," she said, smiling.

It was Maria's smile all right, with those big dark eyes giving out flashes of silver like they always did. Her shimmering hair and her lips that always looked swollen-up. "It's great to see you too," he said smiling.

It was Jessie's smile all right, with those mesmerizing green eyes that had always set Maria's pulse racing. And he was just as handsome as ever, or even more so. Kevin was handsome, all right, but not like Jessie. And she had that same deep-down feeling she'd always got when she looked at him- the feeling that she wanted to kiss him and have him hug her. That hadn't changed one tiny bit. So why was she hesitant? She didn't know why, only that something was holding her back. Was it her guilty conscience over Kevin?

Jessie felt shocks of desire as he looked at her. He wanted to just grab her and kiss her, but something he didn't understand was holding him back. Was it because he noticed she wasn't wearing the Elgin watch he gave her? Or was it his own guilty conscience over Mary Jane?

"You seem...kinda different, Jessie."

"So do you, Maria. I hardly recognized you,-and you sure talk different."

"Ah've worked real hard to get rid of the hillbilly talk and the image."

"I liked your hillbilly image."

"You don't like ma new image?"

"Oh yeah, I didn't mean that."

"Like ah told you in my letters, Jessie, I want to become educated and be a real lady, like my aunt. And if I graduate with good grades, ah'm going to UCLA."

"Golly."

"Don't you want me to go to college?"

"Oh, sure. That's great, Maria. I'm goin' to art college."

"I know. You told me in your letter, and that's good Jessie. Ah know you will be a good artist." A silence. "Ah don't like bein' so far away from home, and ah do miss Mama and Bear Trap Canyon and Marble Springs. Ah ain't, ah mean, ah haven't been home for a whole year, and ah miss it terribly."

"I don't like you bein' so far away either, Maria, but I know you have to do it."

"Yes. Ah do." Silence. "Would you like a soda pop?"

"Sure."

"You like Coca Cola?"

"Sure."

"It's not as good as Mr. Switzner's root beer, but it's okay," she said, smiling, and then she got up and left the room.

Jessie sat in the big chair and fidgeted. He couldn't understand what was going on. He was sitting there talking to the girl he loved like they were cousins or something and Maria was acting strange too. Was it because what he'd done had changed everything? Did she know about Mary Jane? How could she know? Well, it didn't matter. He had to tell her anyway, didn't he?

Maria too did not understand what was going on. She had known the moment she saw Jessie that she still loved him, so why the uncertainty? And why was Jessie acting so strangely? It wasn't like him. Maybe he'd changed. Or did he somehow know about Kevin? How could he know? She took two bottles of Coca-Cola out of the refrigerator and opened them. Maybe someone told him about Kevin. Well, she had to tell him anyway, so it didn't matter, did it?

When she re-entered the room, she gave Jessie a bottle of Coca-Cola and resumed her seat. They smiled at each other and both took drinks. Then both started to speak simultaneously, stopped, and laughed.

It was great to hear her laugh, Jessie thought.

It was wonderful to hear his laugh, Maria thought.

"Ladies first," Jessie said, grinning.

Maria smiled and then diverted her eyes. "Ah have to tell you something Jessie."

"Okay."

She struggled to begin. "Ah have been going with a boy here in Los Angeles."

The pain that shot through Jessie was far worse than when the steer kicked him in the stomach. It took a minute for him to collect his thoughts and respond. "Is this for gettin' perspective?"

"Well, we been going pretty steady. Ah guess you seen that ah took off the Elgin watch you gave me."

Now what he felt was probably more like what a ranch steer feels when a cowboy slaps a red-hot branding iron on his backsides.

"When you didn't come ta see me, ah thought you didn't want me anymore, Jessie."

"I know, Maria, but I do want you."

"You do?"

"Oh, yes, I love you, Maria, and you're the only girl I'll ever love," said Jessie in an emotional, husky voice.

"Oh, Jessie, ah love you too with all my heart!" blurted Maria as tears sprang to her eyes.

They may have hesitated for one or maybe two seconds, then leaped out of their chairs and met in an emotional embrace in the middle of the room. It was a dramatic reunion for the two teen-age lovers. They grasped each other in an eager embrace, hugging and kissing and whispering endearments. What might have happened if Mr. and Mrs. Hunter hadn't come home at that moment was anybody's guess.

But they did and, after a somewhat reserved welcome to Jessie, reminded Maria they were going downtown to the theater that evening. They were sorry they hadn't been able to get another ticket so Jessie could go. Jessie thanked them, but said he had to drive back to the Grapevine to run his paper route Monday morning.

So again, Jessie and Maria didn't get to be alone for long. It really upset Jessie, because he wanted desperately to be alone with her and do all the exciting things they did when they had been together in Bear Trap Canyon.

Mrs. Hunter invited Jessie to dinner, but it was torture for him to be so near Maria and not be able to touch her. When dinner was over, Mrs. Hunter reminded Maria they had to leave shortly. This, of course, told Jessie his stay was over. He thanked them for dinner, and they said it was good to see him again.

Maria walked out to the Ford with Jessie, and they had a few moments alone. "Ah'm sorry, Jessie, that we didn't have more time alone, but the important thing is we both know that we still love each other."

"Yes. That is the important thing, Maria." Should he tell her about Mary Jane? He'd promised himself that he would. But he only had a few minutes, and he couldn't very well explain all that in a few minutes.

"Jessie, ah have to ask you a question."

"Okay."

"You got a girl down on the Grapevine?"

"No!" said Jessie without hesitation.

"Oh, Jessie, ah knew you didn't. Ah told Patsy you didn't, and ah was right." She threw herself into Jessie's arms and told him again that she loved him and that he was the only boy she would ever truly love. She promised that she would put her Elgin watch back on and never take it off again.

Jessie drove back down the Grapevine feeling good, even if he hadn't had much private time with Maria. The important thing was that he hadn't lost her. There was no question that she still loved him and he still loved her. It hurt badly when she told him about the guy she was going with, but he figured he deserved that, considering what he'd done with Mary Jane. He felt some remorse for not telling her about that, but since everything turned out okay, it was probably best that he didn't. He sensed that Alvin was right. She might not have understood.

As Jessie steered the Ford around the Grapevine switchbacks on his way home, Maria was sitting in the theater in Los Angeles, but she wasn't paying much attention to the performance. She was thinking of her reunion with Jessie, the boy she loved. And she did love him truly; there was no longer any doubt about that. She'd hadn't been sure until she saw him again, but now she knew. She felt guilty about not being completely truthful about her relationship with Kevin: it was a little more than she'd let on. And it was going to be real hard to stop going steady with him. But she had no choice now; she had to break it off.

Chapter
~24~

As always, Miss Trembell's Christmas play was the big social event on the Grapevine the fall of 1938. The play that year was "all right," conceded Jessie and his friends, but not as good as when they done it. It didn't seem possible that little Ruth was old enough to play Mary and skinny Dwane to play Joseph. They had both been little kids when the gang was at Grapevine School.

"But that's the way life goes fellows," said Jessie as they gathered around the punch bowl after the play was over. "Us older guys move on out, and the young kids take over."

Danny nodded and said, "Yeah. But ya know, Ruth sure is getting pretty. If she wasn't so young I might take her out."

"You gotta get yourself a car, Danny, if yer gonna take out girls," said Bobbie.

"Yeah, I know, and I'm gettin' me one in March. I'll be sixteen, and I've saved almost a hundred dollars from workin' in the root beer stand."

"Yer dad gonna let ya?" asked Bobbie.

"Well, he ain't said yet, but I think he will."

"I'll be sixteen in May, and Jessie is gonna sell me his Model A, and I'm gonna run the paper route," announced Billy triumphantly.

"Yer gettin' Jessie's paper route?" asked Gerald.

Jessie nodded. "That's right. I'm letting my little brother take over because after I graduate in June me and Alvin are going to work for the GP."

"Wow!" exclaimed Gerald. "The GP pays six bucks a day. How'd you get on?"

Alvin preempted Jessie with, "My dad knows one of the big shots in Los Angeles, an' he said he'd get me and Jessie summer jobs as roustabouts in the oil fields as soon as we turn eighteen."

"That's exactly what I'm gonna do when I'm eighteen, go to work for the GP and get me a car," Jack pronounced.

"You still gonna go to art college, Jessie?" asked Gerald.

"Yeah, I am. I'm just workin' for the summer, then I go to college up at San Francisco in the fall."

"Why are ya goin' way up there?" asked Bobbie.

"Well, they have a real good art college up there."

"That's a long way from Grapevine," said Jack.

"Yeah, I don't like that part, but if I'm gonna be an artist, I want to be a good one."

"Oh, you're gonna be a good artist, Jessie," said Jack. "I saw your paintings in that art show an' you really are good."

"They were good. I saw them too," put in Bobbie.

"You ain't gonna have a car anymore, Jessie?" asked Gerald.

"Nope. Billy needs it for the paper route, and I need all my money to help my dad pay the tuition at college."

"Next year, when I graduate, I'm joining the Army Air Corps and work on those big airplane engines," said Gerald, filling his cup again from the punch bowl.

Taking the dipping ladle from Gerald, Bobbie filled his cup too and said, "I'm gonna do what Jack is an get me a job with the GP. I need a car of my own. My dad hardly ever lets me take the car."

"My dad's the same. An' Agnes likes to go out," complained Alvin.

"Alvin, how is everything goin' with you and Agnes?" asked Bobbie, who sorta liked Agnes and would like to have her for his girl.

"Great. Since we got in high school, we don't fight like when we were little kids at Grapevine school."

"Oh," said Bobbie.

"Jessie, who are you gonna bring to the New Year's party at the Tavern?" asked Jack.

"I guess I'm not gonna bring a girl because Maria can't come."

"I thought you said her uncle was gonna bring her down for the Christmas holidays," said Alvin.

"He was, but I got a letter yesterday from Maria, and she said her uncle couldn't bring her."

Jack shook his head. "I'll tell ya, I sure wouldn't want a girl that lived so far away you never get to see her. You really gotta be stuck on that girl, Jessie."

Yes, Jessie was stuck on Maria. He'd made a vow he intended to keep this time, so he was the only one of the gang that didn't have a date for the big New Year's party at the Tavern. Even Gerald, who still wasn't all that keen on girls, took Andrea Bartling.

Jessie was surprised at how grown up and pretty Andrea looked in a white satin evening gown. He danced with her once, and she really snuggled up close. Then when Frank and his band played Auld Lang Syne as 1939 came in, everybody kissed to celebrate the new year. Andrea's kiss was a lot more than a fifteen-year-old ought to be giving, Jessie thought. But after he'd kissed a couple other girls, he guessed that's the way young girls were kissing these days.

Jessie graduated from Kern County Union High School in June of 1939. It was a big event for him and his family. His parents told him that from now on he had to make his own decisions regarding his life and his actions and assume full responsibility for it. He would be expected, however, to abide by family rules of behavior as long as he lived at home.

Mr. Rascoe wasn't the philosophical type, but he did say to his son: "I'll give you advice, Jessie, if you ask for it. Otherwise, at eighteen, you're an adult and old enough to judge for yourself what is right and what is wrong. You're resourceful, and you got good instincts, use them. You're gonna get in trouble; that comes with living life. But if you remember your Boy Scout motto of being prepared and apply common sense, you'll do just fine, and remember, you reap what you sow in this life. And you're not going to sow much of value if you don't understand responsibility and accountability."

One of Jessie's first adult decisions was to go to Los Angeles to see Maria. Her high school didn't get out until a week after Jessie's, and he and Alvin had to report to their oil field job before she would be home for the summer. Besides, he had something important to ask her.

He had thought about it the whole year and come to the conclusion that it was time to ask Maria to marry him and replace the Elgin watch with a diamond ring. He didn't want to take any more chances on losing her, so he went to Bakersfield and bought one. It was a blue-white diamond in a Tiffany setting and cost him almost fifty dollars. That hit his discretionary college fund hard, but it was worth it. He'd just have to save more during the summer.

He tried to call long distance to the Hunters to let Maria know he was coming, but no one answered the phone so he just went anyway.

It was an easier drive than last fall when he'd driven the Grapevine ridge route to Los Angeles, because the Griffith Company had finished widening a good portion of it. But he'd gotten a late start, and it was after nine o'clock in the evening when he got there. After he'd knocked on the door several times, Mr. Hunter finally came to the door in a robe. He didn't seem too pleased to see Jessie and told him that Maria was out on an engagement. He suggested that Jessie call again in the morning.

It was disappointing to Jessie that Maria wasn't there. He'd practiced his engagement speech on the drive down, and now he could hardly wait to say it and give her the ring. Then, as he sat in the Ford waiting, an uncomfortable feeling began to gnaw at him.

All kinds of thoughts started going around and around in Jessie's head. What kind of an engagement was she on? Who was she with? Could it be that guy, Kevin? She'd promised not to go with him anymore. She hadn't said any more about him in her letters, so he'd decided not to ask, but lately she hadn't written much. She said that was because she was working hard to get good grades so she could go into UCLA. But he shouldn't be imagining things. He knew Maria loved him; he was sure of that.

When Jessie's eyes suddenly popped open several hours later, he realized he'd fallen asleep. He pulled himself up in the seat and glanced out. A car had just parked up the street a ways and turned off its lights. There was enough reflection from the Hunters' porch light that he could tell there were two people in the front of the car.

Jessie felt a terrible ache growing down deep inside. Was it Maria in that car? Who else could it be? Maybe it was some one else because the car was up the street a bit from the Hunters. He sat watching for some time with growing anxiety. Every so often he'd get a glimpse of movement in the darkened car. What were they doing? Were they doing something? Could they have been making love? Finally, he couldn't stand it any longer, and just as he'd decided to get out of the Ford and go find out, the door of the other car opened and a tall guy wearing a football letter sweater got out, walked around, and opened the passenger side door. Jessie held his breath. The girl stepped out.

It was Maria.

Jessie felt as though he was suddenly paralyzed. He sat there in the Ford, dumbfounded, experiencing the worst emotional shock of his life as he watched the guy and Maria walk arm in arm up the sidewalk and onto the Hunters' front porch. Then they stopped and kissed before Maria finally went into the house.

Jessie drove back to the Grapevine in a daze. He was hardly aware of what he was even doing, he was so upset. Nothing he'd ever experienced before compared to how he felt. It was like the end of the world.

He had already turned the paper route over to his brother Billy in preparation for his departure to the oil fields. So he lay in bed most of that next day trying to make some kind of sense out of what had happened. How could it be? How could Maria do that? How could she kiss another guy like that if she loved him? How could she? Then suddenly Hallie Lamont's warning came crashing into his thoughts: "She's nothing but a little tramp!"

This time, Jessie was sure what he felt was worse than a red-hot branding iron on a steer's backside.

When Jessie left for the oil fields a few days later, he looked so despondent that his mother felt his forehead to see if he had a fever. He didn't, but she made him drink a glass of warm milk before he got on the company bus that took him and Alvin to the Lost Hills oil fields.

"What's the problem, Jess?" asked Alvin as they bounced along in the company bus.

Jessie turned from looking out the bus window and said, "I had a surprise to tell you, Alvin. But the surprise was on me. I don't know. I just seem to make one dumb mistake after another."

"What did you do this time?"

"It's the worst mistake I've made so far."

"I know, but what is it?"

Jessie turned and looked out the bus window. "She dumped me for that guy in Los Angeles, Alvin."

"What?"

Jessie turned back to face Alvin and told him the awful story of what happened in Los Angeles.

When he was finished, Alvin squinted his eyes for a moment and said, "Golly, Jess, I didn't know you were gonna propose to Maria."

"I was saving it for a big surprise, Alvin. But the surprise was on me."

"Well, it just proves what I been saying. You just don't know what a girl is gonna do. Whenever I think I got Agnes figured out, she does somethin' that boggles my mind."

"I'll tell ya, Maria did more than boggle my mind. She broke my heart. I guess I should have listened to Hallie. She said she was a little tramp."

"Well, I don't blame you for bein' sore, but I don't think Maria is a tramp. Just because she kissed some guy don't make her a tramp, Jess."

Jessie looked back out the window.

"Did you tell her about Mary Jane?"

"No."

"What you did was a lot worse than kissing somebody."

The bus driver down shifted as the bus started up the side of one of the rolling hills.

"I know it is, Alvin. But I'm a changed man. I promised myself I'd never do anything like that again. Besides, she told me she loved me, and she was gonna break it off with that guy. Yeah, she broke it off all right."

Alvin let out an audible sigh. "That's tough, Jess. What'a ya gonna do now?"

"I wrote her a letter and told her she broke my heart and I never want to see her again."

"Ya did?"

"Yeah. It's all over. After all this time, I finally found out she doesn't really love me."

"Well, I don't know about that, but I do know that girls are hard to understand sometimes."

"You can say that again."

"I'm mad at Agnes too, so what'a ya say, Jess, that we forget girls and just have fun this summer out in the oil fields?"

"That sounds like a great idea, Alvin. Let's not even talk about girls for the whole summer."

"Yeah! Who needs "em anyway? We're oil field workers, out in the real world!"

The old Tejon Pass Stage stop and cattle water trough.

The Grapevine creek bridge

Boy Scout troop 34 on campout in 1937

The "Grapevine gang" in their Model T Ford

Chapter
~25~

The oil field roustabouts from Grapevine were out in the real world all right. Oil field pipeline ditches were dug by hands with pick and shovel. And that's what roustabouts on the GP oil field gang did: dig ditches in the Lost Hills oil fields where the daily temperature ran over a hundred degrees in the shade - except there wasn't any shade.

Lost Hills is a part of the eastern slopes of California's Coast Range Mountains. They are the lower mountains, with few trees, referred to as foothills. In the early spring, they are covered with green grass and vivid wildflowers. By early summer; however, that all turns to a scorched brown under a blistering sun.

The oil wells in Lost Hills were drilled with a steel-and- diamond drilling bit. The bit was on the end of a long steel shaft that was rotated by a gasoline engine. As the hole was dug, steel pipe, called casing, was then lowered into the well hole. To do this, a wooden derrick had to be erected so the casing could be hung, and then lowered into the hole.

After the drillers struck oil, a pump was installed to pump the oil up from the well through the casing, and out into steel

pipe lines that ran across the hills and valleys to collection centers. From there, pipelines went to huge storage tanks where
the big steam-powered pumping stations pumped the oil to
the refineries.

New oil wells were constantly being drilled, which required
new pipelines, and older lines were being re-routed or
repaired. So roustabouts Jessie Rascoe and Alvin Pyeatt found
out quickly how they were going to earn their "big money," in
the Lost Hills oil fields.

That it was going to be a tough summer was evident from
the outset. Their hands swelled with blisters from swinging a
pick and shovel, and by the end of the day, they were so tired
and sore they sure enough didn't want to talk about girls. All
they wanted to do was fall into bed in the bunk house, in Lost
Hills where the oil field workers were housed.

But after a while, their muscles hardened, the blisters
went away, and they began to feel like real oil field roustabouts. They also began to feel the need for a little recreational diversion, but in Lost Hills there wasn't an awful lot
of recreational opportunity. Where they were housed was
sure enough lost in the hills, and there was no means of
transportation.

At quitting time on the Friday of their third week, the gang
boss walked up and said, "You boys take that ole Chevy pickup
and go on over to Devil's Corner Saturday night and have a
little fun."

"Gee, that's really nice of you, Mr. Jackson," said Alvin.

"Yeah, thanks a lot, Mr. Jackson," added Jessie.

"Where is Devil's Corner?" asked Alvin.

"It's northwest of Lost Hills. Take the blacktop that goes
north out of Maricopa. Follow it across Turkey Trot Ridge and
on down into the valley about ten miles, and you'll come to it.
There ain't much there, but some young folks hang out there
on Saturday nights at the Inferno Cafe. Just don't get drunk
and wreck the pickup."

"Oh, we won't, sir. Me an Alvin only drink soda pop,"
assured Jessie.

Jackson, a big man with a sun-browned, leathery face, nodded. "Well, yer ahead of the game then. Incidentally, yer both good workers."

The boys thanked him for the compliment. It was the first time the boss had said anything other than dig a ditch here or dig a ditch there.

The GP roustabouts put on their best jeans and shirts and headed out late Saturday afternoon for Devil's Corner. They were pretty happy to get away for a change of scenery and curious about the Inferno Cafe at Devil's Corner. It sounded adventurous and exciting after three weeks of pick and shovel in a ditch on the side of a lost hill.

After about an hour of driving down the narrow blacktop that meandered through the sun-scorched hills, they found their destination. It was a small town on the northern rim of the oil fields, and if you weren't paying attention, you might drive right past it and not realize it.

The Inferno Cafe was right on the main road that went through the town so it was easy to find. A sign out front read: "Home cooked food, cold beer, and pop." Jessie and Alvin were a little disappointed since it didn't look nearly as exciting as they had imagined. It did, however, live up to its name: Inferno. It was hot.

Inside, there were some oil field workers in jeans and brogans, and a few young girls wearing bright summer dresses. A lunch counter stretched across one side with a dozen or so tables on the opposite side, covered with red-and-white checkered oil cloth. Toward the rear, a jukebox emitted flashing lights and loud music. In front of the jukebox was a small dance floor. A couple of big fans on pedestals whirred at full speed, which, for the most part, just pushed a lot of hot air around. But it was better than the outside air that was well over the one hundred degree mark.

Heads turned when Jessie and Alvin entered and took a seat at one of the vacant tables. After looking over the newcomers, everyone went back to what they were doing. A waitress wearing a red smock made her way through the tables and handed them a one-page paper menu that had catsup spilled on it. Then she told them the best thing on the menu was the T-bone steak, so they ordered that and orange pop.

The roustabouts' declaration of forgetting girls for the summer had not been tested in the oil fields, and it didn't look as though it would be tested at the Inferno Cafe either.

"Looks like all the girls here are with someone," observed Alvin.

"Yeah, but I don't care," replied Jessie.

"Me either."

The waitress arrived with their orange pop, and they both took a drink.

"Hey look, Jess, that little blonde over there by the jukebox just smiled at us."

"Yeah, I saw her."

"Is she with someone?"

"Well, she was talking to that big guy in the red shirt. I don't see him now."

"Maybe he left."

"Yeah, and look. She's smiling at us again."

"I bet she'd like to meet us."

"I think you're right."

"Oh, oh. That big guy in the red shirt just came back."

"Yeah, and now look, she's smiling at him. Ya see that, Alvin? That's just the way girls are. One minute they're smiling at you, and the next minute it's somebody else. They're all alike."

"Yeah, ain't it the truth? They're all alike."

The waitress arrived with their T bone steaks, and as she set them down, the guy with the red shirt turned to speak to someone and the cute blonde smiled at them again.

The two roustabouts shifted their attention to the steaks. When it was gone, they ordered homemade apple pie a la mode. The ice cream was almost all melted by the time it got to them, but it was good anyway.

About that time, two new patrons came into the cafe, and all heads turned, Jessie's and Alvin's included. When they saw the newcomers, their mouths popped open. They were shapely, pretty girls who wore identical red-and-green polka dot dresses and red ribbons in their hair. They had dark eyes, long dark hair, and were so much alike it was impossible to tell them apart. They seemed to know several of the patrons, and as they visited, Jessie and Alvin watched incredulously.

"Ain't that somethin'?" said Alvin.

"Yeah," agreed Jessie. "I bet they're identical twins. A friend of my mother had identical twin girls and you couldn't tell them apart."

"Yep, they look exactly alike."

The two roustabouts watched the twins visit for a while and then make their way across the room to the table next to theirs. The waitress hadn't cleaned off the dirty dishes from the last customers yet, so the girls just stood there.

Alvin and Jessie glanced at each other and then jumped to their feet. "Would you like to sit at our table until yours gets cleaned?" offered Alvin.

Both girls smiled demurely and nodded. With chairs scraping across linoleum, the girls were seated. Alvin smiled and said, "I'm Alvin Pyeatt, and this is Jessie Rascoe."

"We're the See sisters," the girls said, in sing-song unison.

"I'm Jan," said one sister.

"I'm June," said the other.

Jessie and Alvin glanced back and forth between the girls.

"You look exactly alike," said Alvin.

The girls nodded.

"How can you tell which is which?" asked Jessie.

"You can't," they both said in voices exactly alike.

The two roustabouts stared, and Alvin laughed. "I bet that causes some confusion."

Both sisters laughed. "Oh, it does, and sis and I have great fun," said June.

"Do you always dress alike?" Jessie asked.

"Not all the time," said Jan.

"It depends on who we're with," said June.

"Can your folks tell you apart?" Alvin asked.

"Mom can, but Papa can't," replied Jan with a smile.

"That's pretty neat," Alvin said.

"Yes," said June, giggling. "We can do all kinds of things, and no one knows for sure which one did what."

The roustabouts looked at each other in amazement.

Both sisters laughed.

"Do you guys work in the oil fields?" asked June.

"Yeah," answered the guys in unison, and everyone laughed.

The waitress arrived and cleaned the dishes off the other table, but before the girls could move, another couple sat down. So everyone laughed again, and Jessie asked the girls what they would like a drink. In unison, they said, "One oh two."

Jessie and Alvin weren't familiar with that kind of pop, but the waitress seemed to understand.

"You guys always drink orange pop?" asked one of the sisters after the waitress had departed.

"Not always, but it's what we like best," explained Jessie.

"That's neat. That's what we drink too when we can't get one oh two," said Jan, and both girls giggled.

"Well, didn't you just order one oh two?" asked Alvin.

"Yeah, but Alice ain't gonna bring us one oh two. She'll bring us orange pop like yours," said June.

The guys looked confused. "Well, what's one oh two?" pressed Alvin.

The girls exchanged glances. "Don't you ever listen to the radio?" asked Jan.

Both guys confessed they listened mostly to *The Shadow* or *The Lone Ranger.*

"They advertise Brew One Oh Two on the radio all the time. It's really good beer," said Jan authoritatively. "But in this place, they know we ain't twenty-one, so they won't serve us beer."

"Oh," said the guys.

"But most places don't ask for our I.D. They just think we're twenty-one," said June. "You guys think we look twenty-one?"

Both guys nodded.

"How old are you guys?" Jan asked.

"Uh, we're both eighteen," said Alvin.

"Hey, so are we!" said June.

"Do you live here in Devil's Corner?" asked Jessie.

Both twins nodded. "But we go to high school in Paso Robles," said one of the twins. "They don't have a high school here."

"We're seniors," said the other twin.

"Hey, so am I," said Alvin. "Jessie's goin' to college this year."

"Neat," said June. "What are you goin' to be?"

"I want to be an artist," replied Jessie.

"An artist?"

"Yes."

A nod. "We live in Paso Robles during the school year, but we have to come home to Devil's Corner in the summer," said Jan.

"Paso Robles is great fun, but it's dullsville over here in the summer except on Friday and Saturday night," said June.

The waitress brought the four bottles of cold orange pop, and they all took drinks. The jukebox started up, and one of the girls said, "You guys like to dance?"

The guys looked at each other. Both girls stood up. Both guys jumped up, and all four made their way to the dance floor. By the time they meandered through the tables, the guys weren't sure which See sister he ended with on the dance floor and was embarrassed to ask. But at that point, it didn't seem to be all that important anyway.

The dance floor wasn't big enough to do much more than move around in small circles, and the pedestal fans didn't make much difference. It was still hot. After a few minutes, everyone was perspiring. But the intimacy of dancing with the pretty sisters worked its magic, and by the time they returned to the table, both roustabouts were excited over the See sister he'd danced with, whichever one it was.

"It's always hot as Hades in Devil's Corner this time of year," said Jessie's girl as she watched him wipe the perspiration from his forehead with his handkerchief.

Jessie grinned. "Yeah, me an Alvin noticed that working in the oil fields."

"You ever been to Pismo Beach?" asked the other sister.

Both guys shook their head. "Where is that?" asked Alvin, also wiping off perspiration.

"It's just down the coast from Paso Robles."

"It's really cool there all summer," added the other sister. "And you can drive over there in about an hour."

"Ya can?" Jessie said.

"Yeah," the sisters confirmed.

"You guys got a car?"

Alvin and Jessie exchanged glances. "Uh, sorta. It ain't ours, but we got a Chevy pickup," explained Jessie.

"Swell, we like pickups," said both girls.

"Want'a drive over and cool off?" asked one.

"You can drive right out on the beach over there, and it's really fun at night," coaxed the other.

The guys seemed to hesitate. The See girls got up from the table, and both guys also stood.

"Come on, let's go," said one girl putting her arm through Jessie's as the other put her arm through Alvin's.

Everyone in the Inferno Cafe stopped what they were doing and watched the two couples depart.

Jessie's instincts told him Mr. Jackson hadn't intended that he drive the company pickup to Pismo Beach, but dancing with June, or Jan, or whichever one it was, had sparked that feeling that had been dormant since his emotional disaster over Maria. It was evident that Alvin, too, was captivated by whichever of the girls he was with, so they crowded into the pickup and headed down the road to Pismo Beach; the guys having forgotten all about their declaration of girl abstinence.

Chapter
~26~

The two country boys were captivated by the vivacious personalities of the See sisters - not to mention the excitement of being in the crowded pickup with girls who liked to snuggle up. If there was any concern as to which sister was snuggling with which guy, it was lost in the adventure. When they first started, June sat next to Jessie and Jan next to Alvin. But after they stopped at a roadside diner to get cold pop, it was anyone's guess as to what the arrangement was when they got back in the pick up. But it didn't seem to be a big deal with the girls, so it wasn't with the guys, and everyone was happy.

It was hot, so they had to keep the windows down and the wind noise made it difficult to converse, but they laughed and shouted. By the time they came over that last hill where Highway 101 entered the little sea-side town of Pismo Beach, they had all become quite friendly.

The See sisters were right about Pismo Beach. It was delightfully quaint and the sea breeze refreshingly cool after the heat of Lost Hills. The main street of the little town ran down to the beach where there was a long wooden pier that had food and drink concessions, music, and lots of activity. But the girls directed Jessie to a small store off the main street that had a sign in the window: "Clam Forks for rent."

"The guy that runs this place will sell beer to anyone. Go get us four bottles of Brew One Oh Two, and we'll take 'em out on the beach and drink 'em. It's great fun," assured one of the See sisters.

Jessie and Alvin were apprehensive about trying to buy beer, but the excitement of what lay ahead in this adventure sparked their courage, and they walked boldly into the store and asked for four bottles of Brew One Oh Two. Sure enough, the storekeeper sold them the beer without batting an eye. He did look at Jessie strangely when he asked what a clam fork was.

"You dig clams with it," the storekeeper answered a bit indignantly.

"Where do you dig them?" asked Alvin.

"On the beach. Ain't you guys ever been to Pismo Beach before?" The guys shook their heads.

"Pismo Beach is famous for clams," he said handing them the beer in a brown paper bag. "Arthur Godfrey even comes here to dig clams."

As they walked out of the store, Jessie said, "Who's Arthur Godfrey?"

Alvin shrugged. "I don't know, but it sounds like one of those guys that go around savin' people in big tents."

"Could be."

The girls showed Jessie where he could drive the pickup right out onto the beach sand. By this time, it was dark, and they drove down the wide, smooth beach until all the lights from the pier and the concessions faded into the night.

Finally, they stopped the pickup right there on the beach, and Jessie turned off the engine and the headlights. Everyone got out and stood for a moment, holding hands in the darkness and looking at the sparkling surf in the starlight. It was romantic watching and listening to the thundering waves as they pounded the sand and rolled up the sloping beach in long arches of glittering foam. The tangy sea smell and the salty taste of ocean spray that whipped across their faces added to the unique experience for the two mountain boys.

Both guys admitted that Pismo Beach was really great, and after the twins claimed it was the best beach in those parts, they suggested it was time to open the Brew One Oh Two. That would have been a problem, but Jessie Rascoe had his scout knife, which had a bottle opener. Jessie and Alvin were both apprehensive about drinking alcohol as that had been prohibited by their parents and their scout master. But being roustabouts in the real world now and the enchantment of the See sisters overcame their apprehension.

"Here's to fun at Pismo Beach," said one of the twins, and they all touched bottles and drank. It was the first taste of alcohol for both mountain boys, and it was awful.

"Ain't that great beer?" exclaimed one of the girls.

"Yeah, It's uh, great, huh Jess?" croaked Alvin.

"I love Brew One Oh Two," claimed the other See sister. Jessie nodded.

They all leaned against the pickup and listened to the roar of the surf and watched the waves in the starlight, while they drank the beer. After a while one of the girls, noticing that the boys weren't keeping up, said, "Okay, it's chug-a-lug time."

"Come on, it's bottoms up and ya gotta drink it all without stopping or you're a panty waist," said the other See sister.

Jessie and Alvin were trapped. There was no way out. They had to touch their beer bottles with the girls and drink.

It was a terrible ordeal, and it took a lot of will power to do it without gagging, but they did it.

"Come on, let's go for a walk," said the girl with Jessie as she pulled off her shoes and socks and threw them into the pickup. Jessie followed suit, and she took his hand and pulled him after her, shouting over her shoulder, "See you guys later!"

"Okay," replied the other sister, pulling Alvin in the opposite direction.

After Jessie and his girl had walked down the beach for a while with waves washing up over their bare feet, he noticed his anxiety over what he was doing had pretty well dissipated. And

June- he was pretty sure it was June- began to captivate him more every passing moment. Any thoughts regarding his ban on girls dissolved.

Although Jessie had never been under the influence of alcohol before, his good instincts told him that was probably the reason for his uninhibited feeling. He suddenly halted, put his arms around the girl, and said, "I like you."

"I like you too," she replied.

His arms tightened around her and he pulled her close and kissed her. She responded, returning his kiss eagerly. They stood there together on the starlit beach with the sound of the roaring surf in their ears and the waves washing over their feet for some time, embracing and kissing with growing, eager passion.

"Come on, let's go out in the waves," she said, pulling him toward the surf.

With alcohol-enhanced enthusiasm, they ran through the roaring surf, and it was great fun until a big wave caught them by surprise and sent them tumbling into the cold water. That took their breath away and swept them up the beach into a foamy heap of salt water, sand, and seaweed.

"Wasn't that fun?" the girl said, giggling and pulling seaweed from her tangled hair.

"Yeah, and for sure it was breathtaking," replied Jessie, digging sand out of one ear. "That big ole wave turned me upside down."

"I love playing around on the beach at night, even if the water is cold and sandy, don't you?"

"This is the first time I ever did it."

"You never played around on the beach before?"

"No, but I like it. And it sure enough cools ya off."

She was sitting in the wet sand a short distance from Jessie, so she moved over and put her arms around him. "Yer a good sport, Jessie. I like guys like you," she said and kissed him hard with sandy lips.

That started them off kissing again with renewed enthusiasm, particularly for Jessie since her water-soaked dress revealed some exciting contours. It wasn't long till passions peaked again, but the girl pulled away and said, "I love makin' out on the beach but it's too sandy to go all the way. Let's go get a cabin so we can take a shower first."

Her bold offer shocked Jessie, despite his desensitized condition; it also triggered a flashback to the Mary Jane Brown affair- and his oath to never do that again.

"It'll be fun, but ya gotta use a rubber. I don't want to get pregnant."

Jessie nodded and, after brief consideration, decided that would be okay. In fact, it seemed that when you drink beer whatever you do is okay. "I haven't got any rubbers, June, but I'll get some."

"Okay, Jessie. But I'm Jan."

Another surprise cut into Jessie's state of glow. "You're Jan?" he blurted.

She looked at him as though miffed, then laughed. "It's okay. Guys do that all the time." Jessie laughed too because that didn't seem to be a big deal either. "Sis and I have fun switching off and keeping guys guessing, but we got principles. When we pair off, we don't switch no more. And I picked you, Jessie. You're good-lookin' and you're neat."

"Yer neat too Ju...uh, Jan." They both laughed again.

"Come on, let's go find sis and your buddy," she said taking his hand.

They arrived at the pickup about the same time June and Alvin did, and it was evident they had also been having fun on Pismo Beach. They were both wet and disheveled, but smiling radiantly in the starlight.

They all talked and laughed about having sand and sea-weed in their hair and ears, and the guys' wallets were all wet, but that didn't seem to be a big deal either. After a while, Jan said, "Come on, let's go buy some more One Oh Two and get a cabin."

"There is a swell little place just down from the pier called Seashore Cabins," said June.

"It's against the law to be in there if yer not married, but sis and I can duck down in the pickup while you guys register.

They let ya drive right up to the front of the cabins to park so it's easy then to sneak inside," explained Jan.

It occurred to Jessie and Alvin that the girls knew a lot about how all this was done, but they weren't in a frame of mind to worry about it. Everything worked out pretty much as the sisters said.

The night clerk at the Seashore Cabins apparently didn't suspect they were smuggling girls into the cabins although he did ask them how come they were all wet. They both laughed, and Alvin explained that they got caught by a big wave while wading in the surf.

The guys rented two of the cabins at two dollars apiece. They were small but cozy with just one room, a bed, and a small shower and toilet. Everyone gathered in one to snicker over the success at fooling the night clerk.

"How about you guys go getting some more Brew One Oh Two and some snacks while we shower and clean up, okay?" said one of the girls.

As they went out the door, Jan whispered a reminder to Jessie that they sold rubbers at the drug store there on the corner of Main Street and Highway 101. Jessie acknowledged with a return whisper and a leaping pulse.

As soon as they were out of the cabin and going down the road in the pickup, Alvin blurted, "Oh man, I can't believe all this, can you, Jess?"

"Me either. I heard about guys and girls doin' stuff like this, but I never thought we'd be doin' it."

"And ya know what? June told me right out that she would do it in the cabin if I used a rubber. How about that?"

Jessie laughed. "Me too, Alvin! Jan told me the same thing. All we gotta do is get some rubbers. I hope they will sell us some."

"Sure they will. We look twenty-one now."

"Yeah, but we don't look so good in these wet clothes."

"Aw, they won't even notice. Man, we're livin' dangerously tonight, Jess!"

"That Brew One Oh Two sure makes you feel reckless, don't it?"

"Yeah. I almost gagged at first, but it makes ya feel good all right."

Jessie glanced at Alvin. "Did you know your girl was June?"

"Did you know yours was Jan?"

They looked at each other across the seat of the pickup and laughed.

"Those girls are somethin', Jess."

"They are. I guess ya gotta get out in the world to meet girls like them."

"Yeah, I guess. You, uh, okay about this, Jess?"

"Well, we're breakin' all the rules, and I know we shouldn't."

"Yeah, I know. But I want to. Don't you?"

Silence.

"Yeah, I do."

The store keeper at the clam fork place told them beer was cheaper by the case so they got one and a block of ice to cool it. Then they got ham sandwiches and potato chips at one of the concessions. At the drug store, they bought two three-packs of condoms without a hitch.

By the time the guys returned to the Seaside Cabins, the girls had showered, washed their dresses, and hung them on the window sill to dry. The sight that greeted Jessie and Alvin provoked instant revival of their sexual appetite. The See sisters were sitting in the middle of the bed, each draped in a bed sheet, with their hair pulled back in pony tails. They looked beautiful, and there was no question that the devilish smile on their faces promised more exciting things to come.

"You guys go take a shower in the other cabin then we'll drink beer and have a bed picnic," instructed one of the twins.

"Yeah, and make it a quick shower," said the other with a promising smile.

The guys had never heard of a bed picnic, but it sounded exciting. They eagerly rushed across, took a quick shower, hung up their wet clothes, and wrapped themselves in the bed sheets for their return to the other cabin.

It was daring fun to slip out into the misting, sea night dressed in a sheet. But then, when they arrived for the bed picnic, they found themselves again facing the twins without a clue as to which was which. The only difference was that one had a red ribbon on her pony tail, the other a blue.

The girls just sat there in the middle of the bed, draped in the sheets, drinking beer and smiling demurely. Then they laughed, and one girl reached out and took Jessie's hand and the other took Alvin's.

"I knew it was you, June," said Alvin as they opened more beer and spread the sandwiches on the bed where they all sat cross-legged.

She laughed. "Sure you did."

They all laughed, and the other girl held up her beer bottle and said, "Here's to more fun and games at Pismo Beach."

"I'll drink to that," said Jessie, and everybody joined in and took a big draft of the beer. The beer seemed to taste a little better to the guys than it had the first time, and of course, it added even more zip to their exuberance. Everything that was said seemed to be hilarious, and the two roustabouts declared that bed picnics were great.

When the sandwiches were gone, Jan said, "We don't have to be home till two o'clock tomorrow, cause that's when our parents get back from church in Paso Robles. They go over there every Saturday afternoon and come back Sunday."

Everyone knew that was the signal, and shortly thereafter they paired off into separate cabins where Jessie and Alvin found that the See sisters were even more exciting in a soft, dry bed than on a wet, sandy beach. When the promise to never again go all the way with a girl other than Maria crossed Jessie's thoughts, his alcohol enhanced emotions sent it sailing off into space.

It was a daring, unique experience for the two guys from Grapevine to spend their first night in bed with a girl in a quaint seashore cabin, with the sounds of the Pismo Beach surf roaring through the window.

Along about midnight, they gathered back in one cabin, ate what was left of the potato chips, and drank more Brew One Oh Two as they laughed at just about everything that was said since it all seemed to be hilarious. Then sometime around two o'clock Jan said, "Hey, less go out on'a beach and skinny dip."

"Less do it!" agreed June.

By this time, the two mountain boys were in rare condition since they had consumed a considerable amount of alcohol.

"That's a great idea!" said Alvin.

"Let's go!" agreed Jessie.

"They ain't nobody out there this time'a night. Come on!" said Jan leaping off the bed. The other three followed in eager pursuit. The four bed-sheeted skinny dippers looked like four ghosts in the night running across deserted Pismo Beach. They stopped at surf's edge, dropped the sheets, and plunged into the starlit surf.

They whooped and howled when their naked bodies hit the cold water. Fortunately, the antifreeze properties of alcohol displaced the effects of the cold water, and they romped and splashed around in the big waves while stopping often to embrace and kiss.

Every so often a big wave would break over their heads, separating the lovers and sending them tumbling into the churning sea water. When they recovered, there in the darkness and roaring surf, it was impossible for the guys to identify which girl was his since they even looked exactly alike naked. But after a while, it didn't seem to be all that important because everybody liked everybody. So they just took whichever girl turned up, and all had a roaring good time until the Pismo Beach night policeman showed up on the scene and spoiled all the fun.

Driving his 1936 Ford V-8 right out onto the beach, the policeman shined his spot-light out over the waves and on the nude swimmers. That got their attention, but in their high spirits they decided to play a little game of hide-and-seek, ducking in and out of the waves. The policeman on the beach was persistent, and after a while, the hide-and-seekers were getting waterlogged.

They huddled and tried to debate a strategy, but the noise of the surf and the big waves prevented any real discussion, so

Alvin finally instructed, "You guys jus' stay here. I'll go an' talk to 'em."

"Alvin'ze part injun. He'ze real brave and knows how'ta talk with anybody," explained Jessie to the See sisters as they crouched down in the ocean water.

Alvin listed slightly to starboard as he followed a great circle route up the beach to where the policeman stood. They spoke briefly, and then he reversed his course and, listing now to port, plodded back to where the others waited. He explained as best he could that they were all in violation of an ordnance prohibiting nude bathing and therefore under arrest. Everyone was a bit distressed, of course. But Jessie said that he was sure some kind of compromise could be worked out, so they agreed to surrender.

The policeman, a kindly looking, grey-haired man in an ill-fitting green uniform, was good enough to turn his back while the girls came out of the surf and got into the sheets. But after that, things didn't go well. He wasn't nearly as kindly as he looked.

When he shined his flashlight on the twins, he did a double-take and growled, "You girls been drinking, haven't ya?"

"Oh, no, we ain't had nussing but orange pop, ossiffer," giggled one of the sisters.

"Oh yes, you have. I can smell it. And I'll bet you aren't of age either, are ya?"

"Sure we are," slurred the other sister.

The policeman swung his flashlight to the guys. "You two boys are in a heap of trouble. You not only violated our indecent exposure ordinance, you been drinking alcohol on a public beach and contributing to the delinquency of a minor."

"This beech ain't public. They ain't nobody here," observed one of the girls.

The officer swung his flashlight back to the twins. "An' you two girls are in deep trouble too, so don't give me any of your lip."

Despite their intoxication, the gravity of the situation began to register on the two guys from Grapevine. To make matters worse, the time had come when their stomachs gave notice of a rebellion over all the Brew One Oh Two they'd consumed.

"Osifeer, isn't there some way we could...uh, work thish out?" asked Jessie in the best voice he could muster.

"We thought it'd be all right to, uh, swim without clothes, cause...bein at night'n all," explained Alvin, trying to stand as still as he could, but the beach kept swaying back and forth. Then before the policeman could respond, Alvin felt his stomach begin its ascent, and he spun around and ran toward the surf as fast as his legs would carry him.

He didn't make it. About half way there he began to throw up. About three or maybe four seconds later, his best friend followed suit. Both the girls stood there giggling and watching the guys. "They ain't done mush drinkin' before," explained one of the twins to the policeman.

"Well, it serves 'em right."

"Mr. Policeman, we're both eighteen, honest injun. So don't put'em in jail fer uh, contribitin' to a minor."

"They're real nice guys," said the other twin in her most appealing voice.

The officer turned his flashlight on that twin for a moment and then over to the other. Each girl's hair seemed to hang in exactly the same entanglement, while the wet, sandy sheets clung to each in the same fashion. "You girls identical twins?"

"Yes, sir," they both answered, grinning.

"You sure do look alike, but you don't look eighteen."

"We are eighteen," the girls insisted.

"When's yer birthday?" he snapped.

"May six, nineteen twenty-one," they replied in unison.

The policeman thought a moment, and then nodded. "Okay. Where you staying?"

"Right there," said one pointing up at the Seaside Cabins that were just visible in the darkness.

He looked at them suspiciously. "You got two cabins?"

"Oh sure. We're in one and they're in'a other," replied one girl quickly.

"Yeah, sure. Lucky for you we ain't got a jail here, or I'd throw all of you in it right now. Anyway, if I arrest you, I gotta drive you all the way down to the county seat, and I don't want to do that at three o'clock in the mornin'. So tell ya what, you get them two boys up there quietly to bed, and then you two get to bed in the other cabin and you stay there till you all sober up, ya hear?"

"Yes, sir," said both sisters. "You ken count on it."

"Oh, I'll be counting on it all right cause I'm gonna be watchin' an' if you make a wrong move you will all go to jail. I promise."

It wasn't easy, but they did it. The girls managed to get the guys, who were pretty subdued and embarrassed over getting sick, up to the cabins and into bed. As instructed, the girls went to bed in the other cabin. There wasn't much else to do anyway because the lovers had lost all of their romantic zeal.

The next morning, the big lovers from Grapevine were in bad shape. They felt terrible and could hardly hold up their heads. They both were still throwing up every so often. It was the dreaded "dry heaves." They lay side by side on the bed in their cabin, confident they were on the verge of death, while the girls did some sun bathing on the beach. But noon was check-out time, and besides, the girls had to be home by two o'clock at the latest. So there was nothing to do but brave the agony and start off down the road toward Devil's Corner.

It ended up that Jan drove the pickup back, with the guys piled against each other on the opposite side of the seat. From Devil's Corner, they were on their own, but somehow they made it back to the bunkhouse.

The next morning when they reported to work, the gang foreman looked at them and said, "You two look like you been in one hell of a wreck. I hope it wasn't the pickup."

"No, sir, we didn't wreck the pickup. It's there in the garage," said Jessie in a raspy croak.

Jackson nodded then broke into a smile. "Okay, then you must have met the See sisters." The roustabouts who looked like they had been in a wreck glanced at each other, but felt too awful to comment.

Digging ditches under the blistering August sun in the Lost Hills oil fields, may well have been the ultimate punishment for the two lovers who were still suffering their first alcoholic hangover. They weren't sure how they managed to survive the day, but they did. That night they both took an oath that they would never drink beer again if they lived to be a hundred.

By the following day, they were feeling much better and had their first rational discussion on their adventure at Pismo Beach.

"Getting sick on beer was the worst experience of my life. I thought I was gonna die and wished that I'd hurry up and get it over with," admitted Jessie. He and Alvin were sitting on a pile of fresh dirt they had just dug up, eating their lunch from lunch pails.

"Yeah, I know what you mean. I felt the same way. Funny how alcohol works. I was really feelin' great there for a while then all of a sudden it was like the crash of the Hindenburg. I could hardly talk, and things started spinning around. It was awful."

"Well, I ain't gonna drink any more Brew One Oh Two, that's for sure."

"Me either. But the girls drank as much as we did. In fact, they drank a lot more. I wonder why they didn't get sick?"

"Probably because they're used to it."

"I guess so. Boy, that was some kind of party, huh, Jess?"

"Well, I guess the See sisters are what ya call chippies, but we were right there with 'em."

"Yeah, I know we were. One thing for sure, when we broke the rules and the law, we went whole hog."

"We did, and when I think about it, I get a guilty feeling," admitted Jessie.

"What do you feel guilty about, Jess?"

"Well, I know what I did was wrong, but the worst part is that I swore I'd never do anything like that again. And what did I do? I did it again."

Alvin nodded. "Yep, yer right. You broke yer Boy Scout honor."

"Well, I didn't swear on my scout honor."

"Oh."

"But it was still dead wrong, and it makes me wonder if I got any character at all. No wonder Maria dumped me for that football player."

Alvin squinted his eyes for a moment. "Jess, I admit it was morally wrong. But I think that kind of stuff just happens when yer out in the real world like we are now."

"Yeah, I guess so, but that don't make it right."

"I know it don't. But the way I see it is that once you've shacked up with a girl like we did, you sorta graduate into another part of your life. I mean we're not kids any more. We're oil field workers and adults livin' life in the raw. What we do now is up to our conscience."

"Yeah, well, my conscience ain't doin' so good."

Alvin put his foot on the shovel and thrust it into the ground. "Neither is mine," he muttered.

So the conversation went most of that week until Friday when Alvin turned to Jessie and said, "Jess, I come to the conclusion that we gotta accept life as it is and like I always say: do what comes naturally."

Jessie stopped shoveling and looked at Alvin. "You mean what comes naturally this Saturday?"

Alvin grinned. "Yep, that's what I mean."

"Okay, what comes natural for you?"

"Well, I know those girls are sorta…Well, they play around with guys. But I like June. I mean, I'm not in love or anything, but she's neat and a lot of fun. What do you think, Jess?"

"Yeah, they are fun girls all right."

"You want to see them again?"

Jessie hesitated. "Well, if you do…"

Alvin nodded. "Yep, I do."

"You think they will go with us to Pismo Beach again this Saturday?"

Alvin hesitated. "Well, I don't think they liked it too good when we got sick."

"But Jan said she understood, cause she got sick once from drinking too much Brew One Oh Two."

"Aw, they'll go, Jess. Those girls are crazy about us."

"Yeah, yer right, Alvin."

The gang boss gave them the pickup again, and when they entered the Inferno Cafe Saturday afternoon, the place had its usual customers, but the See sisters weren't among them. After two hours of waiting, Alvin took a drink of his third orange pop and said confidently, "I'm sure they'll be here. Probably their parents were late leaving for Paso Robles or something."

"Yeah, that's probably what happened," agreed Jessie.

"If you two are waiting for the See sisters, yer gonna have a long wait," said Alice the waitress, standing beside their table. "They went over to Pismo Beach with a couple guys and won't be back till Sunday."

Between that Saturday at the Inferno Cafe and the time they said good-bye in Bakersfield six weeks later, when Jessie departed for college, the two friends had numerous discussions about their summer experience. One of their conclusions was a confirmation that you never know what girls are gonna do, which they already knew before they went to the oil fields and shacked up with chippies. But they did agree that now they knew a lot more about life in the raw.

Chapter
~27~

The day Jessie departed for college, all his family and friends went to Bakersfield to see him off. His parents, brother Billy, a couple aunts and uncles, some nieces and nephews, and most of the Grapevine gang showed up at the train station. As far as anyone knew, Jessie was the only one on the Grapevine ever to go to a real college. That wasn't unusual in those depression years as few could afford it, but with his saving from the root beer stand, paper route, and the oil field job, Jessie had enough for his first two years. He planned to earn the rest with summer jobs.

It was a marvelous occasion that left Jessie with a lump in his throat as he waved good-bye from a window of the Santa Fe Chief when it pulled out of the station. He felt honored, yet strangely sad to leave the Grapevine. The truth was he'd had some pretty serious second thoughts right up to the time he climbed on the train.

After all, Bakersfield had a great junior college. So why was he going away? Well, because he was sure that his dad was correct: if you're going to do something, do it right. He didn't want to go to a far-off place, but he wanted to be a good artist and was convinced the college in San Francisco was the best. So in late August of 1939, Jessie Rascoe left his family and friends with regret, but with great expectations for the future.

Across the Atlantic Ocean, Nevil Chamberlain, prime minister of Great Britain, came home from a meeting with Adolf Hitler, with great expectations as he waved an agreement he had made with Adolf Hitler that guaranteed no war. The world praised Mr. Chamberlain as a man of wisdom who had brought peace through negotiations, instead of through force.

Poor Mr. Chamberlain and the rest of the gullible diplomats in Europe couldn't believe it when Adolph Hitler's Nazis war machine rolled over Poland in the fall of 1939. It began on September 1, and two days later, Great Britain and France declared war on Germany and the Second World War was under way.

World War I had been over for twenty years, but it was still pretty fresh in people's minds. Most folks in the United States sympathized with Great Britain and France, but they just didn't want to get involved in another European war. The isolationist politicians said that we should stay out of it, and that was what most people wanted to hear.

But at the urging of President Roosevelt, Congress passed the first peace-time draft in history. They also passed the Neutrality Act of 1939, which made it possible for nations fighting the Axis to buy war supplies from the United States. At least that added a little zip to the economy and put some people back to work making war machines.

Out on the Grapevine, Alvin, Jack, and Gerald were starting their final year at Bakersfield High, and Bobbie, Danny, and Billy were juniors. Frank and Bud had graduated from Bakersfield Junior College that spring and Frank joined the navy because he didn't want to get drafted. Bud joined the Army Air Corps for the same reason. They were the first from the Grapevine to join up, and that broke up the dance band, so the Tavern at Frazier Mountain Park didn't have dancing anymore on Saturday nights.

Miss Trembell had nine new students that fall because the construction crews were still working on the Grapevine ridge route. She had to double up in three grade rows, and she admitted to Mr. Carver that the new kids weren't well disciplined. But as always, she ran a tight ship, and it wasn't long till she had everything in good order.

In Los Angeles, Maria Hunter had suffered a terrible blow when she received Jessie's letter saying he never wanted to see her again. She was depressed for a while, and it took a lot of counseling from her friend Patsy before things got back to normal. She told Patsy that even though she'd lost him, she knew she would love Jessie forever. But when Kevin Blake gave her his football ring to wear, it helped heal Maria's heart, and it also told everybody they were going steady again for their senior year at Lincoln High.

Hallie Lamont was in her third year of college at UCLA and getting her usual high academic marks. But flying had become her real love, and she'd already earned her commercial pilot's license. Nobody around the Grapevine seemed to know if she was still keeping company with that big jerk George Simmons.

The San Francisco College Jessie had elected to attend was a liberal arts school that had a notable art department. Jessie's art teacher at Bakersfield High had gotten her degree there and assured him it was the place he should attend to become a good artist. After he got there, however, Jessie wasn't all that sure his teacher had given him good advice. The college was inspirational in that it sat on top of one of those hills right in the city, and he could look out and see the Golden Gate Bridge and Alcatraz Prison on its little island in the bay. But the view was about the only thing Jessie liked about it.

Jessie's major problem was that for the first time in his life he was alone and away from home, family, and friends. He'd had a taste of being away in Lost Hills, but he'd been with Alvin. Now, he was all alone in a sea of strangers in a huge, noisy city that was so different from what he was used to it was like being on an alien planet.

To make matters worse, he was homeless. There were no campus dormitories, so he was on his own to find a place to live. The college had given him a list of places to look, but housing in the city by the bay was far too expensive for Jessie's limited budget.

There was no doubt about his resolve to become an artist, and he'd earned the money the hard way. But now he began to question why he hadn't just gone to Bakersfield Junior College. If he had, he wouldn't be way up in San Francisco all by himself with no place to live and he'd be at home in his old room and have Alvin to talk to about things.

Adding to Jessie's depression, he'd found himself thinking about Maria. Despite his new maturity and understanding of girls and life, he couldn't forget her, and he knew, deep down, that Hallie was wrong: Maria wasn't a tramp.

And what about beautiful Hallie? Well, it was always thrilling to think about her, but even before his newfound maturity, he'd known that she'd just played games with him. He also knew that Hallie was smart and wasn't nearly as bad as she appeared. But she was a rich guy's girl.

Jessie recognized that he was bad homesick, but there was no way he could go home until the Christmas break. God, that wouldn't be for three whole months! Could he wait that long? He didn't think he could, but what choice did he have? He couldn't quit, could he?

No, he couldn't. In the scouts you learn not to quit. ...although the trail be hard and long you'll always hear us singing a song... Thinking of the boy scout fight song gave Jessie's determination a little boost. He was able to resist the urge to quit and managed to get through his first two weeks of college.

He was sitting on the concrete steps in front of the college on the first day of his third week, watching the fog roll in over the Golden Gate Bridge-and fighting off an overwhelming urge to go back to the YMCA where he was staying temporarily, get his gear, and go home.

It was an awesome sight to watch that mammoth red bridge structure dissolve into the swirling, grayish mist that swept through the Golden Gate, devouring Alcatraz Island and all else in its path. It seemed to mirror the feeling that he, too, was being consumed by some inexorable force and he had no choice but to run- run away fast before it pulled him into its clutches. He suddenly knew that he had to leave, and it had to be now- right now!

Jessie leaped to his feet, resolute and determined. He snatched up his books, spun around, and collided with another student, sending them both sprawling down the steps with their books and papers bouncing in all directions.

Jessie fell on top of the other student, so his only injury was his embarrassment. Underneath him, the other accident victim was a tall, lanky girl with long arms and legs. She had absorbed the brunt of the crash and was crunched into the rough cement steps. When they finally untangled themselves and were sitting there, Jessie said, "I'm really sorry! Are you all right?"

Grasping one arm to her side, the girl hissed through clenched teeth, "You clumsy oaf! Why don't you watch where you're going?"

"I'm sorry."

"Christ! My arm...it feels like it's broken."

"I didn't mean to bump into you, I was just going...You think it's broken?"

She nodded, still grimacing. He leaned over her and looked, but she was holding it against her side in such a way that he couldn't see the alleged injury. "I know some first aid, and I can probably tell if it's broken if you let me look at it."

She glanced across at him. Her large, wide-set eyes were a dark brown but appeared now to be emitting red sparks. "Don't you touch me! Just see if you can find my glasses!"

"Glasses?"

"Yeah, glasses, you know, the kind you use to see with?"

"Oh, sure, they must be right here someplace," he said, glancing around the steps where their books and papers were scattered. The morning class period had already begun, so there were no other students. He spotted the glasses laying several steps below. They had thick black frames that appeared undamaged, except that both lenses were broken out and the pieces scattered over the steps. He reached down, picked up the frames, and announced, "Here they are."

She reached out with one hand.

"Well, they're..."

"Just give me the damn glasses!" she snapped.

Jessie placed them in her hand. She put them on and looked up at him strangely. "You're not only a clumsy oaf, you're a sadistic clumsy oaf!"

"I'm not clumsy, and I'm not sadistic. I said I'm sorry. It was an accident, you know."

"It may have been an accident, but it was sadistic to give me the glasses when you knew the lenses were broken out."

"I was going to tell you they were broken, but you didn't give me a chance."

"Now what am I going to do? I don't have another pair with me."

"You can't read without them?"

She gave a cynical sneer. "Read? I can't see my hand in front of my face without them."

"Oh."

"And my arm is killing me."

"It's...bleeding some too. You probably should go to the college infirmary and have them look at it."

"They got an infirmary?"

"The brochure says they do."

She paused before answering. "I guess I don't have any choice."

"You want me to help you?"

"I don't want you to even come near me."

"Look, I'm just trying to help you doggone it!"

"Your help I can do without."

Jessie stood beside the girl on the steps. He felt guilty over what had happened and sorry for her as she sat there in her lensless black-framed glasses, holding her arm. He had a sudden flashback to the time he'd broken Carlo's arm. That was kind of an accident too, the same as this, and if she refused his help, what else could he do? And now that he'd made up his mind to quit the college, he was eager to leave.

"On second thought, you are the perpetrator, so you do have an obligation to help me."

"I'm not a perpetrator."

"Yes, you are. You caused the accident that injured me and destroyed my property."

"Look, you're not being very nice. I offered to help you, didn't I?"

She was silent for a moment, and then said, "Yes, you did."

"Okay then, let's get on with it. I want to get out of here as fast as I can."

"What? You got a hot date?"

"No, I don't have a hot date. I'm leaving this stupid college, and I'm leaving today."

The girl looked up at him. "That figures. You're obviously like all males. If things don't go just right, cut and run."

"That's not true, I'm not-"

"Never mind. Come on and help me up. My arm is killing me. It feels like it really is broken."

Jessie retrieved their books and papers and led her to the front office. There, a clerk directed them to wait in the infirmary while she tried to find the nurse, who also taught a class in anatomy.

The infirmary doubled as a storage room, so Jessie had to move some boxes out of the way and borrow a couple chairs from a vacant classroom so they could sit down and wait for the nurse.

The girl sat holding her arm and looking pale. She wasn't a pretty girl. In fact, she was downright homely. Her face was plain, and her hair, a sort of washed-out brown, hung down around her face in a disheveled mess. Her most distinguishing feature was a set of large brown eyes that were too far apart in her face, which was accentuated by the black frames of her lenseless glasses. She wore a baggy sweater over a long pleated skirt, which made her look shapeless and gangly.

After they sat silently for a while, he said, "My name is Jessie Rascoe."

"You must be a bohunk."

"A what?"

"Never mind. I'm Peggy Barton," she muttered, keeping her head down.

"How do you feel now?"

She glanced at him from across the room. "My arm is broken, and I can't see. How do you think I feel?"

"You really can't see anything without your glasses?"

"No. I can see you, but you're just a fuzzy blur."

"That's probably just as well," said Jessie in an attempt to introduce a little humor into the grim ambiance.

"Probably."

"I'm the nurse. What's the problem here?" interrupted the voice of a heavy-set woman who blustered into the small room.

After a short explanation and a shorter examination, the nurse speculated that Peggy Barton probably did have a broken arm. "But you will have to go to the hospital and get an x-ray. You'll need a cast anyway, and we don't do that here. I'll get Archie, the janitor, to run you over there in the woodie."

"He's going with me," grumbled Peggy, nodding at Jessie.

The nurse glanced at him.

"He's my seeing-eye dog," she explained sarcastically.

The nurse shrugged.

The "woodie" was an old LaSalle station wagon that took them up and down the hilly streets of San Francisco. It was slow going because of the fog, but Archie finally reached the hospital, which was on the opposite side of town. There, Jessie sat in the waiting room while they did whatever they were doing to Peggy.

He felt bad about breaking the girl's arm, and he told himself that no matter how nasty she got, he did have an obligation to see this thing through and get her settled before he left town and headed for home.

After a two-hour wait, she came back to the waiting room with her arm in a big L-shaped plaster of Paris cast. "It was broke, huh?" he asked.

"Great observation."

"Well, how do you feel? I mean, does it still hurt?"

"Only when I laugh."

"Then don't laugh," he snapped, rolling his eyes.

"I won't."

Archie, the woodie driver, had gone back to the college so they took a taxi back across town to where Peggy lived. It pained Jessie to pay out a dollar and twenty cents cab fare, but he felt obligated.

She lived in one of those classic old San Francisco apartment buildings on Powell Street that was right on the cable car tracks. She claimed she couldn't see to get to her apartment, so Jessie led her up the stairs to the top floor. He opened the door with her key, and they entered a large, luxurious apartment.

"Hey, this is nice," Jessie said, glancing around at the lush furnishings. "Is this your apartment?"

"No, but I got squatter's rights. Make yourself at home while I get my other pair of glasses."

He nodded, and she disappeared into one of the bedrooms.

Jessie glanced around the apartment. It was large with several interconnecting rooms. The floors were covered with thick carpeting, and all the furnishings looked expensive. He walked across to a picture window and was looking out at the swirling fog when she returned to the room.

She halted at the entrance with a strange look on her face and stood there staring at him through glasses that were so thick they looked like the bottoms of Coke bottles. "You don't look like a bohunk."

"I don't even know what you're talking about," he said.

"Where you from?"

"I'm from the Grapevine."

"You mean where the ridge road is? That Grapevine?"

Jessie nodded.

"I didn't know anyone lived up there."

"A lot of people live up there."

"Well, what are you doin' here?"

Jessie hesitated. "Well, you asked me to bring you-"

"No, I mean what are you doing at the college?"

"I'm studying to be an artist, or at least I was."

"So you came up here to become an artist and you're quitting after only two weeks? You sure don't want to be an artist very badly."

"That's not true. I do want to be an artist. I just don't like it here. That's all."

"Oh. I'm quitting because I don't like it here," she mimicked.

"Well, what's it to you?"

"Nothing. I don't care. Why don't you like it here?"

"Because."

"Because why?"

"Well, because I don't think it's a very good art school, and I don't have a place to live."

"That's just more excuses. Like I said, you're a typical male quitter. Go where the grass looks greener. No loyalty to anything or anyone, just whatever looks the easiest, right?"

"No, that's not true!"

"Yes, it is and you know it. You're a quitter and a coward."

"And you're a genuine weirdo, that's what you are!" blurted Jessie as he stomped out of the apartment.

A little smile eased across Peggy Barton's face as she watched Jessie Rascoe stomp out the front door, slamming it.

Chapter

~28~

As much as Jessie wanted to quit school and go home, the girl's charge that he was a quitter and a coward affected him to such a degree that he couldn't bring himself to pack his gear and leave. He walked in the fog along Fisherman's Wharf all that afternoon thinking about it, finally admitting to himself that the weirdo girl was right. It would be quitting before he gave it his all, so he had no choice but to stick it out. The next morning it took all the determination he could muster, but he returned to class.

He was standing in the hallway later that afternoon reading the bulletin board when Peggy Barton walked up to him and said, "Change your mind?"

Jessie turned and looked at her. She was wearing another bulky sweater over a dull-colored long dress that made her look shapeless and even taller than she was, which was almost his height. Her arm cast was cradled in a white neck sling. Her eyes, magnified by the thick glasses, appeared huge and challenging.

He nodded.

"So you really do want to be an artist?"

He nodded again.

"Then you made a good decision."

"I hope so."

"What changed your mind?"

"You did."

"I did?" She smiled. "Now you owe me double. Here, carry my books," she instructed, thrusting them at him.

He took the books and frowned at her. "I got another class."

"I know. I'm in the same one."

"You are?"

"Yes. For someone who wants to be an artist, you're not very observant."

"I was feeling too bad to notice anything."

"You okay now?"

"No, but I'm gonna stick it out, for a while anyway. If I can't find a place to live soon though, I'll have to quit anyway."

"You'll find something."

"How is your arm?" he asked as they walked together down the hallway, which was bustling with other students.

"It only hurts when I laugh."

"I told you: don't laugh."

"Well, the good news is that I can use it as an excuse to goof off in this stupid class."

"Why do you want to do that?"

"I'm just not interested."

"Why are you taking it then?"

"It's an elective that fits my schedule, and it's easy."

"It may not be as easy as you think."

"I can do it standing on my head."

Jessie glanced at her. She walked with sort of a lope, taking long strides. She probably could stand on her head. "What are you studying?" he asked.

"What makes the world go round: business and management."

"I guess that stuff is all right if you like it."

"I love the subject, but studying about it is a real drag."

"Then why are you doing it?"

"It's a long story."

Jessie shrugged as they entered the classroom and took seats next to each other. Sure enough, the girl paid no attention in class, working crossword puzzles instead.

When Jessie walked into the YMCA that evening after classes, there was a message in his mailbox about a room for rent. He called the number from the pay phone in the office and was told by a Mr. Helms, the manager, that if he were interested he should come over and look at it. Jessie wanted to know how much, but Mr. Helms told him they would discuss that when he got there.

With mixed feelings, Jessie hopped a cable car and went to the address the manager had given him. To his surprise, it was the same apartment building where Peggy Barton lived.

"It ain't much, mind you, but it's got everything you need," advised Mr. Helms, as he escorted Jessie into the basement of the building. Indeed, it wasn't much: one room and a small bathroom on one end of the basement next to a coal-fired furnace. But it did have everything Jessie needed, including a small electric hot plate.

"The apartment caretaker used to live here. He was a bachelor an' liked it real good," said Mr. Helms.

"It looks fine, Mr. Helms. How much is the rent?"

"Tell you what, you willing to keep an eye on the furnace?"

Jessie glanced over at the iron furnace. "Well, I don't know anything about furnaces, Mr. Helms, but I can sure keep an eye on it for you."

"That's all ya really gotta do, and shovel a little coal once in a while in the winter time. It don't get real cold here in Frisco. The rent is five dollars a month."

"What?" blurted Jessie.

Mr. Helms looked surprised. "That too much?"

"Oh no! I mean, I thought it would be a lot more. I'll take it, Mr. Helms. I haven't found anything as good as this for anywhere near that price."

Mr. Helms smiled. "Well, of course, that's a special price in consideration of your tending the furnace."

"That's fine, Mr. Helms. I really appreciate it, and I'll take good care of the furnace."

"Well, I hope you become a good artist."

Jessie looked at Mr. Helms curiously. "How did you know I'm studying art?"

"Oh, Miss Barton told me. She's the one gave me your name and said you'd be a reliable man to keep an eye on the furnace."

For the first time since he arrived in the city by the sea, Jessie felt better about things. It was comforting to know that he now had a home he could afford. And it was right on the cable car line and walking distance to the college. It did concern him that now he would be even more beholden to Peggy Barton. Fortunately, he only had one class with the weirdo, which was the art history course that met three days a week, so it was Wednesday before he saw her again.

"Thank you for giving Mr. Helms my name," he said when he accidently met her on his way to class.

"Now you owe me double."

"I was afraid you were gonna say that."

"Well, you do. That job of tending furnace is a cinch since we hardly ever need it. And don't forget that you were the cause of my broken arm."

"How could I forget? You keep reminding me! How does it feel?"

"It doesn't hurt anymore, but this cast is a pain in the neck. Here, carry my books."

Jessie carried Peggy's books to class that Wednesday and again on Friday. He didn't particularly like her. She was different from any girl he'd ever known. She talked and acted more like a guy than a girl, and all she ever did in class was work crossword puzzles.

During the next few weeks, Jessie's desire to go home diminished. The room in the basement worked out well. It was comfortable and efficient, and he only had to fire up the furnace during an occasional cold spell, which wasn't often. His classes became more enjoyable each passing day, and he began to make a few friends. He also noticed there was a cute girl in his drawing class.

His concern that Peggy might become a real pest at the apartment was ill founded. She kept to her apartment on the top floor when she was there. On occasion, he would see her coming and going at odd hours and couldn't help but wonder where she went. He was sure it wasn't on a date because what guy in his right mind would want to date her? And when he'd asked her what she meant by "squatter's rights" for that luxurious place upstairs, her answer was so ambiguous it didn't make any sense. But then a lot about Peggy Barton didn't make any sense.

They had only the one class in art history together, but he did have lunch with Peggy almost every day in the college cafeteria. Peggy bought her lunch, but Jessie fixed his own in the basement room and brought it in a brown paper bag because he couldn't afford cafeteria prices. The reason they ate together was because Peggy's favorite lunch was a blue plate special that came with a small bottle of milk. Since she detested the milk, she gave it to Jessie, who liked milk. It was a practical arrangement and the scene of some lively discussions.

"You decided yet if this is a good art school?" she asked one day as they sat opposite each other at a chrome table in the noisy cafeteria.

Jessie nodded as he chewed on a peanut butter and jelly sandwich and then took a drink of his free milk. "Yeah. You were right. It's a good school, I gotta admit."

"I'm always right."

Jessie rolled his eyes.

"I hope you get to finish."

He looked at her. "Oh, I'll finish all right. I admit I was discouraged at first, but not anymore."

She nodded. "I believe you, but the problem I'm referring to is that European war. We're gonna be involved. You can count on it."

"No, we're not. That's their war, not ours."

"You're wrong. Hitler is gonna pull the whole world into this thing, and sooner or later you'll have to go."

"Not me. I'm not gonna fight no dumb war."

"You'll have to. When we get in it, you have to fight for your country. You don't have any choice."

"I'd fight for my country all right, but I ain't fighting in no European war. They got us in the last one, and my dad had to go over there and nearly got himself killed. They're always fighting each other. It's only been twenty years since their last stupid war."

"What are you, an isolationist or something?"

"I'm not gonna fight their war. That's all."

"I don't blame you for not wanting to go to war, but you can't be an isolationist anymore. The world is too economically interrelated. What affects one country affects us all, and Hitler and his bullies have to be stopped."

"It's not my problem."

"It is your problem, or it's gonna be. You'll see."

"How come you know so much about it?"

"Because I'm smart-that's why. Most of the world's problems have always been because of macho, stupid males who want to be big men. If females were in control of things, we'd have a different world. The female of the human species is intrinsically smarter and should be running things. Then we wouldn't be having wars every few years."

"If you're so smart, how come you're here wasting your time when you admitted you detest what you're doing?"

"I'm here to accomplish a far, far better thing than I can explain to the likes of you."

"Like what?"

"You wouldn't understand."

"Try me."

She was dressed, as usual, in one of her baggy sweaters and a long drab dress with her hair hanging in scraggly curls down around her face and shoulders. She finished a bite and put her fork down. "I'm here to qualify for...shall we say, a certain position I'm going to have one of these days. A position where

I can prove what women can do at the helm of a great ship of commerce. But I gotta have a stupid college degree. So I'm getting a stupid college degree. Now, you see, I told you, but the dumb look on your face tells me you don't understand."

"You didn't tell me anything, and you know it."

She laughed, which always seemed to improve her appearance a little. In a way, Jessie felt sorry for her because she was such an ugly duckling. Granted, looks aren't everything, he'd counsel himself. But then, poor Peggy didn't have much else going for her either. Besides being homely as a mud fence, she had an obnoxious personality to boot.

"Ya know what?"

"No. What?"

"You look nice when you smile. You should do it more often."

She looked at him in surprise, and then quickly recovering, said, "Fallacious flattery will get you nowhere."

Jessie laughed. "I sure ain't trying to get anywhere with you, Peggy."

"Yeah. I know the type of girl your kind goes for: cutesy, brainless, and big boobed- isn't that right?"

Jessie was getting used to Peggy, but her insults still rankled him. "No, that's not right!" he snapped.

"Oh, yes it is. I've noticed you drooling over that brainless blonde in art history."

"I haven't been drooling over her, and at least she pays attention in class."

"She's so dumb she'd better pay attention."

"That's more than you do. How do you expect to pass the course?"

"I don't need to pay attention to pass that simple course. All you have to do is memorize the names and dates of some broken-down pieces of ancient junk."

"Yeah, sure. We'll just see what you do on the next exam," said Jessie taking another bite of his sandwich.

"I'll get a better grade than you or the dumb blonde."

"You wanna bet?"

"Sure, I'll bet. I'll bet you a dinner at the Saint Francis Hotel. Loser pays the tab."

"The Saint Francis! I can't afford that."

"If you're so sure you'll win, what have you got to lose?"

"Oh, I'll win the bet all right, but you shouldn't ever bet something you can't afford."

"You're just all mouth, aren't you?"

"Okay, you asked for it. I'll bet ya!" blurted Jessie, as he stood up and stomped out of the cafeteria while Peggy smiled one of those smiles that made her look a little less homely.

Chapter
~29~

*

Since Jessie's real love was painting, he was eager to get started, but the art school required first-year students to complete all the prerequisites first: basic design, drawing, color theory, and art history. He enjoyed art history, but it required a lot of memorizing, and that required a good deal of study. He did that and got a B+ on his test paper, and the dumb blonde who paid attention in class got a C+. He was pleased until he found out Peggy got an A.

"I can't believe it," he said as they were leaving class after the professor had returned their papers.

"Okay, see for yourself. It's in that folio you're carrying." He stopped in the middle of the hall and extracted the paper that sure enough had a big red A on the cover.

He was incredulous. "How did you get an A?" he challenged suspiciously.

"I told you before; I can do this stuff standing on my head if I want to. But I don't like it, so I only do enough to get by. But our little bet gave me incentive, so I did it."

Jessie shook his head. "I still don't understand. Did you cheat somehow?"

"No. I'm not above doing a lot of things, but I'm not a cheat. I hate people who cheat."

Jessie shook his head. "I can't imagine how you did it, but I guess I lose the bet."

"I have to admit that in a way it wasn't fair, I-"

"I knew it! You're admitting you cheated."

"You didn't let me finish, big mouth. I told you I don't cheat. I was going to say that it wasn't fair because I'm so much smarter than you and the dumb blonde that there was no way either of you could win."

"Jesus," muttered Jessie. "And I gotta take her to dinner."

"That you do. Make a reservation for seven o'clock Friday, and I'll meet you there," she instructed.

"Okay, I'll be there."

"You got a suit?"

"Yeah, I got a suit."

"Good. You have to wear one to get in that place. And bring plenty of money. It's expensive."

That Friday Jessie was there at seven o'clock sharp wearing his high school graduation suit. He sat nervously at his reserved table in the dining room of the Saint Francis Hotel, waiting for Peggy to show. The room was huge and beautifully decorated, with sparkling chandeliers and real oil paintings on the wall, which he identified as either genuine, or good copies of French impressionists. The waiters all wore tuxedos, as did many of the patrons. It was the first time Jessie had ever been in such a place, and he was not only uncomfortable, but he was worried about what all this was going to cost.

After forty-five minutes of waiting, he was about to walk out of the place when he saw Peggy being escorted to the table by the maitre d'. She was dressed as usual, in one of her long, drab dresses with her hair, as usual, hanging down around her face. The only difference in her appearance was that her arm cast was gone.

Jessie stood up while the maitre d' seated her, and then he grumbled, "You're late."

"Of course. I'm supposed to be."

"Why are you supposed to be late when you're the one who said seven o'clock?"

"I know you come from the sticks, Jessie, but try not to show it." Jessie shook his head and sat down. "I got the cast off, and oh, does it feel good not to be carrying that load around anymore."

"Yeah, I see. I'm glad."

"You're probably as happy about it as I am, aren't you?"

He looked at her and couldn't help smiling. "Yes. I'm glad it's off, Peggy, for both our sakes."

"You look presentable in a suit."

"Thanks. You look your usual. How come you never dress up?"

"What's the matter with what I'm wearing?"

"It's okay, But it's what you wear all the time."

"So?"

"Well, you told me to wear a suit, so I thought you would dress up too."

"You mean something glitzy and slinky, like the dumb blonde would wear?"

"You could take a lesson or two from the dumb blonde."

"When and if you ever get past the impressionable, adolescent stage of life, you will realize that fancy clothes are superfluous. It's what's in your brain that counts. And I've got a lot there, so I don't have to worry about how I look. I can just be who I am."

"I hope 'who I am' will be a little less obnoxious tonight, since I'm treating you to dinner."

"No, you're not. I won it. You owe me dinner."

When he first met Peggy, her brashness and cutting insults had upset and flustered Jessie. Although he could hold his own in his world, he'd never been challenged in the kind of arena Peggy hosted. But as he became more accustomed to her sharp tongue and wit, he got so he could at least maintain his composure in their many verbal jousts.

"Yeah, and I'm paying my debt, even if it means I won't have food money for two weeks, or longer. How come you picked the most expensive place in town?"

"I'm trying to get some class into that hayseed image of yours, but it's probably hopeless."

"Probably."

"Cocktails?" asked the waiter who appeared beside the table.

"Yes. Bring us a bottle of Chevel Bordeaux '35," she said before Jessie could open his mouth. The waiter nodded and left.

"You could take a lesson in etiquette yourself. I'm paying the bill, so I'm supposed to do the ordering," Jessie said.

"I know, but since I'm the guest of honor, so as to speak, I get to order."

"Well, you'll have it all to yourself anyway, because I don't drink alcohol."

"You don't drink anything?"

"No. Oh, I drank some beer last summer, and it made me real sick."

"No wonder. Only peasants drink beer."

"Then my peasant days are over."

"Not likely."

The waiter returned with the wine and after his bottle-opening ceremony, poured a sample into Peggy's glass. She tasted it and nodded, and before Jessie could protest, he poured two glasses.

"Don't be a boor," she chided. "Have a drink of the wine. It won't kill you, and Chevel is the best Bordeaux you can get."

Jessie couldn't even guess what a bottle of wine cost, particularly in the Saint Francis Hotel. But the thought of it upset him so much he reached out, picked up the wine, and took a drink. Surprisingly, it didn't taste all that bad.

"You're supposed to have a toast before you drink," she reprimanded.

"Why?"

Peggy rolled her eyes.

He shrugged. "I do have to admit it's pretty good." It surprised Jessie how tasty the wine was and how smoothly it went down. But a little voice of caution reminded him of that horrible experience at Pismo Beach, and he told himself he would be careful.

"There may be hope for you," she said holding out her glass. "Here's to getting the cast off my arm."

"Hey, I'll toast that," said Jessie, touching her glass with his. They both took sips of the wine.

A group of violinists appeared and began to stroll through the dining room playing dinner music. The two college students sat quietly for a while listening to the music.

"That was great. I like violin music," said Jessie when the violinists took a break.

"Yes, so do I. You know, there may be a little class under all that hayseed after all."

Jessie looked across the table at Peggy. She had on one of her half-smiles. "Am I supposed to say thanks for the compliment?"

"You should say what you think."

"A friend of mine used to tell me that too, but I still believe you shouldn't say exactly what you think if it will hurt someone's feelings."

"The truth shouldn't hurt anybody's feelings."

"But sometimes it does. And how do you know for sure what you say is true?"

"If you don't know it's true, then keep your big mouth shut. Was your friend a girl?"

"What?"

"The friend who told you to say what you think."

"Oh, Yeah."

"A girlfriend?"

"Sort of."

"What's that mean?"

"It means she's a rich girl and she has a rich boyfriend."

"What's the matter with rich girls?"

"Nothing, but they go with their own kind."

"Not always."

Jessie smiled. "That's true," he said as the time Hallie asked him to be her boy friend flashed through his memory.

"I see you're drinking the wine."

"I'll admit it's better than peasant's beer."

"It should be. It's top of the line."

"Yeah, and I bet the cost is top of the line too."

"Never mind. You lost the bet so don't complain. Males are all alike, can't stand to lose."

"I got a question, Peggy. Since you have such a low opinion of males, why do you even bother with us?"

She hesitated a moment. "I generally don't bother, because I am convinced that most men are stupid, dishonest, and deceitful. You could be an exception, but I doubt it."

Jessie grinned. "And what if I am an exception?"

She gave him one of her smiles that made her look almost pretty. "I'll cross that bridge when I get to it."

Jessie laughed. "You're a nut, Peggy, ya know that? What is it with you? Some guy walk out on you or something?"

"He didn't walk out! I kicked him out!" she flared and then took a big gulp of wine.

"Oh ho! So that's it!" It was the first time Jessie had seen her flustered since the day he'd knocked her down the steps.

"Don't look so smug!" she snapped, her face flushed.

"Well, since the cat's out of the bag, why not tell me about it?" he said, smiling.

"I'll tell you. He was a cheating, no-good louse who was playing both ends against the middle for his own selfish gain. I hate cheating. But I'll have the last laugh on the little jerk."

Jessie was surprised. He would never have guessed that Peggy's secret was an unfaithful lover because who in his right mind would even be interested in her?

"You want to talk about it a little bit?" Jessie coaxed.

"There's nothing to talk about. Besides, what would you know about anything?"

"It might surprise you what I know."

She looked at him suspiciously. "Don't tell me the rich honey played for a while then dumped you."

Jessie shifted in his chair. "Sorta."

She studied him for a moment. "Were you in love with her?"

Jessie shifted again and said, "I was in love with another girl."

Peggy gave an exaggerated nod. "Unh-huh. That doesn't surprise me. Like all men, you were playing both ends against the middle. Right?"

"No. That's, uh, not right. I mean I wasn't playing...Well it's complicated...but I really was in love with the other girl."

"So what happened?"

Without looking at her, Jessie said, "She dumped me for another guy."

Peggy looked surprised. "So you bombed out with both girls?"

Jessie nodded. "I guess you could say that."

They both took drinks of the wine.

"You really were in love with the other girl?"

"Well, I thought I was. But I've decided that I don't understand the subject of love."

She stared at him with her huge, wide-set eyes, magnified by her thick glasses. "Hummm. There may be more to you than meets the eye. I've come to that same conclusion about love."

"Were you in love with your guy?"

"Yeah, or like you, I thought I was. But never again for me. From now on, my relationship with men will be void of that kind of emotionalism."

Jessie knew now that the tough-skinned Peggy Barton had a sensitive spot, and it had to do with being hurt by a man. Even though it was difficult to even imagine a man being interested in her, Jessie could relate to how she felt. "Well, I've told myself the same thing, and I found out you can have a relationship with someone without getting all emotionally involved."

She nodded. "Absolutely. Look at us, we got a relationship, and we aren't wallowing in emotionalism."

Jessie laughed. The wine seemed to make him more tolerant of her than usual. "Our relationship has emotionalism all right, Peggy, but it ain't the kind you wallow in."

She laughed, and it was like her smile: it made her seem almost pretty.

The group of strolling violinists started up again, came to their table, and played a romantic number. For a while conversation ceased, and they listened to the music and drank the wine. When the violinists moved off, the waiter reappeared, poured the last of the wine into their glasses, and asked if they wanted another bottle or wished to order dinner.

Jessie noticed that same mellow feeling he'd experienced at Pismo Beach was settling in, so he asked the waiter to please bring the dinner menus.

"Jessie?"

"Yeah?"

"There's...another reason I wanted you to take me to dinner."

"Another reason?"

"Yes, I mean other than just to collect the bet."

"You will destroy your image if you tell me you like my male company," he said smiling.

"Don't flatter yourself!"

"Your image is saved."

"Come on," she said, finishing off her glass of wine and getting up from the table just as the waiter arrived with the menus. Jessie had learned to be prepared for most anything from this girl, but he wasn't prepared for this antic.

"We've decided to have dinner elsewhere," she said to the astonished waiter. "Pay the man for the wine, Jessie, while I get my coat," she added, and walked off toward the coat room.

Jessie sat there and watched her walk calmly out of the Saint Francis Hotel dining room without a backward glance. He looked at the scowling waiter and, thanks to the affect of the wine, shrugged and asked for the bill.

When Jessie saw the bill for the one bottle of wine, it took a good deal of the edge off his glow. It was only slightly less than the total amount of money he'd brought for the entire evening. Keeping enough to get home on the cable car, he put what little was left on the tray as a tip and walked out of the dining room with the waiter glaring after him.

He found Peggy waiting for him in the foyer. "All taken care of?" she asked casually.

He nodded. "Yeah, and it took care of my finances for the next six months. I got twenty cents left to get us home on the cable car."

"I told you to bring lots of money."

"Yeah, so you did. But I didn't know there was a bottle of wine in the world that cost that much."

"Come on, clod from Grapevine, we're goin' back to my apartment for dinner, and I'll tell you the real reason why I condescended to come here with you."

Chapter
~30~

The Bordeaux wine had its effect on Jessie, but he felt confident he had things under control and knew what was going on. But what was going on didn't make any sense. He'd used up a whole month's spending allowance from his meager budget on one bottle of wine, he hadn't had any dinner, and he was now standing in the front room of Peggy's apartment, wondering why.

"Here, open this while I get things going in the kitchen," instructed Peggy, handing him a bottle of wine. "There's an opener and some glasses in that buffet in the dining room," she added and disappeared into another room.

Jessie's warning system told him he shouldn't drink any more wine, but he obeyed her instructions anyway, and as he prepared to open the bottle, he noticed the label: Chevel Borbeaux '35.

"Peggy!" he bellowed.

"What's wrong?"

"This is Chevel Bordeaux '35!"

"I know. I love it," she said, appearing in the doorway.

"But...this stuff cost..." Suddenly, even with his dulled senses, a light came on in Jessie's head: the luxurious apartment; the expensive furnishings; the fancy car he'd seen her in. "Peggy, are you rich or something?"

"No," she said, and disappeared back into the kitchen.

"Well then, how can you afford all this?" he shouted after her.

"I can't. Like I told you, I got squatter's rights!" she shouted back.

As usual, her answer told Jessie nothing, but he'd come to expect that. She was a strange unpredictable weirdo, although he had to admit, she was an intriguing one. It had been a shock to discover that she'd been involved with a man. He'd assumed that she didn't have those kinds of feelings. But her admission had cast her in a new light, and Jessie suspected more surprises Were coming. In a way, she reminded him of Hallie Lamont, except of course, Hallie was a sensuous, beautiful girl. Peggy was the homeliest girl he'd ever met with zero sex appeal.

When he finally got the bottle open, he took it and two glasses into the kitchen where she was stirring a kettle at the stove. She had pinned up her hair and wore a bright orange apron.

"Hey, that apron is colorful. You ought to wear it all the time."

"Is that the artist speaking, or the Grapevine clod?"

"Your choice."

"I'll take the wine."

"I know I shouldn't, but I'll have some too," he said and poured two glasses.

"It won't hurt you, and we're gonna have dinner in a few minutes." Then, shifting the stirring ladle to her other hand, she took the wine and held it up to him.

He touched her glass with his and said, "To whatever it is you're cooking, I'm starved."

She nodded. "I'll drink to that. So am I."

They took a drink, and she went back to her cooking. He straddled a kitchen stool behind her and said, "Are you gonna tell me why you suddenly decided to walk out of the Saint Francis Hotel?"

"Because I knew you couldn't afford it."

"Well, if you were so concerned about that, why did we go there in the first place?"

"Cause you lost the bet and you're the kind who needs to meet his commitments."

"So you had this planned all along?"

She faced him and nodded. "I'll have you know that it took hours of my valuable time to prepare this dinner. All I need to do now is add a couple things and warm it up. Go set the table. The dishes are in that buffet. And light the candles."

"Peggy, you're not just a plain weirdo- you're an unpredictable weirdo."

"So you've told me."

"I never called you unpredictable before."

"True. I like it."

A few minutes later they sat down opposite each other at a polished rosewood table and began their candlelight dinner.

She called the main course "Biff Borgan Yo." It was a tasty beef dish cooked in red wine with vegetables, served over a bed of wild rice and fresh mushrooms. With it, she had hot San Francisco sourdough bread and a tossed green salad.

"Peggy, my mom is a great cook, but this is some of the best stuff I've ever tasted," Jessie said as he wolfed down the food. Of course, the late hour and the wine enhanced Jessie's enthusiasm and his appetite.

"Thank you. Compliments are welcome, but I have to confess that I only do this sort of thing on rare occasions."

"I'm honored. Where did you learn to cook like this?"

"I could say that it's just another of my many talents, but the truth is I don't know how. If you can read, you can cook."

Jessie broke off a piece of sourdough bread. "What's reading got to do with cooking?"

"Read a cookbook. It tells you exactly what to do. I bought it in the bookstore for a dollar and sixteen cents."

"That's how you made all this?"

"Yes...disappointed?"

"No. It's great no matter what. And it was nice of you to do it. But for some reason, I got the feeling there is more to all this than you're telling me."

"Why would you think that?"

He looked down the long table at her. "Because I've gotten to know you pretty well in the last couple months, that's why."

She took a sip of her wine and said, "Are you implying I have ulterior motives?"

"Yes."

"Typical male reaction - no appreciation."

"I said I appreciate the dinner, but what's the catch?"

"I do have something I want to discuss."

He nodded, chewing a piece of sour-dough bread. "See? I knew it. Okay, what'a ya want?"

"Not yet. Let's finish dinner first, then I'll explain."

"Good idea, I don't want to spoil what's left of this good dinner, and the wine. Ya know, I've never drunk any wine before in my whole life, but I got to admit it's good stuff."

"It's my favorite."

"And the wine also comes from squatter's rights?"

"Yes."

He looked down the table at her.

She hesitated. "I'm sort of doing what you're doin' downstairs. I'm baby-sitting for a...relative."

"That's the kind of relative to have."

"Yes."

Jessie still didn't understand, but he accepted it as just more of Peggy Barton and went back to the Biff Borgan Yo.

She had finished eating and was leaning back in her chair watching him when he swiped up the last of the sauce in his plate with a piece of sourdough. "You read a recipe well. Maybe you ought to consider another line of work."

"No thanks."

"Okay. So tell me the catch," he said, wiping his mouth with a napkin.

"A question first, then I'll explain."

"Okay."

"How do you feel about me?"

Jessie hesitated, cautious. "I'm not sure what you mean."

"Well, do you like me?"

He smiled. "Now what am I supposed to say to that?"

"Say it the way it is."

"Okay. Yeah, I like you, Peggy."

"All right. So that means you're attracted to me."

Jessie hesitated, suspicious. "If you mean am I attracted to you romantically, the answer is no."

"But you're intrigued, right?"

Another hesitation. "Yeah, I guess you could say that."

She nodded. "So that means you're attracted."

"No, it doesn't."

"Yes, it does. Attracted is a synonym for intrigued."

Jessie laughed. "It may be, Peggy. But let me tell it to you straight, I ain't attracted to you."

"Yes, you are."

Jessie shook his head. "Okay, Peggy. What's all this leading up to?"

"A proposition."

"A proposition?"

"Yeah. Even from Grapevine, you ought to know what a proposition is."

"A proposition for what?"

"For sex, what else?"

Jessie's mouth opened, and he stared at her for a moment, unable to come up with a single word of reply.

"I knew you would be surprised. But after I explain, I think it will make sense to you."

He continued to stare at her.

"I think you're a hick from the sticks, and you think I'm a weirdo, so our relationship can be strictly sexual. We have both sworn off love, so we aren't going to get all involved. I have the feeling you're a sexy guy, and it may not show, but I'm a sexy girl."

Jessie shifted in his chair and shook his head. "I'll tell ya, Peggy. I was prepared for something bizarre, but this is beyond anything I could have imagined. Are you serious?"

"Yes, I'm serious. It's a perfect arrangement for both of us."

He shook his head again. "Let me get this straight. You're proposing an arrangement whereby we just use each other for sex purposes. We have it whenever we want it, like cattle or squirrels or something?"

"Well, that's putting it a bit crudely."

"You're the one who's being crude, Peggy. Is this some kind of a game you're playing?"

"No, it's not a game."

"Then you're crazy."

"You're not looking at it with the right perspective. It's a practical matter. Since we're both stuck here for the next four years, or until you have to go to war, it will save both of us a lot of time and trouble."

Jessie shook his head. "First off, I ain't goin' to no war. Secondly, it's a crazy idea that couldn't possibly work."

"Why won't it work?"

"For one thing, Peggy, I'm not physically attracted to you, Sorry."

"Oh yes, you are."

"I'm not, believe me."

"You just don't realize it."

"Oh sure. I'm secretly mad about you, but I don't know it. Wowzville!"

"I didn't say that."

"I'm a little woozy from all that wine all right, but I'm functioning well enough to tell ya, Peggy, hurt feeling or not, I ain't attracted to you sexually, believe me."

"Oh yes, you are."

Jessie laughed and got up from the table. "Peggy, thanks for the dinner. I gotta go. It's getting late."

"Hold on. The least you could do is hear me out after I slaved to fix your dinner when you were supposed to take me out to dinner."

"That was your idea. Okay, just for a minute. But I can tell you, you're wasting your time."

"We'll see. You go on in the front room and put some records on the phonograph. We'll have our cordials in there, and I'll explain it. It's quite simple," she said, scooping up the dishes into a tray and disappearing into the kitchen.

Thinking about it as he carried out her instructions in the living room, it occurred to Jessie that he'd just experienced another first in his adventure with life in the raw: the homeliest girl he'd ever met propositioned him for sex. He didn't know if he should be flattered or insulted.

After he got the music started, he sat down on a large sofa to wait for her and the cordials, whatever they were. Although he felt a bit tipsy from the wine, he considered himself in full control of his faculties and capable of dealing with her explanation, which could only be some kind of psychological gobbledegook.

He was wondering why she was taking so long when she suddenly appeared before him. Peggy had shocked him before, but this time she gave him the full treatment. His eyes grew large, and his pulse leaped.

She stood before him dressed in a beautiful, transparent, black negligee that revealed every curve of her naked body in a strikingly sensuous way. What a figure she'd been hiding behind those baggy dresses and shapeless sweaters! From her long neck down, the filmy gown molded a tall, voluptuous body with large upturned breasts and protruding nipples that made bulging tents in the material. The gown parted just below her hips, revealing long shapely legs. She had taken off her glasses and combed her hair out, which gave her a completely different look about the face and eyes: a sensual, sexy look, totally alien to the weirdo Peggy Barton.

Jessie was not only dumbfounded, he was instantly sexually aroused. How could he not be?

She stood before him for a moment; giving him time to absorb what she obviously knew was a sensual sight that would speed the pulse of any red-blooded heterosexual male. Then she sat down next to him on the sofa.

Whenever Jessie's thoughts turned to his love life and sex, he always thought of Maria. That was probably because they'd had their first sexual experience together. But since his arrival at college, so much of his time and energy had gone into school work, his sex thoughts had gone on hold. Now, as he looked at Peggy, those thoughts came back in an avalanche.

"I gather the absence of comment indicates you like what you see?" she said in a husky voice.

Jessie just nodded.

"And you're sexually attracted?"

"Yeah, I am that."

"Then I've made my point."

"Yeah, I got to admit that too."

Peggy Barton smiled and slowly put her long arms around Jessie, and then gently brought her lips down upon his.

Chapter
~31~

Jessie Rascoe experienced a whole new world of sex on the sofa with Peggy Barton. The ugly duckling who disdained the male of the species turned out to be a passionate lover with an insatiable appetite for sex.

Projecting her frank, extroverted personality into her love making, she gave Jessie a sexual experience he'd not had in his earlier relationships. It was a unique and astonishing revelation to find that behind her anti-male behavior, baggy clothes, and black framed glasses, Peggy was a sensuous woman who made passionate love with erotic abandon. When the warning voice in his head told Jessie to put on a rubber, Peggy said it wasn't necessary. She knew when her safe time was, whatever that meant. Besides, she explained, doing it with a rubber was like washing your feet with socks on.

When passion was finally exhausted, they lay with entangled, perspiring bodies on the sofa and listened to pounding pulse and heavy breath for some time before Jessie spoke. "I don't know what to say Peggy...except that was an experience the likes of which this country boy never imagined."

"Pretty good, wasn't it?"

"I've never been so surprised in my whole life."

"Surprised?" She smiled.

"Yeah. It was like you suddenly turned into a different person."

"I told you that you were sexually attracted to me even if you didn't realize it."

He laughed. "I couldn't possibly dispute your analysis."

"I wasn't all that surprised about you. Despite your hicksville manner, I suspected you were gonna be good, and I was right, as usual. Among my other talents, I'm an expert on sex. It's an obsession I've had since I first discovered that boys and girls are different."

"That's a strange obsession considering you don't like men."

"Jessie?"

"Yeah?"

"I have a confession to make. That's a smoke screen. I don't dislike men. I got burned by one because I made the mistake of falling in love. But that's over. Oh, I'm still struggling to get it out of my craw...like my little flare-up there tonight at the Saint Francis. But the truth is I like men. Or more appropriately put, I like sex, which means men. But the type man I'm attracted to is not attracted to me and since I'm selective of who I go to bed with, I have to go through these little charades. But the black negligee works every time."

"It sure worked on this selection."

"Yes. Aren't you glad?"

Jessie smiled. "Yeah, I am."

"Well, after I got to know you, I sensed that you were a sexy guy. I can tell by that certain look and you had it. Oh, you're a little inexperienced, but that's all right because it's going to be great fun teaching you."

"Peggy, you sure about not getting pregnant?"

"Like I told you, I'm an expert on sex, and that includes how not to get pregnant. It's one of the advantages of an affair with an older woman."

"You're not much older than me."

"Than I. And I'm twenty-five, and you're what? Eighteen?"

"Yer kidding!"

"It takes time to develop talent like mine."

"I can't believe you're twenty-five, but the price is right, and you got yourself an eager pupil."

She rose up and leaned over him so that her shapely breasts were just above his face. "We both had our shot at love and flunked. Now, it's gonna be just lots of good ole raw *sex*," she whispered in a low, husky voice. Then she swung off the sofa, pulling him with her. "Come on, let's go to the bedroom. I need more room to work on you."

Jessie had never heard a girl be so frank about sex, and it was both embarrassing and stimulating. She caught the look on his face and laughed. "That's what I love about you Jessie. You're a tiger with a touch of naivete, but you won't be when I'm finished with you."

On the big oversized bed in her luxury apartment in San Francisco, Peggy Barton kept her promise to expose Jessie Rascoe to an expanded sexual agenda, the likes of which the college boy from the Grapevine could never, ever have imagined.

When they had exhausted their passions this time, Peggy produced robes, and they retreated barefoot to the front room. There, they sat at the rosewood table again, drank some more wine, and Jessie finished off what was left of the Biff Borgan Yo.

"I've been trying to find someone like you, ever since I got rid of that jerk," said Peggy from her end of the table.

"Am I a promising pupil?"

She looked at him and smiled. "I got the feeling you're gonna be a great pupil, Jessie. And someday some lucky girl will owe me."

He looked down the table. Her hair was in wild disarray, and she'd put on her black-rimmed, thick glasses. It wasn't an attractive sight. But the robe had fallen open in the front exposing the cleavage of her swollen bust. "I'm a little woozy from both the sex and the wine, but I got a feeling that you may be right."

"I'm always right. And it will probably be that little hillbilly who will owe me."

"What?"

"You're still in love with her."

Her claim surprised him. "What makes you think that?"

"I can tell. But that's fine with me. She can have the love-struck hayseed. I want the Grapevine stud."

Jessie couldn't deny Peggy's claim that he was still in love with Maria, but all he could think of to say was: "Looks like you got yourself a Grapevine stud, Peggy."

Jessie was doing well in his first year of college with pretty good grades, but he knew they could be better. His academic problem was related to Peggy. If he didn't go up to her apartment and have sex on her oversized bed, she would come down to his room in the basement and have sex on his little bed, or in the chair where he was trying to study. It didn't matter to Peggy, as long as they did it.

One day he looked up the word *nymphomaniac* in the dictionary. It read: "excessive sexual desire by a female." That definition fit Peggy all right. When he asked her if she thought she might be one of those, she laughed and replied, "It takes one to know one, Jessie."

It concerned him that he just might be a male nymphomaniac because he had to admit that he liked sex a lot and was powerless to resist her. Oh, he would try to resist sometimes when he knew he should be studying, but when she slipped out of her clothes, all studying would cease abruptly.

Jessie realized that, as Alvin had said, having an affair with a girl these days didn't make you the lone Ranger. People did it. But he had to ignore the moral issue and pretend that love had nothing to do with it. It was an addiction, and he did it just like an ole bull. But deep down, Jessie was having a problem with that rationale because of the passion he experienced when he and Peggy had sex. Wasn't passion an integral part of love?

When he went home for Christmas, Jessie discovered that he did, indeed, Miss Peggy. Oh, it was great to be home and see his family and all his friends, particularly Alvin. But when the holidays were over and it was time to go back to college, he could hardly wait to see her.

Peggy met him at the train station with the fancy car that belonged to her relative. They were so eager, they did it right there on the front seat of the car in the parking lot. Then they went home to her apartment and did it some more.

So it went all the rest of that school year. Except for the days Peggy disappeared, they saw each other in their art history class, and at lunch in the cafeteria where they continued to verbally spar over a variety of subjects.

Sometimes when he was listening to Peggy expound on a subject with her quick intellect and blunt objectivity, Jessie's thoughts would divert to beautiful Hallie Lamont. She was like that too. How similar the two girls were, yet so different. "Hey, you're not listening!" would bring him back to reality.

Jessie sometimes got irritated, particularly over Peggy's insistence that war was imminent and he should sign up for one of those military reserve programs that would exempt him until he finished college. He refused, convinced that America would not get in the war. But even when they got in a hot debate, it didn't interfere with their sex lives.

Peggy continued to be mysterious in her private life, coming and going at odd hours and sometimes disappearing for a day or two without explanation. Nor did she offer any further explanation of how she managed to finance her rather luxurious life-style.

In one of her more serious moments, Peggy did tell Jessie that she had lived in Europe with her mother for several years, and that was why she was late starting college. He knew there was more to the story, and he was curious about the real reason why she was even going to college. There was no question that she was smart. In fact, it seemed like a waste of time for her to even be there. But Peggy had asked him not to question her about her private life, and although he was curious, he respected her wishes and avoided the subject.

On the last night before Jessie caught the train home for the summer, she surprised him with another Biff Borgan Yo dinner, including a couple bottles of Chevel Bordeaux '35.

"I'm breaking my rule of only fixing one of these dinners per lover. But I've decided I'll take you again next semester, so you got one coming," she said in her usual matter of fact way.

When they sat down at the rosewood table with the candles burning, Peggy was dressed in a beautiful new evening gown that revealed her tall, shapely figure to perfection.

"I'm impressed, and I'll sign up for another semester. But I have a question," said Jessie.

She looked at him suspiciously.

"You really look great when you dress up, why don't you do it more often?"

"I've just never been interested in clothes, and I detest pretentiousness." She gave him one of those smiles that added to her beautiful dress. "Besides, I'd rather be naked anytime."

He laughed. "Yeah, I'm with you. Here's to next semester."

She held up her glass and said, "To next semester, and tonight."

"I can sleep on the train all the way to Bakersfield, so I'll drink to that."

"You'll have to, 'cause you're not getting any sleep tonight."

"I know," he said, taking a sip of the wine.

"Are you gonna miss me?"

"Miss what?"

"You want me to show you what?"

He grinned. "No, I already know what, and I want to eat the Biff Borgan Yo I got coming to me before it gets cold."

"I can always warm it up?"

He looked at her for a moment and said, "Yeah, I am gonna miss you, Peggy, something awful. You gonna miss me?"

She dropped her eyes. "Yes," she said with a strange look on her face, and for just an instant she looked frightened. Then she leaped up and ran around the table. He barely had time to get out of his chair before she threw herself into his arms. A moment later they were pulling and tearing their clothes off as they fell onto the front room carpet in a heap of flailing arms and legs and gasped words of passion.

Peggy warmed up the Biff Borgan Yo a couple times that night as they ate and drank wine between sessions of sex, but the subject of missing each other didn't come up again. Finally, they got a couple hours' sleep before Peggy drove him across the Bay Bridge to Oakland where he was catching the train to Bakersfield.

Before he got on the train they stood there on the platform facing each other, both at a loss for words. When the conductor shouted "all aboard," they came into each others arms and clung together for a moment. Then Jessie pulled away and ran to the train, glancing back as he swung up the ladder. He was certain that behind those black-framed glasses, there were tears in the weirdo Peggy Barton's eyes.

Chapter
~32~

Although Jessie had gotten over the worst of his home-sickness by the end of his freshman year in college, he still missed his family and friends, and when he rode home from the train station with his parents, he experienced a surge of nostalgia. Everywhere he looked, he saw something that reminded him of those wonderful days on the Grapevine with all his friends.

It was a great homecoming, and of course, his mom and dad and brother Billy asked lots of questions about college, and what they didn't ask he volunteered, except about Peggy Barton. He didn't mention her.

Billy told him that all the gang was going to get together on Saturday at their secret cave behind old Fort Tejon. It seemed that most of the gang was getting ready to leave the Grapevine for one reason or another. Some were joining one of the military services, and others were going to summer jobs or something, so they all wanted to meet one last time before leaving.

When he crawled through the entrance to the cave that next day, it seemed to Jessie it had shrunk considerably. It wasn't nearly as big as he remembered, and the fire was awful smoky. But it was still great to sit there on the rocks again with his friends, listening to the fire crackling, and to watch Alvin, as he always did, jump up every so often and throw wood on the fire, sending sparks flying.

"It wouldn't be the same if you weren't throwing wood on the fire, Alvin," he said smiling.

"Yeah," laughed Jack. "The ole firebug himself. You ought to become a fireman, Alvin." Everyone laughed.

"Well, you guys never knew how to keep a fire goin'," said Alvin.

All his friends looked about the same as when Jessie had seen them last at Christmas, yet something was different. Jessie couldn't put his finger on it, but he sensed it was because some were leaving the Grapevine and might not return for a long time, if ever.

"Are you goin' back to that art college next year, Jessie?" asked Gerald, sitting on one of the rocks with his red hair jutting in all directions.

"Yeah, I sure am, Gerald."

"Do you like it there?"

Jessie nodded, staring into the flames of the fire. "It's really great. I didn't like it at first, but I do now."

"Will they draft ya up there in that college, Jessie?" asked Danny, who didn't seem nearly as fidgety as Jessie remembered.

"Well, my counselor says they aren't supposed to draft us as long as we're in college."

"Yeah, but the guy at the navy recruiting office said that could change any minute, so I ain't takin' any chances on ending up in the infantry. I joined the navy," announced Bobbie proudly with his usual buck-toothed grin.

"You really did? You joined the navy?" asked Jessie.

"Yeah, I sure did, and I'll be gettin' called here pretty soon," confirmed Bobbie.

"I thought you were goin' to go to work for the GP?" said Jack, leaning against a rock with his hair hanging in his eyes, as always.

"I was, but I talked to Frank when he was home on leave an' he says the navy is the only way to go, and we're all gonna have to go sooner or later anyway."

"I don't know," countered Jack. "I heard a Congressman make a speech on the radio, and he says this is not our war and we should stay out of it."

"Yeah, but a lot of people say we can't stay out of it," said Bobbie.

"Well, it sure doesn't look very good. Almost every morning I deliver my papers there's some bad stuff about that guy Hitler on the front page," said Billy, who Jessie could tell had grown up a lot since he'd taken over the paper route.

"Yeah, my dad says there ain't no way we can stay out of it now that France surrendered to Hitler," agreed Danny.

"What are you gonna do, Jack?" asked Jessie.

"I'm gonna wait a while and see what happens. Meanwhile I'll be goin' to Bakersfield Junior College, but I'm working for the GP this summer in the oil fields."

"Hey, that's great, so is Alvin and me, right, Alvin?" said Jessie, glancing across at his friend.

Alvin hesitated a moment then said, "I... would'a told ya sooner, Jess, but I didn't actually know myself till yesterday. I ain't working for the GP this summer. I joined the Army Air Corps."

"Hey, all right, Alvin!" exclaimed Gerald. "That's what I'm gonna join. I want to work on those big airplane engines."

"Well, I didn't know for sure till yesterday when I got a notice that I passed the entrance examination."

"That's great. Maybe I'll get to work on your plane."

"You really did join up, Alvin?" asked Jessie, the disappointment evident in his voice and on his face.

"Yep, I did, Jess. You know, I've always wanted to fly one of those fast army pursuit planes. They require two years of college before you can get in the Army Air Corps cadet program. But I took the two-year college equivalency test and passed it by one point. How about that, Jess?"

"Uh, that's great, Alvin," Jessie said trying to compose himself from the shock that Alvin was one of those who would be leaving the Grapevine. "You'll be a real good pilot, Alvin. I know that. And Gerald, you'll do good too, 'cause you're already a great mechanic."

Except for the crackling fire, it was quiet for a moment in the secret cave behind old Fort Tejon.

Finally Gerald spoke. "Ya know Bud Carver joined the Air Corps too, and he's already flying."

"Yeah, and he an' Penny are gonna get married soon as he graduates from cadets," added Billy.

"Guess who else is getting married?" put in Danny.

"Who?" asked Bobbie.

"Maria Hunter," replied Danny, in the same way he'd always announced news items that he knew about before anyone else.

Danny's news struck Jessie about like that night George laid a haymaker on him at the Tavern. He just sat there staring at Danny.

"She is?" said Alvin. "How do you know?"

"She came to the store with that guy She's gonna marry. He was wearing a football sweater, and she was wearing a big diamond ring. They were on their way over to the Bear Trap to visit her folks."

All the guys knew the story about Jessie and Maria, of course. It had been a gossip item for a long time, so everyone sitting there focused on Jessie to see what he was going to say.

Jessie realized all eyes were watching him as he struggled for composure. The disappointment of his best friend leaving and now hearing that Maria was getting married was a double shock. As much as he'd tried, he still hadn't been able to forget her. He forced a smile and said, "Hey, guys, we all had trouble with our love life, right?"

Smiles broke out all around, and Bobbie blurted, "You can say that again! Alvin and me took turns being dumped by Agnes, and Jack got dumped by Elinor twice!"

Everyone burst out laughing.

Jack said, "Yeah, and I dumped Ruth for Irene, and she dumped me for Billy. The only one around here that hasn't had girl trouble is Gerald. He can take 'em or leave 'em."

"Well, I like girls, but I don't understand 'em, so I just stick with engines. I can understand them," said Gerald, grinning.

Everyone laughed for a minute or two, and then Alvin looked at Jessie and said, "I gotta tell on us Jess, okay?"

"Sure, why not. It's a great story."

"This one you guys ain't gonna believe," began Alvin, and then told a modified version of his and Jessie's romantic adventure with the See sisters. Sure enough, no one believed it.

When the guffawing and laughing was over, Jack turned to Jessie and said, "Well, how is your love life up at that art college, Jessie? I hear they got lots of pretty girls at college."

Jessie laughed. He knew for sure they wouldn't believe the story of his "arrangement" with Peggy, even if he told it, which he wouldn't. "Ya don't have much time for girls in college, fellows," he pronounced.

"Now, I find that hard to believe, Jessie," said Jack. "You were always a busy beaver all right, but you're a lover, and I can't believe you haven't got something goin' up there."

"Yeah, come on, Jessie, 'fess up," put in Bobbie. They have any girls up there like Hallie Lamont?"

Jessie shook his head.

"Man, now there is a girl I could go for," announced Gerald. "I still never seen a girl as pretty as her."

"Ain't it the truth! Remember when we were all in love with her?" recalled Alvin.

"Well, I seen her not long ago," said Danny. "And I can tell ya she is still as good lookin' as she ever was."

"Where'd you see her, Danny?" asked Jessie.

"At the store. Did you hear what she did? She flew an airplane from Los Angeles over the mountains and landed out in a field there by the ranch headquarters."

"She did?" said Gerald.

"Yeah, I heard about that," added Bobbie. "I didn't know she was an airplane pilot."

"I knew she was, didn't you, Jess?" asked Alvin.

Jessie nodded. "Yeah, I knew she was, and I'd bet she is a good one."

"She is some kind of girl all right, but I sure don't know why she has that big jerk George for a boyfriend," added Danny.

"She's back with him again?" asked Jessie.

"Yeah, I guess. He was with her when they came to the store."

Jessie winced silently. He had accepted that his relationship with Hallie could never be more than fascination. But it upset him to hear that she was still with George. His thoughts flashed back to when she asked him to be her boy friend, and he turned her down for Maria. And Maria broke his heart. Well, he'd learned some things about girls and life this past year, but there was a lot he hadn't learned- like how did he really feel about Peggy?

"Hey, you know what?" said Bobbie, interrupting Jessie's thoughts. "Miss Trembell's got a boy friend."

"No foolin'?" said Jack.

"Yeah. He comes up from Bakersfield in a big Packard and takes her out."

"Yeah, I seen 'em goin' down the road," confirmed Danny.

When the reminiscing and Grapevine gossip had run its course, they all crawled out of the smoky cave, shook hands, and promised faithfully to write each other. They agreed to meet at the cave for another reunion whenever they were all back on the Grapevine again.

Alvin had his dad's car, so after they left the cave, he and Jessie drove on down to their secret place on Grapevine Creek to have a private talk.

"This is really a neat place, ain't it?" said Jessie, as he stretched out in the sweet-smelling grass beside the creek where he and Alvin had come so many times in the past.

"It sure is. And I really have missed our talks,"
replied Alvin, sitting down next to Jessie.

"Me too."

"I hate leavin' Jess, but I thought it over a lot an I gotta go. I really do."

"Well, I'm disappointed. I was really lookin' forward to our havin' another great summer together in the oil fields, with an overnight at Pismo Beach."

"Yeah, with those little minks, the See sisters!"

They both laughed.

"Weren't they something?"

"They sure were," agreed Alvin, lying back in the grass.

A blue jay landed in an oak tree next to the creek and let out a loud squawk. Another one answered from an oak tree across the creek. They squawked back and forth for a minute or two and then flew off.

"I understand why you gotta go, Alvin. You always wanted to be an airplane pilot."

"Yep, I always did. Any chance you joinin' up too?"

Jessie shook his head. "No, it would be great being together, but I want to be an artist like you want to be a pilot."

Alvin nodded. "Yeah, I know you do, Jess, and I know you like it at that art school."

"Yeah, I really do."

"I hope this war gets settled before you have to go. But Jess, I don't think it will."

"Well, you may be right, but I ain't goin' until I have to."

"I don't blame you. Uh, I saw the look on yer face when Danny said that Maria's gettin' married. You still got feelings for her?"

Jessie nodded.

"You gotta forget her, Jess."

"I know, and for the most part, I have. And with her getting married, I don't have any choice anyway."

"Yep. That's the way life goes. How about at college- you got anything goin' up there?"

Jessie didn't answer, and Alvin squinted at him. "You got somethin' goin'. I can tell. Come on, out with it."

"Yeah. I didn't want to tell all the guys, but I do."

"Hey, all right. Tell me about it."

"Alvin, you wouldn't believe it."

"Whip it on me!"

"I live in the same apartment building with a girl, and we're havin an affair."

Alvin's black eyes grew large. "Wow! You're living with her?"

"Not exactly," replied Jessie, and then explained in some detail his and Peggy's arrangement.

When he'd finished, Alvin said, "That's wild, Jess. Does everybody do that at college?"

Jessie smiled. "No, I don't think so. I sort of fell into a special deal."

"Man, if I had a special deal like that, I might change my mind and go to college instead of joining the army. Tell me about this girl. What's she like?"

Jessie pulled a dandelion from the grass and looked at it. "She's isn't what you would imagine. She's little older. She's twenty-five."

"Twenty-five? Hey, she is old! How do you feel about her?"

Jessie blew on the dandelion and watched the little blossoms spin down into the grass. "I don't know. That's the honest truth. I just don't know."

Alvin studied his friend a moment. "Jess, are you gettin' in love again?"

There was a long hesitation. "I don't know the answer to that either, Alvin. Peggy says I'm still in love with Maria, so I couldn't be in love with her. She is real smart. Maybe she's right."

Alvin shook his head. "You sure always got a complicated love life, Jess."

"Yeah, it seems like it."

"Well, that's the way life goes. Me and Agnes split up again, an she's goin' with a new guy that just moved up to Lebec. But I still can't seem to forget her either. Oh well, just wait till I come home in my Air Corps uniform with gold bars on my shoulder and silver wings on my chest. I'll have more girls than I know what to do with, right, Jess?"

"Right, Alvin."

They glanced across the creek at a truck on the Grapevine. It had bales of cotton from Kern County Cotton farms stacked so high on the truck it looked like they would fall off. The engine was screaming as it struggled up the grade.

"One thing's for sure, Jess, I know I'm gonna miss that sound and the ole Grapevine."

"Yeah. Me too, Alvin."

Alvin and Bobbie left the Grapevine that summer of 1940: Alvin to the Army Air Corps and Bobbie to the U.S. Navy. Poor Gerald couldn't pass the physical examination because of his bad eye. He'd gotten a piece of metal in it working on an engine when he was a little boy. They classified him 4-F, and he was devastated. Billy ran the paper route in the Model A Ford, and Danny ran the root beer barrel.

Jessie and Jack worked for the GP in the Lost Hills oil fields that summer, and the ditch digging seemed harder than it had the year before and the sun hotter. The gang foreman told Jessie that one of the workers had wrecked the Chevy pickup, so he couldn't loan it to them on the weekend to go to Devil's Corner. But he said the See sisters didn't live there anymore anyway because they had gone to Hollywood to get into movies.

So it wasn't nearly as exciting in Lost Hills, California, as it was across the Atlantic Ocean in England.

Few in America, let alone Jessie Rascoe and his friends, were aware of the significance of the Battle of Britain that raged over the skies of England that summer of 1940.

Hitler's Nazi war machine had over run most of Europe and was poised to invade the British Isles, the last remaining obstacle in his conquest to dominate Europe. That domination seemed almost certain at that time since the German Luftwaffe was overwhelmingly superior to the British Royal Air Force in terms of numbers of aircraft and experience of air combat crews. All that Hitler needed was for the Luftwaffe to destroy the Royal Air Force fighter command so his Nazi invasion fleet could easily cross the channel and conquer England. After that, the rest would be easy because even if the United States entered the war, they would have no bases from which to strike Nazi Europe.

President Roosevelt and the U.S. War Department were well aware of this vital fact but they could do nothing to prevent it from happening. All eyes and hopes now focused on a small group of Royal Air Force fighter pilots and their aircraft, the Hawker Hurricane and Supermarine Spitfire.

The British pilots were heavily outnumbered and faced highly experienced Luftwaffe pilots flying fighters that were equal or superior in performance. They attacked England in aggressive swarms of fighters in overwhelming numbers. The RAF pilots met the oncoming armadas of fighters with courage only possible when one fights for survival over the roof top of one's home and loved ones.

Almost daily in cities and towns across the English countryside, families watched the huge air battles rage overhead as their sons and husbands fought valiantly against the swarms of enemy aircraft. When a trail of fire and smoke followed the long erratic death plunge of a falling aircraft, they could only hope it was one of the enemy.

The brave British pilots fought gallantly and well against overwhelming numbers, and although they destroyed the enemy in equal numbers to their losses, the enemy could afford to lose more because they had more. And the Nazis attacked the RAF air bases in mass attacks destroying aircraft and facilities vital to keeping the fighters in the air.

Hitler's invasion fleet was poised to invade, but then in a series of heavy attacks to finally destroy the RAF, the Luftwaffe suffered massive losses as the RAF pilots fought an unyielding all out battle to the death.

The heavy Nazi fighter losses during those battles in the late summer of 1940 caused Hitler to lose faith in the Luftwaffe's ability to protect his invasion fleet. So he called off the invasion. The Battle of Britain was over. The rest is history.

But as Winston Churchill said in praising the Royal Air Force fighter pilots who fought the Battle of Briton: "Never in the history of human conflict have so many owed so much to so few."

Chapter
~**33**~

Jessie's 1940 summer hadn't been all that exciting, but the thought of seeing Peggy again was exciting. He found himself really anxious to see her, so he was disappointed when she didn't meet him at the train station. Then when he arrived at the apartment, Mr. Helms told him Peggy Barton didn't live there any-more, but she had left a letter for him:

Dear Jessie,

As much as I hate to admit it, you were right.

I was wasting my time in college since my heart wasn't really in it. The only thing I was interested in was you. But I'm going to do the thing now that does interest me. It just came a little sooner than I had anticipated.

I hate these admissions, but I have to make another. I couldn't keep emotion out of our relationship. Naturally I wasn't about to admit that to you. But I have to admit it now and take my lumps because I know it wouldn't work.

After all you're a clod from Grapevine, and I got big fish to fry.

The truth is, I don't think my ego could handle another rejection. And I know it would be, because you're still in love with the mountain girl.

Sorry I couldn't keep it simple, but I couldn't. It sure plays hell with a great relationship. We were really good together, weren't we?

XOX! XOX! XOX!

Peggy

P.S. I know you will be a fine artist someday.

P.S.#2 Get a college deferment. The war is coming!

P.S.#3 No one will be using the apartment this year so move up there an think of me once in a while when you're in that big bed!

When Jessie finished reading the letter, he just stood there staring at it. "Here is the key to the apartment, Mr. Rascoe," said Mr. Helms.

Jessie glanced at the key. ""I don't understand, Mr. Helms. You mean I just live there without paying any rent or anything?"

"That's right. It's all been arranged."

All Jessie could think to say was, "What about the furnace, Mr. Helms?"

"Don't you worry about the furnace. I'll get someone to take care of that."

Jessie shook his head. "I can't believe this."

Mr. Helms looked at Jessie curiously then said, "Mr. Rascoe, do you know who Miss Barton really is?"

"What do you mean?"

"Well, not many know this, but Peggy Barton's full name is Peggy Barton Dumont, and she's the sole heiress to the Dumont business empire."

Jessie lived that whole school year in Peggy Barton DuMont's luxury apartment. He never saw her again though his curiosity required that he look up the Dumonts in the library, and sure enough, Mr. Helms knew what he was talking about. The multi-million-dollar Dumont industrial empire was inherited by Peggy when her father died earlier that summer. An article in the newspaper files said that Miss Dumont had assumed control of the vast Dumont holdings, which made her one of the youngest female chief executives of a major corporation in the United States.

It did explain a lot of Peggy's strange behavior and her mysterious comings and goings. It seemed incredible to Jessie that his crazy little nympho would be running a giant corporation. But when he thought about it, he could imagine her doing it all right.

That first night when Jessie crawled into her big luxurious bed where they'd made love so many times, he did think of her, and he knew he was going to miss her. But how he really felt about her was irrelevant now, since he would probably never see her again. But Peggy Barton Dumont had left her mark on Jessie. If not for her, he would have left college, and in the year they were together, she had, indeed, taught him a lot of things besides how to make love. Strange about life, Jessie thought. It's like the ole Grapevine: a lot of twist and turns.

Other than a lean period in his love life, it was a good year for Jessie in that he enjoyed living in the apartment and really got into his painting. He dated a couple of the female art students, but nothing clicked. So he just put most of his time and effort into his studies and his painting, and before he realized it, the school year was over.

By the time Jessie went home to the Grapevine the summer of 1941, England had won the Battle of Britain, but Germany had continued to bomb England unmercifully, attacked Denmark and Norway, and started the assault on Russia. On the other side of the world, the Japanese had pushed well into French Indochina and although they were engaged in a political dialogue with the United States, their aggressive intentions in the Pacific were obvious. It was becoming more and more evident that the United States would be pulled into the conflict, even though most people still didn't want to hear it, including Jessie.

It was hard not to hear about it, however, because war news was in the newspapers and on the radio daily. Jessie ignored it as much as he could, but the letters he got from Alvin and his friends kept it before him.

Jack, Danny, and Billy were in Bakersfield Junior College. Frank Grover was on the battleship *USS Arizona* out in some place called Pearl Harbor. Bobbie got assigned to a brand new aircraft carrier named *Yorktown* and was heading out to the Pacific. Bud Carver was an Air Corps pilot now and flying the big new B-17 Flying Fortress. Gerald had been classified 4F because of his bad eye and had gone to work at the Bakersfield Airport working on airplane engines for Buckner's Flying Service. Alvin was still in flight training at Luke Army Air Field in Phoenix, Arizona. His letters were full of excitement about flying the Curtis P-40 pursuit plane. That was the plane flown by the famous "Flying Tigers" in China. Alvin was scheduled to get his gold bars and silver wings that fall.

Jessie worked for the GP again that summer, but instead of the oil fields, he was assigned as a boiler washer. It was hard work cleaning and scraping the inside of those huge steam boilers, and the company moved him around to the different pumping stations that needed their boilers cleaned. But it paid an extra dollar a day, so now Jessie was making $8.00 a day, which was big money. His brother Billy had made enough on the paper route that year to buy a 1934 Chevrolet and he let Jessie use the '31 Ford so he could drive home once in a while and get some of his mom's good home cooking.

One Saturday, about the middle of the summer, Jessie stopped off at the root beer barrel to get the latest Grapevine gossip from Danny.

"Guess who I just seen?" Danny blurted as he filled the root beer glass from the spigot.

Jessie smiled. "Who?"

"Maria Hunter."

Jessie's smile waned. "You just saw her?"

"Sure did."

"Was she goin' over to the Bear Trap?"

"Yeah, she was goin' over to see her folks. I can't get over how she growed up. Ya know when she was a little girl she wasn't very pretty. But you should see her now! She's really good lookin'."

"She is, huh?" muttered Jessie.

Danny handed Jessie the glass of root beer.

Jessie nodded. "Uh, did she get married to that guy?"

"I don't know. I just talked to her for a second when she came to get the mail for her folks."

"Was she alone?"

"I didn't see anybody else. She got engaged last year, ya know, and might be married now. You remember that girl Sylvia that got on the bus at DiGeorgia Farms? Well, she got married. Seems like everybody is joining the army or navy or gettin' married."

"Yeah, I guess so."

After he visited a while with Danny, Jessie headed the Model A up the Grapevine toward the Lebec pumping station where he was staying in the company bunkhouse. He was thinking about Maria when he came to the cutoff that went to Bear Trap Canyon, and he just turned off and drove on down the road.

When he stopped at the ranch gate, the watchdog Juan Martinez came out of his cabin and nodded at Jessie in his usual stoic manner. He was a little more wrinkled, and there was more gray in his black hair. But otherwise, he looked the same.

"How have you been, Martinez?"

"Me good. You grow up now."

"Yes, I'm in college."

"What you be?"

"I'm gonna be an artist."

Martinez nodded. "That good."

Jessie was surprised. Most people sort of scoffed when he told them he was going to be an artist.

"You got Indian spirit. Make you a good artist."

Jessie had not forgotten his saying that he had Indian spirit that day he'd saved Maria's life when the rattler bit her. It had given him a feeling of kinship toward the old breed that he still felt. "Thank you, Mr. Martinez."

He nodded. "She go Bear Trap too."

"Who go to Bear Trap?"

"Wild one...Not so wild no more."

"Oh, yeah."

"She mighty pretty now."

Jessie nodded.

"You go Bear Trap too," he said with the hint of a smile, unfastened the gate, and swung it open.

Jessie waved, put the Ford in gear, and drove on through the gate. As he maneuvered the Ford down the bumpy, twisting road, Jessie tried to rationalize what he was doing. It didn't come out well. In fact, it irritated him. What was he doing? Maria was probably already married to the other guy, so why was he moping around over there? He knew why, but he wasn't going to admit it even to himself.

When he arrived at the Pete Miller Meadow, he pulled over and stopped. It was still as beautiful as ever. The willows rustled softly in an afternoon breeze, and a pair of doves swooped down and landed on the rocks where the crystal clear spring water bubbled out. He got out of the car got a drink by cupping his hands, then lay down on his back in the soft grass where he and his Bear Patrol had pitched their tents. He stared up at a cloudless blue sky and thought about Maria and those wonderful times they had been there together. After a while, he got back in the Ford and drove on up to the Hunter homestead. He just couldn't help it.

The old red barn looked exactly as it had the last time he was there: about to fall down. He stopped the car, got out, and stood for a moment looking at it. Then, as though time suddenly went backwards, the rickety side door opened, and Maria stepped out of the barn, just as she had done that time long ago.

Jessie knew instantly that he felt the same as always about Maria. A surge of galvanizing emotion raced through him, and it took all the restraint he possessed to keep from rushing over and grabbing her in his arms.

A stream of sunlight hit her hair and the silver in her dark eyes flashed as she stood staring at him. She wore a pair of tight-fitting jeans and a sleeveless blouse that revealed her marvelous body that he remembered so well, and dreamed of so often. That magic attraction he'd always felt for her was as strong as ever.

Then the barn door opened again, and a tall, good looking guy wearing a football sweater stepped out and looked at Jessie in a not-so-friendly way. It was the same guy Jessie had seen that night kissing Maria in front of her uncle's house- the guy she had dumped him for.

"Hello, Jessie," she finally said in a voice so soft her swollen lips hardly moved.

"Hi, Maria," Jessie managed to choke out.

Maria looked at the guy. "This is my fiance', Kevin Blake." Pause. "This is Jessie Rascoe."

"Fiance?" Jessie blurted. "I mean, I heard you already got married," he stammered.

"We're getting married after we finish college," said the guy, moving up next to Maria and putting his arm around her waist.

"Oh," said Jessie.

Awkward silence.

"We're visiting my folks," Maria explained, her eyes glued to Jessie.

"Are they all right?"

"Yes," she nodded, as Kevin tightened his arm around her.

Another silence.

"I...came over just to...see the ole canyon. I haven't been here in a couple years."

"It looks about the same," she replied.

"Yeah, it looks about the same."

Another silence.

"Well, I guess I better be getting on down the canyon."

Jessie turned to get into the Ford, hesitated, and glanced back at Maria. Their eyes met, and from the depths of those dark eyes, Jessie saw something that struck him like a thunderbolt. It was as though he and Maria were suddenly alone. Everything else just disappeared, and no one could see or hear them. For a precious moment, they were back in the time of their love: lying in the wildflowers at Marble Springs, professing their love for each other with all the emotion their exploding hearts could give.

The trance was over in seconds, and Jessie stumbled into the Ford and drove on out of Bear Trap Canyon in a daze. When he got back to the Lebec pumping station, he went in, flopped down on his bed in the bunkhouse, and thought about what had happened.

He was so emotionally affected by the experience; he found it difficult to think in a rational manner. The whole thing had been such a shock he wondered if he hadn't just imagined it. But no, it wasn't his imagination. There was no doubt about what he saw: Maria did still love him, and she had said it with her eyes just as clearly as if she had spoken the words. He'd seen that look in Maria's eyes too many times in the past to have been mistaken. But then, why was she marrying that guy. Why? It didn't make any sense- no sense at all.

The more Jessie asked himself that question, the more he found himself confused and frustrated. Then a few days before he had to leave for college, Jessie had another emotional encounter almost as disturbing as the one with Maria. He was in the company boarding house having late afternoon supper with several other workers when he was surprised to see Danny enter the room. "Hi, Danny, what are you doin' here?"

"Hi, Jessie, I got something for you. Finish your supper, and I'll wait outside for you."

Even though he wasn't quite finished, Jessie's curiosity made him get up and follow Danny out of the dining room.

"You'll never guess who came by the root beer barrel today," he said, smiling and holding a note for Jessie to see but not receive until he played his guessing game.

"I don't know. Who, Danny?"

"You'll never guess!"

"I know. you said that. Who?"

"Hallie Lamont, that's who!"

That news spurred excitement in Jessie all right, but it also gave him a touch of anxiety. And an instinctive feeling that as much as he would love to see Hallie again, it would probably complicate things.

"Jessie, that girl just gets better lookin' every time I see her."

"What did she say?"

"Well, not a lot. She just asked if you were here for the summer, and I said you were but I thought you were going back to college this week." Jessie nodded. "Then she wrote a note and asked me if I'd make sure you got it today."

"Did you say she wrote me a note?"

"Oh, yeah...Here it is," Danny said, handing Jessie the note.

Jessie,

Please come out to the ranch tonight or tomorrow. Any time will do. I'd like to see you. I'll be there alone.

Hallie

Later, as Jessie pulled on a clean pair of jeans, his instincts told him it would probably be best if he didn't see Hallie. But there was no denying the excitement he felt and there was no denying that he had to go.

When the big iron-encrusted front door to the Lamont hacienda opened to Jessie's knock, he knew his instincts had been right. The sight of Hallie sent his pulse leaping, as always.

"Hello, Tiger," she said with that mesmerizing smile of hers.

"Hello, Hallie," he replied. "You're as beautiful as ever."

"I can't say the same for you, Jessie. You're even better looking than ever."

He grinned. "I never could figure out why you always said that."

"Because it's patently true," she said, stepping up and taking both his hands in hers, then examining him a moment. "I can see that college agrees with you."

"Yeah, it does," he said as they stood holding hands and staring at each other.

She wore a sleeveless, off-white summer dress that made her tanned shoulders and arms take on a golden cast to match the waves of her yellow blond hair. Jessie had forgotten how hypnotizing it was to look into her eyes. Their intense cerulean blue had no equal in his paint box.

"It's been too long, Jessie."

He nodded. "I know."

"Have you been okay?"

"Yes...and no."

She nodded, smiling.

"And you?"

"Yes...and no."

They both laughed.

"I can see we have a lot to talk about. Come on, let's get comfortable," she said, leading him off down the hallway. "Dad is in Bakersfield. He said to tell you hello."

She took him to that same room where she'd told him she wanted to be his girl. As they entered, she said, "Have a seat and I'll get us a drink. Has college corrupted you yet?"

"Yes, I'm afraid so."

"Okay, what'll it be?"

"Would you happen to have any Bordeaux wine?"

Her eyebrows went up. "Well now, you have been keeping good company. I was sure, if anything, you'd ask for a beer."

"Only peasants drink beer," he said.

"Oh, Jessie, we do have a lot to talk about!"

They did talk about a lot. They sat opposite each other in the big living room for some time, sipping wine and pouring out their lives to each other. She told him she had graduated from UCLA and loved flying. He told her all about his life at college and how he loved his art studies, particularly the painting. He didn't mention Peggy or Maria. Nor did she mention George. Finally, at a pause in the conversation, she said, "I guess we covered everything but the gut issue, haven't we?"

He knew what she was referring to.

"You want to go first?"

"Ladies first."

She laughed. "You always were a gentleman." Her smile dissolved, and she looked down at the wine glass in her hand. "I'm going to break it off with George. I have to."

"I've heard that before."

"I know. I've said it before, but this time I really mean it. I've got to get away from him. I know it's not going to be easy. George and I have been together for some time. It's been a good relationship in many ways. I can't deny that. But I have no choice now."

"Why don't you have a choice?"

"Because I've come to realize how much alike we are and I hate it!"

"You're not like him, Hallie."

"I have been, and if I don't change, I know I'll end up just like her." She paused and averted her eyes. "I'll probably end up there anyway."

"Like who?"

She hesitated and then took a big drink of the wine. "My mother."

"Your mother?"

"Yes, She was a bitch and a tramp."

Jessie was dumbfounded. He had always wondered about Hallie's mother since she'd never mentioned her, but to call her own mother a bitch and a tramp?

"My father is not only a very kind and considerate man, he is very smart and successful here at the ranch. His weakness was my mother. He fell in love, married her, and gave her most anything she wanted. But she was a self serving bitch who made his life hell for years. Then one day when I was nine years old, I came in from playing on day and my father was sitting on the sofa with tears in his eyes. She was standing there in front of him with her suitcase. She turned to me and said, 'I'm leaving your father and going away with another man. Do you want to go with me or stay with him?' I was so devastated I couldn't speak. I just stood there. She said, 'suit yourself,' and walked out. I've not seen her since."

Jessie struggled to find a response. "I...I don't know what to say, Hallie."

"There isn't much to say."

"That must have been really difficult for you."

"I cried for a long time, but I don't any more."

"I'm sorry."

"Lately, it's dawned on me just how much like her I am, and it frightens me. I see in myself that same egocentric, selfish bitchiness, and George is the same way. That's probably why we've gotten along so well. You know, birds of a feather?"

"Well, I won't comment on George, but I'll tell you what I've always told you, Hallie: you're not as bad as you think."

She gave him a weak smile. "Yes, you always said that, despite the selfish, awful things I've done to you."

"You didn't do anything bad, except tease me."

"What about trying to separate you and Maria just for the fun of doing it?"

"That was as much my fault as yours."

"No, sweet Jessie. That was all Hallie Lamont. I don't know if what I'm going to do will change anything, but I'm going to give it all I've got, and we'll see."

"What are you gonna do?"

"I've got my commercial pilot's rating now, and I've joined the ATA. I leave day after tomorrow for Hertfordshire, England."

Jessie looked at her incredulously. "What did you join?"

"The ATA. It's the Air Transport Auxiliary of the British Royal Air Force. They have a women's section that does most of the ferry flying for the RAF."

"Hallie, there's a war goin' on over there! That's a pretty drastic thing to do just to get away from a guy."

"Well, it's more than just getting away from George. It's to see if the leopard can change her spots and at the same time do something to help those fighting the Nazis."

Jessie shook his head. "Hallie, there's gotta be another way to do this thing besides getting into the middle of a war. That's not our war."

"It's going to be. It's inevitable and only a matter of time before we're in it."

"Lots of people say that, but I don't believe it."

"I'm afraid it's true. And I really want to do it. It's an opportunity to find out just what Hallie Lamont is all about."

They sat quietly for a moment before Jessie said, "I think that's a pretty drastic way of doing it, but I admire you for your courage and determination."

"Thank you. It was important for me to tell you because, Well, you know. We got a special relationship, haven't we?"

"We do, Hallie."

"I'm serious when I say that I have a real thing for you, Jessie. It's like I told you long time ago: there is some potent chemistry between us."

He looked at her for a moment and said, "Yeah, I know. I have the same feeling when I'm around you."

"Then I'm still ringing your bell?"

He nodded. "Yeah, you sure are. But I have to tell you, I saw Maria Hunter a couple weeks ago, and she rung my bell too. Big time."

"I don't like hearing that, But it does ease my conscience some."

"Well, your conscience can rest at ease, because you didn't break us up. She found another guy in Los Angeles, and they're engaged. But I think she's still in love with me."

"Why do you think that?"

"Well...because of the way she looked at me."

"The way she looked at you? Come on, Jessie, you're past that puerile stage."

He shrugged. "I don't know that I am."

"You are. And although I was wrong to do what I did, I still think I was right about her. I think you are better off without her because Jessie, to be a real artist takes total dedication. That is where all your energies and devotion should go."

"I know. But she turned me inside out when I saw her."

"I suspect that was some nostalgia from your first big love. It's hard to get over that. God, I should know. I have the same problem with George. But I'm determined."

"Yeah. If you're willing to get into a war to get away from him, I guess you are."

"This time I need you to write me...would you?"

"Yes. I will...If you will write to me."

"I will. I have to. You're my security blanket now."

"You don't need a security blanket, Hallie. You got plenty of self-confidence."

"I do normally, but this emotional thing is different. I got a tough row to hoe, and I know it."

"I think you will do just fine."

"If I make it, Jessie, I'm coming after you."

He smiled. "I doubt I'll be too hard to catch."

A while later, in the darkness beside the 1931 Ford, they embraced, and Jessie said, "I'm awful sorry about your mother, but I want to tell you something and I want you to listen."

She nodded.

"I know that you're a good person. You're not your mother. You are Hallie Lamont, and you're a special girl."

"Thank you, Jessie, that means a lot to me."

They kissed tenderly.

"Good-bye, Jessie."

"Good-bye, Hallie."

Chapter

~34~

Patsy Cline could always tell when her best friend, Maria Hunter, had a problem. She got a hound-dog look on her face, and her lips would stick out even more than they usually did. When she walked into their favorite soda fountain on a Saturday afternoon and flopped down in the booth opposite Patsy, she had that look.

"I have a feelin' you got a problem, right?"

Maria nodded.

"Well, you're engaged to one of the best-lookin' guys on campus, who is crazy about you, so it couldn't be a man problem, or could it?"

Maria nodded again.

"Don't tell me, let me guess: Jessie Rascoe?"

Another nod.

Patsy let out a big sigh. "All right, what happened?"

"Well, you know Kevin and I drove over to Bear Trap Canyon to see my folks last weekend, and he came over and I saw him."

"Jessie?"

"Yes. It was awful, Patsy. I almost died."

"What'a ya mean?"

"Oh, Patsy, when I saw him, I thought I was going to explode. My heart started beating so hard I could hear it, and my knees got weak and I almost fell down. And I could tell that Jessie was feeling the same way."

"Aw, it's like that when you see an old boy friend, specially if you...you know, been intimate."

"All I know, Patsy, is that I got an awful pain, and now I'm so confused I don't know what to think."

"I had that same feeling when I met Bill once after I started goin' with Frank. But I got over it before long, and you will too."

"God, I don't know, Patsy."

"Sure you will. You're in love with Kevin now. You said so. And you're gonna get married and live happily ever after with him."

Maria dropped her eyes and stared at the table top.

"Don't be crazy, Maria. You're engaged to marry Kevin Blake, who is handsome, a football star, and a nice guy and he's rich. You got the world by the tail, and you're still pining over that hayseed from Hicksville? That doesn't make any sense."

"I'm a hayseed from Hicksville too, Patsy."

The Irish girl with red hair and freckles looked down and twisted the straw in her root beer float. "Sorry, Maria, that didn't come out very well, did it?"

"It's okay. I know what you mean, and in a way, you're right. It doesn't make any sense. I know I'm very fortunate to have Kevin, and he treats me good. But...I guess I've never gotten over Jessie and..." Maria's voice chocked off as tears began to run down her cheeks.

Patsy jumped up, ran around to the other side of the booth, and put her arms around Maria. "It's okay. Don't cry. You'll be all right. I went through the same thing with Bill, and I still got feelings for him. That's just natural. But I know it's over. He's got somebody else now, and I got somebody else. That's just the way it is. And it's the same with you. You live in a different world now from Jessie, and you're not the same person you were when you were in love with him a long time ago."

"You want somethin', honey?" asked the waitress who appeared beside the booth.

"Bring her a strawberry ice cream soda," said Patsy glancing up at the waitress.

The waitress looked at Maria and nodded. "Man trouble?"

"What else?" replied Patsy, while Maria wiped at her tear-stained eyes with the back of her hand.

The waitress departed, and Maria sobbed, "I know all that, Patsy, but I still can't help what I feel."

"Maria, are you telling me you think you still love that guy more than you love Kevin?"

Maria's teary eyes grew large as she stared at her friend with uncertain, agonizing emotions churning around inside. What was the answer to that question? Did she still love Jessie Rascoe? She had always said that she would never stop loving him, hadn't she? Yes. But like Patsy said, that was a long time ago. She was a different person now, and she did love Kevin. That had come naturally after Jessie told her he never wanted to see her again. Her folks, her aunt and uncle, and everybody else liked Kevin and said he was a fine boy from a fine family. And he'd given her a big diamond engagement ring.

They had gone through about the same intimate routine that she and Jessie had. Of course, being a city boy, Kevin knew all about condoms and since they were engaged, it seemed all right to go all the way in their love making.

Patsy kept reminding her that when you're engaged to a boy and doing intimate things with him, that means you're in love. She knew that Patsy was right, so what was her problem? Her problem was that seeing Jessie had struck her like an exploding bomb. The feelings that seared her insides and squeezed her heart was like nothing she had ever experienced with Kevin and two years of confidence that she truly loved Kevin had been shaken. Did she still love Jessie? If she did, what was she going to do about it?

"I loved Jessie with all my heart for a long time, and my heart tells me I still do," she finally said in a hoarse voice. "But you're right, Patsy, I'm not the same person I was then and I got to do what's right now. I promised Kevin I would marry him, and I can't go back on my promise."

"I knew you would do the right thing, Maria."

A few days after his reunion with Hallie, Jessie went back to college in San Francisco still harboring a distressing emotional uncertainty. He wished that he could discuss his dilemma with Alvin, but he was over in Arizona learning how to fly P-40 pursuit planes. They wrote letters back and forth, but it wasn't the same as lying in the grass beside Grapevine Creek and talking about their problems.

So Jessie started his third year of college in the fall of 1941 with some personal problems that weighed heavy on him. That was offset to some degree when Mr. Helms again handed him the key to Peggy Barton Dumont's luxury apartment and told him it was his again for the school year.

When he entered the apartment, a letter was on the kitchen counter, and Jessie knew before he opened it whom it was from.

> Dear Jessie,
> Oh how I wish I could be there to greet you properly. My guess is we wouldn't even make it to the sofa.
> I still miss you something awful. It's all I can do to keep from coming after you. And if I didn't hate cheating so much, I would. The guy I'm with now is okay, but not like you, lover! Other than some time for sex, I'm totally immersed in my work, and I love it. Someday when I can trust myself to be around you, I want to tell you about it.
> Enjoy the place, especially that big bed, and keep up the good work. You're going to be a fine artist. I'm sure of it.
> The apartment is yours again this year and next year too, as long as you continue your art studies.
> But you better sign up in a reserve program that will let you stay in college because war is coming, Jessie.
> XOX! XOX! XOX!
> Peggy

P.S. There's a couple of cases of Bordeaux in the pantry. Enjoy!

The emotional upset Jessie suffered over the dilemma in his love life continued to plague him as he tried to get back into the swing of college life. Since he was now in his third year of study, his courses demanded more attention and application than he was giving them. Finally, after his painting teacher accused him of not concentrating on his work, Jessie had a heart-to-heart with himself and resolved that since there was nothing he could do about Maria, Hallie, or Peggy, he would stop thinking about them and devote all his time and energy to his studies.

That worked reasonably well, and he at least got back into a routine. Then, one Saturday morning in late October, he answered the front door bell and found himself staring into the smiling face of an Army Air Corps second lieutenant with gold bars on his shoulders and silver wings on his tunic.

"Alvin!"

"Hi, ole buddy!"

"Golly! What a surprise! What are you doin' here?"

"I came to see my ole pal, that's what I'm doin' here," said Alvin as the two friends hugged warmly.

"But I mean, what are you doin' in San Francisco?"

"I'm shipping out, Jess. I'm over at Hamilton Army Air Field at the Port of Embarkation. It's just a few miles across the Golden Gate Bridge."

"Shipping out?"

"Yep, I'm on my way to Hawaii. How about that?"

"They're sending you to the Hawaiian Islands?"

"Yep, I'm going to a P-40 squadron at Bellows Army Air Field on Oahu Island."

"I didn't know they had army airplanes over there."

"They sure do, and they got a big Navy base over there too."

"Hey, you really do look great in that uniform, Alvin."

"Yeah and you should see how the girls look at me now."

"I'll bet! Gosh, it's good to see you. How long can you stay?"

"Unfortunately, not long. I gotta be back on base before midnight, but we got all afternoon."

"Well, come on in and see my castle."

"Criminy, this is even better than you told me in your letter. And this belongs to that girl, Peggy?"

"I guess it does. I'm getting to use it, and it's really great."

"She lets you stay here free?"

"Yeah, she does."

"Do you see her anymore?"

"No. She's a millionaire, Alvin."

"Well, how does it feel to have an affair with a millionaire girl?"

"I don't know, because I didn't know she was rich until after she left," said Jessie.

Alvin shook his head. "I can tell you, that is one the Grapevine guys would never believe."

Jessie laughed. "That's for sure."

"How do you feel about her, Jess?"

Jessie hesitated. "I liked her, a lot, Alvin. But, well she's from a different world and...Hey, come on, let's have a drink and celebrate, okay?"

"You bet! This calls for a special celebration."

Jessie broke out a bottle of the Bordeaux wine, and they sat down on the big sofa and celebrated being together again. They sipped wine and reminisced about those great times on the Grapevine and exchanged the latest on all the gang: where they were and what they were doing. Jessie brought Alvin up to date on his progress at the art school, and Alvin expounded on his flying and the Army Air Corps.

"I love it, Jess. And you wouldn't believe how much fun it is to fly the P-40. It will go over three hundred miles per hour! If we get in a war, those Japs won't have a chance against that baby."

"We're not gonna get in a war, Alvin."

"I think we are, Jess."

"Hallie agrees with you."

"You see Hallie?"

"Yeah, I did," said Jessie, and then told Alvin the whole story of his visit with Hallie and with Maria over in Bear Trap Canyon.

"Jess, you always did have a tangled-up love life. And not with just one girl, you got three girls! What are you gonna do?"

Jessie smiled. "Well, Peggy left to be a millionaire, Hallie is in England flying for the RAF, and Maria is getting married, so I don't think I'm gonna do anything."

Alvin laughed. "Yeah, you got a point. But ain't that something that Hallie went to England to fly in the RAF?"

"Yeah, it's something all right. I got a letter from her just a couple days ago, and she says it's pretty rough over there. I guess the Nazis have really caused a lot of destruction and killed thousands of people with their bombing. A lot of folks are homeless and everything is rationed, clothes and food and everything."

"Did she say what kind of planes she's flying?"

"No, but I guess it's tough flying. She says the weather over there sure isn't like it is in Southern California."

"Boy, ya gotta hand it to that girl. I mean she always had things pretty good. Giving all that up to go over there and help those folks says something about her."

"Yeah, it does. She's a brave girl, in more ways than one. She...well, she lost her mother when she was real young, and she never really got over it. I think, though, that Hallie has changed. Of course, I never could find much fault with her anyway,-except for her choice of a boyfriend."

"How well I remember! He's the big jerk who knocked me across the dance floor at the Tavern."

"Yeah and me too." They both laughed.

After a sip of wine, Alvin said, "So you're back carrying the torch for Maria?"

"Well, I know I'm still in love with her. But I know I got to forget her."

"Yep, she's marrying the other guy, Jess. But I'll tell ya somebody who ain't marrying the other guy." Alvin paused with a grin.

Jessie looked at him curiously. "Who?"

"Agnes, that's who! Me and her got engaged."

"Hey, all right! You two finally got back together. That's great!"

"It sure is. Agnes matured a lot in the last year. She's goin' to Bakersfield Junior College now. Anyway, when I was home on leave I saw her one day and we sorta realized that we really do love each other, and before my two weeks' leave was up, we got engaged."

"Well, congratulations, ole buddy. Agnes is a neat girl."

Alvin looked at his friend. "Yeah, she is."

"I'm happy for you, Alvin. When are you getting married?"

"We wanted to get married before I left, but her folks wanted her to wait for another year. If the war doesn't start, I'll come back on leave, and we'll get married and you're gonna be best man. Then she can go with me to Hawaii, and we'll live in a little grass shack on Lala Kahooki, Hawaii. Wouldn't that be neat?"

"That would be. And you will because the war isn't going to start."

"I hope you're right. But whatever happens, you stay in college and finish your art studies, Jess."

"Hey, I'm a lover not a fighter, remember?"

Alvin laughed. "Are you ever! I just hope that one of these days you get your love life straightened out."

Jessie nodded. "Me too."

When they had finished the bottle of wine, they got on the cable car in front of the apartment and rode it down to Fisherman's Wharf. There, they had a great seafood dinner at Grotto Number Nine, drank more wine, and reminisced some more.

When time came for Alvin to leave, they were both feeling the effects of the wine. "Well, I'm feelin' no pain, but we ain't in quite the shape we were that night on Pismo Beach, huh, Jess?"

"I'll never forget that night, Alvin. But that was in our youth when we used to drink that ole beer that only peasants drink."

They both laughed, and then stood silently in the San Francisco mist for a long moment there beside the taxi cab that would take Alvin back to his base.

"So long, Jess."

"So long, Alvin."

The War

Chapter
~35~

Second Lieutenant Alvin Pyeatt was wearing tennis shoes and a pair of swimming trunks as he ran in the grass alongside the runway at Bellows Army Air Field, on the Island of Oahu. He liked running in the early morning because everything was quiet and peaceful, just like it was back on the Grapevine where he used to run in the grass beside the Grapevine Ranch barbed-wire fence.

It was a cool, bright morning, although a few clouds were building up over the mountains to the east. He'd been in the Hawaiian Islands for a little over a month and loved it. Hawaii was just like it said in the geography books: a peaceful, beautiful place, with swaying palm trees and lush green mountains that rose out of a sea of sparkling, aqua blue water. It was a world apart from the oak and willow trees of the Tehachapi Mountains and the polliwogs of Grapevine Creek. As his thoughts went to the Grapevine, Alvin felt a twinge of homesickness. But then he remembered the letter he had just received from Agnes, and the homesickness was replaced by excitement. She had written that she didn't want to wait any longer. She wanted to get married as soon as they could and come to Hawaii and live in a little grass shack on Lala Kahooki, Hawaii. He had written back that he would get leave as soon as possible and come home for the wedding. After his morning run, he would write to Jessie and tell him to get ready to be his best man.

His thoughts were interrupted as his peripheral vision picked up an object moving just below the face of a cloud. It prompted him to slow to a walk and focus on the object. But whatever it was, it disappeared behind one of the clouds, so he picked up his pace. A moment later he saw it again; only now there were several objects, this time moving toward the airfield. Now he could see clearly that it was a formation of aircraft coming in fast. Strange, he thought. A formation at this time on a Sunday morning?

Curious, Alvin watched the planes approach. They must be a formation of aircraft from the Kaneohe Marine Base, and they were obviously going to give the army airbase a little early morning buzz job. The marine pilots and the army pilots often mixed it up in competitive aerial dogfights to see who was the "hottest." But buzzing the airbase was a no-no, and it surprised Alvin that they would do it. He stopped and watched as the formation began its run on the airfield.

When the first bomb hit and exploded in a giant mushroom of fire and smoke, sending dirt and debris high overhead, Alvin watched in shocked incomprehension. Then, as another series of giant explosions shook the earth where he stood, the reality of what was happening exploded in his brain, and he blurted, "Jesus Christ!"

From that moment on, Alvin knew what he had to do: get to a P-40! He began to run as fast as his legs would carry him on a beeline dash across the runway toward his squadron's aircraft parking area.

As he ran, he could hear explosions and see giant clouds of smoke and fire erupting all over the airbase. He knew before he ever saw the red ball on the wing of a low-flying aircraft, that the attacking planes were Japanese. He also knew that all the guessing and speculating was over. Jessie was wrong. America was going to get into the war, and he and Agnes would not be living in a little grass shack on Lala Kahooki, Hawaii.

Alvin could hear bullets whining past and more explosions all around him, but he held his course straight to the fighter parking area. He was only yards away on a dead run when a bomb struck directly in the parking area and with a tremendous explosion sent pieces of aircraft flying in all directions, knocking Alvin off his feet and onto the cement ramp. He scrambled up, his legs bloody, and dashed on toward the remaining aircraft.

He detoured around a burning aircraft, raising his arm against the searing heat. He spotted a P-40 that wasn't damaged and ran to it, jumped onto the wing, and pulled back the canopy. Glancing inside, he saw what he wanted: the red warning tag that indicated the plane was armed and ready to go.

Second Lieutenant Alvin Pyeatt jumped into the cockpit of the Curtis P-40 Warhawk, dressed in his jogging shorts with blood running down his skinned legs. He flipped the master switch and began the starting sequence. Within seconds, the Allison engine roared to life. He pulled the crash straps down over his bare shoulders, fastened his seat belt, and advanced the throttle. The P-40 wouldn't budge. "Damn!" he shouted. He'd forgotten to remove the parking chocks! He cut the throttle and started to unfasten the seat belt when he saw a figure dash out of the smoke and flames. It was one of the line crew, and he too had blood all over his face and part of his clothes was burnt away. He ran up to the front of the aircraft and jerked the parking chocks clear. As he jumped back out of the way, he gave Alvin a thumbs-up signal and disappeared into the smoke.

Another gigantic explosion sent pieces of debris bouncing off the P-40 as Alvin advanced the throttle and roared out of the parking area. Twice he had to jam on the brakes and swing the tail around to keep from crashing into chunks of wreckage that littered the ramp. With all the smoke and fire obscuring his vision, he could only hope that he was headed in the right direction. Since he had no flight helmet, he had no earphones to talk to the control tower, although he doubted it was still there.

Finally, he broke into the clear and saw the taxiway that would lead to the runway where he could take off. He advanced the throttle and started down the taxiway just as a string of bombs hit directly in front of him. Again he had to cut the engine and swing the tail of the aircraft around. "To hell with the runway!" he shouted and rammed the throttle as far open as it would go. Down the taxiway Second Lieutenant Pyeatt drove the P-40 at full power. Overhead flashed the shadow of a Japanese bomber as it roared past. Directly ahead more explosions and smoke and more Japanese aircraft on their bombing run.

Alvin didn't waver; he held the throttle open, hurtling down the narrow taxiway toward a huge chunk of wreckage ahead. At the last instant. he hauled back on the stick and the P-40 staggered into the air, clearing the wreckage by inches.

As his pursuit struggled to gain speed, he saw two attacking aircraft headed straight toward him, and he could see their tracer bullets flashing past his canopy. He lowered the nose, retracted the landing gear, and held the aircraft down close to the ground, letting his speed build. The two Japanese aircraft were directly ahead now and coming right at him with their wing guns blazing. They flashed past him so close he could see the pilots in the cockpit. It occurred to Alvin that they must have been so preoccupied that they hadn't even seen him. It was the only possible explanation of why they missed him- that or a miracle.

Alvin held the P-40 down low as he headed toward the mountains at full throttle. He reasoned that the Japanese pilots were so busy bombing and strafing the airbase they might not notice him. If he could make it across to the mountains and get some altitude before they saw him, he would gain the advantage of surprise and position. As soon as he was over the first ridge, he pulled up into a steep climb and headed for the clouds.

It only took a couple minutes to climb up through the scattered clouds, and when he topped out, there were no other aircraft in sight. He banked back toward the airbase continuing his climb. When he was over the mountains, he could see the airbase below and ahead with blazing fires and huge columns of smoke billowing into the morning sky. Japanese aircraft were everywhere, still attacking in waves.

Now it was time to give the sneak attackers some of their own medicine. He flipped his gun switch to arm and tightened his seat belt, which reminded him that he wore no parachute, and although it was against army regulations to fly without one, he somehow doubted it mattered at this point. Alvin pushed the stick forward and dove the P-40 toward the nearest enemy aircraft he could see.

One-quarter Tejon Indian, Alvin Pyeatt may well have fired the first American airborne shot, of billions to come, during World War II. But it wasn't a good shot. He was so eager to shoot that he fired while he was still out of range. When the Japanese pilot saw the tracers flying off into space, he banked away, and Alvin had his first lesson in aerial combat.

Alvin snapped the P-40 into a steep bank and pulled back hard on the stick, which, at high speed, immediately blacked him out, and he had his second lesson in aerial combat.

By the time his vision cleared a few seconds later, his target had disappeared, so he picked out another attacking aircraft and dove after it. This time he held his fire until he was close enough to see the rising sun insignia on the Japanese plane, and this time when he jammed down on the firing button, he saw his tracers pouring into the enemy aircraft, sending pieces of metal flying. An instant later there was a flash of fire, followed by an explosion, and the Japanese bomber erupted into a giant fireball and began to disintegrate, spewing a shower of blazing pieces that marked its twisting fall to earth.

"I got him! I got him! I got the son of a bitch!" shouted Alvin in the cockpit of the P-40. But his jubilance was interrupted by the sound of an explosion and a violent shudder as the cockpit filled with chunks of flying metal, pieces of plexiglass, and acrid smoke. At that same instant, he felt a searing pain in his side and shoulder, and the inside of the canopy was splattered with bright red blood.

Alvin slammed the stick over, sending the aircraft into a banking dive just as another series of explosions ripped through the aircraft. Glancing back, he saw a trail of smoke pouring out of his fighter and two Japanese aircraft directly behind him, their guns blazing.

Alvin knew that both he and the P-40 were hit bad, but somehow that didn't seem to matter. He was immune to the pain, and his only thought was to fight back. But he also knew that he had to shake his pursuers as they were so close that within seconds their deadly fire would disintegrate his aircraft just as he had the Japanese bomber.

Alvin's peripheral vision picked up the cloud off his left wing and he slammed the Warhawk into a steep bank and dove into the billowing mass. For several seconds he plunged through the swirling mist and then jettisoned out. He scanned the sky and saw his attackers coming straight toward him. Alvin smiled. It was exactly what he wanted.

The two Japanese aircraft and the American P-40 hurtled toward each other head on, with all guns blazing. As his friends on the Grapevine always said, there was no one braver than Alvin Pyeatt. He sat unflinching in the shattered cockpit of the P-40 with the wind whipping his black hair and the blood pouring from his wounds. His Indian eyes squinted with determination as he held the machine gun firing switch down hard while the opposing aircraft closed at tremendous speed.

One of the Japanese pilots recognized that a collision was imminent and broke off the frontal attack. The other one, probably a Japanese Alvin Pyeatt, did not. And in that last instant, just before the blinding flash and oblivion, the American Alvin Pyeatt grinned. It was as though he was back at the ranch water trough charging that ole Hereford bull.

Seaman Frank Grover was standing next to the boarding ramp of his ship, dressed in navy blues and talking to his buddy while they waited to go ashore on liberty. They had just been paid a few days earlier and were going into Honolulu to do some Christmas shopping. They paid no attention to the formation of aircraft approaching from the east because there was always airplanes coming and going from the Pear Harbor Naval Air Station and nearby Hickam Army Airfield.

Frank didn't even hear the bomb. All he knew was that some tremendous force suddenly picked him up and hurled him over the side of the battleship *Arizona*. The force of the blast left Frank in a spinning swirl of flashing lights and horrendous noises as he plummeted through space toward the water far below.

By the time Frank struck the aqua-blue water of Pearl Harbor, it had already turned into a sea of black, burning oil. All around him, pieces of flaming debris were falling into the water, and he could hear one gigantic explosion after another, intermingled with cries of agony from somewhere in the smoke and chaos.

As Frank struggled to regain his breath and swim away from the burning oil, a thought pierced the jumble of noise and confusion: his ship, the mighty battleship *Arizona* was going down, and his prized saxophone, the one he'd played all those years in his Grapevine dance band, was going down with it.

Hallie Lamont strained to see through the mist and rain that whipped around the small windshield on the Tiger Moth trainer she was flying. She reached up and pushed her goggles back on her helmet, but now the rain-saturated wind stung her eyes so intensely she could see even less. She pulled the goggles back down and stuck her head out into the slipstream of the open-cockpit aircraft. A dark shape loomed out of the mist ahead, prompting her to ram the throttle forward and jerk back on the stick. She caught a glimpse of a building as it skimmed by, just a few feet below.

Hallie's heart pounded in her rib cage and her gloved hands on the controls oozed perspiration even though her body was numb from the cold. She had been "scud running" now for nearly two hours in the small bi-wing RAF trainer aircraft, and the tension and cold were taking their toll-not to mention that she was nearly out of fuel. If she didn't find her destination airfield soon, she would have to make a forced landing and hope for the best. God, she hated to do that, because it would probably mean a crash. Although that frightened her, her real concern was wrecking the aircraft and letting Commander Gower down. Every aircraft was precious to Britain's war effort.

Pauline Gower was the commander of the small group of women pilots in the ATA who ferried aircraft for the RAF all over England and Scotland regardless of weather. Praised for their dedication and bravery, they were an honored group who made a valuable and significant contribution to the RAF as Britain struggled to survive the vicious Nazi onslaught.

But when the female pilots first appeared in the early days of the war, praise was sparse. Most male pilots had little confidence in their female counterparts and openly ridiculed them. In their opinion, flying was a man's business, and the "skirts" should stick with what they were made for. But Commander Gower and her small band ignored the ridicule and did the job, which for the most part was ferrying trainers and utility aircraft in rotten weather.

Suddenly, a small break appeared in the mist ahead, and a moment later Hallie spotted the river. She glanced up at her compass and checked the magnetic heading. Yes! It should be the check-point she was looking for. She put the Tiger Moth in a right bank and lined up on the river. She knew from studying the chart that the airfield was just north a few miles. All she had to do now was follow the river.

But was there enough fuel? She glanced up at the wing tank gauges. The needles bobbed on empty.

She looked out into the swirling mist again. Although the clouds had raised some, she was still forced to stay low, skimming along the tree tops as she followed the river bank, straining to identify some landmark, some indication of the RAF air base that was her destination.

A few minutes later, she glanced up at the wing fuel tank gauges again. The needles had stopped bobbing, which meant the tanks were empty. Now, Hallie had to accept the reality that the engine would quit momentarily, and she must prepare for a forced landing. She banked away from the river hoping to see an open field, but all she saw was mist-shrouded trees. She had tightened her crash straps and braced herself for the imminent crash when the trees suddenly parted and out of the mist, directly over the nose of the aircraft, appeared the runway. All she had to do was retard the throttle and land the Tiger Moth.

After she landed and parked the trainer, Hallie cut the mixture control and watched the propeller come to a stop. She sat there in the open cockpit with the rain running down her face, too exhausted to pull herself out of the cockpit. She couldn't help wonder just how much longer the flying gods would be this kind to her.

"Great day for ducks, but not so good for flying, eh?" she heard a voice say.

With an effort, she pushed her flying goggles up onto her helmet and glanced out at a ground crewman, dressed in a bulky rain slicker. He was standing beside the cockpit looking at her curiously. "Can I 'elp ya, miss?"

She managed a smile and said, "No thank you, corporal, I think I can make it now." She pulled herself out of the aircraft, retrieved her travel bag from the front cockpit, threw the parachute over her shoulder, and walked through the misting rain across the wet ramp to a small metal hut labeled Flight Operations.

Another RAF ground crewman in a rain slicker walked up beside the Tiger Moth and said to the corporal, "What do you suppose makes a skirt want to do this kind of bloody flying?"

"It's beyond me, mate."

"And that one sure doesn't 'ave to do it. She's a looker."

When she entered the operations hut, two other female ATA pilots were standing next to a pot-bellied, coal-fired heating stove in the center of the room. "What kept you, Hallie?" said one, a tall, blonde girl dressed in winter flight gear.

"I stopped off for tea," Hallie replied as she dropped her parachute onto the bare wooden floor and pulled off her flight helmet, spilling her hair down over the collar of her winter flight suit.

"I sure could have used some bloody tea," muttered the other female pilot, a small-framed woman with short curly hair. "I nearly froze my tail off."

"Tell me about it," said Hallie, pulling off her gloves and moving up next to the stove where the other women stood. "I'm frozen solid."

"That's what I call cruddy flying," said the tall girl.

"Yeah. There must be a better way to serve the crown," muttered the other.

"How long have you been here?" asked Hallie, holding her hands up to the stove.

"About a half hour. I was getting worried about you. I landed short of petrol. You must'a been getting real low."

"I was on fumes," replied Hallie, stamping her feet to regain some feeling.

"I still don't know what motivates you, Hallie. With your looks you could have it all. Why you stick around here risking your neck is beyond me."

"Well, my best guess is that it's got something to do with a man," said the tall girl.

Hallie smiled at the two British pilots who were not only her flying mates, but had also become her good friends.

"Did you 'ear the news?" bellowed a burly RAF sergeant with a handle-bar mustache, who had suddenly tromped into the room.

The three womens standing around the stove looked at him curiously. "What news?" asked one of female pilots.

"The bloody Japs just bombed Peal Harbor in the Hawaiian Islands!"

Seaman Bobbie Murts lay on his bunk in the bowels of the big aircraft carrier *Yorktown*, reading a letter from home. It was from Elinor, and she wrote great letters, telling all the news from the Grapevine. The big news was that Alvin came home looking great in his new Air Corps uniform and he and Agnes got back together and got engaged.

It was good to hear about his friends and the Grapevine, but it made Bobbie homesick. In fact, he'd begun to think he'd made a mistake in joining the navy. It wasn't nearly as exciting as he'd imagined, and all he'd done so far was work in the bottom of the ship. Besides, here it was almost 1942, and there wasn't any war. Jessie was probably right. He should have listened to him and stayed on the Grapevine and gone to work for the GP.

"Attention! Attention all personnel!" suddenly blared the loud-speaker over his bunk. "This is the captain speaking. I have an announcement of vital importance! We have just been advised by Fleet HQ that the Japanese have bombed Pearl Harbor! Repeat, the Japanese have bombed Pearl Harbor! This ship is now on full combat alert! All personnel report to your combat duty stations immediately!"

Chapter
~36~

Jessie Rascoe spent all day Sunday December 7, 1941, working on a design project that was due Monday. So when he arrived at the college Monday morning December 8, 1941, he was surprised to see students and teachers standing around in groups talking excitedly.

"It means war!" declared a professor.

"What means war?" asked Jessie.

The professor looked at him. "Where have you been, Mr. Rascoe?" Didn't you hear? The Japanese bombed Pearl Harbor!"

Pearl Harbor? That was in the Hawaiian Islands! That's where Alvin was! When the significance of that registered on Jessie, he was stunned. Alvin was in Hawaii! He was one of those who said war was coming, and it did, right were he was.

Jessie stood there with the other students listening to the teacher expound on the terrible consequences of what the Japanese had done. But what did it mean to Jessie Rascoe? He'd always said that if war came he would do his duty. But, quit school and join the army? Just the thought of that was unacceptable. He just couldn't do that. How could he quit college now? Maybe he could still sign up for one of those reserve pro-grams and stay in school, like Peggy had told him to. Others he knew had done that, so why not him?

President Franklin Roosevelt called the sneak attack by the Japanese a dastardly act and said that December 7, 1941 was "a date that would live in infamy." The United States declared war on Japan on December 8. On December 10, Germany and Italy declared war on the United States, and the United States in turn, declared war on them. And America joined World War II.

The transformation of the United States from December 6, 1941, to December 8, 1941, was phenomenal. From an almost universal mind set of rejection to becoming involved in the war, the citizens of America reversed themselves over-night. They were outraged by the attack and reacted accord-ingly. Military recruiting stations in every city in every state were overwhelmed with volunteers standing in line around the clock to enlist.

Jessie spent the next few days in a fog of uncertainty as to what he should do. He worried about Alvin but reminded him-self that brave Alvin could handle war if anyone could. Then he was surprised when a messenger brought him a note:

Dear Lover,

I want to remind you that I told you war would come. Now do what I also told you and sign up for a college deferment before they change the rules. This will be a long war, and you will get your chance to serve. So listen to me because you should also know by now that I'm always right!

I hate to tell you that I miss you terribly. But I got to keep on course for now. Hopefully we can visit one day without my wanting to jump you.

Peggy

The note from Peggy boosted Jessie's morale considerably and solidified his uncertainty about what to do: he would heed her advice and apply for the exemption.

A few days after Jessie had made his decision to stay in college, he received a letter from his father with the worst news Jessie Rascoe had ever heard: His life long friend Alvin Pyeatt had been killed during the Japanese attack on Pearl Harbor.

Jessie flopped on the big bed in Peggy's apartment and staring at the ceiling all that day. The next morning he quit school and caught the Santa Fe chief to Bakersfield. He went directly to the army recruiting station where he stood in line for five hours. When his turn came, he joined the Army Air Corps. He'd decided that was the best way he could get at the Japanese killers. And that had now become paramount in Jessie Rascoe's mind. Nothing else mattered. He hated it, but there was no other choice. He could only focus on one objective, and that was revenge. His mother had always said that revenge was the Lord's call, not his, but now, like the rest of America, it was strike back at those who had attacked his country and killed his best friend.

Second Lieutenant Alvin Pyeatt was awarded the Distinguished Service Cross posthumously, and his picture was on the front page of the Bakersfield *Californian* with a wonderful eulogy by the reporter Jim O'Day. He was subsequently buried in a military cemetery called the Punch Bowl on Diamond Head Mountain on Oahu, but they had a memorial service in Bakersfield. Almost everyone on the Grapevine came, and the Boy Scouts of Troop 34 were there in full uniform. When Agnes and Jessie met at the service, they just hugged each other with tears streaming down their cheeks. Neither of them could choke out any words.

On December 7, 1941, the United States was ill prepared to fight the well trained and experienced armed forces of Japan and Nazi Germany. However, geographical isolation provided time to prepare. The outrage of the American people over the attack at Pearl Harbor all but eliminated political opposition to a full and rapid shift to a war based economy.

Factories retooled from producing consumer goods to war planes, ships, tanks, and guns. The Great Depression ended almost over night, and the German-American bund also disappeared overnight. Japanese nationals on the west coast were interned in camps. Young Americans overwhelmed the army and navy recruiting stations, and "housewives" and young women came forth and filled the labor requirements in the factories.

The military and political leaders knew they had a monumental task ahead to build an army and navy that could challenge those of Japan and Germany. The Japanese had already overrun most of the Pacific and the Nazi's most of Europe. A large portion of our navy had been sunk or seriously damaged at Pearl Harbor, and Nazi submarines patrolling our east coast and sunk our merchant ships at will, and we had no way of stopping them.

The Army Air Corps was faced with the daunting task of building and training an air force from almost scratch. Chief of the Army Air Corps, General Henry "Hap" Arnold, and his staff established a procurement program for the aviation industry to design and produce bomber aircraft that could strike the enemy and fighters that could protect the bombers and destroy enemy fighters.

The training of pilots, navigators, bombardiers, and air crew was assigned to the Air Corps Training Command with the basic objective of turning out air crew with the skill and determination that would match or exceed that of the enemy. This was a formidable assignment since the German and Japanese air crews had superior aircraft and years of air war experience.

The training philosophy adapted by the Army Air Corps, particularly for the pilots who would fly and command the aircraft, was an intense, demanding program that required a maximum effort and the total dedication of a superior candidate. A candidate who, when trained, would unhesitatingly fly his bomber to the target and drop the bombs regardless of enemy opposition. And fighter pilots who would attack the enemy aggressively, regardless of enemy opposition.

That training program was established, and it did the job. But it was brutally intense and demanding. Only applicants with perfect health and a minimum of two years college, or pass an equivalency test, were selected. They were then subjected to physical and aptitude screening and testing programs designed to weed out all but the best possible applicants. Additional psychological and motor-skill tests, applied under nerve-wrenching pressure, identified only a small percentage of the original applicants as the final selectees.

Jessie Rascoe was a final selection. In a sense, it was a nightmare for the country boy who wanted to be an artist. But Jessie was totally focused on his goal with a determination to persevere he had learned in his youth and as a boy scout.

Jessie was assigned to a training squadron at Santa Anna Army Air Base in California, where nearly thirty thousand aviation cadet applicants were sent from all parts of the country to be screened. Those selected would receive a three-month "Preflight" training course. Those not selected (the majority) were sent to army training centers to be trained as crew members for transport and bomber aircraft.

The training at Santa Anna included military basic training, drill, physical education, and aviation related academics, such as aerodynamics, theory of flight, meteorology, map reading, internal combustion engines, Morse code, and radio.

The cadets were subject to strict military discipline at all times, and any violation was grounds for instant dismissal. They marched at attention and in lock step formations to and from academic classes and to the mess facilities, physical training, and of course, formation drill. Bugle calls directed all basic activities such as reveille, assembly, and taps.

By applying himself totally in the academics and steeling himself to obey and perform without hesitation, Jessie managed to graduate from Pre-flight training.

To speed up the initial phase of aviation cadet training, the army contracted with civilian flight schools all over the country to conduct the primary flight training program for the Army Air Corps. One of those schools was the Mira Loma Flight Academy at Oxnard, California. This was the school Jessie was assigned after completing Pre-flight.

At Mira Loma, the cadets were divided into flights of about twenty. The long training day began at 0400 hours and ended at lights out at 2100 hours. The cadets marched to and from all training functions, which alternated with academics and flight training.

Jessie began his flight training in a fabric-covered Stearman PT-17 bi-wing trainer. It had two open cockpits with the instructor flying in the front and the cadet in the rear cockpit. Both wore helmet, goggles, and a white neck scarf. They communicated through a "Gosport," which was just a rubber tube and required a raised voice to be affective.

With the roar of the engine in his ears and the wind in his face, Jessie discovered on his first flight why Alvin and Hallie loved flying. It was a wonderful revelation for him and dispelled his pre flight fear that he would not do well.

Unlike his struggle in pre-flight, Jessie took to flying from the outset, and it turned out to be an experience far more exciting than he could have imagined. There was still plenty of discipline and rules, but he discovered the unique thrill of escaping the "surly bonds of earth" and being alone in a whole new world of magnificent beauty. There were principles and procedures to follow, but he discovered the technique involved depended to a large degree on the intrinsic skill of the artist, who in this case was the pilot.

In a way, it was like being at his easel. But the artist of this medium honed his skills in a majestic studio in the sky: soaring, diving, and climbing in the limitless blue, with mountains and canyons of clouds that were painted by the master himself in multicolors and a thousand subtle grays that no painter could match.

So cadet Jessie Rascoe excelled in his flying and was the first in his class to solo the PT-17, which gave him the title of "Hot pilot" and the honor of wearing his flight goggles up on the top front of his leather flight helmet. Before solo the cadets wore their goggles around their neck when not flying.

That evening Jessie sat down and wrote letters to his family and friends, one of which was to Hallie Lamont. He'd had a letter from her just before the Japanese attack on Hawaii. She was stationed at a place called Hatfield Air Base in Hertfordshire, England. But Alvin's death and the agony of his first two months in the army had dissuaded his answering.

> Dear Hallie,
> March 3, 1942
> I hope this finds you sometime, someplace, and that you are all right. I'm sorry it took so long to answer your letter.
> Alvin was killed on Dec 7 in Hawaii. He was my friend. He was a brave man, and he died a brave hero.
> I enlisted in the Army Air Corps. I didn't want to, but I had to join. It's the only way I can hope to even the score with those murderers. The only good news I have is that I love the flying. You were right, Hallie. Flying is wonderful. I truly love it.
> In a sense, I almost feel guilty that it's just a means to an end. But I know now that we are facing evil, so it has to be done.
> I struggled with the stuff you have to go through in pre-flight, but I'm doing great now. I'll graduate late this year and hopefully get shipped out soon afterward to the Pacific.
> I'm sorry this isn't a very nice letter, but I want you to know that I'm very proud of you for what you are doing. You're a good person and a brave girl. I think of you often. I hope it all works out that we will see each other again someday.
> Take care of yourself.
> Love, Jessie

Jessie's primary flight class graduated in early May of 1942 and was sent to basic flight school at Gardner Army Air Field at Taft, California. Introduction at Gardner by the Commandant of Cadets went something like this: "Okay, you are now away from the feather merchants (civilians) and back in the army and now you do it the army way because we own you."

In basic training, Jessie flew the BT-13, a low wing all metal trainer that seemed like a giant after the little PT-17. In this trainer, he began to learn more advanced maneuvers and night flying.

As the commandant had promised, it was the army way, and military discipline was strict. The instructors were all officers and tasked to be critical and demanding of the trainees. Several cadets were unable to make the transition and were "washed out."

The airspace was filled with trainers day and night, which, despite ridged precautions, was inherently high risk and collisions and accidents were inevitable. Two cadets in Jessie's class had a mid air collision and were killed. Another cadet apparently became disoriented and crashed during a night solo training flight and was killed.

Jessie again excelled and graduated at the top of his class.

After basic training, each cadet was evaluated for his flying skills and aptitude and assigned to advanced training in either bombers, fighters, transports, or night fighters. Jessie had chosen fighters and because of his superior record was assigned to fly the army's most advanced and fastest fighter, the Lockheed "Lightning" P-38. That training was at Williams Army Airfield, Chandler, Arizona.

Jessie was elated and wrote to Hallie the day he received the assignment:

> August 15, 1942
> Dear Hallie,
> I am in much better spirits since my last letter. I was just told I'm going to fly the P-38 fighter! How about that? I was lucky.
> Some of my classmates who wanted to fly fighters got stuck in bombers. They are unhappy guys.
> As you probably know, the P-38 is the fastest of all fighters. I can hardly wait to fly it.
> How are you doing? And where are you now? I'll be at Williams Field for the next couple of months then some operational training.
> After that I'll be off to the Pacific where I plan to shoot down a bunch of rising suns!

I think about you a lot, Hallie. I hope you are ok. Write me. Address on envelope.

Love,

Jessie

At Williams Field, Jessie flew a twin engine trainer called the T-9. It was specially designed to train pilots to fly the twin engine P-38 fighter.

Jessie's instructor, a Mr. Limi, was an RAF exchange pilot from England. He had flown Spitfire fighters in the Battle of Britain where a few hundred fighter pilots beat off the Nazi Luftwaffe (air force) and saved Britain from Hitler's planned invasion. Mr. Limi told Jessie he was a "natural" and would be a great fighter pilot.

After learning the characteristics and technique of twin engine flying, Jessie was ready to fly the twin engine, twin tailed P-38 the German Luftwaffe called, "The forked tail devil."

There was no dual instruction given in the P-38. It only had one seat, and that was for the pilot. After hours of study and a blindfold cockpit test to confirm that he knew where every instrument and lever was, Jessie was cleared for his first flight.

The flight was even more thrilling than Jessie had imagined.

Instead of the traditional single engine all other fighters had, the P-38 had two powerful engines, and when Jessie pushed the throttles forward for takeoff he was slammed back in his seat by the acceleration. When the fighter lifted off the runway, the climb skyward was breath taking. Jessie was thrilled and knew at that moment that he would use this awesome flying machine to destroy the enemy.

Jessie graduated in early December, 1942, and was given leave for the Christmas holidays. He came home wearing his "pinks and greens" (army olive green blouse and light grey trousers) with the gold bars of a second lieutenant on his shoulders and silver wings on his tunic.

Maria Hunter and Kevin Blake held hands as they stood on the departure platform at the Southern Pacific railway station in Los Angeles. The platform was crowded with young high school and college men, some wearing suits, others in jeans and letter sweaters they had earned in various sports. Families, friends, and girlfriends were quietly embracing; others were laughing and talking nervously as they waited to board the troop train that would take them to an army training camp.

"I wish we could have gotten married before I left," said Kevin looking at Maria lovingly.

"Yes, but you don't want to defy your folks. They are already terribly upset about your joining the army."

"Yeah, I know, and I didn't like upsetting them, but I want to do my part, and with all my best friends joining I'd look like a slacker if I didn't join up."

"I think they understand that, but the additional shock of your wanting to get married was just more than they could deal with right now."

"I guess so," Kevin said, tightening his arm around Maria. "You're so sweet and considerate. I know one thing for sure, I'm really gonna miss you."

"And I'm going to miss you too, Kevin."

Kevin Blake was tall and handsome with dark wavy hair and brown eyes. Off the football field, he was mild mannered and soft spoken and liked by almost everyone, particularly the girls. But Kevin had eyes only for Maria. He looked at her lovingly and said, "Maria, I love you more than anything in the whole world."

Maria tightened her arms, holding him with all her might. "I...I'll be waiting for you, Kevin, for as long as it takes."

"All right you bunch of feather-merchants, let's get this show on the road!" barked a sergeant dressed in army olive drab.

Kevin's parents and Maria's aunt and uncle moved up from where they had discreetly retreated to give the lovers a last moment of privacy. Hurried good-byes had to be said in raised voices to overcome the noise and confusion of the train-boarding process and the hissing steam from the locomotive.

Maria's last glimpse of Kevin through tear-stained eyes, left her feeling a terrible pain that she'd never experienced before, and she knew it was of her own making. As her mother had said to her, "you always pay the penalty for dishonesty." The dishonesty she would pay for was in deceiving Kevin...and herself.

But that was the way it would have to be. She had made her decision, and there was no changing that now. She had known since that day she'd seen Jessie at the barn that she should tell Kevin the truth, but she couldn't bring herself to do it. He was so sweet and so much in love, and it wasn't as though she didn't love Kevin. She did. But as she had discovered, not the way she loved Jessie. Despite the years of absence and her own resolution to accept the fact that she was a different person now, those terrible moments of emotional agony that day she saw him at the old barn had told her differently. They told her what she had always known, deep down: that she loved Jessie like she could never love anyone else, ever. But it would be a lost love. Her mother had also always told her two wrongs don't make a right. She couldn't break her promise to Kevin now. Not now, it was too late. She would pay the penalty for her deception, but she would wait for Kevin, no matter how long it took, and marry him when he came home.

Jessie was happy to be home and see his parents and his brother who peppered him with questions about the Air Corps. Mr. and Mrs. Rascoe were proud of their son and dragged him around the Grapevine and Bakersfield showing him off to their friends and relatives. They were all proud that Jessie was now an officer and a pilot in the United States Army. But privately the Rascoes were like parents all across America whose young sons were going off to war: they understood why they must go, but that knowledge didn't negate the worry over the consequences of war.

Jessie's brother Billy had also joined the Army Air Corps and was waiting for his call to pre-flight. Jack had joined the Naval Air Corps and was home in his all-white naval cadet uniform. Bobbie also got Christmas leave and was dressed in his navy blues and wearing several campaign ribbons on his tunic. He told some exciting stories about his ship, *The Yorktown*, which had fought in the big Battle of the Corral Sea in the South West Pacific. It was the first naval battle in history that was decided by aircraft and not ships, and the ships involved (aircraft carriers) did not even see each other.

Danny had joined the marines, but he was still in training and didn't make it home for Christmas. Frank was assigned to another ship after the *Arizona* was sunk at Pearl Harbor. He was somewhere in the Pacific. Bud's B-17 group had been sent to England and was flying bombing missions over Germany. Penny and Virginia were both working in a war factory in Bakersfield, as were Irene and Patty. Ruth had joined the WAVES. After Alvin was killed, Agnes left the Grapevine and never returned.

Jessie and four of the old gang came to Miss Trembell's Christmas program, three of them looking mighty handsome in their uniforms. Gerald was there too, but he was dressed in civilian clothes. At intermission, Miss Trembell had the boys in uniform and Ruth, the only girl there in uniform, come up to the front of the room and they received a standing ovation.

After the Christmas play was over, the five guys had one token drink of punch, then slipped out, and drove up to the Tavern in Frazier Mountain Park to get a beer. It was Saturday night, and Johnny Lashburn, who drove the high school bus during the week, was the bartender. Johnny knew that a couple of them weren't twenty-one yet, but he served them anyway and said it was on the house.

"By God, if you're old enough to fight a war, you're old enough to drink!" he declared. Then he got a glass of beer for himself, and they all raised their glasses and toasted their hero, Second Lieutenant Alvin Pyeatt.

"You know it sure seems strange to see you boys all drinking beer instead of soda pop like I served you all those years," said Johnny nostalgically.

"To tell the truth, Mr. Lashburn, I still like pop better," said Bobbie. "But in the navy everybody thinks you're a sissy if you don't at least drink beer."

"Well, we're all proud of you boys. I can tell you that."

"It sure is quiet for a Saturday night," said Jessie, glancing around. There were only three other patrons: two older men and a woman, obviously well beyond draft age, drinking beer at the far end of the bar. The dance floor on the opposite side of the room, where Frank's dance band had played on Saturday nights, was dark and deserted. "You don't have dancing anymore, Mr. Lashburn?"

"No, we sure don't, Jessie. Not since the war started. Everybody's either in service or gone to the city to work in the war factories. It's not like it was in the good ole days. This past Halloween I didn't even get to shoot my shotgun." The five boys and Johnny laughed.

It had been a tradition, when all the gang lived on the Grapevine, to go up to Frazier Park on Halloween night and try to let the air out of the tires on the high school bus, which Johnny parked in his front yard. Of course Johnny knew they were coming and would be waiting with his shotgun. He would let them sneak up close, then step out from his hiding place, and blast away. The boys would scatter, and of course he never hit any of them. It was great fun, and they would laugh about it later, claiming that ole Johnny Lashburn couldn't hit the broad side of a barn with the door closed. Their final Halloween act would then be to sneak over to the volunteer fire department and ring the brass fire bell, but then everybody expected that too on Halloween night.

"Mr. Lashburn, I gotta know something," said Jack. "Did you ever actually shoot at us with that shotgun?"

"That's my secret," said Johnny with a smile.

Everybody laughed.

"Well, I sure miss the old days," said Gerald. "And I wish I could be in the service with you guys."

"You're working on army airplane engines, aren't ya, Gerald?" asked Jack.

"Yeah, Mr. Buckner got an army contract, and I overhaul the engines."

"Well then, you're doin' your share, Gerald. You can't help it if they won't let you in the army," assured Billy.

"Yeah, and what you're doing is important, Gerald," added Jessie.

"You like the Air Corps, Jessie?" asked Gerald.

"Well, I don't care for the military stuff, but I know ya gotta have it when you're fighting a war. I love the flying though. I didn't think I would, but I do. It's kind of like painting: the pilot is the artist. Once you leave ole Mother Earth yer up there alone in the wild blue yonder, doin' your thing."

"Well, aren't there other guys in the plane with you, like navigators and gunners and stuff?"

"No. They are in the bombers but not in the one I'm flying."

"Jessie is flying the P-38, "Lightning," said Billy. "That's a pursuit plane, and it's the best. That's the one I want to fly too."

"Is it fast, Jessie?" asked Bobbie.

"It's real fast, and it's got four machine guns and a twenty-millimeter cannon that I'm gonna use to blow a bunch of those damn Japs to hell," said Jessie in a way that caused everyone there to look at him in surprise. They had never heard Jessie Rascoe speak that way before.

Chapter

~37~

In early January 1943, Second Lieutenant Jessie Rascoe reported to an operational training unit at Muroc Army Air Base near Landcaster, California. There, on the western edge of the Great Mojave Desert, he received four week's training in aerial gunnery and combat fighter tactics in the P-38.

As Jessie had all through his cadet training, he excelled again in scoring high marks in his gunnery and tactical training. As the final day of his training approached, the squadron commander called him into his office and asked him to stay on as an instructor.

"We need instructors of your caliber, Lieutenant. We don't have enough of them, and it's affecting the quality of our training," he explained.

"No sir. I don't want to be an instructor," replied Jessie.

"You would be making a major contribution to the war effort, Lieutenant. If the new pilots don't get good tactical training here, they won't do well when they get in combat. This is going to be a long, tough war, and you will get your chance to fly combat. Right now we need you more right here."

"I'm sorry, Captain, but I can't wait. I've got to get into combat right now. I have to go overseas."

The captain's eyes narrowed as he pulled a cigarette from a package on his desk and lit it with a Zippo lighter. "You realize I don't have to get your approval. I can just cut the orders, and you stay whether you like it or not," he said, the smoke bubbling out as he spoke.

"Yes sir, but please don't. I have a score to settle an' I can't do it here as an instructor."

The door to the office swung open, and a staff sergeant stuck his head in. "Excuse me, sir, but you said to advise you when that replacement aircraft arrived."

"Okay, Sergeant," said the captain, getting up from his desk. "I want you to give this some more thought, Rascoe, and we'll talk about it again later."

"Yes, sir," said Jessie, saluted, did an about face, and left the office.

"Where is the new bird, Sergeant?" asked the captain as he walked into the outer office.

"He just pulled up onto the parking ramp, sir."

"Jesus, Mary, and Joseph, would you look at that!" exclaimed one of a group of pilots as Jessie and the captain emerged from the training squadron's operations shack.

All eyes turned and locked on the pilot of the new P-38 who had climbed out of the cockpit, jumped down off the wing, and was walking across the flight ramp towards the Quonset. He looked like any other pilot in a flight suit, carrying his parachute over his shoulder, except when he reached up and pulled off his flying helmet, he had long yellow hair.

For a moment Jessie stood watching, unable to believe what his eyes were reporting to his brain. It couldn't be! She was in England, thousands of miles away. Then he started to walk toward her, slowly at first, still uncertain. When she saw him emerge from the group of gawking pilots, she slowed her gait, as she too, wasn't sure if her eyes were playing tricks. Then she shrieked, "Jessie!" dropped the parachute and bolted, throwing herself into his arms with such force it nearly knocked him down.

"Hallie!" he croaked hoarsely, grabbing her and holding her in a bear hug.

"Oh, Jessie, Jessie!" she whispered in his ear as they clung to each other.

"That guy is not only one of the hottest pilots I've ever seen, he's also the luckiest," said the captain as he and the others watched enviously.

"And that is the best-looking dame I've ever seen," added one of the pilots. "Where the hell did she come from?"

"She came out of that P-38!" exclaimed another pilot.

"She couldn't have! They don't let dames in the Air Corps."

"I'm telling ya, I saw her taxi up and get out of it!"

All the pilots turned to the captain. He shook his head. "She's not in the army. She's in an outfit called WAFS: Women's Auxiliary Ferrying Squadron. They work for Air Transport Command, and they ferry new aircraft from factories to operational units."

"Wow! Ain't that something!"

"I still can't believe it!"

"Yeah, what's this war coming to?"

After some introductions, a lot more gawking, and some official paperwork on the transfer of the P-38, the captain let Jessie borrow his jeep, and he drove Hallie over to a bar and restaurant just off the air base.

"God, it's good to see you!" she said as they got out of the jeep in front of a low, wooden building that had several clumps of desert cactus in front and a hand-painted sign over the front door that read "Rosie's Place."

Jessie walked around, took her hand, and they stood there in front of the restaurant looking at each other.

"It is good, isn't it, Hallie?"

"Yes, I've never been so surprised, or so glad, to see anyone in my whole life," she said in a voice that was almost a whisper. "I came home rather suddenly, so I didn't have a chance to write and I had no idea where you were."

He held her at arm's length and looked at her. "I couldn't believe my eyes when I saw you. And you're just as beautiful as ever Hallie, but there's something different."

"Still good enough to kiss?"

"Yeah," he said hoarsely, pulling her into his arms gently and then tightening his arms around her. They kissed softly at first, and then emotions rose to a feverish pitch.

"Hey, you two! If you're gonna do that, go out in back! I don't want my place to get a bad reputation," barked a heavy-set woman who came out through the front door of the restaurant.

They terminated the kiss, both with quickened breath and racing pulse. "Yeah...okay, Rosie," Jessie managed to rasp.

Rosie was large, with a mop of blond hair and a round, homely face, but the face turned on a warm, friendly smile. "I'm only joshing, kids. Kiss all you want. If you'd like, there is a big hammock out back, and it's private back there," she added looking curiously at Hallie, who wore an Air Corps flight suit but without insignia. "You in the army, girl?"

"No," Hallie replied in a husky voice, her pulse still racing. "I'm, uh, in the WAFS."

"You are?"

Hallie nodded, struggling to collect her emotions.

"Hey, that's great! I heard about you girls, but you're the first one I seen. Did you fly a plane to the air base?"

"Yes."

"What kind?"

"P-38."

"Christ! I always said that we women can do anything that men can...well, not quite everything...fortunately," said Rosie, breaking out in another smile. "I gotta go to town, but I'll be back in a couple hours. I sure would like to talk to you."

"Unfortunately, I have to catch a courier at seventeen hundred at base ops," said Hallie, glancing at Jessie.

"You do?" said Jessie.

"Yes, damn it."

Jessie glanced at his watch. It was almost fifteen hundred. "You really gotta leave?"

She nodded. "Yes. There is a B-25 that's going to fly me back to Long Beach where I got another ferry flight first thing in the morning. Well, we've got two hours, not much to make up for a year and a half, is it?"

"It sure isn't, Hallie. Not the way I feel."

"I know. Isn't that good ole fate for you? Ever since that day at the water trough, we knew our time would come, and it's finally here, and I gotta leave. Damn!"

"You wouldn't happen to have a water trough in the back there, would you, Rosie?" joked Jessie.

"No, but that hammock will hold two," she said, laughing.

"We just may take you up on that."

"Help yourself. But first go in there an' tell John I said the drinks are on the house." Rosie climbed into a faded old Ford truck and drove away.

Rosie's Place looked like her truck: as though it had been sandblasted and baked in the desert too long. But inside the weathered walls, it was homey and looked like a World War I aviation museum of sorts. Pictures of Eddie Rickenbocker, Frank Luke, Billy Mitchell, and other famous fliers and airplanes were hanging on the walls beside broken wooden propellers and other aviation memorabilia.

Two men sitting at the bar wearing cowboy hats and shirts glanced at Jessie and Hallie when they walked in, and then turned back to their beers.

"This is a pretty popular place in the evenings. We come over after flying and drink beer," explained Jessie as he and Hallie took a table off to one side of the bar room.

"I thought you said only peasants drink beer?"

"I'm afraid some things have changed since I told you that Hallie: like a year in the army."

"Well, you're just as mesmerizingly handsome as ever, particularly with those silver wings on your tunic. But I do see a change in you too, Jessie."

"Not for the best, I'm afraid."

"Not many things going on now are for the best. I was real sorry to hear about your friend Alvin."

Jessie's green eyes darkened. "I'm going to even the score for that, Hallie. You can count on it."

"I'm afraid there will be a lot of scores to settle before this thing is over."

He nodded. "I'm sure that's true. Was it pretty bad over in England?"

"So bad it's hard to describe. The terrible bombings are not as frequent as they were there for a while, but it's still awful. The people here squawk about a little rationing, but it's nothing compared to the rationing and conditions over there. Surprisingly though, moral is remarkably high."

"I guess they have been hardened to it."

"Yes. The Brits are resolved not to bow to the Nazis."

"How was the flying?"

She shook her head. "Let me put it this way: I learned a lot about flying in lousy weather. And I found out what it means to be cold and stay cold. But, Jessie, I was right. It was exactly what I needed. Both the living and flying conditions were difficult, and there was no special consideration for Hallie Lamont, the 'good-lookin, American skirt.' But the Brits were great, particularly those wonderful, brave, female pilots I flew with. And who will be my friends forever...the ones who survive."

"Hi, Lieutenant. Can I get you something?" interrupted Rosie's bartender, a thin little man wearing a soiled white apron.

"Yeah, you sure can, John. We're having a hello and good-bye party."

The bartender glanced at Hallie. "You just meet?"

"No, we're lovers who never get to make love. Bring me a margarita," she said. The bartender looked at her curiously.

"I'll have one too," added Jessie.

"Okay, two of John's special margaritas coming up for lovers who don't make love."

"Well, where are you stationed?" Jessie asked.

"I'm assigned to the WAFS detachment in Long Beach, and I ferried the P-38 over here from the Lockheed plant in Burbank. It was my first ferry flight in the Lightning."

"You flew it without a check out?"

"No, they gave me a written exam and a cockpit check."

"You get a piggy back?" (P-38 with the radios removed so a student can squeeze into that space and be taken for an orientation flight.)

"No, they didn't have one available."

Jessie laughed. "I'd love to fly with you, Hallie. I got a feeling you're good."

Hallie smiled. "I am. It just came natural. Oh, I got myself in serious trouble several times over there in that terrible weather. But I managed to survive, although probably because the flying gods were smiling on me."

"No, I'm sure it's more than that. How do like the P-38?"

"Oh, Jessie, I love it. It's by far the most exciting aircraft I've ever flown. How about you?"

"It's the greatest, and it's just what I need to do what I gotta do."

She looked at him anxiously. "You shipping out soon?"

He nodded. "I hope so."

"That frightens me."

"Now you're gonna get a taste of how I felt when you went to England."

She gave him a melancholy look. "Did you really worry about me?"

"Yes, I did, Hallie. I really did."

She reached across the table and squeezed his hand. "If I could, I'd ship out right with you."

"Well, I got to admit I'd like to have you with me, but I wouldn't want you flying combat."

"I know, but I'd like to even some scores too."

"You're doing your part and then some."

She looked at him silently for a moment. "You've gotta come back, Jessie. You've got to."

"I'll come back, Hallie. Fortunately, I've had a year to get over my seething urge for revenge. So I'm not going to be foolish, but I am determined to blow away some of those sons of bitches."

Hallie looked at Jessie with surprise.

Jessie dropped his eyes. "Sorry," he muttered.

"I guess it's just that I don't recall ever hearing you swear."

He glanced at her and grinned. "I guess my Boy Scout days are history."

"No. You're adjusting to reality."

"Yes, that I am."

"You're a good pilot too, aren't you?"

"Yes, I'm good," he replied.

"I'm prejudiced, of course. But I know that you're resourceful and imaginative, and when you put your mind to something, you have a lot of determination. I know you hated to give up your painting, but when you did, you applied those same attributes and emotions to your flying, didn't you?"

He nodded. "Yeah, I guess so. I had, and still have, a difficult time adjusting to the military side of the challenge, but I took to the flying from the first rattle out of the box. In a way, it was a big surprise. I never thought I'd be very good at flying, but you were right, Hallie, like you were about a lot of things."

"And you were right about some things too."

The bartender appeared beside the table. "Here ya go. Two of John's special margaritas, guaranteed to make lovers love."

They both laughed. "Shall we have our margarita's first?" she asked.

"I hate to waste the time, but if you insist."

They picked up the glasses and touched them across the table.

"To you, Hallie. I'm really proud of you."

"Thank you, Jessie. Having you say that is important to me, since you were part of the reason I went in the first place."

"Did you find out what you wanted to know about yourself?"

"Yes, I think so. Oh, there's still some missing pieces, but at least I've got a different perspective on things."

"I knew you would be all right."

"It wasn't easy...none of it, but it was good for me. I can't tell you how many times I almost quit, but I knew if I did, I'd be right back where I started."

"And George?"

She hesitated. "I don't know. I guess you could say that I got him out of my system. I haven't seen him, and I don't intend to. I was surprised to hear that he joined the marines. I can't imagine George Simmons doing something like that. At any rate, right now, I feel pretty good about myself."

"That's great, Hallie."

"Yes, and even though my contribution was small, I helped fight the Nazis. But when the Japs bombed Pearl Harbor, I knew I had to come home. Then I found out they were organizing the WAFS over here in the States, so I wrote to Nancy Love who heads it up. She replied right away that they would like to have me because of my experience in the ATA. I wired back that I was on my way."

"I seem to remember you once told me you stopped trying to help other people because it gets you into a lot of trouble," said Jessie with the hint of a smile.

She looked across the table at him. "And it sure enough got me into trouble...a bunch of times."

They both laughed.

"I told you that you were a better person than you thought, Hallie."

"There is hope, isn't there?"

"Yeah, I'd say so."

"And what about you, Tiger? Are you over her yet?"

Jessie hesitated and looked down at the margarita glass in his hand. Finally he said, "No, I'm not over her. Frankly, I haven't had time in the past year to give it a lot of thought. Air Corps flight training takes every ounce of your energy and thought. But I'm still hung up on Maria, and I can't lie to you about that, Hallie."

"I sensed that. But it's okay. Our time just isn't quite here yet. Oh, you wouldn't have to drag very hard to get me out to that hammock. That desire has smoldered in me ever since the first time we kissed in the Rose Station water trough. But I realize, despite my proclamation, that I, too, need more time. Both of us do. We still have some things to settle and a small matter of a war to fight."

He reached across the table, took her hands in his, and held them tightly. "I want you to know that I've never experienced emotion any more powerful than what I'm feeling at this moment for you, Hallie. But considering what I just told you, it's not right for me to say any more."

"I know, Jessie darling...I know."

Chapter

~38~

The day after Jessie's meeting with Hallie, the training squadron commander told him that he was keeping him as an instructor whether he liked it or not. Jessie was devastated and went back to the tar papered building they called a BOQ and did what he'd always done when he was upset: flopped down on his bed and stared at the ceiling. After a couple hours, he got up and walked the two miles to Rosie's place.

"That's tough, kid," consoled Rosie after he'd told her his problem, while sitting at the bar drinking beer. "But ya know the captain's got a point. You can do a lot of good right here training those other new pilots that aren't as gifted as you. And look at it this way, now you can see that pretty girl you're in love with."

He looked across the bar at the big blond woman. "How do you know I'm in love with her, Rosie?"

"Aw, that's easy. I seen how you looked at her."

"How do you know that wasn't the look of lust?"

"Hey, if there ain't no lust, there ain't no love!"

Jessie laughed and it made him feel better. "Yer a character, Rosie."

"I've had a lot of experience in these matters, and I know there's a difference between lust and love all right, but nothing say's you can't lust for the one you love."

"Well, I don't deny my lust for Hallie all right. But I got another lust to satisfy, and I sure as hell can't do it here in the damn Mojave desert. Give me another beer, would ya?" he said, pushing his empty mug across the bar.

"You got the hots to get over there and be a hero?" she asked, thrusting the beer mug under the spigot and pulling the handle.

"No, I don't care about being a hero. I just want to send some Japs to hell."

"By God, I'll drink to that."

"But I can't do it sittin' here."

Rosie scraped the excess foam from the beer mug and pushed it across the bar to Jessie. "You know any big shots anywhere? Somebody that's important. That's the only way I know you can get the army to do somethin' it don't wanna do."

Jessie shook his head. "No, I'm just a country guy, Rosie."

The next morning when Jessie checked into training operations the sergeant said, "Here are some orders for you, Lieutenant Rascoe. And the captain said he doesn't want to see you. Just get the hell out of here."

Jessie tore open the envelope and read the orders directing him to the Port Of Embarkation at Hamilton Army Air Field in San Rafael, California, for overseas shipment.

"But he said to tell you good hunting."

"Tell the captain I owe him one."

When Jessie arrived at the POE he was given three days leave before embarkation processing began. He called the General Petroleum Oil Company at Rose Station and got a message to his father that he was shipping overseas. Mr. Rascoe had been saving his gas ration coupons so he got a few days off from work, and he Mrs. Rascoe drove to San Francisco to see Jessie. They met and had dinner at Grotto #9 on Fisherman's Wharf where Jessie and Alvin had gone. They just had the one evening together, but it was a grand occasion for both Jessie and his parents, despite the underlying distress of a mother and father whose son was going off to war and might never return.

Mr. and Mrs. Rascoe were like tens of thousands of other parents whose sons were going to war. They were deeply concerned but forced themselves not to expose their feelings. Jessie had also counseled himself to keep his demeanor upbeat. It all worked until departure time, which was unavoidably emotional.

When Jessie checked in for overseas processing at the embarkation center, he was surprised to meet one of his fellow cadets from primary flight school, Donald Benilli, who was also on the same shipment.

"Hey, Jessie! You made it!" said Benilli as the two shook hands warmly.

"Yeah, I managed to squeak through."

"Yeah sure, ole hot pilot Rascoe squeaked through."

"What did you end up flying, Don?"

"The P-38 Lightning! And is it ever a beauty. What did you get?"

"I got the P-38 too!"

"All right! It doesn't surprise me that you would get the hottest fighter in the Army Air Corps!"

"Give me your attention please! Would you all please form a line and move into the processing room," announced an orderly who started the commissioned officers' overseas processing. The process required a full day and consisted of a complete physical examination, a review of records, assignment of pay allotments, completion of last will and testament, and required inoculations depending on area of assignment. Once completed, each officer was issued orders designating the major command to which he was assigned and the APO number (overseas address).

Jessie, Donald, and ten other fighter pilots were assigned to the Fifth Fighter Command, Fifth Air Force, in the South West Pacific Theater of Operations. They were given a priority shipment code, which meant they would be flown to their overseas destination by aircraft instead of by surface vessel.

The Consolidated Vultee B-24 was a four engine bomber the Army Air Corps used extensively in World War II. It was called the "Liberator," and it saw service in all combat theaters. Because it could carry sizable loads over a long range, the Army Air Corps converted some for passenger use to transport priority personnel to the combat zones quickly. Seats were installed for a dozen passengers in the bomb bay, and it was called the LB-30.

The LB-30 was noisy and cold but it would reach Australia in five days instead of the month required by ship and that was fine with Jessie. From Hamilton Army Air Field in San Rafael, California, the B-24 flew to Hickim Army Air Field on Oahu, Hawaii for refueling and overnight crew rest.

Jessie saw remnants of wreckage from the December 7th attack when he and the other pilots offloaded at the airfield. After he and the others were checked into the visiting officers' quarters, Jessie hired a cab to drive him to the military cemetery on Oahu where after a lengthy search, he found the simple grave marker of Second Lieutenant Alvin Pyeatt, U.S. Army Air Corps.

Jessie stood there looking at the vivid green slopes of Diamond Head Mountain, with gently swaying palm trees and sparkling aqua blue water caressing its shore line. It was a beautiful, stirring sight. But Jessie's thoughts were somewhere else: they were on Grapevine Creek and its crusty oaks, whispering willows, and the sound of crows squawking and tree squirrels scampering.

The LB-30 took off and climbed out over Pearl Harbor early the next morning and set a course for Christmas Island, a tiny U.S. Island south of Hawaii. It was rather austere compared to Hawaii. After another overnight and refueling, the next stop was enchanting Pago Pago in the Samoa Islands. During the overnight there, the pilots all had dinner at a local native restaurant, which wasn't quite as it was in the Hollywood movies, but exciting anyway.

The next day's flight took them to the beautiful Fiji Islands where thoughts and discussions focused on dancing native girls in sarongs, sailing ship, and *Mutiny on the Bounty.* They didn't see any dancing girls, but it was exciting just to be at a place they had read about in history books.

The travel adventure ended the next day when the LB-30 landed at the Royal Australian Air Force Base in Brisbane, Australia.

Chapter
~39~

"Welcome to Australia, gentlemen! Would you please sound off as I call your name?" said an American army first lieutenant who greeted Jessie and his fellow fighter pilots when they crawled out of the LB-30 Liberator.

After the lieutenant had called the roll from a clipboard, he pointed to an army truck parked on the concrete ramp and said, "That will take you and your gear to the Allied Transient Officers Quarters where you will be billeted for a while."

"Lieutenant, we have priority orders to report to HQ, Fifth Air Force Fighter Command at the earliest possible date,"

said Jessie as the twelve pilots retrieved their B-4 bags from a pile of luggage tossed out of the LB-30 onto the flight ramp.

"Sure, Lieutenant. Everybody's got a priority these days. The Aussies run the transient camp where you're going and will provide all your logistical needs. One of our officers there will contact you with your shipping orders, When they come. Happy landings!" The lieutenant smiled as he strolled off across the ramp with his clipboard.

"I don't like the sound of that," muttered Jessie.

"Neither do I. It sounds too much like typical army stuff," replied Second Lieutenant Donald Benilli searching for his B-4 bag in the pile.

Benilli was tall with a huge mop of black hair, the same color eyes, and a handsome Italian profile. Being full-blooded Sicilian and raised in New York City, he was also streetwise and glib tongued.

"My Uncle Vincent warned me about the army, and I would'a joined the navy, but I even get seasick on the Stanton Island Ferry," said Benilli, finding his bag and jerking it free.

"I smell hurry up and wait," grumbled Jessie.

"Me too. But look at the bright side- Aussie girls love Yanks," said Benilli bobbing his eye brows.

"How do you know?" asked Jessie.

"That comes right from the horse's mouth."

"Was it an Australian horse?"

"Don't tell me guys from Grapeville don't like girls?"

"It's Grapevine. And I like girls all right, but I been waiting over a year to kill Japs, and I want to get at it."

"Me too. And I got a New York feeling we're gonna get our chance, but since waiting in the army is inevitable, we might as well take advantage of whatever little compensations present themselves. That same horse also told me that you don't have to waste a lot of time with Aussie girls: they either like you or they don't. And they like Americans cause we're big spenders from the east."

"Then they won't like me."

"How come?"

"I'm a little spender from the west."

After the group of pilots and their baggage were crammed into the back of a canvas-covered GI truck, it rumbled out into the Australian countryside over winding roads for nearly an hour. Finally, it stopped at a guard gate that was the entrance to a hastily built tent city. The camp housed arriving military personnel waiting for assignments to the South West Pacific area.

After the American pilots had checked into the Allied Transient Officers Quarters, the Aussie corporal in charge said,

"I say, chaps, there isn't much in the way of entertainment 'ear at the camp, but it's only a forty-five minute ride on the rail to Ipswich. They got a couple of lively pubs there, and sometimes you can get styke and iggs at the Ipswich Cafe."

"What is styke and iggs?" asked one of the pilots.

The corporal looked surprised. "Don't you 'ave styke and iggs in America, sir?"

The pilot shook his head.

"We're replacement pilots with priority orders, Corporal. You know how soon we'll be shipping out?" asked Jessie.

The Corporal, a big fellow wearing the traditional wide-brimmed Australian bush hat, smiled. "Ay haven't the foggiest, Leftenant. Shipping orders are all hush-hush. But it shouldn't be long, what with the bloody Japs about to overrun Port Moresby in New Guinea, and the blighters bombed us up at Darwin, ya know."

The officers' quarters were bare GI tents, canvas cots, and wool blankets. But in February, it was summer down under, and the inside of the tents were like ovens.

Dropping their B-4 bags on the cots, the twelve pilots decided to take the corporal's advice and head for Ipswitch, which was the closest Australian civilization.

The "rail" was a narrow-gage railroad over which a half-dozen wooden cars were pulled by a small, coal-fired locomotive. It stopped in front of the camp on its way down the track to Ipswich. The cost of two schillings seemed reasonable, and other than sooty smoke boiling into the open windows and the hardwood seats, it offered a better view of the countryside than the back of a canvas covered GI truck.

The train station at Ipswich occupied the center of the small town that had one main street between two rows of white washed, clapboard buildings.

"This town looks like something out of a Hemingway novel," observed one of the pilots.

"Looks more like a Monogram western to me," said Benilli as he and Jessie stood with the other pilots on the wooden train platform.

"Well, I don't see any Aussie lassies, so they must all be in that Down Under Pub there across the street," said another of the pilots.

"Yeah, man, let's go see," said another.

"I hear Aussie beer is even better than their girls," said still another.

"No beer could be better than girls," corrected Benilli.

The American pilots fell in behind Benilli and walked across the dusty street and into the Down Under Pub. By this time, it was late afternoon and the pub, one large room with a bar running the full length, was noisy and packed with Aussie and American soldiers and a few civilian men wearing broad-brimmed hats. A hand-painted cardboard sign behind the bar read: "Beer Call 4 to 6 today."

"Hey, pushing and shoving is New York stuff. You wait here," said Benilli to Jessie and shouldered his way through the crowd. He was back with two bottles of beer before any of the other pilots got near the bar.

"I learned how to do that when I was nine years old," said Benilli handing Jessie a beer. They touched bottles and took a long draft.

"Wow! That is good stuff," exclaimed Benilli.

"It's good, but it's warm."

"That's the way the Aussies drink it. Besides, the barkeep says it gets drunk up before they have time to cool it since they only get enough beer to be open two hours a day."

"That's because of the war?"

"I guess so. But let me tell you the really bad news. They don't allow women in the pub."

"Why would they do that?"

Benilli shrugged.

"Hey, Benilli, if Aussie girls are better than this beer, lead me to 'em," laughed one of the pilots.

"I'm forced to drink to that," agreed the Sicilian from New York.

And drink they did. But what the Americans did not realize was that the Australian beer had three times the alcohol as

American beer, and drinking it on empty stomachs added to the effect: the first drinkers were seeing double before the last ones reached the bar.

So the combat pilots to be had a roaring good time on their first night in Australia. They didn't meet any of the alleged pretty Aussie girls, but they mixed with the Aussie men in fine style. Naturally there was a disagreement or two, and one gigantic Aussie sergeant lifted an American soldier off his feet by the shirt collar and held him there while he swung his fists wildly about until he was exhausted. Then, laughing, the sergeant dropped him in a heap on the floor.

A couple of the American pilots got alcohol vertigo and crashed onto the barroom floor. Jessie was reminded of the time with Alvin at Pismo Beach. But he managed to stay on his feet and, for a while, forgot about killing Japs.

They turned the cardboard sign around to the closed position at six sharp and all those still standing sang "O'Riley's Bar."

"Twas a cold winter's evening the guests were all leaving, O'Riley was closing the bar.

When he turned round and said to the lady in red, 'Get out you can't stay where you are.'

She shed a sad tear in her bucket of beer as she thought of the cold night ahead.

When a gentleman dapper stepped out of the crapper and these are the words that he said:

'Her mother never told her, the things a young girl should know, about the ways of Army men and how they come and go.

She lost her youth and beauty and life has dealt her a scar.

So think of your mothers and sisters, boys, and let her sleep under the bar.'"

By this time, the pilots needed food badly, and so did most of the pub's other customers. That translated to a long waiting line at the only place open, the Ipswich Cafe.

Benilli thought of bucking the line, but the gigantic Aussie sergeant let it be known there would be none of that. Those who could stood in line. Those who couldn't lay down on the ground, and when the line moved, their buddies would kick them, and they would crawl forward to maintain their positions.

"Uh, scuse me. How come thish is the only resserand open in this town?" Benilli asked an American soldier who was in line in front of him.

"They got shom other cafes, but they take turns opening on account of food rationing. I jus' hope they got enough fer this bunch."

"If they don't, I'm dead," groaned Jessie.

They didn't. After nearly an hour of waiting in line, the owner of the cafe came out and was apologetic but claimed that he didn't have a scrap of food left in the place.

It was another two hours before the next train took the decimated warriors back to camp. There, some crashed on their cots. Some didn't make it to their cots. Others rummaged through their bags to find remnants of candy bars or anything else that was edible.

All in all, it was an experience that those who were lucky enough to eventually go home would always remember, but the next day was an experience none of them wanted to remember. Their hangovers were horrendous, and of those who made it to the mess hall, only a skinny pilot from Nebraska could stomach the mutton stew.

Later that day they did get some good news, at least it sounded like good news. "You fighter pilots with priority shipment orders are restricted to the base," advised an American captain who showed up at their sweltering tent. "We don't know when your orders will come, but when they do, you have to be ready to go at a moment's notice."

"I think that ground pounder lies," growled one of the pilots contemptuously, referring to the non-flying officer as he walked away.

An Irish pilot by the name of O'Malley won all the cash in the first two days of poker. After that, they played with IOUs and lay on their cots in undershorts and waited. Benilli told Jessie he thought some kind of mutiny was in order. Jessie agreed and was headed out the tent door determined to track down whoever was in charge, when he ran into the ground-pounder captain.

"Okay, you guys with the priority orders, you're shipping out pronto! Get your gear and be ready to go in ten minutes."

"All right. Finally!" How are we goin'?"

"By train," said the captain.

"They got a train that goes-"

"No questions, Lieutenant. These shipments are classified. Just get your gear and get down to the train depot on the double."

"I don't like the sound of that, Kemo Sabe," said Benilli as they stuffed their few belongings into B-4 bags.

"I don't either, Tonto," mumbled Jessie.

They hurried to the train station, then sat on their B-4 bags for another four hours in the blistering sun before the train finally clattered into the station in a flurry of coal smoke and hissing steam. It looked exactly like the train they had taken to Ipswich that first day. A small engine pulling a half dozen cars with open windows and wooden seats, and every seat was taken. Besides the twelve pilots with priority orders the train was crammed with troops, both American and Australian.

For the next two days and nights the train rattled along, swaying and jerking on its narrow-gauge track. Fortunately, the small steam engine had to stop often to take on water, so everyone jumped off for a few minutes to stretch. It also stopped twice a day at a Aussie mobile army kitchen where the troops had their choice of mutton stew or mutton stew.

"What do they make mutton stew out of?" asked Benilli from where he and Jessie stood in line with their GI mess kits at the first mess stop.

"I think it comes from sheep."

"You mean baa baa sheep?"

"Yeah. They got a lot of them in Australia."

"I thought they make wool outta sheep?"

"They do, but when the sheep get too old for wool, they grind 'em up for mutton stew," said one of the other pilots standing in line behind Benilli.

When they finally reached the head of the line and saw the pot of mutton stew swimming in mutton fat, Benilli stepped out of line and said, "I think I'll pass. I still got a couple candy bars in my B-4 bag."

"Me too," agreed Jessie.

Since the troop train offered no sleeping accommodations and all seats were taken, those who could sleep sitting up got cat-naps between jostling water stops at night. Those who couldn't got no sleep. In either case, they were all covered with a layer of coal soot the next morning.

"You look like the lead guy in one of those old minstrel shows," said Benilli.

"And you look like my partner," grinned Jessie, his teeth showing white in a soot-blacked face.

"I hope we get to where we're goin' today."

"I heard an Aussie say we got a long way to go yet, and I'm out of candy bars."

"Me too."

"What do you suppose that is growing out there?" Jessie asked.

"That's sugar cane."

"How do you know that?"

"I asked one of the Aussies."

"Well, there's a shit load of it. We been traveling through it since dawn."

"I got it figured that we're headed north up the coast of Queensland," pronounced Benilli."

"Is the war goin' on up there?"

"I don't think so. The fighting is all over in New Guinea."

"You suppose this train goes to New Guinea?"

"No, the Coral Sea is between Australia and New Guinea."

"Oh."

"They are probably taking us to a seaport up the coast somewhere, and we'll go across on a boat," Jessie speculated.

"A boat? Christ! I hate boats! I get seasick on the Staten Island ferry."

"So you told me. I've never been on a boat."

"You never been on a boat? Grapeville must really be in the boons."

"Grapevine."

"Hey, the Coral Sea. That's where they had that big sea battle, isn't it?"

"Yeah, one of my friends from Grapevine was on the carrier *Yorktown* in that battle. But the way it's going, the war will be over before I ever get in any battles."

"Ya know, if we're on priority orders, I wonder how long it would take to get there on regular orders?"

"No wonder we're not winning the war."

Late that afternoon, the train finally reached its destination, the small, sunbaked town of Townsville on the northwest coast of Queensland. There, the pilots were loaded into a truck and taken to another transient holding area, a weathered, wooden barrack that had shed most of its whitewash. The barrack, a short distance from the town, was just one large room with several rows of iron cots. On one end, there was an open cement shower stall with several adjacent toilets.

"Uh, Sergeant, why are the cot legs immersed in tin cans?" asked one of the pilots, when the Aussie sergeant escorted them into the barrack, which was like walking into a blast furnace.

"Them cans got oil in 'em to keep the fire ants from crawling in yer bed. They will sure enough set you on fire," said the sergeant.

With blackened faces and weary from little sleep, the fighter pilots took showers, ate mutton stew, and fell onto the iron cots with little comment about the stew, the heat, or the fire ants.

It seemed they had just closed their eyes when an Aussie leftenant awakened them and instructed they to pack their B-4 bags and be ready to go in ten minutes.

"Same ole army crap," growled one of the pilots. "Hurry up and wait, hurry up and wait. I'd bet ten bucks as soon as we get packed they'll tell us to go sit on our bag and wait."

The pilot lost his bet as an Aussie truck rolled up to the barrack a few minutes later, loaded the twelve half asleep Americans, and rumbled off into the night with only two tiny beams of light showing from the covered headlights.

After a two hour jostling ride the truck slowed and stopped. "I say, chaps, get yer bags and follow me," instructed a voice that then led them stumbling through the blackness down a dirt trail. "Where the hell are we going?" grumbled someone.

"No talking please," whispered the phantom voice.

After a half hour, the phantom abruptly stopped. It was quiet, but Jessie could hear water lapping nearby and then the muffled sound of an engine going chug, chug, chug. It sounded to Jessie just like one of those old two cycle water pumps the farmers used back home in the Kern County cotton fields.

The sound of the engine got louder and then suddenly stopped.

"Righto, chaps, follow me," instructed the voice who then led them down an embankment and out onto what appeared to be a dock. Sure enough, an open-sided boat appeared out of the blackness, and the voice encouraged them to get aboard.

After some confusion and a touch of profanity, the twelve Americans were aboard the boat. The chug-chug engine started, and the boat moved out.

"I'm in trouble," groaned Benilli.

Jessie smiled in the darkness. "Yeah, probably. Because I wouldn't be surprised if we're going across the Coral Sea in this thing."

"Oh no! It couldn't be. It's a long ways to New Guinea from here! I'll never make it. I get sick on the-"

"Staten Island ferry," cut in someone.

But then the chug-chug engine began to slow as the boat approached something ahead. Jessie could make out a large shape looming through the misting darkness, and as the shape formed, he could see that it was a large three engine flying boat rocking gently in the water.

"What is that?" someone asked.

"Okay, chaps, get your bags and carefully move forward. We will load through the rear hatch of the flying boat."

"Oh, man, I'm glad to see that thing, whatever it is," groaned Benilli.

The pilots boarded the aircraft and were seated on an aluminum bench facing each other on both sides of the hull. A crewman held a flashlight so they could see to fasten seat belts riveted into the bench. In the V- hull below their feet, water covered with a layer of raw gasoline sloshed gently. The smell was overwhelming.

"Hey, that's gasoline!" said one of the Americans.

"Righto. This is an old captured German Dornier DO24, and it's a bit weary. It would be better chaps if you didn't smoke," advised the Aussie crewman.

"Jesus, I guess!" groaned someone.

The crewman then stepped back out of the hull and slammed the bulkhead door. Jessie thought of how they did that in submarine movies when it was about to blow up.

After a while, the engines started, and the DO24 began to move gently at first and then roared across the water for what seemed an eternity before finally lifting off.

The flying boat droned through the night for what seemed like another eternity to the pilots who were entombed in what might as well been a gasoline tank. The noise prohibited any talk, and someone got sick, which added to the aroma.

Finally, the engines slowed and the German flying boat began to descend. After a while it touched down smoothly, gradually came to rest, and the engines stopped. The bulkhead door popped open, and the crewman said, "We're here. You can come on out now for offloading."

One of the Americans fell into the gasoline and vomit in his hurry to get out. They were all scrambling to escape their entombment as they climbed out of the flying boat and into what looked like a whaling boat. The air was heavy and hot even though it was early morning. Jessie could see they had landed in a small bay.

"Where are we?" he asked the Aussie.

"Your at the Isle of Enchantment, ole chap. Port Moresby, New Guinea."

As he looked out across the bay, Jessie could see the hulks of several sunken ships and other wreckage along the shore line.

"This looks like the south side of the tracks to me," said Don Benilli.

"Yeah, I guess," muttered Jessie.

At the time of Jessie's arrival in New Guinea in March of 1943, Port Moresby, on the southeast tip of the island, was the only major foothold apart from Australia, that the Allies held in the South West Pacific. Japanese forces had overrun everything else in that section of the Pacific.

The defending American and Australian forces in the Port Moresby area had fought against heavy enemy ground assault that advanced to within a few miles of the vital seaport. Japanese bombers had attacked at will until late 1942 when the allies finally had adequate air defenses to turn the tide, but the damage to the port from those assaults was evident.

The whale boat wove its way through the ship wreckage and nosed up to a battered dock where a number of walking patients, with crutches and bandages, American and Australian, waited for their turn to ride in the Dornier back to Australia.

As Jessie stepped onto the dock, his eyes met with one of the patients. His face looked like someone had reshaped it with a meat cleaver. His eyes were dark, sunken, and lifeless. A pair of Army Air Corps silver wings hung on his crumpled khaki shirt.

Chapter
~40~

The twelve American fighter pilots were loaded on a truck and taken to Fifth Air Force Headquarters, which was housed in a colonial looking building, surrounded by a grove of palm trees. It was a part of the governmental complex used by the Australians who governed that section of New Guinea at the outbreak of World War II.

The building had originally been painted a colonial white. Now it was a dirty grey and scarred with shrapnel holes and surrounded with narrow trenches in the ground called "fox-holes," for personnel shelter during air raids. Scattered about were several sandbagged anti-aircraft batteries, their black gun muzzles pointed skyward.

Inside the building, khaki-clad administrative personnel scurried between rooms filled with rusted furniture. The pilots were lined up before one of the desks, and a ground pounder captain checked their names off a list and assigned them to various squadrons in the Fifth Fighter Command. They were then herded into a room for an indoctrination briefing by an Australian official who represented the governmental authority.

"Welcome to Port Moresby, chaps," said the ruddy-faced Australian with a handlebar mustache. "Sorry it's a bit sticky, but as you know, it's summer in this part of the world. To be truthful, it's a bit sticky here summer and winter," he said with a smile. "Just a touch of geography on New Guinea as it's not one of those places that's very well known.

"Next to Greenland, it's the world's largest island, about 1500 miles long and as wide as five hundred miles. Rugged mountains as high as sixteen thousand feet run up the center of much of the island. Most of the low lands are covered with bloody awful jungle, swamps, and rain forests. It's estimated that the natives speak over six hundred dialects. No one knows how many natives there are because much of the interior has never been seen by white man. But we do know that some of those sports in the interior are cannibals and headhunters, so you might want to avoid that area.

"Now just a few cautions, lads. The gov'nor would prefer if you didn't fraternize with the local natives. That shouldn't be a problem as they're a bit strange and I doubt you'll find your-selves attracted to the native lassies. To avoid Jap patrols, you might want to stay within the perimeter and watch where you walk at night because there's a bloody lot of poisonous snakes about.

"We recommend you wear long-sleeve shirts and pants at night to keep down mosquito bites as the blighters all carry malaria and dengue fever. And as your flight surgeon will advise, it's important that you take quinine tablets daily. It's bloody awful-tasting stuff, but it beats the alternative. Good luck, chaps."

As they walked out of the briefing room, Benilli said to Jessie, "My doubts about this neighborhood just got confirmed when that Aussie said snakes. I hate snakes."

"You don't have snakes in New York?"

"We've got snakes all right, but they're not the kind he was talking about."

Assigned to the same squadron, the ninth Fighter Squadron of the Forty Ninth Fighter Group, Jessie and Benilli picked up their B-4 bags and were driven in a mud-splattered jeep down a muddy road to an airstrip a few miles east of Port Moresby. It had been bulldozed from the jungle and matted with steel planking called PSP (pierced steel planking). There, they boarded a C-47 "Gooney Bird" transport that was shedding its OD paint and dripping oil from both engines. The cabin was crammed with aircraft engines and crates of aircraft parts.

When the two fighter pilots climbed aboard, a lanky first lieutenant, wearing a crushed service cap, stepped out of the flight compartment and said, "Hey, either one of you ever flown a Gooney?"

The fighter pilots shook their heads.

"Aw, it doesn't matter. All ya do is pull up the landing gear, and my crew chief can do that. But regulations say I gotta have a co-pilot, so if you guys want to get to Dobodura today, I'll need one of you to fill in. My co-pilot just keeled over this morning, and now the doc says he's got malaria."

With Jessie in the co-pilot's seat and Benilli in the radio operator's seat, the lanky pilot took off from Port Moresby and began a climb over the mountain Range that loomed ahead. "It's gonna take a while to climb this ole baby over the mountains, but don't worry. She'll make it," assured the Gooney pilot. "I usually have a couple of P-39 Aircobras escort me when I go to Dobodura, but I guess they didn't have any to spare today. The Japs bomb and strafe over there quite a bit, but there is usually clouds so if we get jumped I'll dive into one."

Jessie and Don Benilli got their first aerial view of the rugged mountains and dense jungles of New Guinea when the C-47 topped out over the Owen Stanley Mountain Range at 13000 ft. The pilot called Horanda control at Dobodura and was advised there was no alert on and he could land at the air strip, which was another of those bulldozed out of the jungle by the army engineers and covered with PSP.

After they had landed and parked the C-47, the pilot said, "Look down the strip there. Ya see that revetment area? That's where the ninth fighter squadron P-38s are parked, and their bivouac area is back in the jungle. I sure envy you lucky guys getting to fly that bird. I give my hat and ass to fly that airplane." Jessie and Benilli thanked the Gooney pilot for the ride and, with B-4 bag in hand, walked down the air strip to the revetment area and then into an enclave of scattered tents back in the jungle. They stopped before a tent with a home made sign that read: Orderly Room. It was a typical army pyramidal tent, but raised off the jungle floor on fifty five-gallon fuel drums under a wooden floor and frame. The canvas sides were rolled up for ventilation. Inside were two rusted metal desks cluttered with papers, and a couple of rusted filing cabinets. The lone occupant was a sergeant wearing soiled khakis, pecking on a GI typewriter.

"This the Ninth Fighter Squadron Orderly Room?" asked Benilli, as he and Jessie entered.

"Yeah," answered the sergeant keeping his eyes on his typing.

"We're supposed to report to the commander," said Jessie.

"He ain't here," muttered the sergeant, frowning at the typewriter. Glancing up, his eyes widened. "Hey, you guys replacement pilots?"

"Yes we are, Sergeant," answered Benilli emphasizing *sergeant.*

The message didn't register. "There's a couple of war-weary pilots sure gonna be happy to see you guys, cause they get to go home now. But us poor enlisted slobs will be in this shit hole until we rot...or the Japs get us."

"That's the way the cookie crumbles," said Benilli sarcastically. "Where can we find the commander?"

"He's down in his tent," said the sergeant turning back to the typewriter.

"Which tent is that?"

"It's the one down next to the lister bag," muttered the sergeant, starting his pecking again.

"What's a lister bag?" asked Benilli when the two pilots were out of the orderly room tent.

"It's a canvas bag that holds drinking water."

"Never had any of those in New York either."

"Weren't you ever in Boy Scouts?"

"Naw, we never did that sissy stuff."

"That sissy stuff taught me some things that I suspect are gonna come in handy in this neighborhood."

They found the tent opposite the lister bag. There were two men inside wearing pilots' wings on crumpled khakis and sitting with their feet propped up on a homemade table.

Jessie knocked on the wooden door frame.

The pilots inside looked at them, and one said, "I hope you guys are who I think you are."

"We're replacement pilots Rascoe and Benilli, reporting as ordered, sir," said Jessie.

"Come on aboard, Rascoe and Benilli," said the captain, who was tall and muscular, with dark hair and a cigar stub in the corner of his mouth. He swung his feet off the table and ignoring the new pilot's salute, adjusted his cigar and said, "I'm Thomas O'Shea, C O of this outfit. We don't bother with saluting here in the combat zone," he added, scrutinizing the newcomers with intense, piercing eyes.

The other pilot, trim and handsome with a Clark Gable mustache, wore the silver bar of a first lieutenant. He shook hands with the two newcomers and said, "I'm Bob Heinricker, the operations officer. Glad to see you fellahs. Benilli? You wouldn't happen to be from New York would you?"

"Yes, sir," replied Benilli.

"You know Richard and Mario Amodeo?"

"No, sir, I don't think so."

"No? Great guys. I was in boot camp with them."

"I'm from New York city," Benilli explained.

"Well, we won't hold it against you. Pull up a couple of those canvas chairs and take a load off. You just get in from the states?"

"Yes, sir, in a roundabout way," said Jessie.

Heinricker smiled. "Ipswich, the choo choo, Townsville, and the flying gas tank, and all on priority orders."

The new pilots smiled.

"Par for the course. But what I want to know is what's goin' on back in the good ole USA?"

Benilli shrugged. "It's goin.' Everything is rationed, gas, meat, sugar. And ya can't get new cars, or new tires, or much of anything else new."

"Never mind that stuff. I want to hear about dames. Is it true there are more women working in the factories now than men?" asked Heinricker, twisting the end of his mustache.

"That's what I hear," agreed Benilli.

"I'll bet those damn four-F's (classification of physically disqualified men) working in factories get to screw a different babe every night," groaned Heinricker.

"Yeah, don't you wish you were a four-F instead of a big war hero?" said O'Shea.

"Uh, do I have to answer that, boss?"

"Lieutenant Heinricker just became the squadron's third ace," O'Shea informed.

"Congratulations, Lieutenant Heinricker. That means you shot down five Japs, right?" said Jessie.

"Yeah, that's the magic number to become a hero. We call them nips or meatballs. They got big red balls on their birds. The sign of the rising sun."

"And thanks to you, there's five less of the son's of bitches," said Jessie in a low voice, almost as though he were talking to himself.

Heinricker looked at Jessie, hesitated, and nodded. "Yeah, we're doing pretty good since we got our P-38s. Captain O'Shea's got five too, and Lieutenant Bong's got nine. He is now the top ace in the fifth Air Force."

"The squadron was flying P-40s up till a couple months ago, and although the Warhawk is a good fighter, the Lightning is better," said Captain O'Shea, pulled out a Zippo lighter and flamed his cigar stub.

"Lets get back to talkin' about dames," said Heinricker, as he dug out a pack of cigarettes and offered it to the newcomers. They both declined. "Haven't seen non-smokers since the last replacements arrived," he said, firing a cigarette also with a blazing Zippo lighter. "I'll give ya two weeks, and you'll be puffing like soot-clogged chimneys."

"Speaking of women. Not that I think you'd be inclined, but the native women are strictly off limits," advised O'Shea.

"Yeah, they told us at headquarters," said Benilli.

"The good news is that you get to go to Sydney for a week every three months, and the Aussie girls love Yanks," consoled Heinricker.

"Well, that's what I keep hearing, but so far I haven't been assaulted by one," complained Benilli.

"Wait till you get to Sydney! Man you get a battle star for every week you survive down there," emphasized Heinricker.

"How much P-38 time you guys got?" asked O'Shea, removing his cigar and tapping the ashes into the cap of a ninety-millimeter anti-aircraft shell on the table.

"I got about a hundred hours, Captain," said Benilli.

"About the same," said Jessie.

A loud thunderclap echoed through the open tent, and seconds later the rain came down in a torrent.

"You get a lot of thunderstorms?" asked Benilli, raising his voice to overcome the noise of the pouring rain.

"Is the Pope Catholic?" shouted Heinricker. "But it'll be over before you can answer that question."

"Where did you get your combat training?" shouted O'Shea.

"Muroc," shouted Jessie.

"San Diego" shouted Benilli.

O'Shea nodded and leaned back in his chair signaling an end to conversation while the rain roared on the canvas tent. After a few minutes, as though from a signal, the rain ceased as quickly as it had began.

O'Shea removed the cigar from his mouth and rolled it in his fingers a moment. "Okay. We're pleased to have you join the Flying Knights Squadron, the top fighter squadron the fifth fighter command. I'll want to give you a thorough briefing tomorrow morning over in operations. Meantime let me show you where you'll be bunking."

The captain led Jessie and Benilli down a path that meandered through the trees where army pyramidal tents were all raised on fifty-five gallon fuel drums to discourage unwelcome visitors. They had a coat of jungle mold that added another layer of green to the army olive drab.

O'Shea took the newcomers into one of the moldy tents where a lone figure sat on a GI cot in one corner. The floor was rough cut wood with folding cots in each of the four tent corners. Mosquito nets hung from wooden frames over the cots. There were foot lockers at the foot of each space and a rusted steel locker at the opposite end. Items of personal equipment and clothing hung from the wooden tent frames and the tent poles.

The lone occupant was tall and thin with shaggy brown hair and eyes. He wore only a pair of GI OD boxer shorts. His mosquito net had been folded up on top of the rack to allow a place to sit on the cot. The cigarette in his mouth giggled as he rubbed a Colt 45 pistol with an oil-soaked cloth.

"I got a couple new tent mates for ya, Rascoe and Benilli," said O'Shea, adding: "Ralph Wander."

Wander laid the 45 down on his cot, got to his feet, and shook hands with the two new pilots. "Welcome aboard, Rascoe and Benilli. Those two cots with no junk on 'em are now unoccupied so help yourself." Wander then sat down and continued wiping the colt.

"Okay. Ralph is a flight leader and has three nips to his credit, so whatever he tells you is good stuff. Your other tent mate is Lieutenant Larry Carbon He's on the flight schedule today and will be back later. I want you to come over to the operations tent tomorrow morning for the briefing. Meanwhile, Ralph will show you where things are around camp," O'Shea said, nodded, and walked out of the tent.

"Go ahead and put your stuff in the lockers. Everything has been cleaned out and the stuff divided up, except those Aussie flying boots, and you guys can flip a coin for those. They are brand new. George never had a chance to wear them," said Wander, pulling a fresh cigarette out of a package on his bed and lighting it from the butt of the one he was smoking.

"Uh, did George leave?" Benilli asked.

"Yeah, he and Austin. That's why we got two empty cots."

"Where did they go?"

"They got shot down yesterday."

"Shot down...and killed?"

Wander picked up his shoulder holster from the bed, rammed the 45 into it, and fastened the safety strap. "Yeah."

A momentary silence in the moldy tent in the New Guinea jungle.

"Look, it takes a while to understand how it works here, but you'll get the hang of it after a while." Wander hesitated, took a deep pull on his cigarette, and let the smoke tumble out in little puffs as he talked. "When a squadron mate goes down in flames it rips yer guts. But we drink a toast to him, divide up the spoils, and go on with the business of shooting down nips."

Chapter
~41~

R alph Wander's explanation of how the pilots react to the death of one of their squadron mates brought a sudden and shocking awareness of the reality of aerial warfare to Jessie. He understood it was their way of dealing with the emotional challenge, but it affected him with an emotional challenge he'd not anticipated. Yes, he'd come there to kill Japs, or nips, or whatever the hell they call them. And all he wanted was to get to it but...He glanced down at the flying boots. They were a beautiful tan color and glistening with polish- they had never been worn. They were the spoils.

"Let me get some clothes on, and I'll take you over to the quartermaster, and you can get an air mattress and a cover. You can use the mattress cover as a sheet until you can get some real sheets. I wrote home and had my mother send me a couple. There's no laundry facilities here, so ya gotta wash them in the river, but it's worth the effort because those wool GI blankets are hot and scratchy."

"No laundry?" Benilli muttered.

Wander shook his head. "All we wear here is khakis, so when they get so filthy ya can't stand them any more, ya throw 'em away and go get new ones from the quartermaster. They charge ya a buck quarter for a set, but who cares since they run a tab and ya don't have to pay until the war's over, if it ever is."

The two new war pilots followed the war pilot down the New Guinea jungle trail in numbed silence. At the quartermaster tent, they were each issued an air mattress and cover, two GI blankets, a flashlight, and two bug bombs.

"You need the flashlight to go to the privy after dark. It's just down the trail a way. Watch out for snakes and spiders. When you get in your sack at night, be sure and tuck in the mosquito net all around and then spray inside with the bug bomb," said Wander, glancing at his wrist watch. "Okay, let's go see if they got anything you can stomach for supper."

The officers' mess was a larger moldy tent within a wooden frame that was screened to keep out mosquitos and other winged intruders. A number of pilots dressed in soiled khaki's, were seated at wooden picnic-style tables eating and talking. Wander led his two followers to an empty table where an enlisted server brought them metal trays of food.

Wander groaned. "Bully Beef and dehydrated potatoes again. Just dump lots of catsup on it," he muttered as he scooped spoons of catsup from a large tin can on the table. "It's the only way you can eat it, and we got lots of, is canned catsup."

"What is Bully Beef?" asked Jessie.

"Probably ground up Aussie sheep," replied Wander.

"Any where around here I can buy candy bars?" asked Benilli.

"No. There's a candy bar in some of the K rations, but it's worse than the Bully Beef."

"What is that bowl of pills for," asked Jessie pointing to a bowl of white pills that was on all the mess tables.

"That's quinine, and it's God awful stuff, so take it with catsup too," advised Wander.

"You gotta take that stuff?" asked Benilli.

"Your supposed to take one a day. Nobody keeps track, but you better take it because if moderates the affects of malaria or Dinghy fever if you catch it. Otherwise. you're in serious trouble."

A husky, dark-haired pilot wearing sweat-stained khakis with a 45 pistol holster strapped under the left shoulder walked up and sat down at the table.

"Meet the other member of our little jungle home, Larry Carbon," said Wander. The new pilots shook hands with Carbon and exchanged hellos.

The mess server dropped a tray of the bully beef on the table in front of Carbon. He shook his head and said, "Pass me the can of catsup. I swear, this stuff is worse than the horse meat they used to serve back on the reservation."

"Larry claims to be one half Black Foot Indian," explained Wander.

Carbon smiled. "That's true fellows, but the reservation I'm talking about was college. The food there was almost as bad as it is here."

"We must have gone to the same college," said Benilli. "I survived on candy bars."

"Well, I guess ya can't have everything. I gripe about the lousy food, the mold, and stuff, but man, I get to do my fighting up there," said Carbon, jabbing his index finger upward. "It's hard to imagine what it must be like for those poor infantry guys out there fighting in the mud, bugs, and snakes."

"Jesus, don't even mention snakes," groaned Benilli.

"How did it go today, Larry?" asked Wander.

Carbon nodded as he chewed a mouthful of Bully Beef. "We escorted a formation of B-25s that hit shore installations along the north coast west of Buna Bay. The weather was good, and they plastered the target. The Japs put up some pretty heavy flak, but no bogies showed so everybody came home."

"That's good to hear for a change," muttered Wander.

"What's a bogie?" asked Benilli.

"That's what we call a meat ball flying machine."

After they had eaten as much of the Bully Beef as could be tolerated, Carbon said, "One thing I can't complain about is our shower. It works, and there's plenty of hot water, so that's where I'm headed. See ya later, guys."

Carbon left, and Wander said, "Let's go on over to the club. After dinner most everybody goes there so you'll get a chance to meet most of the squadron."

The Flying Knights Officers' club was also wedged into the jungle. It was wood framed with screened open sides. The floor was a concrete slab and the sides and roof, rough-cut wood. There were several home-made wooden tables and GI folding chairs. The tables were covered with GI blankets where the pilots could write letters, play cards, or just sit and talk. The ceiling was draped with parachutes that gave it a festive look. The insignia of the Flying Knights was painted on the front of a bar that filled one corner of the room. On the back side of the bar was a rack filled with silver cups, each engraved with a pilot's name and varying numbers of stars. Each star represented survival of an R and R in Sydney, Australia.

Wander led the new pilots around the club introducing them, and then they sat down at a table with several pilots including the top scoring ace in the Fifth Air Force, Lieutenant Dick Bong. After introductions, Benelli asked Bong what he thought was the key to his success. Bong, cherub faced, with a pug nose and tousled blond hair, shrugged his shoulders and said, "All ya have to do is get your gun site on 'em and push the shooter button."

There were immediate guffaws from the other pilots at the table. Bong grinned.

Benilli smiled. "It sounds good to me."

"Never mind that stuff. Tell us what's going on back in the good ole USA," said one of the pilots.

Jessie strived to focus on the questions and discussions, but the earlier shock of the two pilots that were killed kept popping back into his thoughts. Finally, he asked, "Can I get a drink at the bar?"

"No, it's closed because we're out of booze," replied one of the pilots. "But our Fat Cat is goin' down to Australia in a couple days."

"Fat Cat?" questioned Benilli.

"That's what we call our B-26 Marauder. It got all shot up on a mission and crash-landed on our strip one day, and they just pushed it off into the jungle. So our mechanics fixed it up, and we use it to fly to Australia when we need booze. It brings back a plane load, and sometimes it brings some real meat and real potatoes. And even sometimes some real fruit and vegetables."

Jessie slept little his first night in the New Guinea jungle. The primitive conditions didn't particularly disturb him, nor did the jungle noises that, although different from those in Bear Trap Canyon, were just night sounds that he'd heard many times on overnight camp outs. What kept Jessie awake and tossing through most of the night was a lingering concern about his reality-shock over the death of the two pilots and the almost casual way it was treated. But then what had he expected? It was the reality of war...wasn't it?

The next morning when Captain O'Shea met with Jessie and Benilli he began with a tactical briefing: "We've had a rough row to hoe trying to stop the Japs' advances here in this section of the South West Pacific. They came within a hair of pushing us out of New Guinea, but the tide has turned a bit now. We held at Port Moresby, and now we just blasted a major Jap resupply attempt. Fifth Air Force aircraft sunk fourteen supply ships, eight war ships, shot down over fifty aircraft, and killed over 3500 troops in the Battle of the Bismarck Sea. And the Flying Knights, being the first squadron to be sent to this advanced base at Dododura, played a major role in that great victory. General Kenny is expecting us to keep on performing with these new P-38s, and so far we have done that. Living conditions here are primitive, but the engineers did built us a damn good air strip. We still get regular air attacks so we run two schedules. We keep one flight on alert during daylight, and the rest of the squadron alternates on a mission flight schedule. The alert flight gets scrambled when Horanda control calls that they have picked up incoming unidentified on radar."

O'Shea paused, flipped his Zippo to life, and fired his cigar. After a moment, he continued: "Lieutenant Heinricker prepares the daily mission schedule and assigns pilots and the number of flights that will fly the next mission. That ranges from one to four flights depending on the type mission that fighter command lays on us. It's a challenge because the nips will attack in waves of bombers and fighters, and we are often outnumbered badly." Pause. "Any questions?"

"Yes, sir. When will we be on the schedule?" asked Jessie.

"I want you both to spend a few days getting acclimated. Get all your personal equipment, parachute, may west, forty-five, survival kit, and then get a few hours of non combat flying here in the local area. Then I'll have Heinricker put you on the regular schedule. Anything else?"

There wasn't.

"Okay. By the way, new officers get the job of censoring all the enlisted mail, till the next new officers come, then you're off the hook. Don't butcher their letters too badly."

Lt. Alvin Pyeatt, USAAF

**The above is a watercolor by the author, and
can be seen in color at his website, richardckirkland.com**

Lt. Jessie Rasco training to fly a P-38 fighter plane

**The "Flying Kinghts", fighter squadron in New Guinea.
Captain Richard Bong, WWII top ace, directly under the nose.
Lt. Jessie Rascoe, top left wing, second from end.**

Chapter
~42~

The day after Captain O'Shea's briefing, the new pilots were scheduled for local orientation flights. When Jessie strapped himself into the P-38, completed the starting procedure, and heard the deep roar of the high-powered Allison engines, a twinge of confidence zipped through him- confidence that had waned since that first day when the reality of war had hit him like a kick from an ole steer. He sat in the tiny cockpit listening to the sound and savoring the feeling as he watched the various needles and indicators come to life.

It was good to be back in the cockpit of the Lightning. Despite his rationale that flying was just a tool to effect his revenge, he had developed a personal relationship with this beautiful aircraft. When he took off, hurtling down the runway and up into the sky, confidence surged, and he laughed aloud.

He kept the fighter in a steep climb that propelled it high into the New Guinea sky where he skimmed past a billowing cumulus cloud, rolled over and dove back through it, then out the opposite side, and through another, rolling out on top into the blue sky. And after wheeling, soaring, and diving through the clouds and the New Guinea sky for some time, he landed at Horando air strip, and a rejuvenated Jessie Rascoe crawled out of the Lockheed Fighter.

Three days later Jessie and Benilli were on the combat mission schedule. The sixteen pilots scheduled to fly the mission gathered in the ops tent for a pre-mission briefing.

"Okay, we're gonna escort a couple squadrons of B-25s on a low-level bombing mission to Lae," said Captain O'Shea. They will attack on the deck and drop delayed-fused bombs. Intelligence says there is a moderate possibility we will be intercepted by nip fighters. I'll lead red flight and take blue flight with me for low cover. Lt. Heinricker will lead green and take yellow flight with him for top cover. If they have patrols up, they will probably be at altitude and will try to come down on the bombers, so everybody keep a sharp eye. Rendezvous will be over Buna Bay at 0930."

"Bob, I want you at angels twenty over the target so you can bring your flights down once we spot 'em. We'll maintain strict radio silence until we hit the target or spot a bogie. Any questions? Okay, let's go get 'em."

As the pilots filed out of the briefing tent, Captain O'Shea pulled Jessie and Benilli off to the side. Removing his cigar, he said, "I suspect you're both anxious to mix it up with the nips. But this is your first combat mission, so you want to remember the briefings you got on aerial combat tactics. You're flying wing today, and as new pilots, you'll fly wing until you get some combat experience. Your job as a wingman is to protect the element leader. He will pick the target and attack. You make sure he doesn't get blindsided. And whatever you do, *don't* take off on your own to play hero. You understand?"

"Yes, sir," said both new pilots.

O'Shea studied them for a moment, then crammed the cigar back into the corner of his mouth, and said, "Okay, both your element leaders are experienced combat pilots, so they know what it's all about. You just stay with them and don't forget to keep your head on a swivel: look, look, look in all directions. It's the one you don't see that will get ya. Good luck."

When the pilots had strapped themselves into the cockpit and started their engines, O'Shea edged his P-38 out of the parking area and started it rolling down the taxiway toward the takeoff end of the runway. As he taxied past the other parked aircraft, each P-38 pulled out in its assigned order.

"Horando tower, this is Captive lead with sixteen chicks for takeoff, over," O'Shea transmitted as he reached the takeoff position on the runway.

"Roger, Captive, you're cleared into position for takeoff. You goin' in pairs?" asked the control tower operator from his crude perch atop four palm trees lashed together off to one side of the runway.

"Roger, takeoff in pairs," replied O'Shea, swinging his fighter onto the runway followed by his wing man.

"Roger, Captive. Good luck and you're clear to go."

"Captive on the roll," replied O'Shea, advancing the twin throttles on the two powerful engines. A few seconds later O'Shea's element of two ships pulled into position, advanced throttles, and roared off down the jungle runway behind their leader, followed by pairs of the remaining fighters in turn until all sixteen were airborne.

After takeoff, the squadron leader throttled back and made a slow, wide circle around the airfield to allow the other fighters to join the formation, which became four flights of four. Each flight with a leader with a wingman, and his element leader with a wingman.

As soon as the formation was formed, O'Shea began his climb to altitude and turned toward the rendezvous point where his fighters would catch up with the slower flying bombers. After twenty minutes of flying, he spotted the formation of B-25 "Billy Mitchell" twin-engine bombers. They were flying at ten thousand feet now but would go down to low altitude as they neared the target to drop the delayed fuse bombs they carried.

As the fighters closed in over the bombers, two of Captive's four-ship flights, yellow and green, broke away and began to climb to their assigned "top cover" position. The combat strategy was to insure that high-flying enemy aircraft couldn't surprise the formation by diving on it from above.

During the en route flight, the fighters flew weaving-S patterns above the slower flying B-25s. In this way, they could maintain vigil over the formation while keeping up speed to respond to attacking enemy aircraft.

When the formation neared the target area, Lieutenant Woodson, Jessie's element leader, flying a few yards ahead and off Jessie's left wing, glanced across and gave a hand signal that meant to arm guns and give them a short test firing. Jessie acknowledged the signal, flipped the arming switches, and squeezed the firing buttons. The rattle of his four fifty-caliber machine guns and the dull thump of the twenty-millimeter cannon, spurred an excitement in Jessie. Finally, he would meet his enemy. In a few minutes, he would have his chance to find out just how good a war pilot Jessie Rascoe was.

Jessie had known since they were boys together that he wasn't as brave as Alvin. Nobody was. But Jessie knew that he was skilled enough in his flying to do what he'd vowed to do.

"Bogies! Two o'clock high!" The words shot through Jessie's earphones like an explosion. He glanced off his right wing and saw them coming: a formation of several aircraft swooping down on the bombers at high speed.

"Let's go, Captive, red and blue!" snapped the squadron leader, and Jessie's blue flight went into an immediate right bank for an intercept as the distance between the enemy formation and the P-38s closed rapidly.

Jessie knew from aircraft-recognition classes that they were Mitsubishi Zeros: they had low wings, sleek aerodynamic lines, black engine cowling and bird-cage canopy. A flash of intense color drew his eyes to the fiery red ball on the Zeros' fuselage and wings: the insignia of the rising sun: the meatball! For an instant he stared hypnotically with the strange feeling that it was all happening in slow motion.

The spell was shattered by a stream of fire balls that arched across his canopy as the opposing formations closed.

In seconds, the formations merged into a melee of turning, twisting aircraft with deadly machine-gun fire spewing in all directions across the horizon, while pitched voices filled the radio waves:

"Red two! Red two! One o'clock!"

"Blue three, take the one on the left!"

"Watch out, Bill! There's one on your tail!"

"Son of a bitch! I'm hit!"

"Captive, yellow and green, from red leader, get down here! We're up to our ass in alligators!"

"Roger, red lead, we're on our way," replied Heinricker.

"Watch out, they're goin' after the bombers!"

"I got 'em! I got one! See 'em burning?"

"Blue four, yer left engine is trailing smoke!"

Jessie stuck with his element leader like glue through a series of aerial maneuvers as Woodson banked and turned in an attempt to gain firing position on an enemy aircraft in the giant aerial dogfight. But the nimble Zeros were like a pack of elusive foxes, darting here and there, taking snap shots, then zipping into evasive maneuvers.

When a stream of fireballs filled the sky in front of him, Jessie glanced out and saw two Zeros diving from his three o'clock high position with their guns blazing. "Blue three! Blue three! Two bogies at two o'clock!" he shouted at his element leader through his throat mike.

He glanced across at Woodson, anticipating a right bank into the attacking enemy, but surprisingly, Woodson rolled the fighter into a left bank as though he'd not heard the transmission. Jessie shouted again, "Blue three! Blue three! Two o'clock! Bogies at two o'clock!"

Jessie saw Woodson glance back, but the attacking Zeros, diving from above with superior speed, were now in point-blank range and sending a hail of machine-gun fire into the American fighters.

"Blue four! Get 'em off! Get 'em off!" screamed Woodson over the radio as the Zeros poured a fusillade of machine-gun fire into his Lightning sending pieces of metal spewing and a burst of smoke and fire belching from Woodson's aircraft.

Jessie could hear the sound of explosive rounds striking his aircraft. Then a flash of fire and a terrible pain in his head as an explosion shattered the front canopy and showered the cockpit with pieces of plexiglass and shredded metal. He slammed the yoke over, rolling the aircraft into an inverted position and a vertical dive. A blast of air tore at his face through the shattered canopy, and the severity of the maneuver brought a black curtain down over Jessie's eyes from the high G-forces.

As the aircraft plummeted, all Jessie could see was spinning lights in a sea of blackness. The shrill scream inside his skull was so intense and painful it was impossible to think. His senses told him there was something he had to do. What was it?

"Pull out, blue four! Pull out!" came the voice from afar. Jessie heard, but what did it mean?

"Pull out, Jessie! Pull out!" the voice came again.

Comprehension pierced his brain, and Jessie pulled back on the yoke with such force that he was again hurled into a sea of blackness.

When the blackout lifted and his vision cleared, Jessie could see the jungle flashing by a few feet below. His aching brain told him he had pulled out of the dive with only inches to spare.

Jessie pulled his flying goggles down over his eyes as protection against the terrible wind force coming through the shattered canopy. The fighter was skimming along just above the trees, trailing smoke from the left engine. No sound in his earphones meant that his radio was dead.

Jessie knew the P-38 was badly damaged. Most of the instruments were inoperative, and it required brute force on the controls to maintain level flight. He could smell raw fuel and acrid smoke, and the coolant temperature gauge on the left engine was pegged in the red. In a daze, he cut the mixture control on that engine and hit the feathering switch. In seconds, the three-blade prop came to a stop and the smoke thinned. Now he could see that the cockpit was spattered with a red liquid. It seemed almost inconsequential that it was his own blood.

A shadow passed across the cockpit, and Jessie was certain it was one of the attacking Zeros come to polish him off. But when he glanced up, he saw the twin tails of another P-38 flying just off his left wing. It was a welcome sight. He caught a glimpse of the pilot signaling for him to follow, and he recognized Don Benilli. He acknowledged with a nod, which sent another jab of pain through his throbbing skull.

Donald Benilli had seen Jessie's aircraft diving toward the jungle with smoke pouring from one of the engines, so he had pulled away from his element leader and followed Jessie knowing that he was in serious trouble. After trying to contact him, he realized Jessie's radios were inoperative and signaled him to follow, and then headed back toward Dobodura.

It was an ordeal for Jessie to keep the severely damaged P-38 flying as he followed Benilli toward Dobodura. He could feel himself growing weaker by the minute as blood poured from his head wound, splattering everywhere from the force of the wind. Even the control yoke was slippery in his hands.

Swarms of black specks began to cloud his vision, and Jessie knew that he must summon all the determination he possessed or suffer the ultimate humiliation of being shot down and killed on his first combat mission.

After nearly an hour of flying, Benilli began calling Horanda tower. When he finally got a response, he advised that he was escorting a badly damaged Captive fighter to the air strip.

"Roger, Captive. Do you have radio contact with your chick?"

"Negative, Horanda. His radio is dead, and he's pretty bad shot up. He may have to land gear up."

"Roger. Captive, try to get him to land on the far side, so if he blows up, it won't close our main runway because we got returning combat aircraft shortly."

"Horanda, I got no way of directing him, and his canopy is shot away, and he's struggling to keep in the air."

Through the haze before his eyes, Jessie caught a glimpse of Benilli signaling him, and he knew he was trying to tell him something, but it didn't register. And it didn't matter anyway because he could go no farther, his strength was gone. Bail out, Jessie, a voice told him. Bail out... He glanced at the canopy release lever. Did he have the strength to pull it? Wait... Altitude? Did he have enough altitude to bail out? He forced his heavy eyes up and looked out over the nose of the fighter. What? The air strip? Was it? Yes! It was dead ahead! Could he make it? Jessie shook his head violently, and blood splattered and his head spun. You can make it Bear Patrol leader...You can make it!

It seemed incidental to Jessie's numbed senses that the landing gear would not extend. That meant a crash landing and the bird was saturated with leaking fuel. Like playing Russian roulette...stay off the PSP...put her in the mud...yeah. Land in the mud.

"Looks likes he's gonna make it," said the Horanda tower operator to his sergeant as he spotted the P-38 diving over the trees and heading for the landing strip.

"Yeah, I see 'em," replied the sergeant, punching the crash rescue alarm switch that would activate the fire truck and emergency rescue team. "Nothing we can do but have the fire fighters put out the fire as soon as possible and scrape him off the runway before the other aircraft get here."

"Here he comes, but hey, it looks like he's gonna try to land in the mud beside the PSP."

"By God he is. I hope he makes it."

The tower operators watched as the aircraft swept over the trees at the far end of the runway, leveled momentarily, and then struck the New Guinea ground off one side of the runway. The propeller stopped abruptly, its blades twisted like a pretzel as the plane leaped back into the air for a second, then slammed down again, and began a ripping, grinding slide, with broken pieces spewing in all directions. Finally the battered fighter ground to stop with a piece of torn aluminum flashing in the sun as it hurtled on down the airfield.

The tower operators watched intently. Then the sergeant blurted, "Ah shit!" as an explosion sent a giant fire-ball mushrooming into the sky.

Chapter
~43~

When his aircraft slammed down and began its death skid, Jessie's numbed senses had focused on one objective: get out of the aircraft the instant it stopped. When all the grinding and screaming of tortured metal finally ceased, he used his last drop of adrenaline to pull himself free of the mutilated cockpit and leap out onto the ground. Then he ran, stumbling, falling, running again, until he felt the blast of heat from the explosion.

Jessie sat with his back against a palm tree a short distance away, blood streaming down his face, and watched the beautiful P-38 being reduced to globs of molten metal by the burning high-octane fuel. The fire truck arrived and began to spray the fire with white foam, which seemed to have little effect on the burning aircraft.

When the rescue medics arrived a moment later and saw the blood-splattered pilot leaning against a nearby tree, the attempted to put him on a stretcher.

"I'm all right," he muttered, waving them off.

"You got a pretty bad gash on your head that's going to require attention, Lieutenant," said one of the medics.

Jessie shook his head and struggled to his feet. "I...I don't need any help...I...I..." He hesitated and then fell flat on his face.

The medics scooped him up, put him into the GI ambulance, and drove off across the landing field to the medical aid station.

The aid station was like all U.S. Army facilities in the New Guinea jungle: a GI tent that had turned from olive drab to a moldy green color. The medics carried Jessie in and laid him on a portable medical table where the army doctor on duty sewed up the gash on his forehead with a dozen or so stitches.

"You're not gonna be quite so handsome with the scar you're gonna have, but your mama will still love you," said the doctor as he pulled the last stitch tight and snipped off the end of the suture with his scissors. "You hurt anywhere else?"

The fog had cleared enough for Jessie to comprehend, but he was having trouble bringing the doctor's image into focus. It occurred to him that it was like the time Hallie's boyfriend George Simmons laid a haymaker on him. "I don't think so, but everything looks a little fuzzy," he replied, as he attempted to sit up.

The doctor put his hand on Jessie's chest and pushed him back down. "Hold on there, ace. As much as I know you want to get back to all that fun you were having, you got a concussion, and you're also a little low on red stuff. Head wounds bleed profusely, so if we got any of your type blood around here, I'll give you a refill." The doctor reached for Jessie's dog tags around his neck and read the imprinted blood type. "Yeah, I think we got some of that."

After his blood transfusion, they carried Jessie in the ambulance to an army medical holding station where the casualties were kept temporary. Serious cases were then air evacuated to the field hospital in Port Moresby. Jessie was diagnosed as less serious and kept there. He slept for two days, during which he relived the disastrous experience of his first combat mission over and over in tortured dreams.

It was the morning of his third day before he could open his eyes and see things clearly again, and the first thing he saw was the face of Don Benilli. "Hey, Jessie, how long you gonna goof off in this luxurious resort?"

Jessie sat up on the cot and stared at him for a moment. "Jesus, Don, am I ever glad to see you. And you're in focus."

"I got in focus just for you."

"Those are the magic words, Lieutenant," said the army doctor standing beside Benilli. "If you're in focus, you're out of here. Hold still and look straight ahead." He shined a small flashlight in Jessie's eyes. After a moment, he snapped the flashlight off, stuck it in his shirt pocket, and said, "No trip to beautiful Port Moresby for you. Give those stitches a few more days, then have a medic pull them out and you'll be as good as new."

A while later, as Benilli drove Jessie back to the squadron, he glanced across the jeep and said, "Look at it this way, Jessie, you won't have to take off your pants to show people your battle scar."

"I don't mind the scar, but I'm sure glad to get out of there. That concussion stuff is scary," said Jessie holding on to the bouncing jeep.

"Well, I'll tell ya, I about had heart failure when I saw your bird explode. It didn't look like you had time to get out."

"I almost didn't. I figured she was gonna blow when I belly landed, but I didn't have any choice. The controls were shot up so bad I barely had control, and when I decided to bail out, I was too low. You saved my ole bacon, Don. I couldn't have made it if you hadn't...Thanks, friend...I owe you."

"No, you don't, Jessie. You would have done the same for me."

"Yeah, that's true," said Jessie, as the jeep fish-tailed down the muddy jungle road.

"I didn't fire a damn shot," muttered Jessie.

"Well, I fired, but I was so busy trying to keep those bastards off my tail I don't think I hit anything."

"Don, did Woodson make it back okay?"

Benilli hesitated. "No, he bought the farm, Jessie. He was on fire when he crashed into the jungle."

Jessie sat staring out through the windshield of the jeep for several moments without speaking. "I...I never saw him again after I got hit."

"Two others, one in green and one in blue flight, got hit pretty bad too, but everybody made it home except Steve Woodson. Captain O'Shea got a confirmed kill, Bob Heinricker got one, and Dick Bong got two and a probable."

Jessie nodded. "You see him go down?"

"What?"

"You see Woodson go down?"

"No, but Carbon did and he said there was no chute"

Benilli turned the jeep off the main road and into the entrance of the Ninth Fighter Squadron Bivouac area.

"I don't understand why he did it."

"What did he do?"

"Uh...nothing...nothing."

As Benilli pulled up and stopped in the jeep parking area, he said to Jessie, "Captain O'Shea wants to see you over in his tent."

"Yeah, I figured he would."

"It wasn't your fault, Jessie."

Jessie turned and looked at his friend. "No, it wasn't, Don, but I'm not sure O'Shea is gonna believe that."

"I don't know. He's pretty upset."

Jessie nodded. "Thanks again, Don, sincerely."

"Well, I caught some hell for breaking off from my element leader, but he admitted that it was acceptable when a buddy is in trouble."

When Jessie knocked on the tent frame, O'Shea and Heinricker were as usual, talking and smoking with their feet propped up on the table. "Welcome home! I see you got a little souvenir," said Heinricker glancing at the bandage on Jessie's head.

"It's okay," said Jessie.

"Well, it's good enough for a Purple Heart and a little goofin' off time."

Jessie gave a little smile and said: "Congratulations on your victory."

"Thank you. Like shootin' fish in a barrel." Heinricker ground out his cigarette. "See ya later," he said, and walked out of the tent.

O'Shea took the cigar out of his mouth. "Sit down, Rascoe," he said, motioning to a canvas chair across from where he sat.

Jessie nodded and sat down.

"They tell me you made one hell of a crash landing. Are you okay?"

"Yeah, I'm fine, Captain."

O'Shea reached up and took the cigar out of his mouth. "Okay, tell me what happened?"

Jessie hesitated and shook his head. "Two of them came down on us from above and behind, and the next thing I knew my canopy was gone and I didn't see much after that."

"You on his wing when they jumped you?" snapped O'Shea.

"I was on his wing!" Jessie snapped back.

"Don't get smart with me, Lieutenant!"

Silence.

"We learn how to defeat the enemy and stay alive by correcting mistakes, and it's my job to do that. You may be a hot pilot, but you don't know fuck all about combat yet. So don't give me any bullshit."

"Yes, sir."

"Okay. Now tell me what happened. Did you see the meatballs before they opened fire?"

"Yes, sir, I saw them."

"Did you warn Woodson?"

"Yes, sir, several times."

"What did he do?"

"He banked away."

O'Shea's dark eyes narrowed. "Woodson banked away?"

"Yes, sir."

O'Shea slowly put the cigar back in his mouth and looked out through the open side of the tent for a moment. "When he did that, did you think it was a mistake?"

"Yes, sir."

The only sound in the musty tent for a moment was the distinctive, distant roar of a B-25 taking off from Horanda air strip.

"All right. I respect your reluctance to criticize Woodson since he paid the supreme penalty for his mistake. It shows you got some character, Rascoe. But I gotta know these things. Christ knows why he did it. Maybe he was distracted or something. He was a good pilot, but who knows...it's easy to second-guess. Any one of us can make a mistake. In the business of aerial combat, it's gotta be the judgment of the combatant at that critical moment. If you judge correctly, you win- if not, well, you don't get many second chances. I'll have the flight leaders do a review of combat tactics, and we'll leave it at that, except that I have the God-awful job of writing the letter to Woodson's family."

"Was he married?" asked Jessie.

"No. But he was crazy in love with the girl he was engaged to marry, and he only had a couple months to go."

"Damn."

"Yeah...Shitty luck of the draw." O'Shea paused then added, "I'll tell Heinricker to keep you off the mission schedule for a few days."

"I'm ready anytime."

"How about the head wound?"

"I'll get the stitches out in a couple days."

"Okay, but make sure you're ready. I hate writing those letters."

"Yes, sir."

"How did it go?" asked Benilli, when Jessie entered the tent after his talk with the squadron commander.

Jessie flopped on his cot and muttered, "Okay."

"He didn't blame you, did he?"

Jessie shook his head.

"I'll tell you who was as much to blame as the nip that shot him down, and that's the bitch he was engaged to," growled Wander from where he lay on his cot.

Jessie glanced at Wander and said, "What'a ya mean?"

Swinging his legs off the cot, Wander sat up. "He got a Dear John letter from her a couple days ago, and it really tore him up."

"Jesus," muttered Jessie.

"She kissed him off?" asked Benilli.

"Yeah. She's gonna marry the other guy. Some Four-F son of a bitch sittin' back in the states making big dough and livin' the life of Riley."

"That's a bummer," said Carbon.

"He tell you about it, Ralph?" asked Jessie.

Wander nodded and fired a cigarette. "Yeah. We were good friends. He was really upset. That letter ripped his guts out. He shouldn't have been flying, and I told him that. But he said he was okay and made me promise not to tell anyone."

It was quiet in their moldy jungle tent for a while with each pilot engrossed in his own thoughts. Outside, one of the jungle birds let out a loud screech, and another one answered with another shriek.

Jessie knew the death of Steve Woodson was not his fault, but the combination of that, and the disastrous experience of his first combat mission seemed to open a crack in his confidence. His dreams were plagued with images and sounds, as though he was still there: the piercing noise of explosions... the acrid smoke chocking him...pieces of metal and glass spewing...the blast of wind...his blood, red and sticky, everywhere... The crash and his desperate effort to escape incineration... And the God-awful aftermath.

Chapter
~44~

J essie was off the flight schedule all that week until finally he asked O'Shea to please put him back on and the CO agreed. The next day he was scheduled to fly on Larry Carbon's wing. The mission was escorting B-24s to bomb Japanese installations on the north-east coast of New Guinea.

"If we get jumped just stay on my wing, Jessie, and keep your eyes open and your head on a swivel," instructed Carbon as they prepared to climb into their aircraft.

"You can count on it, Larry."

Carbon nodded. "Okay, let's go, tiger."

After takeoff, the sixteen P-38's joined in formation and climbed to 20,000 ft. on their route to the rendezvous point where they met the formation of B-24 "Liberators." The long-winged bombers with the big twin tails were grouped in several formations that stretched for miles.

Carbon's red flight took up their protective position, which was a pattern of lazy eights over the formation. Although they were flying at high altitude and on oxygen, Jessie was perspiring with anxiety. He kept his fighter close on Carbon's wing while anxiously searching the sky for enemy aircraft.

As the formation approached the target area two hours later, black puffs of anti-aircraft fire, referred to by air crews as ack ack or flak, began to fill the sky. Following their standard procedure, the fighters test fired their guns, increased engine RPM, tightened crash straps, and intensified their vigil of watching for enemy aircraft.

Since on this day of war no enemy aircraft challenged the bombers, the P-38s skirted along the edge of the primary target away from where the black cloud of anti aircraft fire was concentrated. To drop their bombs on the target, the bombers had to fly over the target and therefore through the black cloud. The escorting fighters did not. If, however, enemy fighter appeared, the P-38s would pursue them wherever they were, in the black cloud, or anywhere else they went.

As the P-38s circled the target area, Jessie watched the anti aircraft shells exploding all around the bombers as they held their course over the target. It seemed impossible that they could fly through it without being struck. Then he could see the gigantic explosions far below as one after another the bombs struck the Japanese facilities. Flashes of exploding bombs and then huge columns of black smoke boiled into the sky as more explosions occurred.

Then another flash caught his eye, and Jessie glanced across to see a huge ball of fire engulf one of the B-24 bombers. It had taken a direct hit by ack ack, exploding in flames and spewing burning pieces that left zigzag trails of smoke and fire. As the bomber fell in a bizarre series of twisting and turning gyrations, it shed more flaming parts and a long trail of black smoke that marked its path to the earth far below.

After they landed back at Port Moresby and parked their aircraft, Carbon and Jessie crawled down off the wing of their aircraft with their parachute over their shoulder and walked off down the path toward the personal equipment shack where the parachutes were stored.

"The next worst job in this war business, other than being a poor infantry slob, is being on a bomber crew. I wouldn't trade places with those guys for all the squaws in Sydney."

Jessie nodded. "They get hit like that often?"

Carbon nodded. "Yeah, too often... Come on, let's put our chutes away and get a drink. The beefer came back from Australia today, and we got fire water!"

Jessie nodded. "Yeah, I could use some."

The Flying Knights were assigned a series of supply-barge strafing missions along the New Guinea coast, and Jessie finally got to fire his guns. But strafing supply barges was a far cry from what Jessie was there for, and the doubts continued to hang in his mind and plague his sleep.

It was his fifteenth mission before Jessie even saw an enemy aircraft again. On that mission, he was flying wing in the top cover flight and again never got to fire his guns. What made it even worse was he could hear the radio chatter from the two lower flights that had tangled with enemy fighters, and Don Benilli shot down his first Zero.

That night Carbon dug out a bottle of Aussie schnapps in honor of Benilli's victory, and the four of them sat on their cots in their moldy jungle tent in a fog of cigarette smoke and celebrated.

"You keep doing that, Don, an' you'll be an ace in no time," said Wander, a cigarette dangling from his lips. "Heck, I been in the squadron over six months, and I only got three kills. Now old eagle-eye Carbon has four to his credit, but he's got an advantage over us palefaces. He's got injun eyes. That's his secret."

"Injun eyes?" asked Benilli.

"Injun eyes better than pale faces. We got eagle eyes: the better to see Japs with," Carbon replied.

"Are you really an Indian, Larry?" asked Benilli.

Carbon nodded. "Well, me half-breed. Half Black Foot and half paleface."

"My best friend was quarter Tejon Indian," said Jessie.

"Tejon? Where are they?" asked Carbon.

"That's a tribe out in the Tehachapi Mountains in California. Alvin and me grew up there. He was killed when they bombed Pearl Harbor. He shot down the first Jap of the war."

"Yeah. I remember reading about him," said Carbon. "He was your friend?"

Jessie nodded. "And I haven't shot down shit."

"Aw, you'll get plenty of chances," assured Carbon. "Me, I only got a couple more months, and I'm outta here and back to the reservation and my little squaw, Cindy."

"You really live on a reservation, Larry?" asked Benilli.

"Yeah, it's called Saint Louis, Missouri."

The four pilots laughed.

"But what I wanta know, Benilli, is how come Italians from New York are called wops?" asked Carbon.

Benilli took a drink of his schnapps. "I thought everybody knew that: it's because they import a lot of Italian snow tires in New York."

Carbon looked suspicious. "Okay, I'll bite. What's an Italian snow tire?"

"Dago through snow, dago through mud, and when dago flat, dago wop, wop, wop."

After the laughter and more Aussie schnapps, Benilli said, "Okay. I'll tell you philistines the real story. When my grand pappy came over from Sicily as an immigrant, he was part of a group who was on a quota system and didn't have passports. So when they got to Ellis Island, they put tags on them: WOP, which meant: 'without passport.' And the name sort of stuck."

"That really true?" asked Carbon.

"Honest injun," grinned Benilli.

"Well, I wish this injun had some tequila instead of this schnapps shit. But it's alcohol and that's all that counts," he added, sticking a cigarette in his lips. "Neither of you guys started smoking yet, have you?"

Rascoe and Benilli both shook their heads.

"Give them a little more time. I didn't smoke either for my first couple months," said Wander.

"I thought injuns only smoked war pipes," said Benilli.

"This injun want smoke love pipe and the sooner the better," replied Carbon. "But I would like to get one more nip before I leave. I'd be heap big medicine if I went home an ace."

"All I want is a chance to shoot at a fuckin' Jap," said Jessie, taking another big gulp of the schnapps.

"Jessie, you have been snake bit, haven't ya?" drawled Carbon, the effects of the schnapps now evident.

"I got sixteen missions now, and I ain't had a chance to shoot at one lousy Jap!"

"Speaking of snakes, look at that big mamoo out on that log," said Wander.

They all looked out through the open side of the tent, and there on a rotting log lay a huge jungle snake, not an uncommon site in the New Guinea jungle.

"Oh shit! Look at the thing!" shrieked Benilli.

"Snakes bother you, Donald, my boy?" asked Carbon, reaching up and pulling his forty-five out of the holster where it hung on his mosquito net post. "I'll take care of it for you, ole buddy."

The others watched as Carbon took aim at the snake.

"Larry, you know what Capt'n O'Shea said about shooting yer gun in the camp," warned Wander.

"Well, I don't want that damn snake crawling in my pal Donald's bed tonight, so I'm gonna blow its damn head off."

"Yeah, I'm with you, Larry. Shoot the bastard!" encouraged Benilli.

At the sound of the first shot, which made a lot of noise but never came close to the snake, there were cries from other nearby tents. "Stop shooting in the camp!" someone yelled.

"Aw, fuck you guys and the horses you rode in on!" muttered Carbon, getting up and stumbling out of the tent. He walked across the short distance to where the snake lay on the log, put the forty five up next to the snake's head and pulled the trigger. When he staggered back into the tent, smiling broadly, there were parts of the snake hanging on his gun and spattered over the front of his crumpled khakis.

Wander shook his head. "Ya see what happens to you if you stay in the jungle long enough?"

"Naw, I'll tell ya what really happens to ya. Come on, Ralph," slurred Carbon, putting his arm around Wander neck, and the two pilots broke into song:

"Beside a Guinea water fall, one bright and sunny day, beside his battered Lightning, the young pursuit'er lay. His parachute hung from a very high limb, he was not yet quite dead; so listen to the very last words the young pursuit'er said:

I'm goin' to a better land, a better land I know, where whisky flows from coconut groves; play poker every night.

We'll never have to work at all, just sit around and sing... And we'll have a crew of pretty women, oh death where is thy sting!

Oh death where is thy sting...oh death where is thy sting-a-ling-ling. Oh death where...is...thy...sting!"

Fortunately, none of the four pilots were on the flight schedule that next morning, so they stayed in their sacks nursing hangovers until late in the day. Since all were hungry by then, they had no choice but to straggle over to the mess tent for dinner, even though the odds were it would be the dreaded Australian bully beef.

No one ever knew for sure just what the Aussies, who supplied most of the sustenance for the American forces in New Guinea, used to make bully beef. It may not have been quite as bad as its reputation, but as a steady diet, it became all but uneatable. Jessie was reminded of his dad's stories about the infamous "spam" of World War I. The New Guinea GI cooks tried to camouflage it, even baking it in a pie, but it still required gobs of GI catsup to be edible.

"It tastes kind of like stale cow shit," said Carbon.

"What does stale cow shit taste like?" asked Wander with a straight face.

"A little like undercooked horse shit," replied Carbon, sitting across the table, also with a straight face.

"You guys don't have any class. You got to use your imagination. Pretend it's Steak Diane and you're at the Ritz on Park Avenue," said Benilli.

"Well, I ain't ever been on Park Avenue, so I pretend it's Bear Trap scout stew," said Jessie.

"Bear Trap? Rascoe, that sounds worse than the reservation," said Carbon. "That where you're from?"

"Well, I lived near Bear Trap Canyon. My girl lived over there, and I used to go there on Boy Scout camp outs."

"And you'd sneak out of camp at night and screw the little Bear Trap girl, right?" accused Carbon.

Jessie grinned. "Not exactly."

"Well, that's what I used to do. Only I was in a Catholic boy's camp, and there was a Catholic girl's camp right next door."

"And you were screwin' those little Catholic girls?" asked Benilli, looking incredulous.

"Naw, I was trying to get a nun to kick the habit," replied Carbon winking at Jessie.

"I'm not sure I want to eat my Steak Diane in such coarse company," said Benilli.

Jessie's tent home in the nNEw Guinea jungle at Dobodura

The Flying Knights Officer's club at Dobodura,
built by the pilots from scrap materials

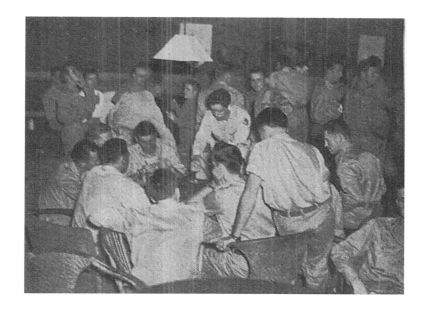

Flying Knights relaxing and playing cards
after a combat mission.

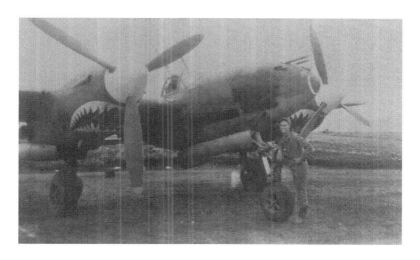

Lt. Jessie Rascoe and his P-38 at Dobodura.

Chapter
~45~

"Hear ye! Hear ye, all good knights of the air, the flight schedule for the morrow is hereby posted!" said Bob Heinricker who had entered the mess tent that was crowded with pilots seated at the wooden tables and involved in various methods of trying to eat the Australian Bully Beef.

Heinricker pinned the schedule on the bulletin board, walked over to where Jessie sat, and put his hand on his shoulder. "You got promoted, my boy. You're leading my element tomorrow in red flight."

Jessie looked at Heinricker in surprise. "Thank you for the vote of confidence, but you know, I have yet to even shoot at a nip."

Heinricker shrugged. "You will. Probably not tomorrow though because intelligence says there's no reported Jap fighters in that area, so we probably won't get intercepted. Some big brass are going on a sightseeing tour, and they wouldn't have scheduled that if there was any risk. But then you never can tell. The whole nip air force may be waiting for us."

"I'd take on the whole damn nip air force just to get a shot at one of the little bastards," grumbled Jessie.

Early the next morning the pilots selected for the mission gathered in the operations tent for the pre-mission briefing, which normally was an informal affair, often conducted in the revetment aircraft parking area by whoever was leading the squadron that day. On this occasion, it was in the briefing tent and more formal than usual as a major from HQ gave the briefing.

The major stressed the requirement for top performance since the squadron would be protecting high-level VIP officers from McArthur's staff who were being flown in a C-47 transport to survey a possible amphibious landing area near the Japanese base at Lae. He did say that intelligence reported little chance of an enemy aircraft attack, but anything was possible and the Flying Knights squadron was selected because of its outstanding record.

Flying his first mission as an element leader, Jessie re-briefed his wing man again as they prepared to climb into their aircraft in the revetment area. He was a new pilot to the squadron, Richard Turney. He was handsome with dark curly hair, a quick smile, and like most newcomers, eager to challenge the enemy.

"As the major said, we probably won't get into a fight today, but if we do, just stick on my wing, Richard. And keep your eyes open," he instructed, feeling almost foolish and certainly inadequate since it was gnawing at Jessie that he still had not fired at an enemy aircraft.

Lieutenant Heinricker led the squadron with red flight. After takeoff, red and blue flight stayed low making lazy S turns over the slow-flying Gooney Bird while the other two flights, green and yellow, climbed to altitude for high cover. The gooney flew from Dobodura out to the Soloman Sea and, then turned west just offshore along the white sandy beaches of New Guinea's northeast shoreline.

When the formation approached the designated area the pilots went through their usual pre combat preparations and sharpened the watch for bogies. But their only opposition was a few token bursts of flak, as intelligence had predicted. The transport circled the area a few times and headed back.

As usual, after leaving the target area, the formation loosened, and the pilots relaxed as much as possible within the small confines of the tiny P-38 cockpit.

Jessie, leading Heinricker's red flight element, had just flipped off his gun sight and reset the salvo switches on his drop tanks when the radio erupted: "Bogies! Bogies! Six o'clock!"

He glanced back over his shoulder and saw the attacking formation. Jessie knew they were Zeros: Mitsubishi A6M fighters, Japan's finest at that point in WWII. They had that same low-wing, sleek profile indelibly etched in Jessie's mind from his disastrous first mission.

"Captive, drop your tanks!" barked Heinricker over the radio. The P-38's were normally equipped with two sixty five gallon external fuel tanks to extend range. If enemy fighters were encountered, the tanks were jettisoned to prevent an explosion and provide better maneuverability.

Jessie switched the fuel selector to internal tanks, rearmed, and punched the salvo switch. Feeling the tanks release, he glanced across at his wingman to verify he'd heard Heinricker's order. He saw Turney's tanks tumble away, spewing fuel, their aluminum skin flashing in the morning sun. He also saw streams of tracer fire from the Japanese fighters.

It was like a repeat of the day Woodman was killed: machinegun fire across the canopy of his P-38. But this time Jessie slammed his fighter into a tight bank that brought him head on with the lead Zero that was spitting fire from its wing guns. He jammed down on the firing button and heard the roar of his guns that on the P-38 were mounted in the nose of the gondola, which allowed the smell of burning gunpowder to penetrate the pilot's cockpit.

Knowing that the Zero could not match the concentrated fire power of the P-38, Jessie held his head-on attack. He could see his glowing tracers streaking across the distance and plunging into the Japanese aircraft followed by flashes of twenty-millimeter cannon exploding and sending pieces of metal and plexiglass spewing. Then a sudden flash of red orange followed by a fiery explosion engulfing the Zero as it snapped into a tumbling, twisting plunge with a column of flame and black smoke marking its path to the Soloman Sea, ending in a volcanic geyser of foam and flame.

For an instant, Jessie experienced a unique, exhilaration that electrified his entire being. In the span of a few seconds, it was done. He had finally accomplished the thing that had possessed him-the thing he had agonized over-and now he'd done it! Now he knew that he could challenge the Japanese enemy and defeat him.

"You got 'em, red three!" came a transmission. Glancing across at his wingman, Jessie acknowledged with a thumbs-up signal.

Pitched voice transmissions filled his headset as the American and Japanese fighters merged in a giant, deadly melee of swooping, turning, and diving aircraft amid streaks of red tracers crossing the sky.

"Captive lead to squadron! Keep 'em off Top Cat! Keep 'em off Top Cat!" Top Cat was the call sign of the VIP transport.

"Top cover, get down here. We're up to our ass in alligators!" shouted Heinricker.

"Blue lead! Bogie at nine o'clock!"

"Frank! There's one on yer tail!"

"Christ, they're all over the place!"

"Scotty! Two o'clock! Two o'clock!"

"Red three, you're trailing smoke!"

"I'm shuttin' 'er down. Cover me, Larry!"

"Take the one on the left, Bill!"

"I'm hit! I'm hit!"

"Who's hit?"

"Red two! Red two's hit! Get 'em off!"

"I got the bastard!"

"Bogie at four o'clock high!" Came a warning from Jessie's wing man, Turney.

Jessie glanced over his shoulder and saw the attacking Zero on a steep-angle dive, with wing guns blazing. He also saw pieces of aluminum from his own wing flying off and a string of bullet holes suddenly appear. He snapped the fighter into a hard climbing bank to meet the Japanese fighters. An instant later the Zero flashed past, and Jessie rolled with him, jamming on full power.

"Stay with me, Turney!" he instructed.

"I'm with ya, red three!" replied Turney.

The Japanese pilot made the mistake of thinking his high-speed dive had propelled him out of range and wasn't expecting Jessie to close the gap so quickly. But with full war emergency power, the swift Lightning closed on the diving Zero, and when the silhouette of the Mitsubishi filled his gun site, Jessie fired all four fifties and his 20MM cannon. The stream of explosive projectiles pierced the Zero's cockpit canopy, disintegrating it, spewing pieces of aluminum and plexiglass that fluttered and flashed in the bright sun.

Since the Zero had no cockpit protective armor, the Japanese pilot was killed instantly, and the fighter fell off on one wing and into a slanting dive to a fiery explosion in the Soloman Sea. Again Jessie felt an exhilaration. He'd sent another son of Nippon to hell!

But Jessie's elation was interrupted when he caught a glimpse of two Zeros closing on a lone P-38 that was trailing smoke from one engine. Jessie put the P-38 on an intercept course at full power. The superior speed of the Lightning again came into play, and he closed the distance quickly. But the two Zeros were in firing position on their wounded prey and were blazing away while the American pilot screamed over the radio for help.

Jessie was still out of range for accuracy, so he pulled the nose up slightly and fired a long burst, which fortunately sent glowing tracers arching over the Zeros, and they instantly broke off the attack. Jessie winged over after them.

When the image of one of the fleeing Zeros filled his gun sight, Jessie squeezed the firing switch again and watched a deadly concentration of firepower slam into the Zero. The Japanese pilot pulled up into a steep climb as a fire ball erupted from the interior of his aircraft, and an instant later a forked object separated from the flaming fighter and drifted out into the blue sky. Jessie recognized that it was the pilot jumping free of the inferno.

The forked object seemed to float out into space, almost as though it was happening in slow motion. As Jessie watched, he felt a strange, ambivalent fascination: the forked object was a Jap son of a bitch, but it was also a man-a pilot, like himself.

"That's another confirmed, red three," came the voice of Turney.

Jessie nodded there in the P-38 cockpit, banked steeply, and dove after the other Zero, who also made a fatal mistake by going into a high-speed climb, which was to the advantage of the more powerful Lightning. Within seconds, the Zero's silhouette filled his gunsight, and Jessie fired. The Zero belched fire almost immediately and within seconds turned into a flaming torch that began a series of wild barrel rolls, trailing burning pieces and black smoke as it went into its final death plunge.

"Red Three! Red Three! I got one on my tail!" came the cry through Jessie's earphones. He glanced back and saw that a Zero had come down from above and was in deadly position behind Turney.

"Split S, Turney! Split S!" Jessie screamed over the radio as he pulled his fighter into a climbing bank.

Turney obeyed, snapping the P-38 onto its back and then diving away, with the attacking Zero after him. Jessie rolled over also and dove after the Zero. As the three fighters plunged, the Zero was firing at Turney, and Jessie was firing at the Zero. He could only hope that he would score a vital hit before the Zero scored one on his wingman. Jessie knew the P-38 would accelerate faster in a dive than the Zero, but he also knew that the Zero could pull out of a dive much quicker than the P-38 and required less altitude. Since they were at low altitude, Jessie had only seconds before he must pull out of the dive.

Closing to point-blank range, Jessie could see hits all over the Mitsubishi but with no apparent effect as the Japanese pilot continued to fire on Turney. Because the Japanese fighters lacked self sealing fuel tanks, usually a single burst of fire into the fuselage would cause an explosion, but this one seemed immune. Then suddenly one wing ripped from the fuselage as a burst of Jessie's cannon fire cut through the Zero's wing spar. The severed wing fluttered off like a falling leaf flashing the red ball wing insignia as it spiraled in the sunlight.

With the loss of a wing, the remainder of the Japanese fighter went into in a series of violent gyrations, shedding pieces, then plunged into the sea sending a plume of fire and smoke shooting skyward.

With the Soloman Sea filling his windshield, Jessie hauled back on the control yoke with all his might. The blood surged from his head, and blackness closed down around him while he wondered if the wings on the Lockheed P-38 would rip off from the G-forces.

After a few seconds he knew the wings were still on, but all he could see was a black cloud. Now he must recover his vision before another Zero shot him out of the sky. He shook his head violently to speed up the process, but it seemed an eternity before the blackness began to turn grey. As his vision cleared, Jessie saw blue green water just below that suddenly erupted into churning foam: machine gun and cannon fire from an attacking Japanese fighter.

Jessie reacted, by banking the Lightning sharply away from the foaming water. He glanced back and saw his attacker's wing guns blazing and, an instant later, black holes spewing metal walking up the P-38's right wing. Jessie instinctively cringed as he anticipated the god-awful explosion, noise, smoke, and blood when the Zero's projectiles reached his cockpit, but they didn't. Because of his steep diving angle, the Zero pilot had to cease firing at that critical moment and pull out of his dive or crash into the sea. Fortunately for Jessie, this son of Nippon was not suicidal. And Jessie learned another lesson about the business of aerial warfare: It could turn from victor to victim in a split second.

Jessie knew his fighter's wing fuel tanks had taken hits, and he could smell fuel. But unlike the Japanese Zero, the P-38 had self-sealing tanks. So Jessie slammed on full power and into a high-speed climb, searching the sky to see where his attacker had gone. Unable to spot him Jessie continued to climb for altitude.

"Captive! They're after Top Cat! The Gooney Bird!" someone shouted over the radio.

"I'm on fire! I'm on fire!" screamed someone else.

"Get out, Jim! Bail out!" came another frantic transmission.

"Red four! Red four! You read?" Jessie called his wing man. No answer.

"Red four! Turney! You read me?" repeated Jessie into his throat mike.

Jessie was clawing for altitude in a maximum climb when he heard the transport pilot again shout over the radio: "Captive! Captive! This is Top Cat. I'm under fire! I'm under fire!"

Jessie searched the sky frantically trying to locate the transport. Then a flash of sunlight off metal drew his eyes down, and he spotted the C-47 flying just above the sea. The wise Gooney pilot had dove down to just above the water and was turning and banking frantically to escape the withering fire of two attacking Zeros.

Jessie had enough altitude now to dive on the attackers who were low over the water firing at the transport. As soon as the first Zero was in his sights, Jessie fired. His tracers arched across the distance and ripped into the first Zero. The Japanese pilot overreacted by slamming into a steep bank striking the water with a wing tip, which caused the aircraft to cartwheel wing over tail until it flopped into the sea upside down and sank. The other attacking Zero pulled off the transport and sped away.

Jessie turned back toward the transport: "Top Cat, you okay?"

"We got holes and injuries, and I just had to shut down my right engine. But I think we can make it if you can keep 'em off us."

"I'll be right here, Top Cat," replied Jessie. "Captive, any Captive! This is Captive red three!"

"Captive red three, this is Captive red leader. Where are you, Jessie?" came Heinricker's reply.

"I'm on the deck with Top Cat. He's in trouble."

"I'm lookin,' I can't see you."

"I see him!" said someone. "He's down low over the water! I got ya, Jessie!"

"Who's got me?"

"Me, red four!"

Jessie breathed a sigh of relief at hearing from his wing man. "Okay, red four, get over the Gooney and watch for bogies."

"Roger, Jessie. I'm coming."

"Red three, this is Red lead. I got you now, Jessie. Top Cat, this is Captive Red leader. You read me?"

"Roger Captive red leader. Top Cat reads you."

"Okay. We got ya covered now. How are you doing?"

"We're beat up and on one engine, but I think we can make it to Horando. Request you call them and see if they have a Duck (Catalina Flying boat) around anywhere that could head out to meet us in case we have to go in the drink. Also have medical aid standing by as we have VIP wounded aboard."

"Roger Wilco, Top Cat...All Captives from Captive red leader form up over the Gooney and check in."

The remaining pilots called in. Two were missing. One had lost an engine in the fight and headed home. One had been shot down in flames and crashed into the Soloman Sea.

"Anybody see a parachute or a rubber boat?" asked Heinricker.

"Captive lead, Yellow three. I saw him go in. No chute. No boat"

"Shit! All right. We still got a way to go to get Top Cat home, so lets keep a sharp eye."

Chapter
~46~

Up to that point in World War II, no American fighter pilot had shot down six enemy aircraft on a single mission. Jessie Rascoe was not only an instant ace, he was an instant national hero. And having saved the top brass in the transport was the icing on the cake.

After Fifth Air Force Headquarters officially confirmed his feat, Jessie was promoted to first lieutenant and ordered back to the states to be awarded the United States highest decoration: the Medal Of Honor. It was to be presented by President Franklin D. Roosevelt in Washington, D.C.

On the long flight home, Jessie had time to reflect on what had happened and how he felt about it. He knew with a certainty that the crack in his confidence had been welded shut and would not crack again. He realized that he faced instant death in every engagement he would have with the enemy, but now he knew that he could meet and defeat his enemy. His flying skill, keen eye sight, and disciplined dedication gave him an advantage in the deadly game of aerial combat, and all he'd needed was the opportunity. That opportunity had come, and he had performed.

Jessie also realized that his terrible obsession to kill Japanese had come and gone. Oh, he would shoot down many more of them because they were the enemy who had killed his friend and attacked his country. But he would not be haunted by that venomous obsession he'd harbored before, and because he recognized that, it was like he'd shed a burden.

For the second time Jessie Rascoe had his picture on the front page of the Bakersfield *Californian* newspaper. The first time was when he saved Maria Hunter's life when the rattler bit her at Pete Miller Meadow.

It was a great story because they put Alvin's picture next to Jessie's and told about the two best friends who lived out on the Grapevine, and how they had been Boy Scouts together and received the nation's two highest awards for valor serving their country. It was the kind of story people wanted to hear during those terrible war years, and it ran on the front page of most every newspaper in the country.

They had a parade in Bakersfield, and Jessie's mom and dad rode with him in the mayor's white Cadillac convertible down Chester Avenue, the main street. Everyone on the Grapevine, was proud of him, and Miss Trembell organized a special program at the Grapevine School in Jessie's honor.

He received dozens of letters and telegrams of congratulations. One was from Peggy Barton Dumont. It sounded just like her:

Jessie Rascoe, Grapevine, California.

Congratulations. You are my hero and America's hero.

I knew you would be as good a fighter as you are a lover!

XOXOXOX Peggy

He also got a telegram from Hallie Lamont. After he read it, Jessie was more excited about going to Washington, D.C.:

Jessie Rascoe, Grapevine, California.

Proud of you beyond words. I am now stationed near Washington, D.C. Will arrange to see you there.

Love, Hallie.

Jessie didn't hear anything from Maria Hunter. But then, why would he? She was engaged to be married.

When President Roosevelt put the beautiful Medal of Honor around his neck at a special ceremony in the White House, with all kinds of dignitaries in attendance, Jessie was humbled and deeply honored. Even though he knew that his driving motivation to shoot down enemy airplanes hadn't been just patriotism, it had included cold-blooded revenge. But then Jessie reminded himself that he'd resolved that issue which allowed him to accept the medal with at least an eased conscience.

After the awards ceremony, there was a grand reception that evening at the White House, and Jessie was scheduled to attend. He would have preferred to skip that part as he was eagerly waiting to hear from Hallie. He had no idea where she was, but since she'd said in her telegram that she would contact him there, he could only assume that she knew where he was and how to find him.

The special affairs major assigned to oversee Jessie's participation told him that he couldn't skip the reception because he was scheduled to stand in the receiving line, whether he liked it or not.

"You ever done this before?" asked the major.

"No, sir, and I don't want to do it now," admitted Jessie, as they stood in the glittering grandeur of the White House Grand Ballroom, waiting for the receiving line to form.

"All you have to do is stand up there and smile and say 'How do you do' and 'Thank you' when they congratulate you on your medal. President Roosevelt won't be attending, but some of his staff will, along with a lot of VIPs. You will be introduced in the receiving line by General Kristian. He's General Hap Arnold's right hand man over at the Pentagon."

"You sure there is no way I can get out of this, Major?"

"No way. Come on, I'll present you to the general."

General Kristian was tall and handsome and looked too young to be a two-star general. He shook Jessie's hand and gave him a warm smile. "General Arnold would like to have been here to meet you personally, Lieutenant Rascoe. But he asked me to convey his congratulations."

"Thank you, sir," replied Jessie.

"No, Lieutenant, thank you," said the general. "Your feat of destroying six enemy aircraft on a single mission and saving the lives of those in the transport was not only an outstanding personal accomplishment-it's a vital morale booster for all of our troops, whoever and wherever they are."

As the major promised, the receiving line was made up of presidential advisors and other VIPs, big military brass, their ladies, other honored guests, and First Lieutenant Jessie Rascoe. It was all somewhat overwhelming, but Jessie kept smiling and tried to speak properly as the seemingly endless line filed by. They all congratulated him on his award and said he was a real American hero, but Jessie was ill at ease and could hardly wait to have it finished.

The end of the receiving line was finally in sight, when a handsome, young army brigadier general stepped up and congratulated him. Jessie wasn't surprised when he turned to meet the general's lady. He expected to see a beautiful woman. In fact, she was breathtakingly beautiful. The most beautiful girl Jessie Rascoe had ever seen. She was dressed in a low-cut gown that revealed an equally stunning figure. Her hair a beautiful yellow blond color and she had eyes that were such a vivid blue they drew you right into them.

"Hallie!" he blurted, causing heads to turn up and down the receiving line.

"Hello, Tiger," she said in that wonderful voice of hers, which sent shock waves through Jessie. For a moment he was so surprised he just stared at her. Oh, how beautiful she was! How could he have turned this girl down for that disloyal hillbilly, Maria?

"I understand you and Miss Lamont are old friends, Lieutenant?" said the handsome general in a calm voice and a forced smile. It was one of those moments when Jessie had to use all the restraint he possessed to keep from grabbing Hallie in his arms. He gave the general a wooden nod in answer to his question.

"Congratulations, Jessie, I knew you could do it. And like everyone else in our country, I'm extremely proud of you," Hallie said softly, holding out her hand to him.

He took her hand and held it tightly. "Hallie, you've surprised me before, but this is your best!" I sure wasn't expecting you'd come here. I thought-"

"I told you I'd be in touch," she said with one of her intoxicating smiles.

"Excuse me, Lieutenant. We seem to be holding up the line," said the general, putting his hand on Hallie's shoulder as though to nudge her along.

Jessie held on to her hand. "Hallie, when can we...?"

"As soon as the receiving line is over," she said, with her eyes saying much more. The general was smiling too, but his eyes weren't.

The minute the receiving line broke up, Jessie looked around and spotted her standing beside the general in a group of other high-ranking army officers, all of them with their eyes on her. And no wonder, she was like a sparkling jewel in their midst. Jessie stood there for a moment, watching her with churning emotions.

"Would you care for a cocktail, Lieutenant?" asked a waiter.

"Yes, I believe I would," replied Jessie, picking one off the waiter's tray and gulping it down without even looking to see what it was.

About that time Hallie looked over and saw him. She turned, said something to the general, and then walked over to where Jessie stood while the general glared.

"Jessie, you're so handsome in your uniform with that beautiful sash and medal around your neck, I can hardly stand it," she said, taking one of his hands and squeezing it.

Jessie smiled. "Even when I was wearing Boy Scout jodhpurs you said that, Hallie."

"Yes, I remember. And you were the best-looking Boy Scout I ever saw, but you're in a class of your own now," she said, looking up the scar across his forehead. "You're a real American hero, Jessie, and I can't tell you how proud I am."

"And I can't tell you how glad I am to see you, Hallie."

She nodded and looked at him intently. "Yes. It is good, isn't it?"

"Know what I wish right now..? That we were back at the ole Rose Station water trough."

She laughed that great laugh of hers. "So do I, Tiger."

"But as usual, we're cut off at the pass...unless I can find a vacant broom closet or something around here," said Jessie glancing around as if he were searching for one.

She laughed again and said, "Who would ever have thought we'd be looking for a place to make love in the White House?"

Smiling broadly, Jessie shook his head. "Not in a million years. I was anxious to see you, but I didn't realize just how much until I saw you in that receiving line."

"I know exactly what you mean."

As they stood looking at each other, the cocktail waiter appeared, and they both exchanged their empty glasses for full ones. She held up her glass, touched his, and said, "To you, my love,- the pride of America."

"And to you, brave Hallie, for all that you have done."

After they drank, he said, "Hallie, what'a ya say we just walk out of here?"

"As much as I'd like that, I don't think you can just up and walk out of this little shindig."

"Why not? They won't miss us?"

She smiled. "I don't think we would get very far."

Jessie glanced across at the general who, sure enough, was watching. "The general?"

She nodded. "You have to really be somebody, or have top-level connections to get in and out of this place. It's almost as bad as the Grapevine Ranch."

"Did he bring you?"

"Yes."

"Must be nice to know a general with that kind of horsepower."

"It comes in handy."

He hesitated before asking, "Just a friend?"

"You could say that. He's in a position to get invitations to almost any function in Washington."

"You do this often, then?"

"Oh, a few times."

"You see him much?"

"Now and then. I'm doing a lot of flying, Jessie. I travel almost constantly."

It pleased him to hear that she traveled a lot, and didn't see the general often. "You like what you're doing, don't you?"

"Oh, I do! I love it. The WAFS are doing great work. We ferry every kind of aircraft they make from the factories to the fighter and bomber bases all over the United States. One day I fly a P-38 fighter to Florida, pick up a P-47, and fly it to Kansas. It's very demanding, but fun, and I feel as though I'm doing my part for the war effort."

"That's great, Hallie. And I'm really proud of you."

"Thanks. I'm feeling pretty good about myself now."

"Yeah. I can see that, and it shows."

"And I can see even more change in you since we met in California."

"Along with all the bad stuff, the army and war does make you grow up and face reality, whether you like it or not."

Hallie nodded. "I wasn't actually in the shooting war in England, of course, but close enough to understand what you're saying." She paused. "Frankly, I think I could fly combat... and I would if they'd let me."

Jessie shook his head. "No, it's not something I'd want you to do. Aerial combat is the ultimate challenge in flying all right...and a fascinating game,... but a deadly one. I got a feeling you could play the flying game all right. But...there is another part that I wouldn't want you to experience."

She looked into his eyes intently. "Some time, Jessie, I want you to tell me about it, about the part you're omitting. And the scar...how it happened...all of it, okay?"

He nodded. "Sure, Hallie."

"Are you going back?"

"Yes."

"Voluntarily?"

"No, I have to go back because I'm only here on leave. But I'd go back anyway. Although I've satisfied my driving obsession, in a sense. But I still have a job to do."

"Yes, and I suspect it's not going to be easy."

"I think you're right."

"You know what I'd like right now?"

"The water trough?"

"The next best thing," she said, taking his hand as the dance music started on the opposite end of the ballroom.

"I'd prefer the trough, but okay. Let's do it."

They placed their cocktail glasses on a waiter's tray and, holding hands, walked across to the dance floor where a few couples had begun to dance. Jessie's pulse leaped when she came into his arms and he felt the softness of her touch and smelled that special fragrance Hallie always had. As they danced, the emotion burgeoned, and it took all the restraint he possessed to keep from kissing her right there on the dance floor.

Although the place was full of beautiful, exquisitely dressed ladies and handsome young men in their uniforms, few were as striking as Jessie and Hallie as they danced in the grand ballroom of the White House. This was evidenced by the number of guests who stopped whatever they were doing just to stare at them. Jessie wore a class-A summer uniform with his silver wings and the beautiful blue sash of the Medal of Honor around his neck. Hallie's stunning evening gown was the same color as Jessie's Medal of Honor sash.

"Hallie," he whispered hoarsely in her ear, as they danced, "the chemistry is brewing."

"I know."

"Powerful chemistry."

"I told you that a long time ago."

"I remember."

They turned and looked at each other, then came together as closely as they dared, and danced silently, savoring the emotion. When the music stopped, she said in a husky voice, "I think we better go get ourselves a drink and cool off."

"It'll take more than a drink to cool me off."

She smiled, took his hand, and led him off the dance floor.

They selected cocktails from a waiter's tray and moved back against one wall of the ballroom, trying to appear as inconspicuous as possible.

"Are we gonna be able to meet somewhere after this is over?"

"No...I'm sorry, Jessie. I have to go back tonight. I have a ferry flight to Detroit first thing in the morning."

"Cut off at the pass again."

"I know. I'm just as disappointed as you. When I found out you were coming to Washington and Tony, uh, General Browne, got us an invitation, I tried to rearrange my schedule, but it was just impossible. They really keep us busy."

"There's gotta be a way. Do you live here in Washington?"

"No. I live in Wilmington, Delaware. That's where I'm stationed now."

"Where is that?"

"It's about a three-hour drive from here."

"Well, maybe I could go with you. How are you getting there?"

"The way I came."

"The general?"

She nodded.

"I thought you said that after you broke off with George that you weren't going to get into any more involvements."

"So goes the best-laid plans of mice and women."

"But...?"

"I'm not in love with him, Jessie. I'm waiting for you, remember?"

"Well, if you're waiting for me, how come you're involved with another guy?"

"It comes with the territory of waiting for a guy who is hard to catch."

Jessie gazed at beautiful Hallie Lamont. "Yeah, but every time you catch me, you cut and run."

She laughed. "It seems that way, doesn't it?"

"It sure does," said Jessie. "Like I told you in California, you've changed all right, and it shows. But you're still the same beautiful, *unpredictable* girl you always were."

She smiled in her mesmerizing way, reached up, and touched his face. "I can't catch you until you're available, Tiger."

"I'm available."

"I know: you're available to make love. And that's tempting, believe me. But you're not really available. You're still in love with Maria, aren't you?"

Jessie wanted desperately to say no, but the words wouldn't come out. He took a big gulp of his drink and looked at the polished hardwood floor of the grand ballroom.

"It's okay, Jessie. I can wait. I know that in your heart you still don't have the answer. You're not sure which of your loves is the true one. But you will. You'll settle it one of these days. Meanwhile, be careful over there. You've already proven yourself. I know you're good. You have to be to do what you did. But please don't get reckless. You must come home because I know something you don't: I know which one."

"Excuse me," interrupted General Browne, stepping up next to them. "I think we should leave now, Hallie. It's a long drive to Wilmington"

"Yes, Tony. I guess it is time to leave," said Hallie, taking the general's arm.

Chapter
~47~

After the celebrations in Washington were over, the army gave Jessie a few days at home before he was to report to the port of embarkation for shipment back to his fighter squadron in New Guinea.

It was good to see the Grapevine again and be with his parents for a few days, but it wasn't as enjoyable as Jessie would have liked. There wasn't a single one of the old gang at home. His brother Billy and Jack were still in flight training, and everyone else had shipped out in one service or the other, except Gerald. He had taken a job where they built Liberty ships up at the big Kaiser Shipyards near San Francisco. Even the Grapevine girls were all gone. They were either working in a war plant somewhere or had joined one of the services.

To make matters worse, he couldn't shake the emotional upset that had plagued him since his meeting with Hallie. The more he thought about it, the more he was convinced that he'd acted like a fool in Washington. All he'd had to do was tell her he loved her, and she would have kissed the general off. So what did he do? He stood there like a dummy and let her believe that he was still in love with a girl he hadn't seen in years and who was probably already married the other guy! Christ! He may have learned how to shoot down Japs, but he sure hadn't learned much else!

But then what difference did it make? He would be returning to New Guinea in a few days and the war and the Japanese Zeros, and he would have to defeat a lot more of the sons of Nippon before anything would matter. He knew now that he could do that all right, but he also knew that one little mistake, like Lieutenant Woodson...The reality was that it probably didn't matter which girl he truly loved, or did he love either one?

His parents suggested several things he might want to do, but nothing seemed of interest. He realized they were worried, and he'd overheard his father tell his mother that no doubt Jessie was suffering from battle fatigue.

He wasn't suffering from battle fatigue. How could he? He'd only been in two battles: one he lost and one made him a hero. As he lay on the bed in his old room, staring at the ceiling, it occurred to Jessie he was behaving just the way he had when he was sixteen and couldn't decide which girl he wanted. He got up, crawled into his old '31 Ford, and headed for Los Angeles to find Maria and settle it once and for all.

No one seemed to know if she was married, but Mr. Switzner did say that Mr. Hunter told him she was still living down south. So with some extra gas-ration stamps his father had saved, he drove to Los Angeles and presented himself at the Hunters' front door.

Maria's aunt and uncle congratulated him on his award of the Medal of Honor, but hastened to tell him that Lieutenant Kevin Blake, who was engaged to their niece Maria, had also distinguished himself on the battlefields of North Africa.

At least now Jessie knew that Maria wasn't married, and he could face her and settle it. Mr. Hunter said he didn't think it proper for him to give out Maria's address where she shared an apartment with her girlfriend Patsy Cline. But he did tell Jessie that both Maria and Patsy worked on the assembly line at the big Lockheed Aircraft plant over in Burbank.

It gave Jessie a good feeling to know that Maria was working at the plant where they made the P-38 fighter that he flew. But as he drove across the city toward Burbank, other feelings began to brew in the pit of his stomach, conflicting feelings that he didn't want to even try to decipher. But he'd come this far, and he was determined to see it through.

Because the United States expected Japanese military forces to attack the west coast during the early days of the war, essential war production facilities in the Los Angeles area were camouflaged and under heavy security. One of the more extensive camouflaging of a major facility was the huge Lockheed Aircraft plant in Burbank. It was almost impossible to distinguish from the air and nearly as hard to find by surface means.

When Jessie finally found the plant and the visitor's office, he was told they had thousands of workers, and unless he knew where she worked and had an official reason to see her, they couldn't help him. Even if they could, he wouldn't be allowed in the plant without special permission from plant security, which was very tight.

He was standing in the noisy, crowded office, trying to decide what to do when a distinguished-looking man with a handful of papers appeared beside him and said, "Excuse me, young man, aren't you Lieutenant Jessie Rascoe?"

Jessie looked at the man and nodded. "Yes, I am."

"May I shake your hand?" he said extending his. "My name is Kelly Johnson, and it's an honor and a pleasure to meet you. In my opinion, few pilots have distinguished themselves as you have."

"Thank you, sir. It's an honor to meet you too, Mr. Johnson," said Jessie. "Are you the Kelly Johnson who designed the P-38?"

"I am. I take it you approve of my creation?"

"It's a great airplane, Mr. Johnson."

"Well, you certainly proved what the P-38 can do in the South West Pacific. That was some feat, Lieutenant. I know you have been asked this question many times, but I've got to hear it first-hand. How did you do that? What was the key to your being able to get six of 'em in one shot, so to speak?"

Jessie smiled. "That's easy. My secret is the P-38 Lightning."

Johnson laughed. "I suspect there is more to it than that, but I must admit that is what I wanted to hear." Glancing at his wrist-watch, he added, "Lieutenant Rascoe, I'm late for a meeting, but I sure would like to buy you a beer and do some talking later. Any chance of that?"

"I'd like that, Mr. Johnson, but I have a sort of previous appointment."

"I understand. Here, take my card and call me if you have some spare time. And if there is anything I can help you with let me know."

"There is, sir," Jessie said.

"Fire away."

"I'm trying to find my, uh, a friend who works here, and I can't seem to-"

"He works at this plant?"

"Yes, sir. He's a girl."

"I understand," nodded Johnson, smiling. "Follow me, Lieutenant," he directed, as he barged through the outer door into the inner offices, with Jessie following.

"Bill!" he bellowed to a grey-haired man in one of the offices. "Meet Lieutenant Jessie Rascoe. This is Bill Wyman, and he'll make sure you get to see whoever you want."

"The Jessie Rascoe that shot down-"

"He's the one."

"You bet I'll take care of him. It's a real honor to meet you, Lieutenant. You are the hero of this factory. I'll tell ya," said Wyman.

Johnson shook hands with Jessie warmly and said, "Good luck and good hunting, Lieutenant Rascoe."

It took a while to locate where Maria Hunter worked and then they had to get a special security badge for Jessie. Finally, he was escorted into a huge production building where hundreds of people, mostly women and older men, were working on two long lines of P-38s in various stages of construction.

The foreman of the section where Maria worked, a skinny little man with thick glasses, looked at Jessie and said, "She's over on ship number 1793, working in the cockpit."

Uh, Lieutenant, would you mind signing this production routing slip for me? My kids would sure be thrilled."

Just seconds from facing Maria, Jessie's thoughts weren't geared to giving his autograph, but he managed a smile and signed the production routing slip.

"Thank you, Lieutenant. I'll be the hero when I come home with this tonight. Follow me, sir, and I'll take you to where the young lady is working," said the foreman.

"That's all right, just point out which one is 1793."

The foreman smiled. "She's a sweet girl and a good worker. Just follow that red line on the floor, the numbers are on the nose of the gondola."

"Thanks," said Jessie. With rising emotions, he walked down the red line painted on the concrete floor that ran between the two rows of aircraft in the huge, noisy factory.

When Jessie reached number 1739, he could see that someone was in the cockpit, but he couldn't identify the person. He climbed a steel rollaway ladder to the wing and walked up to the cockpit. He could clearly hear his own excited heartbeat over the sounds of rivet guns and other machines.

Maria was sitting in the pilot's seat, dressed in jeans and a denim shirt with a blue bandanna on her head and working intently on the forward instrument panel. She sensed someone was watching her and turned to see. When their eyes met, Jessie Rascoe and Maria Hunter felt as though their hearts would leap out of their bodies. They both experienced emotion so profound they just stared at each other for several seconds, unable to utter a word.

"Hi, Maria," he finally said.

"Oh, Jessie...Oh, Jessie..." her voice choked off and her eyes filled with tears.

"It's okay, Maria. Don't cry," he said, kneeling down beside her and putting his hand on her shoulder.

She lowered her head and sobbed uncontrollably for a moment. Then abruptly, she pulled herself up, leaped out of the cockpit, and threw herself into his arms. He grasped her, and they clung to each other hungrily, oblivious to all but each other as if they were the only two people in the world.

They stood there on the wing of the Lightning, in the huge building that had giant American flags hanging from the steel ceiling beams. The workers up and down the long assembly line stopped what they were doing and watched with smiles on their faces.

When Patsy Cline realized that it had suddenly become quiet at her work station, she glanced up from where she was bucking rivets on the lower gondola of P-38 line number 1795. "What's goin' on?" she asked the girl opposite her who held the rivet gun.

"Take a look at Maria," said the girl.

Patsy glanced across the production line to number 1793. "Oh, Jesus Christ!" she blurted. "That poor girl. Now she is really in trouble."

"Well, that's the kind of trouble I'd like to have," said the riveter.

"You don't understand, Kathleen."

"What don't I understand, Patsy?"

"She's in love with that guy."

"So? Who wouldn't be?"

"But she's engaged to another guy."

"As good lookin' as this one?"

"Yes."

"Christ. And all I can find is a four-F'er who is half blind and has a wooden leg."

All activity around P-38 line number 1793 had stopped, and the workers were watching Jessie and Maria when the company public relations crew, having been tipped off by Kelly Johnson, came hustling down the aisle and immediately began taking pictures.

"Who is the army guy?" asked one of the workers.

"That's Jessie Rascoe, the P-38 ace," said one of the photographers.

"Oh wow!" said Kathleen. "Did you know that, Patsy?"

"Yeah, I knew that."

Then a roar of approval went up among the factory workers as the two on the wing kissed passionately.

"This is great stuff!" cried the Lockheed director of publicity, standing beside the camera crew. "Keep shooting! Keep shooting!"

It was a major disruption on the assembly line at the Lockheed Aircraft plant in Burbank, California, that day. But no one was unhappy about it, except perhaps Patsy Cline, and even she told Kathleen that maybe it was for the best after all.

Maria was in such an emotional state she clung to Jessie as he signed more autographs and answered questions while trying to get himself and Maria away. Her supervisor gave her the rest of the day off, and Patsy whispered to her that she would spend the night with her sister.

Maria and Jessie had both known the moment they saw each other in the cockpit of the P-38 that their love was as strong as it had ever been. When they were finally alone in Maria's and Patsy's apartment in Burbank, they just stood in the middle of the room clinging to each other.

"Jessie, I never stopped loving you," she whispered.

"I know you didn't, Maria. I saw it in your eyes that day at the barn."

"Oh God, I almost died that day."

"I know, my darling Maria, and so did I. I never stopped loving you. I doubted that for a while...right up to the moment I saw you there at the factory. But not anymore, and not ever again."

"Oh, Jessie! My darling! My darling!" she gasped, clinging to him.

He responded by tenderly taking her face in his hands, forcing the work bandanna off, cascading her hair down over her back. He looked into those dark, quick-silvered eyes and saw what he'd always seen in Maria's eyes: love- wonderful, true love! For a moment, Jessie held her there, wondering how in the world it could have happened? How had they lost each other for so long?

"Maria, I never want to lose you again," he said in a husky, emotional voice. "I love you as I'll never love anyone, ever."

"Oh, Jessie, I love you," she replied in an equally emotional voice. "It was a terrible thing I did to you, and I will have to pay the price for that selfishness. But I love you and only you, and there will never, never be anyone else for me either."

"I can't imagine you being selfish, Maria."

"I was though. I wanted too much and lost you and deceived poor Kevin, and myself."

"It's okay, Maria. It's over now, and we've found each other again. That's all that counts," said Jessie, tightening his arms around her.

She shook her head and pulled away. "No. It's like my mama says: two wrongs don't make a right. I gotta do what's right, Jessie, no matter how much it hurts. And the first thing I have to do is tell you everything."

"You don't have to tell me anything, Maria. The past doesn't matter. It's the future that counts," he said, reaching out and pulling her back to him. "I know now that I only care about you," he said, pulling her into a crushing embrace and kissing her greedily.

She responded, returning his kisses with fiery passion. For several minutes they clung to each other in a hungry embrace, grasping at each other, kissing and groping as their pent-up passions soared.

Maria abruptly pulled away, breathing heavily. "No, Jessie, No. I...I have to tell you," she gasped. "I have to!"

They stood apart, staring at each other, both with racing pulse and heavy breath.

She reached out, took his hand and guided him into the apartment kitchen that had a small breakfast nook. "Would you like a beer?" she asked, her voice still choked with emotion.

He nodded and sat down at the table. She opened a small refrigerator, took out two bottles of beer, and opened them.

"It's not as good as Marble Springs water, but it has a little more zip after a long day at the plant...an' I guess everybody in the Army drinks beer now, don't they?"

"Yeah, or anything else we can get."

"Oh, Jessie. I was so proud of you when I read in the papers about what you had done. I wasn't surprised though, because I knew you were strong and brave," she said, sliding into the breakfast nook across from him. "And you were over there fighting the war, and I didn't know where. I was so worried I could hardly stand it, and..." Maria's voice choked off and again tears began to roll down her cheeks.

He reached across and took one of her hands in his. "It's all right, darling. Everything is okay now. You got to remember that."

She nodded and wiped at the tears. Then she reached across and touched the scar on his forehead with the tips of her fingers. "Are you...are you all right now, my darling?"

He nodded. "It looks a lot worse than it was. The doctor that sewed me up promised that my mom would still love me. And now that I know you still love me, I'm just fine. Let's drink to us," he said, holding up the bottle of beer. "Come on, bottles up."

They touched the beer bottles. "To our love forever," he said, and they both drank.

"You're the same beautiful, sweet girl I fell in love with a long time ago, Maria, but you sure talk different," he said with a smile.

"Yes, and God knows how hard I worked at it. I wonder now if it was worth the price."

"Why do you say that?"

"It's a part of what I must tell you. I wanted desperately to shake the hillbilly image and educate myself. And I always told myself that I was doing it for you, because I wanted you to respect me and I was afraid of...well, I was afraid someone else would take you away from me."

"Hallie Lamont?"

She cast her eyes down and nodded.

"I know now that it is you I truly love, Maria."

"I know, but it was in my mind that I had to pull myself up. Then once I got into that world I became immersed in it, and when you're young and naive...Somewhere along the line I lost sight of my goal. I began to think more about me and material things. Just to *say* that I was going to UCLA became more important than the reason for being there. And I became enthralled with the status it gave me to be going with a rich boy who was a football star."

"Kevin Blake?"

"Yes. And I..."

"You don't have to tell me any more, Maria."

"I got to, Jessie. I hate it, but I gotta tell you all of it and hope and pray you'll understand. You see I was his girl, and he was loyal to me even though every girl on campus would have killed to get him. Kevin loved me and treated me like a queen. The tragedy is that I didn't love him...At least not like I love you." Maria paused and took a draft of the beer. Jessie followed suit.

"Oh, I'd convinced myself there for a while that I loved him and that I was a different person now and you were something that happened a long time ago. And everyone was happy about it: all my friends and my aunt and uncle...my folks...all but Mama. She knew. And she asked me if I was sure I loved Kevin, and I even lied to my own mama." She paused again, her eyes moist with tears. Taking a deep breath, she continued. "I deceived them... and myself. And the worst part is..." Maria hesitated and looked away. "We made love...all the way... And I promised to marry him."

"None of that matters now, Maria."

"But...now he's off fighting the war in Europe, and that's what I have to tell you, Jessie. I...I love you with all my heart, and I'll never love anyone like I love you, but I have to marry Kevin Blake when he comes home."

Chapter
~48~

Jessie sat in the breakfast nook stunned, feeling as though his heart had been ripped from his body. It was an amplification of the agony he'd felt that day long ago when he saw Maria kissing Kevin Blake, except it was a thousand times worse since he'd suddenly lost her again after the joy of having just found her.

"I'm sorry, Jessie, my love. I'm so sorry. I can understand now why people commit suicide."

"No, don't do that, Maria," he said in a hoarse voice.

"Oh, Jessie, my heart is breaking," she cried as tears spilled down her cheeks.

"I know you are sincere in your belief that you're doing the right thing, Maria. But if you don't love Kevin, then it's not fair to him, or you, to get married and live a lie."

"I...I know," she sobbed. "But I promised Kevin I'd marry him, and I've been so dishonest that I swore I'd not break that vow, no matter what. All I can hope is that the love I can give him will be enough. Patsy says that because he is so much in love with me that in time I'll love him as much as I do you."

Maria's rationale churned in Jessie's brain, fighting a tug of war between raging jealousy and a love that forbade him to say or do anything that would hurt her. Finally, he pulled himself out of the breakfast nook. "I have to go, Maria. I have to," he muttered, struggling to control his voice.

"I...know darling. I know."

He walked into the front room, picked up his service cap, and opened the front door. She had followed and stood silently behind him. He hesitated, turned, and looked at her for what he perceived as the last time. She looked like he remembered her from those wonderful days long ago: dressed in blue jeans and shirt, hair tumbling down her back, swollen lips, beautiful eyes, but filled now with tears.

"Good-bye, Maria. I'll always love you."

She tried to answer, but her voice choked as more tears spilled down her cheeks. Then suddenly she threw herself into his arms and clung to him as though she were drowning in a violent sea. Jessie's surprise vanished quickly and he grasped her to him in a vice grip.

They held each other in the doorway for some time without words. Then they began to kiss, and their kisses became feverishly passionate. They groped and grasped each other urgently with their hands and hungry mouths-kissing and fondling and uttering endearments as sexual desire consumed all resistance like dry grass before a raging fire.

Jessie swept Maria off her feet, kicked the front door shut, and carried her into the bedroom. No words were spoken as they frantically tore at their clothes. When she was naked, the sight of her body sent Jessie's passion spinning with that same intense desire that he'd always felt for her. She was the only girl he would ever truly love, and he would take her now regardless of the consequences.

Maria too, was experiencing feelings that made rational thinking impossible. She had known when she threw herself into Jessie's arms that she had lost her will to resist, and she knew they would make love. She couldn't help herself any more than Jessie could.

What Maria could not have imagined was that her deep love for Jessie would now translate into sexual desire. Her experience with Kevin had been more obligation than desire. Now she was experiencing a passion so intense and insatiable that she found herself reacting in a way foreign to anything she had felt previously. It was as though she had suddenly become a wild animal-a starved wild animal.

They smothered each other with greedy embraces, fondling and kissing lips, eyes, and each other's bodies until both were filled with an urgent passion that was so overwhelming, there was no thought of using a contraceptive. When he entered her, Maria immediately felt an extraordinary sensation moving through her body. It was like nothing she had ever experienced before, and it burgeoned with explosive intensity.

From her first intimate encounters with Jessie as a teenager, Maria was aware that she harbored sexual desire, but concerns over morality and pregnancy had inhibited her. Those inhibitions were now obliterated by the erotic avalanche that consumed her, and she responded in a manner she could never have imagined. Her only conscious thought was to satisfy the urgent, compelling need that mushroomed within.

The earth moved for Maria, for the first time in her life. She lost all consciousness of reality, being only vaguely aware of primitive cries escaping her lips. As Maria experienced her first orgasm in Jessie's arms, he too cried out when the earth moved as never before in his sexual encounters. Jessie knew in that wonderful moment, that he had experienced the ultimate in emotion with the girl he loved.

With their bodies entangled, the lovers lay without moving or speaking for some time as their pounding hearts and gasping breath gradually subsided.

"Are you all right?" he eventually whispered.

She reached over, took one of his hands in hers, and squeezed it. "I don't know. I think so."

"I couldn't help myself, Maria."

"I know...neither could I."

They lay with only the sound of breathing for some time, still holding hands tightly. "I knew a long time ago when we were teen age lovers that someday I would experience what I just did, and I knew that it would be with you, my darling Jessie. But I didn't know it would be like this." Maria then raised to a sitting position. "What I just experienced was beyond anything I imagined. It was so...intense, so moving that I still feel as though I'm floating in space. God, Jessie, in a way it's frightening."

"It's because you're in love, Maria. That's why. When you make love with the one you love, it's different."

"Sex is like that because we're in love?"

"I've always believed that. I came to doubt it for a while, but after what I just experienced, I know now that I was right all along. Maybe we had to go through all those things that happened to us before we could realize just how strong our love is."

She lay back and put her arms around him tightly. "Jessie, if that is true, I swear, it was worth all we had to go through. I feel as though I have suddenly stepped into another world, a world I had no idea existed. In a way, it's hard to believe I'm the same person."

"You are the same person and so am I. It's just that we have found the real Jessie and Maria that belong together."

"Yes. God, I shudder to think how close I came to letting you walk out that door."

"That is frightening, but now we know. We know how much we really mean to each other."

She nodded. "I know now what I must do. No matter how much it hurts, I must do it. I must tell Kevin the truth."

"It's the right thing to do, Maria. You can't live a lie. It's not fair to him or you."

"I... I know that now. It will hurt him badly, but I have to do it. I have to. I have no choice," she whispered.

They lay quietly for a while just holding each other. Then Maria slipped on a bathrobe, and Jessie put on his pants, and they went into the kitchen barefoot and sat down in the breakfast nook with two bottles of beer and talked about their lives during their long separation.

Maria told him how much her life had changed living in Los Angeles, and how difficult it had been at first, but that she had worked hard to change her image and qualify to attend UCLA. She told him she and her friend Patsy had both quit college to take jobs at Lockheed because they wanted to help in the war effort. But they both planned to return after the war and finish.

He told her a little about New Guinea and the war, about art college, the terrible loss he felt when Alvin was killed, and about discovering how much he loved to fly. He didn't mention Peggy or Hallie, and she avoided any further discussion of Kevin.

At a break in the conversation, Maria said, "Jessie, I have to ask you something. Have you...made love to many girls?"

"Not many."

"But some girls?"

"Yes. But not like that, Maria. Besides, it doesn't matter now. There will never again be anyone else for either of us."

"Yes. Oh yes, my darling! But...I have to ask one other question. once you have made love the way we did and that happens, will it be like that all the time?"

"I think it will, Maria. As long as you're with the one you love."

"Well, I'm with the one I love," she said.

He looked into her beautiful eyes. "And I'm with the one I love."

They downed the last of their beer, slipped out of the breakfast nook, and returned to the bedroom. There, after a frenzy of erotic kissing and caressing, they had another sexual experience that was as intense and moving as their first. Again for some time afterward, they lay together in Maria's bed with racing pulses and gasping breath, savoring the wonderful experience.

After they lay quietly for a while, they got up, and Maria, dressed in a bathrobe, made a salad and a tuna casserole.

Jessie, barefoot and wearing only his pants, sat in the breakfast nook drinking beer and watching her. They talked more about those great times in Bear Trap Canyon, stopping often to kiss.

After dinner, she slipped out of the breakfast nook, untied her robe, and let it fall to the kitchen floor. They went immediately to the bedroom and made love again, with the same wonderful results.

The next morning when Jessie awoke, it took a moment to orient himself, but when it came to him where he was, he felt a sudden panic. Maria was gone. He leaped out of the bed and hurried out of the bedroom. He found her in the kitchen, barefoot, dressed in jeans, wearing an apron and tending a skillet of frying potatoes.

Jessie stood there for a moment watching her. The sight filled him with an emotion as powerful as their sex had the night before, and he wanted to savor it and record it in his mind so that he would never forget it. He grabbed her from behind and whispered, "Maria, let's get married, right now!"

She dropped the spatula and turned around to face him. His hair hung down over his face, and he was stark naked. "Oh, Jessie, darling!" she cried and wrapped her arms around him.

"I mean it, Maria. I got three days left on my leave. We can drive to Tijuana and get married in a few minutes."

She clung to him desperately for a moment before answering. "I want to marry you more than I want to breathe, Jessie darling, but I can't...I can't."

He looked at her, puzzled. "Why can't you?"

"I know now that I have to break my engagement with Kevin, and I will, but I can't do it in a letter, Jessie. That would be the easy way, but I can't do it, not while he's over there fighting the war."

The emotion that had gripped Jessie when he proposed going to Tijuana had been so acute that now her rejection cut him like a knife. He stood in the kitchen staring at her with his heart aching and his thoughts in disarray.

"Oh, Jessie, I'm sorry, darling. Please try to understand."

"But I don't understand, Maria. I have to go back to the war too."

"Oh God, I know. I know! And I can't stand to even think about it," she cried and tightened her arms around him.

"I don't want to lose you again, Maria."

"We will never lose each other again, never!"

"If you really mean that, you'll marry me now."

"Oh, Jessie, Jessie, I do mean it."

"Then let's go to Mexico."

She hesitated, then said in a low voice, "All right, Jessie."

They held each other for a moment silently. Then he reached down and tilted her face toward him. "I can't take a chance on losing you again, Maria. I just can't. You have to write him." Jessie paused as a sudden jab of guilt sliced through him. Yeah, say it: she has to write him a Dear John letter, like the one that killed Steve Woodson.

"I...I understand, darling," she said with tears in her eyes.

"I...guess I better go take a shower and get some clothes on."

"There's clean towels in the bathroom," she said, wiping at her eyes as she turned back to the frying potatoes.

When he returned to the kitchen, she gave him a little smile and said, "Breakfast is ready except the eggs. How do you like them?"

"Any way except scrambled," he said. "We get scrambled eggs over in New Guinea, but they're dehydrated and taste the way I imagine ground-up chalk would taste."

"Is it bad over there?" she asked, breaking eggs into the frying pan.

Jessie hesitated. Is it bad over there? Yeah, it's bad. The food stinks. The jungle stinks...the snakes...the mosquitoes... shoes turn green overnight. It's war. People are getting killed, and getting Dear John letters. Finally, he replied, "Tokyo Rose plays great music on the radio."

"I read about her. Does she really talk to you on the radio?"

"Yeah. She speaks good English, plays great American music, and has a kind of sexy voice. She's always telling us some guy back in the States is stealing our girl, while we are fighting the war and that we'll be getting a Dear John-" *Like the one Kevin Blake will be getting!* "We all laugh at her, but I guess there is more truth to what she says than we realize."

Maria set a plate of bacon and eggs and hash brown potatoes in front of him.

"Maria?"

"Yes?"

He got up from the table, stepped across to where she stood, and put his arms around her. "I'm wrong and you're right, darling. You can't do that to him...to Kevin...not in a stinking Dear John letter."

She grasped him tightly. "Oh, Jessie, I love you with all my heart and soul, and I promise I'll wait for you for as long as it takes."

"And I'll come back to you, Maria. I promise."

They stood for several minutes holding each other.

"I got an idea. Let's drive up to Santa Barbara and stay in one of those hotels they got on the beach."

"Oh, Jessie, let's do it!"

"But first, I gotta eat this great breakfast you fixed," he said, kissed her, and slid back into the breakfast nook.

It was a wonderful fairy-tale two days. Maria got time off from Lockheed, and Patsy's boyfriend gave Jessie some black market gas-ration stamps so they could buy gasoline to drive to beautiful Santa Barbara. They checked into a grand old oceanfront hotel as Mr. and Mrs. Jessie Rascoe and spent the night making love.

The next day they went swimming, walked on the beach, and had a delightful seafood dinner at a quaint little seashore café, but at dusk the beach was closed and patrolled by armed soldiers. No lights were allowed, and all windows had to be covered with blackout curtains. But Jessie and Maria didn't mind because they spent their evenings in the hotel making love.

It was like two days of heaven for the two lovers. But they weren't in heaven; they were on finite earth where things come to an end, and where a war was going on.

Back in Burbank, they sat in Maria's breakfast nook for a few minutes and talked before Jessie's departure.

"That was the most wonderful two days of my life," she said, taking one of Jessie's hands and holding it on the table. "No matter what happens, I'll never feel cheated now."

"Me either. But now I have to go back."

"Oh, I'd give anything if you didn't have to."

"I know, but I do, Maria. I have to go back and fight the war because it has to be done. I'm just like the rest of the guys who don't want to do it, but do. They put their lives on the line because they know they are right. The Nazis and the Japanese have to be defeated. And Kevin is over there doing his part, so I understand why you have to wait until he comes home to tell him."

"I know, darling. I know."

A few minutes later, on the doorstep of her apartment, they held each other for a long emotional moment.

"Good-bye, my darling Maria."

"Good-bye, my darling Jessie."

Chapter
~49~

Jessie dreaded returning to New Guinea. His driving obsession to avenge Alvin's death was gone. The need to kill Japs was gone. He told himself it was probably a combination of having destroyed the six Japanese Zeros and the emotional effect of rediscovering his love for Maria. But whatever the reasons, he didn't want to go back to war. All he wanted now was the war to be over so he could go home to Maria and his painting.

But the war was far from over, and Jessie knew that he had to go back to New Guinea and fight it, regardless. Like his brother, his friends, Jack, Bobbie, Danny, Bud, Frank-all of them, all around the world. They had to fight and defeat the aggressors. He knew that he could defeat the enemy pilots, and he would do that until it was over, or until a Japanese Jessie Rascoe won the duel.

So it wasn't the same Jessie Rascoe in the converted bomb bay of a B-24 bomber on his way back to war, and his thoughts were not the same either. He relived those wonderful days and nights with Maria over and over, as though to ensure that no matter what the future held, he would have those memories locked within.

When his thoughts went to Hallie Lamont, he felt a pang of guilt, but he reminded himself that he needn't worry too much about Hallie. He was sure that beautiful Hallie had found in her flying what she'd been searching for. He'd seen it when they were together this time. The jerk George was history, and the handsome general, or someone like him, would be waiting. Hallie would always be his beautiful princess, but Jessie was now sure that no girl could ever replace Maria in his heart. It was Maria he would come home to.

And if he didn't...? Then Kevin Blake would come home to her, wouldn't he? But then Kevin had the same problem Jessie did: he had to survive the war. In a strange twist of emotions, Jessie hoped that one of them would, since he couldn't stand the thought of what Maria would face if they were both killed.

When Jessie arrived back at his squadron at Dobodura, the hero's welcome he got from his squadron mates was enhanced by the half dozen bottles of American whiskey he'd brought.

"Jessie, we are glad to see your smiling, scarred face again, ole buddy, but we're happier to see those bottles of good ole Jack Daniel's whiskey," said Robert Heinricker that evening when they all gathered in the squadron Officers club. "Some damn stoolie told the group commander about our Fat Cat Marauder, and they took it away from us so now we are bone dry of drinking material."

"It warms my heart to know how much you guys missed me," said Jessie, putting the six bottles of whisky on the bar top.

"Enough talk, let's get those bottles opened! That is sippin' whiskey!" exclaimed Benilli.

"Jack Daniel's is sure enough good whiskey," agreed a new pilot from Georgia, Bill Kirkwood, who had been assigned to Jessie's tent when Larry Carbon had completed his combat tour and went home. "But I'll tell ya, fellah's, there is nuthin' as good as Georgia white lightnin'. And mah pappy makes the best on the mountain," declared the boyish-featured Georgia pilot.

"What's white lightning?" asked Jessie as he placed the bottles of Jack Daniel's on the bar top.

"You never had any white lightnin'?"

"I have, an' it will knock your head right off your shoulders," said Wander, who had volunteered to be bartender and was in the process of opening the bottles.

"Aw, you must'a got some of that rotgut bootleg stuff. Good white lightnin' is smooth as silk," defended Kirkwood.

Most of the squadron pilots had showed up at the club that evening as the word had spread about Jessie's return with the Jack Daniel's. Now they crowded around the bar with their Battle of Sydney cups waiting for a share of the coveted American whiskey.

When Wander had given everyone their share, Heinricker held his cup high and pronounced, "Here's to all Knights of the air, past and present, and welcome back our gracious host, Ace Jessie Rascoe!" All cups went up with a "Hear hear!" And the celebration began.

"So tell us what all happened, Jessie. Did you get to see the president?" asked Benilli.

Jessie nodded. "Yeah, I saw him."

"Did he pin the medal on you?"

"Well, he put it around my neck. It was on a sash."

"That must'a made you feel purty good, huh?" said Kirkwood.

"Yeah, it did."

"I heard there's a ton of women workers in Washington, D.C.," said Benilli. "You make out with any of them?"

Jessie smiled. "Well, I didn't have a lot of spare time in Washington, but I did get a chance to visit the National Art Gallery and-"

"Hold!" said Heinricker, waving his hand. "Never mind that shit. Don't tell me a big, good-lookin' hero like you didn't get jumped by one or more of those babes, right?"

"Yeah! That's right, Jessie!" said Benilli. "Smile if you got some."

Jessie couldn't help but smile.

"See! See! Look at him smiling, guys. He got some, and I want to hear every detail."

Jessie laughed and took a drink of the whisky. "Well, you guys wouldn't believe it anyway."

"Whip it on us," said Kirkwood, pulling out a bag of Bull Durham tobacco and starting to roll a cigarette.

"Can you really roll one of those?" asked Jessie.

"Sure," grinned the Georgian. "Ah been rollin' mah own since ah was twelve."

"He can not only roll his own, I seen him do it with one hand while flying formation," said Wander.

"It takes a little practice," Kirkwood admitted, then licked the piece of brown cigarette paper to seal in the tobacco, and stuck it in his mouth.

"That's gotta take a LOT of practice," agreed one of the pilots.

"Hey, come on, Jessie!" said Heinricker. "Tell us the story about the beautiful babe that raped you."

"Well, okay, if you really want to hear it," said Jessie, taking a big slug of the Jack Daniel's.

A crowd of pilots gathered as Jessie told them an enhanced version of his meeting Hallie Lamont in the receiving line at the White House. He changed her name and omitted certain personal details, of course. He was interrupted several times for additional toasts and, then urged back to the story. The periodic toasts enhanced Jessie's artistic talents and imagination, and he described Hallie's beauty in detail, extending the story, adding suspense with a long dialogue of sexual innuendo. By the time he was ready for the conclusion, most of the pilots' imaginations had also been enhanced by the Tennessee sipping whiskey. Finally, came the suspenseful, but awful ending, when the beautiful girl walked off with the general.

A chorus of guffaws erupted and Heinricker said, "Jessie, my boy, I can't believe a Flying Knight who can knock nips down by the half dozen would possibly let that happen!"

"You're right, Bob," slurred Wander.

"Well, I don't believe Ish too awful to be true," slurred Benilli.

"Hey, guys, ya got to admit it's one heck of a story," said the non intoxicated voice of Dick Bong, who had become the top ace of the entire South West Pacific. The farm boy from Wisconsin, did not, however, fit the image of a hard-drinking ace fighter pilot. Soft spoken and slightly aloof, he was one of the few non drinkers in the squadron.

"Hey, listen to that you, non believers? And I thank you, Richard, for your expression of confidence in my honesty," slurred Jessie nodding at Bong and grinning.

Bong laughed. "Well, let's say I found it to be a fascinating story."

"You're a gentleman and a scholar, Richard. You sure you wouldn't like a dash of the Jack?"

"No thanks. I just never got into the habit. Oh, I tried some beer once when I was in college, and it made me sick."

Jessie laughed as his thoughts flashed back to the See sisters and his first taste of beer at Pismo Beach.

"Okay, troops, we got an early mission in the morning, so the bar closes in ten minutes," announced Heinricker.

"Mission? Mission? Who cares? Besides I think I'm gonna get into another line of work," announced one of the pilots. "I've had a belly full of war!"

"Yeah me too!" said another, and a group formed a circle and began to harmonize:

"Oh I wanted wings till I got those godamn things,
And now I don't want'em anymore.
Oh they taught me how to fly and sent me here to die
I've had a belly full of war.
You can save those Zeros for your godamn heroes,
Distinguished Flying Crosses do not compensate for losses.
Oh I wanted wings till I got those godamn things,
And now I don't want 'em anymore."

Fortunately, Jessie was not scheduled to fly the next morning after the Jack Daniel's party, but was summoned to meet with Captain O'Shea in his headquarters tent. After the squadron commander had fired up his usual cigar and crammed it into the side of his mouth, he propped his feet up on the table. "You look a little green around the gills this morning, Rascoe. You and the boys have a welcome-home party?"

"I'm afraid so, Captain," replied Jessie in a raspy voice.

"Other than a hangover, how do you feel?"

"I'm fine."

"Then you're ready to go back to work?"

"Yes, sir."

"Okay, I'll tell Heinricker to put you back on the flight schedule tomorrow, and I've promoted you to flight leader. I think you're ready for that."

"Yes, sir. Thank you for your confidence."

O'Shea nodded, pulled his feet down off the table and looked at Jessie. "There is another reason I wanted to see you. This may not be necessary, Jessie, but I'm gonna warn you anyway because I don't know how seriously you're taking all this hero stuff. But I do know how the nip pilots are taking it: they couldn't care less that you got a big hero badge. They will shoot your ass down just the same. You get my point?"

"Yes, Captain. I got it."

"Okay, and I want to caution you that with all this publicity you got, everybody from MacArthur on down is gonna be watching you, expecting more glorious deeds. The war correspondents particularly are gonna be lookin' for another big story, and if you get caught up in that bullshit, they'll get their story all right: your obituary. Comprendo?"

"I got the picture, Captain O'Shea."

"I hope you have, Jessie. I sincerely do."

That evening Jessie wrote a ten-page letter to Maria, most of which was about how much he loved her and missed her already and how wonderful their three days together had been. He assured her he would come home and not to worry. Then he wrote to his folks to let them know he'd arrived back safely. He started three letters to Hallie and tore up all three. Nothing he wrote sounded right. He decided to let it lie for a while until he could figure out what to say to her.

The next day Jessie flew his first mission in a brand new P-38 assigned to him. One of the ground crew who specialized in "nose art" had painted six Japanese flags and the name MARIA on the side of the fighter.

Jessie led Yellow flight in a sixteen-ship formation that flew cover for two squadrons of B-25 Billy Mitchell bombers. They were to strike Japanese ground installations at Finschhafen on the northeast coast of New Guinea.

After takeoff from Horanda strip, the fighters joined with the bombers at the rendezvous point and followed their standard procedure of weaving a protective lazy-S pattern above the bombers. Then, just before they reached the target, the fighters pulled off, avoiding the target area and the anti-aircraft fire but keeping close enough to engage any enemy aircraft that attacked the bombers.

This time the Japanese fighters did not attack, so the P-38s flew around the perimeter of the target area watching the bombers.

Jessie looked down from inside his tiny cockpit and watched the fiery explosions trailing the B-25s, as they swept low over the mottled jungle dropping their bombs. It seemed impossible for them to fly through the blanket of black clouds, which were exploding shells and the streams of antiaircraft fire coming up at them from the enemy batteries. But each bomber swept through, holding its course and leaving a trail of destruction from the exploding bombs.

Then, one B-25 began to spew a trail of smoke from one of its engines, but the bomber held its course across the target and dropped its bombs. Jessie watched in wrenching fascination as the pilot pulled up after his bomb run with black smoke pouring from the crippled engine. Seconds later the smoke erupted into a blazing inferno that stretched the length of the aircraft. The bomber seemed to hang in space for an instant, then nosed down, and dove into the jungle with a gigantic, fiery explosion.

Since no enemy aircraft challenged the bombers, there was no action on the part of the fighter escort. The B-25 that was shot down was the only loss on the mission, and intelligence reported excellent results.

That night as he lay in his cot under the mosquito net, listening to the jungle sounds, Jessie thought of the times he and Alvin used to lie in their pup tents listening to the night sounds in Bear Trap Canyon, and he thought of his Maria and all the wonderful times they had together. Then he thought about the wives or girl friends of those brave men who died in the B-25 bomber and the terrible news they would be receiving.

Jessie led Yellow flight on three more B-25 escort missions that week with no enemy opposition. Then the squadron was assigned to cover a large formation of B-24 heavy bombers that would strike major installations deep into enemy territory at Wewak on the north west coast of New Guinea.

It was Jessie's first mission of escorting a large fleet of heavy bombers, and it was an inspiring sight to see them in a massive formation that stretched over the horizon. His squadron and several others weaved their protective cover over the armada as it winged its way toward the enemy. The B-24 Liberator, with its long, slender wing and big twin tails, flew in a uniquely graceful way that seemed to belie its deadly capabilities.

After three hours of flying, the armada approached the target area. The fighters pulled off to the side of the bomber formation, test-fired their guns, and armed their auxiliary fuel drop switches. They had just completed that when radio silence was broken with a shrill voice shouting: "Bogies, ten o'clock!"

"Drop your tanks, Captive!" barked Captain O'Shea, and seconds later the morning sky was filled with tumbling auxiliary fuel tanks. "There they are. Let's go get 'em!"

A large number of Japanese fighters swooped down on the bombers, who returned fire in deadly streams from their turret and waist guns. To pursue the attackers now required that the P-38s fly into that hail of anti aircraft fire, but no one flinched. They attacked the enemy with guns blazing.

Jessie, leading Yellow flight, glanced across at his wingman to make sure he was in position. The Georgia mountain boy gave him a thumbs-up. Then Jessie nosed his fighter down and swooped onto an attacker's tail as the Japanese pilot came off his run on a B-24. Jessie held his fire until the Zero filled his gunsight, then pressed the firing button that activated the deadly arsenal on the P-38. The concentrated fire power of four fifty caliber machine guns and a 20MM cannon ripped into the enemy aircraft, and seconds later it mushroomed into a blazing ball of fire and began to disintegrate.

Jessie was watching the Japanese fighter that he had recognized as a Nakajima KI 43 "Oscar" begin its death plunge when his headsets cracked: "Jessie! We got bogies on our tail!" He recognized Kirkwood's voice and glanced back to see two more Oscars in a diving attack with wing guns blinking fire.

"Yellow lead! Yellow lead! You got two of 'em on your tail!" someone else warned.

Before Jessie could respond he heard that awful sound of lead ripping through aluminum. He rolled the Lightning into a bank toward the attacking aircraft. This required the Japanese pilots to adjust their angle of attack, and that allowed Jessie to temporarily escape their fire then pull up into a high speed climb that the Ki 43 could not match.

"Stay with me, Kirk!" he shouted over the radio.

"I'm with ya!" replied the Georgian.

The Japanese pilots continued to fire on the P-38s, but now they were out of range, and the Oscars banked away for greener pastures.

Watching them in the mirror on top of his canopy, the instant he saw the Oscars break, Jessie whipped the Lightning into a 180 degree turn and dove after them at full power.

The P-38 closed the distance quickly on the two enemy aircraft. Jessie lined his sight on the nearest Oscar and jammed his thumb on the firing button, but his aim was high and the tracers arched over the canopy of his target. The Japanese pilot, seeing the tracers, banked his nimble fighter into a wing over and dove away, with Jessie and his wing man in hot pursuit. (Using tracers was at the pilot's discretion. Some pilots had their guns loaded without tracers, to keep the enemy from knowing they were being attacked. Most pilots however, including Jessie, preferred to use them.)

At that same instant, the other Japanese pilot saw the P-38s and also slammed his aircraft into a dive. Now all four fighters were in a loose formation dive with both P-38s firing at the Oscars.

Knowing they could terminate their dive quicker than the P-38s, the two Japanese pilots suddenly pulled out of their dive, and Jessie was faced with an Oscar fighter directly in his path. His reaction was also a violent pull-up. But it was not in time, and the two fighters met in a clash of crushed aluminum and the scream of a runaway engine as one of Jessie's propeller's ripped off as it sliced through the Oscar's's wing, and then went spinning out into space, its blades still whirling and spewing pieces of torn Ki 43 aluminum. The Oscar, with one wing ripped off, spun wildly as it tumbled, shedding bits and pieces along its path.

Loss of the propeller, and with huge chunks of the engine nacelle torn away by the collision, caused a severe drag on that side of the fighter. The controls jerked erratically, and the P-38 yawed and pitched as Jessie fought to keep it from going out of control. He could smell raw fuel, and clouds of black smoke poured from the mutilated engine.

"Who is that trailing smoke?" said someone over the radio.

"It's Yellow lead," replied Jessie.

"Is it as bad as it looks, Rascoe?"

Jessie recognized O'Shea's voice. "I don't know how it looks, but it's bad where I am."

"You gonna make it?"

"I don't know."

"Where's your wingman?"

"I lost him."

"Ah'm here. Uh, Yellow two. Ah lost ya, Jessie," came the voice of Kirkman.

"Okay, Yellow two, you see him now?"

"Uh, yeah. Ah see 'em! You puttin' out a lot of smoke, Jessie."

"Yellow two, get over there an cover him."

"Roger, sir."

"Captive lead to all flights. Looks like the bogies have departed. We lose anybody?"

"Captive lead, we lost green four."

"You lost Johnson?"

"Yes."

"Damn! Any sign of a chute?"

"No, he went straight in."

There was silence for a moment on the combat frequency of the Flying Knights Fighter Squadron.

"Green lead, you saw him go in?"

"I saw him...and the explosion."

"Shit! Mark the spot on your chart."

"Roger."

"Anyone else in trouble?"

"Blue lead here. Blue three has one feathered, but he's all right."

"Okay. Have blue four cover him and send him home."

"Roger wilco."

"How you doin', Jessie?"

"I'm doin."

"Yellow two, you covering Jessie?"

"Ah'm on his wing, but it sure looks bad. He lost his right prop, and he's trailing a lot'a smoke."

"Head down the coast, Jessie. You'll have a better chance there if you have to bail out. Good luck."

"Roger wilco."

"The rest of you Captives form up over the bombers. I don't think the nips will be back, but keep a sharp eye," instructed Captain O'Shea.

The two wounded P-38s headed for home with their escorts, while the remaining flights returned to their protective positions again, weaving over the bombers in lazy-S turns as they started the long flight home.

With Kirkman following off his right wing, Jessie headed east down the New Guinea coast of the Soloman Sea. It was all

Japanese territory but better than the jungle if he had to bail out, which looked probable.

It was like a re-creation of Jessie's first disastrous mission except this time he had to wrestle with the badly damaged fighter for over two hours, knowing that he could lose control at any moment and crash or attempt a bailout. Either way, Jessie would be in serious trouble. But he'd promised Maria he would come home to her, so with dogged determination he kept the wounded P-38 flying until he reached Horanda strip at Dobodura. Fortunately, this time he managed to land the crippled Lightning, but was so exhausted the crash rescue crew had to lift him out of the cockpit.

After he was taken by jeep back to his squadron bivouac, Jessie walked down the trail to his tent, dug out a bottle of Jack Daniel's whiskey he had saved, and took a big gulp straight from the bottle.

When Kirkman entered a few minutes later, he looked at Jessie and said, "Sorry Jessie."

"Just gimme a damn cigarette, Bill."

Kirkman raised an eye brow. "You want a cigarette?"

"Yeah."

"You want ta roll yer own or a tailor made?"

"I don't give a damn. Just gimme a cigarette!"

Kirkman reached into his shirt pocket and handed Jessie a pack of cigarettes.

Jessie dug one out and put it to his lips.

"Keep the pack. Ah got plenty," said Kirkman handing Jessie his Zippo cigarette lighter. "But ah want ma Zippo back. Ya gotta get yer own lighter."

Jessie lit the cigarette, took a puff, and choked.

"They take a little gettin' used to."

Jessie nodded and took another gulp of Jack Daniel's and another puff of the cigarette. This time he didn't choke.

"Ah'm sorry ah lost ya in that dogfight, Jessie."

"It wasn't your fault, Bill, so don't worry about it."

"That bird of yours is a mess. What happened?"

"I'm knockin' down nips now with my props," Jessie grumbled, took another gulp from the bottle of whiskey and handed it to Kirkman. Then he flopped down on his cot and fell into an exhausted sleep.

Chapter
~50~

In a tortured dream, Jessie was back fighting for survival in the cockpit of his damaged P-38 when his eyes popped open to see Captain O'Shea standing beside his cot.

"I need to talk to you, Rascoe."

Jessie swung his legs off the cot and sat up. O'Shea stood without speaking for a moment, the usual cigar in the corner of his mouth. He was dressed in his sweat-stained flight suit with his forty-five pistol strapped under one arm.

"You awake?"

"Yeah, I'm awake."

"I'm glad you made it, Jessie, although I don't know how you managed to keep that bird in the air. It's so beat-up we may have to scrap it. What in hell did you do?"

"It was easy, Captain. I crashed into a Oscar."

"Jesus!"

Was he as bad off as you?"

Jessie nodded. "Yeah, poor bastard lost a wing."

"That's a tough way to get a kill. Unfortunately, you're only gonna get probable credit since no one else saw it and your gun camera is a mutilated mess."

"So it goes."

"Well, Kirkman saw you shoot down the other Oscar, so at least you'll get credit for him."

Jessie nodded.

"Are you okay?"

"Yeah."

"Well then, get your tail over to intelligence and give Lt. Spence you're combat report," said O'Shea. Removing his cigar, he tapped the ashes off and put it back in his mouth. "And congratulations on number seven," said the commander and walked out of the moldy tent.

Jessie's depressed state of mind got a boost when later that day he received several letters at mail call; most of them were real letters from Maria and not V mail. Although the government encouraged families to write V mail, it was photo copy and didn't seem personal enough for the news hungry warriors in the combat zones.

Jessie, like everyone, savored mail and devoured Maria's letters, reading them over and over. She wrote just the way she talked and always included wonderful expressions of her love. Her letters always gave Jessie's morale a big boost, and on this day he needed it.

Two days later, Jessie was back on the flight schedule, and when he arrived at his newly assigned aircraft for an early morning mission, he was surprised to see that his name with seven miniature Japanese flags, and MARIA II, painted on the side of the gondola.

"How does it look, Lieutenant?" asked his crew chief, Sergeant Charles Kurtz.

Jessie was pleased although he was still smarting over the loss of his first Maria. After hesitating, he said, "It looks great, Charles. It really does. Thanks."

"Captain O'Shea's orders," said the sergeant.

"It was?"

"Yes, sir."

Jessie nodded. "I hope I can keep from wrecking this one at least for a while."

"You'll do fine, Lieutenant. You're gonna be one of the top aces in the squadron."

Dressed in a crumpled flight suit with a faded yellow Mae West life jacket around his neck, Captain O'Shea walked up to Jessie and his crew chief, removed his cigar, and said, "I thought you said you didn't smoke, Rascoe."

"A recent bad habit acquisition," said Jessie taking a puff of his cigarette.

O'Shea nodded. "So it goes. I expect we'll get some action today. You sure you're okay?"

"I'm fine, Captain."

The commander nodded. "Okay, then let's get to it."

At the earlier briefing, the intelligence officer advised that reconnaissance aircraft had brought back pictures of scores of newly arrived fighter aircraft on the big Lae airfield. It was the objective of the Flying Knights squadron to sweep in at low altitude with two flights and destroy the aircraft by strafing them in their parking areas while the other two flights came in at high altitude to protect the lower flights from any enemy patrols that might be airborne.

After takeoff, the squadron flew out to the Soloman Sea, turned west, and followed the New Guinea coast line. As they approached the area two hours later, the squadron split into two groups of two flights each. Yellow and Green flight began their climb for higher altitude while Red and Blue remained at low altitude.

A few minutes before reaching Lae, O'Shea gave another hand signal, and the two lower flights armed and test-fired their guns and jettisoned their auxiliary fuel tanks. Now it was the squadron leader's job to lead his two attacking flights to the target, which was a test of his navigation skills because at low altitude navigation is more difficult.

O'Shea gave another hand signal for his two flights to drop back into trail for their strafing run. Jessie glanced across at his wingman, Dick Turney, who gave a thumbs up signal as he eased back on power to drop into a trailing position.

A short time later the two flights were in trail for their strafing attack, and shortly after that, the Japanese airfield appeared ahead. Squadron leader O'Shea's navigation had brought them on target.

Jessie could see that sure enough the airfield ahead was packed with aircraft and they had taken the Japanese by surprise as there was no antiaircraft fire visible. He could see O'Shea open fire on his strafing run, and immediately an aircraft on the airfield erupted in flame and smoke, and as the other ships in red flight streaked across the airfield, several more aircraft exploded and began burning.

Jessie swooped down over the airfield firing his guns that raked several aircraft causing explosions that sent flaming pieces shooting skyward. He watched the fiery trail of his cannon fire walk down the airfield, across another aircraft, and into a building that suddenly erupted with a huge explosion that mushroomed into the sky in a gigantic cloud of fire and smoke that engulfed the P-38, pelting it with debris.

For an instant, it flashed through Jessie's mind that he had just destroyed MARIA II. Then blue sky reappeared in his windshield, and his earphones cracked with Heinricker's voice from his top cover position: "Captive lead you got bogies diving on you!"

"Bogies! Bogies!" shouted someone else.

"Green and Yellow, drop your tanks!" snapped Heinricker.

The attacking Japanese Zeros had been on patrol but had not seen the approaching enemy aircraft until the lower flights struck the airfield. Now they came swooping down on the strafing aircraft who, at low altitude, were vulnerable. But the Captive top cover dropped their external tanks and dove on the enemy flights, which then became a giant aerial engagement of the two enemy forces.

A quick check told Jessie that MARIA II had not been disabled by the explosion he'd flown through. Hearing the call of bogies, he put his fighter into a full power climb, scouring the sky around him, watching for aircraft. "Blue two, where are you?" he called for his wingman, but now the radio crackled with aerial dogfighting transmissions.

A flash of metal in the sun drew his eyes to a P-38 with a Zero swooping down from a high speed dive. Seconds later he heard the pilot call for help and recognized it was Captain O'Shea.

"I'm in trouble! I got one on my tail!" transmitted O'Shea.

"I'm on 'em!" barked Jessie as he swooped down on the enemy aircraft.

The squadron leader banked sharply to cut inside the attacker's fire, but in seconds, the quick-turning Mitsubishi had pulled inside the Lightning and began to fire. Jessie dove from his altitude advantage and opened fire, but not in time as O'Shea's left engine belched a column of black smoke.

Jessie's machine gun and cannon fire slammed into the Zero, killing the pilot instantly. He slumped over his controls, dove straight in the ground, and disintegrated.

"Get the hell out of here, Red leader! I'll cover you," instructed Jessie.

"I'm goin'!" O'Shea replied as he applied full war emergency power to his good engine and feathered the prop on his smoking engine.

Jessie held a protective position off the crippled leader's wing as they raced away from where the aerial battle raged.

"Captive lead, this is Yellow lead. You covered?"

"I'm okay, Bob. Jessie's covering me, and we're headed out of here."

"Roger. You gonna make it?"

"I think so."

"Blue leader! Blue leader from Blue two! Where are ya?" came Turney's frantic transmission.

"Blue two, I'm covering Red leader. Find a Captive and get on his wing!"

Sweeping his eyes from side to side watching for bogies, Jessie picked up two enemy aircraft that had seen the smoke from O'Shea's engine and were on a steep diving attack.

Jessie banked head on into the attacking fighters. "Red lead, we got a couple coming down on us. Hold your heading!" instructed Jessie.

"Roger wilco."

"Your mistake, guys," muttered Jessie as his gun site zeroed-on the lead aircraft. When he opened fire, his prediction was validated. The deadly, concentrated fire power of the Lightning struck the lead Zero head-on sending pieces of the engine and structure flying, including a large piece of engine cowling that flew off and slammed into the other Zero who was following his leader closely.

The lead Zero erupted into a flaming mass, leaving a trail of burning aircraft piece on its course to the jungle. The other Zero pitched violently into an erratic flight path and then seemed to just wander off across the jungle. Jessie winged over in pursuit to finish the job. Then a frantic transmission cut into his plans.

"I got another one on me, Jessie!"

Jessie banked around and slammed on full power. He could see another enemy aircraft was indeed on O'Shea's tail and firing. O'Shea was banking and turning frantically to keep out of the enemy fire, but with only one engine, he could not escape the Zero.

Jessie realized that he could not get in firing range in time to save his commander. His only chance was a long shot. He pulled the nose up and fired a long burst. He watched his tracers arch across the distance, falling behind the Zero. Raising the nose again slightly, he fired another long burst. This time the fireballs lobbed across and plunged directly into the aft section of the Zero. The Mitsubishi burst into flames, continued on for a short distance, then nosed down, and plunged into the jungle.

"You okay, red lead?" Jessie called.

"I think so. Let's get the hell out of here," O'Shea replied.

In scattered groups of ones and twos, the Knights returned to Dobodura and landed back at Horanda Air strip. O'Shea landed on one engine. Green three couldn't get his landing gear down and crash landed in the mud. Miraculously there were no losses, and the Flying Knights had successfully destroyed numerous aircraft and facilities on their strafing attack and shot down another seven enemy aircraft, despite being outnumbered.

Several of the P-38s had damage in the form of Japanese bullet holes. One that didn't was MARIA II, and Jessie Rascoe added three more confirmed aerial kills to his score.

As the pilots gathered around the de-briefing tent, smoking and talking about the mission, O'Shea walked up to Jessie with a solemn look on his face and said, "You are a hell of a shot, Rascoe, and I owe you," said the commander.

Jessie nodded. "Well, you would do the same for me, Captain...Wouldn't you?"

The two pilots smiled. "Yeah, I sure as hell would," said O'Shea.

It was uplifting to the fighter pilots when they scored a major victory, as they had this day, without a loss. That evening someone came up with three bottles of Aussie Schnapps, and a celebration was on. Schnapps was awful stuff compared to Jack Daniel's, but no one complained as everyone was in high spirits. Even Captain O'Shea showed up and joined in the party.

Georgian Bill Kirkman was celebrating his first victory and Donald Benilli his fourth. "Just think, one more, and I'm an ace! Can you imagine how those New York babes are gonna swarm around me then?" said Benilli.

"I thought you said they already swarm around you?" replied Jessie as a group of pilots stood next to the bar drinking the Schnapps.

"Yeah, but those were Forty-second Street babes. It will be Broadway babes for big ace Benilli!"

"What's the difference?" asked Dick Turney.

"Well, I'll tell ya, Forty-second Street babes are good. But it's kinda like plain ole Bourbon compared to Jack Daniel's. The Broadway babes are just a little smoother."

Everyone laughed, and Wander proposed a toast. "Well, here's to you new guys. You're doing great, and I swear, if he continues ole hot pilot Rascoe is gonna catch Dick Bong."

"You're right, Ralph," said Bong as he had overheard Wander and stepped up to the group. "Congratulations, Jessie." The way you are going you're gonna pass me for sure."

"Not likely," replied Jessie with a smile.

"I think you got a handle on it."

"Beginner's luck."

Bong smiled. "I don't think so."

"Neither do I. He zipped right past me and is now the second leading ace in the Fifth Air Force," said Bob Heinricker.

"Yeah! And that goes double for me because he sure as hell saved my ass today," said the squadron commander holding up his mug. "Hear's to ya, Jessie!"

After more toasts to Jessie and the other victors of the day, a group huddled together and harmonized with another of the Flying Knights' special songs created by the pilots themselves:

"It's down to Sydney from Guinea I go
Down to Sydney from a place called Lae
When an M P sergeant sais pardon me please
There's blood on your tunic and mud on your knee
I said listen here sergeant, you bloody damn fool
I just came back from a place called Lae
Where shrapnel is flying and comforts are few
And good men are dying for dastards like you
Dinky die...Dinky die
And good men are dying for bastards like you."

The celebration continued until all the Schnapps was gone. Then some made it back to their tents, and others had to be carried. Jessie made it on his own, but it seemed that he had barely shut his eyes when it was morning and Bob Heinricker was shaking him. "Come on, Ace, wake up. Your fans are calling."

"What?"

"Colonel Johnson from Fifth Air Force headquarters and a couple big mouth correspondents await your presence."

"Aw, come on, Bob, I'm hammered. Tell 'em I flew the dawn patrol or something."

"It won't fly, ace. You gotta come."

With Heinricker's help Jessie dressed, dumped a canteen of water over his head, and stumbled up the path to the officers' club where the dignitaries awaited.

It was evident the colonel was not pleased at the sight of his new double ace, but he explained that Lieutenant Rascoe was suffering a bit from battle fatigue.

Jessie answered the usual questions as best he could considering he had a splitting headache and was having trouble focusing his thoughts. Then he gave them his favorite line about how he was just a country boy who shot birds on the fly and that's the way he now shot down nips.

The correspondents loved it and ran off to file their stories on the new double ace at 5th Air Force. Jessie stumbled back down the path and crashed in his sack.

David Blake, chairman of the board of the Blake Corporation, looked down the sparkling dinner table and focused his eyes on one of his guests: Maria Hunter. It concerned him that his future daughter-in-law wasn't from the social stratum he would have preferred for his son. But she was a pretty girl, and there was a kind of homey quality about her that he liked, which went a long way toward making up for her lack of pedigree. Besides, he knew Kevin worshiped her, and he'd promised his son that he and Mrs. Blake would make her feel like part of the family until Kevin returned from the war. So Maria was included on occasion in their social functions.

"How are you doing over at the aircraft plant, Maria?" he asked.

Maria glanced down the table at him and said, "Just fine, Mr. Blake. We just rolled out Lightning number five thousand."

"Is that right? That is impressive. I didn't realize Lockheed had reached that kind of production." Blake turned to one of his guests at the table and said, "Fred, did you know they were cranking out those kind of numbers at Lockheed?"

"Yeah, I did. David. That aircraft has turned out to be a really fine pursuit plane and particularly in the South West Pacific. I hear that MacArthur is squalling for all of them he can get."

"There was a story in yesterday's *Examiner* about one of the Army Air Corps Pilots over in New Guinea that just became a double ace in a P-38," said another of the guests at the dinner table.

Maria sat at the table struggling with conflicting thoughts swirling through her. She wanted to shout that she knew that P-38 pilot and that she loved him and he loved her, but of course, she couldn't. Actually, she felt ashamed that she was even there pretending to be the faithful fiancé of the Blake's son, when she knew that she was going to call off the engagement as soon as Kevin came home. But the Blake's had been so nice to her, she didn't have the heart to disappoint them. It was deceitful and dishonest, and she hated it.

Brigadier General Anthony Browne pulled himself up on one elbow and looked across the hotel room at Hallie Lamont as she reached for a bathrobe hanging in the hotel closet. Her beautiful, slender body gleamed with perspiration, the nipples on her breasts swollen from the intensity of the sexual experience she had just enjoyed.

"You're a beautiful woman, Hallie."

"And you are a handsome and delightful lover, Tony," she replied, flipping her hair back as she slipped into the robe.

"After the way we just made love, I can't believe that you're not in love with me."

She laughed. "A little male ego there, General?" she said, pulling the bathrobe around her and fastening the tie.

He smiled. "Generals certainly got ego, but it's more than that. I'm desperately in love with you, Hallie, and I just find it hard to accept that your only interest in me is sexual."

"I like you, Tony, and we have a lot of fun together. But I'm not ready to tell you that I'm in love with you."

"I know, but I guess this is where the ego comes in because I can't accept it. And I don't understand how someone as sophisticated as you could think she is in love with some young guy who hardly knows which end is up."

"What young guy?"

"You know."

She smiled. "Who do I think I'm in love with?"

"That hotshot pilot, Rascoe."

She hesitated. "Well, I can't honestly deny or confirm that either. But in any event, that young hotshot just shot down three more Zeros, so I think he knows which end is up."

"Yeah. I heard, and I meant that relatively."

"I know," she said, leaned down, and kissed him.

"Does that mean I'm in the running?"

"I think so, but love is a strange phenomenon, Tony. There's no logic to it."

"I know. Can you stay over tonight?"

"No, sorry. In fact, I've got to shower and get dressed now because I have to be back on base tonight. I'm ferrying a B-17 to Kansas tomorrow morning."

"You are? You're piloting a Flying Fortress?"

"Yes."

The general pulled himself up in the bed and looked at the young woman across the room. "That's also hard to accept."

"What is?"

"That a beautiful little girl like you could fly one of those big bombers."

She laughed. "It's got nothing to do with looks or size, Tony. The B-17 doesn't care who flies it, as long as they know how."

The general shook his head. "You are an amazing girl, Hallie. I just hope I've got more of what it takes than that hotshot pilot."

Hallie smiled.

Patsy Cline looked up from where she sat reading a book when the front door to the small apartment swung open. It was Maria, and Patsy knew by the look on her face that something was wrong. Maria had been depressed a lot lately. In fact, she hadn't been herself since her reunion with Jessie Rascoe. Patsy almost wished he'd never showed up. Oh, she liked him, and he was terribly handsome, even with that scar on his forehead, but he sure had played havoc with Maria's life.

"What's wrong, Maria?" said Patsy as Maria flung herself into a sofa chair.

"Oh, Patsy, I hate myself for what I'm doing! I feel obligated to go to the Blakes' when they invite me, but it's so dishonest that I..."

"Well, why don't you just make an excuse not to go?"

"I've thought about doing that, but they are so nice to me and they treat me like one of the family. I just can't disappoint them. Tonight at dinner, Mr. Blake and a guest were talking about Jessie, and I almost blurted out that he was the boy I love. But I caught myself and then I felt terrible. It was awful, Patsy."

"That's wild. Why were they talking about Jessie?"

"Well, his picture was in the Examiner because he just shot down some more Japanese airplanes."

"Wow! What did you say?"

"I didn't say anything. I just sat there feeling like some kind of traitor or something."

"Yeah, I can imagine."

"I just feel so dishonest..."

"Well, I can see you gotta talk this out," said Patsy. "You want a beer?" she asked, getting up from the chair.

"I guess so."

When they had settled with their beers, they both took a drink, and Patsy said, "Maria, you better quit beating yourself up over this, or you are gonna come unglued. Make up your mind what you're going to do, and do it!"

"Yes, you're right. And that is what I'm going to do!"

"Okay, then, do it. What are you gonna do?"

"I got a letter from Kevin today, and he's coming back from overseas on a special project, and he'll get a few days to come home. So when he gets here, I'll tell him."

"Good. What are you gonna tell him?"

"You know. That I love Jessie, and we're going to be married when he comes home."

"If he comes home."

"Oh, Patsy, please don't say things like that."

"I'm sorry, Maria. You're right. I shouldn't have said that. You know how I am. I always put my foot in it."

"He has to come home. He just has to."

Chapter
~51~

The tents in the Flying Knights bivouac area had low-voltage electricity powered by a central gasoline generator. Each pilot was allowed one low-wattage light-bulb hung in his clothes locker to reduce the mold that formed overnight on shoes and clothes. Each cot also had a line hooked to a set of earphones that could be used to listen to Armed Forces Radio in the evenings. One of the favorite programs was Tokyo Rose because she played all the latest American music.

Late one night, a few days after Jessie had become a double ace, he was lying in his mosquito-netted bed listening to Tokyo Rose. She was playing some of the great music that Frank Grover and his band had played at Frazier Park. Jessie paid little attention to her occasional pitch about how poor American boys were being misled by American propaganda and back home their girls and wives were being seduced by four F's and draft dodgers. Then suddenly, she said: "The Ninth Fighter squadron pilots in New Guinea are not Flying Knights at all. They are nothing but butchers, and their newest butcher, Lieutenant Jessie Rascoe, will pay the penalty for his vicious action at Lae."

"Jessie! You hear that?" shouted Benilli as he was also listening.

"Hey! Stop shouting. I gotta fly in the morning," growled Wander, who was awakened by Benilli's shout.

"It's Tokyo Rose. She's talking about Jessie!"

"She is?" said Kirkman.

"Yeah, plug in your headset."

"Well, she's just put on another record, but she sure enough was talking about me and the squadron. Jesus, how do you suppose she knew that?" said Jessie.

"Aw, those war correspondents wire stuff like that back to the states, and it gets sent all over. Then it ends up on Tokyo Rose's radio show, and she blabs it all over the place," informed Wander. "Now you guys shut up. I gotta get some sleep."

Although Jessie had listened to Tokyo Rose often at night and realized it was just propaganda. This time it was personal, and it struck a chord that disturbed him. He took off the headsets and repeated her charge in his thoughts. In a sense, he was a butcher, wasn't he? Yeah. No question about that, but then so were the Japanese pilots who were trying just as hard to butcher him. So? It's the name of this game, Rascoe. Not like the games of your boyhood, this challenge isn't earning Boy Scout merit badges. It's a game of kill or be killed. It's a game you play to win if you ever want to go home to Maria, and someday, maybe, become an artist.

The next day the squadron was scheduled to seek and destroy Japanese resupply barges along the enemy occupied north east coastal area. Jessie was assigned to lead yellow flight, and Don Benilli would lead green flight. As the two friends stood talking and smoking before mission briefing, Lieutenant Heinricker walked up and said, "Good news for you two, you're out of here tomorrow on R and R for a week of booze, women, and debauchery in Sydney."

"Hot diggidy dog!" exclaimed Benilli. "Get ready all you Aussie babes, Benilli is on his way!"

"Leave a couple for me, Benilli. I got an R and R coming up," said one of the other pilots.

"Hey, when Jessie and I leave Sydney, those gals will never want to see any of you clods again, right, Jess?"

"Right on, Don," replied Jessie with a grin.

"Meanwhile, let's go mutilate some Jap supply barges," said Heinricker. He then led the group of sixteen pilots down the path to the personal equipment tent where they each picked up his personal parachute, which had attached a one man rubber life boat and a jungle survival kit.

A short time later the squadron of sixteen P-38's took off from Dobodura's Horanda air strip in pairs, joined in formation, and began a search along the North West coast of New Guinea. Red and Yellow flight flew at low altitude to spot the barges while Blue and Green covered them from high altitude.

After about an hour of flight, Jessie came on the radio with: "Okay, little red riding hood, the big bad wolf can see you down there." He had spotted a group of Japanese supply barges tied up in a cove. They had camouflage netting stretched over them to escape detection during daylight hours, but Jessie's sharp eyes had detected them.

"Yellow leader, you got 'em spotted?" came Heinricker voice.

"I got 'em, Bob."

"Okay. You lead, we'll follow. Captive leader to squadron: Yellow is going in first, then I'll go, and when we're finished, we'll take high cover, and Blue and Green, you can work 'em over."

"Okay. Yellow flight get in trail and give it on 'em !"

Following Jessie, the fighters formed in trail and one after the other went into shallow dive strafing runs, raking the barges with their blistering fire.

"Yellow lead to squadron. Watch it. They got anti aircraft!" barked Jessie as lines of fire balls began to stream skyward from one of the barges. But one after the other, the P-38's saturated the barges with machine gun and cannon fire, ripping them to pieces as multiple fires and explosions sent columns of black smoke boiling into the sky.

Then a P-38 coming off its strafing run took a direct hit from anti aircraft fire and instantly belched smoke and flames. The Lightning flew on for a short distance, then nosed down, and dove straight into the Soloman Sea with an eruption of fire and sea foam.

"Who went in?" barked Heinricker.

"I think it was Green lead," replied someone.

"Green leader from Red leader, you read, Benilli?"

No answer.

"He ain't gonna answer."

"What? Who called?"

"Yellow lead, It...was green lead...Benilli," confirmed Jessie Rascoe in a voice filled with agony.

"You see it, Jessie?"

"Yeah."

"Was there a chute?"

"There was no chute."

"Any one else see anything?"

No answer.

"Fuck!" Silence. "Red element, drop down and make a few passes just in case."

After red element had flown over the water where Benilli had crashed, the squadron assembled and returned in silence to Horanda airfield.

After the squadron landed all the pilots gathered at the debriefing tent except Jessie who went straight to his tent, dug out his last bottle of Jack Daniel's, and took several big gulps straight from the bottle. Then he lit a cigarette, flopped down on his cot, and smoked the cigarette while he stared at the moldy tent ceiling. Jessie was torn with a wrenching agony akin to that he had experienced when Alvin was killed. Benilli had, in a way, replaced the void that Jessie had felt with the loss of his best friend, Alvin Pyeatt.

"You want to write the letter to his parents?" asked O'Shea who appeared at the entrance to the tent.

"No, but thanks for asking. I think it would mean more coming from his commander."

"Okay...I'm sorry about Benilli. I know you and he were good friends."

Jessie swung his legs off the cot and took another drink of whiskey. "Want a shot?" he said, handing the bottle to O'Shea.

"Yeah, I do," said the captain taking a drink from the bottle. "Your R and R in Sydney might help," said O'Shea handing the bottle back to Jessie.

"I don't want to go to Sydney now."

"I think you should, Jessie."

Jessie shook his head and took another drink of the Jack Daniels.

"Well, I do. So your goin', and that's an order. Wander is also due, so he you can go together," said the commander, turned, and walked out of the tent.

Chapter
~52~

A few days later Jessie and Ralph Wander got R and R orders. They packed their B-4 bags and hitched a ride on a Gooney Bird that flew them over the Owen Stanley Mountains to Port Moresby. There, they caught another ride to Sydney, Australia, on one of the many C-47 transports, called "Bully Beefers," that flew supplies and troops between Australia and New Guinea. The only requirement to get a ride was to be in a U.S. or Aussie uniform.

The metal bucket seats on the C-47 were anything but comfortable, and with no cabin insulation, the noise prohibited conversation. That was fine with Jessie because he was depressed, with his thoughts continuing to dwell on the death of Benilli.

After landing at a Royal Australian Air Force Base, Jessie and Wander were required to check in at a military desk where they received a pamphlet of R and R rules and instructions to use the prophylactic stations after sexual exposure. The pamphlet included the locations of all the prophylactic stations in Sydney, which were open twenty-four hours. Then they walked out of the military terminal to the taxi cab waiting area.

"What is that?" said Jessie, pointing at several small cars with huge black bags on their top.

Wander smiled. "Petrol (gasoline) is severely rationed in Australia, so most of the taxi's run on coal dust, which is stored in those big black bags."

"Coal dust?"

"Yeah. They don't run very well, and they gotta get up speed to go up a hill, but most of the time they get ya where yer goin'."

Both their heads were bumping against the ceiling of the tiny cab, and it wasn't very fast, but as Wander said, it got them to their destination in Sydney, which was an apartment building called the Buckingham Flats near King's Cross.

Since Flying Knights rotated on R and R constantly, the squadron rented a large flat in the building, paid for by the pilots. It had four bedrooms, a couple bathrooms, kitchen, dining, and living room. The flat included a housekeeper who came each morning and cleaned up after the parties that generally lasted most of the night. She would also fix breakfast around noon for the pilots and their female room mates who came back to life about that time. She cooked real eggs sometimes for breakfast and occasionally real meat for dinner. That service had to be ordered the night before, otherwise, she would go home in the late after noon.

Liquor, milk, eggs, and an ice cream were delivered every morning. A large refrigerator held the fresh milk and ice cream, which, other than alcohol, was most in demand.

There were always four Flying Knights on R and R with two coming and two going. Often those going would leave a female room mate, who would stay over for another week of R and R fun with an incoming pilot, depending on chemistry and persuasive talents.

There was such a candidate when Jessie and Wander arrived at the flat. Her name was Claire, and she was a petite little girl with wavy brown hair and eyes. She looked a bit weary, but when the outgoing pilot introduced her, she put on a smile and sort of came to life. Having been on R and R before, Wander knew the scenario, and after a couple drinks of Aussie scotch with Claire, he had himself a room mate for his week of R and R.

Jessie went into one of the vacated rooms, dropped his B-4, and flopped down on the bed. It had a real mattress and soft blankets, crisp white sheets, and smelled fresh and clean. It reminded him of his bed back home on the Grapevine. As he laid there, his thoughts turned to home and family and...Maria. What would she be doing at this moment far away? Would she be at work? Would she be asleep? Would she be thinking about him?

"Hey, Jessie. Claire has a girl friend if you want a date tonight. We're all gonna hit some of the hot spots. You want to join us?" asked Wander, stepping into the room.

Jessie shook his head. "I'm gonna lie here for a while, soak in the bath tub, then gorge on ice cream."

"I admit that sounds good. But, uh, Jessie, if you're gonna want some female action, yer better off with one of these girls because we know they are okay. I mean, they don't have the clap or anything."

"Oh, okay. Thanks, Ralph. I'm just gonna hang around here and relax."

"Uh, Jessie, I know how it is to lose a friend. My advice for what its worth, is to get yourself a woman, get drunk, forget about everything else, and have a ball."

"I appreciate the advice, Ralph, but I'm gonna just relax tonight."

"Okay. See ya later."

Jessie did exactly what he told Wander he was going to do. The ice cream wasn't as good as he remembered Mr. Switzner's, but it was good. He ate so much that he had no space for dinner, went to bed, and slept in the clean, soft bed till late morning the next day.

When Jessie opened his eyes, it was as though he had slept through a time warp that had swept away the war, the Zeros, the dank, muggy jungle, and all that went with it. He could see bright sunlight through the window, and the air was cool and fresh. He leaped out of bed, pulled on his pants, went to the bathroom, and then headed for the kitchen and the ice cream.

The flat was quiet as Wander and the other pilots and their room mates had partied till the early hours and were still asleep in their bedrooms. When he walked into the kitchen, he came face to face with one of the room mates dressed in a filmy negligee. She was standing next to the refrigerator eating ice cream from a bowl.

"Good morning," she said with a mouthful of ice cream.

"Uh...yeah. Good morning," Jessie managed.

"You're Jessie Rascoe, aren't you?"

Jessie nodded, unable to pull his eyes from her oversized breast nipples that were plain to see through the sheer material.

"I heard about you," she said, taking another bite of the ice cream. Then added, "I'm Joan."

"Hello, Joan."

"I'm with Lieutenant Barns. He's asleep. You want some ice cream? It's right there in the fridge."

"Yeah, I do," said Jessie, stepping past her to the fridge.

"You're not what I expected."

"What were you expecting?" said Jessie, filling a bowl with ice cream.

She smiled. She was a cute girl with large brown eyes, and a mop of disheveled brown hair. "Oh, I don't know. You just don't fit the image I had, except for that scar on your forehead."

"Sorry about that," said Jessie as he took a big spoon ful of ice cream.

"Yank fighter pilots all love three things: alcohol, girls, and ice cream. I see you like ice cream. What about the other two?"

Jessie nodded since he had a mouth full.

"Alcohol?"

A nod.

"Girls?"

A nod.

"Okay. George, Lieutenant Barns, leaves today."

Jessie looked at her.

"I got no other commitments this next week."

Jessie hesitated.

"You said you liked girls?"

"Uh, Joan, I'm sure it would be fun to spend a week with you, but I can't."

She looked at him uncertainly.

"I'm engaged to a girl back home that I love dearly."

She frowned. "You not only don't look like I imagined you're not behaving like I imagined."

Jessie grinned. "Sorry about that."

"You're funny."

Jessie looked at her a moment. "Funny?"

"Yes. Lots of yanks who come to Sydney on R and R are engaged or married, but they are here to get away from the war for a little while, and that changes the rules."

"How does it change the rules?"

She studied Jessie for a moment. "I'm not sure if you're serious or what?"

"I'm serious. I know all about war, and I can't see why that changes anything. If you're in love and engaged to a girl; that requires you to be faithful."

The girl put the bowl down and shook her head. "Well, maybe big war heros are different from other Yanks. But let me ask you a blunt question, okay?"

"Sure, ask away."

"You attracted to me?"

Jessie smiled. "Of course."

"Would you like to take me to your bedroom right now?"

"Of course."

"So what are you waiting for?"

"I had heard that if an Aussie girl likes a guy she doesn't mince words, and now I can see that's true."

"So?"

"As much as I might like to do that, I can't, Joan. But thank you for the offer."

She shrugged. "Well, if you change your mind, let me know," she said, took the last bite of ice cream, put the empty bowl in the sink, and walked out of the kitchen.

Jessie watched her go. She was...sexy, and he had the impression that what you saw is what you got. And what you got in bed would be...Whoa, Rascoe! Forget it.

After he'd eaten the bowl of ice cream and drank two glasses of fresh milk, he returned to his room and flopped back down on the bed.

Because of the agony Jessie had suffered over Donald Benilli's death, he knew R and R would result in a binge of alcohol and sex, and for that reason, he'd elected not to go. But since O'Shea had ordered him to go, he'd decided to let the chips fall where they may. Strangely, that had all changed overnight. He had no answer why. Ice cream and a soft bed? Whatever. But if he'd wanted a binge, he could have had it in spades with Joan. It made him feel good about himself.

He got out of bed, took a bath, put on his moldy uniform, and started out the front door just as the housekeeper was entering. She was a nice middle-aged lady who told him there was a cleaning shop in King's Cross, just down the street, where they would clean his uniform while he waited.

Sure enough, for one schilling six pence, and a short wait in a dressing room, he was back dressed in his "pinks and greens" without the New Guinea mold. He caught a street car and rode it through the city enjoying the sights. Sydney was much larger than his home town of Bakersfield, and despite severe rationing and shortages of almost everything, the city was bustling with activity. Civilians and both Australian and American service men in uniform were on the streets as were vendors selling post cards and such. There was a noticeable lack of private automobiles, but a few of the little taxi cabs with the black coal bags waddled along here and there.

At the end of the street car line he got off, went into a small shop, and got a cup of iced lemonade and a licorice bar. Then he caught another street car that took him where he could see the sights along the bay and the Sydney bridge. It made him wish he had his sketch book.

Jessie spent the day sightseeing the beautiful city of Sydney returning to the Buckingham Flats in the early evening. He knew from the sounds of music and laughter coming from the flat that the evening party had started.

"Jessie, my boy, it's party time!" said Wander. "Come join us."

"Yeah! Come on, Ace!" said one of the other pilots with his arm around Joan.

Claire, Joan, and another girl where with the three pilots. One couple was dancing to the music of a wind up phonograph that was playing American big band music.

"The girls said hello, and Jessie said hello. Then Wander said, "Oh, I almost forgot, an Aussie lieutenant came by earlier and left a letter for you. It's on your bed."

Jessie went to his bedroom and opened the letter. It had the seal of the Australian Royal Air Force and was a formal invitation to a reception at a downtown hotel that evening. It also had a personal note written in longhand by Brigadier General Enis Whitehead, Commander, Fifth Fighter Command, USAAF. The note encouraged Lieutenant Rascoe to attend.

Jessie was not interested in attending a reception, but Ralph Wander's advice was that if the general suggested he attend, he had better do it. So he shaved, ate a bowl of ice cream, and caught a coal dust cab to the hotel. The cab driver told him it was one of the best hotels in Sydney.

When Jessie presented his invitation the Aussie officer at the entrance to the reception, he said, "Oh, yes. General Whitehead is expecting you, Lieutenant Rascoe."

The ballroom was filled with military officers and their ladies and a few civilians, all in formal dress, but at least it wasn't the reception line thing that Jessie had endured in Washington. General Whitehead and several other high-ranking American and Australian officers were gathered at one end of the ballroom meeting guests.

When Jessie was introduced by the Aussie officer, General Whitehead shook his hand warmly and said, "I apologize for interfering with your R and R, Lieutenant Rascoe, but I hadn't congratulated you on your receiving the Medal of Honor and on becoming a double ace. You're squadron commander told me you were here, so I thought it a good time to meet you and tell you that I consider you an inspiration to the pilots and crews of the Fifth Fighter command and all the allied troops in the South West Pacific."

The general seemed sincere and then introduced Jessie to an Aussie general and other officers and dignitaries and their ladies. One of those was a striking girl with brilliant red hair that looked almost as though it was on fire. One of the civilian dignitaries, a Mr. Manning, introduced her as his daughter, Barbara. She smiled and said it was a pleasure to meet him. She was so striking that after she and her father moved on, Jessie stood watching her as she seemed to radiate in the crowd.

Jessie decided he needed a drink and made his way to the bar, which was on one end of the ballroom. He ordered Aussie Scotch and soda since they didn't offer Jack Daniel's.

He took a drink, and it didn't taste all that great. Actually he'd rather have ice cream, but the scotch had better mellowing power. After receiving more congratulations, he went back to the bar and got another scotch and soda. As he left the bar, he came face to face with the girl, Barbara.

She smiled and said, "I was afraid you were going to leave before I could get a chance to talk to you personally."

"It's my pleasure, Miss Manning."

"How about Barbara?"

Jessie smiled. "Would you like something to drink, Barbara?"

"Yes, I would, scotch and soda, please."

Jessie ordered the drink. He handed it to her, and they moved back and away from the bar.

"Here's to you, Leftenant, you are a real hero," said Barbara, touching Jessie's glass with hers.

After the toast, Jessie said, "Thank you, Barbara. Complements from beautiful girls are always welcome."

"And beautiful girls like complements from handsome heroes."

Jessie laughed.

"I mean that. If it weren't for you and your fellow Yanks, our country would probably be over run by those yellow butchers.

It is your bravery that is stopping them. I know that you have personally destroyed many of their aircraft and that you are one of America's top fighter pilots and have won America's highest decoration for bravery."

"How did you know that?"

"It was in the Sydney paper with your picture."

Jessie smiled. "Was it a good picture?"

"Not as good as the real item."

"Big heroes like flattery."

She laughed. "But I will say that you don't seem to fit the mold of a typical Yank fighter pilot."

"What seems to be missing?"

"I'm not sure. I may need a bit more exposure. How about a drive in the country tomorrow?"

"A drive in the country?"

"Yes, and I'll even do the driving and furnish the picnic lunch."

"How can I loose?"

"You're at the Buckingham Flats, right?"

"That's right."

"I'll pick you up at ten o'clock. See you then," she said smiled, turned, and walked off.

After she disappeared in the crowd, it came to Jessie that he'd just made a date with an Australian girl. What are you doing, Rascoe? You better not do that. It isn't right and you know it. So why the hell did you do it? But he knew why. How could he refuse that girl? Yeah, and she was obviously another Aussie girl who would not mince words, or actions. And that meant...?

Fortunately, the flat was quiet when Jessie returned as the party had moved to a Sydney night club, so Jessie had another bowl of ice cream and went to bed. But his second night of R and R was the antithesis of his first night. He tossed and turned most of the night thinking about his date with the red haired girl. He finally decided he would have to tell her the truth, that he was in love and engaged to a wonderful girl so he couldn't go with her on the picnic.

When Barbara arrived at the flat in an English MG sports car the next morning and Jessie told her he was engaged, she smiled and said about what he'd expected: "What has that got to do with anything? I'm not gonna rape you, Jessie, unless you want to be raped, of course. I just want to spend the day with you because you are a fascinating hero, and I just want to get to know you. So get in the car and let's go."

Her driving was like her outgoing personality, but she handled the little MG well, and Jessie decided to just sit back and enjoy the beautiful scenery along the beaches and countryside where she took him. Finally she pulled over near a deserted section of a white sandy beach. She had brought a blanket, a basket of food and drink, bathing suits, and towels for both.

After they had settled on the beach, she said, "Turn your back while I get into my suit, then I'll turn mine while you change."

Jessie obeyed, and after they had put on their bathing suits, she applied sun tan lotion to herself and Jessie. "I can see you haven't had much sun lately, so you will blister without lotion. The sun is very hot down under."

It came to Jessie as she applied the lotion that he was subjecting himself to some serious temptation. Her bathing suit revealed the body of a Betty Grable. (She was the ultimate in shapely girls and a favorite pin up of American Armed Forces in WWII.)

"Okay, let's go swimming. But not too far out because we do have sharks here." She took his hand, and they ran down the beach and into the waves where they romped and splashed. It reminded Jessie of that time long ago when he and Alvin had romped in the waves at Pismo Beach with the See sisters.

Returning to the blanket, they dried off, and she brought out two bottles of Aussie beer. Jessie opened the beer and handed her one.

"I know you Yanks like your beer cold and your women hot, but you will have to do with the opposite today."

Jessie laughed. "I guess that's true, but you will hear no complaints from this Yank."

"Be honest. You would prefer it the other way around, right?"

"I can't deny that, Barbara."

"Neither can I, but a deal is a deal, so tell me about yourself, and your love."

For some time, they sat on the blanket in the sun, drank beer, and smoked Jessie's American cigarettes while he told Barbara about his life on the Grapevine. It surprised him at how easy it was to talk to her about himself and his love for Maria, probably because she was obviously interested and listened intently. Although he was well aware of her nearness and her sexuality, he became engrossed in telling his story.

Finally Jessie said, "Enough about me. Now I want to hear about you, Barbara."

"I really enjoyed that, Jessie. And I can tell by the way you talk about her that you are truly in love with Maria. I hope someday to enjoy that same kind of love, and as you must now know, I hope that it will be a Yank as I'm fascinated with American men. You have a zest for life and seem to always resonate excitement, as though you are about to charge the dragon. Aussie men are great, brave, and honorable. But in general they are not like American men, and for that, and whatever other reasons, I have this intense attraction to you."

"I wish you could have met my friend Donald Benilli. I think you two would have really meshed."

"Is he in your squadron?"

"He was. He was killed."

"Oh, sorry."

Silence for a moment.

"Now come on, tell me about yourself, Barbara."

"Oh, there is nothing special about me. How about another beer? They are nice and warm."

Jessie laughed. "Yeah, but your beer does have a punch."

She pulled two more beers out of her basket. Jessie opened them, and they touched bottles and drank.

"Okay, I want to hear about the life and loves of Barbara Manning."

"It's not all that exciting. I work in my father's firm, which is nice since it gives me a little edge. Like today, I could skip work to go picnicking with a handsome Yank."

"Come on now. I want more details. You got a special guy?"

"No, it's like I told you. I'm after an American."

"Well, there are lots of them in Sydney on R and R."

"I know, and I've dated a few."

"I can't believe that as beautiful as you are that guys aren't flocking after you."

"I admit that. This mop of red hair is like a homing beam that goes in all directions. The problem is it isn't very discriminating on who it attracts. But I have had some fun experiences with Yanks, although I haven't found the one I want to keep yet. Until now, that is."

Jessie looked into her blue eyes, and what he saw told him they were both flirting with an emotional powder keg. "Barbara, you know you're not playing fair now."

"I'm staying on my side of the blanket."

Jessie smiled. "Yeah, sure. But just looking at you raises a man's blood pressure, not to mention his, well, you know what."

She laughed. "Yes, you're right, and the truth is I know what I'm doing, but I can't help it. I want you, Jessie, and I can't help myself. But you're right. I made a deal, and I will stick with it. Come on. We better go before we both get out of control."

When Barbara stopped the MG in front of the Buckingham Flats and shut off the motor, she turned to Jessie and said, "That was a wonderful day, Jessie, and being with you has given me even more encouragement to find my Yank."

"I'd bet you'll find him, Barbara, but make sure he's the one and not just someone to fill the bill. Know what I mean?"

"Yes, I know what you mean. After you, it's not gonna be easy, but I'll find him...Jessie...One kiss for the road?"

Jessie turned in the seat, and they kissed. Then he got out of the MG.

Barbara smiled at him and said, "Good-bye, Jessie."

"Good-bye, Barbara."

Jessie had enjoyed his day with Barbara so much he was tempted to call her and invite her to dinner or something. But after mulling it for a while, he realized the chemistry between them was too volatile. After all, they were both human, and as Donald Benilli always said, if an Aussie girl likes you, she doesn't mince words or actions.

So Jessie engaged himself in other things, not as exciting as it would have been with Barbara, but enjoyable. He went shopping and bought gifts for Maria and his parents and mailed them. Then he went to the Sydney Theater and saw a stage show, visited the zoo and watched the Kavalla bears, rode the street cars, bought himself a sketch book, and sketched the Sydney Bridge and beautiful Bondi Beach. He did go out once to a night club with Wander and the two other pilots and their girls. Joan insisted he dance with her and told him again that she was available if he desired.

As it turned out, Jessie did enjoy his R and R in Sydney, particularly his day with Barbara. That experience seemed to be special in that his telling Barbara about Maria made her come to life in his thoughts. Although he recognized that Barbara had aroused him sexually, his love for Maria had controlled his behavior.

Chapter
~53~

"I want to hear about all the beautiful Aussie girls you guys jumped in bed with," said Heinricker the day Jessie and Wander returned to Dobodura. It was party time in the officers' club as Jessie and Wander had brought back several bottles of Aussie scotch. Jessie took some razing when he admitted he'd mostly did the tourist thing in Sydney. He didn't mention Barbara. Dick Bong supported Jessie because that was what he did when he went to Sydney since he too had a special girl, Margie, back home. Just about every-body else was more interested in Wander's account about sexy Claire.

Later that night as he lay on his musty cot listening to the jungle night sounds, Jessie realized that Captain O'Shea had been right in forcing him to go to Sydney. It had been a satisfying change that refreshed his whole being, and Jessie felt good about his behavior in Sydney. Oh, he couldn't help thinking about what would have happened if he'd let his sexual desire rule and made love to beautiful Barbara, but he felt virtuous that he hadn't. He'd kept his promise to himself that he would be faithful to Maria no matter what.

"Okay, guys, pay attention to big daddy because this mission is gonna be a tough one," said Lieutenant Heinricker when he briefed the squadron before Jessie's first scheduled mission after his return from R and R. "We are gonna escort B-24's to Holandia on the north west coast, and that will stretch our range to the limit. It will be the longest mission we have flown so far."

There was a groan from the pilots who stood around the operations tent in their flying gear, most with a cigarette between their lips.

Heinricker nodded. "I hear ya. And to make it even more interesting, intelligence sais there will be plenty of bogies to greet us. Now this is important: after you drop your tanks, you can only fight for about ten minutes and then get the hell out of there, and if you don't, you'll be taking a swim in the Bismarck Sea. Captain O'Shea will lead Red Flight, and I'll lead Blue. Bong will lead Green and Rascoe Yellow for high cover. The bombers will be at angels twenty, so we'll be on oxygen for the whole mission. The rescue cat will be in the area, but he will be east of the target area, so if you have to ditch, call him on Dog channel. Any questions?"

"Yeah," said one of the pilots. "I hope the relief tubes are working. That's gonna be a six hour haul, and my bladder and my ass is gonna be hurting."

"That's about right," agreed Heinricker. "Okay. Start engines in ten minutes at zero, oh eight fifteen...hack. We rendezvous with the bombers over Buna Bay at oh nine hundred."

After takeoff and rendezvous with the bombers, the fighters took their assigned positions, reduced their speed, and began the long flight. Nearly three hours later, as they neared the target, the P-38 pilots increased the speed of their lazy S maneuver over the bombers. Each pilot squirmed around in the tiny cockpit, pulled out the rubber hose from under the seat, and relieved himself. Gun sights and gun switches went on followed by a quick test-fire, drop tank salvo switches were activated, and everyone sharpened their watch for enemy aircraft.

"Bogies! Bogies!" suddenly cracked the anticipated call through the headsets of the Flying Knights. Then: "Drop your tanks, Captive!" barked the distinctive voice of Captain O'Shea, and the sky was filled with silver tanks spewing high octane aviation fuel as they tumbled and twisted on their long journey to the New Guinea jungle far below.

Jessie punched off his tanks and glanced across at his wing man, Dick Turney. His tanks also tumbled away as O'Shea snapped, "They are attacking the bombers. Let's go get 'em, Captive!"

A large force of enemy A6M Zero fighters swooped down on the B-24 bomber formation from all directions as the bombers held course over the target to drop their bombs. The turrets and waist gunners of the bombers countered with fifty-caliber machine guns that sent streams of fire spewing in all directions. Lightning fighters attacked the Zeros aggressively despite the bomber fire, enemy fighters, and the black clouds of anti aircraft. Within seconds, a giant aerial battle raged.

A layer of cumulus clouds over the target area resulted in a melee of fighter aircraft of both sides turning and diving around the bombers and through the clouds. Fortunately for both sides, there was no mistaking who was friend and who was foe because of the P-38's distinctive twin booms silhouette. In aerial combat where the fighters for both sides are single-engine aircraft (which all were, except the P-38 in the Pacific), friends often fired on friends. The downside for the P-38 was that the enemy could quickly identify the P-38, which removed one element of surprise.

Jessie winged over and dove after two Zero's that were attacking a B-24 from the stern. "Take the one on the right, Yellow two," he transmitted to his wing man Dick Turney.

"Roger, Yellow lead," replied Turney.

Jessie could see that the two Zeros were pouring a stream of fire into the B-24 and had apparently killed the tail and top gunner as there was no return fire, and the Zeros' 20 MM cannons were carving huge chunks out of the Liberator. Jessie jammed down on his firing button sending a stream of fire at the Zeros and causing one to break off into a left bank and the other in a right bank with Turney in hot pursuit.

Jessie banked hard raking the fleeing Japanese fighter with his deadly fire, shredding the cockpit and killing the pilot instantly. The aircraft then erupted in flames and spun out of sight into a cloud bank. As Jessie pulled out of his bank and scanned the sky, he glimpsed another Zero in his canopy rear view mirror, and its wing guns were spitting fire. Jessie slammed the Lightning into the nearest cloud bank.

Seconds later he was clear of the cloud and searching for the Zero when a stream of machine gun fire arched across his canopy. He banked sharply and plunged back into the cloud. Seconds later, he popped into the clear to see that he was head-on with another Zero. The Japanese pilot was a second or two late in opening fire, and Jessie's fusillade of fire struck the Mitsubishi full on, turning it into a flaming torch that shed pieces of burning debris as it also plunged into the cloud and disappeared.

"Yellow two, where are you?" Jessie transmitted, but the air waves were now cluttered with calls as the aerial battle raged.

Jessie put Maria II into his favorite tactic: a high-speed climb and topped out over a giant cloud where he could see a group of bombers below. One was trailing the formation with black smoke pouring from an engine and a Zero swooping in to finish off the cripple. Jessie winged over and dove on the attacker. Before he could open fire, the Japanese pilot banked the Zero so quickly that Jessie over ran him, and in seconds the Zero had cut inside Maria II and began firing. It was time to run. Jessie rammed on war emergency power pointing the nose toward the closest cloud.

Jessie heard the 20 mm explosions in the rear of the P-38 gondola as smoke and debris filled the cockpit just as he sliced into the cloud. With his radios disintegrated by the 20 mm, the combat chatter stopped in Jessie's headset, and now it was quiet in the white world of the cumulus cloud. The smoke cleared, and a quick check of instruments told Jessie that he'd taken no serious damage.

As soon as he cleared the cloud, he again pulled into a climb, scanning the sky above for enemy aircraft. In the distance, he could see the bomber formation holding its course through the bursts of black anti aircraft fire. They had dropped their bombs and were now on a return course, but were still under attack by enemy fighters who in turn were being attacked by P-38s.

Jessie dove on the nearest enemy aircraft he could see, a Zero coming off a high-speed attack on a B-24. "You're in trouble, meat ball," muttered Jessie as he hurtled toward the Zero. But the Japanese pilot spotted him at that instant and flipped into a split S, diving away before Jessie could fire. Jessie rolled into a dive on the Zero's tail, but before he could fire, the Japanese pilot pulled out of his dive so quickly that the P-38 hurtled past, and now Jessie had to continue his dive or the Zero would be on his tail and in firing range.

As soon as he was out of range, Jessie banked the Lightning into a sharp one eighty turn and rammed on full power toward the oncoming Zero. "Now you really are in trouble." But the instant Jessie fired, the Zero again snapped the nimble Mitsubishi into another split S and was gone.

Jessie knew now that he was up against an experienced Japanese pilot who flew his fighter with cunning and skill that Jessie hadn't seen in his previous engagements.

Each time Jesse got into firing position, his adversary would split S or snap into a tight turn that cut inside the P-38 forcing Jessie to abort the attack, escaping only because of his superior speed and climb-but with increasing holes in his aircraft from the Zero's guns.

Jessie knew that it would require all his skill to keep the Zero from shooting him down. He could cut and run. But in the heat of the contest, that thought was discarded, and he and his opponent continued their deadly contest.

When the duel brought the two fighters into clouds, Jessie nosed the Lightning into a full-power climb. He risked losing sight of the Zero, but it gave him the advantage to continue the duel. Now, however, Jessie was running out of time. His ten minutes over the target were up, and he had to break off the contest, or he would not have enough fuel for the long flight home.

Jessie decided to make one last attempt to win the contest, but the Japanese pilot had pulled his nimble fighter into a bank the P-38 could not match, and within seconds the two fighters were in a tight circle, canopy to canopy. Jessie could see the Japanese pilot in the cockpit, and for an instant their eyes met, and Jessie experienced the unique emotion of knowing that in a few seconds one of them would be falling in flames.

As the Zero gained firing position with each revolution of their circle, Jessie realized his tactic had been a mistake, and he was in serious trouble with no wing man to assist and no radio to call for help. If he broke off the turn now at this close range, the Zero would be on his tail in seconds and blast him out of the sky. He had one slim chance. Generally, it was a no-no in combat flying to chop throttle, but he had no choice.

Jessie broke from the circle and chopped both throttles. The Zero pilot rolled out of his turn and fired, but he hurtled past the P-38 so quickly his fire was inaccurate. Now in seconds, Jessie was on his tail and firing. His explosive rounds penetrated the Zero's unprotected fuel tank, and the aircraft exploded into a ball of fire.

Watching the Japanese fighter fall in a zig zag trail of fire and smoke, Jessie experienced a new and disturbing emotion. The pilot he'd defeated was probably a Japanese Jessie Rascoe who had met his match, but the American Jessie Rascoe had won this contest by the margin of a razor's edge.

As the formation of bombers and their escort of P-38s began the long flight home, Captain O'Shea called for his scattered chicks to form over the bombers and check in. After a head count, Blue two and Yellow lead were missing.

"Blue two went down," said Heinricker in an emotional voice.

"You see it, Bob?" asked O'Shea.

"I saw it. He was a ball of fire."

"No parachute?"

"No."

Silence for a moment.

"Yellow leader, this is Captive leader. Jessie, you receive?"

"He's here, Captive leader."

"Who's calling, and where is here?" snapped O'Shea.

"This is Yellow two, Turney, sir. I'm on Jessie's wing and we're behind the formation a way, but I have you in sight."

"Okay, Yellow two. Jessie's in trouble?"

"He is pretty bad shot up. The back of his gondola is shot off, so he's got no radios."

"Is he gonna be able to keep up with the formation?"

"I don't think so. His left boom is nearly severed, and he had to shut down his right engine."

"Okay. Yellow three from Captive leader?"

"Roger."

"Drop back and cover your flight leader."

"Roger wilco."

"Blue flight, take high cover. Red and Green low cover. I think the nips have gone home, but keep a sharp watch. Yellow three, call the cat on Dog channel. He is in the area somewhere. Jessie will need him if he has to ditch."

Jessie knew he was in trouble. The Lightning was flying, but he'd had to cut back on his remaining good engine to keep down the terrible vibration that threatened to sever the weakened left boom. Now his oxygen gage showed nearly empty as the tank had been pierced.

Jessie signaled Turney and started his descent to a lower altitude where he wouldn't need oxygen. As he scanned the waters of the Bismarck Sea below, he spotted a Liberator trailing a long column of smoke. He watched as the bomber sunk lower and lower and finally into the water with a foaming white streak across the blue sea. Then the big twin tails pitched up as the nose dug into the water and the fuselage crumpled into a foamy mass.

Jessie watched to see if there were survivors, but a cloud blocked his sight. Hopefully, if there were survivors, the Catalina flying boat would pick them up.

Twice before Jessie had fought to bring back a badly-damaged aircraft. He wasn't certain he could bring this one back, and if not, he too would need the services of the cat. Although unstable, he kept Maria II flying at the lower speeds and altitude and after a grueling three hours landed at Horanda strip without further incident but with his fuel gages reading empty.

"Jessie, even though you knock down nips like tin pins, I'm not sure I can afford you. That's the third airplane you have wiped out, ya know."

"Sorry about that. If it's any consolation, I don't like it any better than you do," said Jessie as the pilots gathered in the debriefing tent after the mission.

There was exuberance among the Flying Knights on this day over the success of the squadron having destroyed a total of eight enemy aircraft, three of which were Jessie's victories. Dick Bong was next with two, O'Shea one, Heinricker one, and the new kid on the block, Dick Turney, scored his first victory.

The only damper to the high spirits was, of course, the loss of Blue two. Any loss was felt deeply by all the squadron, and that evening they met in the O club, raised their silver mugs, and gave him their farewell toast:

"A toast to the host of those who love the vastness of the sky.
We drink to those who gave their all of old,
Then down we roar to score the rainbow's pot of gold.
A toast to the host of men we boast, the Army Air Corps."

After the toast, Jessie went to his tent and by flashlight wrote a long letter to Maria. Mostly about how much he loved her and missed her and reminisced about those wonderful days back in Bear Trap Canyon. Censorship prohibited writing about his combat missions, but Jessie had no desire to do that anyway, nor did he write about the awful living conditions in the jungle. Sometimes Maria would tell him about reading articles in the paper about his shooting down enemy aircraft, but she seemed to sense not to ask about those things in her letters.

After he finished the letter to Maria, Jessie listened to Tokyo Rose play some of the great big bands songs. It kept him from thinking about how close he'd come to being shot down this day, but after Rose signed off, those thoughts came flooding back. And so did Captain O'Shea's warning: "Don't get cocky, Jessie, or some nip will flame your ass."

Had he gotten too cocky? Maybe so...He hadn't meant to. He was good, and he knew it. His skill, keen eye sight, and quick reflexes had come naturally, but then the Zero pilot he'd met today had also been good- almost too good. Okay, Jessie... Okay. Lesson learned.

Jessie was assigned a new P-38, and his crew chief, staff Sergeant Charles Kurtz, painted thirteen miniature Japanese flags and the name Maria III, on the gondola. The next morning the squadron intercepted a formation of Japanese "Val" dive-bombers, and Jessie shot down two. So Kurtz had to add two more Japanese flags as Jessie had became a triple ace with fifteen confirmed kills and within one victory of Dick Bong.

A few days later, Jessie and Bill Kirkwood were standing beside the operations hut talking while they waited for take-off time, when a small convoy of jeeps pulled up and stopped. When he saw Captain O'Shea and Heinricker with the visitors, Jessie said, "Probably more war correspondents, or USO celebrities, coming to rub elbows with the boys on the firing line."

"Yeah, you're probably right," said Kirkwood, digging a bag of Bull Durham tobacco out of his flight suit pocket. He then rolled a cigarette, licked it tight, and tucked it between his lips. Jessie fired Kirkwood's cigarette, then his own, and put the Zippo lighter back in his flight suit pocket. They smoked and continued their discussion when O'Shea suddenly appeared and barked: "Ten-Hut!"

It surprised the two pilots as military protocol was rarely observed in the combat area. They turned and found themselves facing a big man with dark glasses and a dilapidated, gold-encrusted service cap. He wore starched khakis, and four silver stars were on each side of his shirt collar.

Jessie realized that he was facing the Man himself: General of the Army, Douglas MacArthur.

The two pilots snapped to attention and then, as an afterthought, snatched the cigarettes from their lips and saluted.

"Sir, this is Lieutenant Rascoe and Kirkwood," said O'Shea.

"At ease," said the general, then nodded to Kirkwood, and turned to Jessie. "I have been wanting to meet and congratulate you, Lieutenant Rascoe, on winning the Medal of Honor. And I understand you have recently distinguished yourself even more."

"Thank you, sir," Jessie replied.

"You are the one to be thanked, Lieutenant. All of my combat troops face the enemy with courage and determination. But I have always felt that you knights of the air are a special breed of combatant. As they say in your corps, 'You live in fame or go down in flame.'" The general paused and, then added, "Perhaps a bit dramatic, but true, is it not, Lieutenant?"

"Yes, sir, I believe it is," said Jessie.

"Where is your home, son?"

"I'm from Grapevine, sir."

"Grapevine? Hummm. Although I haven't spent much time in the States in recent years, I used to pride myself on knowing my geography. But I must say, I'm not familiar with Grapevine. Where is that?"

"Oh, it's just a wide place in the road, General."

"I see. Well, brave young men from wide places in the road all over America, doing their duty with honor, will win this war, Lieutenant. Make no mistake about that. Keep up the good work, Lieutenant Rascoe."

As they watched General MacArthur and his entourage depart, Kirkwood turned to Jessie and said, "Makes ya feel like ya just had an audience with God, doesn't it?"

"Sure does," muttered Jessie. "Brass don't do much for me as a rule, but that guy sure does. Maybe it's just the mystique, but he is impressive."

"Well, ya hear a lot of criticism about him deserting his troops in the Philippines and running off to where it's safe in

Australia. You know, the 'Dougout Doug' thing. But he was ordered to do that by President Roosevelt, and he's got a tough job on his hands. Everybody knows all the priorities go to the European war. He has to fight this one with leftovers."

"Leftover clods from Grapevine and hicks from Georgia. Huh, Bill?"

Kirkwood grinned. "Yes, suh!"

Chapter
~54~

As much as Jessie tried, he found it difficult to keep down his apprehension over his score of victories. He told himself that scores didn't matter. All that was important was shooting them down so he could go home. But a competition had developed between him and Dick Bong for the top ace position in the Fifth Air Force. The military news-paper *"Stars and Stripes Down Under"* kept a box score, and there was speculation throughout Fifth Air Force fighter command on whether Jessie Rascoe would overtake Dick Bong. Even "Tokyo Rose" talked about the two pilots on her nightly radio program. But she said they weren't Flying Knights, they were "Forked-Tailed Butchers."

Fifth Air Force scheduled B-24s to again strike the big Japanese stronghold at Holandia in the northwest section of New Guinea. It would be another of those long missions made possible by the availability of a larger external "drop" fuel tank.

The Flying Knights were assigned to cover the B-24s, and all P-38s were equipped with the new external fuel tanks that would allow them to cover the bombers to the target and if necessary defend them and still have enough fuel for the return.

Jessie would lead green flight with a new pilot, Don Nichols on his wing. It would be the young pilot's first mission, which brought memories of Jessie's disastrous first mission. He knew this was going to be rough one as intelligence reported that reconnaissance flights showed the base was loaded with enemy fighters.

"Stay on my wing no matter what, Don. We are gonna get some action today."

"You can count on it. I'll be right there with you," declared the handsome pilot.

As the pilots milled around, talking and smoking in the revetment parking area before the mission, Dick Bong walked up to Jessie and said, "Jessie, I'm gonna do my best to keep ahead of you, but I won't be surprised if you leave me in the dust."

"Nobody is gonna leave you in the dust, Dick."

"Well, whatever happens, good luck."

"Thanks, Dick, and good luck to you."

A few minutes later, the sixteen Flying Knights took off with Captain O'Shea leading the squadron, Heinricker leading blue flight, Bong leading yellow, and Jessie Green.

At the rendezvous point, they intercepted a formation of three B-24 squadrons of the famed Ninetieth Bomb Group, who called themselves the "Jolly Rogers." This group of heavy bombers presented a unique appearance with a huge white skull, with bombs for cross bones, painted on the twin stabilizers of their Liberators.

The Flying Knights established high and low cover and escorted the Jolly Rogers up the North West coast of New Guinea. As the formation neared the target, they were confronted with a line of billowing cumulus clouds, not uncommon in that area. The bombers' formation went into a shallow dive to a lower altitude where they would have visual reference to the target. That required flying through cloud layers, which made it more difficult for the fighters to keep sight of the bombers and maintain their assigned position.

Although the target area was partially covered with clouds and rain showers, the B-24s lined up on their bomb run amid bursts of anti-aircraft fire and began dropping "sticks" of bombs that rained down on the target.

Then came the anticipated radio call: "Bogies! Bogies!" as the defending Japanese fighters attacked the formation.

"Drop your tanks, Captive!" barked O'Shea.

Jessie salvoed his drop tanks and glanced across at his wing man. Nichol's tanks tumbled away, and he gave Jessie a thumbs-up signal. Glancing out at the nearest group of B-24s, Jessie saw several Zeros in a diving attack. He rolled MARIA III into a quick bank, rammed on full power, and lined up on an enemy fighter coming off his firing run.

Jessie closed the gap quickly, and as soon as the Zero filled his gunsight, he fired. He could see his tracers plunging into the aircraft, but it seemed to have no effect, and the Japanese pilot pulled into a left bank. Jessie followed, raking the Zero with his fire. Then suddenly the Zero snapped into an erratic course and began tumbling wildly, shedding pieces.

Jessie glanced over at Nichols who held his wing position. He gave Jessie a smile and a thumbs-up just as a line of black holes appeared in his wing.

Jessie swore under his breath as he realized that he and Nichols had momentarily let down their guard, and a Zero had swooped into firing position on their tail. Now they were in serious trouble.

Nichols did the only thing he could, rolling sharply into a dive with the Zero hot on his tail. "Green lead! Get 'em off! Get 'em off, Jessie!" he shouted over the radio.

Jessie slammed the Lightning into a steep bank, pulled the nose up, and jammed down on the firing button. It was a difficult shot, but Jessie's trajectory was near perfect: his tracers ached across the distance and sliced across the nose of the Zero causing him to break off the attack.

Jessie had a brief moment of relief that his wingman had escaped. Then came that horrible noise of lead penetrating metal as pieces of Maria III began to fly off in crazy patterns, and the awful smell of burning incendiary projectiles and acrid smoke filled the cockpit.

Jessie pulled back on the yoke violently and kicked full left rudder. He caught a glimpse of the attacker, who was so close that Jessie's violent maneuver caused the Japanese pilot to bank away to avoid a collision. Kicking full opposite rudder, Jessie cranked the yoke at the same time, swinging the fighter's nose into firing position. His guns roared and caught the Zero dead center. It burst into flames, and for a moment he watched the furiously burning Zero whose destruction made him the leading ace in the South West Pacific.

But his moment of victory was short-lived as Jessie knew his fighter was crippled badly. "Green two, Green two, where are you? I need help!" he shouted into his throat mike, but it was a futile call because no sound in his ear phones told him his radios were dead.

A quick glance at his instruments also told him that his left engine was also dead. He cut the mixture control on that engine and hit the propeller feathering switch just as another shower of fire balls spewed over his canopy. He rolled the P-38 into a dive and plunged into the nearest cloud.

When Jessie pulled out of the dive, he was flying along the base of the clouds in a driving rain storm. With only one engine operating and no radio, he knew he was on his own and had no choice but to head back to base at Dobodura. Glancing at his bobbing compass, he banked to an east heading that would take him out to the Bismarck Sea where he could follow the coast east to Buna Bay and then south to Dobodura, but a huge black thunderstorm blocked his way. He banked back to the west. It was difficult to maintain his heading with the compass bobbing and swinging as he maneuvered to avoid the thunderstorm. Then suddenly it was quiet in the cockpit as the right engine quit, so now he had no operating engines.

One glance at his instruments told him why: the oil pressure on that engine also read zero. The lubrication system had apparently taken a Jap bullet, and the oil had drained. Jessie knew now that he was in serious trouble. He glanced at the altimeter: it read two thousand feet. Below him was thick jungle in all directions. No chance for a crash landing. There was only one option: it was time to leave Maria III.

Jessie rolled down the left side window, hit the canopy release, and unbuckled his crash straps. As he pulled himself out of the cockpit, a transient thought exploded in his head: he was bailing out in the New Guinea northwest territory the Aussie survival expert had said to avoid at all cost.

The slipstream hurtled Jessie down off the left wing, and the instant he was clear of the aircraft, he pulled his parachute rip chord. His parachute slammed open seconds before he came crashing down into the thick jungle tree tops.

That evening in the O club at the Flying Knights squadron in Dobodura, New Guinea, the pilots held their Battle of Sydney cups high and gave a final toast to their squadron mate, Jessie Rascoe, who had been shot down the same day he'd become the leading fighter ace in the Fifth Air Force.

The new pilot, Don Nichols, inherited the feather pillow Jessie had brought back from Sydney. Two days later Dick Bong shot down two Betty bombers and was again the leading fighter ace in the Fifth Air Force.

The Flying Knights flight operations and a P-38 at Dobodura.

The above is an oil painting by the author, and can be seen in color at his website, richardckirkland.com

Fligying Knight aces in front of Richard Bong's P-38 "Marge." Right to left: Lt. Jessie Rascoe, Lt. Larry Carbon, Major Gerald Johnson, Major Richard Bong, and Major Thomas McGuire.

The above is a oil painting by the author, and can be seen in color at his website, richardckirkland.com

Lt. Jessie Rascoe shooting down a Japanese Zero fighter.

The above is a watercolor by the author, and can be seen in color at his website, richardckirkland.com

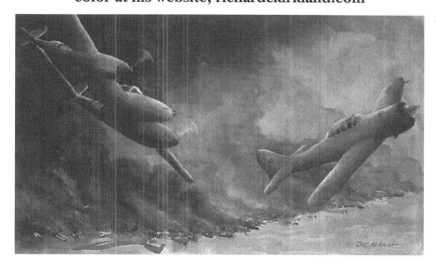

Lt. Jessie Rascoe shooting down another
Japanese Zero Fighter.

The above is a watercolor by the author, and can be
seen in color at his website, richardckirkland.com

Chapter
~55~

"Oh God, Maria! Are you sure?" said Patsy Cline, staring at her friend across their kitchen table.

"Yes, I'm sure, Patsy."

"How did it happen?"

"What do you mean?"

"Well, didn't he use something?"

Maria shook her head.

"Why didn't you make him wear a rubber?"

"I just didn't, Patsy. Those two days together were so romantic and so wonderful that-"

"Yeah. Well, it may have been romantic and wonderful, but what are you gonna do now? Criminy, you're in a real jam, Maria."

"I know, but I'm going to have Jessie's baby, and that's what really counts."

"But you're not married. What's everyone gonna say?"

"I can't help what anyone says."

"Oh, Maria, sometimes you're just impossible. You got to face reality. You're pregnant, and you're gonna start showing and everybody's gonna know, and you'll lose your job, and what are your folks and your aunt and uncle gonna say?"

"I don't know what they will say. But I do know that I'm going to have Jessie's baby, and we'll get married when he comes home. Kevin will be here in a couple of days, and I'll tell him. I hate to hurt Kevin, but I have no choice. And after I've told him, I'll tell my aunt and uncle and my folks."

Patsy shook her head and took a drink of beer from the bottle she held. "That's really gonna be rough, Maria. I don't think any of them are gonna take it very well."

"I know. And I know Jessie and I were wrong to do what we did, but it was like we were married. We just didn't do it legally."

"You gonna tell Kevin you're pregnant?"

"Yes, I have to."

"And then what if...Now don't get upset, Maria. But just what if Jessie don't come home?"

Eula Rascoe opened the front door and saw the army officer standing there. He was a handsome young man in full dress uniform with rows of decorations on his tunic. But Eula knew with a sudden and paralyzing certainty that he'd come to deliver a terrible message.

"I'm Captain Jud Brander. Are you Mrs. Rascoe?"

She nodded and heard herself say, "Come in please," her words sounding strange and hollow as though someone else had said them.

"Thank you," said Brander and stepped into the front room of the Rascoe residence at the Rose Pumping Station of the General Petroleum Oil Company. He took off his service cap and said, "I'm here representing General Jerry Jakobs," the captain said holding his service cap in his hands.

Eula nodded, feeling a gripping, awful numbness spreading through her.

"Is Mr. Rascoe at home?"

She shook her head, staring at the officer, waiting for the words that must inevitably come.

"I have some things to discuss with you and Mr. Rascoe. Will he be home soon?"

"No. He's at work. Just tell me, please."

"Well...uh..."

"For God's sake, say it, Captain!"

"Ah, Mrs. Rascoe, I'm sorry to have to tell you this, but your son, First Lieutenant Jessie Rascoe, has been listed as missing in action over enemy territory in the South West Pacific theater of operations."

A bolt of searing pain shot through every fiber of the mother's mind and body, leaving her paralyzed with agony and despair.

"I'm terribly sorry. Are you all right, ma'am?"

She nodded woodenly.

"Ah...General Jakobs directed me to personally explain things to you in consideration of your son being a Medal of Honor holder. You will, of course, also receive an official telegram from the War Department."

The mother reached out and grasped the door facing.

"I'm terribly sorry, Mrs. Rascoe. The general asked me to convey his personal sympathy and to express the deep regret he, the Army Air Corps, and the whole nation feel at the loss of one of America's bravest heroes."

Eula Rascoe tried to speak, but no words would come out, and she just stood staring blankly at the army officer. Then her legs folded from under her.

A few days after notification of next of kin was completed, the War Department released an official statement to the press and radio stating that Lt. Jessie Rascoe, recipient of the Medal of Honor, was listed as missing in action in the South West Pacific Theater of Operations. Once again Jessie Rascoe got his picture on the front page of the Bakersfield *Californian*.

When Kevin Blake stepped from the train into the crowd of people on the boarding platform at the Los Angeles Southern Pacific depot and saw his fiance, his pulse leaped. It was the moment he had dreamed about so often during those long terrible months of heat, sand, and death in North Africa. He could hardly believe that it was a reality: a moment even more wonderful than he'd imagined, and a surge of emotion sweep through him.

She was waiting for him: his beautiful, precious Maria. The girl he'd fallen in love with the first time he'd met her. Kevin had relived that moment many times during those awful desert nights, lying in his hand-dug trench. Oh, how many times he'd thought of all the fun things they had done together, and how he'd laughed to himself when he recalled how his high school friends had teased him about the little hillbilly gal when he'd first started dating her. But it hadn't bothered Kevin, because he knew how warm and sweet she was and how much he loved her.

When he took her in his arms and held her there on the station platform, Kevin told himself there would be no more waiting. He would marry Maria now. Right now!

As Maria stood with Kevin's arms around her, she was certain she would never again experience any worse pain than she felt at that moment. The love and emotion that Kevin exuded as he held her in his arms was so evident and so powerful that Maria felt her heart would break. Where, oh, where would she get the strength to tell him? How could she do it? Oh God, how?

Maria didn't have the opportunity to be with Kevin alone that day and evening because of parents and friends, so she was unable to tell him the awful truth. She would have to do it the following day when they planned to be together. That night she was so distressed that she slept little, finally falling asleep in the early hours only to be shaken awake by Patsy who was trying to tell her something that she could not understand or accept. It was a front page article in the morning *Los Angeles Examiner* about Jessie. It was something that left her numb and unable to comprehend.

Hallie Lamont slid the canopy back on the P-47 Republic Thunderbolt fighter, and crawled out of the cockpit onto the wing. She pulled her leather helmet off and shook her head, sending waves of hair tumbling. Then she turned back, lifted her parachute out of the cockpit, and threw it over her shoulder.

"You need some help there, little lady?" asked one of the army ground crewman standing near by watching the shapely female ferry pilot as she climbed down off the wing of the thunderbolt, at Langley Army Air Base, Virginia.

"No thank you, Sergeant, I can manage," she replied, smiling.

The sergeant shook his head and grinned. "It always amazes me to see one of you little girls climb out of that big fighter."

"We don't discriminate, Sergeant-little fighters or big fighters, we fly them all," said Hallie as she headed toward flight operations.

"You sure do," said the sergeant. "But I'm still amazed."

An olive-drab staff car, with a silver star on the front on the front license plate and a yellow-and-black checkered flag on the finder, came speeding out across the ramp and pulled up beside Hallie. The driver jumped out and swung open the back door. A trim, handsome brigadier general dressed in class-A uniform stepped out.

"Tony! What a pleasant surprise!" said Hallie. "What are you doing here?"

The handsome general hesitated, looking at her in a curious sort of way. "Oh, I just popped in to see you. Generals do that, you know."

Hallie smiled. "I'm pleased you did. But how did you know I was landing here?"

"Oh, generals got ways of knowing those things."

"So they do. Well, it's good to see you, but I have a feeling you have something on your mind."

"Sergeant, would you put Miss Lamont's parachute in the trunk please."

"Yes, sir," said the sergeant and took Hallie's parachute.

"Is this official or personal business?" asked Hallie as he guided her into the back seat of the staff car.

He got into the car after her and said, "Some of both."

"You sound sort of solemn. I hope I haven't violated any army rules or something."

He gave her a weak smile and replied, "No, nothing like that. Driver, take us to the officers' club."

"I should check into ops first, Tony."

"All been taken care of."

Hallie leaned back against the seat and looked at him suspiciously. "I know-you want to recruit me for some kind of secret spy mission and send me to Casablanca."

"How did you know?"

A few minutes later the car pulled up in front of the base officer's' club, and the general escorted Hallie inside and into a private meeting room.

"The plot thickens," said Hallie "Anthony, what's this all about?"

The general sat down next to her in on the sofa. "Hallie, I'm sorry to have to tell you this, but we got a TWX earlier this morning that Lieutenant Jessie Rascoe was shot down on a combat mission in the South West Pacific Theater of Operations."

Hallie sat still with her large cerulean blue eyes staring at the general for a long silent moment. Then she slumped over in the chair and began to sob. The general put his arms around her and held her in his arms while she cried.

Peggy Barton Dumont's secretary glanced at the man dressed in a stylish business suit standing before her desk at the international headquarters of Dumont Industries in San Francisco.

"I'm Mr. James. I have an appointment with Miss Dumont."

"I'm sorry, Mr. James. Miss Dumont has cancelled all her appointments for today."

James frowned. "I don't understand. I talked to her earlier, and she instructed me to get here as soon as possible to review those Martin contracts."

The secretary, a small woman with bulging eyes, appeared nervous. "I...I uh, know Mr. James, but something has come up. I'm sorry."

A loud crashing noise came through the door from inside the office that sounded like a vase or glass object of some kind smashing against the wall.

James's eyes grew large. He glanced at the secretary. "Do you think Miss Dumont is all right? I mean, should we call someone?"

The secretary, looking increasingly upset, started to speak when another loud noise came through the door.

"Does this,uh, happen often?" asked James.

The secretary shook her head. "No. She was fine earlier when I gave her the mail and morning newspaper. Then a few minutes later she buzzed me and said she was not to be disturbed under any circumstances."

Chapter
~56~

When Jessie crashed down through the thick mass of vegetation and jerked to a sudden stop, the words to one
of the Knights squadron songs flashed through his thoughts:
"Beside a Guinea waterfall, one steamy jungle day. Beside his
battered Lightning, the young pursuiter lay. His parachute
hung from a very high limb, he was not yet quite dead..."

Jessie could see things: trees, branches, foliage all around
him. He glanced up and saw more of the same. And sure
enough there was his parachute! It hung from a high limb all
right, just like the verse in the song: the long nylon shroud
lines disappearing into the blanket of jungle foliage so thick
that only a few cracks of sunlight shone through. He looked
down where his feet dangled, and far below was another swath
of intense greenery.

As Jessie stared, he realized he was fortunate to have escaped
without broken bones or worse. The down side being that he
was dangling in space far above the jungle floor. He dug into
his flight suit pocket, pulled out his cigarettes and Zippo, and
lit one. He took a deep puff and glanced down again. It looked

dark, foreboding. The only sound was the chirping of a jungle bird and the dripping of rain water on the foliage.

As he dangled in the parachute harness smoking and thinking, Jessie realized that he was in serious trouble. He knew he was in the interior of the northwest jungle. How far had he'd flown into it trying to get around the thunderstorm? What was it the Aussie survival expert had said? "No white man has ever penetrated that impregnable jungle with its deadly fever, snakes, crocodiles, and head-hunting cannibals."

He took another puff on the cigarette and tried to focus his thoughts. Okay, he was in trouble all right. But trouble was no stranger, and like his dad always said, he had good instincts when it came to dodging the bullet-but this kind of bullet?

The loud screech of a bird echoed through the jungle and cut into his thoughts. Probably a mating call, and the odds in that game had just changed, hadn't they? Yeah, in Kevin's favor.

Come on Rascoe, remember your old Boy Scout fight song. You don't give up without a fight! And thanks to those years you're no stranger to the wilderness, and that's all the jungle is, a different kind of wilderness. You can use your knowledge of the outdoors. You can survive the jungle, despite its worst adversities. No, you haven't won yet, Kevin.

Jessie began to formulate his plan for survival. He had his parachute, Mae West, life jacket, one-man rubber boat, survival kit, and forty-five pistol. So it was just a matter of keeping a cool head, set his escape plan, and follow it. Okay, first things first. It was a long drop into the jungle below, with or without his parachute. Since it and the attached equipment would be vital to his survival, he'd have to get the canopy of the chute unhooked from its entanglement above.

He finished the cigarette, dropped it, and watched it spiral down and disappear into the darkness below. It was going to be a long fall for him too, but there was no alternative. He braced himself and jerked on the shroud lines. Nothing happened except another loud screech from a bright-colored bird that came diving out of the branches. He jerked again, violently, and still nothing happened. Then, without warning, down he plummeted with the collapsed parachute into a tangled heap in the jungle below.

A thicket of jungle growth provided a soft landing, and Jessie was congratulating himself on his good fortune when his first jungle adversary made its presence known: swarms of mosquitoes that attacked in black clouds.

Struggling to free himself from the entanglement, he searched his memory for the Aussie survival expert's advice on combating one of the jungle's worst predators that carried debilitating malaria and dengue fever.

Mud! That was it! The Aussie had said, "If you can't take cover, plaster your face and hands with mud to protect yourself."

When Jessie finally pulled free of his entanglement, he stuffed the parachute back into its harness so it could be carried. He glanced around. Every direction looked the same: greens of every shade with foliage, trees, vines, and thickets so dense that visibility was limited to a few feet. Since there was no earth, there was no mud. It was as though he was standing on a thick, wet sponge in a steam bath. But he had to find mud!

Jessie picked a direction and sloshed off through the jungle, stumbling and clawing his way through the wet, slimy vegetation that was alive with swarms of mosquitoes and insects. Within minutes, he was soaked with perspiration from the suffocating heat and humidity.

After traveling a short distance, Jessie encountered another adversary: rain forest leeches. Suddenly he was covered with the slimy creatures that attached themselves to his skin tenaciously. At first, he frantically tore them off but soon discovered that it was hopeless. They reappeared faster than he could pull them off.

The perspiration poured down Jessie's face and stung his eyes. He could hear his heart pounding and his breath came in gasps. He was so repulsed by the hideous leeches that he sensed a rising panic-something he'd never experienced before. He ceased clawing at the leeches and stood motionless for a moment. Keep calm. Don't panic. Don't panic.

He took deep breaths and forced himself to stand still for a moment, but it was impossible to curb the burgeoning emotion. His brain would only accept the overwhelming demand that he get out of there. Get out! Quickly! Go! anywhere away from this!

A huge green snake slithered through the foliage grass just a few feet away. Jessie watched the snake hypnotically for a moment, then turned, and plunged into the jungle in a desperate, frantic effort to escape. Losing all track of time and direction, he thrashed through the endless vegetation, stumbling, falling, struggling on until finally, late in the day, he emerged from a thicket and out onto a river bank.

He stood for a moment gasping for breath and staring at a group of crocodiles that scrambled off the bank and disappeared into the dark water. Then he collapsed into gooey, foul-smelling river mud. Jessie lay face down in the mud for some time, exhausted and despondent, unable to move and unable to regain enough composure for any kind of rational thought.

Finally, he pulled himself to a sitting position. His head spun, and his ears rang with weird sounds. Mosquitoes and various other insects were buzzing around him in swarms.

He ignored the insects and began to pull the leeches off his face and body. He'd just removed the last one when a sudden thunderclap echoed through the jungle, followed by rain that came down in a torrent. It was like a gift from heaven, and he stripped off his flight suit and stood there naked, savoring the feel of the cool rainwater over the raw skin where he'd torn off the leeches.

The downpour stopped as suddenly as it had started, and the insects returned as quickly as they had departed. But the interlude and the fresh rainwater cleared Jessie's besieged brain, and he knew what had to be done. He put his flight suit back on, zipped it up, and pulled his flight goggles down over his eyes. Ignoring the awful stench, he scooped up the river mud and plastered it over his face and hands so there was no part of his skin exposed. The mud was awful, but it gave him protection from the leeches and insects.

He sat down on a log next to the river and fished out a cigarette. When he flipped his Zippo it flared to life, but the cigarette was so soggy with water, mud, and perspiration it would hardly burn and the smoke tasted terrible. He hurled it into the river, and an instant later the water boiled and the cigarettes disappeared. As Jessie watched, the hint of a smile eased across his mud-plastered face. Did the Aussie survival expert know that crocodiles liked water-logged cigarettes?

The humor he saw in the incident seemed to bring Jessie a calming clarity. He sat on the log in the small clearing for a while and watched the river water. It was a dark, dirty brown with streaks of slimy-looking green scum that occasionally swirled into little eddies. It was probably from the tails of the crocodiles swimming around waiting for another cigarette-maybe they were getting ready to come out of the water for something to eat a little more juicy than cigarettes. What did the Aussie say about crocodiles? Avoid them -they can be dangerous. Probably like an ole ranch bull.

So far his jungle-escape plan had not gone well. He'd acted like a tenderfoot scout on his first campout. Thrashing off through the jungle with no real plan until panic had nearly scuttled him. Luckily he'd stumbled onto the river bank. Jessie promised himself that would not happen again. From this moment on, he would keep his cool regardless of the circumstances. Emotion would not rule him. He would reason out a plan and follow it.

He glanced around. The river bank was in a small clearing in the rain forest. The canopy of vegetation above was so thick only glimmers of sunlight sifted through. It would be impossible to see an aircraft above- or to be seen. That meant he must transit the jungle until he found a place where he could be seen by overflying aircraft. But then aircraft didn't fly over this remote area.

He pulled another cigarette from the pack and fired it. Strangely, it tasted better this time. He muttered aloud, "It's all a matter of attitude, Rascoe."

After he'd finished the cigarette, he opened his parachute harness and unfastened the survival kit. He zipped the kit open and surveyed its contents. It looked intact, with the usual survival items, which included a bottle of quinine tablets, a packet of K-rations, and two fruit bars. Not much for an extended stay. He pulled out the cloth map of New Guinea and opened it. He had no idea now where he was so the map was of little use.

So now what? Okay, all rivers lead eventually to the sea, and that would get him out of the jungle. And he had the means: the one-man rubber lifeboat attached to his survival kit. Jessie remembered that he'd removed it from his kit because it made him sit too high in the cockpit. But Captain O'Shea had ordered all pilots to keep their one-man boats whether they liked it or not. "Thanks, Tom," he said, reaching out and touching it.

That would be his plan then. He would paddle down the river in the boat until he came to the coast. There, he had his best chance of being spotted and rescued. And a good chance of running into Japs. What about the headhunters? And the crocodiles? He flipped the snap on his shoulder holster, pulled out his forty-five, and checked the clip. It was full and had two spare clips attached to the holster.

He'd never fired a pistol in his youth, but fortunately one of the first things the army taught him was how to shoot a forty-five. By imagining the target was a Jap, he learned to shoot pretty well. But the Japs he would encounter wouldn't be paper targets, nor would the crocodiles or headhunters.

But he would take it as it came. He shoved the pistol back in its holster, re-packed the survival kit, and began to prepare for his first night in the jungle. He made a hammock out of his parachute by tying it between two trees. This would allow him to sleep off the ground and avoid most of the crawly and slithering things, many of which were poisonous.

After his hammock was prepared, he sat down on the log again and opened one of the K-Ration packages. When he peeled the heavy protective wax paper away, he saw a faded stamp on the side of the box. He looked at it for a moment and then smiled. It was difficult to read, but it looked suspiciously like: U.S. Army 1918. After he ate a piece of the "hard tack" cracker, he was convinced the date was accurate. Not exactly like the good ole hunter's stew he used to have on scout camp outs, but it was nourishing, and that was what counted.

As Jessie chewed on his 1918 ration, he thought about Maria. His sweet, beautiful Maria. It wouldn't be so good for her, would it? No. Now she would really be in a fix. What would she do? What could she do? The army would report that he was missing in action-a nice way of saying he was dead. Maria, his mother and father, family, Hallie, Peggy, and all his friends would believe that he would not be coming home, ever.

It was a depressing reality, but he reminded himself of his resolution to stay calm, think positively, and not let anything interfere with his determination to survive. And he would survive. He had to. He'd promised Maria; it was a promise to keep.

Eating with mud-plastered hands and face wasn't easy, but minor in the scheme of Jessie's sustenance problems. He recognized the meager rations in his survival kit would last only a few days. His sustenance would then depend on his ability to procure wild game, fish, and fruit. The survival expert said there was a lot you could eat in the jungle- if you knew what was eatable. In the Tehachapi Mountains, he would know. In the New Guinea jungle? In the morning he would read the survival manual. It would tell him.

After he finished eating the hard tack, he cut a small piece off the fruit bar with his sheath knife to balance his ration and kill the taste of one of the quinine tablets. He knew the quinine would not keep him from coming down with malaria or dengue fever, but it could moderate the severity. The mosquitoes had bitten him hundreds of times earlier that day, so it was all but certain he'd been infected. He could only hope the fever would not be severe enough to keep him from functioning.

When night settled in Jessie's jungle camp, it was pitch-black. He was tempted to build a fire for psychological reasons, but he didn't need the heat and probably couldn't find anything dry enough to burn anyway. He washed the mud off his hands and face with river water, climbed into his improvised hammock, and covered himself with the nylon parachute.

It was hot and suffocating in his nylon cocoon, but better than the mosquitoes and millions of other flying insects that came out after dark in such swarms that the sound of their wings echoed through the jungle like the whine of a thousand high-pitched motors. It was a far cry from night sounds at the ole Pete Miller Meadow in Bear Trap Canyon.

Chapter
~57~

Jessie managed to get some fitful sleep his first night in the jungle, despite the conditions and his anxieties. Awakened the next morning by a piercing scream, he clawed his way out of the nylon cocoon, grabbed his forty-five and listened. When the scream came again, he realized it was some kind of jungle bird or animal.

Glancing up, he could see a few rays of bright sunlight sifting through the jungle canopy. He thought it might just be an omen of good fortune when reality returned as a swarm of mosquitoes swooped down upon him. He put on his cloth flight helmet and goggles, swung out of the hammock, and holding his breath to avoid the smell, plastered himself with the awful mud.

His breakfast was another small piece of hard tack, a bite of the fruit bar, and another quinine tablet washed down with a drink of water from his canteen. He made a mental note that when the next downpour came, he should remember to refill the canteen with rain water.

After breakfast, Jessie sat down on the log with his survival kit to again take stock and solidify his strategy. He looked at each item and reviewed its use. The packet of beads was supposed to be for bartering with the natives to get them to help him, but if the natives in this area had never seen a white man-? Think positive, Jessie, positive. Out of the seven hundred native tribes in New Guinea, he ought to be able to find one friendly tribe. Compass: He should have used it yesterday instead of stumbling through the jungle without direction. Well, he'd promised himself that wouldn't happen again. Signal mirror: It would be critical when he reached the coast where he could spot a friendly aircraft. Waterproof matches: If he could find something to burn in a rain forest. Fishing kit: The survival expert said that all the rivers had fish-good-and he'd seen worms for bait in the gooey mud. Survival manual: It would give him rules to follow in the jungle and tell him what and where he could find things to eat. He removed it from the water resistant bag and leafed through the pages of instruction that had pictures of various plants and berries, small animals, and fish that were edible. He would study it carefully, but now he was anxious to get started, so he put it back in the kit and turned his attention to the boat.

The label on the boat cover read "Boat-one man," and as strange as it sounded, Jessie knew this was the only way he could escape the jungle. He had no idea how far it was to the Bismarck Sea, but he would get there. He glanced at the river. Was it large enough to lead to the sea? Well, if it didn't, he would find one that did.

He removed the boat from its cover, and when he pulled the CO2 lanyard, Jessie felt a surge of confidence. It popped open and inflated, just as the instructions said it would.

After he packed his parachute and other gear in the boat, it occurred to him that the nomenclature should have read "boat one SMALL man." It was a tight squeeze to get his tall frame into the space provided. After he'd crawled in and pushed off into the river, it also occurred to him that the only thing between his posterior and the crocodiles was a thin piece of rubber.

He pulled out his forty-five and held it ready. But apparently the crocodiles didn't like rubber boats because nothing happened, and after a while, he put it back in its shoulder holster.

He tried to keep track of his heading with the compass, but it was difficult as the river meandered through the jungle in all directions and was covered with a canopy of thick vegetation. He found it impossible to identify any landmarks for reference, and sometimes it appeared as though he was floating in a giant swamp of dark, stagnant water with no definition and no end. The current was so slow that it often seemed that his boat was not moving at all.

Fortunately, the mosquitoes were not as bad during the day, and the only leeches he had to cope with were a few that occasionally dropped from the foliage above. The boat kit included a small rubber paddle that he used to steer and keep him away from the vegetation that hung almost to the water line.

He kept a sharp watch for crocodiles, but all he saw was an occasional water snake slithering its way across the river and paying him little attention. There were no human signs that he could recognize, but lots of colorful birds and some small animals that scurried through the tree branches. Some looked like monkeys, and others looked more like baby kangaroos.

After several hours of floating through the steamy vegetation and stifling heat, Jessie found himself fighting a growing feeling of suffocation. He decided to go ashore and stretch his legs, but first he had to find a place to go ashore. He'd noticed that for some time, he'd not seen the river bank or any other indication that he was even following a river. All he could see was still, foul-smelling water and foliage that now hung so low that it was becoming increasingly difficult to find a path through it.

Fighting to keep calm, Jessie paddled the rubber boat for hours in whatever direction gave the least resistance, searching for some indication of river current or solid ground.

The shadows were darkening, signaling the approach of nightfall when Jessie spotted what appeared to be a river bank. But as he approached, he saw that it was only a large growth of some form of water plant. He stopped paddling and just sat there in the boat, dripping with perspiration while a wave of depression swept through him and waves of aquatic insects swarmed over him.

He flinched when a loud thunderclap echoed down through the jungle canopy, followed by a torrential downpour. The rainwater felt cool and soothing, and he pulled off his flight helmet and goggles and let the water cascade over his face, washing off the remainder of his anti-mosquito mud, most of which had already been removed by his own perspiration. But at this point it didn't seem to matter. What difference were a few more mosquito bites? But it did matter and Jessie knew it. If he was going to let himself become despondent after only one day of his survival plan, there was no way he'd make it.

The rainstorm lasted only a few minutes, but it was a welcome relief from the flying predators and it cooled him and boosted his spirits. He pulled one of the precious few remaining cigarettes from his flight suit pocket and fired it. The flame of his Zippo flared in the gathering darkness, telling Jessie that in a few minutes it would be pitch black and he had no option other than to spend the night in the rubber boat. Could he do it? His legs already felt as though they were paralyzed, and he sensed the rising rebellion of his senses. Don't think about it, Jessie. Just do what has to be done, he told himself.

He stubbed out the cigarette, put the butt back in the pack, and began to prepare for nightfall. The boat was half-full of rain water, and the mosquitoes were back in full force. He put his helmet and goggles back on and began to bail out the water with his canteen cup. When he'd gotten most of it out, he tied the boat between two tree limbs to keep it from drifting into the foliage, which was alive with insects. Then he enclosed himself in a small tent fashioned with the parachute. It was suffocating and since he was soaked, like a steam bath, but it kept out most of the crawly things and the flying intruders.

Jessie's second night in the New Guinea jungle was a torturous ordeal. He slept little, and when dawn finally seeped into his tomb, he was exhausted, and every muscle in his body seemed to ache. He forced himself to eat a piece of the hard tack and take one of the quinine tablets. Then he untied the boat and began to paddle, forging through the maze of vines, trees, and swamp vegetation, determined to find the river channel.

By mid-afternoon he felt weak and light-headed and could hardly paddle the boat. His forehead was so hot that even the mosquitoes seemed to shy away, and Jessie knew that the ache in his body was not just from being cramped up in the boat. He knew because now he could feel the fever. The mosquitoes had done their job: he was infected with one or more of the jungle fevers. He could only hope it would not incapacitate him totally.

He tried to reason what to do, but it was difficult to even think with the montage of spinning images and disjointed thoughts that began to swirl through his aching head. He must paddle on...paddle on. Don't stop. Must keep focus...just keep paddling...keep paddling. Eventually he would come to something...something.

It was late afternoon, and darkness was settling through the jungle when the rubber boat came to a halt. Jessie tried to paddle, but the boat wouldn't move. Ahead he could see a wall of hanging vines and thick foliage. Then he picked up a glint from something shiny in the last rays of light. He stared at it for a moment until he was sure it was what it looked like: a beautiful bank of slimy, gooey, river mud.

Jessie was so weak he had to roll out of the boat and crawl up onto the muddy river bank on his hands and knees. He pulled himself to a sitting position, leaned against a tree trunk, and just sat there for a moment watching his little one-man boat float off down the slow moving river with all his survival gear. But in the scheme of things, it didn't seem to matter now.

Jessie dug into his flight suit pocket and pulled out the mutilated cigarette package. It held the butt of his last cigarette. When he flicked his Zippo, it flared and Jessie saw something that drew his eyes-there was a human footprint in the

mud beside where he sat. He took a deep pull from the cigarette and looked at the footprint again. Yes, it was human all
right. A little smile formed. He'd done it! He knew he could.
That footprint was his deliverance- wasn't it?

Chapter
~58~

From where she sat in the breakfast nook of their apartment, Patsy Cline glanced across at Maria. "Maria! You can't mean that!" she cried.

Maria dropped her eyes and stared at the table. "I mean it, Patsy. I haven't slept in two days thinking about it, but I've made up my mind. I'm not going to marry Kevin."

Patsy rolled her eyes, reached into her purse, and took out a pack of cigarettes. She lit one and blew out a cloud of smoke. "Maria, the wedding is the day after tomorrow. Your folks are here. Everything is arranged. I can't believe you're even considering calling it off."

Maria looked up. "I can't go through with it, Patsy. I just can't."

"You *can* go through with it! You have to. You simply have to face the truth. I know how tough it's been, but you gotta accept what is: Jessie is not coming home."

"I just don't believe it. I can't. But even if it's true, I can't marry Kevin. It would be an unforgivable thing to do- a terrible, dishonest thing that I can't live with. I... I..." Maria's voice choked off, and her eyes filled with tears.

Patsy watched her friend's head drop and her shoulders began to shake as she sobbed silently. "Maria, honey,

listen to me. You and I couldn't love each other any more if we were sisters, right?" Maria nodded. "If there was the slightest doubt in my mind about this, I'd cut out my tongue before I'd say it, but there isn't. It is *not* the wrong thing to do. Kevin's family loves you, your family loves him, and he loves you dearly. And you admitted to me that you love him in a way. Maybe not like Jessie, but in time you will. How could you not? And he'll be a good husband, and a good father."

Maria sat motionless staring at the table top. "I... know that, Patsy," she whispered. "But the deception...I can't tell him I'm pregnant. It would kill him. And to have Jessie's baby that Kevin will think is his, I can't live with that."

"You have to, Maria. You have no other choice."

"Yes, I do. I can have my baby and hope for a miracle that Jessie will someday come back to me."

Patsy hesitated and took a puff of her cigarette. "That's not only foolish, Maria, it's very selfish."

Maria looked at her friend with red eyes.

"If you marry Kevin, the only person who will suffer is you, for a while. If you don't marry him, lots of people will suffer, including your own child."

Maria dropped her eyes and began to cry silently again.

"Isn't that true, Maria?"

Finally: "Yes."

"Then you know what you must do, don't you?"

No answer.

"Maria?"

She nodded.

A second lieutenant wearing an Army Air Corps class-A uniform braked his 1937 Chevrolet to a stop in front of the Grapevine General Store. He turned off the engine and got out of the car just as the front door of the store swung open and a sergeant wearing the uniform of a United States Marine walked out. The two men stopped and looked at each other for a moment then broke into big smiles.

"Billy! You son of a gun, how are you?" said the marine sergeant.

"Danny! Criminee, what a neat surprise! I didn't know you were home," said Billy as the two men shook hands warmly.

"I just got in this morning on furlough. It's great to see you and hey, look at those shiny gold bars and silver wings. I guess I oughta salute you, huh?"

"Yeah, sure, Danny. So far all I've done is fly trainers around in circles, but look at the decorations on your uniform."

"I'm sure you'll get your shot at 'em, Billy."

"I hope so. I gotta score to settle with the bastards."

The smiles on both men dissolved. "Yeah, I guess you do. I...I can't tell you how bad I felt when I heard about Jessie, Billy. You know, we were all like brothers."

"I know, Danny. I know. But he got a bunch of 'em before they got him, and I'm gonna get some more."

"I know you will, Billy. What say we go up to the Tavern at ole Frazier Park and have a couple beers?"

"Sounds great. Come on, I'll drive us."

It was Saturday morning, and Johnny Lashburn had just opened the Tavern when he heard the first customer of the day enter. He looked up from behind the bar and saw the two soldiers. He recognized them, but it took a moment to make sure they were who he thought they were.

"Billy and Danny!" he bellowed. "Come on in. It's great to see you."

"Hi, Johnny," they both said, walking up and shaking hands with their old high school bus driver.

"You still driving the ole bus?" asked Billy.

"Yep. Still drive 'er and tend bar here on the weekends. But I'll tell ya, it ain't like it used to be. Seems like these new kids just don't have the zip you boys did, or maybe I'm just getting old," said Lashburn, laughing.

"I sure have missed those days," said Danny.

"It's great to see you boys again. How about a beer? It's on the house."

"You said the magic words, Johnny," laughed Billy.

"Two beers on the house coming up!" said Lashburn, sliding a mug under the spigot and pulling the handle.

"The ole place looks great," said Danny, glancing around as he stuck a cigarette in his mouth and offered the pack to Billy.

"No thanks. Haven't got the habit yet," grinned Billy.

"You will," said Danny, taking a deep draw on his cigarette.

"I guess it can get pretty rough over there, huh?"

"Yeah."

"Where were you, Danny?" asked Lashburn as he set the glasses in front of them.

"Guadalcanal," muttered Danny, picking up the beer glass.

"Christ, that was a tough one, wasn't it? I read about it in the papers. I ain't supposed to, but by God, I'm havin' a beer with you boys!" declared Lashburn as he filled a glass for himself.

Danny nodded and held up his glass. "Here's to the guys from Grapevine that didn't make it."

The three touched glasses and drank.

"I'm sure sorry about your brother, Billy. He was a fine young man and a real hero," said Lashburn.

Billy nodded.

Lashburn shook his head. "What a twist of fate that both Jessie and Alvin would earn medals of valor, but neither of them make it back."

"Yeah, that's three out of our old gang that didn't."

"I thought Bobbie was still listed as missing in action?" said Lashburn.

"He is, but his ship went down the same as Jessie's plane went down in the jungle, which means...well, you know."

"Damn war sure has torn up our lives," said Lashburn as all three took another drink of beer. "I saw Quincy Carver the other day, and he finally got a letter from his son Bud, through the International Red Cross."

"Where is he?" asked Billy.

"Didn't you hear? It was really bad luck for the poor kid. On his last mission, his B-17 got shot down over Germany, and he's a prisoner of war."

"Gosh no, I didn't know that," said Billy.

"Really a tough break. He and Penny were gonna get married as soon as he got back to the States. Looks like she'll have to wait now till the war's over."

"Well, at least Bud's alive."

"Yeah, but I'll bet it ain't no picnic in one of those prison camps."

"But let me tell you something on the good news side," said Lashburn. "I was standing here at the bar a couple months back and in walks our ole Tavern band leader himself in his sailor suit and lookin' fit as a fiddle."

"Frank Grover?" said Billy.

"Right! He made it home, and he and Virginia got married."

"All right, that is good news."

"Speaking of getting married, I guess Maria Hunter married that rich guy from Los Angeles" said Danny.

"Who would have ever thought that little hillbilly would end up marrying a rich guy?" said Billy. "But you just don't know about how people are gonna turn out. Ya know, I never could figure out why Jessie was always crazy about her. But he was, even when she was a little rag-tag running around Bear Trap Canyon."

"I remember, but she turned out to be a right pretty rag tag," observed Danny.

"Yeah, but she dumped Jessie for the rich guy."

"Well, I always thought Jessie would end up with Hallie Lamont, anyway."

Billy nodded and took a drink of his beer. "So did I. Although I'm not sure Jessie ever figured out which one he really loved."

"I didn't know either of those girls very well cause they didn't ride on the high school bus. But I remember the Lamont girl because she came to the Tavern a couple times, and I thought she was the prettiest girl I ever seen."

"Yeah, she sure is some kind of good lookin'," agreed Danny. "I guess all of us were sweet on her at one time or another."

"Ain't it the truth," said Billy.

"Ya know she's a WASP pilot and ferries bombers and fighters and everything else the Army Air Corps has," said Lashburn.

"What a gal!" agreed Danny.

It was quiet in the Tavern for a moment.

"Fill 'er up again, Johnny," said Billy, sliding his glass across the bar.

"Yeah, mine too," said Danny.

"Sure thing, boys," said Lashburn, putting the beer glasses under the spigot. "Are you gonna have to go back to your outfit, Danny?"

"Nope, I'm all through. No more action for this kid. They used medal plates and screws to patch up the holes made by Jap lead. So I get my discharge as soon as I finish rehab."

"Are you okay?"

"Oh sure. A little stove up, but I'm lucky just to be alive, so I ain't complaining."

"Hey, you two bums, how come you're wasting us feather merchants' tax dollars lollygagging in this here saloon?" came a voice as the front door of the Tavern flew open.

"Gerald!" shouted Billy and Danny simultaneously.

Dressed in a dapper civilian suit with a fedora that didn't quite conceal his red hair, a smiling Gerald walked into the Tavern and shook hands warmly with his old friends from the Grapevine.

"Mr. Switzner told me you guys were up here, so I hightailed it up the ole Grapevine as fast as that Chevy would go."

"Just look at the rags this guy is wearing!" exclaimed Danny.

"Well, you soldier boys get all the glory, but us four-Fs get all the dough and the dames."

Everyone laughed.

"How about a beer, Gerald?" asked Lashburn. "But feather merchants gotta buy their own."

"Not only is this feather merchant buying his own, he's buying for the whole house," proclaimed Gerald.

"Since the total house is four, four beers on the feather merchant coming up!" announced Lashburn.

"You really do look great, Gerald! Things must really be good at the shipyards," said Billy.

"Tell you a secret, guys," said Gerald, lowering his voice and glancing around the Tavern. "We send a liberty ship down the shoot every twenty-four hours."

"Holy mackerel!" exclaimed Lashburn. "How can you do that?"

"Old man Kaiser knows how to build ships, I'll tell you. If producing those babies makes a difference in the war, those other guys don't stand a chance."

"He does all that up in San Francisco?" asked Billy.

"Yep. He's got the biggest ship construction facility in the world up there in the Bay Area and you wouldn't believe all the man-starved dames that work there. They will even go out with me, they're so hard up."

"Geeze, they really are hurting!" joked Danny, which brought a laugh.

"Yeah, I make big money and have all the dates I want, and I'd trade it in a second for that uniform you guys are wearing," said Gerald.

"No one here that doesn't know that, Gerald. It isn't your fault they won't take you, and what you're doing is important cause those liberty ships get all the war stuff we need to where we need it," said Danny.

"That's right, Gerald, and I'll drink to that," said Lashburn, sliding the full glasses out onto the bar.

They all picked up the glasses, touched them together, and drank.

"Wow! It's great to see you guys. I had no idea you were here. One of my workers, a cute little blonde, wanted to come to Bakersfield for a visit, so she furnished the gas ration coupons, and I furnished the car to drive down in. Sure glad I did."

"You reckon an old beat-up marine can get a job up there?" asked Danny.

"Sure, come on up," replied Gerald. "That reminds me, you could never guess who I saw over at the Navy Yard here a couple weeks ago. Ensign Jack! He was on his way to the Pacific to shoot down Japs."

"Good for Jack! He got his navy wings, right?" asked Danny.

"Yep, and guess what? He got married!"

"Yer kidding!"

"Nope. You remember that girl he dumped Ruth for?"

"The one that lived in Bakersfield? The sexy-lookin' one?"

"Yeah. That one, Ritina."

"Well, it wasn't Ruth he dumped, it was Patty."

"I thought it was Ruth."

"No, it was Patty. Ruth was goin' with Bobbie. But didn't Ritina join the waves?"

"She did, and now she's gotta salute Jack and say, yes, sir, and no sir, and all that stuff you guys do."

More laughter.

"Billy, you sure look great with those silver wings. Are you goin' over soon?" asked Gerald.

"Yeah, I'm on two weeks' leave. Then I head for the port of embarkation," replied Billy.

"What kind of plane do you fly?"

"Fighters, just like Jessie. Only I'm flying the new P-47 Republic Thunderbolt."

"That's great Billy! I,uh, sure hated it about Jessie. I couldn't believe it. I was so upset I couldn't go to work for two days."

"I plan to even the score some, Gerald," said Billy.

"This may sound corny, but it's all a four-F can say: get one for me, Billy."

"You keep the ships coming down the chute, Gerald, and I'll get one for you!" said Lieutenant Billy Rascoe.

Chapter
~59~

When Jessie opened his eyes, disjointed images spun before him, and shrill noises echoed through his skull. He closed his eyes tightly for a moment and then opened them again. It was the same; only now a strange sound accompanied the high-pitched noises: a steady, deep base of boom, boom, boom! It was a drum-beat. He could hear it clearly now. What? He tried to pull himself up to a sitting position, but his head exploded and the images swirled violently. He aborted the attempt and lay back down. Then out of the swirl a new image appeared. It was a hazy form, but as he watched, it began to take shape transforming into a black face covered with blotches of white paint and tassels of sparkling things. Jessie's senses told him it was a human face, and he knew that it was somehow connected to the footprint in the mud.

The human black face was on the figure of a black man who was naked, but his body was decorated with white and red paint and tassels of feathers and straw. Pieces of bone and wood dangled from his nose and lips. Jessie wanted to speak to him, but all that came out was a hoarse croak.

The black man stepped back quickly, raised the long spear he held, and shouted. The drum beat stopped abruptly, and several similarly painted black men with spears appeared.

They looked at Jessie curiously, grunting and conversing in their native dialect.

Suddenly the natives stepped aside as one of their clan came forward. He was even more elaborately decorated than his associates wearing a headdress that jingled with an array of brightly colored bones and wood. Instead of a spear he held a decorated object that appeared to be some form of scepter. It had a striking resemblance to a human skull.

Jessie's numbed mind struggled to comprehend what he was seeing. This must be their chief or one of their leaders, and these natives must be the ones the Aussie survival expert had talked about. Were they friendly? Was he a guest or a prisoner? He must speak to them- tell them they would be rewarded if they helped him.

When Jessie managed to speak a few words, all conversation between the natives stopped, and all eyes focused on him. Then the leader raised his scepter and grunted a command. Everyone backed away except for the original guard, who remained at a safe distance with his spear held forward prominently.

Although blurred, Jessie could see that he was lying on a reed mat in a thatched native hut. There was an opening at one end where his guard stood. He tried again to rise, but he was so weak he fell back onto the matt. He lay still trying to think, trying to rationalize some plan to communicate with his captors. He could hear native conversations from outside the hut. Then his guard stepped aside, and another native entered.

This visitor was not as tall as the chief but more elaborately decorated and carried his scepter around his neck. It looked like a human jaw bone. His eyes stared from behind circles of thick white paint, and his nose and lips were painted a brilliant red with pieces of white bone piercing his nostrils on both sides. A string of bone and pebbles hung from each ear and similar string of bobbles on a straw hat that also sprouted an array of brightly colored feathers. His body was painted in red and white stripes like a barber pole.

The native squatted and offered Jessie a coconut shell filled with fluid. Jessie raised his head and looked at the fluid. Was it food or poison? The native grunted and thrust it to Jessie's lips. He sensed it was some kind of medicine. If they wanted him dead, all they had to do is run a spear through him. So he drank the fluid.

The fluid was bitter and tasted awful, but Jessie drank it each time the medicine man, or whatever he was, gave it to him over the next few days. It not only put him to sleep, but it was nourishing and reduced the severity of his fever.

Jessie's symptoms were typical of malaria and dengue: burning with fever one minute and shaking violently the next with chills. Between attacks, he would have a period where he could think rationally for a while. He had determined that he was in a primitive New Guinea native village where the people were living in what the Aussie captain had described as a "stone age culture."

He wasn't sure just what his status was. He was guarded constantly, but they continued to feed him the herbal broth. At night, they put a thatched cover over him. It was suffocating and smelled awful but better than the mosquitoes and other insects that came in black clouds at sundown.

His captors continued to tend Jessie, and over the course of a few days, his fever subsided enough that he was able to stand for short periods when the chief and his entourage visited, which always came after a noisy session of drums. However, Jessie's attempts to communicate were hopeless as they just stood watching him with curiosity and uncertainty. The Aussie survival expert said that the interior of the north east section of New Guinea had never been explored. So these natives had probably never seen a white man before and were uncertain as to what to do with him.

Jessie recognized that the chief's scepter was a human skull all right, and he saw others with human bones, so it was apparent that his captors were cannibals. This was confirmed one night when he watched through the cracks in the hut as they dragged a captive into the village, hacked him to death with stone clubs and spears, then cut him into pieces, roasted him over the fire, and ate him.

That night Jessie realized his status was precarious, and there was little hope for survival or escape as he was guarded constantly. It left him with a terrible sense of hopelessness. He lay on the straw mat listening to the natives celebrating their feast. He tried to tell himself that he must not lose hope. But what could he do? They had taken his forty-five, and he was still weak from the fever. God, he wished he had a cigarette. Cigarette! His Zippo lighter! It was in his zipped up breast pocket. They hadn't taken it. It just might work!

The next day when the chief and his entourage appeared, Jessie got to his feet held the lighter up and with a loud cry flicked the little light wheel.

The Zippo flared with flame and with the affect that Jessie had hoped for: the superstitious natives were astonished and drew back in fright. The trick worked like magic. Jessie was transferred to the great spirit house where only gods, chiefs, and high-ranking elders were allowed. Best of all, they produced his forty-five and gave it to him. Jessie's hope for survival skyrocketed.

The Great Spirit House was a large wooden structure built on massive stilts made of palm tree logs. The main floor was ten feet off the jungle floor, under which a number of dug out canoes were kept. The sides were a complex framework of beams under a thatched roof with a steeple at each end. Access was by a long ladder of bamboo lashed with vine. The entrance edifice sprouted the wooden figure of a huge female with large pointed breasts, garishly painted in intense colors.

Despite his weakness, Jessie walked as god-like as he could to his new quarters and up the long ladder. The inside of the spirit house was decorated with all types of figures and symbols carved from wood or human bones, including scores of yawning human skulls. Although the stench was nauseating and the grotesque skulls distracting, it was an improvement in overall living conditions and probably a reprieve from being considered for a village cook out.

A great celebration was held that night with leaping fires, beating drums, and native dancing. Huge fifteen foot long hardwood slit gongs boomed through the jungle with the rhythm of the native dancers as they celebrated the discovery of their new white god.

With his new status, Jessie was revered and treated accordingly. He was assigned a special female native who attended to his needs including an improved diet of prized pieces of pork, fish, sweet potatoes, palm sago starch, and a variety of fruits and nuts. He was also afforded great respect and presented with an array of valuable gifts including carved wooden figures, necklaces, bright feathers, and some poor soul's shrunken head.

Jessie was given free reign now to come and go as he pleased throughout the native village, which consisted of two dozen or so thatched huts in a large clearing and surrounded by dense jungle. On one end of the clearing was the village garden where women carrying infants bound to their back labored most of the day. The older children laughed and shouted and played games like all children while the tribes prized pigs rooted along the jungle rim. Rain-water for drinking was collected from thunder storms in large fired clay containers. The men went on occasional game hunts into the jungle or down the nearby river in their dugout canoes, but for the most part, the women did all the domestic work while the men squatted in groups smoking and talking. Men and women alike only dressed in woven reed clothes for special occasions, but otherwise went naked.

Jessie's primary responsibility appeared to be attending periodic tribal meeting and celebrations. He had no idea what was being said, but it appeared his subjects were satisfied for him to just be there and look godly. The meetings did require some smoking with long-stemmed wooden pipes and sharing an awful alcoholic drink fermented from coconut and other jungle plants. Jessie managed to convey to his subjects that gods didn't partake in alcohol and at least got a pass on the jungle juice.

Jessie's domestic was a young village maiden called Mahzoo. She had huge lips, big dark eyes, and a mop of bushy hair. He guessed her to be twelve or thirteen with developing breasts and colorful rings in her nose and ears. Not wanting to offend the chief, Jessie had accepted her by nodding and smiling, but with some concern over just what services she was expected to perform. His chief concern was solved when he found that the girl was not allowed in the great spirit house.

Since no clothes were worn, washing wasn't on the domestic agenda, nor was shaving. So Jessie washed his flight suit in the nearby river and grew a fine beard, but Mahzoo did about everything else. As Jessie regained his strength, he began to think about escape. He discovered that Mahzoo was quick to learn and could interpret an action or object with the dialect word and pronounce it for him. He knew that if he was going to survive and escape the jungle he would need to have a working knowledge of the dialect, and little Mahzoo would be his teacher.

Over the ensuing months, Jessie regained back most of his strength. He suffered an occasional fever attack, but with the native herbal medicine, he would recover in a few days. But even with his luxurious status as a god, it required all the stamina and determination he could muster to cope with the primitive living conditions and the constant battle with the elements.

Jessie knew he could only survive temporarily in the jungle, and he also realized the volatile natives could turn on him. He had detected indications of jealousy over his status by both the chief and the medicine man. It was a dangerous game that couldn't last. He suspected that he could terrorize his subjects with his forty-five, but that would serve no purpose unless he could first make them understand. So his first step toward escaping the jungle was to learn enough of the dialect to convey his requirements.

It was a slow process, but Jessie had little else to do with his time and spent hour after hour with his young teacher who, as a god's helper, was a tribal celebrity and participated eagerly and happily. After many months, Jessie gained enough knowledge of the dialect to engage in a limited conversation. Now it was time to formulate his escape plan.

He had seen no aircraft fly over, so he knew that he was in the deep interior, which meant it was hundreds of miles to the coast. The native hunting party that had found him on the river bank had taken him via a dugout canoe to their village in a section of New Guinea that was not on anyone's military agenda. His only chance of escape now was to reach the Bismarck Sea, via the river network.

Jessie formulated his speech in the dialect that would tell the chief and his council that their white god had to make a pilgrimage to the great water, and their fine boatmen would have the honor of taking him there. He practiced his speech over and over and was finally ready to make his pitch.

The morning he'd planned to address the chief and his council he was awakened by shrieks of terror and shouting. For a moment, he thought it was some kind of quarrel, but when he glanced out of the spirit house, he could see that the village was under attack by an enemy war party.

Dressed in war paint and screaming like banshees, the attackers were running around clubbing and spearing the terrorized villagers. Women and children alike were being cut down and butchered, their heads chopped off as prizes.

Jessie grabbed his forty-five, slammed a cartridge into the chamber, took aim on the closest warrior, and fired. The sound slammed through the camp like a thunderbolt, and the top of the warrior's head exploded, spewing blood and matter as he dropped in his tracks. Both villagers and attackers fled into the jungle in terror. Even one who had been speared struggled to his feet and stumbled off in panic.

The reaction of the natives was so dramatic it surprised Jessie, and watching the fleeing natives gave him a real god like feeling. He had stopped the slaughter with his index finger.

The attacking warriors fled on through the jungle to where ever they had come from, and gradually Jessie's subjects crept back into the village.

The returning natives including the chief and the council now looked at Jessie in total awe. It was evident that his action with the forty-five had verified his power as a god and dispelled any doubts about his authenticity. Now was the time to make the pitch for his escape. The day after the ritual was completed for the slain villagers, Jessie called for a meeting of the council.

Standing with his forty-five pistol plainly showing in its holster, Jessie gave his prepared speech telling them that their all powerful god must make a pilgrimage to the great water and a crew of their best boatmen would have the honor of taking him.

The announcement was received with mixed reactions as Jessie's command of the dialect was so limited it required much discussion. However, with Mahzoo's help, the chief and council finally got the idea, but then there was more confusion because no one there had ever been to the great water, although they had heard stories about it. Jessie then indicated that was okay because he would guide them. He knew that the river near the village was large enough that it would eventually flow into the Bismarck Sea.

After two days of more discussions, the chief and his council agreed to their god's request, but to get volunteer oarsmen, Jessie had to promise a big reward. He also had to engage in some dishonesty in assuring the council that he would return and protect the village with his god powers. That deception stung Jessie's conscience in a strange way. He realized that in a sense he'd come to feel a kinship to the villagers. They were savage cannibals living in a Stone Age culture. But in their primitive way, they lived and loved and raised their children like all humans. He had become particularly attached to little Mahzoo, almost as though she was his daughter.

After a grand celebration with roaring fires, drums, dancing, and feasting on a roasted pig, the chief and all the village gathered at the river's edge to watch their god's departure. Jessie took off his crash bracelet and put it on Mahzoo's wrist. He could see by the look in her dark eyes that she was emotionally affected. He waved god like, climbed into the dugout canoe, and his six oarsmen pushed off into the muddy river.

Chapter
~60~

Father Patrick McNiff was tall and long-legged, and in his youth he'd been a pretty good soccer player. He still had a full head of hair, although it had receded some and turned from black to jungle grey. But the priest still held himself erect and walked at a fair gait, despite years of difficult living in the New Guinea jungle.

Shortly after World War I, the bishop had convinced Patrick that he could make a major contribution to the church and at the same time enjoy a unique adventure by establishing a parish in far away New Guinea. The priest took the bait and traveled from his native Ireland halfway around the world to the Northwest section of New Guinea and then by a small boat to an isolated native settlement on the Sepik River.

After dumping him and his gear, the boat went back down the river leaving the priest standing on the river bank wondering if this assignment was going to be all the bishop said it was.

And the priest had reason for concern. Patrick was left with the task of trying to establish a mission and convert ignorant, superstitious natives in a harsh, primitive area of rain forest jungle never before inhabited by white man.

It wasn't easy, but Patrick was a dedicated and determined man and now, twenty-three hard years later sat in his home made chair on his home made veranda on the shady side of the rectory at his mission, smoking his pipe. He had selected this location when he built the rectory because a slight rise in the terrain allowed him to see the mission compound on one side, and on the other side, the crocodiles lying on the bank of the Sepik River.

At the sound of a commotion on the river bank, he glanced out to see a number of his native parishioners gathered in a group talking excitedly in their native dialect. "I wonder what that's all about," he muttered to his spinster sister who sat next to him engrossed in her needlework. It was that time of day when things were generally quiet, but he could tell that something unusual had aroused their interest.

Martha McNiff, a stout, matronly woman whose hair had also turned a jungle grey, glanced up and after looking for a moment said, "I don't know, Patrick."

The same bishop had convinced Martha, and she had followed her brother to New Guinea and had the same misgivings when she arrived. But like her brother, she was dedicated and determined, and over the years, they had established a mission that, although primitive, managed to effect a significant improvement in the welfare of the natives, and even convert a few.

Patrick and his sister glanced at each other as the same thought occurred to them: was it the Japanese gunboat that periodically came up the river?

"There is no reason to be concerned, is there, Patrick?"

"No, I wouldn't think so," he replied, hoping that he sounded more convincing than he felt. "If it were the Japanese, we would have been warned by the native drums, but I think I'll walk over and see what's going on," said the priest, getting up from his chair and walking across the rough cut wooden floor to an outside bamboo stairway.

A Japanese gun boat had been patrolling the river on irregular occasions since the Japanese occupied that section of New

Guinea in early 1942. The officer in command, a Lieutenant Fujima, had allowed the mission to continue its work. But he had made it clear to the priest that if he ever found that the mission harbored any allied personnel, he would burn it to the ground and execute everyone.

Father McNiff had faith the mission would be protected from above. But he also recognized it would be prudent to take certain precautions, and being a practical man, he knew the lieutenant would do exactly as he had threatened.

That concern was on the priest's mind when one of his faithful and more astute native assistants came running up to him. "What is it, Mutu? What is going on?" he said to the naïve in English.

"Father, tribesmen come from interior. Bring white man."

"A white man from the interior?"

"Yes, Father. I think so."

The priest frowned. He had never heard of a white man coming from the interior, and although he knew the Americans were fighting the Japanese in Southeast New Guinea, he doubted there would be any this far to the northwest.

As the priest approached, he could tell by their appearance that indeed, these oarsmen were not from the local area. They were somewhat taller and huskier than the local natives and wore different tribal decorations, but one stood out from the others. He was tall and wore a tattered set of filthy clothes. A mop of tangled sandy colored hair hung down on his shoulders, and his face was covered with a long reddish beard. The priest was shocked to see that Mutu was right. He was, indeed, a white man!

"I'm Father Patrick McNiff," he announced in English with an Irish accent.

The tall white man stood on the river bank staring at the priest, who was dressed in clean khakis pants and short-sleeved khaki shirt with a silver cross on a chain around his neck. His full head of grey hair was trimmed and his face clean-shaven. It was a beautiful sight for Jessie Rascoe to see, and for a moment, he was overwhelmed with emotion. "I can't tell you how glad

I am to see you, Father McNiff," he said, stepping forward and grasping the priest's hand. "Despite my appearance, I'm Lieutenant Jessie Rascoe, United States Army Air Corps."

They shook hands warmly and the priest said, "Frankly, Lieutenant, I'm astonished to see you. You have come from the interior?"

Jessie nodded. "Yes, I'm a pilot and had to parachute into the jungle eight months ago and have been living with the natives."

"That is amazing lieutenant. To my knowledge, no white man has ever penetrated that area and lived to tell about it."

"I know that I'm the only one the tribe I lived with had ever seen. They believe I am a white god, so now that my oarsmen have seen another white man, they are confused."

The native oarsmen were looking at the priest strangely, pointing at him and conversing among themselves. Jessie understood enough of the conversation to know they were shocked at seeing another white man.

"Father McNiff, where am I? How far is it to the Bismarck Sea?"

"You are at the Saint Patrick Mission on the Sepik River. By way of the river, it is almost fifty miles to the Sea."

"Are there any Japanese here?"

The priest hesitated. "No, not at the moment. But they have a major facility at the mouth of the river, and they come here on occasion in a patrol boat."

Jessie nodded. "Does my presence here present a danger to you?"

"I'm afraid so, Lieutenant."

Jessie nodded. "I understand, Father McNiff. We will leave shortly."

"I'm sorry, Lieutenant Rascoe. Our mission offers shelter and solace to those in need, but since the war began, the Japanese, they..."

"It's all right, Father McNiff. But would you have a map of the area that I could see?"

"Yes, I do have one in the rectory."

"That will help a lot." Jessie turned and spoke to the oarsmen, telling them he must council with this god and then they would continue their pilgrimage.

"It is amazing that you can speak their dialect that well after only eight months," said the priest. "I speak the local dialect fluently but could not decipher your oarsmen's dialect. I can tell, however, that your natives are quite confused and distressed over seeing me."

"Yes, I know," replied Jessie. "My knowledge of their dialect is limited also, but I recognize they are about to mutiny on me. It has been a very long and difficult trip, and they are desperate to return to their village. So if I could get a quick look at that map I'll be on my way."

"Alright lieutenant, it's only a short distance to the rectory," replied the priest.

As they walked up the incline toward the mission compound, Jessie heard shouts. He glanced back to see his oarsmen paddling the big dugout canoe swiftly back up the river. He ran to the river's edge, pulled out his forty-five, and fired it into the air.

The sound of the shot sent the local natives fleeing in panic but only succeeded in causing Jessie's oarsmen to quicken their stroke to propel the canoe up the river.

Jessie stood on the river bank with mixed emotions as he watched the canoe move swiftly away. It was a wrenching disappointment, yet he understood. These primitive men had become his friends and had labored day after day in the long difficult struggle to find their way through the maze of jungle rivers and swamps to get as far as they had. But now all they wanted was to return to their home, just as he wanted to return to his.

When the canoe went out of sight around a bend, Jessie put his forty-five back in its holster and walked up the bank to where the priest stood. "I'm sorry to have frightened your natives."

"I don't think they have ever heard the sound of a gunshot before, and even I had forgotten how shocking it is."

"I've used my forty-five to maintain authority with the natives all during the time I lived with them."

"You also had God's help, my son."

"I wouldn't dispute that, Father. Is your mission the only civilization between here and the coast?"

"Yes, we are quite isolated. But Lieutenant Rascoe, we have another problem. My assistant, Mutu, will calm the local natives, but that gunshot will be reported by the jungle drum system, and the Japanese will hear about it from their native informants. They know that we have no fire arms here, so they will come to investigate."

Jessie nodded. "All right, Father McNiff, I'll leave as soon as possible. But could you help me get a canoe and some provisions?"

"I will help you any way I can. But I must tell you that a Japanese officer has threatened to burn our mission if I harbor allied personnel."

"Yeah, and I have no doubt he'll do just that."

"I would like to think not, but I must take him at his word."

"All right. Can you get me a canoe?"

"Our native parishioners here at the mission are all loyal, and so are the natives in the area. But down the river the Japanese have paid informants who report anything unusual. So you would be spotted quickly and reported."

"How about the jungle trails to the coast?"

"Between here and the Bismarck Sea, it is thick jungle and a virtual rain forest that is almost impossible to penetrate. The natives in this area all use canoes on the Sepik and other connecting rivers. But even if you got to the coast, it is all controlled by the Japanese. They have a major installation and Naval base at Wewak from which they control the entire area.

I'm afraid you and I are both facing a serious dilemma, Lieutenant. But come, let us go to my rectory. I can think better with a cup of tea."

The mission compound was an area a short distance from the river that had been cleared of all growth but surrounded by thick jungle. More than half of the compound was utilized as a garden filled with plants and vegetables of all sorts. The principal structures were the St. Patrick Chapel and the Rectory, surrounded by several smaller huts. All the structures were elevated on stilts made of palm poles, and access was by bamboo steps. Floors and framing were palm and bamboo and covered with thatch made from woven Kuni grass. A wooden steeple and cross were at the front of the chapel, but the roof of the chapel and the rectory was made of tin that had rusted to a burnt-sienna color. It reminded Jessie of the Hunters' old barn in Bear Trap Canyon.

"Your mission is similar to the village I lived in except for the tin roofs," said Jessie as they approached the rectory.

"Yes, the tin was a gift from a plantation owner when I first established the mission. Usually there is quite a bit of native activity in the mission compound, particularly children, but I'm afraid your gun shot frightened them away. The majority of our parishioners come from a nearby village."

The priest led Jessie up a set of bamboo steps to the rectory, which was constructed similarly to the chapel with palm poles for basic support and siding of hand-cut wood and woven Kuni grass. The interior was surprisingly refined and included Father McNiff's study, a kitchen, dining room, veranda, and three small bedrooms with wooden doors. There was even a small wood stove and a sink with a hand-operated water pump in the kitchen. A combination toilet and shower also had a hand-operated water pump. Rain water, collected in split bamboo troughs around the eves of the roof, was then channeled into large locally made terra cotta containers on the ground.

After they entered the rectory and the priest introduced Jessie to his sister Martha. The matronly missionary stared at him in disbelief.

"I apologize for my appearance, Martha. But I have been living with the natives in the interior for the past eight months."

"You were in the interior?"

"Yes. The natives and living conditions there were very primitive."

"I don't mean to appear incredulous, Lieutenant. it's just that we have never spoken with anyone who was has come from the interior. You were truly blessed. Poor Doctor and Misses Collins went there but never returned," said Martha.

"Doctor and Mrs. Collins were anthropologists that disappeared on an exploration into the interior about ten years ago," explained Father McNiff.

"It was a terrible tragedy, but the Lord works in strange ways because that tragedy provided a blessing as their daughter Stephanie has become a wonderful and dedicated addition to our mission," explained Martha.

"Yes, that was a heavenly gift," agreed the priest.

"Patrick, was that awful noise a gunshot?"

"Yes, but Mutu is calming our parishioners. And Martha, would you please prepare some tea for the lieutenant and I? We have some rather urgent things to discuss."

Martha nodded. "Of course, Patrick."

The priest led Jessie into an adjoining room, which was his study. The room was filled with homemade furniture, a well-stocked book shelf, a home made desk, a picture of the Last Supper, various other religious items, and personal mementoes. On one wall was a large hand-drawn map of Northwestern New Guinea.

"I'm amazed at how resourceful you have been in using natural materials to build your mission, Father McNiff," said Jessie.

"Thank you, Lieutenant. It has been a challenge as the adversities were so forbidding in the early days that at times I almost gave up. But with the help of the Lord, we have persevered and established the only Christian mission in this entire area. Most of the furnishings are hand-made by myself and our parishioners. Oh, we have a few custom pieces of furniture imported from Australia before the war, including a brass tea pot and genuine China tea cups, which I'm sure Martha will use for this special occasion. We have few visitors these days, and I wish yours was under different circumstances."

"Yes, so do I. But I have to tell you, Father McNiff, I'm so thankful to have gotten this far that I feel I can handle whatever comes next," replied Jessie examining the wall map.

"Lieutenant Rascoe, I'm confident the Japanese will come up the river to investigate the reported gunshot, but we do have a warning system. The natives nearby are friendly and always signal via drums when the Japanese patrol boat comes. I doubt, however, that they will come today because it is too late in the day. You see, their base is at the entrance to the Bismarck Sea right here," said the priest pointing to the location on the wall map. "It takes them nearly three hours to reach our mission, so it most likely will be sometime tomorrow morning before they come. The native drums usually gives us about twenty minutes' warning before the patrol boat arrives at our dock on the river."

"I don't want to endanger you and your mission, Father McNiff. But I must get to the Bismarck Sea to have any chance of escaping. What do you suggest?"

"I cannot offer you shelter at the mission, Lieutenant, since I have given my word to the Japanese officer, Lieutenant Fujima. But I have an alternate offer that does not compromise my word. When the Japanese first came to New Guinea in early 1942, there was speculation that we might be taken prisoners, so my native assistant Mutu constructed a safe house in the jungle. Fortunately we didn't have to use it, so I have not seen it, but he claims it cannot be found as it is built high in the trees and only he knows its location. Mutu does speak English, so you will be able to communicate with him. I suggest that for now you hide there until the Japanese have come and completed their inspection. Then we will talk again about your dilemma."

"All right, Father McNiff. I appreciate your taking the risk in helping me at all, so I'll do whatever you say."

"I will have Mutu pack some provisions for you."

"That will help. I have learned how to find edibles in the jungle, but it's difficult and I'm not familiar with this area."

"I understand, it is difficult, but for now we can help you. I assume you've had malaria."

"Yes, and it nearly did me in, but the natives saved me with a jungle herb."

"Malaria comes with living in the jungle. We all have it, but keep it under control with quinine although our supply is nearly gone. Before the Japanese came, we used to get quinine and other supplies and mail from a small steam boat that came up the Sepik River three or four times a year, but the Japanese do not allow that now. Lieutenant Fujima, who is the commander of operations in this area, tells me the Japanese are winning the war and are in control of all of New Guinea. Is that true?"

Jessie shook his head. "No. As of eight months ago, we had pushed them out of the Port Moresby area and back over the Owen Stanley Mountains. And about the time I went down in the jungle, the Japanese had been pushed back from the Buna Bay area also."

"Then the Americans are winning the war?"

"Well, it was far from being won eight months ago, but the Americans and the Australians will defeat the Japanese aggressors. Make no mistake about that, Father McNiff."

"I do not condone war, but I know that the Japanese are the aggressors. They imprisoned many of the island plantation owners on the coast and confiscated their property. My hope is that it will all be over soon."

"So do I, Father McNiff, so do I."

"Patrick, tea is ready," said Martha from the doorway.

When Jessie and the priest walked out of his study into the main room of the rectory, Jessie was surprised to see a young woman with blond curly hair standing beside Martha. She wore an ankle length dress covered with bright colored flowers that had been painted on the material. She had a child like face with rosy cheeks and large sea green eyes that focused on Jessie intently.

"Lieutenant Rascoe, this is our Stephanie, whom God chose to bring to our mission," said Martha.

"I'm pleased to meet you, Stephanie," said Jessie.

The girl just stared at him intently for a moment. "Excuse me," she suddenly said in a youthful voice with a British accent. "I'm being rude, aren't I? It's just that you're not what I had imagined an American soldier would look like."

Jessie smiled. "Judging from my appearance, I can understand that, Stephanie."

"Stephanie is our star teacher. She speaks the local dialect fluently and is loved and admired by all the natives and particularly the children," informed the priest.

"Why did you fire your gun, Lieutenant Rascoe? It frightened the children terribly," said the young missionary.

"I'm sorry. I did that in a kind of desperate effort to stop my native oarsmen from deserting me. I survived for eight months with stone-age cannibals by intimidating them with my gun. Ironically, it didn't work today."

"You came from the interior?"

"Yes."

"Did you hear anything about my mother and father?"

Jessie hesitated.

"Stephanie's parents, Doctor and Misses Collins, were the anthropologists who disappeared in the jungle," explained Father McNiff.

Jessie looked at the girl. "No. I'm sorry Stephanie. I did not hear of them."

"Lieutenant Rascoe will be leaving shortly, so come let us have our tea now," interjected the priest, pointing to a bamboo table and chairs where Martha had indeed set out her brass tea pot with real china cups and saucers and a wooden bowl filled with fruit.

After they sat, Martha poured the tea and then placed each cup on a wooden plate with pieces of fruit and passed them around the table. "We ran out of sugar for our tea some time ago, Lieutenant Rascoe, but our fruit is juicy and sweet. As much as I dislike what the Japanese have done, I do thank Lieutenant Fujima for bringing us tea."

"The Japanese bring you tea?"

Father McNiff answered, "Yes. Although he is strict and very loyal to his country, Lieutenant Fujima has been kind enough to bring us a case of Japanese tea and medical supplies, including quinine. Living here in the jungle and doing the Lord's work has always been difficult, but particularly so since the war started and we lost our outside source of supplies. But we must be thankful for what we have. I remember how it was when we first came. Lord, when I arrived here in 1920, you can't imagine how primitive it was. We had to clear the land and build the mission with our bare hands. The natives were unfriendly and terribly ignorant and living conditions so primitive that it's surprising we even survived. But now let us give thanks."

They bowed their heads, and Father McNiff gave thanks for the food and drink and for delivering Jessie from his long ordeal.

Jessie was suddenly aware of how repulsive he must be with his filthy, ragged flight suit, matted, dirty hair hanging down over an equally filthy, bearded face, and with the 45 pistol obvious in its shoulder holster. No wonder the missionary girl looked at him in disbelief. But as the priest's prayer registered in his thoughts, he was suddenly reminded of where he was. In a sense it seemed bizarre! He glanced around at the three missionaries as though to make sure they were really there. They were, with bowed heads, and they were real. But then how many times had he suddenly awakened at night in that savage place to find he'd been dreaming and the only thing real were the yawning skulls staring at him and the nauseating stench? But this wasn't the spirit house. No! He'd done it! He'd survived! He'd escaped! Suddenly Jessie Rascoe was filled with an overwhelming sense of relief. He sat unmoving for a long moment with his eyes closed and his head down, the long tangled hair covering his face. I will come home to you, Maria. Wait for me. I will come back to you.

"Are you all right, Lieutenant?" came the voice of the priest.

Jessie raised his head and opened his eyes. All three missionaries were watching him curiously. "Yes, I'm fine. I'm having a little trouble believing this is all real."

"Lieutenant Rascoe was an airplane pilot whose aircraft came down in the interior jungle, and he lived there with the natives for the past eight months," explained the priest. "We are giving him temporary sanctuary because that is what we do as missionaries. But since Lieutenant Fujima has forbidden us to harbor Americans, Lieutenant Rascoe will be leaving shortly."

Although Mutu was from the nearby tribal village, he was taller and huskier than his contemporaries and considerably more literate since he was one of the children who had attended the mission school since childhood. He spoke the native dialect and over the years had become fluent in English, but he had trouble pronouncing *lieutenant*. "Just call him Mister Jessie, Mutu," suggested Father McNiff.

"Awright, Father. Come, Mister Jessie, we go to tree house," he said with a toothy smile as the three men stood at the entrance to the jungle trail.

"I'm ready, Mutu," replied Jessie with a reed sack over his shoulder that Martha had filled with fruit and vegetables, a patched mosquito net, and a few quinine tablets.

"Now don't let any of the other villagers see you, Mutu. We don't want anyone to know where the safe house is located."

"No body know but Mutu, Father."

"Good. As soon as Mister Jessie is settled, return to the mission."

"Me do, Father."

"I'm confident the Japanese will come tomorrow or shortly there after. As soon as they have inspected the mission and returned to their base, Mutu will come for you. I cannot harbor you at the mission, but I'll help you any other way I can."

"I understand, Father McNiff. I appreciate what you're doing for me, but don't take any more risk that will endanger you and your missionaries. I have survived this long in the jungle, so if necessary I'll survive some more."

"The Lord be with you," said the priest as Mutu and Jessie disappeared into the jungle.

It was difficult for Jessie to keep up with Mutu as he worked his way through the thick foliage. He realized that it would be impossible to find his way back alone. It reminded him of those first horrific days when he parachuted into the jungle a lifetime ago.

After nearly an hour of travel, the big native finally stopped. "Awright, Mister Jessie, now we climb."

Jessie glanced up but could only see small patches of sunlight through a thick umbrella of foliage. Mutu grasp a hanging vine and used it to help him walk up a large slanting tree trunk that carried him up through the foliage umbrella and out of Jessie's sight. Then the vine dropped back down. "Mister Jessie, you come."

As he grasp the vine, a memory popped into Jessie's thoughts: It was that time long ago when he and Alvin had scrambled up an old oak tree to escape the long horns of a bull.

"Okay, Mutu, here I come," he said, grasped the vine, and walked up through the foliage.

"You do good. Now we climb some more," said Mutu, grasping a bamboo ladder lashed in place and extending up through another layer of foliage.

Again Mutu disappeared, and Jessie followed. This time when he climbed up through the foliage, he came out onto a bamboo platform lashed into a large fork in the tree that held the tree house. He and Alvin had built a tree house once in the fork of a big black oak, but not like this one that had obviously taken many hours of labor to construct.

It was large enough to accommodate several people. Built primarily of bamboo, which was lashed together with vine. The sides and roof were woven Kuni grass. The overhang was slanted to capture rain water in a terra cotta container. It was primitive but functional.

"You built this by yourself, Mutu?"

He smiled. "I do that, Mister Jessie."

"That took a bunch of work. My hat is off to you."

"What mean hat is off, Mister Jessie?"

Jessie laughed, and it surprised him. It had been forever since he remembered laughing. "It means good, Mutu."

The big man smiled. "Awright, Mister Jessie. I go now. I come back when Japanese go home."

"Okay, Mutu."

Chapter
~61~

Father McNiff terminated his prayer when he heard the sound of boots on the bamboo stairway to the rectory. His native friends down the river had sent the drum message warning him of the approach of the Japanese patrol boat. But he had remained in his study so as to appear surprised when they arrived. He got up and walked into the living room just as the Japanese officer came through the rectory doorway.

"Oh, come in, Lieutenant Fujima. It's good to see you again," he said, hoping he sounded more convincing than he felt.

The Japanese lieutenant came to a halt just inside the doorway while his armed escort stopped just outside, but in sight. Fujima was somewhat taller than the average Japanese male. He stood trim and erect, dressed in a naval officer's uniform. After staring at the priest with narrowed eyes for a moment, he said in perfect English, "I do not think you are as pleased to see me as you profess, Father McNiff."

The priest forced a smile. "I can assure you that I am, Lieutenant, as we are almost out of tea, and I was counting on your generosity to solve that terrible problem."

"What I bring you on this visit will depend more on your cooperation than my generosity," snapped Fujima.

"You may count on my cooperation as you have in the past. Come, let us go to the dining room. Martha was just preparing morning tea, and I'm sure she has some of those coconut cookies that you enjoy so much," said the priest, motioning with his arm.

The Japanese officer smiled. "I am not fooled by diversionary tactics, Father McNiff. But your clumsy attempts amuse me, and I do have a taste for those cookies your sister makes."

"I am just a humble priest working in a primitive land with primitive subjects, Lieutenant Fujima. What would I know of diversionary tactics?" said the smiling priest as the two men walked into the adjoining dining area.

"Hello, Lieutenant Fujima," said Martha as pleasantly as she could. "It's nice to see you again."

Fujima gave a slight bow. "A chip from the same block? Is that the correct adage?"

Martha glanced at her brother. The lieutenant smiled. "It's nice to see you too, Miss McNiff."

Martha forced a smile and said, "Please have a seat. The tea and cookies will be ready in a moment."

As Martha left the room, Father McNiff and Fujima took seats across from each other at the bamboo table.

"I have taken the liberty of inviting Miss Collins to join us for tea," said Fujima removing his service cap and placing it on the table.

"I believe she is teaching a class at the moment."

"My men will find her."

The priest nodded. He'd known that Fujima would insist on Stephanie's presence as he had at his previous visits. It concerned him because of the way the Japanese officer treated her. Although he had made no direct overture, his interest in the girl was obvious, but it had not disturbed Stephanie. She treated him in her usual straight forward, innocent way, as though he were a welcome friend come visiting. That also concerned the priest because the girl

had no conception of deception and might unintention-
ally expose the American officer. He had cautioned her
and Martha as sternly as he could about the danger to the
mission, but deception was not Father McNiff's long suit
either. He could only pray the Lord would see it his way in
this situation.

Just as Martha entered the room carrying the tray of tea and
cookies, Stephanie came through the outside door escorted by
one of Fujima's men. The lieutenant stood and bowed as she
entered the room. "Good morning, Miss Collins. You are as I
remember: like an exquisite, blooming flower. But you appear
somewhat flushed. Is there something wrong?"

Stephanie looked at the Japanese officer for a moment
without answering. She was experiencing an emotional conflict with herself over the deception regarding the American,
and it was visibly evident.

"Yes," she said in a quiet voice.

"Is it something I should be concerned with, Stephanie?"

"Oh, no. It's a personal matter that I will have to solve
myself. But it's very kind of you to offer," she added.

Fujima hesitated. "A beautiful lady should not have such
serious problems that take away that delightful smile you usually have. I do not understand your religion, so it is hard for me
to accept that a lovely girl like you would cast herself away in
such a heathen land. In my country, Miss Collins, you could be
a top geisha in the finest tea house."

Stephanie looked at him quizzically.

Fujima smiled. "I can see by your reaction that you are not
familiar with the Japanese geisha."

"No, I'm not."

"The geisha is a highly honored profession in Japan, and
only the finest, most talented and beautiful young women may
aspire to be one."

"Oh. What does a geisha do?"

"She entertains at a tea house by enchanting men with her
beauty and her entertainment talents. I have found the misun-
derstanding about the geisha common in the west."

"Then you have spent time in the west, Lieutenant?" asked Martha as she poured tea.

"Yes. I studied at the University of California."

"I would guess that is why you speak such fluent English?" said Father McNiff.

The Japanese officer nodded. "I have many friends in the United States. It is a shame their leaders do not understand, or this war would not have been necessary."

"I am nonpolitical, Lieutenant. But I do believe that you attacked them first," said the priest.

"A strategic necessity. War was inevitable due to the arrogance of the American leaders and their lack of understanding of Japan's needs."

The priest cleared his throat and said, "Well, have some of those coconut cookies, Lieutenant. Martha just baked them this morning."

"I do enjoy them," said Fujima taking a bite of the cookie. "It astounds me how you can make these taste so sweet without using sugar."

"I use sago starch combined with an herb and the coconut meat," explained Martha. "But without tea, they will not be nearly as tasty," she added, glancing at Fujima.

The Japanese officer smiled briefly and then turned solemn. "As I have told your brother, Miss McNiff, my generosity regarding tea or anything else, will depend upon your cooperation. I have reason to believe there are enemy agents in this area. White men."

Although the missionaries were familiar with the lieutenant's tactics, in the past they had shown little emotion to his threats since they'd had nothing to hide. Now they did. They were concealing an American pilot who would be considered an enemy agent. And in doing so, they had committed themselves to a course that was a violation of their basic beliefs and teachings. It was an alien condition for them, and they faced a shrewd and perceptive adversary. Would the Japanese officer detect the deception by their reaction?

The crack of a thunderbolt suddenly stabbed through the rectory almost as though it was timed to distract the lieutenant as well as the missionaries. The moment of truth that Lieutenant Fujima had counted on was lost, as though from divine intervention, as Father McNiff would later proclaim.

"White men in this area?" said Father McNiff as quickly as he could collect his wits.

"Yes. White men, Australian or American. Only a white man would possess a fire arm. Isn't that correct, Father McNiff?"

"White men do not come to this area, Lieutenant Fujima. You know that."

"I do not know that, priest."

"I gave you my word of honor, Lieutenant Fujima, that we would not harbor your country's enemy at this mission," said Father McNiff. "If you wish to search our mission, you may."

"My men are doing so as we speak," snapped the Japanese officer as a downpour of rain struck the rectory.

A cold chill ran up Father McNiff's spine. He was certain the Japanese could not find Jessie in the jungle tree house, but if they should uncover some evidence that he'd been at the mission...?

Across in the mission compound, Fujima's armed men could be seen scurrying into the chapel and the other grass-roofed buildings to escape the downpour. With the sound of rain on the tin roof making conversation all but impossible, the four people in the rectory dining room sipped tea and watched through the open sides of the rectory as the rain came down in a torrent. After a few minutes, it ceased as suddenly as it had begun.

"You seem nervous, Father McNiff. Is there some reason for that?"

The priest took a sip of tea and replied, "Yes. I think you would be nervous too, Lieutenant, under the same circumstances."

"I would not be nervous if I had nothing to hide."

"There is nothing in this mission I wish to hide."

"I hope so. Because the orders from my superior are quite explicit, as I have told you before. It would be a tragedy and a most distasteful task for me," said Fujima, looking at Stephanie.

Martha gasped audibly. Stephanie paled, and another cold chill ran up Father McNiff's spine. He took a big gulp of tea to steady his voice. He'd never told the women of Fujima's threat to execute the missionaries, and he didn't want them to know if he could avoid it. "I understand your superiors' concern, but I assure you, Lieutenant, we are just missionaries and offer no threat of any kind."

"I do not know that, Father McNiff. And if you are harboring and aiding enemy agents, you are no longer missionaries."

It was quiet in the rectory for a moment or two with only the sound of rain water dripping from the bamboo eaves.

"Tell me again just how you make these wonderful cookies, Miss McNiff?"

Martha swallowed hard, cleared her throat, and relayed the procedure she used to make the cookies. She was just finishing when one of Fujima's men entered the room and snapped to rigid attention before the lieutenant. They conversed rapidly in Japanese for a moment, and then two other men entered and began a room-to-room search of the rectory. After a few minutes, there was another conversation with Fujima, and the men saluted smartly and departed.

The lieutenant carefully lifted his cup and took a sip of tea. "I am going to assume that the enemy agents in this area have not come to your mission, Father McNiff."

The priest gave a silent prayer of thanks- and a silent sigh of relief.

"I am pleased that my men found no evidence of such a presence. I am also pleased that I could instruct the sergeant to bring up a case of our finest tea and the box of medical supplies you asked for."

"Oh, that's very kind of you, Lieutenant, and we are grateful," blurted Martha as a flood of relief spread through her.

"Yes, that is good of you, Lieutenant Fujima," added Father McNiff.

"And you, Miss Collins? Are you not pleased?"

"Yes, I...am pleased," replied Stephanie softly.

"That's better, Miss Collins. I do hope you solve your personal problem so that I can again enjoy that wonderful smile that accentuates your vibrant beauty."

Stephanie dropped her eyes.

"Come now, Miss Collins, is it so abhorrent to you that a Japanese man would find you attractive?"

Stephanie forced herself to look at him and to her surprise she saw sincerity in his eyes. "No, it is not abhorrent to me, Lieutenant Fujima. It is just that you...you frightened me."

He nodded. "Yes. I can understand that. I wish it were not that way. I genuinely do." Fujima's voice trailed off, then he straightened up in the chair, downed the last of his tea, and rose to his feet. He put on his service cap and, looking at Martha, said, "Thank you for your hospitality. Miss McNiff, your coconut cookies were even better than at my last visit."

"Thank you, Lieutenant Fujima. I have some left. Would you care to take them with you?"

"I would indeed. Our cook is somewhat limited in his culinary repertoire."

Martha wrapped the remaining cookies in one of her few linen napkins and gave it to the Japanese officer.

"I do not wish to leave on, what you call, a sour note. But I must for your sake. Although I am not a Christian, I know you are devoted and do good work here. But I will do my duty if you involve yourselves in harboring my country's enemies."

A few minutes later Father McNiff stood on the wooden dock at the river's edge and watched the sleek Japanese patrol boat back out into the muddy waters of the Sepik River, machine guns bristling from its deck and the rising sun flag flapping at its stern.

"Praise the Lord, they go," said Mutu, standing beside the priest.

"Yes, Mutu, we thank the Lord, but I am concerned. Have your boys watch it closely for a while until we are sure it's returning to its base on the Bismarck Sea."

"Yes, Father, we watch. You think it not go home?"

"I have the uncomfortable feeling that Lieutenant Fujima is still suspicious."

"What he do, Father?"

"I don't know. I don't know." The priest was confident in his belief that what he was doing had the Lord's blessing, yet the Japanese officer was deadly serious in what he threatened-and oh, Lord, what a terrible thing that would be.

"I must go to the chapel and pray for guidance, Mutu, for I am uncertain of what action he wishes me to take."

"You want Mister Jessie to stay at tree house?"

"Yes, until we are sure that Lieutenant Fujima is not planning some kind of trick."

Chapter
~62~

Mutu reported to Father McNiff the day after Lieutenant Fujima's departure that the drum net confirmed the patrol boat had returned to the Japanese naval base on the Bismarck Sea.

Mutu then brought Jessie back to the mission where the three men gathered on the rectory veranda to discuss Jessie's disposition.

"How was your overnight stay in the tree house?" asked Father McNiff.

"It was like the Ritz compared to my previous lodging," replied Jessie.

"What is Ritz, Mister Jessie?" asked Mutu.

"Oh, that's a fancy hotel back in the States."

Mutu looked unsure. "That where you live?"

"No, only rich people live there, Mutu. I live out on the ole Grapevine."

Mutu looked puzzled. "You live on Grapevine?"

Jessie smiled. "It's not the kind of grapevine you're thinking of, Mutu. It's where my home is."

Mutu nodded. "You go there when war over?"

"I sure hope so."

"Do you smoke, Jessie?" asked Father McNiff.

"I did."

"Well, I can only offer you native tobacco. It leaves much to be desired, and since we are short of matches and kerosene, getting it lighted is a chore."

"I've tried the native tobacco, and that convinced me to quit smoking," said Jessie.

"A wise decision," said the priest as he packed his pipe from a pouch. Then rising from his chair, he went out the open door, down the outside stairs, and across to an earthen oven in the yard. There, he lit his pipe from the banked coals.

"We have candles, but Father McNiff, he only use at night and sometimes for mass," explained Mutu as they waited for the priest's return.

Puffing on his pipe, Father McNiff returned, sat down, and said, "The Japanese allow us to operate here simply because there is no strategic value to this place. No army is going to cross or even venture into this impregnable jungle, and there are no resources here that they want. Their only interest is making sure I'm not running an intelligence operation. I had a short-wave radio before the war. But Lieutenant Fujima confiscated it and told me that if he ever found one again he would burn the mission to the ground."

The priest paused for a moment. "Lieutenant Fujima has a phobia about enemy intelligence agents, and I sense that he believes now that there are some here. So he will pressure his native agents to increase their vigilance. The truth is, Jessie, I can not envision any way for you to escape this area now."

"Father McNiff, I appreciate your counsel, but I must try to escape. I have no other choice."

"But how can you escape?"

"The only way I can see is by canoe down the river."

"Can that be done, Mutu?" asked the priest.

"No can do, Father. Natives down river work for Japanese. They catch Mister Jessie quickly."

"I'll go at night and hide in the jungle in the daytime."

"No. They catch you, day or night."

"And the worst is that they will know you were here, Jessie, and I fear the consequence of that would be catastrophic."

"I don't want that to happen, Father McNiff."

"I can't break my word to Lieutenant Fujima that I will not harbor allied personnel at the mission. But I believe my conscience could accept your being at the tree house at night and spend your days here at the mission."

Out on the mission grounds, a group of laughing native children passed by on their way to one of the huts where Stephanie was conducting a class. Then a particularly loud bird called out from across the way at the jungle's edge.

"I sincerely appreciate that, Father McNiff. But I'm not sure it's right for me to endanger you and all you have worked for."

"I understand your concern, but I honestly believe it is a workable solution. Think about it, my son."

Jessie nodded. "I will."

"Meanwhile, would you like to get rid of that beard and freshen up a bit, Lieutenant?"

"I sure would, Father McNiff."

"All right, I have a strait razor. It's a bit dull but will do the job. You ever use one?"

"No. My grandfather is the only one I ever saw use a straight razor."

"I'll do the job for you then, and Martha is a pretty good barber if you would like to get rid of some of that hair. She cuts mine and does a good job."

"You're on, Father McNiff!"

"All right, a little refurbishment will probably help your morale, and then we will continue this discussion."

It took some time, but the priest managed to shave off Jessie's beard, and afterward Jessie knew why men wore beards before the invention of safety razors. Then Martha cut his hair, and he bathed in the rectory shower. Father McNiff gave him a clean set of khaki pants and shirt to wear.

"By jove, my clothes fit you pretty well, and you look like a new person, Lieutenant," said Father McNiff when Jessie walked out into the dining area.

"And I can tell you I feel like a new person. Martha, this is a better haircut than I get from our squadron barber."

"My, you do look different, Lieutenant Rascoe," agreed Martha.

At that moment Stephanie walked into the rectory, and when she saw Jessie, a look of surprise crossed her face and her green eyes enlarged.

"It's your surprise visitor," said Jessie with a smile.

"I didn't recognize you, Lieutenant Rascoe."

"I just got an overhaul."

"But...how old are you?"

"How old would you guess?"

"I thought you were about forty, but I'm not sure now."

"How about twenty three. Would you believe that?"

She smiled and said, "Well, you're the first American I've met, so I don't know. But you surely look different than when I saw you yesterday."

Jessie laughed and it felt great. "Thank you, Stephanie. And how old are you?"

"Oh, I'm nineteen, and I've been a missionary for ten years and I love it."

"That's wonderful, Stephanie." She was so lovely and child-like that Jessie had the feeling he should hug her.

"Lieutenant Rascoe is joining us for dinner, so as soon as you are ready, Stephanie, we'll begin," said Father McNiff.

Stephanie went into her room and then returned a few minutes later wearing another of her ankle length hand made dresses. This one was a pale yellow with a variety of brightly colored flowers hand painted onto the material.

"I noticed the beautiful flowers on your dress yesterday, Stephanie, and these are even more so. Do you paint them on the material yourself?" asked Jessie as Stephanie sat down next to him at the bamboo table.

She gave him a beaming smile and said, "Thank you, Lieutenant. Dear Martha makes all my clothes on her foot peddle sewing machine. Then one of my native students paints the flowers on the dress for me."

"That is beautiful work and very creative. Does he make his own paint?"

"Yes, from jungle materials."

"It is such vibrant color. The natives I lived with also made paint from the jungle, but the color wasn't as vivid as your artist makes. And Martha, I'd never guess that dress was hand made. It looks professional."

Martha smiled broadly and said, "We rarely get such complements, Lieutenant Rascoe, and they are most welcome.

I have a peddle sewing machine that Patrick got for me from Australia before the war."

Jessie and Stephanie sat next to each other at the bamboo table with the priest and Martha sitting on the opposite side. Father McNiff explained that Mutu always had his meals with his family in the village.

It was late afternoon, and outside the jungle birds provided a dinner serenade. Martha served a combination vegetable and fruit salad with a spiced dressing and baked sago starch and coconut bread that Jessie found delicious.

"It's amazing, Martha, that you can prepare food like this here in the jungle," said Jessie.

"I'm pleased that you enjoy it."

"Well, even though we live in a primitive, harsh land, we have managed to civilize it to a degree," said Father McNiff. Then he launched into a commentary on life in the jungle and about how they managed to live and do their missionary work.

He explained how the mission garden supplied most of the fruit, yams and vegetables, which was their primary diet. Other fruits, nuts, berries, sago starch, mushrooms, edible insects, snakes, coconuts, and various herbs were acquired direct from the jungle. Their only animal meat came on rare occasions when the mission was given a pig, which was considered a delicacy by the natives.

The native parishioners lived in their own village, which was only a quarter mile from the mission. Many of these natives had accepted Christianity, to a degree.

The missionaries had worked for years to establish a cultural system that outlawed killing each other, headhunting, and cannibalism, which, for the most part, was working. Most of the village children came to the mission school, and that was where the primary emphasis was directed: teaching and educating the children. That was where Stephanie shined and therefore where the most progress had been made.

The tribal elders, steeped in their old ways, continued to resist. But Mutu had played a major role in helping to convince some of the natives to accept Christianity and to allow their children to attend the mission school.

The small huts on the mission grounds were used as classrooms, and all of the missionaries taught although Stephanie carried the primary responsibility. The children and the natives who had been converted attended mass in the chapel. Occasionally there was a wedding in the chapel of those natives who had accepted Christianity.

The priest completed his explanation including praising Martha for all the domestic chores that she performed with dedication and Stephanie for her unique skills in teaching and managing the native children.

Listening to Father McNiff while eating a delicious dinner with silverware and conversation with civilized people in a civilized manner was an experience that Jessie had often thought he would never enjoy again. It reminded him of all the good things in life that he'd missed so desperately during those long months in that primitive environment in the deep jungle.

"Where is your home, Lieutenant?" asked Stephanie.

Jessie turned and looked at her. "What? I'm sorry, Stephanie. My thoughts were elsewhere."

"Don't apologize. I do that often."

Jessie smiled at her. "My home is in the Tehachappi Mountains of California."

"I've heard of California in the United States, but I never heard of the Tehachapi Mountains. Are they big mountains?"

"No, not like the mountains in New Guinea. But they are beautiful, with big oak trees and grassy meadows. And in the spring the wild flowers cover the mountain sides."

"It sounds lovely. I have never been to our mountains, but I'm told that they are beautiful and gigantic."

"Yes, I have flown over them. They are beautiful, and very high, much higher than the Tehachappi."

"You fly airplanes?"

"Yes. Well, I did."

She looked at him with large innocent eyes. "You were fighting in the war?"

"Yes."

"And that is why you carry that terrible gun?"

"Yes."

"I do not like war. The Lord says thou shalt not kill."

"Stephanie, tell Lieutenant Rascoe about the classes you teach," interjected Farther McNiff.

The expression on her face transformed instantly. "Oh, it is so satisfying. Despite their primitive ways and the terrible ignorance of the adults, the children are eager to learn, and they love coming to the mission."

Mutu appeared at the entrance to the rectory and said, "We must go soon, Mister Jessie, or it be too dark."

"This has been so pleasant I forgot how late it's getting," said Father McNiff.

"Oh yes. It has been such a long time since we've had a guest," added Martha.

"Your hospitality and kindness has given me a whole new outlook, and I appreciate it most sincerely," said Jessie.

Chapter

~63~

That evening after Mutu had guided Jessie back to the tree house, he lay on the straw mat under the patched mosquito net, listening to the jungle night sounds and thinking about the events of the past two days. He recognized that he'd been fortunate the oarsmen had rebelled and returned to the interior. Otherwise, they would have continued down river and been taken prisoner or killed by the Japanese.

So what were his options now? Only two and they both had serious problems. If Mutu and Father McNiff were correct, he had little or no chance of escaping down the river on his own and that might well result in the destruction of the mission and something worse for the missionaries. If he stayed as Father McNiff had suggested, there was also a chance the Japanese would find out, which also could be disastrous for the missionaries.

He knew McArthur had been on the offensive eight months ago, so by now he must be moving well up the west coast of New Guinea. It shouldn't be too long before Wewak was taken, and then he could escape down the river. Although Jessie wanted to let the world and Maria know that he was still alive, he realized the option to stay was the better for both himself and the missionaries. He smiled to himself when he thought of how he and Alvin had only spent two nights in their tree house and decided it wasn't as much fun as they thought. But at least he would have some contact with civilization at the mission.

After reconfirming in his mind that his decision was final, Jessie's thoughts turned to Maria, as they had almost every night for the eight months he'd spent in the deep jungle. His beautiful, wonderful Maria what would she be doing at this moment in far away California? Working at the aircraft factory? Sleeping? Thinking about him? He was certain she would still be waiting for him despite the report that he was missing in action. Yes, she would. She would wait. He knew she would. I will come back to you, Maria. I promised I would, and I will. Wait for me, Maria. Wait for me.

When Jessie told Father McNiff he would accept his offer, the priest was pleased. "I believe that is a good plan, Jessie, and one that minimizes the danger to you and our mission. And I believe you will add much to our family and to our mission. I have no idea about the progress of the war, but from what you tell me, it shouldn't be too long before you will be freed."

"It good that you stay, Mister Jessie," said Mutu with a big smile. "Me help you fix up tree house."

"You got a deal, Mutu. I have some ideas how to make it a little more efficient."

"I'm sure also that Martha and Stephanie will be pleased that you are staying. You have made quite a hit with both the ladies."

"Both of them are jewels. You are fortunate to have them, Father McNiff."

"Yes, I fully realize that. Now we do have to settle on a plan to make sure the Japanese gun boat or one of their native canoe groups doesn't surprise us. We generally have that covered by our friends down river who warn us with drums. I have resolved in my mind that the Lord approves of our plan. After all, you will not be living at the mission, and you are not an intelligence agent. I doubt, however, that Lieutenant Fujima would see it that way, so when you're here at the mission during the day, we will want to post a lookout."

"Me take care of that, Father," said Mutu.

"All right then. You are invited to take your meals here at the rectory with us, Jessie. But that will require you help with the garden and our gathering process from the jungle."

"I would be happy to do that and any other chores I can help with here at the mission."

"We accept that offer as there is always much to do. So as soon as you have completed the tree house renovations, I will give you some assignments."

That evening at dinner Father McNiff's announcement that Jessie would be staying brought instant approval by the missionary ladies. Other than the Japanese officer, they'd had no contact with the outside world for nearly two years. Although Jessie wasn't exactly a socialite, he was imaginative and enjoyed talking about life in America and on the Grapevine The missionaries savored his accounts, particularly Stephanie, who listened intently to his every word.

For the next several days after Jessie's announcement that he was staying, he and Mutu made improvements on the tree house including a bed with a straw mattress, a rainwater shower, and a bamboo chair and table. They also built a vine bridge across a small swamp that cut Jessie's commuter time to and from the mission by more than half. Now Jessie knew the way to the mission, so Mutu no longer had to guide him.

When the tree house project was completed, Jessie reported to Father McNiff that he was ready to go to work at the mission.

"I'm sure you're going to be an asset to our mission, Jessie. I've asked Mutu to show you the garden and how we cultivate and rotate the crops, and we will want to enlarge it some. But first I would like you to take a day or two to see how we handle and teach the native children. Stephanie is conducting a class this morning, so why don't you go over and just observe. I'm sure it will be enlightening.

"I'd like to do that Father McNiff; you said her parents disappeared over ten years ago?"

"Yes. The poor girl has no real home except here as her parents had traveled constantly on their expeditions. When they went into the interior, they left her here. We gave her refuge as she kept hoping they would eventually return but never did. I'm confident they were killed by natives in the interior. Stephanie became interested in our work and has become a dedicated and highly efficient missionary."

Since there were no thunder storms in the sky, Stephanie was conducting the class outdoors in a small amphitheater with logs placed in a semicircle. Jessie sat in the rear and watched.

Her students were a group of native children from the village who looked to be from about six years to teenagers. They were naked except for woven straw skirts that at least covered their genitals although the girls' breasts were bare. The skirts were an innovation the missionaries had initiated.

Stephanie wore one of her homemade long dresses with the colorful flowers and a real jungle flower in her hair. She reminded Jessie of a Jungle princess he's seen in a Tarzan movie when he was a boy. He was surprised to see how efficient she was in keeping the students attention and participation. Occasionally there would be a spurt of giggling, but overall they were surprisingly disciplined compared to the native children at his village in the deep jungle.

Stephanie was so fluent in the dialect she conversed with the children as though she was one of them. As a part of her instruction, she would stop now and then and demonstrate a point by using chalk figures on a wooden board. Then she would return to her presentation.

After about an hour, she dismissed the children, and when they had all left, Jessie walked up from where he'd been sitting in the back, and said to her, "You are something, Stephanie."

She looked at him curiously. "What does that mean, Jessie?"

He smiled. "It means I think you are a very efficient teacher. You had those little kids' complete attention and you sure can speak the dialect."

"Oh, thank you. Sometimes you say things I don't under-stand. You are the only American I've ever known."

"Yeah, we are a breed of cat."

Again she looked puzzled.

He laughed. "Uh, tell me how that native artist gets such vivid color in those flowers he paints on your dress?"

"Would you like to see the artist paint the flowers?"

"Yes, I would like that very much."

"All right. I have a dress that needs repainting. The paint dulls after a while because of washing so he repaints it. Come tomorrow afternoon, and you can watch."

"That will be great."

She smiled, and it occurred to Jessie the girl was like a spar-kling diamond in a pile of rough stones she was so out of place in this primitive environment. Yet she seemed to always be happy, enthusiastic, and totally dedicated to her work as a mis-sionary. He couldn't help wonder if she was void of any attrac-tion to the opposite sex.

Chapter
~64~

The next morning Jessie followed Father McNiff and Mutu down the jungle trail to the nearby native village. It was also built on palm tree stilts and was similar to the one where Jessie had lived, although a number of hygienic improvements were indications of the missionaries' influence.

Father McNiff introduced Jessie to the chief and his council and explained that Jessie was a very important visitor to the mission and worthy of honor. Mutu then explained that Mister Jessie was there to help the mission but his presence must be kept secret. This was followed by discussions and finalized by traditional tribal pipe smoking.

Later that afternoon, Jessie and Stephanie returned to the village and to the hut of the artist who repainted the flowers on one of Stephanie's dresses. The young native artist applied the intense paint onto the dress with a bold but affective technique that was fascinating to watch. It was a thrilling experience for Jessie, and it stirred an excitement that had been dormant since he'd left art college a lifetime ago.

"You seemed to be fascinated with the artist's work," said Stephanie as they walked back down the trail to the mission.

"Yes, I was. I wanted to be an artist once...a long time ago."

"Oh. Why didn't you?"

"The war."

She stopped walking turned and looked at him. "Why would the war keep you from being an artist?"

Jessie stood there on the jungle trail looking into her wide innocent eyes. "When your country is attacked and your best friend murdered, you must respond to the attackers, and that means war."

"I know little about war except that it is wrong and people die. Let's not talk about it anymore."

As they began walking again, she said, "Do you think I'm naive, Jessie?"

"Well, you may be a bit naive about things like that, but you are very efficient and talented in what you do, Stephanie."

"That is kind of you to say, and I do love my work. But I realize that there are lots of things I know little about."

They walked in silence for a while, and then she said, "Do you have a girl friend back at your home in California?"

"Yes, I do."

"Are you betrothed?"

"Yes...kinda. We're gonna get married, if she doesn't give up on me and marry the other guy."

"Why would she do that?"

"Well, she may think I'm...not coming home."

"Because of the war?"

"Yes."

"That would be a terrible tragedy for you and your betrothed."

"Yeah, and there's not a damn thing I can do about it."

"Don't swear, Jessie, and you must not lose faith in the Lord, or yourself."

Jessie nodded.

"I've only known you a little while, but I can tell that you're a good person so he'll watch over you. But you must have faith. If your betrothed loves you, she will wait for you to come back to her."

Jessie looked at her. She wasn't telling him anything he hadn't already told himself a thousand times, but she said it with such sincerity and conviction it was believable. It made him feel better.

"Stephanie, you may be bit naive, but you sure know how to boost a guy's morale."

"I'm a missionary, Jessie."

He nodded. Yeah. She was that all right and a delightful, warm person besides. But he couldn't dispel the feeling that even though she professed satisfaction and content with her roll as a missionary, something was missing in this lovely girl's life, and he sensed what it was.

During the following weeks, Jessie became involved in the various aspects of mission life. He counseled himself not to even think about escape, at least for now, and directed his thoughts and energy toward helping the missionaries. He had made the tree house relatively comfortable and shortened his commute to the mission in such a way that he could even make the trip after dark.

The missionaries remained on guard through their native lookouts, and after a while Father McNiff told Jessie that he was reasonably confident the Japanese had not gotten wind of his being there or Lieutenant Fujima would have come by now. After that, he began to enjoy his involvement more than he'd imagined he would.

Although conditions were primitive and the natives, particularly the adults, superstitious and steeped in lore, they were considerably more civilized than those in the interior jungle where cannibalism and head-hunting were routine.

The missionaries' years of hard work had altered the sociological behavior of the local natives significantly. These natives did not attack their neighbors, and there was no head-hunting or cannibalism-at least not that was evident. Some of the elders still maintained their spirit house, which was filled with various carved figures and symbols but no human skulls. They did continue their custom of occasional ceremonial dances with leaping fires and beating drums.

Jessie participated in missionary work by assisting in the overall logistics of the mission, repairing and making improvements in the mission facilities, expanding and working in the vegetable garden, and improving the system of gathering jungle food resources.

Although the native dialect that Jessie had learned in the deep jungle was different than the one spoken locally, it gave him a basis to learn the local dialect. Stephanie and all the missionaries took time to translate, and Stephanie's private instruction gradually brought Jessie enough fluency that he could converse and assist in missionary activities.

Jessie's hit with the children was the introduction of an entertainment period where he performed a juggling act using three wooden balls he'd carved from palm. The children loved his act, and on occasion, a performance for the adult parishioners got the same reviews.

Jessie particularly enjoyed working with Stephanie. She was kind and considerate yet maintained order with gentle but firm discipline. In a way, she was like Miss Trembell, his teacher back at Grapevine school. Stephanie wasn't as pretty as Miss Trembell, but she had an inner beauty and a fresh, youthful vitality that reminded him of a Tehachapi poppy that had just popped open after a spring rain.

His daily working relationship with Stephanie was warm and congenial. But Jessie had become well aware of a growing physical attraction between them, and sometimes their eyes met in a silent but intense exchange. He sensed she was experiencing the same burgeoning emotion as he, and it took all the discipline he possessed not to encourage that and to remember his pledge of restraint. Remember that he loved Maria and only Maria. And even though she may have thought he was not coming home and perhaps even married Kevin, that didn't change anything. He would not break his pledge until the day he knew that she was no longer his.

Jessie's determination to keep that pledge was tested daily over the ensuing weeks. Then about the time he'd reached a point when his determination was weakening, he'd also reached the point where he could perform his duties at the mission and have time to do what he'd wanted to do since the day he watched the native artist paint Stephanie's dress. He would paint!

With Mutu's influence, he was allowed to observe the native process to make the paint, which turned out to be difficult and time consuming. Since there were no written formulas, he spent long hours observing the process of acquiring, grinding, and mixing the pigment and then mixing on a pallet to obtain a variety of vibrant colors.

For a painting surface, he learned how to make substitute canvas from a durable plant leaf, which was stretched over a wooden frame and given several coats of thick pigment. Paint brushes were made from natural hair the natives acquired from monkeys. It was a far cry from the refined materials he'd always used, but Jessie was consumed with the challenge and eager to start painting.

After observing the native artists and numerous failed attempts on his own, Jessie finally produced an acceptable quality of paint, painting surface, and brush. The water-based paint was easy to work with and dried to the same hardness as oil. But it was less forgiving than oil paint, and mixing the hues from the crude pigment and applying them to the equally crude painting surface was a trial-and-error process.

But the challenge so absorbed him that Jessie began to spend all of his spare time painting. He recognized that the diversion of his thoughts and emotions helped significantly to solve his dilemma over Stephanie.

He labored long and hard to develop a painting technique. When a painting failed, which most did in Jessie's view, he would let it dry and try again. After several cycles, the crude surface would deteriorate, and he would start again with a fresh piece. When his supply was exhausted, he would go through the tedious process of making another batch of paint and surface, and begin again.

After many weeks of trial and error, Jessie had learned to control the medium and apply the hues reasonably well, but the results were still not what he envisioned. Then one day, standing before his bamboo easel struggling with a painting, he became so frustrated he kicked the easel into a heap, hurled his palette and brush after it, and stomped off.

Stephanie had been watching and followed him to where he sat on a log with his head in his hands. "Jessie, it serves no purpose to lose your temper," she said softly.

He glanced up to where she stood beside him, surprised. "How do you know I lost my temper?" he snapped.

"I saw you."

"Oh? Are you now the official mission overseer?"

"No. I just like watching you paint. You are usually so engrossed you don't even know I'm there."

"Well, I don't want you watching me anymore. There's nothing to see anyway but a bunch of shit."

"Jessie!"

"And don't tell me not to swear!"

A hurt look crossed Stephanie's face. "I'm sorry, but I have to say what I feel. You are being too demanding on yourself. The paintings that I see you destroy because you are displeased are far better than you think."

"Now you're an expert on painting, right?"

"No, but I believe I have a sense of color and composition. But that's not the point. What is it you're trying to accomplish in your painting?"

Jessie sat silently staring at the ground before him.

"I know you are searching for something in your painting that you haven't reached yet. But your search for that perfection is keeping you from recognizing the good work you're already doing."

"Sure, I'm painting great masterpieces and don't know it."

"Jessie, I just think that you-"

"I don't want to talk about it, Stephanie," he snapped. "And I don't want to hear your advice on how to paint. I can't paint, that's all. But then who could with jungle shit for paint and brushes made from the hair off a monkey's ass."

Stephanie lowered her eyes and quietly walked away. Jessie sat watching her for a moment, then leaped up, and ran after her. He caught her before she'd entered the mission compound, grabbed her by the shoulders, and spun her around to face him. "I'm sorry, Stephanie. I...didn't mean to hurt you. I-"

Her eyes filled with tears, and her lips quivered. "Oh Jessie, I'm sorry too, but I can't help myself. I...I don't know what to do. I am so consumed with emotion for you that I cannot control or understand. Every moment with you is so precious, yet my heart aches. And there is a yearning inside me that...oh, Jessie, I...I'm afraid. I..."

Jessie knew the moment he pulled her into his arms that he'd stepped over the line that he'd sworn not to cross.

Her body trembled, and she clung to him desperately. She lifted her face, and he could see in her eyes the same explosive desire that he felt. They looked at each other for a brief moment and then kissed eagerly and passionately.

"Mister Jessie! The Japanese come!" shouted Mutu as he came running across the compound. "Go to tree house quickly!"

Chapter
~65~

It was late in the day before Mutu came to the tree house and told Jessie the patrol boat had gone back to its base so he could return to the mission. Father McNiff and the two women were in the rectory dining room waiting for him, and when he walked in and looked at Stephanie, she glowed as if she was engulfed in Saint Elmo's fire. She smiled at him with such loving eyes that Jessie felt as though his insides were being ripped out by a buzz saw. He'd known for some time that she had fallen in love, which he'd had little choice but to ignore. What else could he do? But now, as their eyes locked, Jessie knew that he could ignore it no longer.

"Come in, Jessie," said Father McNiff.

Jessie sat down at the bamboo table and said, "How did it go with the Jap officer? Was he suspicious?"

The priest shifted in his chair and said, "Yes, I'm afraid he is, although I'm not sure he was any more so than at his past visit. Oh, he gave us his usual warning, and his men searched the mission, but thank the Lord found nothing. Fortunately he did bring us some tea."

"Do you think he's gotten more information that I'm here?"

The priest hesitated. "I...I'm not sure."

A jungle bird let out a cry, and by the time it faded, Jessie knew with a certainty what had to be done. It wasn't what he would prefer, and he knew the odds were against him. But Jessie also knew there were no alternatives now. He had to leave. It would solve both problems: it would save the mission and this wonderful girl.

"Jessie, uh, my pipe needs relighting. Would you come with me while the ladies prepare the food?" asked the priest, getting up from the table.

It was as though Father McNiff had read his mind. He nodded and followed the priest out of the rectory and down the outside steps with Stephanie's eyes following him. They walked past the outside oven and on down to the river, where the priest halted.

"The Lord forgives little deceptions when it's for a good purpose," he said with a smile as he put the pipe back in his mouth and puffed a cloud of smoke.

Jessie nodded.

After a moment of silence, he said, "Jessie, I will admit that I am concerned, and we must continue our diligence. But more importantly, I want you to understand that I have faith the Lord will protect us and this mission."

"I don't dispute your faith, Father McNiff. But I sincerely believe that the danger is more than you are willing to admit. With me here, you are sitting on a powder keg, and there is another reason why I must leave."

The priest nodded. "Stephanie."

"Yes."

"She is in love with you. That has been evident for some time, Jessie."

"I know, but I'm in love with my girl back home, even though she probably thinks I'm dead."

The priest shook his head. "War is such a tragedy."

"Yeah."

The priest pulled on his pipe for a moment, then removed it, and said, "I've been around you long enough to know that you are a good person, Jessie, and what you propose is the honorable thing and what I would have expected of you. But I want to point out something you must consider. The jungle between here and the sea is all but impassible, so your only chance is the river. And it is watched by partisan natives who will almost certainly capture you, and they will know we harbored you. That will insure our destruction as well as yours...and something even worse for Stephanie."

"They will not capture me, Father."

"I'm afraid they will, my son."

"I won't let them. But even if they do, they will not take me alive, so it won't do them any good. Dead men can't talk."

The priest shook his head. "You can't do that, Jessie."

"Yes, I can. It's nothing more than what I did as a fighter pilot. You fight to win. If you lose, you die. But I will not lose, Father McNiff."

"They would know anyway."

"No, they won't. I'll take a native boat, wear native garb, and have only native food."

"This is a desperate plan, Jessie...desperate," said the priest, shaking his head. "There has to be another way. I can't let you do this."

"There is no other way, Father. Believe me when I say I don't like it any more than you do. But the truth is I should have left some time ago. With me here, you're sitting on a powder keg, and I...well, I've come to appreciate the wonderful work you are doing. I am jeopardizing that, and it's selfish and wrong. Besides, I...I can't trust myself any longer around Stephanie. If I stay here, I'll hurt her bad."

The priest was silent for a moment. "Even though I firmly believe you were sent here for a purpose, I can not dispute what you say and I can see you are determined."

"I am, Father."

"God bless you, Jessie, and may he be with you."

The "Spirit House" of the tribe of stone age natives in the
deep jungle interior of New Guinea, where
Jessie is interned as a "White God".

"A Stone Age" New Guinea native.

Father McNiff's chaple at the isolated Catholic mission in the Sepic River area of New Guinea.

Jessie's tree house in the jungle near the Father McNiff Mission.

Chapter
~66~

Jessie asked Father McNiff to keep Stephanie busy in the village for a couple days while he prepared for his departure. His plan called for traveling down the Sepik River in a native canoe, keeping close to the shore in case he encountered Japanese patrol boats or unfriendly natives. That way he could quickly hide in the jungle along the bank. If he was successful in reaching the Bismarck Sea, he would work his way east along the coast until he reached friendly territory.

Jessie recognized the odds were against him. The Sepik River would take him to the Bismarck Sea all right, if he could elude the partisan natives and the Japanese. But then he had no idea how much of the north west coast was still under Japanese control. The allied forces should have retaken some of that area since he'd been gone. And he knew more now about surviving in the jungle: what was edible and what wasn't, how the natives behaved, and how to deal with them. He could even understand some of the jungle drum-talk and speak enough of the local dialect to be understood. He also had his forty-five with two clips of ammo.

With Mutu's help, Jessie acquired a small native canoe and some jungle food supplies, making sure he possessed nothing that would lead the Japanese to the mission. Father McNiff gave him a general picture of the Sepik River's course as he had traveled it before the war.

On the day before he'd planned to leave, he went to Stephanie's class, did a special rendition of his juggling act, and got a native equivalent to a standing ovation. Jessie realized that he'd become fond of the children. Despite their primitive ways and superstitions, they were just children- quick to laugh and eager to learn. He would miss them.

As he watched Stephanie usher out the last of her pupils, he knew that he would miss her also, more than he wanted to admit. For a moment he experienced an urge to forget the whole plan and stay at the mission- stay with this lovely girl that he'd come to admire, and desire.

She wore one of her brightly painted dresses that matched the flower she always wore, but that was no match for the love in her eyes. "You are a beautiful person, Stephanie. It's no wonder all the native boys love you."

"Thank you, Jessie. And I love them. But I know now there is another love in my heart that surpasses all others." She reached out and taking his hand said, "Oh, Jessie, I know that you are unsure, because of...because of the girl in California. But I believe that you have a love in your heart for me. I must believe that, since I am so hopelessly in love with you. What a wondrous thing it is to be filled with such happiness when I'm with you. It is beyond anything I have ever known."

Jessie had realized that leaving her was going to be difficult, and he had tried to prepare himself. But now, as he looked at her, the emotion burgeoned and exploded like a sky rocket when she stepped into his arms.

All restraint collapsed, and he crushed her to him in a savage embrace. Ater a moment, he found her lips and kissed her with the totality of the emotion that surged through him. Fortunately, they were interrupted by a native helper who came to tell Jessie that Father McNiff needed him.

That evening when he lay on his straw bed in the tree house, he felt sick at heart. Staring into the blackness, he couldn't help but wonder again if he was wrong. If he should stay and let nature take its course. But he knew what course it would take, and that was wrong. Hadn't he already gone over this a hundred times already? Yes, he had. If he stayed, he would have to make a total commitment to Stephanie or destroy her. He could do neither. Even though his rational sense told him that Kevin had probably won, he would never give up hope. He'd promised Maria he would come back to her, and he would-somehow, someday.

With little sleep, Jessie left the tree house before dawn dressed in native garb Mutu had given him. He gave Mutu a note he had written for Stephanie:

Dear Stephanie,

You are a beautiful, wonderful person in every sense. I hate to leave, but I must. I will never forget you.

Love, Jessie

The birds were squawking and singing their pre-dawn wake-up calls as Jessie retrieved the native canoe from where he'd hidden it in the reeds. It was a wooden dugout, which was tricky to handle and required a delicate balance. But with a few lessons from Mutu, the former Eagle Scout had picked up the technique quickly. He climbed in with his gear and pushed off into the muddy waters of the Sepik River.

As planned, he kept close to the shore and for the most part let the current move him down the river. The jungle foliage overhung the river along its bank except an occasional break with a muddy stretch, often occupied by crocodiles. He gave those areas a wide berth, otherwise staying just outside the foliage overhang to keep away from insects and leeches, but close enough to duck into, if necessary.

Jessie's first day on the river went according to plan. He saw nothing but birds, a few snakes, and a couple batches of crocodiles. But his first night gave him a sample of what lay ahead. He camped in a secluded cove on the river bank, sleeping in the dugout with a reed cover he'd fashioned for mosquito and insect protection. It was hot, uncomfortable, and buggy, and he slept little.

He pushed off the next morning at dawn and again met no obstacles till late morning, when he spotted a large native canoe coming up the river. He nosed his dugout into the foliage overhang before any of the natives saw him and then waited silently until they had passed.

Later in the day, Jessie saw another group of natives on the shore, but again he was able to pass by without being seen. Mutu had told him there were several native villages along the river, some friendly, some not so friendly. He had decided to play it safe and avoid them all by waiting till night to pass by.

After his second miserable night in the dugout canoe, he tried to estimate how far he'd come and how long it would take to reach the Bismarck Sea. With only a rough idea from memory of Father McNiff's map and the difficulty of measuring progress because of the way the river meandered through the jungle, it was impossible to determine.

Jessie started his third day shortly after dawn and proceeded without incident until midday, when a huge black cloud covered the sky and rain came down in such a torrent that his canoe filled with water before he could reach shore. He managed to get onto a mud bank, but in the process lost much of his food supply. It was a setback, but Jessie knew he could find more food in the jungle. When the storm passed, he dumped the water out of the canoe and pushed on down the river.

He continued downstream until late afternoon when he estimated that he was close to a boat landing that was indicated on Father McNiff's map. He selected a place to go ashore just upstream of a bend in the river. There he would hide until late night and then push off in the darkness and float past the boat landing- hopefully unobserved.

As he paddled the canoe toward the spot he'd selected, he heard the sound. He knew instantly that it was a powered boat of some kind coming up the river. He swore aloud as he realized he'd let himself get caught where he shouldn't be: in the middle of the river at a bend. His only option was to try to get to the bank before the boat came into sight.

He didn't make it. The boat came around the bend directly in his path.

It was a Japanese gunboat. A daunting gray color, its deck guns glistened in the sun and dirty river water splashing from its bow as it turned sharply and bore down on him.

Jessie stopped paddling and stared at the gunboat for a moment. He could see the rising sun flag, and figures had appeared on the foredeck with automatic weapons. It appeared there was no escape. He'd vowed that the Japanese would not take him alive, and now the chips were down. And Jessie was about to lose.

But he hadn't lost yet! He swung the canoe around and began to paddle furiously back across the river where it made the bend. He glanced back and saw the gunboat closing rapidly. He could see two Japanese crewmen had moved up to the bow with their weapons raised to firing position. Another crewman was on the upper deck standing behind a deck-mounted twenty-millimeter cannon.

"Just hold your fire a little longer," Jessie muttered as he paddled with all his strength toward the upriver side of the river bend. "Just a little more..." He could hear the sound of the gunboat coming closer, so he knew they were following him at full speed. It was just what Jessie wanted. Would the Japanese helmsman realize in time that he was headed for shallow water and turn back? Or would they just open fire?

Jessie got his answer when the twenty millimeter cannon boomed. As he flipped the canoe over, he caught a glimpse of the two Japanese crewmen who seemed to lift from the bow of the gunboat and fly out into space, as though they had been shot out of a cannon.

The Japanese gunboat had come to a sudden stop when it ran aground in the shallow water, just as Jessie had hoped.

He'd done it! He'd tricked them, and he wanted to shout with glee. But now the priority was to get ashore as quickly as possible and hide in the jungle before they could catch him.

When he reached shore, he glanced back and saw the gunboat sunk to its gunwales on the reef. It had struck hard enough to rip the bottom open, but they had launched a dinghy that was coming after him.

Jessie watched for a moment. "Try and catch me now, you yellow bastards," he said aloud, and then plunged into the dense jungle.

Chapter
~67~

It had been over a week since Jessie left the mission. When the native drums sounded the approach of a Japanese gunboat, Father McNiff had the terrible feeling that it would have something to do with Jessie. He said a brief prayer and walked down from the rectory to the river dock. A few minutes later the gunboat came into sight and eased up to the dock. When he saw the look on Lieutenant Fujima's face, he knew that his worst fears might well come to pass on this day.

"Hello, Lieutenant, it's good to see you again," he forced himself to say with a smile.

As the Japanese officer stepped onto the dock, a group of heavily armed men leaped off the boat and formed behind the lieutenant.

"I am not pleased to be here, Father McNiff, for I have an unpleasant duty to perform."

"I hope it's not as serious as it sounds, Lieutenant."

"It is serious...very serious, priest."

Father McNiff nodded slightly and said, "Shall we discuss it over tea in the rectory?"

"I think not. You have decisions to make, and it's best you do it now before we go to the rectory."

The priest nodded again.

"Fortunately, my men do not speak or understand English so we can talk frankly. My superior believes that you, or agents working from your mission, were responsible for the loss of one of our patrol boats. Therefore, he has ordered that I burn the mission and all other facilities to the ground."

"Would it do any good if I gave you my sacred word that we had nothing to do with the loss of your patrol boat, Lieutenant Fujima?"

"Even though we know there was a white man involved in the patrol boat sinking, I don't personally believe you had anything to do with it. But it doesn't matter what I believe."

The priest hesitated. "And our fate?"

"That depends on you, Father McNiff."

"Then there is an alternative?"

The Japanese officer studied the priest intently for a moment. "Yes, there is an alternative. At some personal risk, for which I... will not explain, I interceded with my superior and obtained his approval for a compromise. I will not burn the mission if you agree to these terms: You will affirm your sacred word that you have not, and will not, engage in any action whatever against the Japanese government. And...the missionary girl, Stephanie, will voluntarily come with me as a hostage to insure that you keep your word."

Father McNiff stared at Fujima, speechless.

"You appear shocked, priest. Let me remind you that I have the authority and the justification to burn the mission, execute all its inhabitants, and simply take the girl."

"There is a much higher authority that would see that as unjustified savagery, Lieutenant Fujima."

"Perhaps, but my superior does not recognize that authority, nor do I. In reality, you have little choice but to accept my generous terms, Father McNiff. You have my personal word that no harm will come to Miss Collins. But she will be held as a hostage to guarantee your full cooperation with my government in its occupation of Japanese New Guinea."

The Japanese gunboat backed away from the Saint Patrick Mission's dock in the late afternoon of that spring day in 1944. When it was well into the channel of the Sepik River, the helmsman retarded the twin engines, flipped the gear lever into forward, and advanced the throttles.

As the boat picked up speed, its captain, Lieutenant Saburo Fujima, glanced across the bridge at the Caucasian girl who stood against the rail next to him. He could see the tears rolling down her cheeks as she watched the mission disappear from sight. He felt sympathy for her, but he also felt an excitement.

It was an emotional thing that Saburo experienced when he was around her. He'd felt this strange fascination since the first time he'd seen her at the mission. It was a secret he shared with no one because he, a Japanese samurai, would be ridiculed for having such feelings for a Caucasian girl. Sexual feelings were acceptable, of course, and certainly that desire was evident. But it was more than just sex. It was stupid, but it was true, even though he hardly knew her. A missionary, a Christian, one who looked at him with fear in her eyes, and who was an enemy of his country. He would tell himself it was only because he was so lonely, being stuck in this forsaken, terrible land so far from home. He would reprimand himself and order himself to wipe such thoughts from his mind. But then, the next time he saw her, his emotions would flare with even more intensity.

So Lieutenant Fujima had jumped at the opportunity to suggest to his superior that she be taken as a hostage, and he, of course, would supervise the missionary's disposition.

During his long months living in the jungle, Jessie had learned enough to easily evade the Japanese who pursued him when their gunboat ran aground. But then what? He'd wanted desperately to continue on and try to reach the Bismarck Sea, but without the canoe and all his gear, he realized it was impossible. If he returned to the mission now, it might mean its destruction and execution of the missionaries, and something far worse for Stephanie- sweet Stephanie.

But after a fitful night in the jungle, Jessie realized he had no choice but to return to the mission. He vowed he would only stay long enough to get another canoe and survival gear and then take to the river again. He despised the thought of endangering the missionaries, and he could almost see the hurt in Stephanie's eyes when he returned only to tell her he must leave again. But there was no other rational answer. He must try again to escape the jungle and the Japanese.

It had taken Jessie nearly two weeks to make his way back to the mission by following the river. It had been a difficult and strenuous journey that required forging through dense jungle and snake-infested swamps while avoiding native marauders. He'd been able to find enough edible food to keep him alive, but when he'd finally reached the mission, Jessie was exhausted, bloodied from leaches, and burning with fever. But that was inconsequential to the gut-wrenching shock he'd experienced when Father McNiff told him of Stephanie's abduction.

Jessie lay bedridden with fever for several weeks after his return, and even when the fever finally subsided, he couldn't shake off the despondent mood that gripped him. He knew it wasn't just the fever- It was also the gnawing guilt over Stephanie's abduction. He listened to Father McNiff's assurances that it wasn't his fault and that it was God's will, but that didn't change anything.

"I'm going to have to leave as soon as I'm able, Father McNiff," said Jessie as they sat on the veranda of the rectory.

"You must do what you believe is right, Jessie. But you should recognize now that it is virtually impossible to evade the Japanese and reach the Bismarck Sea."

"I know, but I must try. I have no other acceptable option."

"I believe you do. Although I am deeply saddened by Lt. Fujima's decision to take Stephanie hostage, I do believe he is an honorable man and will keep his word that no harm will come to her. By remaining hidden here, there is little chance he will find you, and therefore you will both be safe. But if you are caught attempting to escape...which is all but certain?"

Jessie sat staring silently at the muddy waters of the Sepik River. "I'm afraid I don't share your confidence the Jap will keep his word that no harm will come to Stephanie."

"I must believe that he was sincere as I cannot accept the alternative. But I fear that if they catch you, that will, in Fujima's mind, release him from his promise."

Jessie lay on his straw mat bed in the tree house that night with Father McNiff's words echoing through his skull, and no matter what rationale he used to discredit the priest's logic, he failed. About the time the first rays of sunlight peeked through the jungle foliage, Jessie realized that no matter what his personal feelings, he would not be going down the Sepik River again.

Chapter
~68~

Jessie gradually recovered from the malaria attack and regained his strength. He then involved himself again with the daily activities of the mission, working in the garden and making repairs to the facilities. Since he'd gained a working familiarity with the native dialect, he helped with the children and the other native parishioners.

The mission remained on constant alert to detect a Japanese or native partisan surprise visit. Mutu kept in drum contact with his friends downstream, and Jessie kept himself on-guard. But the patrol boat didn't come. Although Jessie was constantly thinking of ways to escape, they all had one overiding flaw: the danger to the mission and the lives of the missionaries.

Jessie doggedly directed all his time and energy into mission work to keep his mind occupied, but he became increasingly restless. Then one day he went to the chapel storage room for something and was surprised to find his painting gear where Stephanie had probably put it. He experienced conflicting emotions for a moment, then gathered it up, and took it with him.

The next day Jessie did a painting of the mission. As he stood examining it after it was finished, he felt the same frustration he'd felt that day he'd lost his temper with Stephanie.

But as he stood there, Stephanie's words came flooding back: "Your search for perfection is keeping you from recognizing the good work you are doing."

Even though he was tempted to kick this painting into a heap also, he forced himself to look at it again and admit that it actually wasn't all that bad. He just hadn't reached what he was striving for yet.

So Jessie forced himself to keep painting even though he continued to be frustrated and impatient with the results and constantly on the verge giving up. Then one day he finished a painting, and when he backed off to look at it, he was so disgusted he dropped his palette and brushes and walked off leaving the painting standing on its bamboo easel.

As he sat on one of the outdoor class logs sulking, a thunderstorm struck. "Good, the rain will save me the time of throwing the damn thing in the river," he muttered. But a few hours later, when he returned to gather up his gear, Jessie was stunned by what he saw. The rain had not ruined the painting. Instead, it had softened the brush work, adding a degree of abstraction to the composition, yet retained the vibrant realism and color Jessie wanted.

The revelation hit Jessie like a thunderbolt. He'd found his answer! Then he remembered the portrait of Stephanie that was one of the few paintings he'd done that pleased him-it had also been accidently rained on!

It was so obvious. Why hadn't he seen it before? He'd been painting too tight, too schematic. He must loosen his technique, soften edges, and paint with more emotion, not frustration.

From that time on, Jessie progressed steadily, failing occasionally, but continuing to refine the technique he'd discovered. Since he was now a familiar face in the village, he was given liberty to go wherever he wished to paint. Over a period of many months, Jessie sketched and painted a panorama of native life in the New Guinea jungle.

During Jessie's first year at the mission, he had only seen an occasional formation of aircraft in the distance. He reasoned that was because the mission was in an isolated section of the Sepik River Valley. Then in mid 1944, he saw large formations of B-24 bombers escorted by fighters. They would almost always be in formations at high altitude on their way to or from targets on the northwest coast of New Guinea. He could only guess that MacArthur's forces were pushing farther and farther into Japanese-held territory. But how long would it take before those forces recaptured the coastal installations that would free him? And how would he know when they did?

Some vague information would filter through the native communications network, but nothing definitive about what was actually going on in the war. And there had been no word of any kind about Stephanie or Lieutenant Fujima. The patrol boat had not come to the mission for months. It was frustrating, but all Jessie could do was try not to think about it and keep himself occupied with his mission work and his painting.

Jessie had another fever attack in mid-1945. But as Father McNiff had predicted, it wasn't severe, and after a few days in bed he was up and back to his painting, which now occupied all his time other than what he spent on his mission duties.

Chapter
~69~

As the calendar moved into late 1945, Jessie noticed that almost no combat aircraft flew over that area anymore. When he did see one, it would be a transport.

"Father, I believe the Allies have moved up the north coast and have either occupied all the Japanese installations or bypassed them. I see no bombers or fighters anymore, and the patrol boat hasn't come up the river since they took Stephanie," said Jessie one morning as he, the priest, and Martha had tea. Since the Japanese supply had long been exhausted, tea was now made from a jungle leaf that had zip, but the taste left much to be desired.

"The jungle network reports that the military installation at Wewak is still in Japanese hands," replied the priest.

"Yes, and that probably means that it has been bypassed and isolated."

"Oh, my poor child. My poor Stephanie," said Martha with tears forming in her eyes.

"Now, Martha, remember, Lieutenant Fujima gave me his word that no harm would come to her."

"I know, but it's been so long. I...I can't help feeling that something terrible has happened."

"If they have been isolated, that would explain why the patrol boat hasn't come. They must be short of fuel and supplies," speculated the priest.

"I'm going down the river," said Jessie. "I can't stand it any longer. And I think Martha is right. Something has happened."

Father McNiff looked at Jessie and was about to speak when gunshots echoed across the mission grounds. Jessie leaped to his feet and glanced out through the open sides of the rectory. He saw Mutu running up the incline from the river shouting frantically: "Japanese! Japanese soldiers coming! They shooting everybody! Run! Run away quickly!"

Jessie exchanged glances with Father McNiff. "The Japanese are attacking the mission! We've got to run into the jungle!"

The priest looked at him incredulously. "There is something dreadfully wrong here. The Japanese have never done this before. What is-"

Another series of shots rang out, and someone screamed.

"Run! Run!" shouted Mutu again. "They all crazy! Crazy!"

Jessie grabbed the priest by the arm and spun him around. "We got to get out of here Patrick, now!" he shouted as more shots sounded.

Glancing out, Jessie saw a group of Japanese soldiers running from the trees along the west side of the compound and more coming from the opposite side. Suddenly they were everywhere, shouting and firing indiscriminately at anything that moved. A native woman was shot the instant she stepped out of the chapel. Several children ran screaming from one of the hut classrooms and were cut into a bloody heap by a burst of automatic fire. Jessie and the missionaries watched the slaughter in disbelieving horror.

There appeared to be no way to escape now, and it was evident the Japanese soldiers intended to murder every soul at the mission. Jessie swore aloud as he had left his forty-five at the tree house. Without a weapon, he could do nothing. He caught a glimpse of soldiers coming up the outside steps into the rectory. "Lie down on the floor, quick!" he rasped, then snatched one of the bamboo chairs, and positioned himself beside the front doorway.

The missionaries were in a state of shock and just stared at him. "Get down!" Jessie hissed. He could feel his heart pounding as he heard the sound of boots coming rapidly up the outside stairway to the rectory. A Japanese soldier stepped inside, glanced at the missionaries, and raised his automatic rifle to the firing position.

Jessie brought the chair down on the soldier's head with all the strength he possessed. The soldier went down in a heap, and the gun clattered across the wooden floor, with Jessie after it. He grabbed it up and spun around just as the second Japanese loomed in the doorway. Jessie pulled the trigger, and his fire caught the soldier full in the chest, knocking him backward out the door and down the stairway onto the ground below.

The one he'd hit with the chair stumbled to his feet and lunged forward. Jessie's fire struck him in the head sending a shower of bloody matter spewing across the room. Martha screamed and dropped to the floor sobbing. Another burst of gunfire and more screams came from the compound as Jessie ran across to the entrance and glanced out. There were no other soldiers directly in front of the rectory. He whirled around and shouted, "Come on, quick! We've got to run for the jungle!"

Father McNiff looked dazed, but he seemed to understand and staggered across to where Martha was on her knees sobbing violently and praying.

"For Christ's sake, hurry!" shouted Jessie.

"Yes...All right, Jessie," he muttered. "Martha, come. We... we must go."

Jessie leaped across and jerked Martha to her feet. "Martha, please! We must hurry. Do you understand?" Her eyes were large and glistening, but she nodded.

They stepped over the slain Japanese soldier and hurried down the outside stairway. Jessie scooped up the automatic rifle the other soldier had dropped when he'd toppled off the stairway. Then he herded the shocked missionaries into the jungle nearest the rectory, which was on the opposite side from the mission compound where most of the Japanese soldiers had gone and were randomly shooting the fleeing natives.

As soon as he reached the thick foliage, Jessie called a halt and said to Father McNiff, "Our only chance is to hide from them. They are crazed and apparently intent on killing everyone, so we must hurry to the village and make sure they all flee into the jungle."

Father McNiff, although still stunned, managed to mutter, "Yes, Jessie. You are right. We must hurry...hurry and warn my people."

"Here, take one of these guns in case we run into them."

The missionary shook his head. "I can't, Jessie. I can't."

Jessie hesitated and then nodded. "All right, follow me and stay as close together as you can," he said, slinging one gun over his shoulder and holding the other in firing position.

Jessie avoided the beaten path between the village and the mission, keeping out of sight in the jungle foliage. When he and the missionaries arrived at the village, the natives were in a state of terrified confusion.

When they saw Jessie and the missionaries, they swarmed around them talking frantically. Father McNiff was composed now and explained in the tribal dialect that they must evacuate the village quickly and all hide in the deep jungle.

The sound of another round of gunfire served to emphasize his warning, and some of the villagers ran into the jungle in panic. Others hurriedly grabbed prized possessions. Mothers scooped up crying infants, while several of the men tried to herd their squealing pigs into the jungle.

"I'll catch up with you later," said Jessie to the missionaries as they started to leave.

"I go with Mister Jessie. Kill Japanese!" said Mutu, his eyes filled with hatred.

"No, Mutu," said Father McNiff. "You must not kill."

"They kill my friends!"

"They know not what they do, Mutu. Come, we go into the jungle."

"Go with Father McNiff and Martha, Mutu," said Jessie, "They need you to guide them." The big black man hesitated. "Go, Mutu. You must keep them safe."

"You come too, Mister Jessie?"

"Yes. As soon I'm sure everyone has left the village."

"Okay, Mister Jessie. Come quick, we go," he said to Father McNiff.

Jessie watched as they disappeared into the jungle and then quickly went through the village. Once he was satisfied all the natives were gone, he stopped and listened. Other than an occasional shot, the gunfire had ceased. He assumed the Japanese had killed everyone at the mission and were on their way to the village. He checked both guns. They had nearly full clips of ammunition. Now what?

Jessie hesitated. He knew how to shoot a rifle as his father had taught him as a boy. But escaping the rectory had more to do with luck than his ability as a soldier, and these murderers were professionals. His rational brain told him to head for the deep jungle as he'd promised Mutu.

A flurry of shooting in the distance interrupted his thoughts. The mad dogs had found someone else to murder! He discarded one of the Japanese guns, saving the ammo clip, and then hurried back through the jungle toward the mission. He knew it was a risk he shouldn't take, but a terrible fury had began to grip Jessie. These same mad dogs had taken Stephanie, and now they were slaughtering innocent natives, women and children alike. He had a weapon, and the Japs would have a difficult time catching him since he knew every inch of the jungle around the mission, and they didn't.

When he reached the mission compound and peeked out from the trees, he saw the bodies of several natives lying about in pools of blood, including women and children, many of whom he recognized. Without hesitation, Jessie raised the gun, took careful aim at the nearest Japanese soldier, and shot him. Two other soldiers came running out of the mission, and Jessie shot them both before they could return fire. Then he quickly retreated into the jungle.

When Jessie was certain he wasn't being followed, he doubled back through a foliage thicket on the opposite side of the mission chapel where he could hear a Japanese soldier shrieking orders. He slipped up to where he could see three Japanese soldiers in heated conversation. He took aim and opened fire, cutting all three of them down before they could fire a shot.

Again he retreated into the jungle, but this time he had pursuers. That was fine with Jessie, who now had only one objective: kill every one of the sons of bitches. He raced through the jungle, keeping just far enough ahead to be out of firing range. Then he selected a hiding place and waited for his pursuers. When he shot the first two, the others retreated back to the mission.

Jessie scooped up the ammunition from the two dead soldiers and started to work his way back toward the mission when he heard another outburst of automatic gunfire. He cringed as it probably meant they were executing more of the natives for what he had done. The fury surged again, and he hurried on.

As he made his way through the jungle, Jessie kept hearing periodic bursts of gunfire. He circled around and approached the compound from a different direction. When he was in position again to look out through the foliage, the first thing he saw was a soldier crouching behind a bush at the edge of the compound. He inched forward silently. Slipping into position behind a tree, he leveled his weapon. Closing one eye, he drew a bead on the crouching soldier. As his finger tightened on the trigger, a signal flashed to Jessie's brain. The Japanese soldier was wearing a strange looking hat. It wasn't a Japanese soldier's hat: it was an Aussie infantryman's hat.

Jessie opened his eyes and looked again. As he watched, the soldier raised his weapon and fired a volley of shots toward the mission, and several more volleys from other soldiers nearby followed. Jessie could see that they too wore the big, wide-brimmed hat. For a moment, he stood behind the tree watching without comprehension. Then, he realized they were

Australian infantrymen shooting at the Japanese who had taken refuge in the chapel. Someone shouted a command in English. And several of the Australian soldiers stormed out of the trees and into the compound. There was more firing and shouts for a few minutes, and then it became quiet. Jessie just dropped his weapon and sat down on the jungle floor, closed his eyes, and was quiet too.

Jessie opened his eyes at the sound of footsteps and looked up into the barrel of a rifle held by a giant of a man wearing one of those big beautiful hats. "I say, you're not a Jap. Are you Father McNiff, ole chap?" he asked.

Chapter
~70~

"**W**ho did you say you are?" the Australian captain asked skeptically, after the giant infantryman had escorted Jessie to his commander.

Jessie could understand why the captain was having trouble believing his identity claim. After Stephanie left, he'd let his beard and hair grow and was wearing a tattered pair of pants he used for painting: not exactly regulation wear.

"You say you're a leftenant in the American army?"

"Yeah. I may not look it, but I'm Lieutenant Jessie Rascoe, United States Army Air Corps. I went down in the jungle in 1943 and have been here at the mission for nearly two years."

"I'm Captain Robert Cough, fourteenth regiment, Royal Australian Army. Do you have any ID, Leftenant?" asked the captain.

Jessie shook his head. "My ID is long gone, Captain Cough. But Father McNiff will verify my claim."

The captain, still skeptical, asked, "Where is the missionary?"

"He's hiding in the jungle with the rest of the village natives. I'll go get him and the others but..." Jessie glanced around at the carnage. "I...I'd like to spare the missionaries having to see this."

Captain Cough nodded. "As soon as we finish attending the wounded, we'll move the bodies into one of those huts and cover them."

Jessie shook his head. "I'm glad you came, Captain. I just wish it could have been a little sooner."

"So do I, Leftenant. What a bloody shame! All this killing for no reason."

Jessie was surprised at the captain's comment. It was a strange thing to say considering what the Japanese soldiers had done. "For what they did, those mad dog Japs deserved to die, Captain."

"Yes, I suppose they did, but having to kill the poor blighters after the war is over is sad."

"What did you say?" said Jessie. The Australian looked at him curiously. "Did you say the war is over?"

"You didn't know?"

Jessie shook his head.

"The bloody war has been over since August, Leftenant."

Jessie was dumbfounded. He didn't know if he wanted to laugh or cry. "Jesus! It's really over?"

The Australian nodded. "It's over all right, but we haven't been able to convince all the Japs of that, including the ones we just had to kill."

Jessie stared at the Australian officer in disbelief.

"We've had the whole Japanese installation at Wewak isolated for over a year now. Command decided it wasn't worth the loss of lives to take the place. MacArthur just bypassed everything that wasn't of strategic value. The plan was to cut off their supplies and starve 'em out. Then when the war ended, the Japanese high command sent a message to all its military installations that Japan had surrendered and the war was over. But some of them would not believe it, especially in places like Wewak that had been isolated so long. This group escaped up the river in one of the patrol boats. Fortunately, someone remembered there was a mission up here so we came after them. Unfortunately, we were a bit late to stop the slaughter, and since they wouldn't surrender, we had no choice but to kill them."

Jessie stared at the captain with a terrible ache in the pit of his stomach. "But...but why? Why did they kill the natives...the women and children?"

Captain Cough shook his head. "I don't know. But I guess if you'd been trapped, bombed, and starved for over a year...?"

Jessie shook his head, his thoughts spinning and his emotions in disarray. "But the war is over...it's all over? You're sure, Captain?"

The Australian captain recognized that the alleged American officer was in a bit of an emotional fog. He replied patiently, "Yes, Leftenant Rascoe. You 'ave my word on it. It's all over. The Germans surrendered in May and the Japs in August after your chaps dropped a couple of atomic bomb on them."

"They dropped what?"

"Atomic bombs. They made quite a blow."

Jessie didn't understand what the Australian was talking about, but it didn't matter. It was over-the war was finally over! Now what? Stephanie!

"Captain!"

"Yes?"

"You came from Wewak? The Jap base near the mouth of the river?"

"Yes, we did."

"Stephanie, is she there?"

"Is who there?"

"Stephanie. Stephanie Collins."

"Was she a prisoner?"

"No...well, I'm not sure. She was a missionary from here. The Japanese took her as a hostage about a year ago."

Shaking his head, the Australian said, "I really couldn't tell you. There may have been some Allied prisoners there, and she could be in that group, but I don't know their disposition. All I saw was a rag-tag bunch of starved Japanese troops. The place was in terrible condition since their supplies have been cut off for so long. It's still a mess down there."

It required several days for the traumatic experience of the massacre at the mission to settle and rational thinking return. The missionaries suffered acutely over the loss of life, and Jessie had his own private agony over his part in the tragic, senseless killing. But the war was over, and he had to keep reminding himself of that.

The natives killed were all given Christian burials modified to a degree by tribal customs. The Japanese soldiers were buried in a plot next to the mission cemetery. Father McNiff offered prayers for their souls and asked the Lord to forgive them since they knew not what they were doing.

The captain agreed to leave some of his men at the mission for a few days to help repair the damage and get the burials over and the natives resettled. The Australian motor launch was sent back down the river with the wounded. And Jessie went along to find Stephanie. He promised the missionaries that he would return as soon as he found her.

Wewak, on the north-central coast of New Guinea, had been a seaport and trading center before World War II. The Japanese had occupied it in early 1942 during their successful advance down the New Guinea coast, establishing a major military installation. But when the tide of war turned, the allies bombed it and then sealed it off from the outside world. With no incoming supplies or equipment and under constant air attack, the entire facility was a wasteland of destruction, strewn with wreckage, and its harbor littered with the hulks of sunken ships.

When the Australian motor launch pulled into the harbor and Jessie saw the devastation, he was filled with despair at the thought of what terrible consequences Stephanie must have faced.

After docking at the Australian facility, Captain Cough took Jessie to the Allied headquarters, which was in a bombed out plantation building with makeshift repairs. Inside, Cough explained to a U.S. Army major where he'd found Jessie and that he was an alleged Army Air Corps pilot.

Father McNiff had given Jessie a clean set of civilian khakis, and he'd shaved and cut his hair, so he was presentable. But the look on the major's face revealed his skepticism. "You may be who you say you are, Rascoe, but with no uniform and no ID, I can't do anything for you until I can get verification," he advised from behind his makeshift desk.

"Well. how long will that take, Major?" asked Jessie.

"Just give me the information, and we'll start the ball rollin'."

Jessie hadn't forgotten what that meant in the army: waiting, waiting and more waiting. "Look, Major, I can't hang around here waiting. I've got to find Stephanie."

"No, you look, Lieutenant, or whatever you are. You're only one of thousands, ya know. There are Allied units all over the Pacific trying to relocate tens of thousands of displaced persons and prisoners, and more tens of thousands of surrendered Japanese troops. Not to mention all of the Allied troops who want to get the hell out of here and go home."

"Okay, I understand that. All I ask, Major, is that you check with whoever handles the prisoners and see if Stephanie Collins is there."

"Who is she?"

"She was a missionary who was taken hostage. I assume that means she was a prisoner."

"Well, how did she-?"

"It's a long story. Just tell me where I can find out about the Allied prisoners."

"I don't think there were any Allied prisoners here," said the major, turning to his adjutant, a lieutenant, who sat at a cluttered wooden table across from him. "John, were there any Allied prisoners here?"

The lieutenant hesitated, then said, "I don't think so, Major."

"But you really don't know? That's what you're saying, isn't it?" questioned Jessie.

"Well, I guess you could check with the Provost Martial. But I was over at Aussie intelligence when they interrogated a Jap naval officer, and he said there were no prisoners at Wewak. And that Jap spoke better English than I can."

"Lieutenant Fujima?" asked Jessie.

The lieutenant thought for a moment and then nodded. "Yeah, I think that was his name. How'd you know?"

"Where is he?"

"He's in the stockade. They are holding some of the Japanese officers there for interrogation."

"Where is the stockade?"

"It's on the other end of the harbor, but you're not gonna get in there unless you got credentials."

"I'll get in. Just tell me where it is."

The lieutenant shrugged. "Go down to the harbor and follow it around about five miles to the west end. It's in a pile of bombed-out Jap buildings."

"Thanks," muttered Jessie and turned to leave.

"Hold on, Rascoe," said the major. "You better give me some information so I can get you an ID. Otherwise you'll end up in the stockade yourself."

Jessie hesitated. "Okay, Major. But do it quickly, please."

After he had taken the information, the major said, "I don't have a clue how long this will take. Meanwhile, I have to classify you as a displaced person. Here is a card that will get you into the Displaced Persons Barracks where you can get a sack and chow. They will notify you down there when we got an ID and some orders for you."

"What about Stephanie?" asked Jessie.

"If you find her, bring her in here, and I'll give her a card too. How did you say she ended up here as a prisoner?"

Jessie just shook his head. "Like I said, it's a long story."

The major shrugged as Jessie walked off.

Jessie managed to catch a ride on a dilapidated Japanese truck, driven by an Australian corporal who was going right past the stockade. But that was where his luck ended. The captain in charge of the stockade wouldn't give him any information or let him see Japanese prisoners without written permission from the Provost Martial. He also had him driven back to the Displaced Persons Barrack in a jeep with orders to stay there until he got some ID.

Jessie was seething with frustration. But he was also weary and hungry, so he checked into the Displaced Persons Barracks, which was another bombed-out building that had been hastily repaired and crammed with displaced persons including women and children and various pets. But he did get a GI cot to sleep on and a hot meal. It was Australian bully beef, which was just as awful as ever.

Jessie spent the night in an open men's bay with dozens of others classified as displaced. Most were Australian and Dutch civilians who had been caught in the Japanese invasion and occupation of New Guinea and the Dutch East Indies. The beds were GI cots with good ole scratchy GI blankets, but he didn't mind, it reminded him that he was out of the jungle at last and hopefully would be going home soon. He didn't dare think about Maria, not yet. He had to find Stephanie first. He had to.

Although Jessie was impatient and anxious to find Stephanie, he realized that eventually the army would identify him and then he would find her. It made him ill just to imagine what she'd had to endure. But discovering that the Jap officer, Fujima, was there and alive had boosted his hopes that she would be there too, somewhere, if she'd survived the bombings. And if Fujima had kept his word that no harm would come to her. And if he hadn't...?

Despite orders to remain at the barracks, Jessie left the next morning and managed to find the Provost Martial's office. It was in the same building as the Allied headquarters. But he was told that the Provost Martial would not discuss anything with him until he got some ID. It was the last straw, and Jessie snapped. He barged through the inner door and stormed into the office.

"You're going to see me whether you like it or not!" he shouted at the startled major. "I've got to speak to Lieutenant Fujima. He knows where Stephanie is!"

The major got to his feet as two MPs rushed into the room and grabbed Jessie. "Who the hell do you think you are?" snapped the major.

"I'm Lieutenant Jessie Rascoe-that's who I am. And all I want is a little consideration."

"You're not gonna get consideration or anything else until you get some ID. Now you get back to the Displaced Persons Barrack and stay there, or your ass is going into the stockade. You got it?"

Before Jessie could answer, the two MPs grabbed him by the arms and hustled him out of the room.

So Jessie ended up back at the Barrack for Displaced Persons where he had little choice but to lie on his cot with the others and wait. After two and a half years away from the army he had forgotten the army did that better than anything else: make you wait!

When his anger had finally subsided, Jessie realized he'd made a mistake by losing his temper. That had gotten him nowhere. And that was punctuated by the fact that all around him were misplaced persons who had been waiting for nearly four years, but were patiently obeying the rules.

The next morning he was sitting on his cot trying to think of some way he could get some action when a civilian dressed in khakis walked up to his cot. "You're Lieutenant Jessie Rascoe?" he asked.

Jessie nodded.

"My name is Daniel McCabin. I'm a civilian attorney assigned to a special division of the United States War Department. May I have a word with you?"

Jessie got to his feet. "I hope you're here to get me out of this place, Mr. McCabin."

"I understand from the Provost Martial that you want to see Lieutenant Fujima."

Suddenly Jessie could see a ray of hope. "Do you know him?" he asked.

"Yes, I know him," replied McCabin.

"Then you know he is here?"

The lawyer nodded. "Yes. Would you mind telling me your connection with him?"

"I've never met him personally, but I know of him. He took Stephanie Collins as a hostage over a year ago, and I need to see him to find out where she is. Can you help me?"

"How do you know Stephanie Collins?"

"She's a missionary from Saint Patrick Mission."

"There's a Christian mission here?"

"Yes. Well, it's not here in Wewak. It's in the jungle on the Sepik River."

"I wasn't aware of that. How...? Ah...Lieutenant Rascoe, I'm not familiar with the circumstances of how you happen to be in Wewak without identification. Would you fill me in on that?"

"I'm an army fighter pilot that went down in the jungle about a hundred years ago, and it's a long story."

McCabin studied Jessie for a moment. "I think, Lieutenant that you and I need to do some talking. Come on, my quarters aren't anything to write home about, but they're a bit more private."

Chapter
~71~

Daniel McCabin was tall and handsome with dark hair and eyes and appeared young to be a high-powered War Department official, but his admission that he knew Lieutenant Fujima had sparked Jessie's hopes of locating Stephanie. An MP drove them in a jeep to the command and staff quarters where McCabin had a room.

"Like I said it isn't much, but it is private, and I do have a bottle of state side bourbon. Could I offer you a drink, Lieutenant?" asked McCabin after they had arrived.

"Yeah, you sure can," replied Jessie.

"I don't have anything to mix it with but rainwater," said McCabin as he pulled a bottle of whiskey from his traveling bag.

"All I need is the whiskey."

McCabin handed the bottle to Jessie. It was Jack Daniel's Tennessee bourbon. "You got good taste, Mr. McCabin," said Jessie as he unscrewed the cap and took a big gulp. "That hits the spot," he rasped, with tears in his eyes. The attorney smiled.

"Long time between drinks?"

"A long time between drinks of that good stuff. The native jungle juice is not bad tasting, but it's so potent it takes a week to get over the hangover. Sometimes when I got desperate and drank it, I always swore afterward I'd never do it again, but I would." Jessie smiled and took another drink. "I'm feeling better already," he said, handing the bottle to McCabin.

"I have the feeling that you have quite a story to tell, Lieutenant." McCabin took a sip of the whiskey and handed the bottle back to Jessie. "Would you mind telling it?"

"I don't mind, Mr. McCabin, but first I'd like to ask you about Lieutenant Fujima and Stephanie. You apparently know something about it, and I'm very anxious to find her."

"I do not know where she is, Lieutenant, but I may be able to help you find her. I think it best for both of us, however, if you tell me your story first. I have the feeling it will provide some missing pieces."

Jessie nodded. "All right. If you think it will help."

McCabin pulled a pack of cigarettes from his pocket and offered Jessie one.

"That looks good, but I'm out of the habit now, so I'll pass."

"Smart move." McCabin smoked, and Jessie took swigs of the whiskey while he told his story. McCabin listened intently, asking an occasional question. By the time Jessie finished, he was feeling better than when he started-much better. "Ya know, thas'a pretty wild story, don't you think, Mr. McCabin?"

The attorney smiled. "It is. In fact, it's an incredible story. And I was right. You answered a number of my questions, and I believe we can, indeed, help each other. Come on, let's get you something to eat, and then I've got to get a message off to Washington."

When Jessie awoke the next morning, his first thought was that he was having another attack of the fever. His head was splitting, and he felt terrible. He sat up on the cot and looked around. It was a strange room, with boarded walls. Couldn't be his tree house...Where?

He was still trying to focus his thoughts when there was a knock at the door and a face appeared that seemed familiar. "How do you feel this morning?"

"Terrible," he muttered. "What happened?"

The face laughed. "Perhaps a little too much of the Jack?"

Memory returned, and Jessie cringed. "Yeah, I remember now. I never seem to learn. Whether it's Brew One Oh Two, jungle juice, or Jack Daniel's, it all comes out the same if you drink too much. Sorry about that, Mr. McCabin."

"Hey, you deserved a little party if anybody ever did." McCabin stepped into the room and tossed a set of khakis on the cot beside Jessie. "I can't guarantee the fit, or the shoe size, but they are regulation."

Jessie looked at the khakis. They were sure-enough regulation U.S. Army, and the shirt had first lieutenant bars pinned to the collar. He glanced at McCabin in surprise.

"Those bars weren't easy to come by, Lieutenant."

Jessie nodded. "I'm sure they weren't. Thanks. How did you manage that?"

"It wasn't easy. Get dressed. We got things to do."

"What are we gonna do?"

"After some breakfast, we're going over to command and get you an ID."

"Why didn't you tell me you were a Medal of Honor holder?" whined the major at the command center as he handed Jessie an army ID card.

"It didn't occur to me," said Jessie.

The major shook his head. "Well, it would have made things a lot easier."

"Come on, Lieutenant Rascoe, we have an appointment at the stockade," said Daniel McCabin.

When the lawyer and Jessie had departed, the major turned to his adjutant and said, "That McCabin guy must be some kind of a big shot. He sent one little message, and everybody in the whole command jumped through their ass."

"Yeah, nothing like a damn civilian with some authority. You'd think he was a four-star general."

"I was surprised that lieutenant had the Medal of Honor. You know what he got it for?"

"No, sir. I heard McCabin say he was one of the top fighter aces in the Pacific."

"Maybe he's the one that shot down Yamamoto."

"Who?"

"Admiral Yamamoto. He's the big Jap admiral that masterminded the Pearl Harbor attack. Some fighter pilot shot him down."

"Yes, sir, I know about that. But Lieutenant Rascoe wasn't the one that shot him down. That was-"

"Whatever. You got that report ready?"

"Oh, uh, I'll have it shortly, sir."

The captain in charge of the stockade was more accommodating than he had been previously, attending Jessie and McCabbin personally and arranging a private room for their meeting.

"Captain, would you bring Lieutenant Fujima over, but keep him in another room until I call?" said McCabin.

"Yes sir, I'll take care of it personally."

"Thank you. And oh, Captain, post a guard outside this room and make sure no one enters without my permission."

"Yes, sir," said the captain and departed.

After they were seated at a table, McCabin lit a cigarette and said, "Lieutenant Rascoe, I know you are concerned about the missionary girl, Stephanie, and I haven't been much help yet, but bear with me a bit longer, and I will explain. What I'm going to tell you is classified and not to go out of this room."

Jessie nodded.

"What we are dealing with here is a very serious and complex situation involving war crimes."

"War crimes? I'm not sure I understand what you mean."

"War crimes are criminal acts in violation of international law."

"You mean Japanese war crimes?"

"Yes, Japan participated in the Geneva Conventions and therefore is considered to be bound by international laws of conduct that apply during war. Just because a country is at war doesn't mean it is free to do whatever it pleases, including how prisoners of war are treated."

"Lieutenant Fujima is involved in war crimes?"

McCabin hesitated. "Lieutenant Fujima is a key witness in a war crimes investigation, but so far he refuses to cooperate. You may be able to help me change his mind and, at the same time, obtain information about Miss Collins."

Jessie looked at McCabin skeptically. "I'll help in any way I can, but I've never even met Fujima. My only interest in him is to find out what he knows about Stephanie."

The attorney cleared his throat. "This is a rather delicate issue, Jessie. But I must be frank with you. Lieutenant Fujima lived in private quarters here at the Wewak naval base during the last year of the war with a Caucasian female. We know that female was Stephanie Collins."

"What?"

"She was classified as a prisoner of war but assigned to Lieutenant Fujima as a 'domestic.'"

"That son of a bitch!"

"After hearing your story, I realized that she was here under unusual circumstances. We aren't sure what the relationship was between them, but we know she was billeted to his quarters."

Jessie shook his head despondently. "Damn! That poor girl. Do you or your intelligence people know where she is? And I want to know right now, Mr. McCabin."

"No, we honestly do not, but I believe Fujima does. Our problem is that he refuses to discuss it. He speaks fluent English, is intelligent, and fiercely loyal to his superiors, some of whom we suspect are guilty of serious war crimes. He may not have been directly involved, but we are confident he knows a lot more than he is telling."

"I don't understand the connection between Stephanie and war crimes."

It was quiet in the room for a moment. The squealing sound of a bulldozer could be heard somewhere off in the distance.

McCabin shifted in his chair. "I'm going to level with you. We know there were a number of Allied prisoners of war held at this installation. They have disappeared, and we believe the field commander here, Fujima's superior, ordered all the prisoners executed."

"Oh, no!"

"But that may not have included the missionary. And we have no physical evidence. They claim the prisoners were all put on a hospital ship marked with the International Red Cross and transported to a prisoner-of-war camp in the Philippines."

Jessie was stunned, and a terrible fear began to grip him. "But you don't believe that?"

"We have been unable to find any record of such a shipment. However, there is still mass confusion in all this relocation of prisoners and misplaced persons, so it's possible. We've got our people in the Philippines working on it from their end."

"Do you think Fujima knows?"

"Yes, I do."

"Why would he talk to me and not you?"

The lawyer pulled out a fresh cigarette and lit it. After he had blown out a column of smoke, he looked at Jessie and said, "It may sound a little bizarre, but I believe Lieutenant Fujima is in love with Stephanie Collins."

Jessie stared at McCabin a moment. "That IS pretty damn bizarre, Mr. McCabin. What makes you think that?"

"For the most part a gut feeling. But-"

"I think you misread him. He once told Stephanie that she could be a top geisha in Japan. That's more in line with his true feelings about her...the son of a bitch!"

"It could be, but I don't think so. I've had several discussions with him. He is articulate, sharp, and disciplined except when her name comes up. Then he seems to hesitate and even the tone of his voice changes."

Jessie shook his head. "I know Stephanie. She would never have agreed to live with that Jap!"

"Living conditions here at Wewak for the past year were very bad. Supplies were cut off, and the Japanese troops were near starvation, so you can imagine what the prisoners' conditions were like. The officers were probably a little better off, and if my gut feeling about Fujima is right, that could be one of the reasons she was billeted to his quarters."

Jessie shook his head.

"I'm sorry, Jessie."

"Well, what does he say? Does he admit she lived with him?"

"Yes, he admits that but will say no more, other than she was classified as a prisoner of war."

"And shipped out with the other prisoners?"

"He won't answer that question or any others regarding her whereabouts."

Long hesitation. "What do you want me to do?"

"I want you to talk to him about her. Tell him about your relationship. Although Fujima is from a samurai family and hard as nails, I can tell that he is emotional over her. So I believe he will react to you in some way. I'm not sure how. But I need to get him to talk, and this might just do it."

"All I want to do is find her and take her home."

"Okay. Would you talk to him?"

Jessie nodded. "All right, let's get to it."

A few minutes later, Lieutenant Saburo Fujima was escorted into the room, and he and Lieutenant Jessie Rascoe met face to face. After the introduction, McCabin departed the room leaving the two officers staring at each other.

"You are as she described," Saburo said in a low voice.

Fujima's statement startled Jessie. "You knew I was at the mission?"

"Yes, I knew."

"Then why didn't you come after me?"

"I promised her I wouldn't."

Jessie stared at the Japanese officer.

"Did you realize the depth of her love for you?"

Jessie gave a wooden nod.

"I know you did not enjoy that same depth of emotion, Lieutenant Rascoe. She told me you were betrothed to another."

Jessie hesitated. His insides were churning, and he wanted to lash out. Yet strangely, he sensed that the Japanese officer was sincere. He took a deep breath and said, "Look, Lieutenant Fujima, as you know, I have not seen or heard from Stephanie in over a year. All I want to know is where is she?"

"She had remarkable strength of character, yet she was like a delicate, beautiful flower. Just to be near her was such a joy as to brighten the darkest day."

"Lieutenant Fujima! Where is she?"

"When I was told I would meet you, I had no inclination of how I would feel or act. Now, I know it is important I tell you that our relationship was far more than would appear."

Jessie's insides were churning, and he wanted to lash out at the Japanese officer, but he braked his emotions and said, "What does that mean?"

"From the first moment I saw her, I was filled with an emotion that I can not explain, nor will I even try. Because of the dire conditions here at Wewak during this past year, we lived simply, improvising with our meager rations, pretending that a small piece of dried fish was fine sushi. And although her heart ached for you, she adjusted to the conditions and never complained. Despite the circumstances and the terrible uncertainty of what lay ahead, it was a wonderful time for me. And in a sense for her, in that she was so sure of her faith, there was no fear. I could only marvel and wonder about that faith. And if there had been more time, perhaps I..."

"Where is she?"

Fujima's eyes became misty, and he looked away.

Suddenly Jessie's legs felt weak.

"I'm sorry, Lieutenant Rascoe. I will tell you that she never wavered in her love for you." The Japanese officer turned and walked out of the room.

Jessie intended to drink whatever remained of McCabin's bottle of Jack Daniel's as soon as he could get his hands on it, but his insides were tied in such knots that he had to force it down his throat.

"I'm really sorry, Jessie," said McCabin in the command staff officer's quarters. "I can only guess how you must feel. I hope you can take some solace in the knowledge that the person responsible for Stephanie Collins's death will pay the penalty for his crime."

Jessie nodded woodenly. "Can I have one of your cigarettes, Mr. McCabin?"

"Sure." He pulled a pack from his shirt pocket. He lit Jessie's cigarette and then one for himself.

Jessie took a deep draw on the cigarette and let the smoke tumble out. "Even after all this time, the damn things still taste good," he mumbled.

"I don't blame you for wanting one. They do seem to have a soothing effect when you're emotionally upset, but I sure wouldn't go back to 'em if you can help it."

Both men puffed their cigarettes for a moment, and Jessie gulped down another swallow of the whiskey. "You get the information you needed?" he asked in a toneless voice.

"Yes. Fujima gave us a sworn deposition and indisputable evidence that can be documented. The general will be tried as a war criminal and will face the death penalty. He ordered the executions of the Allied prisoners, including Stephanie Collins."

Jessie shook his head. "I don't understand. He must have known the war was all but over. Why would he do that?"

McCabin sighed. "Lord only knows. But my guess is frustration. The Japanese high command and its generals were riding high for all those years while they rolled over everything in their way: Korea, Manchuria, China, Singapore, the East Indies, the Philippines, New Guinea. Then the tide turned on them, and it was bad from then on."

"And a wonderful girl who had dedicated her life to doing good had to pay the penalty."

"Yes. A real tragedy. Unfortunately, a lot of good people paid the ultimate penalty in that war."

"Yeah, I know. What will happen to Fujima?"

"He will stand trial. And even though we know he was only following orders, he refuses to plead not guilty. He insists he is as responsible as his superiors."

Jessie was silent for a moment and then said, "You know, Mr. McCabin, you were right. Fujima was in love with Stephanie. I would never have believed it, but it's true."

Chapter

~72~

Daniel McCabin arranged for the navy to furnish a motor launch that took Jessie and a stock of badly needed supplies up the river to the mission. Everyone was glad and relieved to see Jessie, but what should have been a grand occasion was saddened by the terrible news about Stephanie. The joy that should have been was not. Father McNiff and Martha were devastated, and many of the natives, particularly the children, wept openly. The chief declared a day of mourning, and even the village women didn't work.

McCabin also arranged to have Stephanie's body reburied in the mission cemetery as soon as the legal details could be accomplished. That required some time, and although Jessie was ordered back to the States, McCabin got those orders amended, allowing him to remain at the mission until the reburial was completed. Father McNiff conducted mass, and the village chief sanctioned a special native ceremony never before allowed.

The day the navy motor launch arrived at the mission to take Jessie back down the river to Wewak, where he would be flown to the States and home, he and Father McNiff had their final talk on the veranda of the rectory.

"Will I see you again, my son?" asked the priest.

"I don't know, Patrick. My plans for the future are uncertain, to say the least. But I do know that a part of me is here... and always will be."

"Yes, you will always be with us, Jessie. You have given much to our mission. The parishioners, and the children particularly, will remember and miss you greatly."

"And I will miss them and the mission very much."

"Always remember, Jessie, you have a home here if ever you should desire."

"Thank you, Patrick."

The priest nodded. "I know you must return to the military, and I'm sure you're anxious now to go home and see your family, and your loved ones."

"Yes, I am, but I'm having some trouble I can't seem to get a handle on." Jessie paused, took a cigarette from his shirt pocket, and fired it.

The priest pulled his pipe and pouch from his back pocket.

"It seems strange to see you smoking," he said as he packed the pipe. "And it's even stranger not to have to go out to the oven to light my pipe," he added, striking a match.

After his pipe was glowing in a cloud of smoke, he said, "I realize that your emotions are unsettled, but I must speak now, Jessie, while I have the opportunity, and I must be straight forward."

Jessie nodded.

"After more than two years, I know you pretty well, and I can see clearly that you are assuming an emotional burden that our Stephanie would not want. As tragic as her death was, it was the Lord's will, and you must remember that."

Jessie held the priest's eyes for a moment, then turned, and looked out at the mission compound. He looked at where he had seen her so often in those brightly colored dresses she always wore, her curly, sun bleached hair, and the jungle flower- always the flower. She was herself like a delicate flower.

"I want to accept what you say, but something inside is rebelling."

"Time will heal that, my son."

"I hope so."

"And Jessie, please continue your painting. If Stephanie could say one thing to you now, she would tell you that. Those paintings of native life and the mission are remarkable works of art. I hope that whatever you do, you won't forsake that marvelous talent."

A few days later, as Jessie looked out the window of the transport plane droning its way across the Pacific Ocean toward the United States and home, his eyes picked up a huge thunderstorm in the distance. It hung ominously over the horizon, reminding him of the cloud of uncertainty that hung over his homecoming: the resurrection of the dead.

He told himself to put it out of his mind and remember that he was going home- going home. It was hard to imagine that it was actually happening. But it was, and soon he would be there. Home, the Grapevine, his mother and father, his brother, his relatives and friends, and Maria... Maria?

Would she be waiting? Why would she? Why would she wait for him all this time? The war had been over for months, and he didn't come home. It didn't make any sense, none at all. Face it: Kevin won. But then Kevin had to make it home too. What if? Rascoe! Get off it! Get off it!

When the intercom buzzer sounded in her penthouse office suite in San Francisco, Peggy Barton Dumont flipped the switch, pulled off her thick glasses, and rubbed her eyes. "Yes," she muttered.

"There is a gentleman here to see you, Miss Dumont," came the voice of her secretary through the intercom.

"Well, has the gentleman got a name?"

"No, ma'am. He says it's a surprise."

"I'm in no mood for surprises. What's he want?"

"He says he'd like to take you to the St. Francis for dinner and a bottle of Bordeaux. And it's your turn to pay."

Peggy hesitated a moment as her thoughts spun crazily. She put her glasses back on, got up from her desk, and walked, with weak legs, across to the front door and swung it open. "Oh, Jesus Christ! It is!" she gasped and then threw herself into the arms of an Army Air Corps First Lieutenant dressed in a new class-A uniform awash with decorations.

The two clung to each other for a moment while the secretary and others in the reception room of the world headquarters of Dumont Industries watched curiously.

"Jessie, Jessie!" she shrieked with tears smearing her glasses. "What? Oh, Christ, this has gotta be some kind of story!"

Jessie grinned. "Yeah. I guess it is, Peggy."

"I...I can't believe it," she said, stepping back and examining him. "I've never been so glad to see anybody in my whole life. I mean it. Come on, let's go to my club. We've got a lot to talk about," she said, taking him by the arm.

"Miss Dumont? Your afternoon appointments?" said the secretary.

"Cancel everything until further notice," said Peggy Dumont as she went out the door with Jessie Rascoe on her arm.

Minutes later, they were escorted by a black-tie maitre d' into a mahogany-paneled, thick-carpeted private club in the same building. After being seated at a table with white linen and sterling silver, Peggy ordered a bottle of their best Bordeaux wine.

"I see you still do the ordering," said Jessie grinning.

"Old habits never die, but the guy I'm with now doesn't mind...as long as I'm paying."

"Same ole Peggy." She did look about the same as the day he knocked her down the steps of college: black horn-rimmed glasses, hair hanging down around her face, shapeless dress. And Jessie could tell that she hadn't changed. She was still the same person he'd known a life time ago: she knew who she was and what she wanted in life.

"I guess I am, but you look different, lover. Not just the weariness...and I assume you got that scar falling off a barstool.

But that's not what I mean. You been through some bad stuff, haven't you?"

"Yeah...Well, so have a bunch of guys. But I'm here, alive, and for the most part in one piece."

"Yes, and you're supposed to be dead. The newspapers all gave you headline coverage when you went missing in action. I think you got more coverage than MacArthur or Eisenhower that day."

"I put ole Grapevine on the map. Huh?"

"Were you in a prison of war camp?"

Jessie shook his head. "No."

"Well, what?"

"Long story, Peggy."

"When did you get back?"

"A couple days ago, but they've had me going through a bunch of stuff over at the presidio. I finally got away, and I really wanted to see you, Peggy."

She grinned. "You got the hots for me, lover?"

He gave her a smile.

She reached across and grasped his hands in hers. "I'm glad you came, Jessie. I can't tell you how much it means to me that you're alive and kicking. I nearly died when I heard you were missing. And you can talk to me as long as you want."

"Thanks, Peggy," he said pulling out a pack of cigarettes and offering her one.

She shook her head. "I would guess that came with the territory?"

"Yeah, and some other stuff."

"I can imagine. Well, no. How can anyone who wasn't there really imagine what it was like?"

The waiter arrived and poured the wine. Peggy held up her glass and said, "To you, my love. Welcome home."

Jessie smiled as they touched glasses across the table. "What's this love stuff, Peggy?"

She smiled, and as always, it made her look almost pretty. "If I didn't hate cheating so much, I'd show you what this love stuff is about."

Jessie laughed for the first time in weeks, and it made him feel almost human again. "I'll drink to that."

"Yeah, let's do!"

"I had forgotten how good that wine is," he said after they had drunk.

"Remember how we used to drink it by the bottle, then jump into that big bed? You ever think about that over there in the jungles?"

He nodded. "Yeah, I thought about it a lot more than I'm going to admit."

She laughed. "Me too, lover, but I guess we better stay off that subject or we'll both get in trouble. I can see that you do need to do some talking, and I want to hear your story, Jessie. I got the feeling it's a ripper."

Jessie nodded, ground out his cigarette, and lit a fresh one. He took a sip of the wine and said, "It's hard to know where to start."

"Start at the beginning."

Drinking wine and smoking one cigarette after another, Jessie told Peggy his story.

When he'd finally finished, Peggy shook her head and said, "Jessie, I suspected it was gonna be one hell of a story, but that is beyond even what I could have imagined. And a real, honest-to-God tragedy about the girl, Stephanie."

"Yeah, it was a tragedy, and I'm having trouble getting it settled in my head."

"You mean about her?"

He nodded. "I've come to realize that I have to accept what happened. It's done and it can't be undone. But the problem is that it's still down there, gnawing at my gut that it was my fault. If I just hadn't gone down the river...If-"

"Hold the phone," interrupted Peggy. "From what you've told me, you had no choice. It was the right thing to do. You're part of the tragedy was in good faith, so you can't blame yourself. You played it straight. Now you gotta put it out of your mind, my love."

"Yeah, I know, but getting it out of my thick skull is gonna be the challenge."

"It's easy. Stop feeling sorry for yourself."

He looked at her for a moment. "I knew you wouldn't mince words, Peggy."

"Yes, and you better listen to me. I know you have been through a lot, and you sure as hell have proved who you are in spades. But don't wallow in it. Get on with your life."

Jessie looked at her for a moment then nodded. "You always did know how to cut to the chase."

"Yeah, except how to catch a clod from Grapevine."

"Did you really want to catch me, Peggy?"

"You know the answer to that, clod."

They laughed, touched glasses, and drank.

"Does your family know you're back?"

"No, no one knows I'm even alive, except you. The guy I told you about, McCabin, wants to keep my resurrection classified for the time being because of the sensitive nature of the war crimes charges."

"You're returning from the dead is gonna be some kind of shock for your family."

"I'm anxious to see them, yet I...I wanted to try to get my head straight first."

"I understand. But like I said, don't wallow in it."

Jessie nodded. "I hear ya."

"Good."

"Well, how are you doing, Peggy?"

"I'm doing great, and I love what I'm doing. My companies are gearing up for peacetime production of civilian goods, and it's going to be exciting. Lots of demand for consumer goods now, automobiles, refrigerator, and coffee pots. I operate in a man's world, so it's not easy. The big boys don't think a woman should be in their world. But I'm doing just fine, and I'm excited about the future."

"And your love life?"

"He's a good guy, and I got a feeling you're gonna be getting a wedding invitation here before too long."

"That would be great, Peggy. I'm sincerely happy for you."

"Thanks, lover. Now what are your plans? Will you be getting out of the army?"

He nodded. "Yes. I love flying, and I learned a lot in the army and met some great guys...brave men...some who will never come home again. But I don't think I'm cut out for military life."

"Well, what about your painting? You said you did a lot when you were at the mission."

"I don't think I'll do any more painting. I lost interest."

She looked at him intently. "I'm not so sure about that."

"Besides, artists starve."

"Good ones don't. What did you do with the paintings you did over there?"

"I left them with Father McNiff. He's keeping them for me until I want them, but I don't know that I will."

"Reserve judgement on that for a while. After you get yourself settled, you may see it differently."

"Yeah. First things first...and that means Maria."

"Maria?"

"Yes, and you were right about that too. I was in love with her, and still am."

Peggy hesitated and took a sip of wine. "Jessie, you know me. I tell it the way it is, and I have to do that now. Since you have been listed as missing in action, in other words, killed in action, for over two years now, and the war has been over for nearly six months, it's only natural that Maria would have gone on with her life. It's the only thing she could do."

Jessie nodded. "I know, and I don't have any delusions about that. But I'm almost afraid to go home to get the final conformation."

"Jessie, you are a genuine American hero, and you played it straight all the way. You go on home now, and whichever way the cards fall, you roll with it and get on with your life."

When they parted late that night, they held each other tenderly, and Peggy told Jessie that if he ever wanted a job in her world all he had to do was ask. But her advice was to go back to his painting.

Jessie stayed in a small hotel near Fisherman's Wharf that night and slept late the next morning. After a leisurely breakfast, he took a walk along the wharf. It brought back fond memories of his days at college and reminded him of how good it was to be home. It also reminded him that he wasn't quite there yet.

He watched the bustling activity on the wharf for a while and helped the brakemen turn his cable car around on its wooden turntable at the end of the Powell Street trolly line. Then he went back to the hotel and placed a long-distance telephone call to the General Petroleum Company's Rose Station.

As luck would have it, his dad was on duty. At first, Mr. Rascoe could not comprehend. He thought it was some kind of a sadistic hoax and was indignant. When he finally realized that it truly was his son on the phone, he was so overwhelmed he choked up and couldn't talk.

When Jessie got off the Santa Fe Chief in Bakersfield later that day, a lot of his family and friends also got choked up and couldn't talk, including Jessie. It was a very emotional reunion, and there wasn't a dry eye. His poor mother alternated between crying hysterically and laughing for joy. Jessie's concerns over homecoming seemed to vanish at least for the moment.

Chapter
~73~

The Rascoe residence became the gathering place for Jessie's friends and relatives from all over the Grapevine and Bakersfield who came to welcome home their hero who had risen from the dead. Although Jessie wanted to ask about Maria, he couldn't bring himself to do it since it would almost certainly cast a dark cloud over the joy and excitement of his homecoming. He forced himself to listen to all the news, some of it good and some not.

It was good to hear that his brother Billy had also become an army pilot. He'd been sent overseas in the final days of the European war, too late to fly in combat. But while he was stationed there, he'd met and fallen in love with an English girl, and they were already married. It was hard for Jessie to imagine his little brother being married.

Jack had been a navy pilot assigned to one of the aircraft carriers that saw action in the Battle of the Philippine Sea. He had decided to stay in the navy and was stationed at the big navy base in San Diego. He and his wife already had a baby girl.

Jessie had known before he went down in the jungle that Bobbie had gone down with the *Yorktown* at the Battle of

Midway, but he hadn't known about Frank. He had survived Pearl Harbor and made it home to marry his high school sweetheart, Virginia, only to be killed in the closing days of the war when a kamikaze struck his ship.

On the good news side, Bud had survived the POW camp in Germany and had come home and married his longtime sweetheart, Penny. Jessie's cousin Glenn, who had been in the army and decorated for bravery in the landing on Okinawa, had also made it home and married Penny's sister, Bubbles. Gerald came home and was back working on aircraft engines at the airport after the Kaiser shipyards in San Francisco, shut down. Danny had survived Guadalcanal, but had been pretty badly shot up and was given a medical discharge from the Marine Corps. He was home and working with his dad at the Grapevine store. He was the one who told Jessie most of the news about all the Grapevine gang. Like always, he knew the most about what was going on.

"Agnes and Ted got married too, ya know," said Danny as they sat at the kitchen table in Jessie's house drinking beer, smoking, and reminiscing. Aria was in the navy, ya know, and she got a medal for something."

"Good for Aria."

"The bug hasn't bit me yet, although I wanted to date Alyse. But she wouldn't. She finally married some guy in Los Angeles."

Jessie took a drink of beer. "Uh, you hear anything about Hallie Lamont?"

"Yeah, didn't you hear about her?"

The way Danny said it sent a chill through Jessie. "No. What happened?"

"She had a bad crash in one of the planes she was ferrying, and for a long time, they didn't think she would ever get out of bed again."

"Oh no!" groaned Jessie, as the shock cut through him like a knife.

"I guess it was a miracle she even survived."

"Jesus. Where is she?"

"She's out at the ranch."

"She is? Is she all right now?"

"I don't know, Jessie. She was in some big hospital in Los Angeles for a long time. They finally brought her home, and I guess she's up and around some. But she doesn't go off the ranch anymore. Ole Juan Martinez told me she was awful bad hurt."

Beautiful Hallie, brave Hallie- the girl he'd fallen in love with the first time he saw her a million years ago- the girl who had it all. At least everybody thought she did. He was probably the only person in the world who knew differently. Who knew about the terrible secret of her mother and the struggle she'd gone through to overcome it. Damn! He'd never told her the truth, had he? Never written the letter. Oh, he'd written it, several times, and then tore it up. So he'd never told Hallie that Maria was the one- the one he would come home to. Yeah, come home to three years and a lifetime later, and come home to what?

Suddenly, Jessie became warm and clammy, like he was having a fever attack. "Danny, you know where Maria Hunter is?"

"No, I sure don't. Los Angeles I guess. She married that rich guy down there ya know...Hey, Jessie, are you okay? You look awful pale."

John Bartlet's ambulance was getting a little worse for the wear, but it still ran. So when he got the call to hurry down to Doc Veeyon's place, he started it up and headed on down to Oak Glenn.

"It's Jessie Rascoe, John. He's having an attack of some kind of fever he got over in that jungle he was in," Doc said when Bartlet arrived at Doc's rock house on the side of the hill at Oak Glenn. "They brought him down here to me, but I don't know anything about that stuff."

"That boy sure been through a lot, I guess," said Bartlet.

"He sure has. I think ya better drive him down to that big army hospital in LA. They probably know about this fever he's got. It's bad stuff."

"Okay. I'll get there as fast as the old bus will go. I just got my siren fixed, so it'll be red lights and siren all the way to LA."

Bartlet got Jessie to the army hospital in Los Angeles. But they didn't handle malaria and dengue patients there, so they sent him by air-evac to a special military disease clinic in Seattle, Washington.

In Seattle, they gave Jessie what was called the Atabrine cure. It was awful stuff that came in pills that he had to take every few hours. It made him deathly ill at first, but they kept making him take the pills until he could keep them down.

After a month of the Atabrine cure, the doctor came to his room one morning and said, "We have done all we can, Lieutenant. You are going to be released."

"Does that mean I'm cured?"

The doctor nodded. "We believe so."

"Where do I go from here?"

"We're transferring you to our psychological evaluation and rehabilitation center for a while then you can elect to remain in the army or request a discharge."

"Whatever," shrugged Jessie.

"And uh, Lieutenant, we don't recommend you make any blood donations for the time being. Just in case the cure didn't work, you don't want to pass that stuff on to somebody else."

After two weeks of various testing and counseling, Jessie was released from the rehabilitation center and given thirty days' leave.

He considered going to San Francisco to talk to Peggy. But then what could he say to Peggy that he hadn't already said? Since he still hadn't any idea of what he wanted to do, he couldn't give her an answer on taking a job with her company. Maybe he should he go home and get his old job back delivering news papers up and down the Grapevine. Or how about going back to New Guinea and become a real missionary?

He told himself to get serious, but he still couldn't come up with anything that interested him in the least.

Jessie caught a ride on an army air-evac flight on its way to Minter Army Air Field, near Bakersfield, California. He was sitting in one of the aluminum-framed, canvas-backed seats, listening to the drone of the engines and staring at the floor of the aircraft when a voice interrupted his thoughts. "Would you like a box lunch, Lieutenant?"

He glanced up at a female flight nurse. She was a second lieutenant in uniform-a shapely uniform. She was cute, with blue eyes and a delightful smile, which she turned on Jessie. He accepted the box lunch and returned the smile, but it was cursory. He felt no spark. None at all. Maybe he really should become a missionary, or a monk, or something.

When he finally got home, he lay on the bed in his old room, staring at the ceiling for several days. He knew his parents were concerned, but they pretended not to notice. Then one morning his mother said, "Have you gone to see Hallie Lamont yet?"

Jessie shook his head.

"Mr. Switzner told me recently that she is recovering, but it's a long, slow process. Maybe it would boost her morale if you visited her."

"Whose morale we talkin' about, Mom?"

The mother hesitated. "Perhaps both?"

Jessie smiled.

"Well, at least I got a smile out of you."

"I'm sorry, Mom. I'm okay, seriously. I just got to get some things straight in my head."

"Your father and I understand Jessie, and we know it takes time to forget the terrible experiences you have suffered."

"I'll make it, Mom. Don't worry, okay?"

She nodded. "I'll try."

"I do want to see Hallie. It's just that I...Okay, Mom, I'll go."

That afternoon, Jessie fired up the old Model A Ford and headed toward the Ranch to see Hallie. The truth was, he'd avoided going because of his anxiety over facing her. As he drove down the road, he still didn't know what he was going to say.

Like the ole Grapevine, life sure had its twists and turns. Hallie had played games with him all those years, and then he'd done the same thing to her. Would she still be waiting for his answer, or had she been hurt so bad it didn't matter anymore?

As he passed by the road to the Old Rose Station stage stop, he turned off, drove up, and stopped beside the ranch water trough. He got out of the car and walked up to where a few white-faced Herefords were standing, heads down in the trough. They raised their heads when they heard him coming and looked at him curiously for a moment, and then went back to drinking and switching their tails.

Jessie's thoughts spun into the past to the time Alvin ran the ole bull off, and then Hallie had ridden up on her horse and caught them skinny dipping. It was the first time he had ever seen Hallie. He recalled the other time when he and Hallie had skinny-dipped that night he rescued her from the Hunters' smokehouse. Those had been wonderful, exciting times, but times that were no more.

When he pulled up to the Lamont hacienda a short time later, it looked about the same as he remembered. And he remembered it well, particularly the night they wrecked the Model T and he almost got his head blown off by that big jerk George Simmons.

When the iron-encrusted front door swung open to Jessie's knock, George Simmons appeared in the doorway.

The surprise caused Jessie to stare at him, wondering for a moment if it really was the big jerk. He hadn't seen Simmons since that night at the Tavern when George knocked him across the dance floor. Simmons was leaning on a walking cane.

"I'm Jessie Rascoe."

Simmons nodded. "I recognized you."

Jessie nodded. Simmons stepped out onto the entrance porch beside Jessie and closed the door behind him. "You here to see Hallie?"

"Yes."

"You mind taking a little walk with me first? I need to stretch this leg some."

Jessie hesitated.

"Please, Jessie. I really would like to talk to you before you see Hallie?"

The war had changed everything, but it was hard to imagine big tough George Simmons saying please. Jessie nodded, and they both stepped off onto the brick pathway that led to the ranch headquarters.

"You broke your leg?" asked Jessie.

"The Japs did."

Jessie glanced at Simmons curiously.

"Iwo Jima."

Jessie nodded. Another surprise. "You were in the army?"

"No. I was a marine.

"Tough duty."

"Yeah...I read you were missing in action...Prisoner of War camp?"

"I guess you could call it that."

"So you survived the Japs after all."

"Yeah."

Simmons halted and turned to face Jessie. "You know the story of Hallie and me, so I don't need to go into that. And I assume you know she was badly hurt in a crash?"

"Yes. I heard about it."

"It's been a long, tough struggle for Hallie. But she's walking pretty well now and gets better every day. Hallie's strong willed and she's determined. She and I been doing some riding here lately. A little tough on both of us, but we're making it."

"That's good to hear," said Jessie.

Simmons paused for a moment. "Before you came along, she was in love with me. I know I didn't deserve her, but I did love her and still do. I've learned a lot in the last four years, most of it bad. But I did wake up to the fact that I'd behaved like an asshole most of my life, and when you face death day after day for a while, you learn some things."

"I understand," said Jessie.

Simmons nodded. "I know you do."

"You say you still love her?"

"Yes. Very much. She told me when we broke up before she went to England that she was in love with you. But I know that deep down she loves me, and we'll make it. That is, if...Well, I guess the question is a simple one: Do you love her?"

They had stopped at the end of the walkway and stood facing each other.

"Yes, I love her. I've loved Hallie since I was thirteen years old. But ya know George, I doubt that I love her the way you do."

It was silent for several minutes. "Thank you," said George Simmons in a low, choked voice. Then they walked back down the walkway in silence and stopped beside Jessie's car.

"Good luck, George. I have the feeling it's gonna work out for both of you," said Jessie, opening the car door.

"Jessie?"

Jessie glanced back at Simmons. "Yeah?"

"I'm sorry I hit you that night at the Tavern."

"Me too," said Jessie feeling his chin. "My jaw's never been the same."

They both smiled and shook hands. Then Jessie climbed-into the Model A and drove off down the road toward the Grapevine.

Chapter
~74~

The day after Jessie's trip to the Ranch, he went to Grapevine Creek and sat down in the grass under the big oak tree at his and Alvin's old secret meeting place. It was where they had solved most of their weighty problems since they were old enough to walk down there. As he watched a butterfly making lazy circles around a dandelion and listened to the straining engine of a truck laboring up the Grapevine, his thoughts turned to Hallie.

Although he'd been deeply affected by what happened to her, Jessie had come away from the encounter with George Simmons feeling that it had all worked out right. In a sense, he felt exonerated. And it was uplifting to discover that something good had come out of the war. He would not have believed that possible, but he'd seen it last night with his own eyes. The war had transformed George Simmons into a humble human being, and Jessie knew that everything Simmons said was gospel truth. He was in love with Hallie and she loved him, and they would make it now, together. Jessie knew that too.

He flopped down on his back in the grass and looked up into the freshly budded leaves on the old oak tree. How many times he and Alvin had lay there discussing their secret plans and their problems, which seemed to multiply ten-fold after girls came into the picture.

So now what?

The butterfly came back and circled the dandelion again, and the sound of another truck laboring up the Grapevine echoed across the creek. When the butterfly flew away and the sound of the truck faded, this time, it seemed to signal Jessie that it was time to do as Peggy said: get on with life. He climbed to his feet and took one last look around, then walked out to the highway where he'd parked the Ford, got in, and headed up the Grapevine.

As he approached the turnoff to Bear Trap Canyon road, the old Ford seemed to slow down by itself, as though it knew that was where Jessie was going. But Jessie didn't want to go down that road. He'd just agreed with himself to get on with his life, and driving down that road wasn't the way. But the Ford turned off anyway and took Jessie on down the Bear Trap Canyon road.

"What are you doing, Rascoe?" he said aloud.

When he pulled up to the ranch gate, Juan Martinez came out of his shack just the way he always had, walked up to the car, and looked at Jessie. The old breed appeared about the same, perhaps a little more grey hair.

"Newspaper say Japs kill you. But me know you got injun spirit. Not kill so easy when you got spirit, huh, kid?" he grunted.

Jessie was surprised at first, then he remembered that day long ago when Martinez had told him he had Indian spirit. He smiled and said, "I guess you were right Mr. Martinez."

"Take long time, but I know you come back," said the breed, as though he were confirming a prophecy.

"You did?" Jessie heard himself say.

"Yep."

"How did you know that, Mr. Martinez?"

"Me know spirit. And I proud when you get big honor," he said with a glint in his dark eyes.

"Thank you, Mr. Martinez. Thank you very much, sir," said Jessie.

Martinez gave the hint of a smile, nodded, and pulled the gate open. Jessie waved and gunned the Ford on down the road.

The exchange with Martinez had a strange effect on Jessie. It was almost as though the breed actually knew that he was coming: that it was...preordained. In a sense, it was unnerving, yet Jessie felt good. It seemed to justify his impulse to drive into Bear Trap Canyon, and he enjoyed the rest of his drive over the old road that was just as rough and bad as it ever was.

When he reached Pete Miller Meadow, he stopped and shut off the engine. He walked over to where the ice-cold water came out of the rocks, lay down on his stomach, and got himself a drink. It tasted just as good as he remembered. Then he went over to the little grassy knoll where the Bear Patrol had always camped and lay down on his back in the soft grass.

A blue jay squawked somewhere, and a pair of doves flew in and landed in the tops of the willows. It was the same clump of willows where the rattler bit Maria a lifetime ago.

He knew he shouldn't start thinking about her. But Jessie couldn't help himself, and he lay in the grass for some time thinking of that day he first met Maria and about all the other wonderful experiences they'd had together in Bear Trap Canyon.

After a while, he pulled himself to a sitting position and looked around again at the meadow. It was a beautiful sight, and suddenly he wished he had his painting gear. He'd paint it. Yes, that's what he'd really like to do, wasn't it? Yes! Paint! That's what he'd always wanted to do, for Christ's sake! And that's what he would do!

Jesus! He'd spent all that time agonizing over what he wanted to do and now, presto! The decision was made. No more wallowing in indecision. He knew exactly what he wanted to do. The old magic of the Grapevine was still working, and suddenly Jessie felt an excitement he'd not experienced in a long time. It was as though he'd just walked out of a long dark tunnel into the sunlight.

He got up, took one last look around, crawled onto the Ford, and headed back down the road toward Lebec. He'd only gone a short distance when he braked to a stop, hesitated, and said aloud, "What the hell, it's settled now, so it won't hurt anything. Go on up there."

He turned the Ford around and drove up the canyon towards the Hunters' homestead. One last look won't hurt. Not in his frame of mind.

The Hunters' old red barn looked exactly as it had the first time he saw it: about to fall down. The corrugated tin roof was a little more rusted, but not quite as rusted as the corrugated roof on the mission in faraway New Guinea.

He pulled up next to the barn and stopped. He was sitting in the car looking at it nostalgically when he saw a tow-headed little boy squeeze out through a crack in the weathered boards. He watched as the tot freed himself.

"Hello there," Jessie said.

The boy looked at him curiously.

"You playing in the barn?"

The boy nodded. Jessie climbed out of the Ford and walked over to where he stood. He was a cute little boy with red cheeks, tousled blond hair, and intense green eyes. He wore a miniature pair of bib overalls and tiny tennis shoes.

"What you got in the barn?"

"Truck."

"Oh. You got a truck in there?"

He nodded. "C'mon," he said, reached up and took Jessie's hand and pulled him toward the crack in the barn.

Jessie had to force the board open some more to get through, but he managed. There wasn't much in the old barn except remnants of hay mixed with dirt. The boy guided him to a place on the earthen floor where there was a metal toy truck that was filled with scraps of hay. He sat down beside his truck and Jessie sat down next to him.

"Truck go Rrr," the boy said, pushing the toy in the dirt.

It was the first time Jessie had ever played with a little boy, and it gave him a warm, good feeling. Then, as he watched the boy, Jessie was struck with a shocking revelation: this little boy was Maria and Kevin's son - he knew it without question.

Maria's son! It was all he could do to keep from grabbing the child up in his arms and embracing him. Maria's son! God, this could have been his son... But he wasn't he was Kevin's son.

The barn door suddenly swung open and Mrs. Hunter walked in stopping abruptly when she saw Jessie. She raised her hands to her face and cried out, "Oh my God!"

For a moment Jessie was afraid Mrs. Hunter was going to faint, so he got to his feet and put an arm out to steady her. "I'm sorry I shocked you, Mrs. Hunter."

"Oh Jessie! Jessie!" she wailed, throwing her arms around him and hugging him. "You came back! You came back!"

"God answered Maria's prayers, Jessie. He brought you back."

Jessie looked at Mrs. Hunter curiously. It seemed to Jessie she was overreacting at seeing him, but then perhaps the shock of seeing him pop up in her barn when he was supposed to be dead was a little much and it was just a natural reaction.

"I'm so thankful you came back Jessie. So thankful. We haven't been out of the canyon in so long. When did you get home?"

"Uh, I been back a while," he stammered.

"Oh, this is such a blessing. God has been so good to us. Our boys came home too. Both of them, and now you...Oh, this is so wonderful! I can hardly believe it!" She reached out and took his hands in hers again and held them for a moment. "Jessie, go to her now. Go to Maria."

"Mrs. Hunter, I-"

"She never stopped believing you would come home. Never. She said you would come back to her. No matter what they said. And she believed it with all her heart."

Jessie's head was spinning with confusion as he tried to make some kind of sense out of what Mrs. Hunter was saying.

"Even after the war was over, she said you would come."

"Mrs. Hunter, I don't understand. What...what are you saying?"

The woman looked at Jessie curiously.

"Rrrr," said the little boy pushing his truck through the straw and dirt.

"Where is Maria's husband?"

Mrs. Hunter looked even more shocked. "Oh my God in heaven! You don't know!"

"Know what?"

"Maria didn't marry Kevin, Jessie. She couldn't do it. She cancelled the wedding at the last moment."

Jessie suddenly felt as though a million volts of electricity had shot through him. He stood frozen, staring at Mrs. Hunter as though in a trance.

"She left Los Angeles and has been here ever since, waiting for you to come home. She has not left the canyon once."

Crazy, spinning thoughts-like a fever attack-only it wasn't a fever attack and Jessie knew it wasn't. It was true. She hadn't married!

Then another shocking realization-the boy! He glanced down at him and then at Mrs. Hunter. She nodded. "His name is Jessie Rascoe Jr. He is your son."

Jessie looked at his son and experienced the most profound emotion of his life.

"Truck go Rrrr," said Jessie Rascoe Jr.

Jessie sat back down next to his son. A mist appeared in the old barn clouding his vision, as he watched his son push the truck through the straw and dirt.

Jessie gently touched the top of his son's head. "Where is she, Mrs. Hunter?"

"She is where she always goes to think of you."

When Jessie came up over the last rise on the trail to Marble Springs, his pulse was racing and his breath was short. But he was filled with a joy and an excitement that he'd not experienced since that time long ago when he'd come up that same trail looking for Maria.

When he looked down on Marble Springs, it was just as it had been that day so long ago: the shining granite rocks and the thick green grass, sprinkled with a rainbow of wildflowers. The smell of wild mint and honeysuckle drifting with the gentle breeze. A covey of quail bobbing their way through the grass. Then, when he stepped out into the meadow just above the springs, he looked down and saw her lying in the grass and wildflowers. The emotion was so overwhelming he had to lean against a willow tree for support.

As though she sensed he was there, Maria got up from the grass, glanced across and saw him. She stood a moment watching him as he started out across the meadow toward her. Then she slowly began to walk toward him. She was dressed exactly as she'd been that last time: barefoot, jeans, and a short-sleeved blouse.

As they walked toward each other, their pace quickened. Then Maria broke into a run, her long dark hair dancing across her back as she ran toward him as fast as her legs would carry her. Jessie too, began to run as fast as his legs would carry him. And as they ran toward each other, they both knew that nothing in the past mattered. All that mattered now was their love- a love that would take them through the rest of their lives.

When they met with a collision there in the meadow, where they had first kissed long ago, they fell into a heap in the soft grass locked in each other's arms. And for some time afterward they lay there in the grass at Marble Springs.

EPILOGUE

The *Los Angeles Examiner* carried an art review in the spring of 1947 about a unique painting exhibit of a primitive, native culture from the island of New Guinea.

The paintings and sketches were accomplished on location during World War II. According to art critics, the work was superbly executed by a young artist, Jessie J. Rascoe, using only indigenous, primitive materials. Although Mr. Rascoe was previously unknown, the exhibit drew wide acclaim in art circles, particularly an extraordinary portrait of a young missionary titled *"Stephanie."*

The artist and his wife and son attended the opening of the exhibit in Bakersfield, California. Sponsored by the Dumont Industries Corporation of San Francisco, it was scheduled to be shown in art museums across the country.

Painting of Stephanie in front of Father McNiff Chapel

15798593R00354

Made in the USA
Lexington, KY
17 June 2012